ANN PETRY

ANN PETRY

THE STREET
THE NARROWS

Farah Jasmine Griffin, *editor*

THE LIBRARY OF AMERICA

Published in the United States by Library of America.
Visit our website at www.loa.org.

This paper exceeds the requirements of
ANSI/NISO Z39.48–1992 (Permanence of Paper).

Distributed to the trade in the United States
by Penguin Random House Inc.
and in Canada by Penguin Random House Canada Ltd.

Library of Congress Control Number: 2018952815
ISBN 978–1–59853–601–0

First Printing
The Library of America—314

Manufactured in the United States of America

Contents

THE STREET.   1

THE NARROWS.   307

OTHER WRITINGS   759

   The Great Secret   761
   Harlem.   766
   The Novel as Social Criticism   776

Chronology.   787
Note on the Texts   800
Notes.   802

THE STREET

To My Mother

BERTHA JAMES LANE

Chapter 1

THERE WAS A COLD November wind blowing through 116th Street. It rattled the tops of garbage cans, sucked window shades out through the top of opened windows and set them flapping back against the windows; and it drove most of the people off the street in the block between Seventh and Eighth Avenues except for a few hurried pedestrians who bent double in an effort to offer the least possible exposed surface to its violent assault.

It found every scrap of paper along the street—theater throwaways, announcements of dances and lodge meetings, the heavy waxed paper that loaves of bread had been wrapped in, the thinner waxed paper that had enclosed sandwiches, old envelopes, newspapers. Fingering its way along the curb, the wind set the bits of paper to dancing high in the air, so that a barrage of paper swirled into the faces of the people on the street. It even took time to rush into doorways and areaways and find chicken bones and pork-chop bones and pushed them along the curb.

It did everything it could to discourage the people walking along the street. It found all the dirt and dust and grime on the sidewalk and lifted it up so that the dirt got into their noses, making it difficult to breathe; the dust got into their eyes and blinded them; and the grit stung their skins. It wrapped newspaper around their feet entangling them until the people cursed deep in their throats, stamped their feet, kicked at the paper. The wind blew it back again and again until they were forced to stoop and dislodge the paper with their hands. And then the wind grabbed their hats, pried their scarves from around their necks, stuck its fingers inside their coat collars, blew their coats away from their bodies.

The wind lifted Lutie Johnson's hair away from the back of her neck so that she felt suddenly naked and bald, for her hair had been resting softly and warmly against her skin. She shivered as the cold fingers of the wind touched the back of her neck, explored the sides of her head. It even blew her eyelashes away from her eyes so that her eyeballs were bathed in a rush of coldness and she had to blink in order to read the words on the sign swaying back and forth over her head.

Each time she thought she had the sign in focus, the wind pushed it away from her so that she wasn't certain whether it said three rooms or two rooms. If it was three, why, she would go in and ask to see it, but if it said two—why, there wasn't any point. Even with the wind twisting the sign away from her, she could see that it had been there for a long time because its original coat of white paint was streaked with rust where years of rain and snow had finally eaten the paint off down to the metal and the metal had slowly rusted, making a dark red stain like blood.

It was three rooms. The wind held it still for an instant in front of her and then swooped it away until it was standing at an impossible angle on the rod that suspended it from the building. She read it rapidly. Three rooms, steam heat, parquet floors, respectable tenants. Reasonable.

She looked at the outside of the building. Parquet floors here meant that the wood was so old and so discolored no amount of varnish or shellac would conceal the scars and the old scraped places, the years of dragging furniture across the floors, the hammer blows of time and children and drunks and dirty, slovenly women. Steam heat meant a rattling, clanging noise in radiators early in the morning and then a hissing that went on all day.

Respectable tenants in these houses where colored people were allowed to live included anyone who could pay the rent, so some of them would be drunk and loud-mouthed and quarrelsome; given to fits of depression when they would curse and cry violently, given to fits of equally violent elation. And, she thought, because the walls would be flimsy, why, the good people, the bad people, the children, the dogs, and the godawful smells would all be wrapped up together in one big package —the package that was called respectable tenants.

The wind pried at the red skullcap on her head, and as though angered because it couldn't tear it loose from its firm anchorage of bobby pins, the wind blew a great cloud of dust and ashes and bits of paper into her face, her eyes, her nose. It smacked against her ears as though it were giving her a final, exasperated blow as proof of its displeasure in not being able to make her move on.

Lutie braced her body against the wind's attack determined to finish thinking about the apartment before she went in to look at it. Reasonable—now that could mean almost anything. On Eighth Avenue it meant tenements—ghastly places not fit for humans. On St. Nicholas Avenue it meant high rents for small apartments; and on Seventh Avenue it meant great big apartments where you had to take in roomers in order to pay the rent. On this street it could mean almost anything.

She turned and faced the wind in order to estimate the street. The buildings were old with small slit-like windows, which meant the rooms were small and dark. In a street running in this direction there wouldn't be any sunlight in the apartments. Not ever. It would be hot as hell in summer and cold in winter. "Reasonable" here in this dark, crowded street ought to be about twenty-eight dollars, provided it was on a top floor.

The hallways here would be dark and narrow. Then she shrugged her shoulders, for getting an apartment where she and Bub would be alone was more important than dark hallways. The thing that really mattered was getting away from Pop and his raddled women, and anything was better than that. Dark hallways, dirty stairs, even roaches on the walls. Anything. Anything. Anything.

Anything? Well, almost anything. So she turned toward the entrance of the building and as she turned, she heard someone clear his or her throat. It was so distinct—done as it was on two notes, the first one high and then the grunting expiration of breath on a lower note—that it came to her ears quite clearly under the sound of the wind rattling the garbage cans and slapping at the curtains. It was as though someone had said "hello," and she looked up at the window over her head.

There was a faint light somewhere in the room she was looking into and the enormous bulk of a woman was silhouetted against the light. She half-closed her eyes in order to see better. The woman was very black, she had a bandanna knotted tightly around her head, and Lutie saw, with some surprise, that the window was open. She began to wonder how the woman could sit by an open window on a cold, windy night like this one. And she didn't have on a coat, but a kind of loose-looking cotton dress—or at least it must be cotton, she thought, for it had a clumsy look—bulky and wrinkled.

"Nice little place, dearie. Just ring the Super's bell and he'll show it to you."

The woman's voice was rich. Pleasant. Yet the longer Lutie looked at her, the less she liked her. It wasn't that the woman had been sitting there all along staring at her, reading her thoughts, pushing her way into her very mind, for that was merely annoying. But it was understandable. She probably didn't have anything else to do; perhaps she was sick and the only pleasure she got out of life was in watching what went on in the street outside her window. It wasn't that. It was the woman's eyes. They were as still and as malignant as the eyes of a snake. She could see them quite plainly—flat eyes that stared at her—wandering over her body, inspecting and appraising her from head to foot.

"Just ring the Super's bell, dearie," the woman repeated.

Lutie turned toward the entrance of the building without answering, thinking about the woman's eyes. She pushed the door open and walked inside and stood there nodding her head. The hall was dark. The low-wattage bulb in the ceiling shed just enough light so that you wouldn't actually fall over —well, a piano that someone had carelessly left at the foot of the stairs; so that you could see the outlines of—oh, possibly an elephant if it were dragged in from the street by some enterprising tenant.

However, if you dropped a penny, she thought, you'd have to get down on your hands and knees and scrabble around on the cracked tile floor before you could ever hope to find it. And she was wrong about being able to see an elephant or a piano because the hallway really wasn't wide enough to admit either one. The stairs went up steeply—dark high narrow steps. She stared at them fascinated. Going up stairs like those you ought to find a newer and more intricate—a much-involved and perfected kind of hell at the top—the very top.

She leaned over to look at the names on the mail boxes. Henry Lincoln Johnson lived here, too, just as he did in all the other houses she'd looked at. Either he or his blood brother. The Johnsons and the Jacksons were mighty prolific. Then she grinned, thinking who am I to talk, for I, too, belong to that great tribe, that mighty mighty tribe of Johnsons. The bells revealed that the Johnsons had roomers—Smith, Roach,

Anderson—holy smoke! even Rosenberg. Most of the names were inked in over the mail boxes in scrawling handwriting —the letters were big and bold on some of them. Others were written in pencil; some printed in uneven scraggling letters where names had been scratched out and other names substituted.

There were only two apartments on the first floor. And if the Super didn't live in the basement, why, he would live on the first floor. There it was printed over One A. One A must be the darkest apartment, the smallest, most unrentable apartment, and the landlord would feel mighty proud that he'd given the Super a first-floor apartment.

She stood there thinking that it was really a pity they couldn't somehow manage to rent the halls, too. Single beds. No. Old army cots would do. It would bring in so much more money. If she were a landlord, she'd rent out the hallways. It would make it so much more entertaining for the tenants. Mr. Jones and wife could have cots number one and two; Jackson and girl friend could occupy number three. And Rinaldi, who drove a cab nights, could sublet the one occupied by Jackson and girl friend.

She would fill up all the cots—row after row of them. And when the tenants who had apartments came in late at night, they would have the added pleasure of checking up on the occupants. Jackson not home yet but girl friend lying in the cot alone—all curled up. A second look, because the lack of light wouldn't show all the details, would reveal—ye gods, why, what's Rinaldi doing home at night! Doggone if he ain't tucked up cozily in Jackson's cot with Jackson's girl friend. No wonder she looked contented. And the tenants who had apartments would sit on the stairs just as though the hall were a theater and the performance about to start—they'd sit there waiting until Jackson came home to see what he'd do when he found Rinaldi tucked into his cot with his girl friend. Rinaldi might explain that he thought the cot was his for sleeping and if the cot had blankets on it did not he, too, sleep under blankets; and if the cot had girl friend on it, why should not he, too, sleep with girl friend?

Instead of laughing, she found herself sighing. Then it occurred to her that if there were only two apartments on the first floor and the Super occupied one of them, then the occupant of the other apartment would be the lady with the snake's eyes. She looked at the names on the mail boxes. Yes. A Mrs. Hedges lived in One B. The name was printed on the card—a very professional-looking card. Obviously an extraordinary woman with her bandanna on her head and her sweet, sweet voice. Perhaps she was a snake charmer and she sat in her window in order to charm away at the snakes, the wolves, the foxes, the bears that prowled and loped and crawled on their bellies through the jungle of 116th Street.

Lutie reached out and rang the Super's bell. It made a shrill sound that echoed and re-echoed inside the apartment and came back out into the hall. Immediately a dog started a furious barking that came closer and closer as he ran toward the door of the apartment. Then the weight of his body landed against the door and she drew back as he threw himself against the door. Again and again until the door began to shiver from the impact of his weight. There was the horrid sound of his nose snuffing up air, trying to get her scent. And then his weight hurled against the door again. She retreated toward the street door, pausing there with her hand on the knob. Then she heard heavy footsteps, the sound of a man's voice threatening the dog, and she walked back toward the apartment.

She knew instantly by his faded blue overalls that the man who opened the door was the Super. The hot fetid air from the apartment in back of him came out into the hall. She could hear the faint sound of steam hissing in the radiators. Then the dog tried to plunge past the man and the man kicked the dog back into the apartment. Kicked him in the side until the dog cringed away from him with its tail between its legs. She heard the dog whine deep in its throat and then the murmur of a woman's voice—a whispering voice talking to the dog.

"I came to see about the apartment—the three-room apartment that's vacant," she said.

"It's on the top floor. You wanta look at it?"

The light in the hall was dim. Dim like that light in Mrs. Hedges' apartment. She pulled her coat around her a little tighter. It's this bad light, she thought. Somehow the man's eyes were worse than the eyes of the woman sitting in the window. And she told herself that it was because she was so tired;

that was the reason she was seeing things, building up pretty pictures in people's eyes.

He was a tall, gaunt man and he towered in the doorway, looking at her. It isn't the bad light, she thought. It isn't my imagination. For after his first quick furtive glance, his eyes had filled with a hunger so urgent that she was instantly afraid of him and afraid to show her fear.

But the apartment—did she want the apartment? Not in this house where he was super; not in this house where Mrs. Hedges lived. No. She didn't want to see the apartment—the dark, dirty three rooms called an apartment. Then she thought of where she lived now. Those seven rooms where Pop lived with Lil, his girl friend. A place filled with roomers. A place spilling over with Lil.

There seemed to be no part of it that wasn't full of Lil. She was always swallowing coffee in the kitchen; trailing through all seven rooms in housecoats that didn't quite meet across her lush, loose bosom; drinking beer in tall glasses and leaving the glasses in the kitchen sink so the foam dried in a crust around the rim—the dark red of her lipstick like an accent mark on the crust; lounging on the wide bed she shared with Pop and only God knows who else; drinking gin with the roomers until late at night.

And what was far more terrifying giving Bub a drink on the sly; getting Bub to light her cigarettes for her. Bub at eight with smoke curling out of his mouth.

Only last night Lutie slapped him so hard that Lil cringed away from her dismayed; her housecoat slipping even farther away from the fat curve of her breasts. "Jesus!" she said. "That's enough to make him deaf. What's the matter with you?"

But did she want to look at the apartment? Night after night she'd come home from work and gone out right after supper to peer up at the signs in front of the apartment houses in the neighborhood, looking for a place just big enough for her and Bub. A place where the rent was low enough so that she wouldn't come home from work some night to find a long sheet of white paper stuck under the door: "These premises must be vacated by——" better known as an eviction notice. Get out in five days or be tossed out. Stand by and watch your furniture pile up on the sidewalk. If you could call those broken beds, worn-out springs, old chairs with the stuffing crawling out from under, chipped porcelain-topped kitchen table, flimsy kitchen chairs with broken rungs—if you could call those things furniture. That was an important point—now could you call fire-cracked china from the five-and-dime, and red-handled knives and forks and spoons that were bent and coming apart, could you really call those things furniture?

"Yes," she said firmly. "I want to look at the apartment."

"I'll get a flashlight," he said and went back into his apartment, closing the door behind him so that it made a soft, sucking sound. He said something, but she couldn't hear what it was. The whispering voice inside the apartment stopped and the dog was suddenly quiet.

Then he was back at the door, closing it behind him so it made the same soft, sucking sound. He had a long black flashlight in his hand. And she went up the stairs ahead of him thinking that the rod of its length was almost as black as his hands. The flashlight was a shiny black—smooth and gleaming faintly as the light lay along its length. Whereas the hand that held it was flesh—dull, scarred, worn flesh—no smoothness there. The knuckles were knobs that stood out under the skin, pulled out from hauling ashes, shoveling coal.

But not apparently from using a mop or a broom, for, as she went up and up the steep flight of stairs, she saw that they were filthy, with wastepaper, cigarette butts, the discarded wrappings from packages of snuff, pink ticket stubs from the movie houses. On the landings there were empty gin and whiskey bottles.

She stopped looking at the stairs, stopped peering into the corners of the long hallways, for it was cold, and she began walking faster trying to keep warm. As they completed a flight of stairs and turned to walk up another hall, and then started climbing another flight of stairs, she was aware that the cold increased. The farther up they went, the colder it got. And in summer she supposed it would get hotter and hotter as you went up until when you reached the top floor your breath would be cut off completely.

The halls were so narrow that she could reach out and touch them on either side without having to stretch her arms any distance. When they reached the fourth floor, she thought, instead of her reaching out for the walls, the walls were reaching out for her—bending and swaying toward her in an effort to envelop her. The Super's footsteps behind her were slow, even, steady. She walked a little faster and apparently without hurrying, without even increasing his pace, he was exactly the same distance behind her. In fact his heavy footsteps were a little nearer than before.

She began to wonder how it was that she had gone up the stairs first, why was she leading the way? It was all wrong. He was the one who knew the place, the one who lived here. He should have gone up first. How had he got her to go up the stairs in front of him? She wanted to turn around and see the expression on his face, but she knew if she turned on the stairs like this, her face would be on a level with his; and she wouldn't want to be that close to him.

She didn't need to turn around, anyway; he was staring at her back, her legs, her thighs. She could feel his eyes traveling over her—estimating her, summing her up, wondering about her. As she climbed up the last flight of stairs, she was aware that the skin on her back was crawling with fear. Fear of what? she asked herself. Fear of him, fear of the dark, of the smells in the halls, the high steep stairs, of yourself? She didn't know, and even as she admitted that she didn't know, she felt sweat start pouring from her armpits, dampening her forehead, breaking out in beads on her nose.

The apartment was in the back of the house. The Super fished another flashlight from his pocket which he handed to her before he bent over to unlock the door very quietly. And she thought, everything he does, he does quietly.

She played the beam of the flashlight on the walls. The rooms were small. There was no window in the bedroom. At least she supposed it was the bedroom. She walked over to look at it, and then went inside for a better look. There wasn't a window—just an air shaft and a narrow one at that. She looked around the room, thinking that by the time there was a bed and a chest of drawers in it there'd be barely space enough to walk around in. At that she'd probably bump her knees every time she went past the corner of the bed. She tried to visualize how the room would look and began to wonder why she had already decided to take this room for herself.

It might be better to give it to Bub, let him have a real bed-room to himself for once. No, that wouldn't do. He would swelter in this room in summer. It would be better to have him sleep on the couch in the living room, at least he'd get some air, for there was a window out there, though it wasn't a very big one. She looked out into the living room, trying again to see the window, to see just how much air would come through, how much light there would be for Bub to study by when he came home from school, to determine, too, the amount of air that would reach into the room at night when the window was open, and he was sleeping curled up on the studio couch.

The Super was standing in the middle of the living room. Waiting for her. It wasn't anything that she had to wonder about or figure out. It wasn't by any stretch of the imagination something she had conjured up out of thin air. It was a simple fact. He was waiting for her. She knew it just as she knew she was standing there in that small room. He was holding his flashlight so the beam fell down at his feet. It turned him into a figure of never-ending tallness. And his silent waiting and his appearance of incredible height appalled her.

With the light at his feet like that, he looked as though his head must end somewhere in the ceiling. He simply went up and up into darkness. And he radiated such desire for her that she could feel it. She told herself she was a fool, an idiot, drunk on fear, on fatigue and gnawing worry. Even while she thought it, the hot, choking awfulness of his desire for her pinioned her there so that she couldn't move. It was an aching yearning that filled the apartment, pushed against the walls, plucked at her arms.

She forced herself to start walking toward the kitchen. As she went past him, it seemed to her that he actually did reach one long arm out toward her, his body swaying so that its exagger-ated length almost brushed against her. She really couldn't be certain of it, she decided, and resolutely turned the beam of her flashlight on the kitchen walls.

It isn't possible to read people's minds, she argued. Now the Super was probably not even thinking about her when he was standing there like that. He probably wanted to get back downstairs to read his paper. Don't kid yourself, she thought, he probably can't read, or if he can, he probably doesn't spend any time at it. Well—listen to the radio. That was it, he probably wanted to hear his favorite program and she had thought he was filled with the desire to leap upon her. She was as bad as Granny. Which just went on to prove you couldn't be brought up by someone like Granny without absorbing a lot of nonsense that would spring at you out of nowhere, so to speak, and when you least expected it. All those tales about things that people sensed before they actually happened. Tales that had been handed down and down and down until, if you tried to trace them back, you'd end up God knows where—probably Africa. And Granny had them all at the tip of her tongue.

Yet would wanting to hear a radio program make a man look quite like that? Impatiently she forced herself to inspect the kitchen; holding the light on first one wall, then another. It was no better and no worse than she had anticipated. The sink was battered; and the gas stove was a little rusted. The faint smell of gas that hovered about it suggested a slow, incurable leak somewhere in its connections.

Peering into the bathroom, she saw that the fixtures were old-fashioned and deeply chipped. She thought Methuselah himself might well have taken baths in the tub. Certainly it looked ancient enough, though he'd have had to stick his beard out in the hall while he washed himself, for the place was far too small for a man with a full-grown beard to turn around in. She presumed because there was no window that the vent pipe would serve as a source of nice, fresh, clean air.

One thing about it the rent wouldn't be very much. It couldn't be for a place like this. Tiny hall. Bathroom on the right, kitchen straight ahead; living room to the left of the hall and you had to go through the living room to get to the bedroom. The whole apartment would fit very neatly into just one good-sized room.

She was conscious that all the little rooms smelt exactly alike. It was a mixture that contained the faint persistent odor of gas, of old walls, dusty plaster, and over it all the heavy, sour smell of garbage—a smell that seeped through the dumbwaiter shaft. She started humming under her breath, not realizing she was doing it. It was an old song that Granny used to sing. "Ain't no restin' place for a sinner like me. Like me. Like me." It had a nice recurrent rhythm. "Like me. Like me."

The humming increased in volume as she stood there thinking about the apartment.

There was a queer, muffled sound from the Super in the living room. It startled her so she nearly dropped the flash-light. "What was that?" she said sharply, thinking, My God, suppose I'd dropped it, suppose I'd been left standing here in the dark of this little room, and he'd turned out his light. Suppose he'd started walking toward me, nearer and nearer in the dark. And I could only hear his footsteps, couldn't see him, but could hear him coming closer until I started reaching out in the dark trying to keep him away from me, trying to keep him from touching me—and then—then my hands found him right in front of me—— At the thought she gripped the flash-light so tightly that the long beam of light from it started wavering and dancing over the walls so that the shadows moved —shadow from the light fixture overhead, shadow from the tub, shadow from the very doorway itself—shifting, moving back and forth.

"I cleared my throat," the Super said. His voice had a choked, unnatural sound as though something had gone wrong with his breathing.

She walked out into the hall, not looking at him; opened the door of the apartment and stepping over the threshold, still not looking at him, said, "I've finished looking."

He came out and turned the key in the lock. He kept his back turned toward her so that she couldn't have seen the expression on his face even if she'd looked at him. The lock clicked into place, smoothly. Quietly. She stood there not moving, waiting for him to start down the hall toward the stairs, thinking, Never, so help me, will he walk down those stairs in back of me.

When he didn't move, she said, "You go first." Then he made a slight motion toward the stairs with his flashlight indicating that she was to precede him. She shook her head very firmly.

"Think you'll take it?" he asked.

"I don't know yet. I'll think about it going down."

When he finally started down the hall, it seemed to her that he had stood there beside her for days, weeks, months, willing her to go down the stairs first. She followed him, thinking, It wasn't my imagination when I got that feeling at the sight of him standing there in the living room; otherwise, why did he have to go through all that rigamarole of my going down the stairs ahead of him? Like going through the motions of a dance; you first; no, you first; but you see, you'll spoil the pattern if you don't go first; but I won't go first, you go first; but no, it'll spoil the——

She was aware that they'd come up the stairs much faster than they were going down. Was she going to take the apartment? The price wouldn't be too high from the looks of it and by being careful she and Bub could manage—by being very, very careful. White paint would fix the inside of it up; not exactly fix it up, but keep it from being too gloomy, shove the darkness back a little.

Then she thought, Layers and layers of paint won't fix that apartment. It would always smell; finger marks and old stains would come through the paint; the very smell of the wood itself would eventually win out over the paint. Scrubbing wouldn't help any. Then there were these dark, narrow halls, the long flights of stairs, the Super himself, that woman on the first floor.

Or she could go on living with Pop. And Lil. Bub would learn to like the taste of gin, would learn to smoke, would learn in fact a lot of other things that Lil could teach him—things that Lil would think it amusing to teach him. Bub at eight could get a liberal education from Lil, for she was home all day and Bub got home from school a little after three.

You've got a choice a yard wide and ten miles long. You can sit down and twiddle your thumbs while your kid gets a free education from your father's blowsy girl friend. Or you can take this apartment. The tall gentleman who is the superintendent is supposed to rent apartments, fire the furnace, sweep the halls, and that's as far as he's supposed to go. If he tries to include making love to the female tenants, why, this is New York City in the year 1944, and as yet there's no grass growing in the streets and the police force still functions. Certainly you can holler loud enough so that if the gentleman has some kind of dark designs on you and tries to carry them out, a cop will eventually rescue you. That's that.

As for the lady with the snake eyes, you're supposed to be renting the top-floor apartment and if she went with the apartment the sign out in front would say so. Three rooms and snake charmer for respectable tenant. No extra charge for the snake charmer. Seeing as the sign didn't say so, it stood to reason if the snake charmer tried to move in, she could take steps—whatever the hell that meant.

Her high-heeled shoes made a clicking noise as she went down the stairs, and she thought, Yes, take steps like these. It was all very well to reason light-heartedly like that; to kid herself along—there was no explaining away the instinctive, immediate fear she had felt when she first saw the Super. Granny would have said, "Nothin' but evil, child. Some folks so full of it you can feel it comin' at you—oozin' right out of their skins."

She didn't believe things like that and yet, looking at his tall, gaunt figure going down that last flight of stairs ahead of her, she half-expected to see horns sprouting from behind his ears; she wouldn't have been greatly surprised if, in place of one of the heavy work shoes on his feet, there had been a cloven hoof that twitched and jumped as he walked so slowly down the stairs.

Outside the door of his apartment, he stopped and turned toward her.

"What's the rent?" she asked, not looking at him, but looking past him at the One A printed on the door of his apartment. The gold letters were filled with tiny cracks, and she thought that in a few more years they wouldn't be distinguishable from the dark brown of the door itself. She hoped the rent would be so high she couldn't possibly take it.

"Twenty-nine fifty."

He wants me to take it, she thought. He wants it so badly that he's bursting with it. She didn't have to look at him to know it; she could feel him willing it. What difference does it make to him? Yet it was of such obvious importance that if she hesitated just a little longer, he'd be trembling. No, she decided, not that apartment. Then she thought Bub would look cute learning to drink gin at eight.

"I'll take it," she said grimly.

"You wanta leave a deposit?" he asked.

She nodded, and he opened his door, standing aside to let her go past him. There was a dim light burning in the small hall inside and she saw that the hall led into a living room.

She didn't wait for an invitation, but walked on into the living room. The dog had been lying near the radio that stood under a window at the far side of the room. He got up when he saw her, walking toward her with his head down, his tail between his legs; walking as though he were drawn toward her irresistibly, even though he knew that at any moment he would be forced to stop. Though he was a police dog, his hair had such a worn, rusty look that he resembled a wolf more than a dog. She saw that he was so thin, his great haunches and the small bones of his ribs were sharply outlined against his skin. As he got nearer to her, he got excited and she could hear his breathing.

"Lie down," the Super said.

The dog moved back to the window, shrinking and walking in such a way that she thought if he were human he'd walk backward in order to see and be able to dodge any unexpected blow. He lay down calmly enough and looked at her, but he couldn't control the twitching of his nose; he looked, too, at the Super as though he were wondering if he could possibly cross the room and get over to her without being seen.

The Super sat down in front of an old office desk, found a receipt pad, picked up a fountain pen and, carefully placing a blotter in front of him, turned toward her. "Name?" he asked.

She swallowed an impulse to laugh. There was something so solemn about the way he'd seated himself, grasping the pen firmly, moving the pad in front of him to exactly the right angle, opening a big ledger book whose pages were filled with line after line of heavily inked writing that she thought he's acting like a big businessman about to transact a major deal.

"Mrs. Lutie Johnson. Present address 2370 Seventh Avenue." Opening her pocketbook she took out a ten-dollar bill and handed it to him. Ten whole dollars that it had taken a good many weeks to save. By the time she had moved in here and paid the balance which would be due on the rent, her savings would have disappeared. But it would be worth it to be living in a place of her own.

He wrote with a painful slowness, concentrating on each letter, having difficulty with the numbers twenty-three seventy. He crossed it out and bit his lip. "What was that number?" he asked.

"Twenty-three seventy," she repeated, thinking perhaps it would be simpler to write it down for him. At the rate he was going, it would take him all of fifteen minutes to write ten dollars and then figure out the difference between ten dollars and twenty-nine dollars which would in this case constitute that innocuous looking phrase, "the balance due." She shouldn't be making fun of him, very likely he had taught himself to read and write after spending a couple of years in grammar school where he undoubtedly didn't learn anything. He looked to be in his fifties, but it was hard to tell.

It irritated her to stand there and watch him go through the slow, painful process of forming the letters. She wanted to get out of the place, to get back to Pop's house, plan the packing, get hold of a moving man. She looked around the room idly. The floor was uncarpeted—a terrible-looking floor. Rough and splintered. There was a sofa against the long wall; its upholstery marked by a greasy line along the back. All the people who had sat on it from the time it was new until the time it had passed through so many hands it finally ended up here must have ground their heads along the back of it.

Next to the sofa there was an overstuffed chair and she drew her breath in sharply as she looked at it, for there was a woman sitting in it, and she had thought that she and the dog and the Super were the only occupants of the room. How could anyone sit in a chair and melt into it like that? As she looked, the shapeless small dark woman in the chair got up and bowed to her without speaking.

Lutie nodded her head in acknowledgment of the bow, thinking, That must be the woman I heard whispering. The woman sat down in the chair again. Melting into it. Because the dark brown dress she wore was almost the exact shade of the dark brown of the upholstery and because the overstuffed chair swallowed her up until she was scarcely distinguishable from the chair itself. Because, too, of a shrinking withdrawal in her way of sitting as though she were trying to take up the least possible amount of space. So that after bowing to her Lutie completely forgot the woman was in the room, while she went on studying its furnishings.

No pictures, no rugs, no newspapers, no magazines, nothing to suggest anyone had ever tried to make it look homelike.

Not quite true, for there was a canary huddled in an ornate birdcage in the corner. Looking at it, she thought, Everything in the room shrinks: the dog, the woman, even the canary, for it had only one eye open as it perched on one leg. Opposite the sofa an overornate table shone with varnish. It was a very large table with intricately carved claw feet and looking at it she thought, That's the kind of big ugly furniture white women love to give to their maids. She turned to look at the shapeless little woman because she was almost certain the table was hers.

The woman must have been looking at her, for when Lutie turned the woman smiled; a toothless smile that lingered while she looked from Lutie to the table.

"When you want to move in?" the Super asked, holding out the receipt.

"This is Tuesday—do you think you could have the place ready by Friday?"

"Easy," he said. "Some special color you want it painted?"

"White. Make all the rooms white," she said, studying the receipt. Yes, he had it figured out correctly—balance due, nineteen fifty. He had crossed out his first attempt at the figures. Evidently nines were hard for him to make. And his name was William Jones. A perfectly ordinary name. A highly suitable name for a superintendent. Nice and normal. Easy to remember. Easy to spell. Only the name didn't fit him. For he was obviously unusual, extraordinary, abnormal. Everything about him was the exact opposite of his name. He was standing up now looking at her, eating her up with his eyes.

She took a final look around the room. The whispering woman seemed to be holding her breath; the dog was dying with the desire to growl or whine, for his throat was working. The canary, too, ought to be animated with some desperate emotion, she thought, but he had gone quietly to sleep. Then she forced herself to look directly at the Super. A long hard look, malignant, steady, continued. Thinking, That'll fix you, Mister William Jones, but, of course, if it was only my imagination upstairs, it isn't fair to look at you like this. But just in case some dark leftover instinct warned me of what was on your mind—just in case it made me know you were snuffing on my trail, slathering, slobbering after me like some dark hound of hell seeking me out, tonguing along in back of me, this look, my fine feathered friend, should give you much food for thought.

She closed her pocketbook with a sharp, clicking final sound that made the Super's eyes shift suddenly to the ceiling as though seeking out some pattern in the cracked plaster. The dog's ears straightened into sharp points; the canary opened one eye and the whispering woman almost showed her gums again, for her mouth curved as though she were about to smile.

Lutie walked quickly out of the apartment, pushed the street door open and shivered as the cold air touched her. It had been hot in the Super's apartment, and she paused a second to push her coat collar tight around her neck in an effort to make a barrier against the wind howling in the street outside. Now that she had this apartment, she was just one step farther up on the ladder of success. With the apartment Bub would be standing a better chance, for he'd be away from Lil.

Inside the building the dog let out a high shrill yelp. Immediately she headed for the street, thinking he must have kicked it again. She paused for a moment at the corner of the building, bracing herself for the full blast of the wind that would hit her head-on when she turned the corner.

"Get fixed up, dearie?" Mrs. Hedges' rich voice asked from the street-floor window.

She nodded at the bandannaed head in the window and flung herself into the wind, welcoming its attack, aware as she walked along that the woman's hard flat eyes were measuring her progress up the street.

Chapter 2

A CROWD OF PEOPLE surged in to the Eighth Avenue express at 59th Street. By elbowing other passengers in the back, by pushing and heaving, they forced their bodies into the coaches, making room for themselves where no room had existed before. As the train gathered speed for the long run to 125th Street, the passengers settled down into small private worlds, thus creating the illusion of space between them and their fellow passengers. The worlds were built up behind newspapers and magazines, behind closed eyes or while staring at the varicolored show cards that bordered the coaches.

Lutie Johnson tightened her clutch on an overhead strap, her tall long-legged body swaying back and forth as the train rocked forward toward its destination. Like some of the other passengers, she was staring at the advertisement directly in front of her and as she stared at it she became absorbed in her own thoughts. So that she, too, entered a small private world which shut out the people tightly packed around her.

For the advertisement she was looking at pictured a girl with incredible blond hair. The girl leaned close to a dark-haired, smiling man in a navy uniform. They were standing in front of a kitchen sink—a sink whose white porcelain surface gleamed under the train lights. The faucets looked like silver. The linoleum floor of the kitchen was a crisp black-and-white pattern that pointed up the sparkle of the room. Casement windows. Red geraniums in yellow pots.

It was, she thought, a miracle of a kitchen. Completely different from the kitchen of the 116th Street apartment she had moved into just two weeks ago. But almost exactly like the one she had worked in in Connecticut.

So like it that it might have been the same kitchen where she had washed dishes, scrubbed the linoleum floor and waxed it afterward. Then gone to sit on the small porch outside the kitchen, waiting for the floor to dry and wondering how much longer she would have to stay there. At the time it was the only job she could get. She had thought of it as a purely temporary one, but she had ended up by staying two years—thus earning the money for Jim and Bub to live on.

Every month when she got paid she walked to the postoffice and mailed the money to Jim. Seventy dollars. Jim and Bub could eat on that and pay the interest on the mortgage. On her first trip to the postoffice, she realized she had never seen a street like that main street in Lyme. A wide street lined with old elm trees whose branches met high overhead in the center of the street. In summer the sun could just filter through the leaves, so that by the time its rays reached the street, it made a pattern like the lace on expensive nightgowns. It was the most beautiful street she had ever seen, and finally she got so she would walk to the little postoffice hating the street, wishing that she could get back to Jamaica, back to Jim and Bub and the small frame house.

In winter the bare branches of the trees made a pattern against the sky that was equally beautiful in snow or rain or cold, clear sunlight. Sometimes she took Little Henry Chandler to the postoffice with her and she couldn't help thinking that it wasn't right. He didn't need her and Bub did. But Bub had to do without her.

And because Little Henry Chandler's father manufactured paper towels and paper napkins and paper handkerchiefs, why, even when times were hard, he could afford to hire a Lutie Johnson so his wife could play bridge in the afternoon while Lutie Johnson looked after Little Henry. Because as Little Henry's father used to say, "Even when times are hard, thank God, people have got to blow their noses and wipe their hands and faces and wipe their mouths. Not quite so many as before, but enough so that I don't have to worry."

Her grip on the subway strap tightened until the hard enameled surface cut into her hand and she relaxed her hand and then tightened it. Because that kitchen sink in the advertisement or one just like it was what had wrecked her and Jim. The sink had belonged to someone else—she'd been washing someone else's dishes when she should have been home with Jim and Bub. Instead she'd cleaned another woman's house and looked after another woman's child while her own marriage went to pot; breaking up into so many little pieces it couldn't be put back together again, couldn't even be patched into a vague resemblance of its former self.

Yet what else could she have done? It was her fault, really, that they lost their one source of income. And Jim couldn't get a job, though he hunted for one—desperately, eagerly, anxiously. Walking from one employment agency to another; spending long hours in the musty agency waiting-rooms, reading old newspapers. Waiting, waiting, waiting to be called up for a job. He would come home shivering from the cold, saying, "God damn white people anyway. I don't want favors. All I want is a job. Just a job. Don't they know if I knew how I'd change the color of my skin?"

There was the interest to be paid on the mortgage. It didn't amount to much, but they didn't have anything to pay it with. So she answered an advertisement she saw in the paper. The ad said it was a job for an unusual young woman because it was in the country and most help wouldn't stay. "Seventy-five dollars a month. Modern house. Own room and bath. Small child."

She sat down and wrote a letter the instant she saw it; not telling Jim, hoping against hope that she would get it. It didn't say "white only," so she started off by saying that she was colored. And an excellent cook, because it was true—anyone who could fix good meals on practically no money at all was an excellent cook. An efficient housekeeper—because it was easy to keep their house shining, so she shouldn't have any trouble with a "modern" one. It was a good letter, she thought, holding it in her hand a little way off from her as she studied it—nice neat writing, no misspelled words, careful margins, pretty good English. She was suddenly grateful to Pop. He'd known what he was doing when he insisted on her finishing high school. She addressed the envelope, folded the letter, and put it inside the envelope.

She was about to seal it when she remembered that she didn't have any references. She couldn't get a job without them, and as she'd never really had a job, why, she didn't have any way of getting a reference. Somehow she had been so sure she could have got the job in the ad. Seventy-five dollars a month would have meant they could have saved the house; Jim would have got over that awful desperate feeling, that bitterness that was eating him up; and there wouldn't have been any need to apply for relief.

Mrs. Pizzini. That was it. She'd go to Mrs. Pizzini where they bought their vegetables. They owed her a bill, and when she explained that this job would mean the bill would be paid, why, Mrs. Pizzini would write her out a reference.

Business was slow and Mrs. Pizzini had plenty of time to listen to Lutie's story, to study the advertisement in the paper, to follow the writing on Lutie's letter to Mrs. Henry Chandler, line by line, almost tracing the words on the page with her stubby fingers.

"Very good," she said when she finished reading it. "Nice job." She handed the letter and the newspaper to Lutie. "Me and Joe don't write so good. But my daughter that teaches school, she'll write for me. You can have tomorrow."

And the next day Mrs. Pizzini stopped weighing potatoes for a customer long enough to go in the back of the vegetable store and bring the letter out carefully wrapped up in brown paper to keep it clean. Lutie peeled off the brown paper and read the letter through quickly. It was a fine letter, praising her for being hard-working and honest and intelligent; it said that the writer hated to lose Lutie, for she'd worked for her for two years. It was signed "Isabel Pizzini."

The handwriting was positively elegant, she thought, written with a fine pen and black ink on nice thick white paper. She looked at the address printed on the top and then turned to stare at Mrs. Pizzini in astonishment, because that part of Jamaica was the section where the houses were big and there was lawn around them and evergreen trees grew in thick clusters around the houses.

Mrs. Pizzini nodded her head. "My daughter is a very smart woman."

And then Lutie remembered the letter in her hand. "I can't ever thank you," she said.

Mrs. Pizzini's lean face relaxed in a smile, "It's all right. You're a nice girl. Always known it." She walked toward her waiting customer and then, hesitating for the barest fraction of a second, turned back to Lutie. "Listen," she said. "It's best that the man do the work when the babies are young. And when the man is young. Not good for the woman to work when she's young. Not good for the man."

Curiously enough, though she only half-heard what Mrs. Pizzini was saying, she remembered it. Off and on for the past six years she had remembered it. At the time, she hurried home from the vegetable store to put the precious reference in the letter to Mrs. Henry Chandler and mail it.

After she had dropped it in the mail box on the corner, she got to thinking about the Pizzinis. Who would have thought that the old Italian couple who ran the vegetable store would be living in a fine house in a fine neighborhood? How had they managed to do that on the nickels and dimes they took in selling lettuce and grapefruit? She wanted to tell Jim about it, but she couldn't without revealing how she knew where they lived. They had a fine house and they had sent their daughter to college, and yet Mrs. Pizzini had admitted she herself "couldn't write so good." She couldn't read so good either, Lutie thought. If she could find out how the Pizzinis had managed, it might help her and Jim.

Then she forgot about them, for Mrs. Chandler wrote to her sending the train fare to Lyme, telling her what train to take. When she showed Jim the letter, she was bursting with pride, filled with a jubilance she hadn't felt in months because now they could keep the house. And she need no longer feel guilty about having been responsible for losing the State children that had been their only source of income.

"How'm I going to look after Bub and him only two?" he asked, frowning, handing the letter back to her, not looking at her.

Even on the day she was to leave he was sullen. Not talking. Frowning. Staring off into space. He came into the bedroom where she was putting carefully ironed clothes into her suitcase. He stood in front of the window and looked out at the street, his back turned to her, his hands in his pockets as he told her he wouldn't be going to the station with her.

"We can't afford that extra dime for carfare," he explained briefly.

So she went by herself. And feeling the suitcase bump against her legs when she walked down the long ramp at Grand Central to get on the train, she wished that Jim had been along to carry it. So that she could have kissed him good-bye there in the train shed and thus carried the memory of his lips right onto the train with her—so that it could have stayed with her those first few days in Lyme, helping her to remember why she had taken the job. If he'd come to the train with her, he would have lost that pretended indifference; the sight of her actually getting on the train would have broken down the wall of reserve he had built around himself. Instead of that quick hard peck at her forehead, he would have put his arms around her and really kissed her. Instead of holding his body rigid, keeping his arms hanging limp and relaxed at his sides, he would have squeezed her close to him.

As the train left the city, she stopped thinking about him, not forgetting him, but thrusting him far back in her mind because she was going to a new strange place and she didn't want to get off the train wrapped in gloom, and that's exactly what would happen if she kept on thinking about Jim. It was important that Mrs. Henry Chandler should like her at sight, so Lutie carefully examined the countryside as the train went along, concentrating on it to shut out the picture of Jim's tall figure.

There was low, marshy land on each side of the train tracks. Where the land was like that, there were very few houses. She noticed that near the cities the houses were small and mean-looking, for they were built close to the railroad tracks. In Bridgeport the houses were blackened with soot and smoke from the factories. Then the train stopped in New Haven and stayed there for all of ten minutes. She looked at the timetable and saw that it was a scheduled stop for that length of time. Saybrook was the next stop. That's where she was to get off. And she began to worry. How would Mrs. Chandler recognize her? How would she recognize Mrs. Chandler? Suppose they missed each other. What would she do stranded in some little jerk-water town? Mrs. Chandler had said in her letter that she lived in Lyme, and Lutie began to wonder how she could get to Lyme if Mrs. Chandler didn't meet her or missed her at the station.

But almost the instant she stepped on the platform at Saybrook, a young blond woman came toward her smiling and saying, "Hello, there. I'm Mrs. Chandler. You must be Lutie Johnson."

Lutie looked around the platform. Very few people had got off the train, and then she wanted to laugh. She needn't have worried about Mrs. Chandler recognizing her; there wasn't another colored person in sight.

"The car's over there." Mrs. Chandler waved in the direction of a station wagon parked in the dirt road near the platform.

Walking toward the car, Lutie studied Mrs. Chandler covertly and thought, What she's got on makes everything I'm wearing look cheap. This black coat fits too tightly and the velvet collar is all wrong, just like these high-heeled shoes and thin stockings and this wide-brimmed hat. For Mrs. Chandler wore ribbed stockings made of very fine cotton and flat-heeled moccasins of a red-brown leather that caught the light. She had on a loose-fitting tweed coat and no hat. Lutie, looking at the earrings in her ears, decided that they were real pearls and thought, Everything she has on cost a lot of money, yet she isn't very much older than I am—not more than a year or so.

Lutie didn't say anything on the ride to Lyme, for she was thinking too hard. Mrs. Chandler pointed out places as they rode along. "The Connecticut River," she said with a wave of her hand toward the water under the bridge they crossed. They turned off the road shortly after they crossed the river, to go for almost a mile on a country road where the trees grew so thickly Lutie began to wonder if the Chandlers lived in a forest.

Then they entered a smaller road where there were big gates and a sign that said "private road." The road turned and twisted through thick woods until finally they reached a large open space where there was a house. Lutie stared at it, catching her lip between her teeth; it wasn't that it was so big; there were houses in certain parts of Jamaica that were just as big as this one, but there weren't any so beautiful. She never quite got over that first glimpse of the outside of the house—so gracious with such long low lines, its white paint almost sparkling in the sun and the river very blue behind the house.

"Would you like to sort of go through the inside of the house before I show you your room?" Mrs. Chandler asked.

"Yes, ma'am," Lutie said quietly. And wondered how she had been able to say "yes, ma'am" so neatly and so patly. Some part of her mind must have had it already, must have already mapped out the way she was to go about keeping this job for as long as was necessary by being the perfect maid. Patient and good-tempered and hard-working and more than usually bright.

Later she was to learn that Mrs. Chandler's mother and father regarded this house as being very small. "The children's house." The very way they said it told her they were used to enormous places ten times the size of this and that they thought this doll-house affair cute and just right for children for a few years. Mr. Chandler's father never commented on it one way or the other. So it was impossible for Lutie to tell what he thought about it when he came to stay for an occasional week-end.

But to Lutie the house was a miracle, what with the four big bedrooms, each one with its own bath; the nursery that was as big as the bedrooms, and under the nursery a room and bath that belonged to her. On top of that there was a living room, a dining room, a library, a laundry. Taken all together it was like something in the movies, what with the size of the rooms and the big windows that brought the river and the surrounding woods almost into the house. She had never seen anything like it before.

That first day when she walked into Mrs. Chandler's bedroom her breath had come out in an involuntary "Oh!"

"You like it?" Mrs. Chandler asked, smiling.

Lutie nodded and then remembered and said, "Yes, ma'am." She looked at the room, thinking there wasn't any way she could say what this bedroom looked like to her when all her life she had slept on couches in living rooms, in cubicles that were little more than entrances to and exits from other rooms that were rented out to roomers; when the first real bedroom she ever had was that small one in Jamaica, where if you weren't careful you would bump your head on the low-hanging ceiling, for the dormer window only raised the ceiling right where the window was.

No, she decided, there wasn't any way to explain what this room looked like to her. It ran across one whole end of the house so that windows looked out on the river, out on the gardens in front, out on the woods at the side. It was covered from wall to wall with thick red carpet and right near the four-poster bed was a round white rug—a rug with pile so deep it looked like fur. Muted chintz draperies gleamed softly at the windows, formed the petticoat on the bed, covered the chaise longue in front of the windows that faced the river and the pair of chairs drawn up near the fireplace.

The rest of the house was just as perfect as Mrs. Chandler's bedroom. Even her room—the maid's room with its maple furniture and vivid draperies—that, too, was perfect. Little Henry Chandler, who was two years older than Bub, was also perfect —that is, he wasn't spoiled or anything. Just a nice, happy kid, liking her at once, always wanting to be with her. The Chandlers called him Little Henry because his father's name was Henry. She thought it funny at first, because colored people always called their children "Junior" or "Sonnie" when the kid's name was the same as his father's. But she had to admit that calling a kid Little Henry gave him a certain dignity and a status all his own, while it prevented confusion, for there was no mistaking whom you were talking about.

Yes. The whole thing was perfect. Mr. Chandler was young and attractive and obviously made plenty of money. Yet after six months of living there she was uneasily conscious that there was something wrong. She wasn't too sure that Mrs. Chandler was overfond of Little Henry; she never held him on her lap or picked him up and cuddled him the way mothers do their children. She was always pushing him away from her.

Mr. Chandler drank too much. Most people wouldn't have noticed it, but having lived with Pop who had an unquenchable thirst it was easy for her to recognize all the signs of a hard drinker. Mr. Chandler's hands were shaking when he came down for breakfast and he had to have a pick-up before he could even face a cup of coffee. When he came in the house at night, the first thing he did was to get himself a good-sized drink. It was almost impossible for her to keep full bottles in the liquor cabinet, their contents disappeared in no time at all.

"Guess Lutie forgot to put a new supply in the bar," Mr. Chandler would say when she came in in answer to his ring.

"Yes, sir," she would say quietly and go to get more bottles.

The funny thing about it was that Mrs. Chandler never noticed. After a while Lutie discovered that Mrs. Chandler never noticed anything about Mr. Chandler anyway. Yet she was awfully nice; she was always laughing; she had a great many young friends who dressed just like she did—some of them even had small children about the age of Little Henry.

But she didn't like Mrs. Chandler's friends much. They came to the house to luncheon parties or to bridge parties in the afternoon. Either they ate like horses or they didn't eat at all, because they were afraid they would get too fat. And she never could decide which irritated her the most, to see them gulp down the beautiful food she had fixed, eating it so fast they really didn't taste it, or to see them toy with it, pushing it around on their plates.

Whenever she entered a room where they were, they stared at her with a queer, speculative look. Sometimes she caught snatches of their conversation about her. "Sure, she's a wonderful cook. But I wouldn't have any good-looking colored wench in my house. Not with John. You know they're always making passes at men. Especially white men." And then, "Now I wonder——"

After that she continued to wait on them quietly, efficiently, but she wouldn't look at them—she looked all around them. It didn't make her angry at first. Just contemptuous. They didn't know she had a big handsome husband of her own; that she didn't want any of their thin unhappy husbands. But she wondered why they all had the idea that colored girls were whores.

It was, she discovered slowly, a very strange world that she had entered. With an entirely different set of values. It made her feel that she was looking through a hole in a wall at some enchanted garden. She could see, she could hear, she spoke the language of the people in the garden, but she couldn't get past the wall. The figures on the other side of it loomed up life-size and they could see her, but there was this wall in between which prevented them from mingling on an equal footing. The people on the other side of the wall knew less about her than she knew about them.

She decided it wasn't just because she was a maid; it was because she was colored. No one assumed that the young girl from the village who came in to help when they had big dinner parties would eagerly welcome any advances made toward her by the male guests. Even the man who mowed the lawn and washed the windows and weeded the garden didn't move behind a wall that effectively and automatically placed him in some previously prepared classification. One day when he was going to New Haven, Mrs. Chandler drove him to the railroad station in Saybrook, and when he got out of the car Lutie saw her shake hands with him just as though he had been an old friend or one of her departing week-end guests.

When she was in high school she had believed that white people wanted their children to be president of the United States; that most of them worked hard with that goal in mind. And if not president—well, perhaps a cabinet member. Even the Pizzinis' daughter had got to be a school-teacher, showing that they, too, had wanted more learning and knowledge in the family.

But these people were different. Apparently a college education was all right, and seemed to have become a necessity even in the business world they talked about all the time. But not important. Mr. Chandler and his friends had gone through Yale and Harvard and Princeton, casually, matter-of-factly, and because they had to. But once these men went into business they didn't read anything but trade magazines and newspapers.

She had watched Mr. Chandler reading the morning newspaper while he ate his breakfast. He riffled through the front pages where the news was, and then almost immediately turned to the financial section. He spent quite a while reading that, and then, if he had time, he would look at the sports pages. And he was through. She could tell by looking at him that the effort of reading had left him a little tired just like Pop or Mrs. Pizzini. Mr. Chandler's father did the same thing. So did the young men who came up from New York to spend the week-end.

No. They didn't want their children to be president or diplomats or anything like that. What they wanted was to be rich —"filthy" rich, as Mr. Chandler called it.

When she brought the coffee into the living room after dinner, the conversation was always the same.

"Richest damn country in the world——"

"Always be new markets. If not here in South America, Africa, India—— Everywhere and anywhere——"

"Hell! Make it while you're young. Anyone can do it——"

"Outsmart the next guy. Think up something before anyone else does. Retire at forty——"

It was a world of strange values where the price of something called Tell and Tell and American Nickel and United States Steel had a direct effect on emotions. When the price went up everybody's spirits soared; if it went down they were plunged in gloom.

After a year of listening to their talk, she absorbed some of the same spirit. The belief that anybody could be rich if he wanted to and worked hard enough and figured it out carefully enough. Apparently that's what the Pizzinis had done. She and Jim could do the same thing, and she thought she saw what had been wrong with them before—they hadn't tried hard enough, worked long enough, saved enough. There hadn't been any one thing they wanted above and beyond everything else. These people had wanted only one thing—more and more money—and so they got it. Some of this new philosophy crept into her letters to Jim.

When she first went to work for the Chandlers, Mrs. Chandler had suggested that, instead of her taking one day off a week, it would be a good idea if she took four days off right together all at once at the end of a month; pointing out that that way Lutie could go home to Jamaica and not have to turn right around and come back. As Lutie listened to the conversations in the Chandlers' house, she came more and more under the influence of their philosophy. As a result she began going home only once in two months, pointing out to Jim how she could save the money she would have spent for train fare.

She soon discovered that the Chandlers didn't spend very much time at home in spite of their big perfect house. They always went out in the evening unless they had guests of their own. After she had been there a year and a half, she discovered, too, that Mrs. Chandler paid a lot more attention to other women's husbands than she did to her own. After a dinner party, Mrs. Chandler would walk through the garden with someone else's husband, showing him the river view, talking to him with an animation she never showed when talking to Mr. Chandler. And, Lutie observed from the kitchen window, leaning much too close to him.

Once, when Lutie went into the living room, Mrs. Chandler was sitting on the window-seat with one of the dinner guests and his arms were tight around her and he was kissing her. Mr. Chandler came right in behind Lutie, so that he saw the same thing. The expression on his face didn't change—only his lips went into a straight thin line.

Two weeks before Christmas, Mrs. Chandler's mother came for a visit. A tall, thin woman with cold gray eyes and hair almost exactly the same color as her eyes. She took one look at Lutie and hardly let her get out of the door before she was leaning across the dining-room table to say in a clipped voice that carried right out into the kitchen: "Now I wonder if you're being wise, dear. That girl is unusually attractive and men are weak. Besides, she's colored and you know how they are——"

Lutie moved away from the swinging door to stand way over by the stove so she couldn't hear the rest of it. Queer how that was always cropping up. Here she was highly respectable, married, mother of a small boy, and, in spite of all that, knowing all that, these people took one look at her and immediately got that now-I-wonder look. Apparently it was an automatic reaction of white people—if a girl was colored and fairly young, why, it stood to reason she had to be a prostitute. If not that —at least sleeping with her would be just a simple matter, for all one had to do was make the request. In fact, white men wouldn't even have to do the asking because the girl would ask them on sight.

She grew angrier as she thought about it. Of course, none of them could know about your grandmother who had brought you up, she said to herself. And ever since you were big enough to remember the things that people said to you, had said over and over, just like a clock ticking, "Lutie, baby, don't you never let no white man put his hands on you. They ain't never willin' to let a black woman alone. Seems like they all got a itch and a urge to sleep with 'em. Don't you never let any of 'em touch you."

Something that was said so often and with such gravity it had become a part of you, just like breathing, and you would have preferred crawling in bed with a rattlesnake to getting in bed with a white man. Mrs. Chandler's friends and her mother couldn't possibly know that, couldn't possibly imagine that you might have a distrust and a dislike of white men far deeper than the distrust these white women had of you. Or know that, after hearing their estimation of you, nothing in the world could ever force you to be even friendly with a white man.

And again she thought of the barrier between her and these people. The funny part of it was she was willing to trust them and their motives without questioning, but the instant they saw the color of her skin they knew what she must be like; they were so confident about what she must be like they didn't need to know her personally in order to verify their estimate.

The night before Christmas Mr. Chandler's brother arrived —a tall, sardonic-looking man. His name was Jonathan, and Mrs. Chandler smiled at him with a warmth Lutie had never seen on her face before. Mr. Chandler didn't have much to say to him and Mrs. Chandler's mother pointedly ignored him.

Lutie heard them arguing in the living room long after she had gone to bed. An argument that grew more and more violent, with Mrs. Chandler screaming and Mr. Chandler shouting and Mrs. Chandler's mother bellowing any time the other voices stopped. She drifted off to sleep, thinking that it was nice to know white people had loud common fights just like colored people.

Right after breakfast, everybody went into the living room to see the Christmas tree and open their presents. Lutie went along, too, with Little Henry by the hand. It was a big tree, and even though Lutie had helped Mrs. Chandler's mother decorate it the day before, she couldn't get over how it looked standing there in front of the river windows, going up and up, all covered with tinsel and stars and brilliantly colored baubles.

Everybody got down on the floor near the tree to sort out and open the presents. Lutie happened to look up because Jonathan Chandler had moved away from the tree, and she wondered if he was looking for an ash tray because there was one right on the small table near the tree and he didn't need to go all the way across the room to find one. So she saw him reach into the drawer in the secretary. Reach in and get Mr. Chandler's revolver and stand there a moment fingering it. He walked back toward the tree, and she couldn't figure out whether he had put the gun back or not. Because he had closed the drawer quickly. She couldn't see his hand because he had it held a little in back of him.

Mrs. Chandler was holding out a package to Lutie and she looked at her to see why she didn't take it and then followed the direction of Lutie's eyes. So that she, too, became aware that Jonathan Chandler was walking right toward the Christmas tree and saw him stop just a little way away from it.

Lutie knew suddenly what he was going to do and she started to get up from the floor to try and stop him. But she was too late. He drew the gun out quickly and fired it. Held it under his ear and pulled the trigger.

After that there was so much confusion that Lutie only remembered a few things here and there. Mrs. Chandler started screaming and went on and on and on until Mr. Chandler said roughly, "Shut up, God damn you!"

She stopped then. But it was worse after she stopped because she just sat there on the floor staring into space.

Mrs. Chandler's mother kept saying: "The nerve of him. The nerve of him. Deliberately embarrassing us. And on Christmas morning, too."

Mr. Chandler poured drink after drink of straight whiskey and then, impatiently shoving the small glass aside, raised the bottle to his lips letting its contents literally run down his throat. Lutie watched him, wondering why none of them said a word about its being a shame; thinking they acted worse and sounded worse than any people she had ever seen before.

Then she forgot about them, for she happened to look down at Little Henry crouching on the floor, his small face so white, so frightened, that she very nearly cried. None of them had given him a thought; they had deserted him as neatly as though they had deposited him on the doorstep of a foundling hospital. She picked him up and held him close to her, letting him get the feel of her arms around him; telling him through her arms that his world had not suddenly collapsed about him, that the strong arms holding him so close were a solid, safe place where he belonged, where he was safe. She made small, comforting noises under her breath until some of the whiteness left his face. Then she carried him out into the kitchen and held him on her lap and rocked him back and forth in her arms until the fright went out of his eyes.

After Mr. Chandler's brother killed himself in the living room, she didn't lose her belief in the desirability of having

money, though she saw that mere possession of it wouldn't
necessarily guarantee happiness. What was more important,
she learned that when one had money there were certain unpleasant things one could avoid—even things like a suicide in
the family.

She never found out what had prompted Jonathan Chandler
to kill himself. She wasn't too interested. But she was interested in the way in which money transformed a suicide she had
seen committed from start to finish in front of her very eyes
into "an accident with a gun." It was done very neatly, too.
Mrs. Chandler's mother simply called Mrs. Chandler's father in
Washington. Lutie overheard the tail-end of the conversation,
"Now you get it fixed up. Oh, yes, you can. He was cleaning
a gun."

And Mr. Chandler talked very quietly but firmly to the local
doctor and to the coroner. It took several rye highballs and
some of the expensive imported cigars, and Lutie could only
conjecture what else, but it ended up as an accident with a gun
on the death certificate. Everybody was sympathetic—so tragic
to have it happen on Christmas morning right in the Chandlers' living room.

However, after the accident both Mr. and Mrs. Chandler
started drinking far too much. And Mrs. Chandler's mother
arrived more and more often to stay two and three weeks at a
time. There were three cars in the garage now instead of two.
And Mrs. Chandler had a personal maid and there was talk
of getting a bigger house. But Mrs. Chandler seemed to care
less and less about everything and anything—even the bridge
games and parties.

She kept buying new clothes. Dresses and coats and suits.
And after wearing them a few times, she would give them to
Lutie because she was tired of looking at them. And Lutie accepted them gravely, properly grateful. The clothes would have
fitted her perfectly, but some obstinacy in her that she couldn't
overcome prevented her from ever wearing them. She mailed
them to Pop's current girl friend, taking an ironic pleasure in
the thought that Mrs. Chandler's beautiful clothes Designed
For Country Living would be showing up nightly in the gin
mill at the corner of Seventh Avenue and 110th Street.

For in those two years with the Chandlers she had learned all about Country Living. She learned about it from the pages of the fat sleek magazines Mrs. Chandler subscribed for and never read. *Vogue, Town and Country, Harper's Bazaar, House and Garden, House Beautiful.* Mrs. Chandler didn't even bother to take them out of their wrappings when they came in the mail, but handed them to Lutie, saying, "Here, Lutie. Maybe you'd like to look at this."

A bookstore in New York kept Mrs. Chandler supplied with all the newest books, but she never read them. Handed them to Lutie still in their wrappings just like the magazines. And Lutie decided that it was almost like getting a college education free of charge. Besides, Mrs. Chandler was really very nice to her. The wall between them wasn't quite so high. Only it was still there, of course.

Sometimes, when she was going to Jamaica, Mrs. Chandler would go to New York. And they would take the same train. On the ride down they would talk—about some story being played up in the newspapers, about clothes or some moving picture.

But when the train pulled into Grand Central, the wall was suddenly there. Just as they got off the train, just as the porter was reaching for Mrs. Chandler's pigskin luggage, the wall suddenly loomed up. It was Mrs. Chandler's voice that erected it. Her voice high, clipped, carrying, as she said, "I'll see you on Monday, Lutie."

There was a firm note of dismissal in her voice so that the other passengers pouring off the train turned to watch the rich young woman and her colored maid; a tone of voice that made people stop to hear just when it was the maid was to report back for work. Because the voice unmistakably established the relation between the blond young woman and the brown young woman.

And it never failed to stir resentment in Lutie. She argued with herself about it. Of course, she was a maid. She had no illusions about that. But would it hurt Mrs. Chandler just once to talk at that moment of parting as though, however incredible it might seem to anyone who was listening, they were friends? Just two people who knew each other and to whom it was only incidental that one of them was white and the other black?

Even while she argued with herself, she was answering in a noncommittal voice, "Yes, ma'am." And took her battered suitcase up the ramp herself, hastening, walking faster and faster, hurrying toward home and Jim and Bub. To spend four days cleaning house and holding Bub close to her and trying to hold Jim close to her, too, in spite of the gap that seemed to have grown a little wider each time she came home.

She had been at the Chandlers exactly two years on the day she got the letter from Pop. She held it in her hand before she opened it. There was something terribly wrong if Pop had gone to all the trouble of writing a letter. If the baby was sick, he would have phoned. Jim couldn't be sick, because Pop would have phoned about that, too. Because he had the number of the Chandlers' telephone. She had given it to him when she first came here to work. Reluctantly she opened the envelope. It was a very short note: "*Dear Lutie: You better come home. Jim's carrying on with another woman. Pop.*"

It was like having the earth suddenly open up so that it turned everything familiar into a crazy upside down position, so that she could no longer find any of the things that had once been hers. And she was filled with fear because she might not ever be able to find them again. She looked at the letter for a third, a fourth, a fifth time, and it still said the same thing. That Jim had fallen for some other woman. And it must be something pretty serious if it so alarmed Pop that he actually wrote her a letter about it. She thought Pop can't suddenly have turned moral—Pop who had lived with so many Mamies and Lauras and Mollies that he must have long since forgotten some of them himself. So it must be that Jim had admitted some kind of permanent attachment for this woman whoever she was.

She thrust the thought away from her and went to tell Mrs. Chandler that she had to go home that very day because the baby was seriously ill. She couldn't bring herself to tell her what the real trouble was because, if Mrs. Chandler was anything like her mother, she took it for granted that all colored people were immoral and Lutie saw no reason for providing further evidence.

On the train she kept remembering Mrs. Pizzini's words: "Not good for the woman to work when she's young. Not good for the man." Queer. Though she hadn't paid too much attention at the time, just remembering the words made her see the whole inside of the vegetable store again. The pale yellow color of the grapefruit, dark green of mustard greens and spinach. The patient brown color of the potatoes. The delicate green of the heads of lettuce. She could see Mrs. Pizzini's dark weather-beaten skin and remembered how Mrs. Pizzini had hesitated and then turned back to say: "It's best that the man do the work when the babies are young."

She forgot that Jim wasn't expecting her as she hurried to the little frame house in Jamaica, not thinking about anything except the need to get there quickly, quickly, before every familiar thing she knew had been destroyed.

Still hurrying, she opened the front door and walked in. Walked into her own house to find there was another woman living there with Jim. A slender, dark brown girl whose eyes shifted crazily when she saw her. The girl was cooking supper and Jim was sitting at the kitchen table watching her.

If he hadn't held her arms, she would have killed the other girl. Even now she could feel rage rise inside her at the very thought. There she had been sending practically all her wages, month after month, keeping only a little for herself; skimping on her visits because of the carfare and because she was trying to save enough money to form a backlog for them when she quit her job. Month after month and that black bitch had been eating the food she bought, sleeping in her bed, making love to Jim.

He forced her into a chair and held her there while the girl packed and got out. When Lutie finally cooled off enough to be able to talk coherently, he only laughed at her. Even when he saw that she was getting into a red rage at the sight of his laughter.

"What did you expect?" he asked. "Maybe you can go on day after day with nothing to do but just cook meals for yourself and a kid. With just enough money to be able to eat and have a roof over your head. But I can't. And I don't intend to."

"Why didn't you say so?" she asked fiercely. "Why did you let me go on working for those white people and not tell me _____"

He only shrugged and laughed. That was all she could get out of him—laughter. What's the use—what's the point—who cares? If even once he had put his arms around her and said he was sorry and asked her to forgive him, she would have stayed. But he didn't. So she called a moving man and had him take all the furniture that was hers. Everything that belonged to her: the scarred bedroom set, the radio, the congoleum rug, a battered studio couch, an easy-chair—and Bub. She wasn't going to leave him behind for Jim to abuse or ignore as he saw fit.

She and Bub went to live with Pop in that crowded, musty flat on Seventh Avenue. She hunted for a job with a grim persistence that was finally rewarded, for two weeks later she went to work as a hand presser in a steam laundry. It was hot. The steam was unbearable. But she forced herself to go to night school—studying shorthand and typing and filing. Every time it seemed as though she couldn't possibly summon the energy to go on with the course, she would remind herself of all the people who had got somewhere in spite of the odds against them. She would think of the Chandlers and their young friends—"It's the richest damn country in the world."

Mrs. Chandler wrote her a long letter and Jim forwarded it to her from Jamaica. "*Lutie dear: We haven't had a decent thing to eat since you left. And Little Henry misses you so much he's almost sick——*" She didn't answer it. She had more problems than Mrs. Chandler and Little Henry had and they could always find somebody to solve theirs if they paid enough.

It took a year and a half before she mastered the typing, because at night she was so tired when she went to the business school on 125th Street she couldn't seem to concentrate on what she was doing. Her back ached and her arms felt as though they had been pulled out of their sockets. But she finally acquired enough speed so that she could take a civil service examination. For she had made up her mind that she wasn't going to wash dishes or work in a laundry in order to earn a living for herself and Bub.

Another year dragged by. A year in which she passed four or five exams each time way down on the list. A year that she spent waiting and waiting for an appointment and taking other exams. Four years of the steam laundry and then she got an appointment as a file clerk.

That kitchen in Connecticut had changed her whole life— that kitchen all tricks and white enamel like this one in the

advertisement. The train roared into 125th Street and she began pushing her way toward the doors, turning to take one last
look at the advertisement as she left the car.

On the platform she hurried toward the downtown side and
elbowed her way toward the waiting local. Only a few minutes and she would be at 116th Street. She didn't have any
illusions about 116th Street as a place to live, but at the moment it represented a small victory—one of a series which were
the result of her careful planning. First the white-collar job,
then an apartment of her own where she and Bub would be
by themselves away from Pop's boisterous friends, away from
Lil with her dyed hair and strident voice, away from the riff-raff
roomers who made it possible for Pop to pay his rent. Even
after living on 116th Street for two weeks, the very fact of being
there was still a victory.

As for the street, she thought, getting up at the approaching
station signs, she wasn't afraid of its influence, for she would
fight against it. Streets like 116th Street or being colored, or a
combination of both with all it implied, had turned Pop into
a sly old man who drank too much; had killed Mom off when
she was in her prime.

In that very apartment house in which she was now living,
the same combination of circumstances had evidently made
the Mrs. Hedges who sat in the street-floor window turn to
running a fairly well-kept whorehouse—but unmistakably a
whorehouse; and the superintendent of the building—well, the
street had pushed him into basements away from light and air
until he was being eaten up by some horrible obsession; and
still other streets had turned Min, the woman who lived with
him, into a drab drudge so spineless and so limp she was like
a soggy dishrag. None of those things would happen to her,
Lutie decided, because she would fight back and never stop
fighting back.

She got off the train, thinking that she never felt really human until she reached Harlem and thus got away from the
hostility in the eyes of the white women who stared at her on
the downtown streets and in the subway. Escaped from the
openly appraising looks of the white men whose eyes seemed
to go through her clothing to her long brown legs. On the
trains their eyes came at her furtively from behind newspapers,

or half-concealed under hatbrims or partly shielded by their hands. And there was a warm, moist look about their eyes that made her want to run.

These other folks feel the same way, she thought—that once they are freed from the contempt in the eyes of the downtown world, they instantly become individuals. Up here they are no longer creatures labeled simply "colored" and therefore all alike. She noticed that once the crowd walked the length of the platform and started up the stairs toward the street, it expanded in size. The same people who had made themselves small on the train, even on the platform, suddenly grew so large they could hardly get up the stairs to the street together. She reached the street at the very end of the crowd and stood watching them as they scattered in all directions, laughing and talking to each other.

Chapter 3

A FTER SHE CAME OUT of the subway, Lutie walked slowly up the street, thinking that having solved one problem there was always a new one cropping up to take its place. Now that she and Bub were living alone, there was no one to look out for him after school. She had thought he could eat lunch at school, for it didn't cost very much—only fifty cents a week.

But after three days of school lunches, Bub protested, "I can't eat that stuff. They give us soup every day. And I hate it."

As soon as she could afford to, she would take an afternoon off from work and visit the school so that she could find out for herself what the menus were like. But until then, Bub would have to eat lunch at home, and that wasn't anything to worry about. It was what happened to him after school that made her frown as she walked along, for he was either in the apartment by himself or playing in the street.

She didn't know which was worse—his being alone in those dreary little rooms or his playing in the street where the least of the dangers confronting him came from the stream of traffic which roared through 116th Street: crosstown buses, postoffice trucks, and newspaper delivery cars that swooped up and down the street turning into the avenues without warning. The traffic was an obvious threat to his safety that he could see and dodge. He was too young to recognize and avoid other dangers in the street. There were, for instance, gangs of young boys who were always on the lookout for small fry Bub's age, because they found young kids useful in getting in through narrow fire-escape windows, in distracting a storekeeper's attention while the gang light-heartedly helped itself to his stock.

Then, in spite of the small, drab apartment and the dent that moving into it had made in her week's pay and the worry about Bub that crept into her thoughts, she started humming under her breath as she went along, increasing her stride so that she was walking faster and faster because the air was crisp and clear and her long legs felt strong and just the motion of walking sent blood bubbling all through her body so that she could feel it. She came to an abrupt halt in the middle of the block because she suddenly remembered that she had completely forgotten to shop for dinner.

The butcher shop that she entered on Eighth Avenue was crowded with customers, so that she had ample time to study the meat in the case in front of her before she was waited on. There wasn't, she saw, very much choice—ham hocks, lamb culls, bright-red beef. Someone had told Granny once that the butchers in Harlem used embalming fluid on the beef they sold in order to give it a nice fresh color. Lutie didn't believe it, but like a lot of things she didn't believe, it cropped up suddenly out of nowhere to leave her wondering and staring at the brilliant scarlet color of the meat. It made her examine the contents of the case with care in order to determine whether there was something else that would do for dinner. No, she decided. Hamburger would be the best thing to get. It cooked quickly, and a half-pound of it mixed with breadcrumbs would go a long way.

The butcher, a fat red-faced man with a filthy apron tied around his enormous stomach, joked with the women lined up at the counter while he waited on them. A yellow cat sitting high on a shelf in back of him blinked down at the customers. One of his paws almost touched the edge of a sign that said "No Credit." The sign was fly-specked and dusty; its edges curling back from heat.

"Kitty had her meat today?" a thin black woman asked as she smiled up at the cat.

"Sure thing," and the butcher roared with laughter, and the women laughed with him until the butcher shop was so full of merriment it sounded as though it were packed with happy, carefree people.

It wasn't even funny, Lutie thought. Yet the women rocked and roared with laughter as though they had heard some tremendous joke, went on laughing until finally there were only low chuckles and an occasional half-suppressed snort of laughter left in them. For all they knew, she thought resentfully, the yellow cat might yet end up in the meat-grinder to emerge as hamburger. Or perhaps during the cold winter months the butcher might round up all the lean, hungry cats that prowled through the streets; herding them into his back room to skin them and grind them up to make more and more hamburger that would be sold way over the ceiling price.

"A half-pound of hamburger," was all she said when the butcher indicated it was her turn to be waited on. A half-pound would take care of tonight's dinner and Bub could have a sandwich of it when he came home for lunch.

She watched the butcher slap the hamburger on a piece of waxed paper; fold the paper twice, and slip the package into a brown paper bag. Handing him a dollar bill, she tucked the paper bag under her arm and held her pocketbook in the other hand so that he would have to put the change down on the counter. She never accepted change out of his hand, and watching him put it on the counter, she wondered why. Because she didn't want to touch his chapped roughened hands? Because he was white and forcing him to make the small extra effort of putting the change on the counter gave her a feeling of power?

Holding the change loosely in her hand, she walked out of the shop and turned toward the grocery store next door, where she paused for a moment in the doorway to look back at 116th Street. The sun was going down in a blaze of brilliant color that bathed the street in a glow of light. It looked, she thought, like any other New York City street in a poor neighborhood. Perhaps a little more down-at-the-heels. The windows of the houses were dustier and there were more small stores on it than on streets in other parts of the city. There were also more children playing in the street and more people walking about aimlessly.

She stepped inside the grocery store, thinking that her apartment would do for the time being, but the next step she should take would be to move into a better neighborhood. As she had been able to get this far without help from anyone, why, all she had to do was plan each step and she could get wherever she wanted to go. A wave of self-confidence swept over her and she thought, I'm young and strong, there isn't anything I can't do.

Her arms were full of small packages when she left Eighth Avenue—the hamburger, a pound of potatoes, a can of peas, a piece of butter. Besides six hard rolls that she bought instead of bread—big rolls with brown crusty outsides. They were good with coffee in the morning and Bub could have one for his lunch tomorrow with the hamburger left over from dinner.

She walked slowly, avoiding the moment when she must enter the apartment and start fixing dinner. She shifted the packages into a more comfortable position and feeling the hard roundness of the rolls through the paper bag, she thought immediately of Ben Franklin and his loaf of bread. And grinned thinking, You and Ben Franklin. You ought to take one out and start eating it as you walk along 116th Street. Only you ought to remember while you eat that you're in Harlem and he was in Philadelphia a pretty long number of years ago. Yet she couldn't get rid of the feeling of self-confidence and she went on thinking that if Ben Franklin could live on a little bit of money and could prosper, then so could she. In spite of the cost of moving the furniture, if she and Bub were very careful they would have more than enough to last until her next pay-day; there might even be a couple of dollars over. If they were very careful.

The glow from the sunset was making the street radiant. The street is nice in this light, she thought. It was swarming with children who were playing ball and darting back and forth across the sidewalk in complicated games of tag. Girls were skipping double dutch rope, going tirelessly through the exact center of a pair of ropes, jumping first on one foot and then the other. All the way from the corner she could hear groups of children chanting, "Down in Mississippi and a bo-bo push! Down in Mississippi and a bo-bo push!" She stopped to watch them, and she wanted to put her packages down on the sidewalk and jump with them; she found her foot was patting the sidewalk in the exact rhythm of their jumping and her hands were ready to push the jumper out of the rope at the word "push."

You'd better get your dinner started, Ben Franklin, she said to herself and walked on past the children who were jumping rope. All up and down the street kids were shining shoes. "Shine, Miss? Shine, Miss?" the eager question greeted her on all sides.

She ignored the shoeshine boys. The weather had changed, she thought. Just last week it was freezing cold and now there was a mildness in the air that suggested early spring and the good weather had brought a lot of people out on the street. Most of the women had been marketing, for they carried bulging shopping bags. She noticed how heavily they walked on feet that obviously hurt despite the wide, cracked shoes they wore. They've been out all day working in the white folks' kitchens, she thought, then they come home and cook and clean for their own families half the night. And again she remembered Mrs. Pizzini's words, "Not good for the woman to work when she's young. Not good for the man." Obviously she had been right, for here on this street the women trudged along overburdened, overworked, their own homes neglected while they looked after someone else's while the men on the street swung along empty-handed, well dressed, and carefree. Or they lounged against the sides of the buildings, their hands in their pockets while they stared at the women who walked past, probably deciding which woman they should select to replace the wife who was out working all day.

And yet, she thought, what else is a woman to do when her man can't get a job? What else had there been for her to do that time Jim couldn't get a job? She didn't know, and she lingered in the sunlight watching a group of kids who were gathered around a boy fishing through a grating in the street. She looked down through the grating, curious to see what odds and ends had floated down under the sidewalk. And again she heard that eager question, "Shine, Miss? Shine, Miss?"

She walked on, thinking, That's another thing. These kids should have some better way of earning money than by shining shoes. It was all wrong. It was like conditioning them beforehand for the rôle they were supposed to play. If they start out young like this shining shoes, they'll take it for granted they've got to sweep floors and mop stairs the rest of their lives.

Just before she reached her own door, she heard the question again, "Shine, Miss?" And then a giggle. "Gosh, Mom, you didn't even know me."

She turned around quickly and she was so startled she had to look twice to be sure. Yes. It was Bub. He was sitting astride a shoeshine box, his round head silhouetted against the brick wall of the apartment house behind him. He was smiling at her, utterly delighted that he had succeeded in surprising her. His head was thrown back and she could see all his even, firm teeth.

In the brief moment it took her to shift all the small packages under her left arm, she saw all the details of the shoeshine box. There was a worn piece of red carpet tacked on the seat of the box. The brassy thumbtacks that held it in place picked up the glow from the sunset so that they sparkled. Ten-cent bottles of shoe polish, a worn shoe brush and a dauber, were neatly lined up on a little shelf under the seat. He had decorated the sides of the box with part of his collection of book matches.

Then she slapped him sharply across the face. His look of utter astonishment made her strike him again—this time more violently, and she hated herself for doing it, even as she lifted her hand for another blow.

"But Mom——" he protested, raising his arm to protect his face.

"You get in the house," she ordered and yanked him to his feet. He leaned over to pick up the shoeshine box and she struck him again. "Leave that thing there," she said sharply, and shook him when he tried to struggle out of her grasp.

Her voice grew thick with rage. "I'm working to look after you and you out here in the street shining shoes just like the rest of these little niggers." And she thought, You know that isn't all there is involved. It's also that Little Henry Chandler is the same age as Bub, and you know Little Henry is wearing gray flannel suits and dark blue caps and long blue socks and fine dark brown leather shoes. He's doing his home work in that big warm library in front of the fireplace. And your kid is out in the street with a shoeshine box. He's wearing his after-school clothes, which don't look too different from the ones he wears to school—shabby knickers and stockings with holes in the heels, because no matter how much you darn and mend he comes right out of his stockings.

It's also that you're afraid that if he's shining shoes at eight, he will be washing windows at sixteen and running an elevator at twenty-one, and go on doing that for the rest of his life. And you're afraid that this street will keep him from finishing high school; that it may do worse than that and get him into some kind of trouble that will land him in reform school because you can't be home to look out for him because you have to work.

"Go on," she said, and pushed him ahead of her toward the door of the apartment house. She was aware that Mrs. Hedges was, as usual, looking out of the window. She shoved Bub harder to make him go faster so they would get out of the way of Mrs. Hedges' eager-eyed stare as fast as possible. But Mrs. Hedges watched their progress all the way into the hall, for she leaned her head so far out of the window her red bandanna looked as though it were suspended in midair.

Going up the stairs with Bub just ahead of her, Lutie thought living here is like living in a tent with everything that goes on inside it open to the world because the flap won't close. And the flap couldn't close because Mrs. Hedges sat at her street-floor window firmly holding it open in order to see what went on inside.

As they climbed up the dark, narrow stairs, darker than ever after the curious brilliance the setting sun had cast over the street, she became aware that Bub was crying. Not really crying. Sobbing. He must have spent a long time making that shoeshine box. Where had he got the money for the polish and the brush? Maybe running errands for the Super, because Bub had made friends with the Super very quickly. She didn't exactly approve of this sudden friendship because the Super was —well, the kindest way to think of him was to call him peculiar.

She remembered quite clearly that she had told him she wanted all the rooms in the apartment painted white. He must have forgotten it, for when she moved in she found that the rooms had been painted blue and rose color and green and yellow. Each room was a different color. The colors made the rooms look even smaller, and she had said instantly, "What awful colors!" The look of utter disappointment on his face had made her feel obligated to find something that she could praise and in seeking for it she saw that the windows had been washed. Which was unusual because one of the first things you had to do when you moved in a place was to scrape the splashes of paint from the windows and then wash them.

So she said quickly, "Oh, the windows have been washed." And when the Super heard the pleased note in her voice, he had looked like a hungry dog that had suddenly been given a bone.

She hurried up the last flight of stairs, fumbling for her keys, pausing in the middle of the hallway to peer inside her pocketbook, so that Bub reached their door before she did. She pushed him away and unlocked the door and the can of peas slipped out from under her arm to roll clumsily along the hall in its brown-paper wrapping. While Bub scrambled after it, she opened the door.

Once inside the apartment he turned and faced her squarely. She wanted to put her arm around him and hug him, for he still had tears in his eyes, but he had obviously been screwing his courage up to the point where he could tell her whatever it was he had on his mind, even though he wasn't certain what her reaction would be. So she turned toward him and instead of hugging him listened to him gravely, trying to tell him by her manner that whatever he had to say was important and she would give it all her attention.

"You said we had to have money. You kept saying it. I was only trying to earn some money by shining shoes," he gulped. Then the words tumbled out, "What's wrong with that?"

She fumbled for an answer, thinking of all the times she had told him no, no candy, for we can't afford it. Or yes, it's only twenty-five cents for the movies, but that twenty-five cents will help pay for the new soles on your shoes. She was always telling him how important it was that people make money and save money—those things she had learned from the Chandlers. Then when he tried to earn some of his own she berated him, slapped him. So that suddenly and with no warning it was all wrong for him to do the very thing that she had continually told him was important and necessary.

She started choosing her words carefully. "It's the way you were trying to earn money that made me mad," she began. Then she leaned down until her face was on a level with his, still talking slowly, still picking her words thoughtfully. "You see, colored people have been shining shoes and washing clothes and scrubbing floors for years and years. White people seem to think that's the only kind of work they're fit to do. The hard work. The dirty work. The work that pays the least." She thought about this small dark apartment they were living in, about 116th Street which was filled to overflowing with people who lived in just such apartments as this, about the white people on the downtown streets who stared at her with open hostility in their eyes, and she started talking swiftly, forgetting to choose her words.

"I'm not going to let you begin at eight doing what white folks figure all eight-year-old colored boys ought to do. For if you're shining shoes at eight, you'll probably be doing the same thing when you're eighty. And I'm not going to have it."

He listened to her with his eyes fixed on her face, not saying anything, concentrating on her words. His expression was so serious that she began to wonder if she should have said that part about white folks. He was awfully young to be told a thing like that, and she wasn't sure she had made her meaning quite clear. She couldn't think of any way to soften it, so she patted him on the shoulder and straightened up and began taking off her hat and coat.

She selected four potatoes from the package she had put on the kitchen table, washed them, found a paring knife, and seating herself at the table began peeling them.

Bub came to stand close beside her, almost but not quite leaning against her as though he was getting strength and protection from his closeness to her. "Mom," he said, "why do white people want colored people shining shoes?"

She turned toward him, completely at a loss as to what to say, for she had never been able to figure it out for herself. She looked down at her hands. They were brown and strong, the fingers were long and well-shaped. Perhaps because she was born with skin that color, she couldn't see anything wrong with it. She was used to it. Perhaps it was a shock just to look at skins that were dark if you were born with a skin that was white. Yet dark skins were smooth to the touch; they were warm from the blood that ran through the veins under the skin; they covered bodies that were just as well put together as the bodies that were covered with white skins. Even if it were a shock to look at people whose skins were dark, she had never been able to figure out why people with white skins hated people who had dark skins. It must be hate that made them wrap all Negroes up in a neat package labeled "colored"; a package that called for certain kinds of jobs and a special kind of treatment. But she really didn't know what it was.

"I don't know, Bub," she said finally. "But it's for the same reason we can't live anywhere else but in places like this"—she indicated the cracked ceiling, the worn top of the set tub, and the narrow window, with a wave of the paring knife in her hand.

She looked at him, wondering what he was thinking. He moved away from her to lean on the edge of the kitchen table, poking at a potato peeling with an aimless finger. Then he walked over to the window and stood there looking out, his chin resting on his hands. His legs were wide apart and she thought, He's got nice strong legs. She was suddenly proud of him, glad that he was hers and filled with a strong determination to do a good job of bringing him up. The wave of self-confidence she had felt on the street came back again. She could do it, too—bring him up so that he would be a fine, strong man.

The thought made her move about swiftly, cutting the potatoes into tiny pieces so they would cook quickly, forming the ground meat into small flat cakes, heating the peas, setting the table, pouring a glass of milk for Bub. She put two of the hard crusty rolls on a plate and smiled, remembering how she had compared herself to Ben Franklin.

Then she went to the window and put her arm around Bub. "What are you looking at?" she asked.

"The dogs down there," he said, pointing. "I call one of 'em Mother Dog and the other Father Dog. There are some children dogs over yonder."

She looked down in the direction in which he was pointing. Shattered fences divided the space in back of the houses into what had once been back yards. But as she looked, she thought it had become one yard, for the rusted tin cans, the piles of ashes, the pieces of metal from discarded automobiles, had disregarded the fences. The rubbish had crept through the broken places in the fences until all of it mingled in a disorderly pattern that looked from their top-floor window like a huge junkpile instead of a series of small back yards. She leaned farther out the window to see the dogs Bub had mentioned. They were sleeping in curled-up positions, and it was only by the occasional twitching of an ear or the infrequent moving of a tail that she could tell they were alive.

Bub was explaining the details of the game he played with them. It had something to do with which one moved first. She only half-heard him as she stared at the piled-up rubbish and the sluggish dogs. All through Harlem there were apartments just like this one, she thought, and they're nothing but traps. Dirty, dark, filthy traps. Upstairs. Downstairs. In my lady's chamber. Click goes the trap when you pay the first month's rent. Walk right in. It's a free country. Dark little hallways. Stinking toilets.

She had wanted an apartment to herself and she got it. And now looking down at the accumulation of rubbish, she was suddenly appalled, for she didn't know what the next step would be. She hadn't thought any further than the apartment. Would they have to go on living here year after year? With just enough money to pay the rent, just enough money to buy food and clothes and to see an occasional movie? What happened next?

She didn't know, and she put her arm around Bub and hugged him close to her. She didn't know what happened next, but they'd never catch her in their dirty trap. She'd fight her way out. She and Bub would fight their way out together. She was holding him so tightly that he turned away from his game with the dogs to look up in her face.

"You're pretty," he said, pressing his face close to hers. "Supe says you're pretty. And he's right."

She kissed his forehead, thinking what's the Super saying things like that to Bub for? And she was conscious of a stabbing fear that made her tighten her arm around Bub's shoulder. "Let's eat," she said.

All through the meal she kept thinking about the Super. He was so tall and so silent he was like some figure of doom. She rarely went in or out of the building that she didn't meet him in the hallways or just coming out of his apartment, and she wondered if he watched for her. She had noticed that the other tenants rarely talked to him, merely nodding when they saw him.

He usually had his dog with him when he stood outside on the street leaning against the building. The dog would open his mouth, fairly quivering with the urge to run down the street. She imagined that if he ever satisfied the urge to run, he would plunge madly through the block biting people as he went. He would look up at the Super with something half-adoring, half-fearful in his expression, drawing a little away from him, edging along slowly a half-inch at a time, wanting to run. Then the Super would say, "Buddy!" and the dog would come back to lie down close beside the man.

She couldn't decide which was worse: the half-starved, cringing dog, the gaunt man or the shapeless whispering woman who lived with him. Mrs. Hedges, who knew everything that went on in this house and most of the other houses on the street, had informed her confidentially that the Super's wife wasn't really his wife, that she just stayed there with him. "They comes and they goes," Mrs. Hedges had added softly, her hard black eyes full of malice.

Bub took a big swallow of milk and choked on it. "Sorry," he murmured.

Lutie smiled at him and said, "Don't drink it so fast." And her thoughts returned to the Super. She had to figure out some way of keeping Bub away from him. There were those long hours from the time Bub got out of school until she came home from work. She couldn't get over Bub's saying so innocently, "Supe thinks you're pretty." It wouldn't do to tell Bub point-blank not to have anything to do with him. For after that business with the shoeshine box, he would begin to believe there wasn't much of anything he could do after school that would meet with her approval. But she would figure out something.

Again she thought that every time she turned around there was a new problem to be solved. There ought to be someone she could talk to, someone she could ask for advice. During those years she had worked in the laundry and gone to school at night, she had lost track of all her friends. And Pop didn't believe in discussing problems—"Just goin' out of your way to look for trouble," was his answer to anything that looked like a serious question. Granny could have told her what to do if she had lived. She had never forgotten some of the things Granny had told her and the things she had told Pop. Mostly she had been right. She used to sit in her rocking chair. Wrinkled. Wise. Rocking back and forth, talking in the rhythm of the rocker. Granny had even foreseen men like this Super. She had told Pop, "Let her get married, Grant. Lookin' like she do men goin' to chase her till they catches up. Better she get married."

And she had. At seventeen when she finished high school. Only the marriage had busted up, cracking wide open like a cheap record. Come to think about it, an awful lot of colored marriages ended like that.

Mrs. Hedges had implied the same thing shortly after they moved in. Lutie was coming home from work, and Mrs. Hedges having greeted her cordially from the window said, "You married, dearie?"

Her spine had stiffened until it felt rigid. Did the woman think that Bub was some nameless bastard she had obtained in a dark hallway? "We're separated," she said sharply.

Mrs. Hedges nodded. "Thought so. Most of the ladies on the street is separated."

Some day she would ask Mrs. Hedges why most of the ladies on this street were separated from their husbands. Certainly Mrs. Hedges should be able to explain it, because she knew this block between Eighth Avenue and Seventh Avenue better than most people know their own homes, and she should be able to tell her whether the women were separated before they came there to live or whether it was something that the street had done to them. If what Mrs. Hedges said was true, then this street was full of broken homes, and she thought the men must have been like Jim—unable to stand the day after day of drab living with nothing to look forward to but just enough to eat and a shelter overhead. And the women working as she had worked and the men getting fed up and getting other women.

She made an impatient movement and pushed her plate away from her. Bub was playing with a piece of meat ball, using his fork to slide it from one side of his plate to another, then arranging a neat circle of peas around it.

"How about you going to a movie?" she asked.

"Tonight?" he said, and when she nodded his face lit up. Then he frowned. "Can we afford it?"

"Sure," she said. "Hurry up and finish eating." The peas and the hamburger disappeared from his plate like magic. He was still chewing when he got up from the table to help count out the money for his ticket.

"Listen," she said. "You can't get in alone at night——"

"Sure I can. All I have to do is go up to some old lady and ask her to let me go along in with her. I'll show her my money, so she'll know I can pay my own way. It always works," he said confidently.

Then he was gone, slamming the door behind him, running swiftly down the stairs. She could hear his footsteps going down the stairs. She turned the radio on in the living room and stood listening to the dance music that filled the room, thinking that she would like to go somewhere where there was music like that and dancing and young people laughing.

In the kitchen she sighed deeply before she began washing the dishes. Bub shouldn't be going to the movies alone at night. How had he known how to get in despite the fact kids weren't allowed in the movies alone at night? Probably learned it from the kids in the street or at school. It wasn't right, though. She should have told him to go Saturday morning or in the afternoon after school.

There must be something he could do after school, some place he could go where he would have some fun and be safe, too. Leaning out of a kitchen window to play some kind of game with those dogs down there in the rubbish wasn't exactly wholesome play for an eight-year-old boy. She would have to move into a street where there wasn't a playground or a park for blocks around! He had been so happy about going to the movies. A simple little thing like that and he got all excited. She hoped he knew it was a peace offering for having lost her temper and slapped him out there in the street.

She found she was rattling the dishes noisily to cover up the quiet in the apartment. The radio was on full blast, but under it there was a stillness that crept through all the rooms. It's these ratty little rooms, she thought. Yet she found she kept looking over her shoulder, half-expecting to find someone had stolen up in back of her under cover of the quiet.

Yes, she thought. The trouble is that these rooms are so small. After she had been in them just a few minutes, the walls seemed to come in toward her, to push against her. Now that she had this apartment, perhaps the next thing she ought to do was to find another one with bigger rooms. But she couldn't pay any more rent than she was paying now and moving to another street would simply mean getting a new address, for the narrow dark rooms would be the same. Everything would be the same—the toilets that didn't work efficiently, the hallways dank with the smell of urine, the small inadequate windows. No matter where she moved, if twenty-nine dollars was all the rent she could pay, why, she would simply be changing her address, for the place she moved into would be exactly like the one she moved out of.

She hung the dishtowels on the rack over the sink, straightening them so that the edges were even and stood looking at them without really seeing them. There wasn't any point in getting a more expensive apartment, for the rent on this one was all she could manage. She wondered if landlords knew what it was like to be haunted by the fear of not being able to pay the rent. After a while the word "rent" grew so big it loomed up in all your thinking.

Some people took so much a week out of their pay envelopes and stuck it in books or tucked it in kitchen cupboards in cups or teapots or sugar bowls, so that by the end of the month it would be there in a lump sum all ready to hand over to the agent or the super or whoever collected. But someone would get a toothache or lose a job or a roomer wouldn't pay, and at the end of the month the rent money would come up short. So the landlord took to asking for it every two weeks, sometimes every week if he was especially doubtful about his tenants.

As she remembered, Pop preferred to pay weekly, for on Saturday nights he did a brisk business selling the bootleg liquor that he manufactured, so that on Sunday morning he had the week's rent money ready to turn over to the agent.

From the time her mother died when she was seven until she turned seventeen and married Jim, Saturday nights were always the same. Shortly after she got in bed there would be a furtive knock at the door. Pop would pad up the hall and hold a whispered conversation at the door. Then he would go back down the hall and a few minutes later return to the door. There would be the clink of silver and the door would close quietly. Granny would snort so loud you could hear her all through the apartment because she knew Pop had sold another bottle and she didn't approve of it, even though each knock meant they were that much closer to having the rent money ready.

Pop would further aggravate Granny by announcing loudly as he clinked the silver in his pocket, "That's all right. It's guaranteed to put hair on a dog's back and new life in an old man."

Sometimes Pop would try to get a regular steady job and would return home after a few hours to spend the rest of the day, saying wrathfully, "White folks just ain't no damn good." Then he would start mixing a new batch of his buckjuice as he called it, muttering, "Can't get no job. White folks got 'em all."

Granny would look at him coldly and her lips would curl back as she rocked and frowned, saying, "Men like him don't get nowhere, Lutie. Think folks owe 'em a livin'. And mebbe they do, but not nowhere near the way he thinks."

Lutie found herself wondering if Pop would have been different if he had lived in a different part of town and if he had been able to find a decent job that would have forced him to use all of his energy and latent ability. There wasn't anything stupid about Pop. Life just seemed to have reacted on him until he turned sly and a little dishonest. Perhaps that was one way of fighting back.

Even the succession of girl friends that started shortly after her mother died could have been the result of his frustration —a way he had of proving to himself that there was one area of achievement in which he was the equal of any man—white or black. Though his public explanation of them was simply that he didn't intend to marry again. "It don't work out after the first time. And I gotta keep my freedom."

Granny had observed the procession of buxom lady friends with unconcealed disapproval, which she expressed by folding her lips into a thin straight line and rocking faster and faster. Eventually Granny's baleful eye would discourage even the boldest of them, but a few weeks later some other fat woman would show up to share Pop's bed and board.

Again she was aware of the silence under the sound of the radio. And she went into the living room and sat down close to it, so that the dance music would shut out the silence. She had been so dead set on moving away from Pop and Lil, getting this apartment for herself and Bub, that she hadn't stopped to figure out what was to happen next. Listening to the music she thought she couldn't possibly go on living here with nothing to look forward to. As she sat there, it seemed to her that time stretched away in front of her so far that it couldn't be measured; it couldn't be encompassed or even visualized if it meant living in this place for years and years.

What else was there? She couldn't hope to get a raise in pay without taking another civil service examination, for more pay depended on a higher rating, and it might be two years, ten years, even twenty years before it came through. The only other way of getting out was to find a man who had a good job and who wanted to marry her. The chances of that were pretty slim, for once they found out she didn't have a divorce they lost interest in marriage and offered to share their apartments with her.

It would be more years than she cared to think about before she would be able to get a divorce because it was an expensive business. She would either have to move to some other state and establish residence there and on top of that have enough money to pay for the divorce, or she would have to get sufficient evidence to prove that Jim was living with some other woman and on top of that hire a lawyer. Either way it was done, it would cost two or three hundred dollars and it would take her years and years to save up that much money.

She got up from the chair, thinking, I can't stay here in this little place for another minute. I'll go for a walk. As she changed her clothes, she thought, This is the same thing that happened to Jim. He couldn't stand being shut up in the little house in Jamaica just like I can't stand being shut up in this apartment. Only I have a job that takes me out of here every day and I ought to be able to stand it better. But I can't. It seems like life is going past me so fast that I'll never catch up with it, and it wouldn't matter particularly, but I can't see anything ahead of me except these walls that push in against me.

She didn't intend to go anywhere except for a walk, but she found herself dressing as slowly and as carefully as though she had a special date, putting on a plain black dress and fastening a gold-colored chain around her neck. She reached in her closet for her best coat, which was perfectly plain, too, except that it hung from the shoulders so that it flared loose and full in the back. It was a coat that she had made herself, saving up the money to buy the material, cutting it out on her bed in Pop's apartment, stitching it up on Lil's sewing machine. She only wore it when she was going somewhere special at night or when she went for a walk with Bub on Sunday afternoons.

Tonight wasn't anything special. When she put the coat on,

it was with the thought that wearing it would give her the feeling that she was on her way to a place where she could forget for a little while about the gas bill and the rent bill and the light bill. It would be a place where there was a lot of room and the walls didn't continually walk at you—crowding you.

She reached in a drawer for a pair of white gloves and even as she pulled them on she knew where she was going.

"A glass of beer," she said softly. "I'll get a glass of beer at the Junto on the corner." It would take the edge off the loneliness.

Outside on the street, she felt mildly triumphant, for just once she had managed to walk past Mrs. Hedges' window without being seen. Just once. But no——

"Dearie, I been thinkin'——" Mrs. Hedges' voice halted her.

Mrs. Hedges studied her from head to foot with a calculating eye. "If you ever want to make a little extra money, why, you let me know. A nice white gentleman I met lately——"

Lutie walked up the street without answering. Mrs. Hedges' voice followed her, "Just let me know, dearie."

Sure, Lutie thought, as she walked on, if you live on this damn street you're supposed to want to earn a little extra money sleeping around nights. With nice white gentlemen.

By the time she reached the Junto Bar and Grill on the corner, she was walking so fast she almost passed it.

Chapter 4

JONES, THE SUPER, came out of his apartment just in time to catch a glimpse of Lutie striding up the street toward the Junto. She was walking so fast her coat flared out above her straight slim skirt.

As his eyes followed her swift progress up the street, he wished she hadn't worn such a full coat so that he could have had a better view of her well-shaped hips as she hurried toward the corner. Ever since the night she had first rung his bell to ask about the apartment, he hadn't been able to get her out of his mind. She was so tall and brown and young. She made him more aware of the deadly loneliness that ate into him day and night. It was a loneliness born of years of living in basements and sleeping on mattresses in boiler rooms.

The first jobs he had had been on ships and he stayed on them until sometimes it seemed to him he had been buried alive in the hold. He took to talking to himself and dreaming of women—brown women that he would hold in his arms when he got ashore. He used to plan the detail of his love-making until when the dream became a reality and he was actually ashore, he went half-mad with a frenzied kind of hunger that drove the women away from him. When he was younger, he didn't have any trouble getting women—young, well-built women. It didn't worry him that they left him after a few days because he could always find others to take their places.

After he left the sea, he had a succession of jobs as a night watchman. And he was alone again. It was worse than the ships. Because he had to sit in the basements and the hallways of vast, empty buildings that were filled with shadows, and the only sound that came to his ears was that made by some occasional passer-by whose footsteps echoed and re-echoed in his eardrums. Until finally he couldn't stand it any more and got a job as super in a building in Harlem because that way there would be people around him all the time.

He had been on 116th Street for five years. He knew the cellars and the basements in this street better than he knew the outside of streets just a few blocks away. He had fired furnaces and cleaned stairways and put washers in faucets and grown gaunter and lonelier as the years crept past him. He had gone from a mattress by a furnace to basement rooms until finally here in this house he had three rooms to himself—rent free.

But now that he had an apartment of his own, he had grown so much older he found it more and more difficult to get a woman to stay with him. Even women who wanted a refuge and who couldn't hope to find one anywhere else stayed only three months or so and then were gone. He had thought he would see more people as super of a building, but he was still surrounded by silence. For the tenants didn't like him and the only time they had anything to do with him was when a roof leaked or a windowpane came out or something went wrong with the plumbing. And so he had developed the habit of spending his spare time outside the buildings in which he worked; looking at the women who went past, estimating them, wanting them.

It was all of three years since he had had a really young woman. The last young round one left after three days of his violent love-making. She had stood in the door and screamed at him, her voice high and shrill with rage. "You old goat!" she said. "You think I'm goin' to stay in this stinkin' apartment with you slobberin' over me day after day?"

After her the succession of drab, beaten, middle-aged women started again. As a result he wanted this young one—this Lutie Johnson—worse than he had ever wanted anything in his life. He had watched her ever since she moved in. She was crazy about her kid. So he had gone out of his way to be friends with him.

"Hey, kid, go get me a pack of smokes," and he would give the kid a nickel for going. Or, "Run around the corner and get a paper for me," giving him a couple of pennies when he came back with the paper.

They planned the shoeshine box together and made it in the basement. He brought a hammer and a saw down, fished a piece of old carpet out of the rubbish, got the nails to tack it on with, and showed the kid how to hold the hammer.

"Gee, Mom'll be proud of me," Bub had said. He was sweating and he leaned back on his knees to grin up at the Super.

The man shifted his weight uneasily. He had been standing

close to the furnace at the time and he remembered how difficult it was to keep from frowning, for standing there looking
down at the kid like that he saw the roundness of his head, how
sturdily his body was built, the beginnings of what would be a
powerful chest, the straightness of his legs, how his hair curled
over his forehead.

And he suddenly hated the child with a depth of emotion
that set him trembling. He looks like whoever the black bastard was that used to screw her, he thought, and his mind
fastened on the details. He could fairly see Lutie, brown and
long-legged, pressed tight against the body of that other man,
a man with curly hair and a broad chest and straight back and
legs.

"Damn him," he muttered.

"Whatsamatter, Supe?" Bub asked. "Hey, you look sick."

"Go away," the man motioned violently as the boy stood up.
He had felt that if the child should touch him he would try
to kill him. Because the child was an exact replica of his father
—that unknown man who had held Lutie in his arms, caressed
her breasts, felt her body tremble against him. He watched the
child back away from him, saw that his eyes were wide with
fear, and by a prodigious effort he controlled himself. Don't
scare the kid, he told himself. And again, Don't scare the kid.
You'll scare off the mother if you do and she's what you want
—what you gotta have.

"I got a headache," he muttered. "Come on and let's tack
the carpet on the seat."

He forced himself to kneel down beside him and to hold the
carpet taut while the kid nailed it in place. The kid lifted the
hammer and began swinging it with a regular rhythm, up and
down, down and up. Watching him he had thought, When he
grows up he's going to be strong and big like his father. The
thought made him draw away from the nearness of the boy
who was so like the father—that man who had Lutie when she
was a virgin. He couldn't look at the child again after thinking
that, so he stared at the dust and the accumulation of grime on
the furnace pipes that ran overhead.

Now standing here on the street watching Lutie walk toward
the corner, he was aware that Mrs. Hedges was looking at him
from her window. He was filled with a vast uneasiness, for he

was certain that she could read his thoughts. Sometimes standing out on the street like this, he forgot she was there, and he would stare hungry-eyed at the women who went past. Some movement she made would attract his attention and he would look toward the window to find that she was sitting there blandly observing him.

When Lutie disappeared around the corner, he looked up and Mrs. Hedges leaned toward him, smiling.

"Ain't no point in you lickin' your chops, dearie," she said. "There's others who are interested."

He frowned up at her. "What you talkin' about?"

"Mis' Johnson, of course. Who you think I'm talkin' about?" She leaned farther out of the window. "I'm just tellin' you for your own good, dearie. There ain't no point in you gettin' het up over her. She's marked down for somebody else."

She was still smiling, but her eyes were so unfriendly that he looked away, thinking, She ain't never been able to mind her own business. If he could he would have had her locked up long ago. She oughtta be in jail, anyway, running the kind of place she did.

He had hated her ever since he had dropped a hint to her one afternoon, after months of looking at the round young girls who lived with her. He had said, "Kin I come in some night?" He had made his voice soft and tried to say it in such a way that she would know instantly what it was he wanted.

"You got anything you want to talk about, you kin say it at the window, dearie. I'm always a-settin' right here where folks kin see me." She said it coldly, and loud enough so that anyone passing on the street could hear her.

He was so furious and frustrated that he made up his mind to find some way of getting even with her. There must be, he finally decided, some kind of complaint he could make to the police. He asked the super next door about it.

"Sure," the man said. "Runnin' a disorderly house. Go down to the precinct and tell 'em."

The cop he talked to at the station house was young, and Jones thought he acted real pleased when he heard what he had come for. He began filling out a long printed form. Everything was all right until a lieutenant came in and looked over the cop's shoulder as he wrote.

"What's the woman's name?" he asked sharply, though he was looking right at it where the cop had written it on the paper.

"Mis' Hedges," the Super said eagerly, and thought, Maybe there's something else against her and she'll get locked up for a long time. Perhaps she would spend the rest of her life sticking her fat head out between jail bars. That red bandanna of hers would look real good in a jail-house yard.

The lieutenant frowned at him and pursed up his lips. "How do you know this is true?"

"I'm the super of the building," he explained.

"Ever hear any noise? Do the neighbors complain? People in the house complain?"

"No," he said slowly. "But I see them girls she's got there. And men go in and out."

"The girls room there? Or do they come in from the street?"

"They rooms there," he said.

The lieutenant reached out and took the paper away from the cop and the cop's pen sort of slid across it because he was still writing on it. The lieutenant tore it up into little fine pieces and the pieces drifted slowly out of his hands into a wastebasket near the desk. The cop's face turned redder and redder as he watched the pieces fall into the basket.

The lieutenant said, "That isn't enough evidence for a complaint," and turned on his heel and walked out.

Jones and the cop stared at each other. When Jones started toward the door, he could hear the cop swearing softly under his breath. He went back and stood outside the building. He couldn't figure it out. Everything had been all right until the lieutenant came in. The cop was taking it all down and then suddenly, "Not enough evidence."

He asked the super next door what that meant. "You gotta get people to complain about her. And then take 'em down to the station with you," the man explained.

Jones tried out the people in the house. He talked to some of the women first, keeping his voice casual. "That Mis' Hedges is runnin' a bad place downstairs. She hadn't oughta live here."

All he got were indignant looks. "Mis' Hedges' girls come up here and looked after me when I was sick." Or, "Mis' Hedges keeps her eye on Johnnie after school."

"Them girls she's got in there ain't no good," he argued.

"Good's most of the folks round here. And they minds they own business. You leave Mis' Hedges alone"—and the door would slam in his face.

The men roared with laughter. "Wotsa matter, Poppa? Won't she let you buy nothin' in there?" Or, "Go on, man, them gals is the sweetest things on the block." "Hell, she's got a refined place in there. What you kickin' about?"

And so there was nothing he could do about Mrs. Hedges. He had resigned himself to just looking at the young girls who lived in her apartment and the sight of them further whetted his appetite for a young woman of his own. In a sense Mrs. Hedges even spoiled his daily airings on the street, for he became convinced that she could read his mind. His eyes no sooner fastened on some likely looking girl than he became aware of Mrs. Hedges looming larger than life itself in the window—looking at him, saying nothing, just looking, and, he was certain, reading his mind.

He was certain about her being able to read his mind because shortly after he tried to have her locked up the white agent who collected the rents from him said to him, "I'd advise you to leave Mrs. Hedges alone."

"I ain't done nothin' to her," he said sullenly.

"You tried to get her locked up, didn't you?"

He had stared at the man in astonishment. How could he know that? He hadn't said anything to the tenants about having her put in jail. Thus he began to believe that she could sit in her window and look at him and know exactly what he was thinking. It frightened him so that he didn't enjoy his visits to the street. He could only stand there for a little while at a time, for whenever he looked up at her she was looking at him with a derisive smile playing about her mouth.

"She's always sittin' in the window," he had said defensively to the white agent.

The man threw his head back and roared. "You want her locked up for just sitting in the window? You're crazy." He suddenly stopped laughing and a sharp note came in his voice. "Just remember that you're to leave her alone."

They were all on her side, he thought. And then he remembered that he was still standing on the street and she was looking at him. He wished he could think of a cutting reply to make to her, but he couldn't, so he whistled to the dog and went in the house stifling an impulse to shake his fist at her.

He turned on the radio in the living room and slumped down in the shabby chair near it. He didn't turn his head at the sound of a key being timidly turned in the lock. He knew it was Min, the shapeless woman who lived with him. He had got to know her when she stopped at his door every two weeks to pay her rent. He was living alone at the time, for the last shabby woman who stayed with him had been gone for nearly two months.

Min used to sit and talk to him while he wrote out her rent receipt, and linger in the doorway afterward talking, talking, talking. One day when she came down to his door, the keys of her apartment were dangling loose from her hand. Usually she held them tightly clutched in her palm as though they represented something precious. "I gotta move," she said simply.

Jones held out his hand for the keys, thinking that it was lonesome in his apartment, especially at night when he couldn't see anything if he stood outside on the street and therefore stayed inside the house by himself. Standing up outside like that his feet got tired, too. If he had a window where he could look out and see the street like Mrs. Hedges, it would be different, but the only windows in his place were in the back, facing the yard which was piled high with rusting tin cans, old newspapers, and other rubbish.

"You could stay here"—he indicated his apartment with a backward jerk of his head. The sound of her talking would drive away his loneliness and she might stay a long time because her husband had deserted her. He had heard one of the tenants telling Mrs. Hedges about it. He watched a warm look of pleasure lighten her face, and he thought, Why, she musta fell for me. She musta fell for me.

She moved in with him that same day. She didn't have very much furniture, so it wasn't any problem to fit it into his rooms. A bed, a bureau, a kitchen table, some chairs, and a long console table with ornate carved feet. "One of my madams gave me that," she explained, and told him to be careful with it on the stairs.

They got along all right until Lutie Johnson moved in. Then he began to feel like he couldn't bear the sight of Min any more. Her shapeless body in bed beside him became in his mind a barrier between him and Lutie. Min wore felt slippers in the house and they flapped against the dark paleness of her heels when she walked. There was a swish-swish noise when she moved from the stove to the sink as she was doing now. Whenever he heard the sound, he thought of Lutie's high-heeled shoes and the clicking noise her heels made when she walked. The swish of Min's slippers shut the other sound out and her dark knotted legs superimposed themselves on his dreams of Lutie's long brown legs.

As he sat listening to Min slop back and forth in the kitchen, he realized that he hated her. He wanted to hurt her, make her cringe away from him until she was as unhappy as he was.

"Supper's ready," she said in her soft sing-song voice.

He didn't move out of his chair. He wasn't going to eat with her any more. It was a sudden decision made while he sat listening to the soft clop of her slippers as she went to and fro in the kitchen.

She came to stand in the doorway. "You ain't eatin'?"

He shook his head and waited for her to ask him why, so he could shout at her and threaten her with violence. But she went back into the kitchen without saying anything, and he felt cheated. He listened to the sounds of her eating. The clink of the fork against the plate, a cup of tea being stirred, the loud sucking noise she made when she drank the tea, a knife clattering against the plate. She poured a second cup of tea from the teapot sitting on the stove and he heard the scuffing of the slippers as she walked back to the table.

And he got up abruptly and walked out of the apartment. He couldn't bear to stay in there with her for another moment. He would go down and put coal on the furnace and sit in the furnace room awhile. When he came back up, he would eat, and then go stand outside on the street where he might get a glimpse of Lutie when she came home.

As he stepped out into the hall, the street door opened. Bub bounded in, his face still glowing with the memory of the movies he had seen. He paused when he saw Jones. "Hi, Supe," he said.

The Super nodded, thinking, She ain't home. Wonder what he does up there by himself when she ain't home.

"Mom didn't like that shoeshine box," he said. "She got awful mad."

Jones stared at the boy, not saying anything.

"You goin' to fix the fire?" Bub asked.

"Yeah," he said, and walked quickly toward the cellar door under the stairs. He hooked the door behind him, thinking that he couldn't stand the sight of the kid tonight. Not the way he was feeling.

He put shovel after shovel of coal on the furnace. Then he stared into the fire, watching the blue flame lick up over the fresh coal, and studying the deep redness that glowed deep under it.

His thoughts turned almost immediately to Lutie and he stood there leaning on the shovel oblivious to the intense heat that surged out of the open door. So she hadn't liked the shoeshine box. Too bad. He had thought she'd be so pleased and that she would come down and ring his bell and stand there smiling at him. Tall and slim and young. Her breasts pointing up at him. Mebbe she would have got so she rang his bell often.

"Just to say hello to you," she would say.

"That's mighty nice of you, Mis' Johnson," and he would pat her arm or mebbe hold her hand for a moment.

He wouldn't do anything to scare her. He would just be friendly and give her little presents at first. "Saw this in a store. Thought you'd like it, Mis' Johnson." Perhaps a pair of stockings. Yes, that would be it—stockings. Some of those long, mesh ones. Mis' Greene who lived on the third floor worked downtown—she'd get them for him.

"Oh, you shouldn't have, Mr. Jones," Lutie would say, and put her hand on his shoulder.

"How about me seein' if they fit?" That was it. Playfully. Not doing anything that would scare her.

He leaned harder on the shovel imagining what it would be like. Seeing her there in his apartment with one of her long legs thrust forward—a bare, brown leg with red stuff on the toenails. And he would shake out the long stocking and pull it slowly over her foot. The soft brown skin would show through the meshes as he pulled the stocking up, up over the smooth flesh. He would lean nearer and nearer, as the stocking reached the rounded part of her leg where the fatness of the curve came, until he was pressing his mouth hot and close against that curve. Closer and closer so that he could nibble at it with his mouth, nibble the curve of her leg, and her skin would be sweet from soap and cool against the hotness of his mouth.

He had to stop thinking about it. And as he stood there, he could see all those other women who had lived with him. Of the whole lot only one had been young and she had left at the end of three days. The rest of them had been bony women past fifty, toothless women past fifty, big ones and little ones —all past fifty. At that, none of them stayed very long. Three months, six months, and then they were gone.

All except Min. Min had stayed two years. Talking, talking, talking. At first he had thought it was kind of cheerful to have her around. She kept the place from getting so deadly quiet. Now the sound of her voice shut Lutie's voice out and he could never remember what it sounded like. Min's voice would thrust it away from him the minute he started trying to remember.

The thing for him to do was get rid of her. Min was probably the reason Lutie never even looked at him. Only sort of nodded when she went past. He should have thrown Min out that first night he saw Lutie. He remembered how her long legs had looked going up the stairs ahead of him. Just watching her like that he had wanted her so badly it was like a pain in his chest. Those long legs walking up and up in front of him, her rump moving from side to side as she walked. He remembered how his hand had cupped into a curve—unconsciously, uncontrollably, as he walked in back of her.

And in the living room of the apartment he had stood there the light from the flashlight down at his feet so she couldn't see the expression on his face as he fought with himself to keep from springing on her as she stood in the bedroom playing her light on the walls. She went into the kitchen and the bathroom and he made himself stand still. For he knew if he followed her in there, he would force her down on the floor, down against the worn floor boards. He had tried to imagine what it would be like to feel her body under his—soft and warm and moving with him. And he made a choking, strangled noise in his throat.

"What's that?" she had said. And he had seen the light from her flashlight waver from the trembling of her hand.

He had scared her. He tried to speak softly so that the sound of his voice would reassure her, but his throat was working so violently that he couldn't make any words come. Finally he said, "I cleared my throat, ma'am," and even to his own ears his voice had sounded strange.

After he had given her a receipt for the deposit she left on the apartment, he tried to figure out something he could do for her. Something special that would make her like him. He decided to do a special paint job in her apartment—not just that plain white paint she had ordered. So he put green in the living room, yellow in the kitchen, deep rose color in the bedroom, and dark blue in the bathroom. When it was finished, he was very proud of it, for it was the best paint job he'd ever done. He did something else, too. He scraped the paint from the windows, those long-dried spatters from his brush and then he washed them. The agent nearly caught him at it. Fortunately he had locked the door, but the man pounded on it and shouted for quite a while. "Hey, Jones! Jones! Where the devil is he?" He had stayed quiet inside holding the window cloth in his hand until the man went away.

When Lutie came to get the keys, he got his first good look at her in daylight. Her eyes were big and dark and her mouth was rosy with lipstick. She had a small turned-up nose that made her face look very young and her skin was so smooth and so brown that he couldn't stop looking at her.

"You might have trouble with the door," he had said. "I'll show you how it works." He couldn't wait to see her face when she found out what a wonderful job he had done on the apartment. This way, too, he would again walk up the stairs in back of her. But she said, "You lead the way," and stood and waited until he had to start up ahead of her.

In the apartment she looked at the rooms, and at first she didn't say anything until after she had looked in the bathroom, and then she said, "What awful colors!" He couldn't help looking disappointed, but then she added with surprise in her voice, "Why, the windows have been washed. That's wonderful." And he had begun to feel better.

Tonight she wasn't home and the kid was upstairs by himself. Where could she have gone? Out with some man, he supposed. Some big-chested man like the kid's father. Probably now at this moment they were alone together somewhere. Sweat broke out on his forehead and for the first time he became conscious of the heat from the furnace door. He put the shovel down and shut the door and walked away from the furnace. He had a sudden desire to see what the apartment looked like now that she had been living in it. It would be all right, he decided. She might even come home while he was up there and she would be glad he had stayed with Bub. That was it. He would go up and keep Bub company while she was out. And he would see how the place looked. He would see her bedroom.

He walked up the stairs slowly, deliberately making himself go slow when what he wanted to do was to run up them. He stopped outside the door. There was a thin thread of light reaching out from under the door and the radio was going. Maybe she had come home while he was down in the cellar. In that case he would explain that he just came up to see if Bub was all right, he had thought Bub was up here alone——

Bub opened the door a cautious crack in answer to his ring. When he saw Jones he opened it wide. "Hi, Supe," he said and grinned broadly.

"Thought I'd come up and see if you was all right."

"Come on in."

He walked into the living room and looked around. It smelt sweet with some faint fragrance that came from the bedroom. He looked toward it eagerly. That was the room he wanted to see most of all.

"Your ma ain't home yet?"

Bub shook his head. "I been to the movies," he said. "You shoulda seen it. This guy came out to the West and was going to be a lawyer. And he set up in business and a rich man who got his land crooked——"

The boy's voice went on and on and Jones forgot he was there. He was imagining that Lutie was curled up on the couch where the boy sat. He wouldn't sit by her; he would stay where he was and talk to her. He wouldn't scare her. He would be very careful about that—not make any sudden moves toward her.

"Everything all right?" he'd ask.

"Just fine."

"Brought you a little present," and he would reach in his pocket and bring out some earrings—some long gold-colored hoops.

"You want to fasten 'em on?"

"I'm kinda clumsy," he would say playfully. And then he would be beside her on the couch. Right beside her on the couch. He could pull her close to him, very close. So close she would be leaning against him. He looked down at his overalls. They had been blue once, but they had faded to a grayish-white from much washing. At least they're clean, he thought defensively. But the next time he came up, he would wear his good black suit and a white shirt. He would get Min to starch the collar.

And then he remembered that he was going to get rid of Min. That would be easy. He would fix her so that she'd light out in a hurry and she wouldn't come back. She and her carpet slippers and her whispering voice. He moved his shoulders distastefully. Why would he have to think about her here in Lutie's apartment? He frowned.

"You mad about somep'n?" the boy asked.

Jones shifted uneasily in the chair, made an effort to erase the frown. Now what the hell had the kid been talking about —oh, yes, the movies he had seen. "Naw, I ain't mad. Just thinkin'," he said, and thought, I gotta keep him talking. Keep him busy talking. He took out a cigarette and lit it. "You only see one pitcher?" he asked.

"Nope. Two of 'em."

"What's the other one about? That fust one sounded good."

"Gangsters," the boy said eagerly. "A man who arrested 'em. He pretended to be one, only he was really a cop. They had tommy guns and sawed off shotguns and——"

That'll hold him for a while, he thought. There must be some way he could get to look around in the apartment. He stood up abruptly. "Want a glass of water," he explained, and started walking toward the kitchen before the kid could get up from the couch.

But the kid got the water for him so fast that he didn't get much chance to look around. He saw there were three empty beer bottles and a couple of Pepsi-Cola bottles under the kitchen sink. Even while drinking the water, his mind kept peering into the bedroom. What kind of bed did she sleep on? Perhaps he could open the closet door and just touch her clothes hanging there. They would be soft and sweet-smelling.

Back in the living room the boy went on with his endless telling of the movie, and Jones thought there must be some way he could get to look in the bedroom.

"Your ma need any extra shelves in her closet?" he asked suddenly.

Bub stopped talking to look at the Super. What did he keep interrupting him for? He shook his head, "Naw," he said indifferently. Then he picked up the thread of the story, "This guy that was really a cop——"

Jones lit another cigarette. The ash tray was slowly filling up with butts. His throat and mouth were hot from the smoke. It seemed to him they must be raw inside and the rawness was beginning to go all the way down inside him.

"Let's you and me play some cards," he said abruptly. "You kin get some matches for the stakes," he suggested.

He watched the kid go into the kitchen and he got up quickly and tiptoed toward the bedroom. He was almost inside the door when he heard Bub start toward the living room. He cursed the boy inside his head while he stood in the center of the room pretending to be stretching.

"Pull your chair up, Supe," Bub said. "We can play on top of this table." He moved a bowl of artificial flowers that were on top of the blue-glass-topped coffee table in front of the couch.

"Pull your chair up, Supe," he repeated when the man didn't move.

Jones was staring at a lipstick that was on the table-top. It had been lying close to the bowl of flowers so that he hadn't noticed it. The case was ivory-colored and there was a thin line of scarlet that went all the way around the bottom of it. He kept staring at the lipstick and almost involuntarily he reached out without moving his chair and picked it up. He pulled the top off and looked at the red stick inside. It was rounded from use and the smoothness of the red had a grainy look from being rubbed over her mouth.

He wanted to put it against his lips. That's the way her

mouth would smell and it would feel like this stuff, only warm. Holding it in his hand he got the smell from it very clearly—it was sweet like the soap that round girl had used. The one who stayed three days and then left. He raised the lipstick toward his mouth and the boy suddenly reached out and took it out of his hand, putting it in his pants pocket. It was a swift, instinctive, protective gesture.

"Mom thought she'd lost it," he said, almost apologetically.

Jones glared at the boy. He had been so wrapped up in his own thoughts he had forgotten he was there. And he had been holding the lipstick so loosely that the boy took it away from him without any effort. He hadn't even seen him reach out for it. And he thought again of Bub's father and that the boy had known there was something wrong about his lifting the lipstick toward his mouth. He was conscious of the loud ticking of a small clock that stood on a table near the couch. He could hear it going tick-tock, tick-tock, over the sound of the radio. He leaned forward aware that he had been silent too long.

"Let's get the game started," he said roughly.

He showed the boy how to play black jack. Bub learned the game quickly and started playing with a conservative kind of daring that made the pile of matches in front of him increase steadily. Jones studied him in the blue-glass table-top. There ought to be some way of getting that lipstick away from him. It would be good to hold it in his hands at night before he went to sleep so that the sweet smell would saturate his nostrils. He could carry it in his pocket where he could touch it during the day and take it out and fondle it down in the furnace room.

When he stood outside on the street, he wouldn't have to touch it, but he would know it was there lying deep in his pocket. He could almost feel it there now—warm against him. Mrs. Hedges could stare at him till she dropped dead and she wouldn't know about it. The thought of her made him wish desperately that he could just once get his hands on her. Wished that just once she would come out on the street and stand near him. "She's marked for somebody else." Grinning like an ape when she said it and her eyes cold and unfriendly like the eyes of a snake. No expression in them, but you knew you weren't safe. "Ain't no point in you lickin' your chops, dearie." And her eyes boring into him, going through him, threatening him.

Mrs. Hedges or nobody else was going to get Lutie away from him. He'd seen her first. Yes, sir. And he was going to have her.

He lit another cigarette and, when he inhaled, he was aware that the dry hotness in his mouth and throat had gone all the way down him. He laid the cards he was holding down on the table. He had to have a drink of beer. Had to have it bad.

"Hey, kid, go get me some beer and a pack of smokes"—he reached in his pocket and laid thirty-five cents on the table. "You kin keep the change."

As the boy slammed the door behind him, he wondered why he hadn't thought of it before. He was alone in the place as easily as that—just by sending the kid on an errand. He listened to the boy running down the stairs and then got up quietly and walked into the bedroom.

He stood inside the room without moving. The sweet smell was stronger in here. It came from the side of the room. He fumbled for the light and hit his knee against a chest of drawers. And stood there for a moment rubbing the place and cursing. Then he turned on the light. The bed was covered with a flowered pink spread and the same kind of stuff was at the air shaft. Everything was so close together that he could look all around the room without moving.

The sweet smell came from a can of talcum on the bureau. He picked it up and looked at it. She sprinkled this under her arms and between her legs—that's how she would smell when he got close to her. Just like this. He opened the top of the can and sprinkled some of the powder in his hand. It lay there dead-white against the dark paleness of his palm. He rubbed his hands together and the sweet smell grew stronger in the room.

He turned away abruptly. He mustn't stay in here too long, the kid would soon be coming back. The way he ran down the stairs it wouldn't take him any time to get to the store. Probably ran all the way to the corner. He wished that Lutie would come home while he was there. But the kid ought to come back now, he thought fretfully. She might not like it if she came home and found he had sent the kid out on an errand at night. What was keeping him so long? She'd probably be home any minute, now. Why hadn't he told him to get two bottles of beer? Given him enough money for two bottles and then she and him could have sat out in the living room on the couch drinking beer.

He opened the closet door. It seemed to him that the clothes bent toward him as he looked inside—a blue dress, the coat she wore to work, a plaid skirt, some blouses. He looked closely at the blouses. Yes, there was the thin, white one he had seen one day when she came down the stairs with her coat open. It had a low round neck and the fullness of the cloth in the front made a nest for her breasts to sit in. He took it out and looked at it. It smelt like the talcum and he crushed it violently between his hands squeezing the soft thin material tighter and tighter until it was a small ball in his hands except the part where the metal hanger was near the top.

Then he tried to straighten it out, patting it and smoothing and thinking that he must go quickly. Now. At once. Before the kid came back, so that no one would see the look on his face. He thrust the blouse back into the closet, closed the door, reached up and turned out the light.

He hurried out into the living room intent on leaving before the kid came back. He paused in front of the open bathroom door. It wouldn't hurt to look inside, to see how that blue color looked. There were white towels hung on a rack over the tub. He walked all the way into the small room trying to imagine how Lutie would look with water from the shower running down over her. Or lying there in the tub, her warm brownness sharply outlined against the white of the tub. The room would be hot from the steam of the water and sweet with the smell of soap. He would just be able to see her through the steaminess. Perhaps he could hold her next to him while he patted her body dry with one of those white towels.

Why didn't the kid hurry? He felt a sharp anger against him. She would be coming home at any minute now. She wouldn't like it if the kid was out. He forced himself to look away from the tub and he was conscious that the thirst in him had become red-hot. He sat down on the toilet seat and buried his head in his hands. Instantly his nose was filled with the smell of the talc he had rubbed between his palms.

He began thinking of Min. He would throw her out tonight. He had to get rid of her tonight. He wouldn't be able to stand the sight of her any more after being close to Lutie like this. He heard the kid tearing up the stairs and he reached up and jerked out the light. He was standing in the living room when the kid opened the door.

"Get me a opener," he ordered, and reached for the brown-paper bag Bub was carrying. He followed the boy into the kitchen and stood in the middle of the room under the glaring, unshaded kitchen light while he lifted the bottle to his mouth. He didn't even wait to take it out of the bag, but drank in long swallows—faster and faster. He sighed when he put the bottle down empty. "Thanks, kid," he said. "That's what I needed." He started for the door.

"You goin' now?"

"Yeah. I'll be seein' you tomorrow."

He walked heavily down the stairs. He was tired. And he thought, It's got to be soon. He had to have her soon. He couldn't go on just looking at her. He'd crack wide open if he did. There musta been some way he could have got that lipstick away from the little bastard. He thought derisively of Mrs. Hedges. "There's others interested." Yeah. But not as interested as him.

He opened the door of his apartment, thinking that he was going to throw Min out so hard she would walk on the other side of the street when she passed this house. He set the stage for it by letting the door bang behind him so that the sound went up and up through the flimsy walls of the house until it became only a mild clapping noise when it reached the top floor.

Just inside of the door he stood still because all the rooms were dark. Buddy, the police dog, came toward him whining deep in his throat. Jones fumbled for the light in the foyer, pushing the dog away from him with his foot.

Min wasn't in the kitchen, the bedroom, or the bathroom. A look in each room had merely confirmed what he had already known when he found the apartment dark. Amazing as it seemed, she had gone out. She never went anywhere at night. She always came home from work and stayed in the house until she went back to work the next day. It occurred to him that she might have left him like all the others had. Even though he had come downstairs with the intention of putting her out, the thought of her leaving him was unbearable.

In the bedroom he pulled the closet door open in a kind

of frenzy. Her few clothes still hung there—shapeless house dresses and the frayed coat she wore every day. The run-over felt slippers were on the closet floor, the raised places along the sides mute testimony to the size of the bunions on her feet. But her best hat and coat were gone; and the ugly black oxfords she wore on her occasional trips to church.

Could she have gone off and left him like the others? It was impossible to tell from the contents of the closet—these limp house dresses weren't important to her. She could always buy some others. And the felt slippers, though easy on her feet, were practically worn out. She didn't own a suitcase, so he couldn't tell whether she would be back.

If she had really left him, it didn't look so good for his chances with Lutie. For the first time he felt doubtful about Lutie's having him. Up to now he had been confident that it was only a matter of time and he would have her. This way he couldn't be sure, because if a creature like Min didn't want him there was no reason for him to believe that Lutie would have him.

Yet he still didn't know for sure. He reached in toward the clothes, pushing them into a corner with a wide violent gesture of his arm as if by threatening them they would reveal whether Min had walked out on him. Abruptly he turned toward the living room, for it occurred to him that he could tell very easily whether she had gone for good. Just one glance would be enough to tell him. No. He nodded his head with satisfaction. She hadn't walked out. She'd be coming back. For the big shiny table with the claw feet was still there against the living-room wall. She would never go away and leave that behind her. All he had to do was sit down and wait for her. Because he was going to put her out tonight and the shiny table could go right along with her.

He dozed in the chair by the radio, waiting to hear Min's key click in the lock, wondering where she had gone. This was the first time he had ever known her to go out again after she came home from work. For she did the shopping on her way from work and then cooked and cleaned and soaked her feet for the rest of the evening. She didn't have any friends that she visited. He grew angrier as he waited because he wanted to think about Lutie and instead he found himself wondering uneasily where Min had gone.

Chapter 5

Earlier in the evening, when Min was in the kitchen enjoying her supper, she was quite certain that Jones was planning some devilment while he sat in the living room. Even though he didn't answer when she told him supper was ready, the thought of him sitting there by himself, probably hungry but being stubborn about it, finally brought her to the door to ask, "You ain't eatin'?"

He shook his head and she went back to the kitchen to pour herself another cup of tea and spread butter thickly on a third slice of bread, thinking, He don't know me. He thinks I don't know what's the matter with him.

She had seen him look at that young Mrs. Johnson the night she paid the deposit on the top-floor apartment. He had almost eaten her up looking at her, overwhelmed by her being so tall, by the way her body fairly brimmed over with being young and healthy. Three different times since then she had opened the hall door just a crack and seen him standing out there watching young Mrs. Johnson as she went up the stairs.

"He thinks I don't know what's on his mind," she said to herself.

She knew all right, and she also knew what she was going to do about it. Though she had to find out first from Mrs. Hedges the right place to go. She felt certain Mrs. Hedges would know and would be only too glad to tell her because she was always ready to help folks out. Though Jones didn't think so, because he didn't like Mrs. Hedges. He didn't know that she knew that either. But she had seen him roll his eyes up at Mrs. Hedges' window; his face had been so full of hate he looked like Satan—black and evil.

Jones went out of the apartment and Min got up from the kitchen table, walked softly to the door and looked out into the hall. He was talking to Mrs. Johnson's boy—a right healthy-looking boy he was, too. Maybe she ought to sort of hint to Mrs. Johnson that it wasn't a good idea to let him hang around Jones. Not that there was anything wrong with Jones;

it was just that he had lived in basements such a long time he was kind of queer, got notions in his head about things.

She stayed there at the door until she saw Jones open the cellar door and heard his footsteps go heavily down the stairs. He would be down there long enough for her to get dressed and consult with Mrs. Hedges.

She hastily washed the dishes, thinking that whether he came up out of the cellar before she got back from where she was going would make a bit of difference. She dressed hurriedly, putting on her good dress and her best black coat, even the newish pair of oxfords. She hesitated about a hat. The triangular scarf she tied over her head for going back and forth from work was much more comfortable, but a hat was more dignified. So she pinned a high-crowned black felt hat on top of her head with long hatpins, thus anchoring it against the wind that sometimes blew through the street with such speed and force.

She looked out into the living room with a cautious movement, just to make sure Jones hadn't come in while she was dressing. Sometimes he got into the house so quiet she didn't hear him, but turning around would find he was sitting in the chair by the radio or standing almost behind her in the kitchen. Just like a ghost.

Just to make certain she was by herself, she looked into the kitchen and the bathroom. Then she walked over to the big table in the living room and squatting down carefully so that the coat wouldn't touch the floor she reached way up under the table. When she straightened up, she was holding a thin roll of bills in her hand. It was the money she had been saving for her false teeth. She looked at it, trying to decide whether she should take all of it with her. Yes, she thought, tucking it in her pocketbook, because she had no way of knowing how much she would need.

Before she left the room she patted the table gently. It was the best place to keep money she had ever found. She loved its smooth shiny surface and the way the curves of the claw feet gleamed when the light struck them, but the important thing about it was that secret drawer it contained. Until she got the table she had never been able to save any money. For her husbands could find her money, even if it was only a dollar bill or some silver, no matter where she put it. Almost as though they could smell it out whether it was put in coffee pots, under plates, in the icebox, under mattresses, between the sheets or under rugs.

Big Boy, her last husband before Jones, would snatch and tear it from her stocking, reach hard clutching hands inside her dresses in his eagerness to get at it. But with this table, Big Boy had been frustrated. That was really why he had left her. And she hadn't cared at all about his leaving because he was always drunk and broke and hungry and trying to feed him was like trying to fill up a bottomless pit.

So when Jones invited her to move in with him, she had accepted readily. Because she didn't have any place in particular to go to. Besides, she had the table, and if he turned out to be like the others it wouldn't matter, because the table would protect her money and one of these days she would have enough to buy a set of false teeth. But Jones wasn't like the others. He never asked her for money. That and the fact that he had invited her to come and live with him gave her a secure, happy feeling. He had wanted her just for herself, not for any money he might be able to get from her.

So when she came home from work, she cleaned the apartment and cooked for him and ironed his clothes. She bought a canary bird and a large ornate cage to put him in because she felt she ought to pretty the place up a little bit to show how grateful she was. What with not having to pay any rent, she was saving money so fast she would soon have her false teeth besides all the little things she saw and bought in the stores along Eighth Avenue.

She didn't mind Jones being kind of quiet and his spells of sullenness—those spells he had when both she and the dog had to keep out of his way. In his own silent, gloomy way he was fond of her and he really needed her. She didn't know when she had ever been so happy. It kind of bubbled up in her so that she talked and talked and talked to him and to the dog. And when he and the dog went to stand outside the building, she talked to herself, but quietly so that folks wouldn't hear her and think she was queer.

Everything was fine until that young Mrs. Johnson moved in. Then Jones changed so that he stayed mean and sullen all the time. Kicking at Buddy, snarling at her, slapping her. Only last night when she leaned over to take some beans out of the oven, he kicked her just like she was the dog. She had managed to hold on to the pan of beans, not saying anything, swallowing the hurt cry that rose in her throat, because she knew what was the matter with him. He had been comparing the way she looked from behind with the way young Mrs. Johnson would look if she should stoop over.

So the false teeth would just have to wait awhile longer, because she was going to spend her teeth money in order to stay in this apartment. She closed the door behind her gently. "Bless that table," she said aloud, and went outside to stand under Mrs. Hedges' window.

"Mis' Hedges," she said timidly.

"Hello, Min," Mrs. Hedges said immediately and settled her arms comfortably on the window sill in preparation for a long talk.

"I wonder if I could come in for a minute," Min said. "I got something important to talk over with you."

"Sure, dearie. Just walk right in the door. It's always open. You better ring a coupla times first so the girls won't think you're a customer."

Min rang the bell twice and opened the door, thinking now, If she don't help me I don't know what I'll do. She can tell me if she wants to, but sometimes folks won't do things out of pure meanness. But not Mis' Hedges, she thought hopefully. Surely not Mis' Hedges.

She had never seen the inside of Mrs. Hedges' apartment before and she stopped to look around, surprised to see how comfortable it was. The hall door led into the kitchen and there was bright linoleum on the floor, the kitchen curtains were freshly done up, and the pots and pans hanging over the sink had been scrubbed until they were shiny. There were potted plants growing in a stand under the window and she would have liked to examine them more closely, but she didn't want Mrs. Hedges to think she was being nosy, so she went on through the kitchen to the next room where Mrs. Hedges was sitting by the window.

"Pull up a chair, Min," Mrs. Hedges said. She verified the fact that Min was wearing her good coat and hat and then said, "What's on your mind, dearie?"

"It's Jones," Min said, and stopped, not knowing how to go on. The doorbell tinkled and she started to get up, thinking that it might be Jones, that he had seen her come in and followed her, wanting to know what she was doing there.

"It's all right"—Mrs. Hedges waved her hand indicating Min was to sit down again. "Just a customer for one of the girls. Saw him go past the window." She paused, waiting for Min to go on, and when Min said nothing, simply sat staring at her with miserable unhappy eyes, Mrs. Hedges said, "What about Jones, dearie?"

Once Min started talking, she couldn't seem to stop. "He's got his eye on that young Mis' Johnson. Ever since she moved in he's been hungerin' after her till it's made him so mean he ain't fit to live with no more." She leaned toward Mrs. Hedges in an effort to convey the urgency of the situation. "I ain't never had nothing of my own before. No money to spend like I wanted to. And now I'm living with him where they ain't no rent to pay, why, I can get things that I see. And it was all right until that Mis' Johnson come here to live. He'll be putting me out pretty soon. I can tell by the way he acts. And Mis' Hedges, I ain't goin' back to having nothing. Just paying rent. Jones don't ask for no money from me and he wasn't never this mean until that young Mis' Johnson come here. And I ain't goin' to be put out."

She paused for breath, and then continued: "I come to you because I thought mebbe you could tell me where I can find a root doctor who could help me. Because I ain't going to be put out," she repeated firmly. Opening her pocketbook she took out the thin roll of bills. "I can pay for it," she said. "This was the money I was saving for my false teeth," she added simply.

Mrs. Hedges glanced at the roll of bills and began to rock, turning her head occasionally to look out on the street. "Listen, dearie," she said finally. "I don't know nothing about root doctors. Don't hold with 'em myself, because I always figured that as far as my own business is concerned I was well able to do anything any root doctor could do."

Min's face clouded with disappointment and Mrs. Hedges added hastily: "But the girls tell me the best one in town is up on Eighth Avenue right off 140th Street. Supposed to be able to fix anything from ornery husbands to a body sickness.

Name's David. That's all it says on the sign—just David, the Prophet. And if I was you, dearie, I wouldn't let him see them bills all at one time. Root doctor or not, he's probably jest as hungry as you and me."

Min got up from the chair so eager to be on her way to the root doctor that she almost forgot to thank Mrs. Hedges. She was halfway out of the room when she remembered and she turned back to say, "Oh, Mis' Hedges, I can't ever thank you." She opened her purse and took out a bill. "I'll just leave this," she said, putting it down on a table.

"That's all right, dearie," Mrs. Hedges said. Her eyes stayed for a long moment on the bill and it was with a visible effort that she looked away from it. "Put it back in your pocketbook," she said finally.

Min hesitated and then picked it up. When she looked back into the room, Mrs. Hedges was staring out of the window, brooding over the street like she thought, if she stopped looking at it for as much as a minute, the whole thing would collapse.

Before Min stepped out into the hall, she cracked the door of Mrs. Hedges' apartment and peered out to make sure she wouldn't run head-on into Jones. She stood there listening to make certain that he wasn't coming up the cellar stairs, and she heard heavy footsteps going up and up the stairs, from the second floor to the third. It sounded like Jones. And listening more and more intently, she knew that it was Jones. What was he going upstairs for? She opened the door wider in order to hear better. The footsteps kept going up and up, getting fainter as he kept climbing. He was going to the top floor.

"You're letting all the cold air in, dearie," Mrs. Hedges called out.

Min hastily closed the door and scuttled out into the street. She waved a hasty salute toward Mrs. Hedges' window and almost ran toward the bus stop at the corner. What was he doing going up to that Mis' Johnson's apartment? She shivered. The air wasn't cold, but it seemed to come right through her coat in spite of her going along so fast. It was always colder on this street than anywhere else, she thought irritably, and Jones kept the apartment so hot she felt the cold go right through her when she first went out. And the thought of him set her to walking faster. His going up to Mrs. Johnson's apartment tonight meant Mrs. Hedges had told her about the Prophet David just in time.

The Eighth Avenue bus was so crowded that she had to stand to 140th Street, hanging on to a strap as best she could, for her arms were short and she had to reach to get hold of the strap. The bus no sooner got under way than her feet began to hurt, rebelling against the unaccustomed oxfords. For the stiff leather encased her bunions so tightly that they burned and throbbed with pain until she was forced to shift her weight from one foot to the other in an effort to ease them.

They could keep right on hurting, she thought grimly, because no matter what she had to go through, no matter how much money it cost, she wasn't going to let Jones put her out. She swayed back and forth as the bus lurched, trying to wipe out the thought of the pain in her feet by determinedly repeating, "And I ain't a-goin' to be put out."

It was nice of Mrs. Hedges to tell her where to find a root doctor, she thought. Yet now that she was actually on her way to consult him, she felt a little guilty. The preacher at the church she went to would certainly disapprove, because in his eyes her dealing with a root doctor was as good as saying that the powers of darkness were stronger than the powers of the church. Though she went to church infrequently, because she usually had to work on Sundays, the thought of the preacher disturbed her. But he didn't need to know anything about her going, she decided. Besides, even the preacher must know there were some things the church couldn't handle, had no resources for handling. And this was one of them—a situation where prayer couldn't possibly help.

She climbed awkwardly out of the bus at 140th Street, putting her weight on her feet gingerly to cushion them against the quick stab of pain any sudden, careless movement would bring. Before she was quite off the steps, she was already looking for the root doctor's sign, so that she collided with the passengers waiting to get on. Someone stepped on her feet and instantly hot fingers of pain clawed at her bunions, reached up her legs and thighs, making her draw her breath in sharply.

Then she saw the sign and she forgot about the pain. It was right near the corner as Mrs. Hedges had said—a big sign that

winked and blinked off and on in the dark so that she thought
the words "David, the Prophet" were like a warm, friendly
hand beckoning to her to come in out of the cold. She looked
at it so long her eyes started to blink open and shut just like
the sign. So he really was a prophet. She had thought perhaps
Mrs. Hedges had made up that part about his being a prophet.
That was fine, for he would be able to tell her what the future
looked like for her.

It wasn't a very big place she discovered when she got right
in front of it, though it did have a large window that was sparkling clean. She stopped to look at the objects displayed in the
window. Some of them were familiar, but most of them she
had never seen before and could only conjecture about the way
in which they were used. There were colored candles, incense
burners, strangely twisted roots, fine powders in small boxes,
dream books, lucky-number books, medallions, small figures
of monkeys and elephants, a number of rabbits' feet, monkey's
fur, and candlesticks of all sizes and shapes. The window also
contained a great many statues of the Madonna. They were
illuminated with red lights, and there were so many of the statues and thus so many of the lights that they sent a rose-colored
glow out onto the sidewalk.

She tried to see what the shop looked like inside, but the curtain at the window and another at the door effectively blocked
her gaze. Remembering Mrs. Hedges' warning, she took part
of the bills from her pocketbook, and opening her coat pushed
them deep inside her dress. Then she opened the door.

The air inside was heavy with the smell of incense and she
saw that it came from an incense burner on the counter that
ran along one side of the small shop. Her first confused impression was that the place was full of people, but a second,
careful look revealed five or six women seated on the chairs
that lined the long wall opposite the counter. Three women
were standing in front of the counter and she walked toward it
keenly disappointed that the Prophet wasn't right there behind
the counter instead of the young girl who was waiting on the
customers. The girl looked up at her approach and said, "Yes?"
very quietly.

Min noticed that the girl's eyes were almond-shaped and
then she looked down at the counter. There was a thick book

on one side of it. The rest of the top was covered with trays that held brilliantly colored glistening powders—bright orange, green, purple, yellow, scarlet. She stared at them fascinated, noting how finely ground they were, wondering what they were used for and which one the Prophet would recommend to her. She forgot about the girl behind the counter.

"Yes?" the girl repeated.

Min held on to the counter at a loss for words, suddenly frightened at having actually come to the place. Her fright confused her so that for a moment she couldn't remember why she had come. Jones. It had to do with Jones and she let go the counter. "I come to see the Prophet David," she said in her sing-song voice, the words coming out half-muffled so that she sounded as though she were whispering.

"Won't you sit down?" The girl nodded toward the line of chairs across the room. "Those ladies are waiting to see him, too. He takes everybody in turn."

Min sat down next to a light-complexioned woman whose face was covered with freckles, and glancing at the woman she thought, It's better to have a dark skin; lots of times these light-skinned women have freckles all over them till they look like they've been marked by the Devil's fingertips. The woman kept turning her pocketbook over and over between her hands with a nervous gesture that finally had the eyes of all the women near her following the constant restless motion of her hands. She had a big awkwardly wrapped package on her lap and in order to keep turning the pocketbook between her hands she had to reach over and around the package.

Wonder why she doesn't set the package on a chair instead of holding it, Min thought. And tried to conjecture what was in it—whatever it was bulged here and there, and she couldn't think of anything that would look quite like that after it was wrapped up, so she stopped thinking about it. She moved impatiently in the straight-backed chair, thinking that sitting like this just waiting was enough to drive anybody crazy. The thought that had frightened her when she was standing at the counter returned suddenly. How had she dared to come here?

It was the first defiant gesture she had ever made. Up to now she had always accepted whatever happened to her without making any effort to avoid a situation or to change one. During the years she had spent doing part-time domestic work she had never raised any objections to the actions of cruelly indifferent employers. She had permitted herself to be saddled with whole family washes when the agency that had sent her on the job had specified just "personal pieces." When the madam added sheets, towels, pillowcases, shirts, bedspreads, curtains—she simply allowed herself to be buried under the great mounds of dirty clothes and it took days to work her way out from under them, getting no extra pay for the extra time involved.

On other jobs the care of innumerable children had been added when the original agreement was for her to do the cooking and a little cleaning. The little cleaning would increase and increase until it included washing windows and walls and waxing floors. Some of her madams had been openly contemptuous women who laughed at her to her face even as they piled on more work; acting as though she were a deaf, dumb, blind thing completely devoid of understanding, but able to work, work, work. Years and years like that.

Never once had she protested. Never once, she thought with pride, had she left a job, no matter how much work there was or how badly the people treated her. As long as they paid her, she stayed on in spite of their reneging on her days off, in spite of having to work on Sundays so she couldn't get to church, though when she first started work it was always with the understanding she wouldn't be in on Sundays. Day after day she'd go back until the people moved away or got somebody else. She was never the one to make the change.

It was the same thing with the various husbands she had had. They had taken her money and abused her and given her nothing in return, but she was never the one who left.

And here she was sitting waiting to see the Prophet David —committing an open act of defiance for the first time in her life. And thinking about it that way, she was frightened by her own audacity. For in coming here like this, in trying to prevent Jones from putting her out, she was actually making an effort to change a situation. No. It was better to think of it as being an effort to keep a situation the way it had been before. That is, she was trying to stay there in his house because there she was free from the yoke of that one word: rent. That word that meant padlocked doors with foul-mouthed landladies standing in front of them or sealed keyholes with marshals waving long white papers in their hands. Then she thought if Jones ever found out she had come here, he would try to kill her because he was dead set on having that young Mrs. Johnson.

As she waited, she became aware that the women standing at the counter were spending a long time going through the thick book that was placed so handily right on top of the counter. They turned the pages and talked to the girl behind the counter before they finally put in an order.

When they told her what they wanted, their voices had a firm sound with an underlying note of triumph. "Fifteen cents worth of 492." The girl would take it down from the shelf in back of her or scoop it up from a tray on the counter and then weigh the fine powders on the scales. "Fifty cents of 215"; or, "I guess a dime's worth of 319 will fix it."

Listening to them, Min was filled with envy. She watched them turn away from the counter with the small packages safely tucked away in pocketbooks or thrust deeply into their coat pockets, and she saw such a glow of satisfaction on their faces that she thought if she only knew what to get she'd buy it the same way and go on home without waiting for the Prophet. But she wouldn't know how to use any of the powders after she got them. Some, she knew, were for sprinkling around the house, some for putting in coffee or tea, others were intended to be burnt in incense burners like those in the shop window, but she didn't know one from the other. There wouldn't be any point in her looking through the thick pages of the book on the counter, because the very sight of so much print would only bewilder her.

Then she forgot about the book, because a woman emerged from behind the white curtains that hung at the back of the store. All the women sitting on the chairs moved slightly at the sight of the man who followed the woman from behind the curtains. He was tall and he wore a white turban on his head. The whiteness of the turban accentuated the darkness of his skin. He beckoned toward the row of chairs and the woman sitting nearest the back of the shop got up and disappeared behind the curtains with him. The curtains fell back in place with a graceful movement.

Like the others, Min moved in her chair when she saw him

—shifting her feet, leaning forward away from the chair and then leaning back against it. That musta been the Prophet, she thought. Though she listened intently, she could hear no sound from behind the curtains. No murmur of conversation. Nothing. The quiet in back of the curtains disturbed her so that she wished uneasily she hadn't come. Then, remembering that she was dead set on not being put out, dead set on keeping Jones away from young Mrs. Johnson, she folded her hands over her pocketbook, content to wait her turn; determined to finish this action she had begun.

But her tranquillity was disturbed by the freckled woman who sat next to her. The woman kept turning her pocketbook over and over, first one side then the other, until the constant restless motion was unbearable.

In desperation Min turned toward the woman. "You been here before?" she asked, and saw with relief that the pocketbook stayed still in the woman's lap.

"Sure," the woman said. "I come about once a week."

"Oh"—Min tried to conceal her chagrin, tried to keep it from showing in her face. "I thought if you come once he could fix whatever was wrong on the one trip." She couldn't come every week. It was out of the question, for she never went anywhere at night, and Jones would get suspicious and probably act nastier than ever if she started going out regularly when she'd never done it before.

"Depends on what it is," the woman said. "Some things ain't easy. I ain't got a easy case. Prophet's helped a lot, but it ain't all fixed yet."

"No?" Min hoped if she acted interested but not too interested the woman would tell her about it. Then she could get some idea about her and Jones—whether she'd have to pay weekly visits to the Prophet or whether this one time would be enough.

"No," the woman lowered her voice slightly. "You see Zeke, that's my husband, has got a way of not styin' in bed nights. He just disappears. Goes to bed like anybody else and then all of a sudden he's gone. I've stayed awake all night and I ain't never seen him go. Next day he's there for breakfast and don't know nothing about not being in bed all night. Says he don't know where he's been or nothing."

Min frowned as she listened to her. Sounded to her like the woman's husband was fooling her. Probably with some other woman. "Prophet don't know how to fix it?" she asked and waited impatiently for the answer, beginning to doubt the Prophet's power, beginning even to question his honesty, for it looked like to her anybody ought to be able to see the woman's husband was fooling her.

"Oh, yes, he don't disappear quite so often. Prophet's cut him down a lot," the woman said eagerly. "But he say Zeke ain't co-operatin'." She indicated the bulky package on her lap. "Prophet's goin' to sprinkle his shoes tonight. He put off doing it, but he says ain't nothing else to do now seein's Zeke ain't co-operatin'."

Min wanted to ask more questions, but at that moment the Prophet appeared from behind the curtain and beckoned to the woman. She watched her walk toward the white curtains, thinking that perhaps Mrs. Hedges had been right not to put any faith in root doctors, for surely that woman with the freckles didn't need to come here every week. She was glad she had talked to her, though, for if after the first few minutes of talking to the Prophet she decided he was just stringing her along like he was obviously doing with this woman, why, she wouldn't give him any money—she would just leave and look up another root doctor that was honest.

Sprinkling the shoes evidently didn't take very long, Min thought, for when she looked up again the freckled woman was coming out from behind the curtains. Her face was lit up by such a luminous, radiant smile that Min couldn't help but stare at her, thinking, Well, whatever else he might be able to do the Prophet deserved some credit for making that fidgety woman look so happy. The Prophet beckoned toward the row of chairs.

"It's your turn," said the fat woman sitting next to her.

Min walked toward the curtains in the back, and the nearer she got to them, the more she wished that she hadn't come or that while she was sitting waiting outside she had got up and gone home. Her heart started jumping so that she began to breathe heavily. Then the curtains swished together behind her and she was standing in a small room. The Prophet was already sitting behind a desk looking at her.

"Will you close the door, please?" he said.

She turned to close it, thinking, That's why there wasn't any sound outside. Because there was a solid wall in back of the curtains, a wall that went right up to the ceiling and effectively separated the room from the shop. With the door shut no sound could get outside.

After she sat down across from him, she found she couldn't bring herself to look right at him so she looked at his turban. It was like Mrs. Hedges and that bandanna she wore all the time, you couldn't tell what kind or color of hair headgears like that concealed. And staring at the Prophet's turban she got the sudden jolting thought that perhaps Mrs. Hedges wore that bandanna all the time because she was bald. There must be some reason why nobody who lived in the house had ever seen her without it.

"You're in trouble?" asked the Prophet David.

This was worse than when she had tried to get started on telling Mrs. Hedges about it. She shrank into the chair, wondering why she had thought she could tell a strange man about Jones and Mis' Johnson and herself. The more she thought about it, the more bewildered she became until finally, in the confusion of her thinking, her eyes shifted from his turban and she was looking directly at him.

"Tell me about it," he urged. And when she didn't say anything he added, "Is it your husband?"

"Yes," she said eagerly, and then stopped speaking. Her husband. Jones wasn't her husband any more than any of those others she had lived with in between. She hadn't seen her husband in twenty-five years. She had stayed with the others because a woman by herself didn't stand much chance; and because it was too lonely living by herself in a rented room. With a man attached to her she could have an apartment—a real home.

"Tell me about it," the Prophet said again.

If he's a prophet he ought to know without my telling him, she thought resentfully. Then the resentment left her because his eyes were deep-set and they didn't contain the derisive look she was accustomed to seeing in people's eyes. He sat looking at her and his manner was so calm and so patient that without further thinking about it she started talking. It was suddenly

quite easy to tell him about how she'd never really had anything before and about Jones and young Mis' Johnson.

"And I ain't a-goin' to be put out," she ended defiantly. Then
she added, "Leastways that's why I come to you. So you could
give me something to fix it so I won't be put out."

"Which is more important? Your not being put out or Jones
forgetting about the young lady?"

Min looked at him, thinking hard. "Both," she said finally.
"Because if he loses his taste for young Mis' Johnson, he ain't
goin' to put me out."

"One depends on the other. Is that it?"

"Yes."

"Most of these things do." The Prophet folded the tips of
his fingers against the palms of his hands and stared at them.

Min following the direction of his eyes saw that his hands
were long, the fingers flexible. The skin on his hands was as
smooth as that on his face. Once or twice he looked at her
intently and then went back to studying his hands.

"I can fix things so you won't be put out," he said finally.
"I'll see what I can do about taking Jones' mind off the young
lady, but I won't promise results on that."

He got up to open the wooden doors of a cupboard which
stood directly behind the desk. Its shelves were laden with vials
and bottles and small packages.

"Does he drink coffee for breakfast?" he asked over his
shoulder.

"Yes."

He filled a tiny glass vial with a bright red liquid. The vial
was so small that he used a medicine dropper to fill it with.
Next he put a bright green powder in a square cardboard box
and Min watching him was a little disappointed, for this powder was dull, not shiny like those on the counter outside. He
put two squat white candles on the desk and then, reaching far
back in the cabinet, brought out a cross which he held carefully
in his hands for a moment and then placed beside the candles.

Seating himself behind the desk he said: "These things and
the consultation will cost you ten dollars. I make no guarantee about the young lady. However, I can guarantee that you
won't be put out. Is that all right?"

Min opened her purse, took out two limp five-dollar bills

and placed them on the desk. The Prophet folded them together and stuck them in his vest pocket.

"Now listen carefully. Every morning put one drop of this
red liquid in his coffee. Just one drop. No more." When Min
indicated that she understood, he went on: "Every night at ten
o'clock burn these candles for five minutes. You must clean
the apartment every day. Clean it until there isn't a speck of
dirt anywhere. In the corners. On the cupboard shelves. The
window sills."

Min thought of the dust in the corners of the closet floor
—the unfinished splintery boards in there seemed to attract
it. Then there was the grease she'd let accumulate in the oven.
Soot on the window sills. She'd get after all of it as soon as she
got home.

He pointed at the cross with one of his long fingers. "This,"
he said, "will keep you safe at night. Hang it right over your
bed. As for the powder"—he leaned toward her and talked
more slowly—"it's very powerful. You only need a little of it at
a time. Always carry some of it with you because if Jones should
try to put you out this powder will stop him. Sprinkle a little of
it on the floor if he gets violent and he won't dare touch you."

The cross, the candles, and the small vial of red liquid made
a very neat package, for he put them all into a cardboard box
and then wrapped them in white paper. He handed her the box
of powder. "Put it in your coat pocket," he directed, "for you
might need it tonight. If you'll stop at the counter on your way
out, the girl will give you a medicine dropper."

"Oh, I thank you," she said. "You don't know what you
done for me."

Then he shook hands with her and she thought talking
to him had been the most satisfying experience she had ever
known. True, he hadn't said very much except toward the last
when he was telling her how to use the things. The satisfaction
she felt was from the quiet way he had listened to her, giving
her all of his attention. No one had ever done that before. The
doctors she saw from time to time at the clinic were brusque,
hurried, impatient. Even while they asked questions—is the
pain here, is it often, do your shoes fit—their minds weren't
really on her as a person. They were looking at her feet, but not
as though they belonged to her and were therefore different,

individual, because they were hers. All they saw were a pair of feet with swollen, painful bunions on them—nigger feet. The words were in the expressions in their faces. Even with the colored doctors she felt humble, apologetic.

Even Jones when he was in a good mood never listened to her. She might as well not have been there. All the time she was talking, his mind was on something else, something that set him to frowning and biting his lips. And her madams. And her madams—short ones, fat ones, harried ones, calm ones, drunken ones—none of them had ever listened when she talked. They issued orders to some point over her head until sometimes she was tempted to look up to see if there was another head on top of her own—a head she had grown without knowing it. And the minute she started answering, they turned away. The few times she had a chance to talk to the preacher at the church, he interrupted her with, "We all got our troubles, Sister. We all got our troubles." And he, too, turned away.

But this man had listened and been interested, and all the time she had talked he had never shifted his gaze, so that when she came out from behind the white curtains the satisfaction from his attentive listening, the triumph of actually possessing the means of controlling Jones, made her face glow. The women waiting in the chairs outside stared at her and she walked past them, not caring, for she had got what she came after. And it had been simple and easy and not as expensive as she had expected.

Riding toward 116th Street on the bus, she decided that every time she heard about some poor woman in trouble she would send her to the Prophet David. He was so easy to talk to, his eyes were so kind, and he knew his business. Seeing as Mrs. Hedges had been responsible for her finding him, she really ought to do something in return. As she clung to the bus strap she wondered what she could do. She thought about it so hard that she rode past 116th Street and the bus was at 112th Street before she realized it.

She walked up Eighth Avenue, still thinking about Mrs. Hedges. She stopped to look in the window of a florist shop and then went inside.

"How much are them cactuses in the gray dishes in the window?" she asked.

"Dollar and a quarter."

"Wrap one up," she ordered, and when the clerk reached in to the window for one of the plants she took the remainder of the flat roll of bills from her bosom. Peeling off two dollars she saw there wasn't much left over, but what she'd got in return for spending it was worth far more than she had paid for it.

There was a dim light in Mrs. Hedges' living room, and as Min turned the corner of the building Mrs. Hedges' voice came from the window, "Get fixed up, dearie?" she asked.

"I sure did," Min said. Her voice was so full of life and confidence that Mrs. Hedges stared at her amazed. "I saw you liked plants," she went on. "So I brought you a little present." She handed the package up to Mrs. Hedges.

"Sure was sweet of you, dearie." Mrs. Hedges leaned forward holding the plant and waiting to hear about the Prophet David. But Min walked swiftly toward the apartment house door. There was such energy and firmness about the way she walked that Mrs. Hedges' eyebrows lifted as she craned her neck for a further look.

Jones, dozing in the chair by the radio, heard Min's key go in the lock. It was the sound he had been waiting for, and he got up out of the chair to stand in the middle of the floor stretching to get himself thoroughly awake. The dog got up, too, cocking his ears at the click of the lock.

It was the sound he had been waiting to hear, but it came to his ears with an offensive, decisive loudness. Normally Min's key was inserted in the lock timidly, with a vague groping movement, and when the lock finally clicked back, she stood there for a second as though overwhelmed by the sound it made. This key was being thrust in with assurance, and the door was pushed open immediately afterward. He frowned as he listened because on top of that she slammed the door. Let it go out of her hand with a bang that echoed through the apartment and in the hall outside, could even be heard going faintly up the stairs.

Her unaccustomed actions surprised him so greatly that when she came into the living room, instead of starting immediately to throw her out and her table along with her, he found himself saying, "Where you been?"

"Out," she said, and walked into the bedroom.

And he sat down again, appalled at the thought that she might have taken up with some other man. He slowly clenched his fist and then relaxed his fingers until his hand lay limp along the arm of the chair. Here he was thinking about her again when what he wanted was Lutie. And Lutie wouldn't even look at him while Min stayed here. He saw Lutie again in his mind's eye—her long brown legs, the way her pointed breasts pushed against the fabric of her clothing. The thought sent him striding toward the bedroom, his hands itching to do violence to Min. Even his foot was itching, he thought, for he was going to plant his foot squarely in her wide shapeless bottom.

Min was unpinning her high-crowned hat, looking at herself in the mirror over the bureau as she withdrew the long pins. There was something so smug and satisfied about her and her bland, flat face reflected in the mirror was so ugly that the sight of her standing there contentedly surveying herself sent a wave of fury through him.

He took a hasty step toward her and he saw her eyes shift in the mirror. He turned his head to see what she was staring at, it was something that must be near the bed and he followed the direction of her glance. When he saw the great gold cross hanging over the headboard, he stood still. It was like an accusing finger pointing at him.

Almost immediately he started backing away from the sight of it, retreating toward the living room where he wouldn't be able to see it. Though he didn't believe in religion and never went to church, though he only had contempt for the people who slobbered about their sins and spent Sundays pleading for forgiveness, he had never been able to rid himself of a haunting fear of the retribution which he had heard described in his early childhood. The retribution which, for example, awaited men who lusted after women—men like himself.

Hence to him a cross was an alarming and unpleasant object, for it was a symbol of power. It was mixed up in his mind with the evil spirits and the powers of darkness it could invoke against those who outraged the laws of the church. It was fear of the evil the cross could conjure up that forced him out of the bedroom, made him sit down in the chair in the living room.

He covered his eyes with his hands, for it seemed to him the great gold-colored cross was hanging directly in front of him instead of over the headboard of the bed where he had last seen it. He muttered under his breath and got up once to kick savagely at the dog and then sat down again.

In the bedroom Min smiled as she bent forward to light the fat white candles she had placed on each side of the bureau.

Chapter 6

THERE WAS ALWAYS A CROWD in front of the Junto Bar and Grill on 116th Street. For in winter the street was cold. The wind blew the snow into great drifts that stayed along the curb for weeks, gradually blackening with soot until it was no longer recognizable as snow, but appeared to be some dark eruption from the street itself.

As one cold day followed swiftly on the heels of another, the surface of the frozen piles became encrusted with bags of garbage, old shoes, newspapers, corset lacings. The frozen débris and the icy wind made the street a desolate place in winter and the people found a certain measure of escape from it by standing in front of the Junto where the light streaming from the windows and the music from its juke-box created an oasis of warmth.

In summer the street was hot and dusty, for no trees shaded it, and the sun beat straight down on the concrete sidewalks and the brick buildings. The inside of the houses fairly steamed; the dark hallways were like ovens. Even the railings on the high steep stairways were warm to the touch.

As the thermometer crawled higher and higher, the people who lived on the street moved outdoors because the inside of the buildings was unbearable. The grown-ups lounging in chairs in front of the houses, the half-naked children playing along the curb, transformed the street into an outdoor living room. And because the people took to sleeping on rooftops and fire escapes and park benches, the street also became a great outdoor bedroom.

The same people who found warmth by standing in front of the Junto in winter continued to stand there in summer. In fact, the number of people in front of the Junto increased in summer, for the whir of its electric fans and the sound of ice clinking in tall glasses reached out to the street and created an illusion of coolness.

Thus, in winter and in summer people stood in front of the Junto from the time its doors opened early in the morning until they were firmly shut behind the last drunk the following morning.

The men who didn't work at all—the ones who never had and never would—stood in front of it in the morning. As the day slid toward afternoon, they were joined by numbers runners and men who worked nights in factories and warehouses. And at night the sidewalk spilled over with the men who ran elevators and cleaned buildings and swept out subways.

All of them—the idle ones and the ones tired from their day's labor—found surcease and refreshment either inside or outside the Junto's doors. It served as social club and meeting place. By standing outside it a man could pick up all the day's news: the baseball scores, the number that came out, the latest neighborhood gossip. Those who were interested in women could get an accurate evaluation of the girls who switched past in short tight skirts. A drinking man who was dead broke knew that if he stood there long enough a friend with funds would stroll by and offer to buy him a drink. And a man who was lonely and not interested in drinking or in women could absorb some of the warmth and laughter that seeped out to the street from the long bar.

The inside of the Junto was always crowded, too, because the white bartenders in their immaculate coats greeted the customers graciously. Their courteous friendliness was a heart-warming thing that helped rebuild egos battered and bruised during the course of the day's work.

The Junto represented something entirely different to the women on the street and what it meant to them depended in large measure on their age. Old women plodding past scowled ferociously and jerked the heavy shopping bags they carried until the stalks of celery and the mustard greens within seemed to tremble with rage at the sight of the Junto's doors. Some of the old women paused to mutter their hatred of it, to shake their fists in a sudden access of passion against it, and the men standing on the sidewalk moved closer to each other, forming a protective island with their shoulders, talking louder, laughing harder so as to shut out the sound and the sight of the old women.

Young women coming home from work—dirty, tired,

depressed—looked forward to the moment when they would change their clothes and head toward the gracious spaciousness of the Junto. They dressed hurriedly in their small dark hall bedrooms, so impatient for the soft lights and the music and the fun that awaited them that they fumbled in their haste.

For the young women had an urgent hunger for companionship and the Junto offered men of all sizes and descriptions: sleek, well-dressed men who earned their living as numbers runners; even better-dressed and better-looking men who earned a fatter living supplying women to an eager market; huge, grimy longshoremen who were given to sudden bursts of generosity; Pullman porters in on overnight runs from Washington, Chicago, Boston; and around the first of the month the sailors and soldiers flush with crisp pay-day money.

On the other hand, some of the young women went to the Junto only because they were hungry for the sight and sound of other young people and because the creeping silence that could be heard under the blaring radios, under the drunken quarrels in the hall bedrooms, was no longer bearable.

Lutie Johnson was one of these. For she wasn't going to the Junto to pick up a man or to quench a consuming, constant thirst. She was going there so that she could for a moment capture the illusion of having some of the things that she lacked.

As she hurried toward the Junto, she acknowledged the fact that she couldn't afford a glass of beer there. It would be cheaper to buy a bottle at the delicatessen and take it home and drink it if beer was what she wanted. The beer was incidental and unimportant. It was the other things that the Junto offered that she sought: the sound of laughter, the hum of talk, the sight of people and brilliant lights, the sparkle of the big mirror, the rhythmic music from the juke-box.

Once inside, she hesitated, trying to decide whether she should stand at the crowded bar or sit alone at one of the small tables in the center of the room or in one of the booths at the side. She turned abruptly to the long bar, thinking that she needed people around her tonight, even all these people who were jammed against each other at the bar.

They were here for the same reason that she was—because they couldn't bear to spend an evening alone in some small dark room; because they couldn't bear to look what they could see of the future smack in the face while listening to radios or trying to read an evening paper.

"Beer, please," she said to the bartender.

There were rows of bottles on the shelves on each side of the big mirror in back of the bar. They were reflected in the mirror, and looking at the reflection Lutie saw that they were magnified in size, shining so that they had the appearance of being filled with liquid, molten gold.

She examined herself and the people standing at the bar to see what changes the mirror wrought in them. There was a pleasant gaiety and charm about all of them. She found that she herself looked young, very young and happy in the mirror.

Her eyes wandered over the whole room. It sparkled in the mirror. The people had a kind of buoyancy about them. All except Old Man Junto, who was sitting alone at the table near the back.

She looked at him again and again, for his reflection in the mirror fascinated her. Somehow even at this distance his squat figure managed to dominate the whole room. It was, she decided, due to the bulk of his shoulders which were completely out of proportion to the rest of him.

Whenever she had been in here, he had been sitting at that same table, his hand cupped behind his ear as though he were listening to the sound of the cash register; sitting there alone watching everything—the customers, the bartenders, the waiters. For the barest fraction of a second, his eyes met hers in the mirror and then he looked away.

Then she forgot about him, for the juke-box in the far corner of the room started playing "Swing It, Sister." She hummed as she listened to it, not really aware that she was humming or why, knowing only that she felt free here where there was so much space.

The big mirror in front of her made the Junto an enormous room. It pushed the walls back and back into space. It reflected the lights from the ceiling and the concealed lighting that glowed in the corners of the room. It added a rosy radiance to the men and women standing at the bar; it pushed the world of other people's kitchen sinks back where it belonged and destroyed the existence of dirty streets and small shadowed rooms.

She finished the beer in one long gulp. Its pleasant bitter taste was still in her mouth when the bartender handed her a check for the drink.

"I'll have another one," she said softly.

No matter what it cost them, people had to come to places like the Junto, she thought. They had to replace the haunting silences of rented rooms and little apartments with the murmur of voices, the sound of laughter; they had to empty two or three small glasses of liquid gold so they could believe in themselves again.

She frowned. Two beers and the movies for Bub and the budget she had planned so carefully was ruined. If she did this very often, there wouldn't be much point in having a budget —for she couldn't budget what she didn't have.

For a brief moment she tried to look into the future. She still couldn't see anything—couldn't see anything at all but 116th Street and a job that paid barely enough for food and rent and a handful of clothes. Year after year like that. She tried to recapture the feeling of self-confidence she had had earlier in the evening, but it refused to return, for she rebelled at the thought of day after day of work and night after night caged in that apartment that no amount of scrubbing would ever get really clean.

She moved the beer glass on the bar. It left a wet ring and she moved it again in an effort to superimpose the rings on each other. It was warm in the Junto, the lights were soft, and the music coming from the juke-box was sweet. She listened intently to the record. It was "Darlin'," and when the voice on the record stopped she started singing: "There's no sun, Darlin'. There's no fun, Darlin'."

The men and women crowded at the bar stopped drinking to look at her. Her voice had a thin thread of sadness running through it that made the song important, that made it tell a story that wasn't in the words—a story of despair, of loneliness, of frustration. It was a story that all of them knew by heart and had always known because they had learned it soon after they were born and would go on adding to it until the day they died.

Just before the record ended, her voice stopped on a note so low and so long sustained that it was impossible to tell where it left off. There was a moment's silence around the bar, and then glasses were raised, the bartenders started making change, and opening long-necked bottles, conversations were resumed.

The bartender handed her another check. She picked it up mechanically and then placed it on top of the first one, held both of them loosely in her hand. That made two glasses and she'd better go before she weakened and bought another one. She put her gloves on slowly, transferring the checks from one hand to the other, wanting to linger here in this big high-ceilinged room where there were no shadowed silences, no dark corners; thinking that she should have made the beer last a long time by careful sipping instead of the greedy gulping that had made it disappear so quickly.

A man's hand closed over hers, gently extracted the two checks. "Let me take 'em," said a voice in her ear.

She looked down at the hand. The nails were clean, filed short. There was a thin coating of colorless polish on them. The skin was smooth. It was the hand of a man who earned his living in some way that didn't call for any wear and tear on his hands. She looked in the mirror and saw that the man who had reached for the checks was directly in back of her.

He was wearing a brown overcoat. It was unfastened so that she caught a glimpse of a brown suit, of a tan-colored shirt. His eyes met hers in the mirror and he said, "Do you sing for a living?"

She was aware that Old Man Junto was studying her in the mirror and she shifted her gaze back to the man standing behind her. He was waiting to find out whether she was going to ignore him or whether she was going to answer him. It would be so simple and so easy if she could say point-blank that all she wanted was a little companionship, someone to laugh with, someone to talk to, someone who would take her to places like the Junto and to the movies without her having to think about how much it cost—just that and no more; and then to explain all at once and quickly that she couldn't get married because she didn't have a divorce, that there wasn't any inducement he could offer that would make her sleep with him.

It was out of the question to say any of those things. There wasn't any point even in talking to him, for when he found out, which he would eventually, that she wasn't going to sleep with him, he would disappear. It might take a week or a month, but that was how it would end.

No. There wasn't any point in answering him. What she should do was to take the checks out of his hand without replying and go on home. Go home to wash out a pair of stockings for herself, a pair of socks and a shirt for Bub. There had been night after night like that, and as far as she knew the same thing lay ahead in the future. There would be the three rooms with the silence and the walls pressing in——

"No, I don't," she said, and turned around and faced him. "I've never thought of trying." And knew as she said it that the walls had beaten her or she had beaten the walls. Whichever way she cared to look at it.

"You could, you know," he said. "How about another drink?"

"Make it beer, please." She hesitated, and then said, "Do you mean that you think I could earn my living singing?"

"Sure. You got the kind of voice that would go over big." He elbowed space for himself beside her at the bar. "Beer for the lady," he said to the bartender. "The usual for me." He leaned nearer to Lutie, "I know what I'm talkin' about. My band plays at the Casino."

"Oh," she said. "You're——"

"Boots Smith." He said it before she could finish her sentence. And his eyes on her face were so knowing, so hard, that she thought instantly of the robins she had seen on the Chandlers' lawn in Lyme, and the cat, lean, stretched out full length, drawing itself along on its belly, intent on its prey. The image flashed across her mind and was gone, for he said, "You want to try out with the band tomorrow night?"

"You mean sing at a dance? Without rehearsing?"

"Come up around ten o'clock and we'll run over some stuff. See how it goes."

She was holding the beer glass so tightly that she could feel the impression of the glass on her fingers and she let go of it for fear it would snap in two. She couldn't seem to stop the excitement that bubbled up in her; couldn't stop the flow of planning that ran through her mind. A singing job would mean she and Bub could leave 116th Street. She could get an apartment some place where there were trees and the streets were clean and the rooms would be full of sunlight. There wouldn't be any more worry about rent and gas bills and she could be home when Bub came from school.

He was standing so close to her, watching her so intently, that again she thought of a cat slinking through grass, waiting, going slowly, barely making the grass move, but always getting nearer and nearer.

The only difference in the technique was that he had placed a piece of bait in front of her—succulent, tantalizing bait. He was waiting, watching to see whether she would nibble at it or whether he would have to use a different bait.

She tried to think about it dispassionately. Her voice wasn't any better or any worse than that of the women who sang with the dance bands over the radio. It was just an average good voice and with some coaching it might well be better than average. He had probably tossed out this sudden offer with the hope that she just might nibble at it.

Only she wasn't going to nibble. She was going to swallow it whole and come back for more until she ended up as vocalist with his band. She turned to look at him, to estimate him, to add up her chances.

His face was tough, hard-boiled, unscrupulous. There was a long, thin scar on his left cheek. It was a dark line that stood out sharply against the dark brown of his skin. And she thought that at some time someone had found his lack of scruple unbearable and had in desperation tried to do something about it. His body was lean, broad-shouldered, and as he lounged there, his arm on the bar, his muscles relaxed, she thought again of a cat slinking quietly after its prey.

There was no expression in his eyes, no softness, nothing, to indicate that he would ever bother to lift a finger to help anyone but himself. It wouldn't be easy to use him. But what she wanted she wanted so badly that she decided to gamble to get it.

"Come on. Let's get out of here," he suggested. He shoved a crisp ten-dollar bill toward the barkeep and smiled at her while he waited for his change, quite obviously satisfied with whatever he had read in her face. She noticed that, though his mouth curved upward when he smiled, his eyes stayed expressionless, and she thought that he had completely lost the knack of really smiling.

He guided her toward the street, his hand under her elbow. "Want to go for a ride?" he asked. "I've got about three hours to kill before I go to work."

"I'd love to," she said.

Eighth Avenue was lined with small stores. And as they walked toward 117th Street, Lutie looked at each store, closely reacting to it as violently as though she had never seen it before. All of them provided a sudden shocking contrast to the big softly lit interior of the Junto.

The windows of the butcher shops were piled high with pigs' feet, hog maw, neck bones, chitterlings, ox tails, tripe—all the parts that didn't cost much because they didn't have much solid meat on them, she thought. The notion stores were a jumble of dark red stockings, imitation leather pocketbooks, gaudy rayon underwear edged with coarse yellow lace, sleazy blouses—most of it good for one wearing and no more, for the underwear would fade and ravel after the first washing and the pocketbooks would begin to disintegrate after they had been opened and closed a few times.

Withered oranges and sweet potatoes, wilting kale and okra, were stacked up on the vegetable stands—the culls, the windfalls, all the bruised rotten fruit and vegetables were here. She stole a side glance at Boots striding along cat-footed, silent beside her.

It was a good thing that she had walked past these mean little stores with Boots Smith because the sight of them stiffened her determination to leave streets like this behind her—dark streets filled with shadowy figures that carried with them the horror of the places they lived in, places like her own apartment. Otherwise she might have been afraid of him.

She thought about the stores again. All of them—the butcher shops, the notion stores, the vegetable stands—all of them sold the leavings, the sweepings, the impossible unsalable merchandise, the dregs and dross that were reserved especially for Harlem.

Yet the people went on living and reproducing in spite of the bad food. Most of the children had straight bones, strong white teeth. But it couldn't go on like that. Even the strongest heritage would one day run out. Bub was healthy, sturdy, strong, but he couldn't remain that way living here.

"I ain't seen you in Junto's before, baby," said Boots Smith.

"I don't go there very often," she said. There was something faintly contemptuous about the way he said "baby." He made it sound like "bebe," and it slipped casually, easily, out of his mouth as though it were his own handy, one-word index of women.

Then, because she was still thinking about the stores and their contents, she said, "When you look at the meat in these windows it's a wonder people in Harlem go on living."

"They don't have to eat it," he said indifferently.

"What are they going to do—stop eating?"

"If they make enough money they don't have to buy that stuff."

"But that's just it. Most of them don't make enough to buy anything else."

"There's plenty of money to be made in Harlem if you know how."

"Sure," she said. "It's on the trees and bushes. All you have to do is shake 'em."

"Look, baby," he said. "I ain't interested in how they eat or what they eat. Only thing I'm interested in right now is you."

They were silent after that. So there's plenty of money to be made in Harlem. She supposed there was if people were willing to earn it by doing something that kept them just two jumps ahead of the law. Otherwise they eked out a miserable existence.

They turned down 117th Street, and she wondered whether a ride with him meant a taxi or a car of his own. If there was plenty of money floating through the town, then she assumed he must have a car of his own. So when he opened the door of a car drawn in close to the curb, she wasn't oversurprised at its length, its shiny, expensive look. It was about what she had expected from the red leather upholstery to the white-walled tires and the top that could be thrown back when the weather was warm.

She got in, thinking, This is the kind of car you see in the movies, the kind that swings insolently past you on Park

Avenue, the kind that pulls up in front of the snooty stores on Fifth Avenue where a doorman all braid and brass buttons opens the door for you. The girls that got out of cars like this had mink coats swung carelessly from their shoulders, wore sable scarves tossed over slim wool suits.

This world was one of great contrasts, she thought, and if the richest part of it was to be fenced off so that people like herself could only look at it with no expectation of ever being able to get inside it, then it would be better to have been born blind so you couldn't see it, born deaf so you couldn't hear it, born with no sense of touch so you couldn't feel it. Better still, born with no brain so that you would be completely unaware of anything, so that you would never know there were places that were filled with sunlight and good food and where children were safe.

Boots started the car and for a moment he leaned so close to her that she could smell the after-shaving lotion that he used and the faint, fruity smell of the bourbon he had been drinking. She didn't draw away from him; she simply stared at him with a cold kind of surprise that made him start fumbling with the clutch. Then the car drew away from the curb.

He headed it uptown. "We got time to get up the Hudson a ways. Okay?"

"Swell. It's been years since I've been up that way."

"Lived in New York long, baby?"

"I was born here." And next he would ask if she was married. She didn't know what her answer would be.

Because this time she wanted something and it made a difference. Ordinarily she knew exactly how it would go—like a pattern repeated over and over or the beginning of a meal. The table set with knife, fork, and spoons, napkin to the left of the fork and a glass filled with water at the tip end of the knife. Only sometimes the glass was a thin, delicate one and the napkin, instead of being paper, was thick linen still shining because a hot iron had been used on it when it was wet; and the knife and fork, instead of being red-handled steel from the five-and-ten, was silver.

He had said there was plenty of money in Harlem, so evidently this was one of the thin glass, thick napkin, thin china, polished silver affairs. But the pattern was just the same. The soup plate would be removed and the main course brought on. She always ducked before the main course was served, but this time she had to figure out how to dawdle with the main course, appear to welcome it, and yet not actually partake of it, and continue trifling and toying with it until she was successfully launched as a singer.

They had left Harlem before she noticed that there was a full moon—pale and remote despite its size. As they went steadily uptown, through the commercial business streets, and then swiftly out of Manhattan, she thought that the streets had a cold, deserted look. The buildings they passed were without lights. Whenever she caught a glimpse of the sky, it was over the tops of the buildings, so that it, too, had a faraway look. The buildings loomed darkly against it.

Then they were on a four-ply concrete road that wound ahead gray-white in the moonlight. They were going faster and faster. And she got the feeling that Boots Smith's relationship to this swiftly moving car was no ordinary one. He wasn't just a black man driving a car at a pell-mell pace. He had lost all sense of time and space as the car plunged forward into the cold, white night.

The act of driving the car made him feel he was a powerful being who could conquer the world. Up over hills, fast down on the other side. It was like playing god and commanding everything within hearing to awaken and listen to him. The people sleeping in the white farmhouses were at the mercy of the sound of his engine roaring past in the night. It brought them half-awake—disturbed, uneasy. The cattle in the barns moved in protest, the chickens stirred on their roosts and before any of them could analyze the sound that had alarmed them, he was gone—on and on into the night.

And she knew, too, that this was the reason white people turned scornfully to look at Negroes who swooped past them on the highways. "Crazy niggers with autos" in the way they looked. Because they sensed that the black men had to roar past them, had for a brief moment to feel equal, feel superior; had to take reckless chances going around curves, passing on hills, so that they would be better able to face a world that took pains to make them feel that they didn't belong, that they were inferior.

Because in that one moment of passing a white man in a car they could feel good and the good feeling would last long enough so that they could hold their heads up the next day and the day after that. And the white people in the cars hated it because—and her mind stumbled over the thought and then went on—because possibly they, too, needed to go on feeling superior. Because if they didn't, it upset the delicate balance of the world they moved in when they could see for themselves that a black man in a ratclap car could overtake and pass them on a hill. Because if there was nothing left for them but that business of feeling superior to black people, and that was taken away even for the split second of one car going ahead of another, it left them with nothing.

She stopped staring at the road ahead to look at Boots. He was leaning over the steering wheel, his hands cupped close on the sides of it. Yes, she thought, at this moment he has forgotten he's black. At this moment and in the act of sending this car hurtling through the night, he is making up for a lot of the things that have happened to him to make him what he is. He is proving all kinds of things to himself.

"Are you married, baby?" he asked. His voice was loud above the sound of the engine. He didn't look at her. His eyes were on the road. After he asked the question, he sent the car forward at a faster pace.

"I'm separated from my husband," she said. It was strange when he asked the question, the answer was on the tip of her tongue. It was true and it was the right answer. It put up no barriers to the next step—the removal of the soup plates and the bringing-on of the main course. Neither did it hurry the process.

"I thought you musta been married," he said. "Never saw a good-looking chick yet who didn't belong to somebody."

She saw no point in telling him that she didn't belong to anybody; that she and Jim were as sharply separated as though they had been divorced, and that the separation wasn't the result of some sudden quarrel but a clean-cut break of years standing. She had deliberately omitted all mention of Bub because Boots Smith obviously wasn't the kind of man who would maintain even a passing interest in a woman who was the mother of an eight-year-old child. She felt as though she had pushed Bub out of her life, disowned him, by not telling Boots about him.

He slowed the car down when they went through Poughkeepsie, stopping just long enough to pay the guard at the entrance to the Mid-Hudson Bridge. Once across the river, she became aware of the closeness of the hills, for the moon etched them clearly against the sky. They seemed to go up and up over her head.

"I don't like mountains," she said.

"Why?"

"I get the feeling they're closing in on me. Just a crazy notion," she added hastily, because she was reluctant to have him get the slightest inkling of the trapped feeling she got when there wasn't a lot of unfilled space around her.

"Probably why you sing so well," he said. "You feel things stronger than other folks." And then, "What songs do you know?"

"All the usual ones. Night and Day. Darlin'. Hurry Up, Sammy, and Let's Go Home."

"Have any trouble learnin' 'em?"

"No. I've never really tried to learn them. Just picked them up from hearing them on the radio."

"You'll have to learn some new ones,"—he steered the car to the side of the road and parked it where there was an unobstructed view of the river.

The river was very wide at this point and she moved closer to him to get a better look at it. It made no sound, though she could see the direction of its flow between the great hills on either side. It had been flowing quietly along like this for years, she thought. It would go on forever—silent, strong, knowing where it was going and not stopping for storms or bridges or factories. That was what had been wrong with her these last few weeks—she hadn't known where she was going. As a matter of fact, she had probably never known. But if she could sing —work hard at it, study, really get somewhere, it would give direction to her life—she would know where she was going.

"I don't know your name, baby," Boots said softly.

"Lutie Johnson," she said.

"Mrs. Lutie Johnson," he said slowly. "Very nice. Very, very nice."

The soft, satisfied way he said the words made her sharply aware that there wasn't a house in sight, there wasn't a car passing along the road and hadn't been since they parked. She hadn't walked into this situation. She had run headlong into it, snatching greedily at the bait he had dangled in front of her. Because she had reached such a state of despair that she would have clutched at a straw if it appeared to offer the means by which she could get Bub and herself out of that street.

As his tough, unscrupulous face came closer and closer to hers, she reminded herself that all she knew about him was that he had a dance band, that he drove a high-priced car, and that he believed there was plenty of money in Harlem. And she had gone leaping and running into his car, emitting little cries of joy as she went. It hadn't occurred to her until this moment that from his viewpoint she was a pick-up girl.

When he turned her face toward his, she could feel the hardness of his hands under the suede gloves he wore. He looked at her for a long moment. "Very, very nice," he repeated, and bent forward and kissed her.

Her mind sought some plausible way of frustrating him without offending him. She couldn't think of anything. He was holding her so tightly and his mouth was so insistent, so brutal, that she twisted out of his arms, not caring what he thought, intent only on escaping from his ruthless hands and mouth.

The dashboard clock said nine-thirty. She wanted to pat it in gratitude.

"You're going to be late," she said, pointing at the clock.

"Damn!" he muttered, and reached for the ignition switch.

Chapter 7

THEY CAME BACK over the Storm King Highway. "It's the quickest way," he explained. "But you better hold on tight, baby."

The road kept turning back on itself, going in and out and around until she was dizzy. They went through the abrupt curves so fast that she had to hold on to the door with both hands to keep from being thrown against Boots.

He seemed to have forgotten she was sitting beside him. She decided that he was playing a game, a dangerous, daring game—trying to see how fast he could go around the sudden, sickening curves without turning the car over. He kept his eyes on the road as it wound in and out ahead of them. He was half-smiling as though he was amused by the risks he was taking. As the lurching and swaying of the car increased, she began to believe that it was only staying on the road because he was forcing it to.

The headlights picked up the signs that bordered the road: "Winding Road Slow Down"; "Watch For Fallen Rock." She lost interest in whatever defiance Boots was hurling at the high hills above and the river below. If they should plunge over into the river, Bub would never know what had happened to her. No one would know. The car would go down, down, down into the river. The river would silently swallow it and quietly continue toward the sea. Or these craggy hills might suddenly spew mountains of rock down on them and crush them beneath it.

She thought of the apartment where she lived with a sudden access of warmth, for it was better to be there alive than buried under this silent river or pinioned beneath masses of rock on the highway.

And then they were down. As the road straightened out into a broad expanse of concrete highway, she relaxed against the seat. There was very little traffic. They passed an occasional car, a lumbering heavy-laden truck and that was all.

"How do you get gas?" she asked.

"Pay more for it. There's plenty of it around if you know where to go."

Yes, he would know where to go to get gas and anything else he wanted. He would know where and how to get the money to pay for it with. Money made all the difference in the things you could have and the things that were denied to you—even rationed gas. But there were some things—— "How come you're not in the army?" she asked.

"Who—me?" He threw his head back, and for the first time laughed out loud—a soft, sardonic sound that filled the car. The thought amused him so that he kept chuckling so that for a moment he couldn't talk. "You don't think I'd get mixed up in that mess."

"But why weren't you drafted?" she persisted.

He turned toward her and frowned. The long scar on his cheek was more distinct than she remembered it. "Something wrong with one ear," he said, and his voice was so unpleasant that she said nothing more about it.

As they approached the upper reaches of the Bronx, he slowed the car down. But he didn't slow it down quite enough. There was the shrill sound of a whistle from somewhere in back of them.

A cop on a motorcycle roared alongside, waved them to the curb. "Goin' to a fire?" he demanded.

He peered into the car and Lutie saw a slight stiffening of his face. That meant he had seen they were colored. She waited for his next words with a wincing feeling, thinking it was like having an old wound that had never healed and you could see someone about to knock against it and it was too late to get out of the way, and there was that horrible tiny split second of time when you waited for the contact, anticipating the pain and quivering away from it before it actually started.

The cop's mouth twisted into an ugly line. "You——"

"Sorry, Officer," Boots interrupted. "My band's playin' at the Casino tonight. I'm late and I was steppin' on it. Should have been there a half-hour ago." He pulled a wallet from an inside pocket, handed the cop a card and his driver's license.

The cop's expression softened. When he handed the license and the card back to Boots, he almost but not quite smiled.

Lutie saw that he was holding something else in his hand. It was a bill, but she couldn't see the denomination.

The cop looked at her. "Don't know that I blame you for being late, Mack," he said suggestively. "Well, so long."

And he was gone. Even with cops money makes a difference, she thought. Even if you're colored, it makes a difference—not as much, but enough to make having it important. Money could change suicide into an accident with a gun; it could apparently keep Boots out of the army, because she didn't believe that business about there being something wrong with one of his ears. He had acted too strangely when he said it.

Money could make a white cop almost smile when he caught a black man speeding. It was the only thing that could get her and Bub out of that street. And the lack of it would keep them there forever. She reaffirmed her intention of using Boots Smith. Somehow she would manage to dodge away from his hard, seeking hands without offending him until she signed a contract to sing with his band. After the contract was signed, she would tell him pointedly that she wasn't even faintly interested in knowing him any better.

She contemplated this goal with satisfaction and the old feeling of self-confidence soared in her. She could do it and she would.

Boots started the car. "I'm so late I'll have to dump you at 135th Street in front of the Casino." He was silent for a moment and then said, "Where do you live, baby?"

"On 116th Street. It isn't far from the Junto."

They were silent the rest of the way downtown. Boots took advantage of every opening in the traffic, barely waiting for a light to change to green, soaring past them as they turned to red at intersections.

He parked the car between the no parking signs in front of the Casino. "I'll look for you tomorrow night, baby," he said. "Come by about ten and you can go over some stuff with the band."

"Okay." She got out of the car without waiting for him to open the door.

"Wear a long dress, huh?" he said. He came to stand beside her on the sidewalk.

When he started to put his arm around her, she smiled at him and walked away. "Good night," she said over her shoulder.

He watched her until she reached the corner of the street. "Very, very nice," he said softly, and then turned into the Casino.

Lutie crossed Seventh Avenue, thinking that by this time to-morrow night she would know whether she was going to leave 116th Street or whether she was to go on living there. Doubt assailed her. She had never sung with an orchestra before, she knew nothing about the technique of singing over a mike—suppose she couldn't do it.

A Fifth Avenue bus lumbered to a stop at the corner. She climbed the narrow stairs to the top deck arguing with herself. Spending a dime for car fare was sheer extravagance. But it didn't matter too much, because Boots had paid for the beer she drank at the Junto, so she hadn't dented her budget as much as she had anticipated. But the Eighth Avenue bus only cost a nickel. Yes, and she would have had to stand up all the way home; besides, five cents saved didn't make that much difference.

The bus started down the street with a grinding of gears and a rumbling and groaning that she immediately contrasted with the swift, silent motion of Boots' car. He could spend money carelessly. He never had to stop and weigh the difference in price between two modes of transportation.

She began to compare him with Jim. There was a streak of cruelty in Boots that showed up plain in his face. Jim's face had been open, honest, young. Come to think of it, when she and Jim got married it looked as though it should have been a happy, successful marriage. They were young enough and enough in love to have made a go of it. It always came back to the same thing. Jim couldn't find a job.

So day by day, month by month, big broad-shouldered Jim Johnson went to pieces because there wasn't any work for him and he couldn't earn anything at all. He got used to facing the fact that he couldn't support his wife and child. It ate into him. Slowly, bit by bit, it undermined his belief in himself until he could no longer bear it. And he got himself a woman so that in those moments when he clutched her close to him in bed he could prove that he was still needed, wanted. His self-respect was momentarily restored through the woman's desire for him. Thus, too, he escaped from the dreary monotony of his existence.

She examined this train of thought with care, a little surprised to realize that somehow during the last few years she had stopped hating him, and finally reached the point where she could think about him objectively. What had happened to them was, she supposed, partly her fault. And yet was it? They had managed to live on the income from having State children there in the house in Jamaica and it had been her fault that they lost them.

She began to go over the whole thing step by step. Jim's mother died when Bub was not quite two. There was a mortgage on the house and the mortgage money had to be paid.

"We don't have to worry about a thing, Lutie," Jim had said. "Mom left a thousand dollars insurance money."

So he didn't put too much effort into looking for a job. Somehow the thousand dollars melted away—interest on the mortgage, and taxes and gas and light bills nibbled at it. Mom's funeral took three hundred and fifty dollars of it. They had to have clothes and food.

Six months after the funeral there wasn't any money left in the bank. She found the bank book on the kitchen table. Its pages were neatly perforated with the words "Account Closed." The last entry left a nice row of zeros where the balance would normally have been. Jim started hunting for a job in dead earnest and couldn't find one.

Finally they went into Harlem to consult Pop. It was on a Sunday—a warm spring day. Irene, Pop's girl friend at the moment, gave them beer and they sat around the kitchen table drinking it.

"You got the house," Pop offered. He spoke slowly as though he were thinking hard. "Tell you what you do. You get some of these State chillern. They pay about five dollars a week apiece for 'em. You get four or five of 'em and you can all live on the money."

Lutie sipped the beer and thought about the house. There was an unfinished room in the attic and three small bedrooms on the second floor. Put two kids in each room and they could take six of them—six times five would mean thirty dollars a week.

"He's right, Jim," she said. "It would be about thirty bucks a week." She took a big swallow of beer. "We could manage on that."

There were papers to be filled out and investigators to be satisfied, but finally the children arrived. Lutie was surprised at how easy it was. Surprised and a little chagrined because theirs wasn't a completely honest setup. For they had said Jim worked in Harlem and a friend had verified the fact when inquiries were made. So the State people didn't know that the children were their only source of income. It made her uneasy, for it didn't seem quite right that two grown people and another child should be living on the money that was supposed to be used exclusively for the State children.

She had to work very hard to make ends meet. She tried to make all the meals good, appetizing ones and that meant spending most of her time hunting bargains in the markets and preparing dishes that required long, careful cooking. It was during that period that she learned about soups and stews and baked beans and casserole dishes. She invented new recipes for macaroni and spaghetti and noodles.

It had been nothing but work, work, work—morning, noon, and night—making bread, washing clothes and ironing them, looking after the children, and cleaning the house. The investigator used to compliment her, "Mrs. Johnson, you do a wonderful job. This house and the children fairly shine."

She had to bite her lips to keep from saying that that wasn't half the story. She knew she was doing a fine job. She was feeding eight people on the money for five and squeezing out what amounted to rent money in the bargain. It got so at night she couldn't go to sleep without seeing figures dancing before her eyes, and mornings when she got up, she was so tired she would have given anything just to lie still in bed instead of getting up to cook quantities of oatmeal because it was cheap and filling, to walk twelve blocks to get co-operative milk because it cost less.

She could hear the word "cheap," "cheap," "cheap," whether she was asleep or awake. It dominated all her thinking. Cheap cuts of meat, cheap yellow laundry soap, yeast in bulk because it was cheap, white potatoes because they were cheap and filling, tomato juice instead of orange juice because it was cheaper; even unironed sheets because they saved electricity. They went to bed early because it kept the light bill down. Jim smoked a pipe because cigarettes were a luxury they couldn't afford. It seemed to her their whole lives revolved around the price of things and as each week crawled by she grew a little more nervous, a little more impatient and irritable.

Jim finally stopped looking for work entirely. Though to be fair about it he did help around the house—washing clothes, going to the market, cleaning. But when there wasn't anything for him to do, he would read day-old newspapers and play the radio or sit by the kitchen stove smoking his pipe until she felt, if she had to walk around his long legs just one more time, get just one more whiff of the rank, strong smell of his pipe, she would go mad.

Then Pop almost got caught selling the liquor he concocted in his apartment. So he stopped making it. He couldn't get a job either, so he couldn't pay the rent on his apartment and he came home one night to find one of those long white eviction notices under his door.

He came all the way to Jamaica to tell her about it.

"You can come stay with us till things look up if you don't mind sleeping in the living room," she offered.

"You'll never regret it, Lutie darlin'," he said fondly. "I'll make it up to you." His lips brushed against her cheek and she caught the strong smell of the raw whiskey he had been drinking.

She stood on the little glass-enclosed front porch and watched him walk down the path. He didn't seem to grow any older, no stoop in his shoulders; his step was firm. As a matter of fact he held himself more stiffly erect with each passing year. She sighed as she watched him cross the street heading toward the bus stop. He might hold himself up straighter and straighter as the years slipped by, but he drank more and more as he grew older.

That night after dinner she told Jim. "Pop's been put out of his apartment. He's coming here to stay with us."

"He can't stay here," Jim protested. "He drinks and carries on. He can't stay here with these kids."

She remembered that she had been washing dishes at the kitchen sink and the dishwater slopped over on her legs from the sudden abrupt movement she made. She never wore stockings in the house because it was cheaper not to and the dishwater was lukewarm and slimy on her bare legs, so that she made a face and thought again of the word "cheap." She was tired and irritable and the least little thing upset her.

She couldn't stop herself from answering him and she was too exhausted to be persuasive about it, too incensed by the criticism of Pop to let the whole thing drop and bring it up again later, leading around to it, not arguing but gently showing how she really couldn't do anything else.

"He's my father and he hasn't any other place to go. He's going to stay here with us." Her voice was insistent and she threw the words at him bluntly, using no tact.

Jim got up from the chair where he'd been sitting and stood over her, newspaper in hand. "You're crazy!" he shouted.

Then they were both shouting. The small room vibrated with the sound of their anger. They had lived on the edge of nothing for so long that they had finally reached the point where neither of them could brook opposition in the other, could not or would not tolerate even the suggestion of being in the wrong.

It ended almost as swiftly as it began. Because she said, "All right, I'm crazy." Her voice was tight with rage. "But either he comes or I go."

So Pop came. At first he was apologetic about being there and so self-effacing that she was only aware of him as a quiet, gray-haired figure doing the marketing, wiping the dishes, playing gently with the children. And she thought it was working out beautifully. Jim was wrong as usual.

After the first couple of weeks, Pop started drinking openly. She would meet him at the door with a brown-paper package in his hand. He would come downstairs from the bathroom holding himself very straight and eat supper in a genial expansive mood smelling to high heaven of raw whiskey.

He urged her and Jim to go out at night. "You're nothin' but kids," he said, loftily waving his hands to give his words emphasis and managing to get into the gesture a sense of the freedom and joyousness that belonged to the young. "Shouldn't be shut up in the house all day. Go out and have yourselves a time. I'll look after the kids."

Somehow he always managed to have a little money and he would take two or three limp dollar bills from his pocket and shove them into her reluctant hands. When she protested, his invariable answer was, "Oh, call it room rent if you gotta be formal about it."

They would head straight for Harlem. The trip rarely included anything more than an evening spent drinking beer in someone's living room and dancing to a radio. But it was like being let out of jail to be able to forget about the houseful of kids, forget about not having any money. Sometimes they would stop at Junto's Bar and Grill, not so much to drink the beer as to listen to the juke-box and the warm, rich flow of talk and laughter that rippled through the place. The gay, swirling sounds inside the Junto made both of them believe that one of these days they would be inside a world like that to stay for keeps.

Going home on the subway, Jim would put his arm around her and say, "I'll make it all up to you some day, Lutie. You just wait and see. I'm going to give you everything you ever wanted."

Just being close to him like that, knowing that they were both thinking much the same thing, shut out the roar and rush of the train, blotted out the other passengers. She would ride home dreaming of the time when she and Jim and Bub would be together—safe and secure and alone.

They were always very late coming home. And walking through the quiet little street they lived on, past the small houses that seemed to nudge against each other in the darkness, she used to imagine that the world at that hour belonged to her and Jim. Just the two of them alone traveling through a world that slept. It was easy to believe it, for there was no sound except that of their own footsteps on the sidewalk.

They would tiptoe into the house so as not to wake Pop and the kids. The living room always smelt strongly of whiskey.

"The place smells like a gin mill," she would say, and giggle as they went up the stairs toward their bedroom. Because somehow the fact of having been away for a while, the lateness of the hour, the stealth with which they had come into the house, made her feel young and carefree.

As they went up the stairs, Jim would put his arm around her waist. His silence, the bulky feel of his shoulders in the darkness, turned their relationship into something mysterious and exciting, and she wanted to put off the moment when she would undress and get in bed beside him, wanted to defer it at the same time that she wanted to hurry it.

It got so they went to Harlem two or three times a week. They wanted to go, anyway, and Pop made it very easy, for he insisted that they go and he invariably proffered a crumpled bill or two with which to finance the trip.

And then all the fun went out of it. Mrs. Griffin, who lived next door, banged on the kitchen door early one morning. She was filled with an indignation that thrust her mouth forward in such an angry pout that Lutie was prepared for something unpleasant.

"There's so much noise over here nights 'at my husband and me can't sleep," she said bluntly.

"Noise?" Lutie stared at her, not certain that she had heard correctly. "What kind of noise?"

"I dunno," she said. "But it's got to stop. Sounds like wild parties to me. Las' night it kept up till all hours. An' my husband say if somep'n ain't done about it he's going to complain."

"I'm sorry. I'll see that it doesn't happen any more." She said it quickly because she knew what it was. Pop had been having parties on the nights they went to Harlem.

As soon as Mrs. Griffin left the kitchen, slamming the door behind her, Lutie asked Pop about it.

"Parties?" he said innocently. His forehead wrinkled as though he were trying to figure out what she was talking about. "I ain't had no parties. Some of my friends come out a coupla times. But I ain't had no parties." His voice sounded hurt.

"You must have made a lot of noise," she said, ignoring his denial of having had any parties. "We gotta be careful, Pop. The neighbors might complain to the State people."

She tried to eliminate the trips to Harlem after that. But Jim was unaccountably and violently suspicious of the headaches that came on suddenly just before they were to leave, of the other thin excuses that she found for not going with him. She couldn't bring herself to tell him that she was scared to go off and leave Pop in the house alone.

"You think I'm too shabby to go out with," Jim had said. And then later, "Or have you got yourself another boy friend?"

She wouldn't swallow her pride and tell him about Pop, so they continued going to Harlem two or three times a week. Besides, every time Jim said something about her having a boy friend his face turned resentful, sullen, and she couldn't bear to see him like that, so she stopped making excuses and pretended an anticipation and an enthusiasm for the trips that she didn't feel.

Now when she came home she was filled with a fear that made her walk faster and faster, hastening toward their street in her eagerness to ascertain that the house was dark and quiet. Once in bed, she twisted and turned the rest of the night, impatiently waiting for morning to come when the neighbors would soon inform her if anything had happened while they were gone.

She could remember so vividly the night they returned to find the house blazing with light. She got a sick feeling deep in her stomach, for there was an uproar coming from it that could be heard way up the street. As she got closer, she saw there were two police cars pulled up in front of the door.

They walked into the living room and a cop sneered, "Little late, ain't you? The party's over."

"We live here," Jim explained.

"Christ!" The cop spat in the direction of the floor. "No wonder they won't let you all live near decent people."

Pop was very drunk. He got up from the sofa where he had been sitting and he was rocking back and forth, though he stood very tall and straight once he finally got his balance. The dignity of his reproachful remarks to the cop was ruined by the fact that the fat woman who had been lolling against him kept reaching both hands out toward him. She was so drunk that she was half-laughing and half-crying at the same time. Her words came out in a blur, "Um's my daddy. Um's my daddy. Um's my daddy."

"Ain't got no right to talk like that to a American citizen," Pop said, swaying out of the reach of the woman's clutching hands.

Lutie looked away from Pop. The living room was filled with strange people, with noise and confusion and empty whiskey bottles. The kids were crying upstairs.

It took Jim nearly a half-hour to persuade the cops not to lock everybody up, a half-hour in which she could see his pride and self-respect ooze slowly away while he pleaded, pretending not to hear the gruff asides about "drunken niggers."

Before the cops left, one of them turned to Jim. "Okay," he said. "But let me tell you this, boy. It all goes on the report."

All Jim said to her that night was, "You wanted that whiskey-soaked old bum here. Now you've got him, I hope you're satisfied."

The next afternoon a disapproving white woman arrived and took the children away with her. "They can't stay in a place where there's any such goings-on as there is here," she said.

Lutie pleaded with her, promised her that everything would be different; it couldn't possibly happen again if she would just let the children stay.

The woman was unmoved. "These children belong to your own race, and if you had any feelings at all you wouldn't want them to stay here," she said, going out the door. In less than half an hour she had the youngsters packed and was putting them into a station wagon. She moved competently with no waste motion.

Lutie watched her from the front porch. Damn white people, she thought. Damn them. And then—but it isn't that woman's fault. It's your fault. That's right, but the reason Pop came here to live was because he couldn't get a job and we had to have the State children because Jim couldn't get a job. Damn white people, she repeated.

The house was very quiet and empty with the children gone. Pop fidgeted around for a while, then put his hat and coat on. "Got some business in Harlem," he explained, not looking at her.

As the day dragged along, she kept thinking with dread of what Jim would say when he came home. He had left the house early to hunt for a job. She hoped that this time he would return swaggering with triumph because he had been successful. She kept remembering how he had pleaded with the cops the night before. Getting a job would make him forget about it. He might not notice the absence of the children.

She fed Bub and bathed him and put him to bed a little earlier than usual. It was something tangible to do. She kept listening for Jim's key in the lock. When she heard a slight sound at the front door, it was after nine and she hurried into the small hall. But it was Pop looking shamefaced and apologetic at the sight of her.

"Pop," she said, "now that the kids are gone, you might as well sleep in one of the bedrooms."

"Okay," he said humbly.

She undressed and went to bed, but she couldn't go to sleep. She remembered how she had kept getting out of bed to look up the street, glancing at the clock, listening to footsteps. When Jim finally came at eleven o'clock, she didn't hear him until he opened the front door. He came straight up the stairs and she turned the light on so he would know she was awake.

He stopped in the tiny upstairs hall and opened the bedroom doors—both of them. She strained her ears to get some clue to his reaction when he saw that Bub was in one of the rooms and Pop was in the other. But there was only silence.

Then he was standing in the door. He was still wearing his hat and overcoat and the sight angered her. He came over to the bed and the room was filled with the smell of cheap gin. And, she thought, he reeks of it. That's the way he looks for a job—in bars and drinking joints and taverns.

"Where are the kids?" he demanded.

"Did you have any supper?" she asked.

"What the hell—you heard me. Where are the kids?"

"They're gone. The State woman came and got them this morning."

"I suppose you figured if those little bastards were taken away, I'd have to find a job. That I'd go out and make one. Buy one, mebbe."

"Oh, Jim, don't——" she protested.

"You knew what would happen when you brought that old booze hound here to live."

Perhaps if she kept quiet, and let him go on raving without

answering him, he would get tired and stop. She bit her lip, looked away from him, and the words came out in spite of her, "Don't you talk about my father like that."

"A saint, ain't he?" he sneered. "He and those old bitches he sleeps with. I suppose I'm not good enough to talk about him."

"Oh, shut up," she said wearily.

"Mebbe it runs in the family. Mebbe that's why you had him come here. Because you figured with him here you'd be able to get rid of the kids. And that would give you more time to sleep with some Harlem nigger you've got your eye on. That's it, ain't it?"

"Shut up!" This time she shouted. And she saw Pop go quietly down the hall, his worn old traveling bag in his hand. The sight shocked her. He didn't have any place to go, yet he was leaving because of the way she and Jim were carrying on. "Oh, Jim," she said. "Don't let's fight. It's all over and done with. There isn't any point in quarreling like this."

"Oh, yeah? That's what you think." He leaned over the bed. His eyes were bloodshot, angry. "I oughtta beat you up and down the block." He slapped her across the face.

She was out of bed in a flash. She picked up a chair, the one chair in the bedroom—a straight-backed wooden one. She had painted it with bright yellow enamel shortly after they were married. And she had said, "Jim, look. It makes sunlight walk right into the room."

He had looked at her squatting on the floor, paintbrush in hand, her face glowing as she smiled up at him. He had leaned over and kissed her forehead, saying, "Honey, you're all the sunlight I'll ever need."

It was the same chair. And she aimed it at his head as she shouted, "You come near me and so help me I'll kill you."

It had been a loud, bitter, common fight. It woke Bub up and set him to crying. And it was more than a week afterward before they were able to patch it up. In the meantime the mortgage money was due and, though Jim didn't say so, she felt that if they lost the house by not being able to pay the interest, it would be her fault.

The Fifth Avenue bus lurched to a stop at 116th Street. She climbed down the steep stairs from the top deck, thinking that if they hadn't been so damn poor she and Jim might have stayed married. It was like a circle. No matter at what point she started, she always ended up at the same place. She had taken the job in Connecticut so they could keep the house. While she was gone, Jim got himself a slim dark girl whose thighs made him believe in himself again and momentarily released him from his humdrum life.

She had never seen him since the day she had gone to the house in Jamaica and found that other woman there. The only time she had heard from him was when he had forwarded the letter from Mrs. Chandler—and then all he had done was put Pop's address on the envelope. There had been no messages, no letters—nothing for all these years.

Once Pop had said to her, "Hear Jim's left town. Nobody knows where he went."

And she was so completely indifferent to anything concerning Jim that she had made no comment. She watched the bus until it disappeared out of sight where Seventh Avenue joins 110th Street. This clear understanding she had of what caused Jim to acquire that other woman was because the same thing was happening to her. She was incapable of enduring a bleak and lonely life encompassed by those three dark rooms.

She wondered uneasily if she was fooling herself in believing that she could sing her way out of the street. Suppose it didn't work and she had to stay there. What would the street do to her? She thought of Mrs. Hedges, the Super, Min, Mrs. Hedges' little girls. Which one would she be like, say five years from now? What would Bub be like? She shivered as she headed toward home.

Chapter 8

I T WAS A COLD, CHEERLESS NIGHT. But in spite of the cold, the street was full of people. They stood on the corners talking, lounged half in and half out of hallways and on the stoops of the houses, looking at the street and talking. Some of them were coming home from work, from church meetings, from lodge meetings, and some of them were not coming from anywhere or going anywhere, they were merely deferring the moment when they would have to enter their small crowded rooms for the night.

In the middle of the block there was a sudden thrust of raw, brilliant light where the unshaded bulbs in the big poolroom reached out and pushed back the darkness. A group of men stood outside its windows watching the games going on inside. Their heads were silhouetted against the light.

Lutie, walking quickly through the block, glanced at them and then at the women coming toward her from Eighth Avenue. The women moved slowly. Their shoulders sagged from the weight of the heavy shopping bags they carried. And she thought, That's what's wrong. We don't have time enough or money enough to live like other people because the women have to work until they become drudges and the men stand by idle.

She made an impatient movement of her shoulders. She had no way of knowing that at fifty she wouldn't be misshapen, walking on the sides of her shoes because her feet hurt so badly; getting dressed up for church on Sunday and spending the rest of the week slaving in somebody's kitchen.

It could happen. Only she was going to stake out a piece of life for herself. She had come this far poor and black and shut out as though a door had been slammed in her face. Well, she would shove it open; she would beat and bang on it and push against it and use a chisel in order to get it open.

When she opened the street door of the apartment house, she was instantly aware of the silence that filled the hall. Mrs. Hedges had been quiet, too, for if she was sitting in her window she had given no indication of her presence.

There was no sound except for the steam hissing in the radiator. The silence and the dimly lit hallway and the smell of stale air depressed her. It was like a dead weight landing on her chest. She told herself that she mustn't put too much expectation in getting the singing job. Almost anything might happen to prevent it. Boots might change his mind.

She went up the stairs, thinking, But he can't. She wouldn't let him. It meant too much to her. It was a way out—the only way out of here and she and Bub had to get out.

On the third-floor landing she stopped. A man was standing in the hall. His back was turned toward her. She hesitated. It wasn't very late, but it was dark in the hall and she was alone.

He turned then and she saw that he had his arms wound tightly around a girl and he was pressed so close to her and was bending so far over her that they had given the effect of one figure. He wore a sailor's uniform and the collar of his jacket was turned high around his neck, for it was cold in the hall.

The girl looked to be about nineteen or twenty. She was very thin. Her black hair, thick with grease, gleamed in the dim light. There was an artificial white rose stuck in the center of the pompadour that mounted high above her small, dark face.

Lutie recognized her. It was Mary, one of the little girls who lived with Mrs. Hedges. The sailor gave Lutie a quick, appraising look and then turned back to the girl, blotting her out. The girl's thin arms went back around his neck.

"Mary," Lutie said, and stopped right behind the sailor.

The girl's face appeared over the top of the sailor's shoulder. "Hello," she said sullenly.

"It's so cold out here," Lutie said. "Why don't you go inside?"

"Mis' Hedges won't let him come in no more," Mary said. "He's spent all his money. And she says she ain't in business for her health."

"Can't you talk to him somewhere else? Isn't there a friend's house you could go to?"

"No, ma'am. Besides, it ain't no use, anyway. He's got to go back to his ship tonight."

Lutie climbed the rest of the stairs fuming against Mrs. Hedges. The sailor would return to his ship carrying with him the memory of this dark narrow hallway and Mrs. Hedges and the thin resigned little girl. The street was full of young thin girls like this one with a note of resignation in their voices, with faces that contained no hope, no life. She shivered. She couldn't let Bub grow up in a place like this.

She put her key in the door quietly, trying to avoid the loud click of the lock being drawn back. She pushed the door open, mentally visualizing the trip across the living room to her bedroom. Once inside her room, she would close the door and put the light on and Bub wouldn't wake up. Then she saw that the lamp in the living room was lit and she shut the door noisily. He should have been asleep at least two hours ago, she thought, and walked toward the studio couch, her heels clicking on the congoleum rug.

Bub sat up and rubbed his eyes. For a moment she saw something frightened and fearful in his expression, but it disappeared when he looked at her.

"How come you're not in bed?" she demanded.

"I fell asleep."

"With your clothes on?" she said, and then added: "With the light on, too? You must be trying to make the bill bigger ——" and she stopped abruptly. She was always talking to him about money. It wasn't good. He would be thinking about nothing else pretty soon. "How was the movie?" she asked.

"It was swell," he said eagerly. "There was one guy who caught gangsters——"

"Skip it," she interrupted. "You get in bed in a hurry, Mister. I still don't know what you're doing up——" Her eyes fell on the ash tray on the blue-glass coffee table. It was filled with cigarette butts. That's funny. She had emptied all the trays when she washed the dinner dishes. She knew that she had. She looked closer at the cigarette ends. They were moist. Whoever had smoked them had held them, not between their lips, but far inside the mouth so that the paper got wet and the tobacco inside had stained and discolored it. She turned toward Bub.

"Supe was up." Bub's eyes had followed hers. "We played cards."

"You mean he was in here?" she said sharply. And thought, Of course, dope, he didn't stand outside and throw his cigarette butts into the ash tray through a closed door.

"We played cards," Bub said again.

"Let's get this straight once and for all." She put her hands on his shoulders. "When I'm not home, you're not to let any-one in here. Anyone. Understand?"

He nodded. "Does that mean Supe, too?"

"Of course. Now you get in bed fast so you can get to school on time."

While Bub undressed, she took the cover off the studio couch, smoothed the thin blanket and the sheets, pulled a pillowslip over one of the cushions. He seemed to be taking an awfully long time in the bathroom. "Hey," she said finally. "Step on it. You can't get to heaven that way."

She heard him giggle and smiled at the sound. Then her face sobered. She looked around the living room. One of these days he was going to have a real bedroom to himself instead of this shabby, sunless room. The plaid pattern of the blue congoleum rug was wearing off in front of the studio couch. It was scuffed down to the paper base at the door that led to the small hall. Everything in the room was worn and old—the lumpy studio couch, the overstuffed chair, the card table that served as desk, the bookcase filled with second-hand textbooks and old maga-zines. The blue-glass top on the coffee table was scratched and chipped. The small radio was scarred with cigarette burns. The first thing she would do would be to move and then she would get some decent furniture.

Bub got into bed, pulled the covers up under his chin. "Good night, Mom," he said.

He was almost asleep when she leaned over and kissed him on the forehead. She turned the light on in her bedroom, came back and switched the light off in the living room.

"Sleep tight!" she said. His only reply was a drowsy murmur —half laugh, half sigh.

She undressed, thinking of the Super sitting in the living room, of the time when she had come to look at the apart-ment and he had stood there in that room where Bub was now sleeping and how he had held the flashlight so that the beam of light from it was down at his feet. Now he had been back in there—sitting down, playing cards with Bub—making himself at home.

What had he talked to Bub about? The thought of his being friendly with Bub was frightening. Yet what could she do about it other than tell Bub not to let him into the apartment again? There was no telling what went on in the mind of a man like that—a man who had lived in basements and cellars, a man who had forever to stay within hailing distance of whatever building he was responsible for.

The last thing she thought before she finally went to sleep was that the Super was something less than human. He had been chained to buildings until he was like an animal.

She dreamed about him and woke up terrified, not certain that it was a dream and heard the wind sighing in the airshaft. And went back to sleep and dreamed about him again.

He and the dog had become one. He was still tall, gaunt, silent. The same man, but with the dog's wolfish mouth and the dog's teeth—white, sharp, pointed, in the redness of his mouth. His throat worked like the dog's throat. He made a whining noise deep inside it. He panted and strained to get free and run through the block, but the building was chained to his shoulders like an enormous doll's house made of brick. She could see the people moving around inside the building, drearily climbing the tiny stairs, sidling through the narrow halls. Mrs. Hedges sat on the first floor smiling at a cage full of young girls.

The building was so heavy he could hardly walk with it on his shoulders. It was a painful, slow, horrible crawl of a walk —hesitant, slowing down, now stopping completely and then starting again. He fawned on the people in the street, dragged himself close to them, stood in front of them, pointing to the building and to the chains. "Unloose me! Unloose me!" he begged. His voice was cracked and hollow.

Min walked beside him repeating the same words. "Unloose him! Unloose him!" and straining to reach up toward the lock that held the chains.

He thought she, Lutie, had the key. And he followed her through the street, whining in his throat, nuzzling in back of her with his sharp, pointed dog's face. She tried to walk faster and faster, but the shambling, slow, painful sound of his footsteps was always just behind her, the sound of his whining stayed close to her like someone talking in her ear.

She looked down at her hand and the key to the padlock that held the chains was there. She stopped, and there was a whole chorus of clamoring voices: "Shame! Shame! She won't unloose him and she's got the key!"

Mrs. Hedges' window was suddenly in front of her. Mrs. Hedges nodded, "If I was you, dearie, I'd unloose him. It's so easy, dearie. It's so easy, dearie. Easy—easy—easy——"

She reached out her hand toward the padlock and the long white fangs closed on her hand. Her hand and part of her arm were swallowed up inside his wolfish mouth. She watched in horror as more and more of her arm disappeared until there was only the shoulder left and then his jaws closed and she felt the sharp teeth sink in and in through her shoulder. The arm was gone and blood poured out.

She screamed and screamed and windows opened and the people poured out of the buildings—thousands of them, millions of them. She saw that they had turned to rats. The street was so full of them that she could hardly walk. They swarmed around her, jumping up and down. Each one had a building chained to its back, and they were all crying, "Unloose me! Unloose me!"

She woke up and got out of bed. She couldn't shake loose the terror of the dream. She felt of her arm. It was still there and whole. Her mouth was wide open as though she had been screaming. It felt dry inside. She must have dreamed she was screaming, for Bub was still asleep—apparently she had made no sound. Yet she was so filled with fright from the nightmare memory of the dream that she stood motionless by the bed, unable to move for a long moment.

The air was cold. Finally she picked up the flannel robe at the foot of the bed and pulled it on. She sat down on the bed and tucked her feet under her, then carefully pulled the robe down over her feet, afraid to go back to sleep for fear of a recurrence of the dream.

The room was dark. Where the airshaft broke the wall there was a lighter quality to the darkness—a suggestion of dark blue space. Even in the dark like this her knowledge of the position of each piece of furniture made her aware of the smallness of the room. If she should get up quickly, she knew she would bump against the small chest and moving past it she might collide with the bureau.

Huddled there on the bed, her mind still clouded with the memory of the dream, her body chilled from the cold, she thought of the room, not with hatred, not with contempt, but with dread. In the darkness it seemed to close in on her until it became the sum total of all the things she was afraid of and she drew back nearer the wall because the room grew smaller and the pieces of furniture larger until she felt as though she were suffocating.

Suppose she got used to it, took it for granted, became resigned to it and all the things it represented. The thought set her to murmuring aloud, "I mustn't get used to it. Not ever. I've got to keep on fighting to get away from here."

All the responsibility for Bub was hers. It was up to her to keep him safe, to get him out of here so he would have a chance to grow up fine and strong. Because this street and the other streets just like it would, if he stayed in them long enough, do something terrible to him. Sooner or later they would do something equally as terrible to her. And as she sat there in the dark, she began to think about the things that she had seen on such streets as this one she lived in.

There was the afternoon last spring when she had got off the subway on Lenox Avenue. It was late afternoon. The spring sunlight was sharp and clear. The street was full of people taking advantage of the soft warm air after a winter of being shut away from the sun. They had peeled off their winter coats and sweaters and mufflers.

Kids on roller skates and kids precariously perched on homemade scooters whizzed unexpectedly through the groups of people clustered on the sidewalk. The sun was warm. It beamed on the boys and girls walking past arm in arm. It made their faces very soft and young and relaxed.

She had walked along slowly, thinking that the sun transformed everything it shone on. So that the people standing talking in front of the buildings, the pushcart men in the side streets, the peanut vendor, the sweet potato man, all had an unexpected graciousness in their faces and their postures. Even the drab brick of the buildings was altered to a deep rosy pinkness.

Thus she had come on the crowd suddenly, quite unaware that it was a crowd. She had walked past some of the people before she sensed some common impulse that had made this mass of people stand motionless and withdrawn in the middle of the block. She stopped, too. And she became sharply aware of a somber silence, a curious stillness that was all around her. She edged her way to the front of the crowd, squeezing past people, forcing her way toward whatever it was that held them in this strangely arrested silence.

There was a cleared space near the buildings and a handful of policemen and cameramen and reporters with pink cards stuck in their hatbands were standing in it looking down at something. She got as close to the cleared space as she could —so close that she was almost touching the policeman in front of her.

And she saw what they were looking at. Lying flat on the sidewalk was a man—thin, shabby, tall from the amount of sidewalk that his body occupied. There was blood on the sidewalk, and she saw that it was coming from somewhere under him. Part of his body and his face were covered with what looked to be a piece of white canvas.

But the thing she had never been able to forget were his shoes. Only the uppers were intact. They had once been black, but they were now a dark dull gray from long wear. The soles were worn out. They were mere flaps attached to the uppers. She could see the layers of wear. The first outer layer of leather was left near the edges, and then the great gaping holes in the center where the leather had worn out entirely, so that for weeks he must have walked practically barefooted on the pavement.

She had stared at the shoes, trying to figure out what it must have been like to walk barefooted on the city's concrete sidewalks. She wondered if he ever went downtown, and if he did, what did he think about when he passed store windows filled with sleek furs and fabulous food and clothing made of materials so fine you could tell by looking at them they would feel like sea foam under your hand?

How did he feel when the great long cars snorted past him as he waited for the lights to change or when he looked into a taxi and saw a delicate, soft, beautiful woman lifting her face toward an opulently dressed man? The woman's hair would gleam and shine, her mouth would be knowingly shaped with lip rouge. And the concrete would have been rough under this man's feet.

The people standing in back of her weren't moving. They

weren't talking. They were simply standing there looking. She watched a cop touch one of the man's broken, grayish shoes with his foot. And she got a sick feeling because the cop's shoes were glossy with polish and the warm spring sunlight glinted on them.

One of the photographers and a newspaperman elbowed through the crowd. They had a thin, dark young girl by the arm. They walked her over to a man in a gray business suit. "She thinks it's her brother," the reporter said.

The man stared at the girl. "What makes you think so?"

"He went out to get bread and he ain't home yet."

"Look like his clothes?" He nodded toward the figure on the sidewalk.

"Yes."

One of the cops reached down and rolled the canvas back from the man's face.

Lutie didn't look at the man's face. Instead, she looked at the girl and she saw something—some emotion that she couldn't name—flicker in the girl's face. It was as though for a fraction of a second something—hate or sorrow or surprise—had moved inside her and been reflected on her face. As quickly as it came, it was gone and it was replaced by a look of resignation, of complete acceptance. It was an expression that said the girl hoped for no more than this from life because other things that had happened to her had paved the way so that she had lost the ability to protest against anything—even death suddenly like this in the spring.

"I always thought it'd happen," she said in a flat voice.

Why doesn't she scream? Lutie had thought angrily. Why does she stand there looking like that? Why doesn't she find out how it happened and yell her head off and hit out at people? The longer she looked at that still, resigned expression on the girl's face, the angrier she became.

Finally she had pushed her way to the back of the crowd. "What happened to him?" she asked in a hard voice.

A woman with a bundle of newspapers under her arm answered her. She shifted the papers from one arm to the other. "White man in the baker shop killed him with a bread knife."

There was a silence, and then another voice added: "He had the bread knife in him and he walked to the corner. The cops brought him back here and he died there where he's layin' now."

"White man in the store claims he tried to hold him up."

"If that bastard white man puts one foot out here, we'll kill him. Cops or no cops."

She went home remembering, not the threat of violence in that silent, waiting crowd, but instead the man's ragged sole-less shoes and the resigned look on the girl's face. She had never been able to forget either of them. The boy was so thin —painfully thin—and she kept thinking about his walking through the city barefooted. Both he and his sister were so young.

The next day's papers said that a "burly Negro" had failed in his effort to hold up a bakery shop, for the proprietor had surprised him by resisting and stabbed him with a bread knife. She held the paper in her hand for a long time, trying to follow the reasoning by which that thin ragged boy had become in the eyes of a reporter a "burly Negro." And she decided that it all depended on where you sat how these things looked. If you looked at them from inside the framework of a fat weekly salary, and you thought of colored people as naturally criminal, then you didn't really see what any Negro looked like. You couldn't, because the Negro was never an individual. He was a threat, or an animal, or a curse, or a blight, or a joke.

It was like the Chandlers and their friends in Connecticut, who looked at her and didn't see her, but saw instead a wench with no morals who would be easy to come by. The reporter saw a dead Negro who had attempted to hold up a store, and so he couldn't really see what the man lying on the sidewalk looked like. He couldn't see the ragged shoes, the thin, starved body. He saw, instead, the picture he already had in his mind: a huge, brawny, blustering, ignorant, criminally disposed black man who had run amok with a knife on a spring afternoon in Harlem and who had in turn been knifed.

She had gone past the bakery shop again the next afternoon. The windows had been smashed, the front door had apparently been broken in, because it was boarded up. There were messages chalked on the sidewalk in front of the store. They all said the same thing: "White man, don't come back." She was surprised to see that there were men still standing around, on the nearest corners, across the street. Their faces were turned toward the store. They weren't talking. They were just standing with their hands in their pockets—waiting.

Two police cars with their engines running were drawn up in front of the store. There were two cops right in front of the door, swinging nightsticks. She walked past, thinking that it was like a war that hadn't got off to a start yet, though both sides were piling up ammunition and reserves and were now waiting for anything, any little excuse, a gesture, a word, a sudden loud noise—and pouf! it would start.

Lutie moved uneasily on the bed. She pulled the robe more tightly around her. All of these streets were filled with violence, she thought. You turned a corner, walked through a block, and you came on it suddenly, unexpectedly.

For it was later in the spring that she took Bub to Roundtree Hospital. There was a cold, driving rain and she had hesitated about going out in it. But Bub had fallen on the sidewalk and cut his knee. She had come home from work to find him sitting disconsolately in Pop's kitchen. It was a deep, nasty cut, so she took him to the emergency room at Roundtree in order to find out just how bad it was.

She and Bub sat on the long bench in the center of the waiting room. There were two people ahead of them, and she waited impatiently because she should have been at home fixing dinner and getting Bub's clothes ready for school the next day.

Each time the big doors that led to the street swung open, a rush of wet damp air flushed through the room. She took to watching the people who came in, wondering about them. A policeman came in with a tired-looking, old man. The man's suit was shabby, but it was neatly pressed. He was wearing a stiff white collar.

The policeman guided him toward the bench. "Sit here," he said. The man gave no indication that he had heard. "Sit here," the policeman repeated. "Naw," as the old man started to move away. "Just sit down here, Pop." Finally the old man sat down.

She had watched him out of the corner of her eyes. He stared at the white hospital wall with a curious lack of interest. Nurses walked past him, white-coated internes strode by. There was a bustle and flurry when a stocky, gray-haired man with pince-nez glasses emerged from the elevator. "How are you, Doctor?" "Nice to see you back, Doctor."

The old man remained completely oblivious to the movement around him. The focus of his eyes never shifted from the expanse of wall in front of him.

Bub moved closer to her. "Hey, Mom," he whispered, "what's the matter with him?"

"I don't know," she said softly. "Maybe he's just tired."

Right across from where they were sitting was a small room filled with volunteer ambulance drivers. They were lounging in the chairs, their shirt collars open, smoking cigarettes. The blue haze of the smoke drifted out into the waiting room. The cop went into the room to use the telephone.

She heard him quite clearly. "I dunno. Picked him up on Eighth Avenue. Woman at the candy store said he'd been sittin' there all day. Naw. On the steps. Yeah. Psychopathic, I guess."

The old man didn't move, apparently didn't hear. She found him strangely disturbing, because there was in his lack-luster staring the same quality of resignation that she had seen in the face of the girl on Lenox Avenue earlier in the spring. She remembered how she had tried to tie the two together and reach a conclusion about them and couldn't because the man was old. She kept thinking that if he had lived that long, he should have been able to develop some inner strength that would have fought against whatever it was that had brought him to this aimless staring.

The telephone in the room across from them rang and she forgot about the old man. The woman who answered it said, "Okay. Right away." She turned to one of the drivers, gave him an address on Morningside Avenue, and said, "Hustle! They say it's bad."

Lutie had hoped that she would be able to get Bub into the emergency room before the ambulance came back, so that he wouldn't be sitting round-eyed with fear when he saw whatever it was they brought back that was "bad." She kept telling herself she shouldn't have brought him here, but the fee was so low that it was almost like free treatment.

The big street doors opened suddenly and the stretcher came through. The men carrying it moved quickly and with such precision that the stretcher was practically on top of them

before Lutie realized it. The room was full of a low, terrible
moaning, and the young girl on the stretcher was trying to sit
up and blood was streaming out of the center of her body.

A gray-haired woman walked beside the stretcher. She kept
saying, "Cut to ribbons! Cut to ribbons! Cut to ribbons!"—
over and over in a monotonous voice. It was raining so hard
that even in getting from the street to the waiting room the
woman had been soaked and water dripped from her coat,
from her hatbrim.

There was a long, awful moment while they maneuvered the
stretcher past the bench and the girl moaned and tried to talk,
and every once in a while she screamed—a sharp, thin, disembodied sound. The policeman looked at the girl in astonishment, but the old man never turned his head.

Lutie had grabbed Bub and covered his face with her face so
that he couldn't see. He tried to squirm out of her arms and
she held him closer and tighter. When she lifted her head, the
stretcher was gone.

Bub stood up and looked around. "What was the matter
with her?" he asked.

"She got hurt."

"How did she get hurt?"

"I don't know. It was an accident, I guess."

"Somebody cut her, didn't they?" And when she didn't answer, he repeated, "Didn't they?"

"I guess so, but I really don't know."

"One of the kids at school got cut up like that," he said, and
then, "Why wouldn't you let me look, Mom?"

"Because I didn't think it was good for you to look. And
when people are hurt badly like that, it doesn't help them to
have someone stare at them."

While the interne dressed Bub's knee, she thought about the
girl on the stretcher. Just a kid. Not much over sixteen, and
she had that same awful look of resignation, of not expecting
anything better than that of life. She was like the girl on Lenox
Avenue who had looked down at her brother lying on the sidewalk to say, "I always thought it'd happen."

Lutie sat motionless staring into the dark. She was cold and
yet she didn't move. She thought of the old man, the young
girls. What reason did she have to believe that she and Bub

wouldn't become so accustomed to the sight and sound of violence and of death that they wouldn't protest against it—they would become resigned to it; or that Bub finally wouldn't end up on a sidewalk with a knife in his back?

She felt she knew the steps by which that girl landed on the stretcher in the hospital. She could trace them easily. It could be that Bub might follow the same path.

The girl probably went to high school for a few months and then got tired of it. She had no place to study at night because the house was full of roomers, and she had no incentive, anyway, because she didn't have a real home. The mother was out to work all day and the father was long gone. She found out that boys liked her and she started bringing them to the apartment. The mother wasn't there to know what was going on.

They didn't have real homes, no base, no family life. So at sixteen or seventeen the girl was fooling around with two or three different boys. One of them found out about the others. Like all the rest of them, he had only a curious supersensitive kind of pride that kept him going, so he had to have revenge and knives are cheap.

It happened again and again all through Harlem. And she saw in her mind's eye the curious procession of people she had met coming out of 121st Street. They were walking toward Eighth Avenue.

She had been to the day-old bakery on Eighth Avenue and she stopped on the corner for the stop light. Down the length of the block she saw this group of people. They formed at first glance what appeared to be a procession, for they were walking slowly, stiffly. There was a goodish space between each one of them as though they didn't want to be too close to each other and yet were held together in a group by shock. They were young—sixteen, seventeen, eighteen, nineteen—and they were moving like sleepwalkers.

Then she saw that they had set their pace to that of the girl walking in the very front. Someone was leading her by the arm, and she was walking slowly, her body was limp, her shoulders sagged.

She had cringed away from the sight of the girl's face. She couldn't collect her thoughts for a moment, and then almost automatically the toneless reiterated words of the gray-haired woman in Roundtree Hospital came back to her: "Cut to ribbons! Cut to ribbons!"

She couldn't really see the girl's face, because blood poured over it, starting at her forehead. It was oozing down over her eyes, her nose, over her cheeks, dripped even from her mouth. The bright red blood turned what had been her face into a gaudy mask with patches of brown here and there where her skin showed through.

Lutie got that same jolting sense of shock and then of rage, because these people, all of them—the girl, the crowd in back of her—showed no horror, no surprise, no dismay. They had expected this. They were used to it. And they had become resigned to it.

Yes, she thought, she and Bub had to get out of 116th Street. It was a bad street. And then she thought about the other streets. It wasn't just this street that she was afraid of or that was bad. It was any street where people were packed together like sardines in a can.

And it wasn't just this city. It was any city where they set up a line and say black folks stay on this side and white folks on this side, so that the black folks were crammed on top of each other—jammed and packed and forced into the smallest possible space until they were completely cut off from light and air.

It was any place where the women had to work to support the families because the men couldn't get jobs and the men got bored and pulled out and the kids were left without proper homes because there was nobody around to put a heart into it. Yes. It was any place where people were so damn poor they didn't have time to do anything but work, and their bodies were the only source of relief from the pressure under which they lived; and where the crowding together made the young girls wise beyond their years.

It all added up to the same thing, she decided—white people. She hated them. She would always hate them. She forced herself to stop that train of thought. It led nowhere. It was unpleasant.

She slipped out of the wool robe and got back into bed and lay there trying to convince herself that she didn't have to stay on this street or any other street like it if she fought hard enough. Bub didn't have to end up stretched out on a sidewalk with a knife through his back. She was going to sleep, and she wasn't going to dream about supers who were transformed into wolfish dogs with buildings chained on their backs.

She searched her mind for a pleasant thought to drift off to sleep on. And she started building a picture of herself standing before a microphone in a long taffeta dress that whispered sweetly as she moved; of a room full of dancers who paused in their dancing to listen as she sang. Their faces were expectant, worshiping, as they looked up at her.

It was early when she woke up the next morning and she yawned and stretched and tried to remember what it was that had given her this feeling of anticipation. She burrowed her head deep into her pillow after she looked at the small clock on the bureau, because she could stay in bed for a few more minutes.

And then she remembered. Tonight was the night that she was going to sing at the Casino. Perhaps after tonight was over she could leave this street and these dark, narrow rooms and these walls that pressed in against her. It would be like discarding a worn-out dress, a dress that was shiny from wear and faded from washing and whose seams were forever giving way. The thought made her fling her arms out from under the covers. She pulled the covers close around her neck, for the room was cold and the steam was as yet only a rattling in the radiator.

Immediately she began planning the things she had to do. When she got home from work, she would wash her hair and curl it, then press the long black taffeta skirt which with a plain white blouse would have to serve as evening gown. She wouldn't wear her winter coat, even though it was cold out, for the little short black coat would look better.

The hands of the battered clock moved toward seven and she jumped out of bed, shivered in the cold air, and slammed the airshaft shut.

Pulling her bathrobe around her, she went into the living room. Bub was still sleeping and she tucked the covers tight under his chin, thinking that sometime soon he would wake up in a bedroom of his own. It would have maple furniture and the bedspread and draperies would have ships and boats on them. There would be plenty of windows in the room and it would look out over a park.

In the kitchen she poured water into a saucepan, lit the gas stove, and stood waiting for the water to boil. While she stirred oatmeal into the boiling water, she began to wonder if perhaps she shouldn't wear that thin white summer blouse instead of one of the plain long-sleeved ones. The summer blouse had a low, round neck. It would look a lot more dressed-up. She turned the flame low under the oatmeal, set the table, filled small glasses with tomato juice, thinking that Bub could sleep about fifteen more minutes. She would have just time enough to take a bath.

But first she would look at the blouse to see if it needed pressing. She went into the bedroom and opened the closet door quietly. The blouse was rammed in between her one suit and her heavy winter coat. She reached her hand toward it, thinking, That's just plain careless of me. It must be terribly wrinkled from having been put in there like that.

She took the blouse out and held it up in front of her, staring at it in amazement. Why, it's all crushed, and there's dirt on it, she thought—great smudges of dirt and tight, small wrinkles as though it had been squeezed together. What on earth had Bub been doing with it?

She shook him awake. "What were you doing in my closet?" she demanded.

"Closet?" He looked up at her his eyes still full of sleep. "I ain't been in your closet."

"Will you stop saying 'ain't'?" she said. "Were you playing with my blouse?" She held it in front of him.

He was wide awake now, and he looked up at her with such obvious astonishment that she knew he was telling the truth. "Honest, Mom," he protested, "I ain't had it."

Unconsciously she thrust the blouse a little farther away from her, holding it by the metal hanger and thinking, Well, then who had done this? She knew that she hadn't hung it up wrinkled and dirty. Then she remembered that Jones, the Super, had been in the apartment last night playing cards with Bub. But he couldn't, she thought—what would he be doing with her blouse and when had he done it?

"Bub," she said sharply, "did you go out while the Super was here?"

He nodded. "I got him some beer."

She turned away and went into the kitchen so that Bub wouldn't see the expression on her face, because she was afraid and angry and at the same time she felt sickened. She could picture him, hungry-eyed, gaunt, standing there in her room crushing the blouse between his hands.

She opened the set tubs, dumped soapflakes in—great handfuls of them—and ran hot water on the flakes until the suds foamed up high. She almost let the water run over the top of the tub, because she stood in front of it, not moving, thinking, He's crazy. He's absolutely crazy.

Finally she shut the faucet off and poked the blouse deep into the hot, soapy water. She couldn't wear it again—not for a long time. Certainly she wouldn't wear it tonight.

Chapter 9

BUB STOOD IN THE DOORWAY of Lutie's bedroom, watching her dress. It was nine-thirty, and he kept thinking, If she's going out so late it will be a long time before she gets back home. He didn't want her to know that he was afraid to stay in the house alone. He wished there was some way he could keep her with him without telling her he was scared.

It would be like last night all over again. He hadn't fallen asleep with the light on as he'd told her. After Supe left, he sat on the couch and finally lay down on it, but he wouldn't turn the light out because even with his eyes held tight shut he could somehow see the dark all around him. The furniture changed in the dark—each piece assumed a strange and menacing shape that transformed the whole room.

He leaned against the door jamb, standing first on one foot and then the other in an effort to see how long he could remain on one foot without losing his balance or getting tired. Lutie picked up a lipstick and he watched her intently as she made her mouth a rosy red color. She frowned a little as she looked at herself in the mirror.

"You look awful pretty," he said. She had on a long black skirt that made a soft noise when she walked and a white blouse and a red scarf tied around her waist. "Where you going, Mom?"

"To a dance at the Casino. I'm going to sing there tonight."

He accepted the fact that she was going to sing with a nod of approval, because he loved to hear her sing or to hum, and he took it for granted that other people would, too. But if she was going to a dance, she wouldn't be home until late. The floor would creak and the wind would rattle the windows like something outside trying to get in at him, and he would be in the house alone. When she was here, he never heard noises like that—footsteps in the hall outside and doors that banged with a loud, clapping noise. He never woke up frightened and not knowing why he was frightened like last night. The dark didn't bother him when she was with him, for he knew all he had to do was call out and she would come to him.

"Will you be gone very long?" he asked.

"Not very long. I'll tuck you in bed before I go." She turned away from the mirror. "You start getting undressed now, so I can turn the light out when I go out."

He lingered in the door, watching her fasten the straps on her high-heeled red shoes, wanting to ask her not to turn the light out when she left and remembering that the bill got bigger and bigger the longer the light burned.

"Could I read some before I go to sleep?"

"I should say not. You go right to sleep." And when he still stood there, holding one foot up in back of him, she walked over and patted his shoulder. "Hurry up, honey. I haven't got much time."

He went toward the bathroom reluctantly and spent a long time putting on his pajamas. He examined his shoes and socks with great care as though he had never seen them before and was puzzled as to what they could be used for. He ran water in the bathroom sink and stirred it with a lackadaisical finger, watching the little ripples that formed as his finger moved back and forth, and wishing that he had come right out and told her he was afraid to stay by himself. Perhaps she would have asked him if he wanted Supe to come up and stay until she got back. Supe would come, too. Only she didn't seem to like Supe very much. He washed his face and hands, picked up his clothes, and went into the living room.

Lutie was turning back the covers on his bed and he stood in the middle of the room looking at the way the long skirt sort of flowed around her as she moved. It looked as though the bottom of it bowed up at her, and as she leaned over and then straightened up, the ends of the red sash moved briskly as though the red sash were dancing. He watched it with delight.

"Okay," she said. "I'll put my coat on while you're getting in bed."

He lay down in the middle of the couch and looked up at the ceiling, trying to think of something that would delay her going out. When she wasn't there, he was filled with a sense of loss. It wasn't just the darkness, for the same thing happened in the daylight when he came home from school. The instant he opened the door, he was filled with a sense of desolation, for the house was empty and quiet and strange. At noon he would eat his lunch fast and go out to the street. After school he changed his clothes quickly and, even as he changed them, no matter how quick he was, the house was frightening and cold. But when she was in it, it was warm and friendly and familiar.

There was a kid in school who had to stay home five days with a toothache. He could say he had a toothache. But he wasn't sure how quickly they came on, and he wouldn't want her to know the instant she heard him mention it that he was making it up. Or a growing pain might be better—lots of the kids at school had growing pains. He was trying to decide where the growing pain would be when she came back into the room. She walked over to the hall and clicked the light on.

Then she was bending over to kiss him and he smelt the faint sweet smell of her and he hugged her with both arms and all his strength, thinking if only she would stay just long enough for him to go to sleep. It would be just a little while because he would go to sleep quickly, knowing that she was close by.

He relaxed his arms and lay down, afraid that she might be angry if he clung to her like that, for he remembered how angry she was this morning about her blouse being wrinkled and he might wrinkle this one she had on by squeezing her so tightly. She reached toward the light by the bed and he touched her coat in a light, caressing gesture.

"Good-bye, hon," she said and turned the light out.

Instantly the living room was plunged into darkness. He opened his eyes wide in an effort to see something other than this swift blackness. The corners of the room were there, he knew, but he couldn't see them. They were wiped out in the dark. It made him feel as though he were left hanging in space and that he couldn't know how much space there was other than that his body occupied.

The overstuffed chair near the couch had become a bulge of darkness so that it no longer looked like a chair. It was a strange, frightening object along with the card table in front of the window and the bookcase. It was as though quick, darting hands had substituted something else in place of them just as the light went off. His eyes slowly became accustomed to the darkness and he saw that the dim light in the hall reached a little way into the living room, leaving a faint yellow square of light on the blue congoleum rug. Even that was disturbing, for he couldn't quite make out the familiar plaid pattern in the rug.

"You won't let anyone in, will you?" Lutie asked.

He had forgotten she was still in the room and he looked in the direction of her voice, grateful to hear the sound of it. "No, ma'am."

There was a strained, breathless quality in his voice, and Lutie turned toward him. "Are you all right, hon?" she asked.

"Sure." He had hoped she would notice there was something wrong with him. Then, when she did, he suddenly didn't want her to know he was a coward about the dark and about staying alone. He thought of the hard-riding cowboys, the swaggering, brave detectives in the movies, and the big tough boys in six B in school, and he said, "Sure, I'm all right."

Lutie walked toward the square of light and he saw her clearly for a moment—the shine of the hair on top of her head, the long, soft-flowing black skirt, the short, wide coat.

"Good-bye," she said again, and turned toward him smiling.

"'Bye, Mom," he answered. Then the light in the hall went off. She was still there, though, because he heard her open the door and for an instant the dim light from the outside hall came into the room. He leaned toward it because it left pools of black shadows in the corners of the room, even in the small foyer. Then she closed the door.

The whole apartment was swallowed up in darkness. He listened to the sound of her key turning in the lock. Her high heels clicked as she walked down the hall. He sat up straight in order to hear better. She was going down the stairs. Her footsteps grew fainter and fainter until strain as he would he could no longer hear them.

He lay down and pulled the bedcovers up to his chin and firmly closed his eyes. They wouldn't stay closed. He kept opening them because even with his eyes shut he was aware of the dark all around him. It had a heavy, syrupy quality—soft and thick like molasses, only black.

It was worse with his eyes open, because he couldn't see anything and he kept imagining that the whole room was changing and shifting about him. He peered into the dark, trying to see what was going on. He sat up and then he lay down again and pulled the covers over his head. There was an even stranger quality to the black under the covers. He shut his eyes and then opened them immediately afterward, not knowing what he expected to find nestling beside him under the sheets, but afraid to look and afraid not to look.

Heavy footsteps came up the stairs and he threw the covers back and sat up listening. Maybe it's Supe, he thought. The steps went past the door, on down the hall, and he lay down again disappointed. The stairs outside creaked. A light, persistent sound started in the walls, a scuttering, scampering noise that set him shivering and cowering under the covers, for he remembered the vivid stories Lil had told him about the rats and mice that ate people up.

There was a fight in the apartment next door. At first he welcomed the sound of the loud, angry voices because it shut out the sound of the rats in the walls. There was a crash of china. Something heavy landed against the wall and then plaster dropped down. He could hear it trickle down and down. The voices grew more violent and the woman screamed.

He put his fingers in his ears. The covers slipped down from his head with the movement of his arms and instantly the darkness in the room enveloped and enfolded him. He gripped the covers tight over his head and the horrid sound of the voices and the screaming came clearly through the blanket and the sheets.

"You black bitch, I oughtta killed you long ago."

"Don't you come near me. Don't you come near me," the woman panted.

Someone threw a bottle out of a window on the fourth floor and it landed in the yard below with a tinkling sound that echoed and echoed. There was silence for a moment. A dog commenced to bark and the voices next door started again.

The woman sobbed, and as Bub listened to the sound he became more and more frightened. It was such a lonesome sound and the room quivered with it until he seemed almost to see the sound running through the dark. There was nothing around him that was familiar or that he had ever seen before. His face tightened. He was here alone, lost in the dark, lost in a strange place filled with terrifying things.

He reached up, fumbled for the light, found the switch, and turned it on. Instantly the room lay all around him—familiar, safe, just as he had always known it. He examined it with care.

All of the things that he knew so well were right where they belonged—the big chair, the card table, the radio, the congoleum rug. None of it had changed. Yet in the dark these things vanished and were replaced by strange, unknown shapes.

The sobbing of the woman next door died away. From somewhere downstairs there came the sound of laughter, the clink of glasses. He lay down relaxed, no longer frightened. Mom would be mad when she came home and found him asleep with the light on, but he couldn't turn it off again.

It occurred to him that she wouldn't mind the light being on if he could figure out some way of earning money so that he could help pay the electric bill. He frowned. She hadn't liked the shoeshine box. But there must be some other way he could make money, some way she would approve of. Finally he dropped off to sleep, still trying to think of something he could do to earn money.

At about the same time Bub was falling asleep, Lutie entered the lobby of the Casino where the smell of floor wax and dust and liquor and perfume hung heavy in the air.

At this hour the big dance hall was deserted and lifeless. The bold-eyed girls in the checkroom talked idly to each other. Their eyes constantly shifted to the thick white china plates on the shelves in front of them, as though they were fascinated by the prospect of the change that would be added to the solitary quarter and dime they had placed on the plates earlier in the evening. The rows and rows of empty coat hangers in back of them emphasized the silent, waiting look of the place.

As Lutie pushed her coat toward one of the checkroom girls, she was wondering if Bub was afraid to stay by himself and ashamed to admit it, for she remembered the sudden, frightened look on his face when she woke him up by opening the door last night.

She mechanically accepted a round white disk from the girl and put it in her pocketbook. There was something inexpressibly dreary about the Casino when it was empty, she thought. You could see all of it for what it was worth, and it was never good to see anything like that. The red carpet on the lobby floor was worn. There were dark places on it where cigarettes had been snuffed out. The artificial palms that stood at the entrance in big brass pots were gray with dust. Even the great staircase which led to the dance floor above was badly in need of a coat of paint.

The long black skirt flowed around her feet as she mounted the stairs. She was surprised to discover that she wasn't nervous or excited about singing with Boots Smith's band. Now that she was about to do it, she had regained her old feeling of self-confidence, and she walked swiftly, holding her head high, humming as she walked.

The shiny, polished dance floor looked enormous. Though it would be another hour before people arrived to dance, the colored lights were already focused on it—pale blue, delicate pink and yellow—rainbow colors that shifted and changed until the wide, smooth floor was bathed in the soft, moving bands of light.

As Lutie walked across the floor toward the bandstand where the orchestra was playing softly, she noticed that the Casino's bouncers were already on hand, standing in a small group off to one side. Their tuxedos couldn't conceal their long arms and brutal shoulders. They had ex-prize-fighter written all over them, from their scarred faces and terrible ears to the way in which their heads drew back into their shoulders as though they were dodging punches.

Boots jumped down from the bandstand when he saw her. He met her midway. "You know," he said, "I began to get the feelin' that you wasn't coming. Don't know why." His eyes traveled slowly from the curls piled high on top of her head to the red sandals on her feet. "You sure look good, baby," he said softly.

He linked his arm through hers and walked with her toward the men in the band. "Boys, meet Lutie Johnson," he said. "She's singin' with us tonight. What do you want to start with?" he asked, turning to her.

"Oh, I don't know." She hesitated, trying to think. "I guess 'Darlin'' would be best." It was the song he had heard her sing in the Junto and had liked.

She avoided the eyes of the men in the orchestra because what they were thinking was plain on their faces. The fat pianist grinned. One of the trumpet players winked at the drummer. The others nudged each other and nodded knowingly.

One of the saxophonists was raising his instrument in mock salute to Boots. It was quite obvious that they were saying to themselves and to each other, Yeah, Boots has got himself a new chick and this singing business is the old come-on.

Boots ignored them. He patted out the rhythm with his foot and the music started. She walked over to the microphone and stood there waiting for the melody to repeat itself. She touched the mike and then held onto it with both hands, for the silvery metal was cold and her hands were suddenly hot. As she held the mike, she felt as though her voice was draining away down through the slender metal rod, and the idea frightened her.

The music swelled in back of her and she began to sing, faintly at first and then her voice grew stronger, clearer, for she gradually forgot the men in the orchestra, forgot even that she was there in the Casino and why she was there.

Though she sang the words of the song, it was of something entirely different that she was thinking and putting into the music: she was leaving the street with its dark hallways, its mean, shabby rooms; she was taking Bub away with her to a place where there were no Mrs. Hedges, no resigned and disillusioned little girls, no half-human creatures like the Super. She and Bub were getting out and away, and they would never be back.

The last low strains of the melody died away and she stood holding onto the mike, not moving. There was complete silence behind her, and she turned toward the band, filled with sudden doubt and wishing that she had kept her mind on what she was doing, on the words of the song, instead of floating off into a day-dream.

The men in the orchestra stood up. They were bowing to her. It was an exaggerated gesture, for they bowed so far from the waist that for a moment all she could see were their backs —rounded and curved as they bent over. She was filled with triumph at the sight, for she knew that this absurd, preposterous bowing was their way of telling her they were accepting her on merit as a singer, not because she was Boots' newest girl friend.

"I——" she turned to Boots.

"The job's yours, baby," he said. "All yours. Wrapped up and tied up for as long as you want it."

After he said that, she couldn't remember much of anything. She knew that she sang other songs—new ones and old ones —and that each time she sang, the smile of satisfaction on Boots' face increased. But it was something that she was aware of through a blur and a mist of happiness and contentment because she had found the means of getting away from the street.

As the hands of the big clock on the wall moved toward eleven-thirty, the big smooth floor filled with dancing couples. They arrived in groups of nine and ten. The boxes at the edges of the dance floor spilled over with people—young girls, soldiers, sailors, middle-aged men and women. The tuxedoed bouncers moved warily through the crowd, forever encircling it, mingling with it. The long bar at the side of the dance floor was almost obscured by the people crowding around it. The bartenders moved quickly, pouring drinks, substituting full glasses for empty ones.

The soft rainbow-colored lights played over the dancers. There were women in evening gowns, girls in short tight skirts and sweaters that clung slickly to their young breasts. Boys in pants cut tight and close at the ankle went through violent dance routines with the young girls. Some of the dancing couples jitter-bugged, did the rhumba, invented intricate new steps of their own. The ever-moving, ever-changing lights picked faces and figures out of the crowd; added a sense of excitement and strangely the quality of laughter to the dancers. People in the boxes drank out of little paper cups, ate fried chicken and cake and thick ham sandwiches.

Lutie sang at frequent intervals. There was violent applause each time, but even while she was singing, she could hear the babble of voices under the music. White-coated waiters scurried back and forth to the boxes carrying trays heavy with buckets of ice, tall bottles of soda, and big mugs foaming with beer. And all the time the dancers moved in front of her, rocking and swaying. Some of them even sang with her.

The air grew heavy with the heat from the people's bodies, with the smell of beer and whiskey and the cigarette smoke that hung over the big room like a gray-blue cloud. And she thought, It doesn't make much difference who sings or whether they sing badly or well, because nobody really listens. They're making love or quarreling or drinking or dancing.

During the intermission Boots said to her, "How about a drink, baby?"

"Sure," she said. For the first time she realized how tired she was. She had come home from work and shopped for food in crowded stores, cooked dinner for herself and Bub, washed and ironed shirts for him and a blouse for herself. The excitement of coming here, of singing, of knowing that she would get this job that meant so much to her had completely blotted out any feeling of fatigue. Now that it was over, she was limp, exhausted.

"I'd love to have a drink," she said gratefully.

He gave the bartender the order and led her to one of the small tables at the edge of the dance floor. A white-coated waiter slid a small glass across the table to Boots. Then he opened the bottle of beer on his tray, poured it into a thick mug and placed the mug so squarely in front of Lutie that she wondered if he had measured the distance.

Boots filled his glass from a flask that he took from his pocket. Then he slid the glass back and forth on the table, holding it delicately between his thumb and forefinger. He looked at her and smiled. The long, narrow scar on his cheek moved up toward his eye as he smiled.

"You know, baby, I could fall in love with you easy," he said. And, he thought, it's true. And that if he couldn't get her any other way, he just might marry her, and he laughed because the thought of being married amused him. He pushed the glass back and forth and smiled at her again.

"Really?" she said. It was beginning rather quickly. But it didn't matter because the job was hers and that was the important thing. She searched her mind for an answer that wouldn't entirely rebuff him and yet would hold him off. "I was in love once, and I guess once you've put all you've got into it there isn't much left over for anyone else," she said carefully.

"You mean your husband?"

"Yes. It wasn't his fault it didn't work out. And I guess it really wasn't mine either. We were too poor. And we were too young to stand being poor."

They're all alike, he thought. Money's what gets 'em, even this one with that soft, young look on her face. And he almost purred, thinking not even marriage would be necessary.

It would take a little time, just a little time, and that was all. He leaned across the table to say, "You don't have to be poor any more. Not after tonight. I'll see to that. All you got to do from now is just be nice to me, baby."

He had thought she would give some indication that being nice to him was going to be easy for her. Instead, she got up from the table. There was a little frown between her eyes. The thick mug in front of her was more than half full of beer.

"Hey, you ain't finished your beer," he protested.

"I know"—she waved her hand toward the bandstand where the men were filing in. "The boys are ready to start," she said.

It was three o'clock when the rainbow-colored lights stopped moving over the dance floor. There was a final blast from the trumpets and the orchestra men began stowing music into the cases that held their instruments. The people filed out of the big hall slowly, reluctantly. The ornate staircase was choked with them, for they walked close to each other as though still joined together by the memory of the music and the dancing.

The hat-check girls smiled as they peeled coats off hangers, reached up on shelves for hats. Coins clinked in the thick white saucers. The men crowded around the mirrors adjusting bright-colored scarves around their necks, buttoning coats, patting their hats into becoming shapes, and adjusting the hats on their heads with infinite care.

Boots turned to Lutie. "Can I give you a ride home, baby?"

"That would be swell," she said promptly. Perhaps he would tell her how much the salary was that went with the job. Perhaps, too—and the thought was unpleasant—he would make the first tentative advances toward the next step—the business of being nice to him. At the moment she felt so strong and so confident that she was certain she could put him off deftly, neatly, and continue to do it until she signed a contract for the job.

When they reached the lobby, there were only a handful of stragglers left. Even these were putting on hats and coats, the men ogling themselves in the mirror, the women posing on the circular bench in the center of the lobby. The women pressed their feet deep into the red carpet, enjoying the feel of it under their shoes, admiring the glimpses they caught of their own reflections in the mirrors on the wall.

At the foot of the stairs one of the biggest of the Casino's bouncers laid a hamlike hand on Boots' arm. Lutie stared at him, for at close range the battered flesh of his face, the queer out-of-shape formation of his ears, and the enormous bulge of his shoulders under the smooth cloth of the tuxedo jacket were awe-inspiring.

"Hey, Boots," he said. "Go by Junto's. He wanta see you." The words came out of the side of his mouth. His lips barely moved.

"He phoned?"

"Yeah. 'Bout an hour ago. Said you was to stop when you got through here."

"Okay, pal."

Boots obtained Lutie's coat from the checkroom, held it for her, pushed the big doors of the Casino open, then helped her into his car, not really thinking about her, but wondering what Old Man Junto wanted that was so important it wouldn't keep until daylight.

He drove down Seventh Avenue in silence, conjecturing about it. When he finally remembered that Lutie was there in the car with him, he had reached 125th Street. "Where'll I let you out?" he asked absently.

"At the corner of 116th Street and Seventh."

He stopped the car at the corner of 116th Street, reached across her to open the door. "See you tomorrow night, baby?" he asked. "Same time so we can rehearse some?"

"Absolutely," she said, and felt a faint astonishment because his hands had gone back to the steering wheel and stayed there. He was looking up the street, his mind obviously far away, not even remotely concerned with her.

She watched his car until it disappeared up the street, trying to figure out what it was that had distracted and disturbed him so that he had put her completely out of his thoughts.

The wind lifted the full folds of her skirt, blew the short, full coat away from her body. She shrugged her shoulders. It was too cold to stand on this corner puzzling about what was on Boots Smith's mind.

As she walked toward the apartment house where she lived, she passed only a few people. They were moving briskly. Otherwise the street was dead quiet. Most of the houses were dark.

The cold couldn't reach through to her, even with this thin coat on, she thought. Because the fact that she wouldn't have to live on this street much longer served as a barrier against the cold. It was more effective than the thickest, warmest coat. She toyed with figures. Perhaps she would get forty, fifty, sixty, seventy dollars a week. They all sounded fantastically high. She decided whatever the sum proved to be, it would be like sudden, great wealth compared to her present salary.

A man came suddenly out of a hallway just ahead of her—a furtive, darting figure that disappeared rapidly in the darkness of the street. As she reached the doorway from which he had emerged, a woman lurched out, screaming, "Got my pocketbook! The bastard's got my pocketbook!"

Windows were flung open all up and down the street. Heads appeared at the windows—silent, watching heads that formed dark blobs against the dark spaces that were the windows. The woman remained in the middle of the street, bellowing at the top of her voice.

Lutie got a good look at her as she went past her. She had a man's felt hat pulled down almost over her eyes and men's shoes on her feet. Her coat was fastened together with safety pins. She was shaking her fists as she shouted curses after the man who had long since vanished up the street.

Ribald advice issued from the windows:

"Aw, shut up! Folks got to sleep."

"What the hell'd you have in it, your rent money?"

"Go on home, old woman, 'fore I throw somp'n special down on your rusty head."

As the woman's voice died away to a mumble and a mutter, the heads withdrew and the windows were slammed shut. The street was quiet again. And Lutie thought, No one could live on a street like this and stay decent. It would get them sooner or later, for it sucked the humanity out of people—slowly, surely, inevitably.

She glanced up at the gloomy apartments where the heads had been. There were row after row of narrow windows—floor after floor packed tight with people. She looked at the street itself. It was bordered by garbage cans. Half-starved cats prowled through the cans—rustling paper, gnawing on bones. Again she thought that it wasn't just this one block, this particular street. It was like this all over Harlem wherever the rents were low.

But she and Bub were leaving streets like this. And the thought that she had been able to accomplish this alone, without help from anyone, made her open the street door of the apartment house with a vigorous push. It made her stand inside the door for a moment, not seeing the dimly lit hallway, but instead seeing herself and Bub living together in a big roomy place and Bub growing up fine and strong.

The air from the street set her skirt to billowing around her long legs and, as she stood there smiling, her face and body glowing with triumph, she looked almost as though she were dancing.

Chapter 10

AFTER MIN hung the cross over the bed, Jones took to sleeping in the living room. He could no longer see the cross, but he knew it was there and it made him restless, uneasy.

Finally it seemed to him that he met it at every turn. Wherever he looked, he saw a suggestion of its outline. His eyes added a horizontal line to the long cord that hung from the ceiling light and instantly the cross was dangling in front of him. He sought and found the shape of a cross in the window panes, in chairs, in the bars on the canary's cage. When he looked at Min, he could see its outline as sharply as though it had been superimposed on her shapeless, flabby body.

He drew an imaginary line from her head to her feet and added another crosswise line, and thus, whenever he glanced in her direction, he saw the cross again. When she spoke to him, he no longer looked at her for fear he would see, not her, but the great golden cross she had hung over the bed.

He turned and twisted on the sofa thinking about it. Finally he sat up. Min was snoring in the bedroom. He could almost see her lower lip quiver with the blowing-out of her breath through her opened mouth. The room was filled with the sound. The dog's heavy breathing formed an accompaniment.

It annoyed him that Min and the dog should be comfortably lost in their dreams while he was wide awake—painfully awake. He thought of Lutie's apartment on the top floor. It was like a magnet whose pull reached down to him and drew him toward it steadily, irresistibly. He dressed quickly in the dark. He had to go up and see if she was home. Perhaps he could get another look at her.

He went steadily up the stairs, his thoughts running ahead of him. This time he would tell her that he had come to see her. She would invite him in and they would really get to know each other. The stairs creaked under his weight.

There was no light under the door of her apartment. He hesitated, not knowing what to do. It hadn't occurred to him that she might not be home. He stared blankly at the door and then went past it, down the hall, and climbed the short flight of stairs to the roof. He stood looking down at the dark street, studying the silhouette of the buildings against the sky.

Gradually he began to discern the outline of a whole series of crosses in the buildings. And he crept silently down the stairs and into his apartment. He didn't undress. He took his shoes off and lay down listening to the sound of Min's snoring, and the dog's heavy breathing, and hating it.

He couldn't go to sleep. His mind was filled with a vast and awful confusion in which images of Lutie warred with images of Min. His love and desire for Lutie mixed and mingled with his hatred and aversion for Min. He was stuck with Min. He hadn't been able to put her out. Yet as long as she stayed he was certain he could never induce Lutie to come and live with him. He dwelt on her figure, etching it again and again in the darkness. She wasn't the kind of girl who would have anything to do with a man who had a wreck of a woman attached to him.

There ought to be some way he could rid himself of the fear of that cross Min had put over the bed. But though he thought about it at length, he knew he could never touch it long enough to throw it out of the house. And as long as it remained, Min would be here with him.

The living room had a cold, menacing feel. He kicked the patchwork quilt onto the floor and reached for his heavy work shoes, not turning on the light in his desire to hurry and get out of the room and go down to the cellar where there was warmth from the fire in the furnace. The glow from its open door would keep him company and finally lull him off to sleep as it had so many times when he stayed in furnace rooms.

One of the shoes slid out of his hands and landed on the floor with a loud clump. Min stopped snoring. He heard the bedsprings creak as she turned over. He turned on the light and bent over to lace his shoes up, not caring whether she knew that he was going out. He thought of her with contempt. She was probably sitting bolt upright in bed, her head cocked on one side just like the dog's, trying to figure out what the noise was that had awakened her.

Outside in the hall he opened the cellar door and then paused with his hand on the knob when the street door opened. He turned to see which of the tenants was coming in so late and he saw Lutie standing in the doorway, her long skirt blowing around her. She seemed to fill the whole hall with light. There was a faint smile playing around her mouth and he thought she was smiling at the sight of him and bending and swaying toward him.

His hand left the door in a slow, wide gesture and he started toward her, thinking that he would have her now, tonight, and trembling with the thought. His long gaunt body seemed taller than ever in the dim light. His eyes were wide open, staring. He was breathing so quick and fast in his excitement, he made a panting sound that could be clearly heard.

Lutie saw the motion of his hand leaving the door, saw his figure moving toward her. She couldn't see who or what it was that moved, for the cellar door was in deep shadow and she couldn't separate the shadow and the movement. Then she saw that it was the Super. He was either going down into the cellar or just coming out of it. At first she couldn't tell which he was doing because his lank figure was barely recognizable in the dim light.

He was walking toward her. She decided he was going into his apartment. When she started up the stairs, she would have to pass close by him and the thought filled her with dread. She saw again the tight, hard wrinkles in her blouse and thought of how he must have squeezed it between his hands. For a moment she was unable to move. Her throat went dry and tight with fear.

She forced herself to walk toward the stairs, aware as she moved that her gait was stiff and unnatural almost as though her muscles were rebelling against any motion. He wasn't going into his apartment. He had stopped moving. He was standing motionless in front of her. Somehow she had to pass him, get past him without looking at him, get past him now, quickly, before she thought about it too long.

He side-stepped and blocked her passage to the stairs. He put his hand on her arm. "You're so sweet. You're so sweet. You little thing. You young little thing."

She could barely understand the words, for he was so excited that his voice came out thick and hoarse. But she caught the word "sweet" and she moved away from him. "Don't," she said sharply. The street door was in back of her. If she moved fast enough, she could get out into the street.

Instantly his arm went around her waist. He was pulling her back, turning her around so that she faced him. He was dragging her toward the cellar door.

She grabbed the balustrade. His fingers pried her hands loose. She writhed and twisted in his arms, bracing her feet, clawing at his face with her nails. He ignored her frantic effort to get away from him and pulled her nearer and nearer to the cellar door. She kicked at him and the long skirt twisted about her legs so that she stumbled closer to him.

She tried to scream, and when she opened her mouth no sound came out; and she thought this was worse than any nightmare, for there was no sound anywhere in this. There was only his face close to hers—a frightening, contorted face, the eyes gleaming, the mouth open—and his straining, sweating body kept forcing her ever nearer the partly open cellar door.

And suddenly she found her voice. Someone in his apartment must have opened the door or else it was open all the time. For the dog was loose. He came bounding toward them down the length of the dark hall, growling. She felt him leap on her back. The horror of it was not to be borne, for the man was trembling with his desire for her as he dragged her toward the cellar, and the dark hall was filled with the stench of the dog and the weight of his great body landing on her back.

She screamed until she could hear her own voice insanely shrieking up the stairs, pausing on the landings, turning the corners, going down the halls, gaining in volume as it started again to climb the stairs. And then her screams rushed back down the stair well until the whole building echoed and re-echoed with the frantic, desperate sound.

A pair of powerful hands gripped her by the shoulders, wrenched her violently out of the Super's arms, flung her back against the wall. She stood there shuddering, her mouth still open, still screaming, unable to stop the sounds that were coming from her throat. The same powerful hands shot out and thrust the Super hard against the cellar door.

"Shut up," Mrs. Hedges ordered. "You want the whole place woke up?"

Lutie's mouth closed. She had never seen Mrs. Hedges outside of her apartment and looked at closely she was awe-inspiring. She was almost as tall as the Super, but where he was thin, gaunt, she was all hard, firm flesh—a mountain of a woman.

She was wearing a long-sleeved, high-necked flannelette nightgown. It was so snowy white that her skin showed up intensely black by contrast. She was barefooted. Her hands, her feet, and what could be seen of her legs were a mass of scars —terrible scars. The flesh was drawn and shiny where it had apparently tightened in the process of healing.

The big white nightgown was so amply cut that, despite the bulk of her body, it had a balloon-like quality, for it billowed about her as she stood panting slightly from her exertion, her hands on her hips, her hard, baleful eyes fixed on the Super. The gaudy bandanna was even now tied around her head in firm, tight knots so that no vestige of hair showed. And watching the wide, full nightgown as it moved gently from the draft in the hall, Lutie thought Mrs. Hedges had the appearance of a creature that had strayed from some other planet.

Her rich, pleasant voice filled the hallway, and at the sound of it the dog slunk away, his tail between his legs. "You done lived in basements so long you ain't human no more. You got mould growin' on you," she said to Jones.

Lutie walked away from them, intent on getting up the stairs as quickly as possible. Her legs refused to carry her and she sat down suddenly on the bottom step. The long taffeta skirt dragged on the tiled floor. Bits of tobacco, the fine grit from the street, puffed out from under it. She made no effort to pick it up. She put her head on her knees, wondering how she was going to get the strength to climb the stairs.

"Ever you even look at that girl again, I'll have you locked up. You oughtta be locked up, anyway," Mrs. Hedges said.

She scowled at him ferociously and turned away to touch Lutie on the shoulder and help her to her feet. "You come sit in my apartment for a while till you get yourself back together again, dearie."

She thrust the door of her apartment open with a powerful hand, put Lutie in a chair in the kitchen. "I'll be right back.

You just set here and I'll make you a cup of tea. You'll feel better."

The Super was about to go into his apartment when Mrs. Hedges returned to the hall. "I just wanted to tell you for your own good, dearie, that it's Mr. Junto who's interested in Mis' Johnson. And I ain't goin' to tell you again to keep your hands off," she said.

"Ah, shit!" he said vehemently.

Her eyes narrowed. "You'd look awful nice cut down to a shorter size, dearie. And there's folks that's willin' to take on the job when anybody crosses up they plans."

She stalked away from him and went into her own apartment, where she closed the door firmly behind her. In the kitchen she put a copper teakettle on the stove, placed cups and saucers on the table, and then carefully measured tea into a large brown teapot. Lutie, watching her as she walked barefooted across the bright-colored linoleum, thought that instead of tea she should have been concocting some witch's brew.

The tea was scalding hot and fragrant. As Lutie sipped it, she could feel some of the shuddering fear go out of her.

"You want another cup, dearie?"

"Yes, thank you."

Lutie was well on the way to finishing the second cup before she became aware of how intently Mrs. Hedges was studying her, staring at the long evening skirt, the short coat. Again and again Mrs. Hedges' eyes would stray to the curls on top of Lutie's head. She should feel grateful to Mrs. Hedges. And she did. But her eyes were like stones that had been polished. There was no emotion, no feeling in them, nothing visible but shiny, smooth surface. It would never be possible to develop any real liking for her.

"You been to a dance, dearie?"

"Yes. At the Casino."

Mrs. Hedges put her teacup down gently. "Young folks has to dance," she said. "Listen, dearie," she went on. "About tonight"—she indicated the hall outside with a backward motion of her head. "You don't have to worry none about the Super bothering you no more. He ain't even going to look at you again."

"How do you know?"

"Because I scared him so he's going to jump from his own shadow from now on." Her voice had a purring quality.

Lutie thought, You're right, he won't bother me any more. Because tomorrow night she was going to find out from Boots what her salary would be and then she would move out of this house.

"He ain't really responsible," Mrs. Hedges continued. "He's lived in cellars so long he's kind of cellar crazy."

"Other people have lived in cellars and it didn't set them crazy."

"Folks differs, dearie. They differs a lot. Some can stand things that others can't. There's never no way of knowin' how much they can stand."

Lutie put the teacup down on the table. Her legs felt stronger and she stood up. She could get up the stairs all right now. She put her hand on Mrs. Hedges' shoulder. The flesh under the flannel of the gown was hard. The muscles bulged. And she took her hand away, repelled by the contact.

"Thanks for the tea," she said. "And I don't know what I would have done if you hadn't come out in the hall——" Her voice faltered at the thought of being pulled down the cellar stairs, down to the furnace room——

"It's all right, dearie." Mrs. Hedges stared at her, her eyes unwinking. "Don't forget what I told you about the white gentleman. Any time you want to earn a little extra money."

Lutie turned away. "Good night," she said. She climbed the stairs slowly, holding on to the railing. Once she stopped and leaned against the wall, filled with a sick loathing of herself, wondering if there was something about her that subtly suggested to the Super that she would welcome his love-making, wondering if the same thing had led Mrs. Hedges to believe that she would leap at the opportunity to make money sleeping with white men, remembering the women at the Chandlers' who had looked at her and assumed she wanted their husbands. It took her a long time to reach the top floor.

Mrs. Hedges remained seated at her kitchen table, staring at the scars on her hands and thinking about Lutie Johnson. It had been a long time since she thought about the fire. But tonight, being so close to that girl for so long, studying her as

she drank the hot tea and seeing the way her hair went softly
up from her forehead, looking at her smooth, unscarred skin,
and then watching her walk out through the door with the
long skirt gently flowing in back of her, had made her think
about it again—the smoke, the flame, the heat.

Her mind jerked away from the memory as though it were
a sharp, sudden pain. She began thinking about the period in
her life when she had haunted employment agencies seeking
work. When she walked in them, there was an uncontrollable
revulsion in the faces of the white people who looked at her.
They stared amazed at her enormous size, at the blackness of
her skin. They glanced at each other, tried in vain to control
their faces or didn't bother to try at all, simply let her see what
a monstrosity they thought she was.

Those were the years when she slept on a cot in the hall of
the apartment belonging to some friends of hers from Georgia.
She couldn't get on relief because she hadn't lived in the city
long enough. Her big body had been filled with a gnawing, in-
satiable hunger that sent her prowling the streets at night, lifting the heavy metal covers of garbage cans, foraging through
them for food.

She wore discarded men's shoes on her feet. The leather
was broken and cracked. The shoes were too small so that she
limped slightly. Her clothing was thin, ragged. She got so she
knew night better than day because she could no longer bring
herself to go out in the daytime. And she frequently wished
that she had never left the small town in Georgia where she was
born. But she was so huge that the people there never really
got used to the sight of her. She had thought that in a big city
she would be inconspicuous and had hoped that she would
find a man who would fall in love with her.

It was a cold, raw night when she first saw Junto. The cold
had emptied the street. She was leaning over the garbage cans
lined up in front of a row of silent, gloomy brownstone houses.
She had found a chicken bone and she was gnawing the meat
from it, wolfing it down, chewing even the bone, when she
looked up to see a squat, short man staring at her—a white
man.

"What you lookin' at, white man?"

"You," he said coolly.

She was surprised at the calm way he looked at her, showing no fear.

"You're on my beat," he said. "You got here ahead of me." He pointed toward a pushcart at the curb. It was piled high with broken bottles, discarded bits of clothing, newspapers tied into neat bundles.

"I got as much right here as you," she said truculently.

"Didn't say you haven't." He went on examining her, the chicken bone in her hand, the ragged coat tied around her, the men's shoes on her feet. "Seein's you're going through this stuff ahead of me, I was thinking you might as well make some money at it."

"Money?" she said suspiciously.

"Sure. Pick out the bottles and the pieces of metal. I'll pay you for them. It won't be much. But I can cover more ground if somebody helps me."

Thus, Mrs. Hedges and Junto started out in business together. It was she who suggested that he branch out, get other pushcarts and other men to work for him. When he bought his first piece of real estate, he gave her the job of janitor and collector of rents.

It was a frame building five stories high, filled with roomers. Not many people knew that Junto owned it. They thought he came around to buy junk—scrap iron and old newspapers and rags. When he obtained a second building, he urged her to move, but she refused. Instead, she suggested that he divide the rooms in this building in half and thus he could get a larger income from it. And of course she made more money, too, because she got a commission on the rent she collected. She was careful to spend very little because she had convinced herself that if she had enough money she could pick out a man for herself and he would be glad to have her.

The fire had started late at night. She was asleep in the basement and she woke to hear a fierce crackling—a licking, running sound that increased in volume as she listened. There was heat and smoke along with the sound. By the time she got to the door, the hall was a red, angry mass of flame. She slammed the door shut and went over to the basement window.

It was a narrow aperture not really big enough for the bulk of her body. She felt her flesh tear and actually give way as she struggled to get out, forcing and squeezing her body through the small space. Fire was blazing in the room in back of her. Hot embers from the roof were falling in front of her. She tried to keep her face covered with her hands, so that she wouldn't see what she was heading into, so that she could keep some of the smoke and flame away from her face.

Even as she struggled, she kept thinking that all she needed to do was to get badly burned, and never as long as she lived would any man look at her and want her. No matter how much money she acquired, they still wouldn't want her. No sum of money would be big enough to make them pretend to want her.

There was nothing but smoke and red flame all around her, and she wondered why she kept on fighting to escape. She could smell her hair burning, smell her flesh burning, and still she struggled, determined that she would force her body through the narrow window, that she would make the very stones of the foundation give until the window opening would in turn give way.

She was a bundle of flame when she finally rolled free on the ground. The firemen who found her stared at her in awe. She was unconscious when they picked her up, and she was the only survivor left from that house full of people.

It was all of three weeks before Junto was permitted to see her at the hospital. "You're a brave woman, Mrs. Hedges," he said.

She stared at him from under the mass of bandages that covered her head and part of her face.

"Getting out of that window was wonderful. Simply wonderful." He looked curiously at the tent-like formation that held the hospital blankets away from the great bulk of her body—a bulk increased by dressings and bandages—marveling at the indomitable urge to live, the absolutely incredible will to live, that had made her force her body through so small a space.

"You'll be all right, you know," he said.

"The doctor told me"—her voice was flat, uninterested. "I ain't going to have any hair left."

"You can wear a wig. Nobody'll ever know the difference." He hesitated, wanting to tell her how amazing he thought she was and that he would have done the same thing, but that there were few people in the world that he had come across who had that kind of will power. He touched one of her bandaged hands gently, wanting to tell her and not knowing quite how to say it. "Mrs. Hedges," he said slowly, "you and me are the same kind of folks. We got to stay together after this. Close together. We can go a long way."

She had thought about her scalp—how scarred and terrible looking it would be. The hair would never grow back. She looked steadily at Junto, her eyes unwinking. He would probably be the only man who would ever admire her. He was squat. His shoulders were too big for his body. His neck was set on them like a turtle's neck. His skin was as gray in color as his eyes. And he was white. She shifted her eyes so that she could no longer see him.

"You're a wonderful woman," he was saying softly.

And even he would never want her as a woman. He had the kind of forthright admiration for her that he would have for another man—a man he regarded as his equal. Scarred like this, hair burned off her head like this, she would never have any man's love. She never would have had it, anyway, she thought realistically. But she could have bought it. This way she couldn't even buy it.

She folded her lips into a thin, straight line. "Yes. We can go a long way."

Lutie Johnson made her remember a great many things. She could still hear the soft, silken whisper of Lutie's skirt, see the shining hair piled high on her head and the flawless dark brown of her skin. She thought of her own scarred body with distaste.

When Junto returned to the hospital after his first visit, he had looked at her for a long time.

"There's plastic surgery," he suggested delicately.

She shook her head. "I don't want no more stays in hospitals. It wouldn't be worth it to me."

"I'll pay for it."

"No. I couldn't stay in the hospital long enough for 'em to do nothing like that."

She would die if she did. As it was, it had been hard enough, and to prolong it was something that would be unendurable. When the nurses and doctors bent over her to change the dressings, she watched them with hard, baleful eyes, waiting for the moment when they would expose all the ugliness of her burnt, bruised body. They couldn't conceal the expressions on their faces. Sometimes it was only a flicker of dismay, and then again it was sheer horror, plain for anyone to see—undisguised, uncontrollable.

"Thanks just the same. But I been here too long as it is."

She stayed in the hospital for weeks during which the determination never to expose herself to the prying, curious eyes of the world grew and crystallized. When she finally left it, she moved into the house that Junto owned on 116th Street.

"There's a nice first-floor apartment I've saved for you, Mrs. Hedges," he explained. "I've even put the furniture in."

Before she left the hospital, she decided that she would have to have someone living with her to do her shopping, to run errands for her. So the first few days in the new apartment she sat at the window seeking a likely-looking girl. One girl passed by several times, a thin, dispirited young thing who never lifted her eyes from the sidewalk.

"Come here, dearie," she called to her. Seen close to, the girl's hair was thick and wiry and with a little care it would look very nice.

"Yes'm"—the girl scarcely lifted her head.

"Where you live?"

"Down the street"—she pointed toward Eighth Avenue.

"You got a job?"

"No'm"—the girl looked up at Mrs. Hedges. "I had one, but my husband left me. I couldn't seem to keep my mind on what I was doing after that, so the lady fired me about two weeks ago."

"Whyn't you come here and live with me, dearie? I got this place all to myself."

"I can't pay the rent where I am now. There ain't much point in my coming here."

"If you'll do my shopping for me, you ain't got to worry about no rent."

So Mary came to live with her and she gradually lost her dejected look. She laughed and talked and cleaned the apartment and cooked. Mrs. Hedges began to take a kind of pride in the way Mary blossomed out.

One night a tall young man walked past the window, headed toward the house.

"Who you lookin' for, dearie?" she had asked.

"I come to see Mary Jackson," he said. He glanced at Mrs. Hedges once and then looked away.

"She's gone out to buy something at the store. She lives here with me. You want to come in and set awhile?"

She had looked him over carefully after he uneasily selected a seat in her living room. The big-brimmed, light gray, almost white, hat, the tight-legged breeches, the wide shoulders of his coat built up with padding, the pointed-toed bright yellow shoes, all added up to the kind that rarely got married, and when they did, they didn't stay put. She stared at him until he shifted his feet and moved the light gray hat between his hands, balancing it and inspecting it as though he were judging its merits with an eye to purchasing it.

The street was full of men like him. She stopped her slow examination of him long enough to wonder if a creature like this was the result of electric light instead of hot, strong sunlight; the result of breathing soot-filled air instead of air filled with the smell of warm earth and green growing plants and pulling elevators and sweeping floors instead of doing jobs that would develop the big muscles in shoulders and thighs.

"What you do for a living?" she asked abruptly.

"Ma'am?"

"I said what you do for a living?"

"Well, I——" He balanced the hat on one finger. "I ain't exactly working right now at the moment," he hedged.

"What'd you do when you was working?"

"I was in a restaurant for a while. Dishwasher. Before that I was a porter in a bar." He put the hat down on a table near the chair. "They wasn't much as jobs go. I got tired of cleaning up after white folks' leavings, so I quit." There was a hard, resentful, slightly fierce quality in his voice when he said the words "white folks."

"How you live now?" And when he didn't answer, she said pointedly, "How you manage to eat?"

"Well, I mostly works for the fellow that runs the poolroom a couple of blocks over. He's got a game going in the back. I kind of help around."

Yes, she thought, and you saw Mary, and you think you're going to get yourself some free loving. Only he wasn't. He was going to have to pay for it. Mary would earn money, and she,

Mrs. Hedges, would earn money from Mary's earnings. The more she thought about it, the more pleased she became with the idea, for making money and saving it had become a habit with her.

The street would provide plenty of customers. For there were so many men just like him who knew vaguely that they hadn't got anything out of life and knew clearly that they never would get it, even though they didn't know what it was they wanted; men who hated white folks sometimes without even knowing why; men who had to find escape from their hopes and fears, even if it was for just a little while. She would provide them with a means of escape in exchange for a few dollar bills.

Staring at him with her hard, unwinking gaze, she could see the whole detail of a prosperous, efficient enterprise. She would get several more girls. They would be like Mary—girls that had been married and whose men had deserted them. The street was full of girls like that.

"They's one or two things you and me got to settle before Mary comes back," she said.

"Yes'm?" His face had turned sullen.

"How much can you afford to pay when you comes here to see Mary?"

"Huh?" he asked, startled.

"Mary and me don't live here on air," she said coldly. "If'n you want to sleep with her, it's going to cost you."

That was how it started. As simply and as easily as that. She explained her plan to Junto, so that he would speak to the people at the precinct and they wouldn't bother her.

"But this ain't for white men," she warned. "You can have them in them Sugar Hill joints you run. But they can't come here."

He laughed out loud, something he rarely did. "Mrs. Hedges, I believe you're prejudiced. I didn't know you were that human."

"I ain't prejudiced," she said firmly. "I just ain't got no use for white folks. I don't want 'em anywhere near me. I don't even wanta have to look at 'em. I put up with you because you don't ever stop to think whether folks are white or black and you don't really care. That sort of takes you out of the white folks class."

"You're a wonderful woman, Mrs. Hedges," he said softly. "A wonderful woman."

Yes. She and Mr. Junto had gone a long way. A long, long way. Sometimes she had surprised him and surprised herself at the things she had suggested to him. It came from looking at the street all day. There were so many people passing by, so many people with burdens too heavy for them, young ones who were lost, old ones who had given up all hope, middle-aged ones broken and lost like the young ones, and she learned a lot just from looking at them.

She told Junto people had to dance and drink and make love in order to forget their troubles and that bars and dance halls and whorehouses were the best possible investments. Slowly and cautiously Mr. Junto had become the owner of all three, though he still controlled quite a bit of real estate.

It amused her to watch the brawling, teeming, lusty life that roared past her window. She knew so much about this particular block that she came to regard it as slightly different from any other place. When she referred to it as "the street," her lips seemed to linger over the words as though her mind paused at the sound to write capital letters and then enclosed the words in quotation marks—thus setting it off and separating it from any other street in the city, giving it an identity, unmistakable and apart.

Looking out of the window was good for her business, too. There were always lonesome, sad-looking girls just up from the South, or little girls who were tired of going to high school, and who had seen too many movies and didn't have the money to buy all the things they wanted.

She could pick them out easily as they walked past. They wore bright-colored, short-skirted dresses and gold hoop earrings in their ears. Their mouths were a brilliant scarlet against the brown of their faces. They wobbled a little on the exaggerated high-heeled shoes they wore. They wore their hair combed in high, slick pompadours.

And there were the other little girls who were only slightly older who had been married and woke up one morning to discover that their husbands had moved out. With no warning. Suddenly. The shock of it stayed on their faces.

"Dearie," she would say, and her eyes somehow always

lingered on the hair piled high above their small, pointed faces, "I been seein' you go by. And I was wonderin' if you wouldn't like to earn a little extra money sometime."

She and Mr. Junto had made plenty of money. Only none of it had made her hair grow back. None of it had erased those awful, livid scars on her body.

Off and on during the years he had made timid, tentative gestures toward transforming their relationship into something more personal—gestures which she had steadfastly ignored. For she never intended to reveal the extent of her disfigurement to anyone—least of all to Junto who knew her so well.

Apparently he still wasn't discouraged, because just the other night when he came to see her he brought a wig with him. He tossed it in her lap. The hair was black, long, silky. It was soft under her fingers, curling and clinging and attaching itself to her hands almost as though it were alive. It was the kind of hair that a man's hands would instinctively want to touch. She pushed it away violently, thinking how the hard, black flesh of her face, the forward thrust of her jaws, the scars on her neck, would look under that silken, curling hair.

"Take it away. I don't want it."

"But——" He started to protest.

"There's some things that are personal"—she touched the coarse red bandanna with her hand and glared at him fiercely.

"I'm sorry," he said. He picked the wig up and put it back in the box it had been wrapped in. "I thought you'd like to have it." He groped for words. "We've been friends a long time, Mrs. Hedges. And I guess I thought that between friends anything would be understood. If I did any harm bringing this here, I did it with good intentions. But I understand why you don't want it. I understand better than you think."

That same night was the only time she was ever really mean to Mary. She couldn't get the memory of that soft, fine, clinging hair out of her mind. She kept remembering how Junto said he understood why she didn't want it. And Mary's hair was combed high over her small, pointed face. It was heavy with grease from the hairdresser's. There was a white rose in the center of her pompadour—the rose seemed to nestle there.

"Mrs. Hedges, Tige's got to go back to his ship tonight," Mary had said.

She had been staring out at the street, thinking about the wig. "Who's Tige, dearie?" she asked absently.

"The sailor boy who was here last night."

She remembered him then. He was so young that he swaggered when he walked past her window in his tight-fitting, dark blue sailor pants. So young that his eyes were alive with laughter; his sailor's hat was perched so far back on his head and at such a precarious angle, it looked as though any sudden movement would pitch it off. His hands were thrust deep into the pockets of his short jacket and the bulky wool of the jacket couldn't conceal how flat and lean his waist was and how it tapered up to his wide shoulders in a taut, slanting line. Very, very young.

"Yes?" she said.

Mary patted a stray hair in place, and her eyes had followed the movement of Mary's hand and stayed there on the high curve of the pompadour, on the white rose that seemed to nest in the thickness of the hair.

"He spent all his money last night," Mary went on. "And I want to know can he come in again tonight? He says he'll mail the money back to you." She hesitated, and added shyly, "I like him."

"Of course not," she had said sourly. "You think I'm in business for my health?" She couldn't seem to stop looking at the girl's hair. "You can take him out in the park. Cold night like this will cool you both off."

She turned her head away from the sight of Mary's face. All the life had gone out of it, leaving it suddenly old, drawn, flat. There were deep lines around the mouth. The little fool must be in love with him, she thought.

The boy came out of the house about an hour later. He was dragging his feet. He looked cold, miserable. They been standing up there in that hall, she thought. He had to go back to his ship tonight. Go back to fighting the white folks' war for them.

"Sailor!" she said sharply, just as he reached her window.

"What do you want?"

"Where you and Mary been?"

"We been standing in the hall talking. Where you think we been?"

"How much more time you got?"

"About two hours."

"Listen, dearie, you go ring the bell and tell Mary I said it was all right."

He moved so quickly she had to yell to catch him before he opened the street door.

"Listen, sailor, you send that money back prompt on the first of the month."

"Yes, ma'am. Yes, indeed, ma'am." He paused in the doorway to execute a dance step. And then he bowed to her, taking his flat sailor's hat off in a gesture that made her think again, He's so young—so crazy young.

Her thoughts returned to Lutie Johnson. With that thick, soft hair, Lutie offered great possibilities for making money. Mr. Junto would be willing to pay very high for her. Very, very high, because when he got tired of her himself he could put her in one of those places he ran on Sugar Hill. With hair like that—her face twitched, and she got up from the kitchen table and went into the living room where she sat down by the window.

The window was half open and the air blowing in was cold. The street was silent, empty. As she looked, the wind lifted scraps of paper, bits of rubbish, and set them to swirling along the curb as though an invisible hand with a broom had reached down into the street and was sweeping the paper along before it.

The wind puffed the white nightgown out around her feet. She moved a little closer to the window. She had never felt really cool since the time she was in the fire.

Chapter 11

DESPITE THE LATENESS of the hour, groups of men were still standing in front of the Junto Bar and Grill, for the brilliant light streaming from its windows formed a barrier against the cold and the darkness in the rest of the street. Whenever the doors opened and closed, the light on the sidewalk was intensified. And because the men moved slightly, laughing and talking a little louder with each sudden increase in light, they had the appearance of moths fluttering about a gigantic candle flame.

Boots Smith, who had parked his car at the corner, watched the men without really seeing them. Something must have scared the living daylights out of Old Man Junto to make him send for him at this hour, he thought. He hated to be taken by surprise, and he was still trying to figure out what it was that had upset Junto.

Finally he shrugged his shoulders, started out of the car, and then paused with his hand on the door. It could be only one thing. Somewhere along the line there had been a leak about how he had stayed out of the army. His hand left the door. Okay, he thought. He wasn't going to play soldier now any more than he was that day he got the notice to report to his draft board for a physical examination. He took the notice to Junto early in the afternoon and he had been so angered by it that he had talked fluently, easily, quickly—something he rarely did.

"Fix this thing, Junto." He had slapped the postcard down on the table in front of Junto.

"What is it?" Junto peered at it, his turtle neck completely disappearing between his shoulders.

"Notice to report for a physical. First step on the way to the army."

"You don't want to fight?"

"Why should I?"

"I don't know. I'm asking you."

He had pulled a chair out and sat down across from Junto. "Listen, Junto," he said. "They can wave flags. They can tell me the Germans cut off baby's behinds and rape women and turn black men into slaves. They can tell me any damn thing. None of it means nothing."

"Why?"

"Because, no matter how scared they are of Germans, they're still more scared of me. I'm black, see? And they hate Germans, but they hate me worse. If that wasn't so they wouldn't have a separate army for black men. That's one for the book. Sending a black army to Europe to fight Germans. Mostly with brooms and shovels."

Junto looked at him thoughtfully and then down at the postcard.

"Are you sure that's it?" he asked. "Are you sure that you're not afraid to fight?"

"What would I be afraid of? I been fighting all my life. The Germans ain't got no way of making a man die twice in succession. No way of bringing a man alive and making him die two or three times. Naw, I'm not scared to fight."

"Suppose there wasn't a separate army. Suppose it was all one army. Would you feel differently?"

"Hell, no. Look, Junto"—he remembered how he had leaned toward him across the table talking swiftly and with an energy and passion that sent the words flooding out of his throat. "For me to go leaping and running to that draft board a lot of things would have to be different. Them white guys in the army are fighting for something. I ain't got anything to fight for. If I wasn't working for you, I'd be changing sheets on Pullman berths. And learning fresh all over again every day that I didn't belong anywhere. Not even here in this country where I was born. And saying "yes sir," "no sir," until my throat was raw with it. Until I felt like I was dirt. I've got a hate for white folks here"—he indicated his chest—"so bad and so deep that I wouldn't lift a finger to help 'em stop Germans or nobody else."

"What makes you think life would be better if the Germans ran this country?"

"I don't think it would. I ain't never said I thought so."

"Then I don't see——"

"Of course you don't," he interrupted. "You never will because you ain't never known what it's like to live somewhere

where you ain't wanted and every white son-of-a-bitch that sees you goes out of his way to let you know you ain't wanted. Christ, there ain't even so much as a cheap stinking diner in this town that I don't think twice before I walk into it to buy a cup of lousy coffee, because any white bastard in there will let me know one way or another that niggers belong in Harlem. Don't talk to me about Germans. They're only doing the same thing in Europe that's been done in this country since the time it started."

"But——"

"Lissen"—he stopped Junto with a wave of his hand. "One of the boys in the band come back in uniform the other night. You know what he's doing?"

Junto shook his head.

"He's playing loading and unloading ship in some god-damn port company. That boy can make a fiddle talk. Make it say uncle. Make it laugh. Make it cry. So they figured they'd ruin his hands loading ships. He tried to play when he come by the other night." He had picked the postcard notice up, flicked the edge of it with his thumbnail. "Jesus! He broke down and cried like a baby." It was a long time before he said anything after that.

Then finally he had said slowly: "I've done all the crawling a man can do in one lifetime. I don't figure to do no more. Ever. Not for nobody. I don't figure to go to Europe on my belly with a broom and a shovel in each hand." He shoved the post-card across the table. "What you going to do about this thing?"

Junto had sent him to a doctor who performed a slight, delicate, dangerous operation on his ear.

"You'll be all right in a month or so," said the doctor. "In the meantime mail this letter to your draft board." The letter stated that Boots Smith was ill and unable to report for a physical examination. And, of course, when he was finally examined, he was rejected.

Yeah, he thought. That's what it is. He tried to decide just what would happen to him and to Junto and the doctor. And couldn't. He opened the car door, stepped out on the sidewalk. Well, at least he knew what it was that Junto wanted.

When he pushed the Junto's doors open, his face gave no indication of the fact that he was worried. He glanced at the long bar where men and women were standing packed three deep, observing that the hum of their conversation, the sound of their laughter, almost but not quite drowned out the music of the juke-box.

It was getting near closing time. The white-coated bartenders were hastily pouring drinks and making change. Waiters darted about balancing heavy trays filled with the last drinks that would be served before the wide doors closed for the night.

He paused in the doorway for a moment, admiring the way the excited movement around the bar and the movement of the people at the tables and in the booths was reflected and multiplied in the sparkling mirrors. Then he waved at the bartenders, sought and found Junto sitting at a table near the back, and sat down beside him without saying anything.

"Want a drink?" Junto asked.

"Sure."

Junto beckoned a passing waiter. "Bourbon for him. Soda for me."

The waiter deposited the glasses on the table and moved off to fill the orders from a near-by table of boisterous, clamoring customers who called out to him to hurry before the bar closed.

Junto picked up his glass, sipped the soda slowly. He rolled it around in his mouth before he swallowed it as though it were a taste sensation he was anxious to retain as long as possible. Boots watched him in silence, waiting to learn how he was going to introduce the business about the army.

"That girl," Junto said. He didn't look at Boots as he talked; his eyes stayed on the noisy crowd at the bar. "That girl—Lutie Johnson——"

"Yeah?" Boots leaned toward him across the table.

"You're to keep your hands off her. I've got other plans for her."

So it wasn't the army. It was Lutie Johnson. Boots started sliding the glass of bourbon back and forth on the table, wondering if he had managed to conceal his amazement. Then, as the full meaning of Junto's words dawned on him, he frowned. He had had all kinds of girls: tall, short, wide-fannied, big-breasted, flat-breasted, straight-haired, kinky-haired, dark, light —all kinds.

But this one—this Lutie Johnson—was the first one he'd seen in a long time that he really wanted. He had even thought that if he couldn't get her any other way, he'd marry her. He watched Junto roll the soda around on his tongue and was surprised to discover that the thought of Lutie, with her long legs, straight back, smooth brown skin, and smiling eyes, sleeping with Old Man Junto wasn't a pleasant one.

And it wasn't because Junto was white. He didn't feel the same toward him as he did toward most white men. There was never anything in Junto's manner, no intonation in his voice, no expression that crept into his eyes, and never had been during the whole time he had known him, nothing that he had ever said or done that indicated he was aware that Boots was a black man.

He had watched him warily, unbelieving, suspicious. Junto was always the same, and he treated the white men who worked for him exactly the same way he treated the black ones. No, it wasn't because Junto was white that he didn't relish the thought of him sleeping with Lutie Johnson.

It was simply that he didn't like the idea of anyone possessing her, except of course himself. Was he in love with her? He examined his feeling about her with care. No. He just wanted her. He was intrigued by her. There was a challenge in the way she walked with her head up, in the deft way she had avoided his attempts to make love to her. It was more a matter of itching to lay his hands on her than anything else.

"Suppose I want to lay her myself?" he said.

Junto looked directly at him for the first time. "I made you. If I were you, I wouldn't overlook the fact that whoever makes a man can also break him."

Boots made no reply. He studied the bubbles that were forming on the side of Junto's glass.

"Well?" Junto said.

"I ain't made up my mind yet. I'm thinking."

He fingered the long scar on his cheek. Junto could break him all right. It would be easy. There weren't many places a colored band could play and Junto could fix it so he couldn't find a spot from here to the coast. He had other bands sewed up, and all he had to do was refuse to send an outfit to places stupid enough to hire Boots' band. Junto could put a squeeze on a place so easy it wasn't funny. And he thought, Pullman porter to Junto's right-hand man. A long jump. A long hard way to get where he was now.

Yeah, he thought, Pullmans. The train roaring into the night. Coaches rocking and swaying. A bell that rang and rang and rang, and refused to stop ringing. A bell that stabbed into your sleep at midnight, at one, at two, at three, at four in the morning. Because slack-faced white women wanted another blanket, because gross white men with skins the red of boiled lobster couldn't sleep because of the snoring of someone across the aisle.

Porter! Porter this and Porter that. Boy. George. Nameless. He got a handful of silver at the end of each run, and a mountain of silver couldn't pay a man to stay nameless like that. No Name, black my shoes. No Name, hold my coat. No Name, brush me off. No Name, take my bags. No Name. No Name.

Niggers steal. Lock your bag. Niggers lie. Where's my pocketbook? Call the conductor. That porter—— Niggers rape. Cover yourself up. Didn't you see that nigger looking at you? God damn it! Where's that porter? Por-ter! Por-ter!

Balance Lutie Johnson. Weigh Lutie Johnson. Long legs and warm mouth. Soft skin and pointed breasts. Straight slim back and small waist. Mouth that curves over white, white teeth. Not enough. She didn't weigh enough when she was balanced against a life of saying "yes sir" to every white bastard who had the price of a Pullman ticket. Lutie Johnson at the end of a Pullman run. Not enough. One hundred Lutie Johnsons didn't weigh enough.

He tried to regret the fact that she didn't weigh enough, even tried to work up a feeling of contempt for himself. You'd sell your old grandmother if you had one, he told himself. Yes. I'd sell anything I've got without stopping to think about it twice, because I don't intend to learn how to crawl again. Not for anybody.

Because before the Pullmans there was Harlem during the depression. And he was an out-of-work piano-player shivering on street corners in a thin overcoat. The hunger hole in his stomach had gaped as wide as the entrance to the subways.

Cold nights he used to stand in doorways out of the wind, and sooner or later a white cop would come up and snarl, "Move on, you!"

He had known the shuddering, shocking pain of a nightstick landing on the soles of his feet when he slept on park benches. "Get the hell outta here, yah bum!"

Yeah. He was a piano-player out of work, living on hunger and hate and getting occasional jobs in stinking, smoky, lousy joints where they thought he was coked up all the time. And he was. But it was hunger and hate that was the matter with him, not coke.

He would get a meal for playing in the joint and the hard-faced white man who owned it would toss a couple of dollars at him when he left, saying, "Here, you!" He wanted to throw it back, but he had to live, and so he took it, but he couldn't always keep the hate out of his eyes.

He had played in dives and honkey-tonks and whorehouses, at rent parties and reefer parties. The smell of cigarette smoke and rotgut liquor and greasy food stayed in his nose.

He got so he hated the sight of the drunks and dopesters who frequented the places where he played. They never heard the music that came from the piano, for they were past caring about anything or listening to anything. But he had to eat, so he went on playing.

More frequently than he cared to remember some drunken white couple would sway toward the piano, mumbling, "Get the nigger to sing," or, "Get the nigger to dance." And he would despise himself for not lunging at them, but the fact that the paltry pay he would get at the end of the night's work was his only means of assuaging his constant hunger held him rigid on the piano bench.

White cops raided the joints at regular intervals, smashing up furniture, breaking windows with vicious efficiency. When they found white women lolling about inside, they would start swinging their nightsticks with carefree abandon.

He learned to watch the doors with a wary eye, and the instant he entered a place he located a handy exit before he settled down to play.

When he got the job on the Pullman, he vowed that never again, so help him God, would he touch a piano. And in place

of the stinking, rotten joints there were miles of "Here boy,"
"You boy," "Go boy," "Run boy," "Stop boy," "Come boy."
Train rocking and roaring through the night. No longer hunger. Just hate. "Come boy," "Go boy." "Yes, sir." No, sir." "Of
course, sir."

Naw, Lutie Johnson didn't weigh that much. Even if she
did, he had no way of knowing that he wouldn't come home
some night to find a room full of arrested motion. Even now
he never saw the wind moving a curtain back and forth in front
of a window without remembering that curious, sick sensation
he had when he walked into his own apartment and found the
one room alive with motion that had stopped just the moment
before he entered it.

Everything in the room still except for the sheer, thin curtains blowing in the breeze. Everything frozen, motionless;
even Jubilee, stiff still in the big chair, her house coat slipping
around her body. Only the curtains in motion, but the rest of
the room full of the ghost of motion, and he couldn't move his
eyes from the curtains.

It was a warm night in the spring—a soft, warm night that
lay along the train like a woman's arms as it roared toward
New York. It was a bland, enticing kind of night, and he kept
thinking about Jubilee waiting for him at the end of the run.
He couldn't wait to get to her. Going uptown on the subway,
he thought the train kept slowing down, sitting motionless on
the track, waiting at stations, doing every damn thing it could
to keep him from getting to her in a hurry.

The street had that same soft, clinging warmth. It seemed
to be everywhere around him. He tore up the stairs and put
his key in the door. It stuck in the lock and he cursed it for
delaying him. The instant he got the door open, he knew
there was something wrong. The room was full of hurried,
not quite quickly enough arrested movement. He stood in
the doorway looking at the room, seeking whatever it was
that was wrong.

Jubilee was sitting in the big upholstered chair. She had a
funny kind of smile on her face. He could have sworn that she
had got into the chair when she heard his key click in the lock.

The thin, sheer curtains were blowing in the breeze that
came through the opened windows. Swaying gently back and

forth at the front windows, at the fire-escape window. But the fire-escape window was always closed. Jubilee kept it shut because she said it wasn't safe to sit in a room in Harlem with a fire-escape window open. That was how people got robbed. Even in hot, sweltering weather it was closed. They had argued about it the summer before:

"Christ, baby! Open the window!"

"I won't. It isn't safe."

"But we'll sweat to death in here."

"That's better than being robbed——"

He crossed the room quickly, pushed the curtains aside, and looked down. A man was going swiftly down the fire escape. Not looking up, climbing steadily down, down. He had his suit jacket over his arm. Every time the man passed a lighted window, Boots could see him quite clearly. Finally the man looked up. He had his necktie in his hand. And he was white. Unmistakably—white.

When he turned back into the room, he was so blind with fury he couldn't see anything for a moment. Then he saw her sitting in the chair, frozen with fear.

"You double-crossing bitch!" he said, and pulled her out of the chair and slammed her against the wall.

He pulled her toward him and slapped her. Then threw her back against the wall. Pulled her toward him and slapped her and threw her back against the wall. Again and again. Her face grew puffed and swollen under his hand. He heard her scream, and it pleased him to know that she was afraid of him because he was going to kill her, and he wanted her to know it beforehand and be afraid. He was going to take a long time doing it, so that she would be very afraid before she finally died.

But she fooled him. She ducked under his arm and got away from him. He took his time turning around, because there wasn't any place for her to go. She couldn't get all the way away from him, and it was going to be fun to play cat and mouse with her in this none too big room.

When he turned, she had a knife in her hand. He went for her again and she slashed him across the face.

He backed away from her. Blood oozed slowly down his cheek. It felt warm. And it shocked him to his senses. She wasn't worth going to the clink for. She was a raggle-tag slut, and he was well rid of her because she wasn't worth a good god damn.

He took the knife away from her. She cringed as though she expected him to cut her. He threw it on the floor and laughed.

"You ain't worth cutting, baby," he said. "You ain't worth going to jail for. You ain't worth nothing." He laughed again. "Tell your white boy friend he can move in any time he wants to. I'm through, baby."

The sound of Jubilee's sobbing followed him down the hall. As he went past the silent doors that lined the hallway, he thought, It's funny with all that noise and screaming no one had tried to find out what was going on. He could have killed her easy and no one would even have rapped on the door, and he wondered what went on inside these other apartments to make their occupants so incurious.

He wanted to laugh at himself and at Jubilee. Him riding Pullman trains day in and day out and hoarding those handfuls of silver, so he could keep her here in this apartment, so he could buy her clothes. Bowing and scraping because the thought of her waiting at the end of a run kept him from choking on those "Yes sirs" and "No sirs" that he said week in and week out. He paused on the stairs thinking that he ought to go back up and finish the job, because leaving it like this left him less than a half man, because he didn't even have a woman of his own, because he not only had to say "Yes sir," he had to stand by and take it while some white man grabbed off what belonged to him.

Killing her wouldn't change the thing any. But if he'd had a gun, he would have shot that bastard on the fire escape. He went on down the stairs slowly. He never realized before what a thin line you had to cross to do a murder. A thin, small, narrow line. It was less than a pencil mark to get across. A man rides a Pullman and the woman fools around, and the man can't swallow it because he's had too much crawling to do, and the man spends the rest of his life behind bars. No. He gives up his life on a hot seat, or did they hang in this state? He didn't know, because fortunately the woman cut the hell out of him.

He concealed the slash with his handkerchief, thinking that there was a colored drugstore somewhere around and the guy would fix him up.

The druggist eyed the blood on his face. "Get cut?" he asked matter-of-factly.

"Yeah. Put somep'n on it, will you?"

The druggist applied a styptic pencil. "You oughtta see a doctor," he said. "You're going to have a bad scar." And he thought must have been a woman who cut him. Guys built like this one don't let other guys get close enough to them to carve them with a knife. Probably ran out on the woman and she couldn't take it.

"A scar don't mean nothing," Boots said.

"What was it—a fight?"

"Naw. A dame. I beat her up and she gave me this for a souvenir."

There had been a lot of other women since Jubilee. He didn't remember any of them except that he had kicked most of them around a bit. Perhaps as vengeance now that he came to think about it. He only thought about Jubilee when he happened to see a pair of curtains blowing in a breeze. The scar on his face had become a thin, narrow line. Most of the time he forgot it was there, though somehow he had got into the habit of touching it when he was thinking very hard.

He looked across at Junto patiently waiting for an answer. He wasn't quite ready to answer him. Let him stew in his own juice for a while. There wasn't any question in his mind about Lutie Johnson being worth the price he would have to pay for her, nor worth the doubts that he would always have about her.

Riding back and forth between New York and Chicago he used to look forward to dropping into Junto's place. He was perfectly comfortable, wholly at ease when he was there. The white men behind the bar obviously didn't care about the color of a man's skin. They were polite and friendly—not too friendly but just right. It made him feel good to go there. Nobody bothered to mix a little contempt with the drinks because the only thing that mattered was whether you had the money to pay for them.

One time when he stopped in for a drink, he was filled up to overflowing with hate. So he had two drinks. Three drinks. Four drinks. Five drinks. To get the taste of "you boy" out of his mouth, to shake it out of his ears, to wash it off his skin. Six drinks, and he was feeling good.

There was a battered red piano in the corner. The same piano that was there right now. And he was feeling so good that he forgot that he had vowed he'd never play a piano again as long as he lived. He sat down and started playing and kept on until he forgot there were such things as Pullmans and rumpled sheets and wadded-up blankets to be handled. Forgot there was a world that was full of white voices saying: "Hustle 'em up, boy"; "Step on it, boy"; "Hey, boy, I saw a hot-looking colored gal a couple of coaches back—fix it up for me, boy." He forgot about bells that were a shrill command to "come a-running, boy."

Someone touched him on the shoulder. He looked up frowning.

"What do you do for a living?"

The man was squat, turtle-necked. White.

"What's it to you?" He stopped playing and turned on the piano bench, ready to send his fist smashing into the man's face.

"You play well. I wanted to offer you a job."

"Doing what?" And then, angered because he had answered the man at all, he said, "Sweeping the joint out?" And further angered and wanting to fight and wanting to show that he wanted to fight, he added, "With my tongue, mebbe?"

Junto shook his head. "No. I've never offered anyone a job like that," saying it with a seriousness that was somehow impressive. "There are some things men shouldn't have to do" —a note of regret in his voice. "I thought perhaps you might be willing to play the piano here."

He stared at Junto letting all the hate in him show, all the fight, all the meanness. Junto stared back. And he found himself liking him against his will. "How much?"

"Start at forty dollars."

He had turned back to the piano. "I'm working at the job right now."

It had been a pleasure to work for Junto. There hadn't been any of that you're-black-and-I'm-white business involved. It had been okay from the night he had started playing the piano.

He had built the orchestra slowly, and Junto had been pleased and revealed his pleasure by paying him a salary that had now grown to the point where he could afford to buy anything in the world he wanted. No. Lutie Johnson wasn't that important to him. He wasn't in love with her, and even if he had been she didn't weigh enough to balance the things he would lose.

"Okay," he said finally. "It doesn't make that much difference to me."

Junto's eyes went back to an examination of the bar. There was nothing in his face to indicate whether this was the answer he had expected or whether he was surprised by it. "Don't pay her for singing with the band. Give her presents from time to time." He took his wallet out, extracted a handful of bills, gave them to Boots. "All women like presents. This will make it easier for you to arrange for me to see her. And please remember"—his voice was precise, careful, almost as though he were discussing the details of a not too important business deal—"leave her alone. I want her myself."

Boots pocketed the money and stood up. "Don't worry," he said. "That babe will be as safe with me as though she was in her mother's arms."

Junto sipped his soda. "Do you think it will take very long?" he asked.

"I dunno. Some women are"—he fished for a word, shrugged his shoulders and went on—"funny about having anything to do with white men." He thought of the curtains blowing back from the fire-escape window and the white man going swiftly down, down, down. Not all women. Just some women.

"Money cures most things like that."

"Sometimes it does." He tried to decide whether it would with Lutie Johnson. Yes. She had practically said so herself. Yet there was something—well, he wasn't sure a man would have an easy time with her. She had a streak of hell cat in her or he didn't know women, and he felt a momentary and fleeting regret at having lost the chance to conquer and subdue her.

He looked down at Junto seated at the table and swallowed an impulse to laugh. For Junto's squat-bodied figure was all gray—gray suit, gray hair, gray skin, so that he melted into the room. He could sit forever at that table and nobody would look at him twice. All those people guzzling drinks at the bar never glanced in his direction. The ones standing outside on the street and the ones walking back and forth were dumb, blind, deaf to Junto's existence. Yet he had them coming and going. If they wanted to sleep, they paid him; if they wanted to drink, they paid him; if they wanted to dance, they paid him, and never even knew it.

It would be funny if Junto who owned so much couldn't get to first base with Lutie. He wasn't even sure why Junto wanted to lay her. He couldn't quite figure it out. Junto was kind of nuts about that black woman on 116th Street, talked about her all the time. He had never forgotten the shock he got when he first saw Mrs. Hedges. He hadn't really known what to expect the night he went there with Junto, but he was totally unprepared for that hulk of a woman. He could have sworn from the way Junto looked at her that he was in love with her and that he had never been able to get past some obstacle that prevented him from sleeping with her—some obstacle the woman erected.

"How was the crowd tonight?" Junto asked.

"Packed house. Hanging from the ceiling."

"No trouble?"

"Naw. There's never any trouble. Them bruisers see to that."

"Good."

"That girl sings very well," he said. He watched Junto's face to see if he could get some clue from his expression as to what it was about Lutie Johnson that had made him want her. Because there had been all kinds of girls in and out of Junto's joints and he had never been known to look twice at any of them.

"Yes, I know. I heard her." And Junto's eyes blinked, and Boots knew instantly that Junto wanted her for the same reason that he had—because she was young and extraordinarily good-looking and any man with a spark of life left in him would go for her.

"You heard her tonight?" Boots asked, incredulous.

"Yes. I was at the Casino for a few minutes."

Boots shook his head. The old man surely had it bad. He had a sudden desire to see his face go soft and queer. "How's Mrs. Hedges?" he asked.

"Fine." Junto's face melted into a smile. "She's a wonderful woman. A wonderful woman."

"Yeah." He thought of the red bandanna tied in hard, ugly knots around her head. "She sure is."

He turned away from the table. "I gotta go, Junto. I'll be seein' you." He walked out of the bar, cat-footed, his face as expressionless as when he came in.

Chapter 12

JONES, THE SUPER, closed the door of his apartment behind him. He was clenching and unclenching his fists in a slow, pulsating movement that corresponded with the ebb and flow of the rage that was sweeping through him.

At first it was rage toward Mrs. Hedges and her barging into the hall, shoving her hard hands against his chest, ordering him about, threatening him. If she hadn't been so enormous and so venomous, he would have knocked her down.

He frowned. How had the dog got out? Min must have let him out. Min must have stood right there where he was standing now, just inside the door, looking out into the hall, and seen what was going on and let the dog loose. A fresh wave of anger directed at Min flooded through him. If she hadn't let the dog out, he would have had Lutie Johnson. The dog scared Lutie so she screamed and that brought that old sow with that rag tied around her head out into the hall.

He could feel Lutie being dragged out of his arms, could see Mrs. Hedges glaring at him with her baleful eyes rammed practically into his face, could see the bulk of her big, hard body under the white flannel nightgown, and could feel all over again the threat and menace in her hands as she slammed him against the cellar door.

All of it was Min's fault. He ought to go drag her out of bed and beat her until she was senseless and then toss her out into the street. He walked toward the bedroom and stopped outside the door, remembering the cross over the bed and unable to get over the threshold despite his urge to lay violent hands on her. He couldn't tell by the light, rhythmic sound of her breathing whether she was asleep or just pretending. She must have scuttled back to bed the minute she saw him start toward the apartment door.

His thoughts jumped back to Mrs. Hedges. So that was why he couldn't have her locked up that time he went to the police station. He remembered the police lieutenant, "What's her name?" and his eyes staring at the paper where it was already written down. Junto was the reason he couldn't have her arrested that time. Sometimes during the summer he had gone to the Bar and Grill for a glass of beer and he had seen him sitting in the back—a squat, short-bodied white man whose eyes never apparently left the crowd drinking at the bar. The thought of him set Jones to trembling.

He moved away from the bedroom door and walked aimlessly around the living room. Finally he sat down on the sofa. He ought to go to bed, but he'd never be able to sleep with his mind swirling full of thoughts like this. Lutie's body had felt soft under his hands, her waist had just fitted into the space between his two hands. It was small, yielding, pliant.

His face smarted where she had scratched him. He ought to put something on it—get something from the medicine cabinet, but he didn't move. The reason she had scratched him like that was because she hadn't understood that he wasn't going to hurt her, that he wouldn't hurt her for anything. He must have frightened her coming at her so suddenly.

He could feel his thoughts gather themselves together on Lutie, concentrate on her, stay put on her. Those scratches on his face were long, deep. She hadn't been frightened that bad. It wasn't just fright. It must have been something else. She had fought him like a wildcat; as though she hated him, kicking, biting, scratching, and that awful wild screaming. But she screamed because of the dog, he told himself. But even after Mrs. Hedges came out and the dog left, even after Mrs. Hedges had pulled her out of his arms, she had gone on screaming. He could hear the despairing, desperate sound of her screams all over again, and he listened to them, thinking that they sounded as though she had found his touching her unbearable, as though she despised him. No. It wasn't just fright.

The full significance of what Mrs. Hedges had said to him came over him. That was why Lutie had fought like that and screamed and couldn't stop. She was in love with the white man, Junto, and she couldn't bear to have a black man touch her.

His mind rebelled against the idea, thrust it away. It wasn't true. He refused to admit it was remotely possible. He tried to rid himself of the thought and it crept back again quietly establishing itself. He quivered with rage at the thought of Junto's squat white body intimately entwined with Lutie's tall brown body. He saw Junto's pale skin beside Lutie's brown skin. He created situations and placed them together—eating, talking, drinking, even dancing.

He tortured himself with the picture of them lying naked in bed together, possibly talking about him, laughing at him. He attempted to put words into their mouths.

"Can you imagine, Mr. Junto, that Jones making love to me?"

He couldn't get any further than that because his mind refused to stay still. It seemed to have become a livid, molten, continually moving, fluid substance in his brain that spewed up fragments of thought until his head ached with the effort to follow the motion, to analyze the thoughts. He no sooner started to pursue one of the fragments than something else took its place, some new idea that disappeared just as he began to explore it.

Mrs. Hedges and Min. They were the ones that had frustrated him. Just at the moment when he had Lutie in his arms they had fixed it so she was snatched away from him. If only he could have got her down into the cellar, everything would have been all right. She would have calmed down right away.

Now he would have to begin all over again. He didn't know where to start. Maybe a little present would make her feel better toward him. He must have frightened her a lot. He was certain she had been smiling at him when she stood there in the doorway, holding the door in her hand, the long skirt blowing back around her legs as she looked toward the cellar door.

What ought he to give her? Earrings, stockings, nightgowns, blouses—he tried to remember some of the things he had seen in the stores on Eighth Avenue. It ought to be something special—perhaps a handbag, one of those big shiny black ones.

Junto probably gave her presents. His mind stood still for a moment. What present could he give her that could compare with the things Junto could give her? Junto could give her fur coats and—— He got up from the couch wildly furious, so agitated by his anger that his body trembled with it.

She was in love with Junto. Of course. That was why she had fought him off like a she-cat, clawing at him with her nails, kicking at him, filling the hall with that howl that still rang in his ears. She was in love with Junto, the white man.

Black men weren't good enough for her. He had seen women
like that before. He had had women like that before. Just off
the ship, hungry for a woman, dying for a woman, seeking and
finding one he had known before. A door opened a narrow
crack, "No. You can't come in." The door slammed tight shut
in his face. He had waited and waited outside and seen some
replete, satiated white tramp of a sailor emerge from the same
room hours later.

Yes. He'd seen that kind before. No use for men their own
color. Well, he'd fix her. He'd fix her good. He searched his
mind for a way to do it and was surprised to find that his thinking had grown cool, quiet, orderly. Her fighting against him
as though he was so dirty she couldn't bear to have him touch
her, her never looking at him when she went in and out of the
building, her being frightened that night when she came to
look at the apartment and they were up there together—all of
it proved that she didn't like black men, had no use for them.

So she belonged to a white man. Well, he would get back at
both of them. Yes. He'd fix them good.

He strained his eyes in the dark of the room as though by
looking hard enough in front of him he would be able to see
the means by which he would destroy her. He walked up and
down thinking, thinking, thinking. There wasn't anything he
could think of, no way he could reach her.

But there was the kid. He paused in the middle of the room,
nodding his head. He could get at the kid. He could fix the
kid and none of them could stop him. They would never know
who was responsible. He finally went to sleep, still not knowing what it was he would do, but comforted by the knowledge
that he could hurt her through the kid. Yes. The kid.

When he woke up the next morning, Min was standing by
the couch looking down at him with a curious expression on
her face.

"What you looking at?" he asked gruffly, wondering what
she had been able to read on his face while he lay there asleep,
unaware of anyone watching him, perhaps unconsciously revealing the things he had been thinking about just before he
went to sleep. "How long you been there?"

"I just come," she said. "Breakfast is ready"; and then she
added hastily: "I ate mine already. You can have the kitchen to
yourself."

"How come you ain't gone to work yet?"

"I overslept myself. I'm gettin' ready to go now."

She went into the bedroom. The worn felt slippers made a slapping, scuffing sound as she walked. It was a hateful sound and his anger of the night before returned so swiftly that he decided it must have stayed on the couch with him waiting for him to awaken. He thought of Lutie's high heels clicking on the stairs, of her long legs, and immediately he began puzzling over a way of fixing the kid.

In the kitchen he ate hungrily. Min had made rolls for breakfast. They were light and fluffy. He ate several of them, drank two cups of coffee and was starting on a third cup when his eyes fell on a slender glass vial almost full of a brilliant scarlet liquid. It was lying flat between the bottle of ketchup and a tin of evaporated milk right near the edge of the shelf over the kitchen table.

He stood up for a better look at it, uncorked it, and sniffed the contents. It had a sharp, acrid odor. There was a medicine dropper lying beside it.

He had never seen either of them before. And for no reason at all he thought of the candles that Min burned every night, of the sudden unexpected appearance of the cross over the bed, of her never explained absence one evening.

He picked up his coffee cup, suddenly suspicious. There seemed to be traces of the same acrid odor, fainter, to be sure, but still there in the cup. He smelt the contents of the big enameled coffee pot that was sitting on the stove and put it down, frowning. He still couldn't be sure, but there seemed to be traces of the same odor, diluted down, much fainter, but definitely there. It might be his imagination, and on the other hand it might have been only that his nose was full of the sharp smell of the red liquid and so he thought he found it again in his coffee cup and in the big pot.

She wouldn't dare put anything in his coffee. She wouldn't dare. How did he know? The candles and the cross returned sharply to his mind. For all he knew she had been working some kind of conjure on him all along, trying to bring him bad luck.

He picked up the slender vial and the medicine dropper and went toward the bedroom. He didn't go all the way into the room. He stood in the doorway.

Min was tying a triangular, faded wool scarf over her head. She had her coat on and her movements were slow, clumsy, awkward. Her galoshes were fastened tightly around her feet and he thought nobody but a half-wit would get dressed backward like that. She saw him in the door and she put one hand into her coat pocket, leaving the ends of the scarf dangling loose.

"What's this for?"—he held the bottle and medicine dropper out toward her. "You been putting this in my coffee? You been trying to mess with me?"

"It's my heart medicine," she said calmly.

He stared at her, not believing her and not knowing why he didn't believe her. She didn't shrink away from him, she stared back giving him look for look, and with her hand in her coat pocket she had a slightly jaunty air that made him want to strike her.

"What's the matter with your heart?"

"I don't know. Doctor gave me that for it."

"What do you do with it?"

"Put it in my coffee."

"Why ain't there no doctor's label on it?" he asked suspiciously.

"He said it don't need one. Couldn't mix that bottle up with no other one."

He still wasn't satisfied. "When'd you see him?"

"The night I went out."

He didn't believe her. She was lying. She looked like she was lying. She didn't have nothing the matter with her heart. If it wasn't for that cross—he located it out of the corner of his eye. Yes. It was still there over the bed, and he turned his eyes away from it quickly, sorry that he had looked at it, for he would be seeing the damn thing before him everywhere he looked the rest of the day.

"Well, keep it in here," he said hastily. He entered the room, laid the bottle and the medicine dropper down on the bureau and walked away quickly. "Don't have it out there in the kitchen. I don't want to look at it. Or smell it." He said the words over his shoulder.

When she emerged from the bedroom a few minutes later, the scarf tied tightly under her chin, her house dress wrapped up in a brown-paper bag that she carried under one arm, he refused to glance in her direction.

"Well, good-bye," she said hesitantly.

He grunted by way of answer, thinking that he had been so confused at the sight of the cross he hadn't asked her what the candles were for. They didn't have anything to do with her heart. He hadn't planned to ask her about the cross, because he couldn't have brought himself to question her about it; mentioning it aloud would have given it importance. It would never do for her to know what it had done to him.

He went outside to bring in the garbage cans. He stood against the building looking up and down the street. It had snowed during the night—a light, feathery coating that clung to the brick all up and down the street, gently obscuring the dirt, covering the sidewalk with a delicate film of white. He eyed it, thinking that it wouldn't call for any shoveling. A couple of hours and it would be gone just from folks walking on it.

The Sanitation Department trucks rumbled up to the curb. The street was filled with the rattle and bang of garbage cans, the churning sound of the mechanism inside the trucks as it sucked up the refuse and rubbish from the big metal cans.

There was a steadily increasing stream of women passing through the street. They were going to work. Most of them, like Min, carried small brown bundles under their arms—bundles that contained the shapeless house dresses they would put on when they reached their jobs. Some of them scurried toward the subway entrance, hurrying faster and faster because they were late. Others plodded past slowly with their heads down as though already tired because the burden of the day's work had settled about their shoulders, weighing them down before they had even begun it.

Jones rolled his empty garbage cans into the areaway and returned to stand in front of the building. In the mornings like this he was usually inside working, shaking the furnace, firing it, taking out ashes. The street had a pleasant, lively look this morning. The sun had come out, and what with the light coating of snow he felt a faint stirring of pleasure as he stood there. Just this one day he ought not to do a lick of work in the house, let the fire go out, leave the halls full of rubbish while he stayed outside and enjoyed himself.

As he watched the street, he saw that there were young, brisk-walking women among the plodding, older women. Some of them had well-shaped legs that quivered where the flesh curved to form the calf. His eyes lingered on one of them as she moved toward the corner at a smart pace that set her flesh to jiggling pleasantly.

"Right nice legs, ain't she, dearie?" Mrs. Hedges inquired from the window.

He gave her one quick look of hate and then turned his head away. Even early in the morning she was there in that window like she'd been glued to it. She was drinking a cup of coffee, and he wished that while he was standing there she would suddenly gag on it, choke, and die before his very eyes. So that he could stand over her and laugh. He couldn't remain out here with her looking at him. His pleasure in the morning and in the street faded, died as though it had never been.

There was nothing for him to do but go inside. He wanted to get some more air and look around a bit. He wasn't ready to go in yet. He wasn't going to let her drive him away. He was going to stand there until he got good and ready to go. He was uncomfortably aware of her unwinking gaze and he shifted his feet, thinking he couldn't bear it. He would have to go back in the house to get away from it.

His eye caught the postman's slow progress up the street. His gray uniform disappeared in and out of the doorways. Each time he appeared, Jones noticed how the heavy mail sack slung over his shoulder pulled him over on one side, weighing him down. Watching him, Jones decided he would stay right there until the postman reached this building. That way the old sow wouldn't know she had chased him inside.

Post-office trucks backed into the street, turned and moved off with a grinding of gears. Children scampering to school were added to the stream of people passing by. The movement in the street increased with each passing moment, and he cursed Mrs. Hedges because he wanted to enjoy it and couldn't with her sitting there in the window watching him.

The superintendent next door came out to sweep the sidewalk in front of his building. Jones saw him with relief. He walked over to talk to him, welcoming the opportunity to put even a short distance between himself and Mrs. Hedges. This way she couldn't possibly think she had driven him off.

"Kind of late this morning, ain't you?" the man asked.

"Overslept myself."

"Sure glad this wasn't a heavy snow."

"Yeah. Don't know whether snow or coal is worse." Jones was enjoying this brief chat. It proved to Mrs. Hedges that he was completely indifferent to her presence in the window. He searched for something humorous to say so that they could laugh and the laughter would further show how unconcerned he was. He elaborated on the theme of snow and coal, "Got to shovel both of 'em. One time when white is just as evil as black. Snow and coal. Both bad. One white and the other black."

The sound of the other man's laughter was infectious. The people passing by paused and smiled when they heard it. The man clapped Jones on the back and roared. And Jones discovered with regret that the hate and the anger that still burned inside him was so great that he couldn't even smile with the man, let alone join in his laughter. And the laughter died in the other man's throat when he looked at Jones' sullen face.

The man went back to sweeping the sidewalk and Jones waited for the approach of the postman. He was next door. In a minute he'd turn into this house. Yes. He was coming out now.

"Well, I gotta go."

"See you later."

He followed the postman into the hall, feeling triumphant. It was quite obvious to Mrs. Hedges that he had simply come inside to get his mail, not because of her looking at him. Then he felt chagrined because knowing everything like she did she probably knew, too, that he never got any mail.

The postman opened all the letter boxes at once, using a key that he had suspended on a long, stout chain. The sagging leather pouch that was swung over his shoulder bulged with mail. He thrust letters into the open boxes, used the key again to lock them and was gone.

Jones made no effort to open his box. There wasn't any point, for the postman hadn't put anything in it. He stood transfixed by the wonder of what he was thinking. Because he had found what he wanted. This was the way to get the kid. Not even Junto with all his money could get the kid out of it. The more he thought about it, the more excited he became. If the kid should steal letters out of mail boxes, nobody, not even

Junto, could get him loose from a rap like that. Because it was the Government.

The thought occupied him for the rest of the morning. It was foremost in his mind while he shook down the furnace, carried out ashes, even while he put a washer in a faucet on the second floor and cleaned out a clogged drain pipe on the third floor.

During the afternoon he studied the mail box keys in his possession, taking them out of the box where he kept them and strewing them over the top of his desk. These were duplicates of the keys that the tenants had. He pondered over them. He had to figure out a master key—make the pattern for a master key. He didn't have to make the key himself, the key man up the street could turn it out in no time at all, there wasn't anything complicated about a mail-box key.

He went next door to see his friend, the super, in response to a sudden inspiration.

"Lissen," he said craftily. "Let me borrow one of your mail-box keys for a minute. Damn woman in my house has lost two keys in two days. None of my other keys will work in her box. I thought one of yours might work. She's having a fit out there in the hall wanting to get her mail."

"Sure," the man said. "Come on downstairs. I'll get one for you."

Jones tried the key in the boxes in the hall. With just a little forcing it worked. He looked at it in surprise. Perhaps it would work anywhere on the street. He would have liked to ask the man if it was a master key, but he didn't dare.

He spent the rest of the afternoon drawing careful outlines of the keys. Then he evolved one that seemed to embody all the curves and twists of the others. It was slow work, for his hands were clumsy, sometimes the pencil slipped in his haste. Once his hands trembled so that he had to stop and put the pencil down until the trembling ceased.

The final pattern pleased him inordinately. He held it up and studied it, surprised. This last, final drawing wasn't really a copy. It was his own creation. He was reluctant to put it down, to let it go out of his hands. He picked it up again and again to admire it.

"I shoulda took up drawing," he said, aloud.

He held it away from him, turned it around, until finally, half-closing his eyes and staring at it, he thought he saw a horizontal line across the length of the drawing. He threw it down on the desk in disgust, his pleasure in it destroyed.

Was he going through life seeking the outline of a cross in everything about him? Min had done this to him. There were other things she had done to him which he probably didn't even begin to suspect. He thought of her standing in front of the bureau whispering, "It's for my heart," strangely unafraid, almost as though she had some kind of protection that she knew would prevent him from doing violence to her.

She had changed lately, now that he thought about it. She dominated the apartment. She cleaned it tirelessly, filled with some unknown source of strength that surged through her and showed up in numberless, subtle ways. She was always scrubbing and cleaning the apartment just as though it were hers, and then beaming approval at the result of her effort, so that her toothless gums showed as she smiled at her own handiwork.

Suddenly he laughed out loud. The dog pricked up his ears, scrambled to his feet, and came to where Jones was sitting at the desk and thrust his muzzle into his hand. Jones patted the dog's head in a rare gesture of affection.

Because he was going to fix Min, too. Min was going to take the drawing to the key man and get the master key made. There would be nothing, no scrap of evidence, no tiny detail to connect him with this thing. Even if the kid should say that he, Jones, had showed him how to open the boxes, had given him the key, all he had to do was deny it. He had been Super on this street for years, collecting rents and scrupulously turning them over to the white agents. That alone was proof of his honesty. No one would believe the story of a thieving little kid—a little kid whose mother was no better than she should be, whose mother openly lived with white men.

No. They'd never be able to pin anything on him. It would be the kid. And if things worked out right, it would be Min, too.

When Min came home from work that night, he greeted her cordially but not too cordially, because he didn't want her to wonder what had made him change his attitude toward her.

"Your heart bother you today?" he asked.

"No," she said. She looked at him distrustfully. "Not much anyway," she added hastily.

"I was wondering about it." He hoped she would think that this concern about her heart accounted for his cordiality because he had been going out of the house almost as soon as she came home from work, not saying anything, deliberately waiting until she entered the living room and then brushing past her in order to show his distaste for her, thus making it obvious that he was hastening to get away from the sight of her.

She took off her coat and hung it up in the bedroom, shaking it carefully after it was on the hanger. When she unfastened the scarf around her head, she looked at herself in the mirror and automatically she sought the reflection of the cross hanging over the bed.

"Supper'll be ready in a minute," she said cautiously.

"Okay." He stood up, yawned, went through an elaborate, exaggerated stretching. "I'm good and hungry." He was beginning to enjoy himself.

He went to stand in the kitchen door while she set the table, talking to her companionably as she moved from table to stove. Gradually the faint suspicion, the slow caution in her face and in her eyes lessened, and then disappeared entirely. It was replaced by a quiet pleasure that grew until her face was alive with it. She talked and talked and talked. Words welled up in her, overflowed, filled the kitchen.

He ate in silence, wondering if he would ever be able to get the sound of her flat, sing-song voice out of his ears. It went on and on. He lost all sense of what she was saying, though in sheer self-defense he made the effort to catch it. It was like trying to follow the course of a tortuously winding path that continually turned back on itself, disappeared in impenetrable thickets, to emerge farther on at a sharp angle having no apparent relation to its original starting point.

"Mis' Crane's got three of the smallest kittens. Just born a month ago and the canned milk don't agree with them. So when we got to the rug on the living room we hadn't any of the soap chips. The man at the store said that kind is gone over to the war. And I got bacon there. A whole half pound. Mis'

Crane was surprised because Mr. Crane has it for breakfast every morning. The drippings make the greens have a nice taste, don't they? Them Eighth Avenue stores is the only place that's got ones that have a strong taste. And the collards was fresh in this afternoon so I got it for tomorrow——"

Finally he gave up the effort to follow the train of her thought. She wouldn't know whether he really listened or not. He nodded his head occasionally which satisfied her.

After supper he wiped the dishes, and the fact that he was standing near her, staying there to help her, increased the flow of her words until it was like a river in full flood.

He lay down on the sofa in the living room while she went through such elaborate and long-drawn-out, totally unnecessary cleaning that he couldn't control his impatience as he listened to and identified her movements. She was scrubbing the kitchen floor, washing out the oven, scouring the jets of the gas stove.

Finally she came to sit in the big chair in the living room, her eyes blinking with pleasure as she looked at the canary and talked to him. She was breathless from her scouring of the kitchen and she talked in gasps and spurts. "Cheek! Cheek! Dickie-boy. You going to sing, Dickie-boy? Cluk! Cluk! Dickie-boy!"

"Min," he said, and stopped because that wasn't the right tone of voice. It was too charged with urgency, too solemn, too emphasized. He had to keep his voice casual; make what he was saying sound unimportant and yet important enough for her to get dressed and go out again.

Her head turned toward him as though it were on a swivel. There was a slight rigidity in her posture as she waited for him to continue.

Jones sat up and put his hand on his head. "I got a awful headache," he said. "And I got to have a mail-box key made for one of them damn fools on the third floor. She done lost two keys in two days and I ain't got another one. I was wondering if you'd take the pattern around to the key man and wait while he made it."

"Why, sure," she said. "I'd be glad to. A breath of air would be real nice. Sometimes it seems awful close and shut up inside here, especially after Mis' Crane's having so much room around her and——"

After she got her things on, he gave her the drawing, handing it to her carelessly. When he saw how slackly she held it, he couldn't help saying, "Don't lose it."

"Oh, no," she said. "I don't ever lose nothing. Only today I was thinking that I never lose nothing. Everything I've ever got I been able to keep——"

She had to talk awhile longer and he listened, biting his lips in impatience as she rambled on and on. Finally she left, limping slightly because she hadn't had a chance to soak her bunions. But her face was warm with the pleasure of being able to do something for him.

The key was such a slender little thing, he thought, when Min returned with it and handed it to him; it was so small and yet so powerful.

Min soaked her feet and talked and talked and talked. She undressed and came out of the bedroom to stand near the couch where he was sitting, fondling the key.

"You ain't sleeping in the bedroom tonight?" she asked.

"No," he said absently. He glanced briefly at her shapeless, hesitant figure. This was her way of inviting him to sleep with her again. I think I fixed you, too, with this little key, he thought. And I hope I fixed you good. "No," he repeated. "My headache's too bad."

The next afternoon Jones stood outside the building and waited for Bub. The street was swarming with children who laughed and talked and moved with gusto because school was out.

When Bub ran in from the street, he was moving so swiftly that Jones almost didn't see him. All of him was alive with the joy of movement—his arms, his legs, even his head. Kicking up his heels like a young goat, Jones thought, watching him. A little more and he'd jump right out of his skin.

"Hi, Bub," he said.

"Hi, Supe"—he was panting, chest heaving, eyes dancing. "Hi, Mrs. Hedges"—he waved toward the window.

"Hello, dearie," she replied. "You sure was going fast when you turned that corner. Thought you couldn't put your brakes on there for a minute."

He laughed and the sound of his own laughter pleased him so that he laughed louder and harder in order to enjoy it more. "I can go even faster sometimes," he said finally.

"How about you and me building something in the basement this afternoon?" Jones asked.

"Sure. What'll it be, Supe?"

"I dunno. We can talk it over."

They went into the hall and Jones opened the door of his apartment.

"Thought you said we were going into the basement."

"We gotta talk something over first."

Jones sat down on the sofa with the boy beside him. The boy sat so far back that his legs dangled.

"How'd you like to earn some money?" Jones began.

"Sure. You want me to go some place for you?"

"Not this time. This is different. This is some detective work catching crooks."

"Where, Supe? Where?" Bub scrambled off the sofa to stand in front of Jones, ready to run in any direction, already seeing himself in action. "How'm I going to do it? Can I start now?"

"Wait a minute. Wait a minute: Don't go so fast," he cautioned. This was the easiest thing he'd ever done in his life, he thought with satisfaction. He paused briefly to admire his own cleverness. "There's these crooks and the police need help to catch them. They're using the mail and it ain't easy to get them. You gotta be careful nobody sees you or they'll know you're working for the police."

"Go on, Supe. Tell me some more. What do I have to do?" Bub implored.

"Now what you have to do is open mail boxes and bring the letters to me. Some of them will be the right ones and some won't. But you bring all of them here to me. You gotta make sure nobody sees you give them to me. So you bring them down in the basement. I'll be down there waiting for you every afternoon."

He took the slender key out of his pocket. "Come on out in the hall and I'll show you how she works."

The key was stiff in the lock. It turned slowly. He had to force it a little, but it worked. He had the boy try it again and again until he began to get the feel of it and then they returned to his apartment.

"Don't never open none of them boxes in this house," he warned. He put one of his heavy hands on the boy's shoulder to give emphasis to his words. "This ain't the place where the crooks are working."

He hesitated for a moment, disturbed and uneasy because Bub had been silent for so long. "Here," he said finally and extended the key toward the boy. "You got the whole street to work in."

Bub backed away from his outstretched hand. "I don't think I want to do it."

"Why not?" he demanded angrily. Was the little bastard going to spoil the whole thing by refusing?

"I don't know"—Bub wrinkled his forehead. "I thought it was something different. This ain't even exciting."

"You can earn a lot of money." He tried to erase the anger from his voice, tried to make it persuasive. "Mebbe three, four dollars a week." The letters would yield at least that much. Yes. He was safe in saying it. The boy didn't answer. "Mebbe five dollars a week."

"I don't think Mom——"

"Your ma won't know nothing about it. You're not to tell her anyhow," he said savagely. He made a superhuman effort to control the rage that burst in him. He must say something quickly so that the boy wouldn't tell her anything about it. "This is a secret between you and me and the police."

"No," the boy repeated. "I don't want to do it. Thanks just the same, Supe."

And before Jones realized his intention, Bub had run out of the apartment, slamming the door behind him. He was left standing in the middle of the room still holding the key in his outstretched hand and with the knowledge that the kid could ruin him by telling Lutie what he, Jones, had suggested.

He cursed with such vehemence that the dog walked over to him, thrust his muzzle into his hand. He kicked the dog away. The dog howled. It was a sharp, shrill outcry that filled the apartment, reached to the street outside.

Mrs. Hedges nodded her head at the sound. "Cellar crazy," she said softly. "No doubt about it. Cellar crazy."

Chapter 13

IT WAS TIME for intermission at the Casino. The men in the bandstand got up from their chairs, shoved the music racks in front of them aside, yawned and stretched. Some of them searched through the crowd, seeking the young girls who had eyed them from the dance floor, intent on getting better acquainted with them, even at the risk of incurring the displeasure of their escorts. Others headed straight for the bar like homing pigeons winging toward their roosts.

The pianist and one of the trumpeters stayed in the bandstand. The trumpeter was experimenting with a tune that had been playing in his head for days. The pianist turned sideways on the piano bench listening to him.

"Ever hear it before?" he asked finally.

"Nope," replied the pianist.

"Just wanted to make sure. Sometimes tunes play tricks in your head and turn out to be somep'n you heard a long while ago and all the time you think it's one you made up."

The pianist groped for appropriate chords as the man with the trumpet played the tune over softly. Together they produced a faint melody, barely a shred, a tatter of music that drifted through the big ballroom. Conversation and the clink of glasses and roars of laughter almost drowned it out, but it persisted—a slight, ghostly sound running through the room.

The soft rainbow-colored lights shifted as they slanted over the smooth surface of the dance floor, softening the faces of the couples strolling by arm in arm; making gentle the faces of the Casino's bruisers as they mingled with the crowd. The moving lights and the half-heard tones of the piano and the trumpet created the illusion that the people were still dancing.

Lutie Johnson and Boots Smith were sitting at one of the small tables near the edge of the dance floor. They had been silent ever since they sat down.

"When will my salary start? And how much will it be?" she asked finally. She had to know now, tonight. She couldn't wait any longer for him to broach the subject. The intermission was half over and he was still staring at the small glass of bourbon in front of him on the table.

"Salary?" he asked blankly.

"For singing with the band." He knew what she meant and yet he was pretending that he didn't. She looked at him anxiously, conscious of a growing sense of dismay. She waited for his answer, leaning toward him, straining to hear it and hearing instead the faint, drifting sound of music. It disturbed her because at first she thought it wasn't real, that she was imagining the sound. She turned toward the bandstand and saw that two of the boys were practicing. Boots started speaking when her head was turned so that she didn't see the expression on his face.

"Baby, this is just experience," he said. "Be months before you can earn money at it."

Afterwards she tried to remember the tone of his voice and couldn't. She could only remember the thin, ghostly, haunting music. But he had told her she could earn her living by singing. He had said the job was hers—tied up and sewed up for as long as she wanted it.

"What happened?" she asked sharply.

"Nothing happened, baby. What makes you think something happened?"

"You said I could earn my living singing. Just last night you said the job was mine for as long as I wanted it."

"Sure, baby, and I meant it," he said easily. "It's true. But I don't have all the say-so. The guy who owns the Casino—guy named Junto—says you ain't ready yet."

"What has he got to do with it?"

"I just told you," patiently. "Christ, he owns the joint."

"Is he the same man that owns the Bar and Grill?"

"Yeah."

The music faded away, returned, was lost again. She remembered Junto's squat figure reflected in the mirror behind the bar. A figure in a mirror lifted a finger, shook his head, and she was right back where she started. No, not quite; for this still, sick feeling inside of her was something she hadn't had before. This was worse than being back where she started because she hadn't been able to prevent the growth of a bright optimism that had pictured a shining future. She had seen herself moving away from the street, giving Bub a room of his own, being home when he returned from school. Those things had become real to her and they were gone.

She had to go on living on the street, in that house. And she could feel the Super pulling her steadily toward the stairway, could feel herself swaying and twisting and turning to get away from him, away from the cellar door. Once again she was aware of the steps stretching down into the darkness of the basement below, could feel the dog leaping on her back and Mrs. Hedges' insinuating voice was saying, "Earn extra money, dearie."

"No!" she said sharply.

"What's the matter, baby? Did it mean so much to you?"

She looked at him, thinking, He would like to know that it meant everything in the world to me. There was nothing in his expression to indicate that the knowledge that she was bitterly disappointed would concern him or that he was even faintly interested. But she knew by the eager way he was bending toward her across the table, by the intentness with which he was studying her, that he was seeking to discover the degree of her disappointment.

"I suppose it did," she said quietly.

She got up from the table. "Well," she said, "thanks for the chance anyway."

"Yeah," he said vaguely. He was fingering the scar on his cheek. "Hey, wait a minute, where you goin'?"

"I'm going home. Where did you think I was going?"

"But you ain't going to stop singing with the band, are you?"

"What would be the point? I work all day. I'm not going to sing half the night for the fun of it."

"But the experience——"

"I'm not interested," she said flatly.

He put his hand on her arm. "Wait and I'll drive you home. I want to talk to you, baby. You can't walk out on me like this."

"I'm not walking out on you," she said impatiently. "I'm tired and I want to go home."

"Okay"—he withdrew his hand. "Junto sent you this——" He pulled a small white box out of his vest pocket and handed it to her.

The cover stuck and she pulled it off with a jerk that set the rhinestone earrings inside to glinting as the rainbow-colored lights touched them. They were so alive with fiery color that they seemed to move inside the small box.

"Thanks," she said, and her voice sounded hard, brassy to her own ears. "I can't imagine anything I needed more than these."

She turned away from him abruptly, hurried across the dance floor, down the long, massive staircase to the cloakroom. She took her coat from the hat-check girl, put a quarter on the thick white saucer on the shelf. As she went out the door, she thought, I should have left the earrings with the girl, she probably needs them as badly as I do.

The Casino's doorman, resplendent in his dark red uniform, paused with his hand on a taxi-door and looked after her as she walked toward Seventh Avenue. He thought the long black skirt made an angry sound as she moved swiftly toward the corner.

She was holding the earring box so tightly that she could feel the cardboard give a little, and she squeezed it harder. She tried not to think, to keep the deep anger that boiled up in her under control. There wasn't any reason for her to be angry with Boots Smith and Junto. She was to blame.

Yet she could feel a hard, tight knot of anger and hate forming within her as she walked along. She decided to walk home, hoping that the anger would evaporate on the way. She moved in long, swift strides. There was a hard sound to her heels clicking against the sidewalk and she tried to make it louder. Hard, hard, hard. That was the only way to be—so hard that nothing, the street, the house, the people—nothing would ever be able to touch her.

Down one block and then the next—135th, 134th, 133d, 132d, 131st. Slowly she began to reach for some conclusion, some philosophy with which to rebuild her shattered hopes. The world hadn't collapsed about her. She hadn't been buried under brick and rubble, falling plaster and caved-in sidewalks. Yet that was how she had felt listening to Boots.

The trouble was with her. She had built up a fantastic structure made from the soft, nebulous, cloudy stuff of dreams. There hadn't been a solid, practical brick in it, not even a foundation. She had built it up of air and vapor and moved right in. So of course it had collapsed. It had never existed anywhere but in her own mind.

She might as well face the fact that she would have to go on living in that same street. She didn't have enough money to pay a month's rent in advance on another apartment and hire a moving-man. Even if she had the necessary funds, any apartment she moved into would be equally as undesirable as the one she moved out of. Except, of course, at a new address she wouldn't find Mrs. Hedges and the Super. No, but there would be other people who wouldn't differ too greatly from them. This was as good a time and place as any other for her to get accustomed to the idea of remaining there.

She hoped what Mrs. Hedges had said about Jones not bothering her any more was true, for she knew she couldn't force herself to register a complaint against him. The thought of telling some indifferent desk sergeant about the details of his attack on her was one she didn't relish.

But that's what she should do. Then she thought, Suppose they locked him up for thirty days or sixty days or ninety days, or whatever the sentence was for such things. Then what? He couldn't be kept in jail indefinitely. He was the kind of man who would carry a grudge against her as long as he lived and once out of jail she was certain he would make an effort to strike back at her.

Harlem wasn't a very big place and if he was dead set on revenge he wouldn't have any difficulty in finding her. Besides, there was Bub to be considered, for instead of harming her he might seek to avenge himself on Bub.

No. She wouldn't go to the police about him. She paused for a stop light. Have you got used to the idea of staying there? she asked herself.

From now on they would have to live so carefully, so frugally, so miserly that each pay-check would yield a small sum to be put in the bank. After a while they would be able to move. It would be hard. She might as well get used to that, too.

They would have to live so close to a narrow margin that it wouldn't really be like living; never going anywhere, never buying the smallest item that wasn't absolutely essential, even examining essential ones and eliminating them whenever possible. It was the only way they could hope to move. She thought with regret of the quarter she had so lavishly given the hat-check girl. She ought to go back and tell the girl it was a mistake, that she was angry when she gave it to her, and she tried to picture how the girl's face would look—startled, incredulous at first, and then sullen, outraged.

Nights at home she would start studying in order to get a higher civil service rating. Perhaps by the time the next exam came up, she would be able to pass it. The job at the Casino that had looked like such an easy, pat, just-right thing was out of the question and her common sense should have told her that in the beginning. Yet she found she was thinking of it with regret and of all the things it would have meant—those things that seemed to be right within reach last night when Boots said, "The job is yours, baby."

And she began thinking about him. "All you gotta do is be nice to me, baby." She hadn't done or said anything that would indicate that she had no intention of being "nice" to him. It must have been something else that had made him lose interest in her so quickly.

She tried to remember all the things he had said to her to find some clue that would explain his indifference. For he had been indifferent, she decided. He had sat there at the table to-night, making no effort to talk, absorbed in his own thoughts, and even when he had talked to her he had looked at her im-personally as though she were a stranger in whom he didn't have even a passing interest.

"I could fall in love with you easy, baby." He had said that just last night. And that first night she had met him, "The only thing I'm interested in is you."

When he drove her home last night, he had scarcely spoken. He had made no effort to touch her. She sought a reason and remembered that he had fallen silent after the bouncer at the Casino told him Junto wanted to see him.

She walked a little faster. If Junto owned the Casino, then Boots worked for him. Even so, what could Junto have said to him that would make him lose his obvious desire for her so abruptly? It must have been something else that disturbed him, she decided. Perhaps it had something to do with his not being in the army, for she remembered how he couldn't conceal his annoyance when she persisted in asking him why he hadn't been drafted.

It didn't matter anyway. Perhaps it was just as well the thing had ended like this. At least she no longer had to duck and dodge away from his brutal hands. Even if she had been hired at a fat weekly salary, his complete lack of scruple might have been something she couldn't have coped with.

She pushed open the door of the apartment house where she lived. The hall was quiet. There was no movement in the pool of shadow that almost obliterated the cellar door. And she wondered if every time she entered the hall, she would inevitably seek to locate the tall, gaunt figure of the Super.

The cracked tile of the floor was grimy. The snow that had been tracked in from the street during the morning had melted and mixed with the soot and dust on the floor. She looked at the dark brown varnish on the doors, the dim light that came from the streaked light fixture overhead, the tarnished mail boxes, the thin, worn stair treads. And she thought time had a way of transforming things.

Only a few hours had elapsed since she stood in this same doorway, completely unaware of the dim light, the faded, dreary paint, the filth on the floor. She had looked down the length of this hall and seen Bub growing up in some airy, sunny house and herself free from worry about money. She had been able to picture him coming home from school to snacks of cookies and milk and bringing other kids with him; and then playing somewhere near-by, and all she had to do was look out of the window and see him because she was home every day when he arrived. And time and Boots Smith and Junto had pushed her right back in here, deftly removing that obscuring cloud of dreams, so that now tonight she could see this hall in reality.

She started up the stairs. They went up and up ahead of her. They were steeper than she remembered them. And she thought vaguely of all the feet that had passed over them in order to wear the treads down like this—young feet and old feet; feet tired from work; feet that skipped up them because some dream made them less than nothing to climb; feet that moved reluctantly because some tragedy slowed them up.

Her legs were too tired to move quickly, so that her own feet refused to move at their usual swift pace. She became uneasily conscious of the closeness of the walls. The hall was only a narrow passageway between them. The walls were very thin, too, for she could hear the conversations going on behind the closed doors on each floor.

Radios were playing on the third and fourth floors. She tried to walk faster to get away from the medley of sound, but her legs refused to respond to her urging. "Buy Shirley Soap and Keep Beautiful" was blared out by an announcer's voice. The sounds were confusing. Someone had tuned in the station that played swing records all night, and she heard, "Now we have the master of the trumpet in Rock, Raleigh, Rock."

That mingled with the sounds of a revival church which was broadcasting a service designed to redeem lost souls: "This is the way, sisters and brothers. This is the answer. Come all of you now before it's too late. This is the way." As she walked along, she heard the congregation roar, "Preach it, brother, preach it." Suddenly a woman cried loud above the other sounds, "Lord Jesus is a-comin' now."

The congregation clapped their hands in rhythm. It came in clear over the radio. And the sound mingled with the high sweetness of the trumpet playing "Rock, Raleigh, Rock," and the soap program joined in with the plunking of a steel guitar, "If you wanta be beautiful use Shirley Soap."

A fight started on the third floor. Its angry violence echoed up the stairs, mingling with the voices on the radio. The conversations that were going on behind the closed doors that lined the hall suddenly ceased. The whole house listened to the progress of the fight.

And Lutie thought, The whole house knows, just as I do, that Bill Smith, who never works, has come home drunk again and is beating up his wife. Living here is like living in a structure that has a roof, but no partitions, so that privacy is destroyed, and even the sound of one's breathing becomes a known, familiar thing to each and every tenant.

She sighed with relief when she reached the fifth floor. The stairs had seemed like a high, ever-ascending mountain because she was so tired. And then she thought, No, that wasn't quite true, because the way she felt at this moment was the way a fighter feels after he's been knocked down hard twice in succession, given no time to recover from the first smashing blow before the second one slams him back down again.

And the second blow makes him feel as though he were dying. His wind is gone. His heart hurts when it beats, and it goes too fast, so that a pain stays in his chest. The air going in and out of his lungs adds to the pain. Blood pounds in his head, so that it feels dull, heavy. All he wants to do is crawl out of sight and lie down, not moving, not thinking. She knew how he would feel, because that about summed up what had happened to her, except that she had received, not two blows, but a whole series of them.

Then she saw with surprise that there was a light under her door and she stopped thinking about how she felt. "Why isn't he asleep?" she said, aloud.

But Bub was asleep, so sound asleep that he didn't stir when she entered the room. He is afraid here alone, she thought, looking down at him. He was sprawled in the center of the studio couch, his legs and arms flung wide apart. The lamp on the table was shining directly in his face.

Each time she had come home from the Casino, he had been sleeping with the light on. Yes, he was definitely afraid. Well, she wouldn't be going out any more at night, leaving him alone. She switched the light off, thinking that it would be years now before he had a bedroom of his own. It was highly doubtful that he would ever have one, and there was still the problem of his having no place to go after school.

After she undressed and got into bed, she lay staring up at the ceiling for a long time. She thought of Junto, who could so casually, so lightly, perhaps at a mere whim, and not even aware of what he was doing, thrust her back into this place, and of Boots Smith, who might or might not have been telling the truth, who might for purposes of his own have decided that she wasn't to be paid for singing. And a bitter, angry feeling spread all through her, hardening and congealing.

She was stuck here on this street, in this dark, dirty house. It was going to take a long time to get out. She thought of the Chandlers and their friends in Lyme. They were right about people being able to make money, but it took hard, grinding work to do it—hard work and self-sacrifice. She was capable of both, she concluded. Furthermore, she would never permit herself to become resigned to living here. She had a sudden vivid recollection of the tragic, resigned faces of the young girls and the old man she had seen in the spring. No. She would never become like that.

Her thoughts returned to Junto, and the bitterness and the hardness increased. In every direction, anywhere one turned, there was always the implacable figure of a white man blocking the way, so that it was impossible to escape. If she needed anything to spur her on, she thought, this fierce hatred, this deep contempt, for white people would do it. She would never forget Junto. She would keep her hatred of him alive. She would feed it as though it were a fire.

Bub woke up before she did. He had put the water for the oatmeal on to boil when she came into the kitchen.

She kissed him lightly. "You go get dressed while I fix breakfast."

"Okay."

And then she remembered the light shining on his face while he was asleep. "Bub," she said sternly, "you've got to stop going to sleep with the light on."

He looked sheepish. "I fell asleep and forgot it."

"That's not true," she said sharply. "I turned it out when I left. If you're scared of the dark, you'll just have to go to sleep while I'm here, so you won't be afraid, because this way the bill will be so big I'll never be able to pay it. Furthermore, I don't like lies. I've told you that over and over again."

"Yes, Mom," he said meekly. He started to tell her just what it was like to be alone in the dark. But her face was shut tight with anger and her voice was so hard and cold that he decided he'd better wait until some other time.

It seemed to him that all that week she talked to him about money. She was impatient, she rarely smiled, and she only half-heard him when he talked to her. Every night after dinner she bent over a pile of books placed on the card table and stayed there silent, intent, writing down queer curves and hooks over and over until she went to bed. He decided he must have done something to displease her and he asked her about it.

"Mom, you mad at me?"

They were eating supper. Lutie was startled by his question. "Why, of course not. What made you think I was?"

"You sort of acted like it."

"No, I'm not mad at you. I couldn't be."

"What's the matter, Mom?"

She framed her answer carefully, trying not to let the hard, cold anger in her color her reply. She frowned, because her only explanation would have to be that they needed to save more than they were doing. "I've been worried about us," she said. "We seem to spend so much money. I'm not able to save very much. And we have to save, Bub," she said earnestly, "so that we won't always have to live here."

During the next week she made a conscious effort to stop talking to Bub about money. Yet some reference to it inevitably crept into her conversation. If she found two lights burning in the living room, she found herself turning one of them out, saying, "We've got to watch the bill."

When she was mending his socks, she caught herself delivering a lecture about being careful and watching out for nails and splinters that might snag them. "They have to last a long time and new ones cost money."

If he left a cake of soap soaking in the bowl in the bathroom, she pointed out how it wasted the soap and that little careless things ate into their meager budget. When she went to bed, she scolded herself roundly because it wasn't right to be always harping on the cost of living to Bub. On the other hand, if they didn't manage to save faster than she had been able to do so far, it would be months before they could move and moving was uppermost in her thoughts. So the next day she explained to him why it was necessary to move, and that they had to be careful with money if they were going to do it soon.

Her days were spent in working and at night she cooked dinner, washed and ironed clothes, studied. She found that, in spite of her resolve never again to dream about some easier and more remunerative way of earning a living, and in spite of her determination to put all thought of singing out of her mind, she couldn't control a faint regret that assailed her when she least expected it.

Coming home on the subway one night, she picked up a Negro newspaper that had been discarded by a more affluent passenger. And because of her reluctance to give up the idea of singing, it seemed to her that an advertisement leaped at her from the theatrical pages: "Singers Needed Now for Broadway

Shows. Nightclub Engagements. Let Us Train You for High-Paying Jobs."

She tore it out and put it in her pocketbook, thinking cautiously that it was at least worth investigating, but not permitting herself to build any hopes on it.

The next night after work she went to the Crosse School for Singers. It was on the tenth floor of a Forty-Second Street office building. Going up in the elevator, she somehow couldn't prevent the faint stirring of hope, the beginnings of expectancy.

A brassy haired blonde was the sole occupant of the small waiting room. She looked up from the book she was reading when Lutie opened the door.

Lutie produced the advertisement from her purse. "I came for an audition."

"Have a seat. Mr. Crosse will see you in a minute."

A buzzer sounded, and the girl stopped reading to say, "Mr. Crosse'll see you now. It's that door to the left. Just walk right in."

Lutie opened the door. The walls of the room inside were covered with glossy photographs of smiling men and women clad in evening clothes. A hasty glance revealed that all the pictures were warmly inscribed to "dear Mr. Crosse."

She walked toward a desk at the end of the room. It was a large flat-topped desk and Mr. Crosse had his feet on top of it. As she drew closer to him, she saw that the desk was littered with newspaper clippings, photographs, old magazines, even piles of phonograph records, and two scrapbooks whose contents made the covers bulge. A box of cigars, an ash tray that hadn't been emptied for weeks from the accumulation of soggy cigar butts in it, and an old-fashioned inkwell, its sides well splashed with ink, were right near his feet. A row of dark green filing cabinets stood against the wall behind the desk.

She was quite close to the desk before she was able to see what the man sitting behind it looked like, for his feet obstructed her view. He was so fat that he appeared to be bursting out of his clothes. His vest gaped with the strain of the rolls of fat on his abdomen. Other rolls of fat completely obliterated his jaw line. He was chewing an unlit cigar, and he rolled it to one side of his mouth. "Hello," he said, not moving his feet.

"I came for an audition," Lutie explained.

"Sure. Sure. What kind of singing you do?" He took the cigar out of his mouth.

"Nightclub," she said briefly, not liking him, not liking the fact that the end of the cigar he was holding in his hand had been chewed until it was a soggy, shredding mass of tobacco, and that the room was filled with the rank smell of it.

"Okay. Okay. We'll try you out. Come on in here."

One of the doors of his office led to a slightly larger room. She stood in front of a microphone on a raised platform facing the door. A bored, too thin man accompanied her at the piano. He smoked while he played, moving his head occasionally to get the smoke out of his eyes. His hands were limp and flat as they touched the keys. Mr. Crosse sat in the back of the room and apparently went to sleep.

At the end of her first song, he opened his eyes. "Okay, okay," he said. "We'll go back to the office now."

He lowered his bulk into the swivel chair behind his desk, put his feet up. "Sit down," he said, indicating a chair near the desk. "You've got a good voice. Very good voice," he said. "I can practically guarantee you a job. About seventy-five dollars a week."

"What's the catch in it?" she asked.

"There's no catch," he said defensively. "Been in business here for twenty years. Absolutely no catch. Matter of fact, I don't usually listen to the singers myself. But just from looking at you I thought, That girl is good. Got a good voice. So I decided to audition you myself." He put the cigar in his mouth and chewed it vigorously.

"When do I start working at this seventy-five dollar a week job?" she asked sarcastically.

"About six weeks. You need some training. Things like timing and how to put a song over. Called showmanship. We teach you that. Then we find you a job and act as your agent. We get ten per cent of what you make. Regular agents' fee."

"What does the training cost?"

"Hundred and twenty five dollars."

She got up from the chair. One hundred and twenty-five dollars. She wanted to laugh. It might as well be one thousand and twenty-five dollars. One was just as easy to get as the other.

"I'm sorry to have taken your time. It's out of the question."

"They all say that," he said. "All of 'em. It sounds out of the question because most people really don't have what it takes to be singers. They don't want it bad enough. They see somebody earning hundreds a week and they never stop to think that person made a lot of sacrifices to get there."

"I know all that. In my case it's impossible."

"You don't have to pay it all at once. We arrange for down payments and so much a week in special cases. Makes it easier that way."

"You don't understand. I just don't have the money," she turned away, started past his desk.

"Wait a minute." He put his feet on the floor, got up from the swivel chair and laid a fat hand on her arm.

She looked down at his hand. The skin was the color of the underside of a fish—a grayish white. There were long black hairs on the back of it—even on the fingers. It was a bone-less hand, thick-covered with fat. She drew her arm away. He was so saturated with the smell of tobacco that it seeped from his skin, his clothing. The cigar in his flabby fingers was rank, strong. Seen close to, the sodden mass of tobacco where he had chewed the end of it sent a quiver of revulsion through her.

"You know a good-looking girl like you shouldn't have to worry about money," he said softly. She didn't say anything and he continued, "In fact, if you and me can get together a coupla nights a week in Harlem, those lessons won't cost you a cent. No sir, not a cent."

Yes, she thought, if you were born black and not too ugly, this is what you get, this is what you find. It was a pity he hadn't lived back in the days of slavery, so he could have raided the slave quarters for a likely wench any hour of the day or night. This is the superior race, she said to herself, take a good long look at him: black, oily hair; slack, gross body; grease spots on his vest; wrinkled shirt collar; cigar ashes on his suit; small pig eyes engulfed in the fat of his face.

She remembered the inkwell on the desk in back of him. She picked it up in a motion so swift that he had no time to guess her intent. She hurled it full force in his face. The ink paused for a moment at the obstruction of his eyebrows, then dripped down over the fat jowls, over the wrinkled collar, the grease-stained vest; trickled over his mouth.

She slammed the door of the office behind her. The girl in the reception room looked up, startled at the sound.

"Through so quick?" she asked.

"Yes." She walked past the girl. Hurry, she told herself. Hurry, hurry, hurry!

"Didya fill out a application?" the girl called after her.

"I won't need one"—she said the words over her shoulder.

She boarded a Sixth Avenue train at Forty-Second Street. It was crowded with passengers. She closed her eyes to shut them out, gripping the overhead strap tightly. She welcomed the roar of the train as it sped toward Fifty-Ninth Street, welcomed its lurching, swaying motion. She wished that it would go faster, make more noise, rock more wildly, because the tumultuous anger in her could only be quelled by violence.

She sought release from the urgency of her rage by deliberately picturing the train plunging suddenly off the track in a fury of sound—the metal coaches rushing headlong on top of each other in a whole series of thunderous explosions.

The burst of anger died away slowly and she began to think of herself drearily. She was running around a small circle, around and around like a squirrel in a cage. All this business of saving money in order to move added up to less than nothing, because she had forgotten or blithely overlooked the fact that she couldn't find any better place to live, not for the amount of rent she could pay.

She thought of Mr. Crosse with a sudden access of hate that made her bite her lips; and then of Junto, who had prevented her from getting the job at the Casino. She remembered the friends of the Chandlers who had thought of her as a nigger wench; only, of course, they were too well-bred to use the word "nigger." And the hate in her increased.

The train stopped at Fifty-Ninth Street, took on more passengers, then gathered speed for the long run to 125th Street.

Streets like the one she lived on were no accident. They were the North's lynch mobs, she thought bitterly; the method the big cities used to keep Negroes in their place. And she began thinking of Pop unable to get a job; of Jim slowly disintegrating because he, too, couldn't get a job, and of the subsequent wreck of their marriage; of Bub left to his own devices after school. From the time she was born, she had been hemmed into an ever-narrowing space, until now she was very nearly walled in and the wall had been built up brick by brick by eager white hands.

When she got off the local at 116th Street, she didn't remember having changed trains at 125th Street. She was surprised to find that Bub was waiting for her at the subway entrance. He didn't see her, and she paused for a moment, noting the anxious way he watched the people pouring into the street, twisting his neck in his effort to make certain he didn't miss her. She was so late getting home that he had evidently been worried about her; and she tried to imagine what it would be like for him if something had happened to her and she hadn't come.

At this hour there were countless children with doorkeys tied around their necks, hovering at the corner. They were seeking their mothers in the homecoming throng surging up from the subway. They're too young to be familiar with worry, she thought, for their expressions were exactly like Bub's— apprehensive, a little frightened. They're behind the same wall already. She walked over to Bub.

"Hello, hon," she said gently. She put her arm around his shoulders as they walked toward home.

He was silent for a while, and then he said, "Mom, are you sure you're not mad at me?"

She tightened her grip on his shoulder. "Of course not," she said. She was neatly caged here on this street and tonight's experience had increased the growing frustration and hatred in her. It probably shows in my face, she thought, dismayed, and Bub can see it.

"I'm not mad at you at all. I couldn't be"—she caressed his cheek. "I've been worried about something."

She thought of the animals at the Zoo. She and Bub had gone there one Sunday afternoon. They arrived in time to see the lions and tigers being fed. There was a moment, before the great hunks of red meat were thrust into the cages, when the big cats prowled back and forth, desperate, raging, ravening. They walked in a space even smaller than the confines of the cages made necessary, moving in an area just barely the length of their bodies. A few steps up and turn. A few steps down and turn. They were weaving back and forth, growling, roaring, raging at the bars that kept them from the meat, until the entire building was filled with the sound, until the people watching drew back from the cages, feeling insecure, frightened at the sight and the sound of such uncontrolled savagery. She was becoming something like that.

"I'm not mad at you, hon," she repeated. "I guess I was mad at myself."

Because she was late getting home and she knew that Bub was hungry, she tried to hurry the preparation of dinner. And when she tried to light the gas stove, there was a sudden, flaring burst of flame that seared the flesh of her hand and set it to smarting and burning. Bub was leaning out of the kitchen window intently watching the dogs in the yard below.

"Damn it," she said. She covered her hand with a dishtowel, holding the towel tightly to keep the air away from the burn. It wasn't a bad burn, she thought; it was a mere scorching of surface skin.

Yet she couldn't check the rage that welled up in her. "Damn being poor!" she shouted. "God damn it!"

She set the table with a slam-bang of plates and a furious rattling of knives and forks. She put the glasses down hard, so that they smacked against the table's surface, dragged the chairs across the floor until the room was filled with noise, with confusion, with swift, angry movement.

The next afternoon after school, Bub rang the Super's bell.

"I changed my mind, Supe," he said. "I'll be glad to help you."

Chapter 14

I T WAS ONLY TWO-THIRTY in the afternoon. Miss Rinner looked at the wriggling, twisting children seated in front of her and frowned. There was a whole half-hour, thirty long unpleasant minutes to be got through before she would be free from the unpleasant sight of these ever-moving, brown young faces.

The pale winter sunlight streaming through the dusty windows and the steam hissing faintly in the big radiators intensified the smells in the room. All the classrooms she had ever taught in were permeated with the same mixture of odors: the dusty smell of chalk, the heavy, suffocating smell of the pine oil used to lay the grime and disinfect the worn old floors, and the smell of the children themselves. But she had long since forgotten what the forty-year-old buildings in other parts of the city smelt like, and with the passing of the years had easily convinced herself that this Harlem school contained a peculiarly offensive odor.

At first she had thought of the odors that clung to the children's clothing as "that fried smell"—identifying it as the rancid grease that had been used to cook pancakes, fish, pork chops.

As the years slipped by—years of facing a room swarming with restless children—she came to think of the accumulation of scents in her classroom with hate as "the colored people's smell," and then finally as the smell of Harlem itself—bold, strong, lusty, frightening.

She was never wholly rid of the odor. It assailed her while she ate her lunch in the corner drugstore, when she walked through the street; it lurked in the subway station where she waited for a train. She brooded about it at home until finally she convinced herself the same rank, fetid smell pervaded her small apartment.

When she unlocked the door of her classroom on Monday mornings, the smell had gained in strength as though it were a living thing that had spawned over the week-end and in reproducing itself had now grown so powerful it could be seen as well as smelt.

She had to pause in the doorway to nerve herself for her entry; then, pressing a handkerchief saturated with eau de Cologne tight against her nose, she would cross the room at a trot and fling the windows open. The stench quickly conquered the fresh cold air; besides, the children insisted on wearing their coats because they said they were cold sitting under open windows. Then the odors that clung to their awful coats filled the room, mingling with the choking pine odor, the dusty smell of chalk.

The sight of them sitting in their coats always forced her to close the windows, for the coats were shabby, ragged, with gaping holes in the elbows. None of them fit properly. They were either much too big or much too small. Bits of shedding cat fur formed the collars of the little girls' coats; the hems were coming out. The instant she looked at them, she felt as though she were suffocating, because any contact with their rubbishy garments was unbearable.

So in spite of the need for fresh air she would say, "Close windows. Hang up coats." And for the rest of the day she would avoid the clothes closet in the back of the room where the coats were hung.

Thus drearily she would start another day. It always seemed as if by Monday she should have been refreshed and better able to face the children, but the fact that the smell lingered in her nostrils over the week-end prevented her from completely relaxing. And when the class assembled, the sight of their dark skins, the sound of the soft blurred speech that came from their throats, filled her with the hysterical desire to scream. As the week wore along, the desire increased, until by Fridays she was shaking, quivering inside.

On Saturdays and Sundays she dreamed of the day when she would be transferred to a school where the children were blond, blue-eyed little girls who arrived on time in the morning filled with orange juice, cereal and cream, properly cooked eggs, and tall glasses of milk. They would sit perfectly still until school was out; they would wear starched pink dresses and smell faintly of lavender soap; and they would look at her with adoration.

These children were impudent. They were ill-clad, dirty. They wriggled about like worms, moving their arms and legs in endless, intricate patterns, and they frightened her. Their parents and Harlem itself frightened her.

Having taught ten years in Harlem, she had learned that a sharp pinch administered to the soft flesh of the upper arm, a sudden twist of the wrist, a violent shove in the back, would keep these eight- and nine-year-olds under control, but she was still afraid of them. There was a sudden, reckless violence about them and about their parents that terrified her.

She regarded teaching them anything as a hopeless task, so she devoted most of the day to maintaining order and devising ingenious ways of keeping them occupied. She sent them on errands. They brought back supplies: paper, pencils, chalk, rulers; they trotted back and forth with notes to the nurse, to the principal, to other teachers. The building was old and vast, and a trip to another section of it used up a good half-hour or more; and if the child lingered going and coming, it took even longer.

Because the school was in Harlem she knew she wasn't expected to do any more than this. Each year she promoted the entire class, with few exceptions. The exceptions were, she stated, unmanageable and were placed in opportunity classes. Thus each fall she started with a fresh crop of youngsters.

At frequent intervals the children would bring penknives into the classroom. Her mind immediately transformed them into long, viciously curving blades. The first time it happened, she attempted to get a transfer to another district. Ten years had gone by and she was still here, and the fear in her had now reached the point where even the walk to the subway from the school was a terrifying ordeal.

For the people on the street either examined her dispassionately, as though she were a monstrosity, or else they looked past her, looked through her as though she didn't exist. Some of them stared at her with unconcealed hate in their eyes or equally unconcealed and jeering laughter. Each reaction set her to walking faster and faster.

She thought of every person she passed as a threat to her safety—the women sitting on the stoops or leaning out of the windows, the men lounging against the buildings. By the time she dropped her nickel into the turnstile, she was panting, out of breath, from the cumulative effect of the people she had met. It was as though she had run a gantlet.

Waiting for the train was a further trial. She searched the platform for some other white persons and then stood close to them, taking refuge in their nearness—refuge from the terror of these black people.

Once she had been so tired that she sat down on one of the benches in the station. A black man in overalls came and sat next to her. His presence sent such a rush of sheer terror through her that she got up from the bench and walked to the far end of the platform. She kept looking back at him, trying to decide what she should do if he followed her.

Despite the fact that he remained quietly seated on the bench, not even glancing in her direction, she didn't feel really safe until she boarded the train and the train began to pull away from Harlem. After that, no matter how tired she was, she never sat down on one of the benches.

Her thoughts returned to the street she had to walk through in order to reach the subway. It was as terrifying in cold weather as it was in warm weather. On balmy days people swarmed through it, sitting in the doorways, standing in the middle of the sidewalk so that she had to walk around them, filling the length of the block with the sound of their ribald laughter. Half-grown boys and girls made passionate love on the very doorsteps. Discarded furniture—overstuffed chairs thick with grease, couches with broken springs—stood in front of the buildings; and children and grown-ups lounged on them as informally as though they were in their own living rooms.

When it was cold, the snow stayed on the ground, growing blacker and grimier with each day that passed. She walked as far away from the curb where it was piled as she could, so that even her galoshes wouldn't come in contact with it, for she was certain it was teeming with germs. Lean cats prowled through the frozen garbage that lay along the edge of the sidewalk.

The few people on the street in cold weather had a desperate, hungry look, and she shuddered at the sight of them, thinking they were probably diseased as well; for these blacks were a people without restraint, without decency, with no moral code. She refused to tell even her closest friends that she worked in a school in Harlem, for she regarded it as a stigma; when she referred to the school, she said vaguely that it was uptown near the Bronx.

And now, as she watched the continual motion of the young bodies behind the battered old desks in front of her, she thought, They're like animals—sullen-tempered one moment, full of noisy laughter the next. Even at eight and nine they knew the foulest words, the most disgusting language. Working in this school was like being in a jungle. It was filled with the smell of the jungle, she thought: tainted food, rank, unwashed bodies. The small tight braids on the little girls' heads were probably an African custom. The bright red ribbons revealed their love for gaudy colors.

Young as they were, it was quite obvious that they hated her. They showed it in a closed, sullen look that came over their faces at the slightest provocation. It was a look that never failed to infuriate her at the same time that it frightened her.

Every day when the classes poured out of the building at three o'clock, she hastened toward the subway, and as she went she heard them chanting a ghastly rhyme behind her:

> Ol' Miss Rinner
> Is a Awful Sinner.

When she turned to glare at them, they would be clustered on the sidewalk, standing motionless, silent, innocent. The rest of the rhyme followed her as she went down the street:

> She sins all day
> She sins all night.
> Won't get a man
> Just for spite.

She glanced at her wrist watch and saw with relief that it was now quarter of three. She would have them put their books away and that would occupy them until they got their frowzy hats and coats on.

The order, "Put your books away!" was on the tip of her tongue when Bub Johnson's hand shot up in the air. The sight of it annoyed her, because she didn't want even so much as a second's delay in getting out of the building.

"Well?" she said.

"Bathroom. Got to go to the bathroom," he announced baldly.

"Well, you can't. You can wait until you get out of school," she snapped. All of them said it like that—frantically, running the words together and managing to evoke the whole process before her reluctant eyes.

Bub got out of his seat and stood in the aisle, jiggling up and down, first on one foot and then on the other. All the children did this when she refused them permission to leave the room. It was a performance that never failed to embarrass her, because she couldn't determine whether they were acting or whether their desperate twisting and turning was the result of a real and urgent need. If one of them should have an accident —and she felt a blush run over her body—it would be horrible. The thought of having to witness one of the many and varied functions of the human body revolted her, and with boys—she looked away from Bub determinedly.

"No," she said sternly. It happened every day with some one of the children and every day she weakened and let them go. Somehow they had cunningly figured out this dangerously soft spot of hers. "No," she repeated.

Then, in spite of herself, her eyes crept back toward him. He was still standing there beside his desk. He had stopped twisting and turning. His face was contorted with that look she feared—that look of sullen, stubborn, resentful hate.

"Go ahead," she said. She filled her voice with authority, made it cross, waspish, in the hope that the sound would so overawe the class they wouldn't realize that she had lost again. "Take your books and your coat with you and wait for us downstairs." He would be gone long before the class got down, but it was just as well. It made one less of them to herd down the stairs. She saw that he had left his books on his desk, but she didn't call him back to get them.

Thus, Bub Johnson got out of school early and was able to beat all the other kids to the candy store across the street from the school.

He peered into the smoke-hazy showcases, trying to find something pretty to buy for his mother—something shiny and pretty. And as he looked, he murmured, "Ol' Miss Rinner Is a Awful Sinner."

Last week he had earned three dollars working with Supe—three whole dollar bills that he had put under the radio on the living-room table. Before he left for school in the morning, he put one of them in his pants pocket because he was going to buy Mom a present—today.

He passed by the smooth, fat chocolates; the bright-colored hard candy, the green packages of gum, and came to a dead stop in front of the case that spilled over with costume jewelry: shiny beads and bracelets and earrings and lapel pins.

"You want something?" the short, thin woman who ran the store asked.

"Yup," he said. Her nose was sharpened to a point. Even her glasses had a sharp, pointed look. Her mouth was a thin, straight line. He looked at her hard, remembering what Mom had said about white people wanting colored people to shine shoes. He would have liked to stick his tongue out at her to show her he wasn't going to be hurried.

"What is it you want?"

"I don't know yet. I got to look around."

Each time he moved to look at something in the case she moved, too. Then the store filled up with kids and she walked away from him. By the time she reached the front of the store, he had made up his mind.

"Hey," he called. "I want these." He pointed to a pair of shiny, hoop earrings. They were gold-colored, and they ought to look good on Mom. They were fifty-nine cents. She counted the change into his hand, put the earrings in a small paper bag. The change made a pleasant clinking.

"Hey, look, that kid's got money."

Bub stole a cautious glance at the front of the store. It was Gray Cap, one of the big six-B boys who had spoken. He had five other big boys with him. They could easily take his change and his earrings, too. He edged near the door.

Gray Cap got up from the counter. Bub was sure they wouldn't take his money away from him here in the store. If he was quick—he darted out of the door, running fleetly up the street, heart pounding as he heard the hue and cry in back of him.

He fled toward the corner, plunging into the thick of the crowd crossing the street—slipping, twisting, turning in the midst of it, bumping into people, and going on. He ignored the exclamations of anger, of surprise, of chagrin, that followed in his wake. "You knocked my groceries!" "Eggs in here——" "Boy, watch where you're going!" "If I get my hands on you, you little black devil——" "Ouch! My foot!"

His pursuers ran head-on into the confusion he left behind him. He turned to look—a large lady had Gray Cap by the ear, was indignantly pointing at the groceries spilling out of a brown-paper bag on the sidewalk. Bub chuckled at the sight and kept running.

Two blocks away, he slowed his pace and looked back. The boys were nowhere in sight. He had thrown them off completely. He walked on, not thinking, merely trying to catch his breath. His heart was thudding so hard, he thought it was just as though it had been running, too. He smiled at the idea. It had been running right alongside of him, so that it had to go faster and faster to keep up with him. He could almost see it —red like a Valentine heart with short legs kicking up in back of it as it ran.

He wondered if he ought to start working in this block. Supe hadn't said not to go in other streets, and this one was quite unfamiliar. The sun added a shine and a polish to the buildings; it sparkled on the small muddy streams at the crossings where the snow had melted. Yes, he would try working here where the strangeness of his surroundings offered a kind of challenge, like exploring a new and unknown country. In fact, he would start in that house right across the street—the one where two men were sitting on the steps talking. He felt a quiver of excitement at his own daring.

There was a vast and lakelike expanse of water in the middle of the street. Bub paused to wade through the exact center of it and then ducked out of the way as a passing car sent a shooting spray of water splashing to the curb.

He walked quietly up the steps, past the two men, and paused in the doorway. They weren't paying any attention to him. They were talking about the war, and they were so engrossed he knew they would soon forget he was there behind them. Water dripped down from the roof, gurgled into the gutters.

"Sure, sure, I know," the man in overalls said impatiently. "I been in a war. I know what I'm talking about. There'll be trouble when them colored boys come back. They ain't going to put up with all this stuff"—he waved toward the street. His hand made a wide, all-inclusive gesture that took in the buildings, the garbage cans, the pools of water, even the people passing by.

"What they going to do about it?" said the other man.

"They're going to change it. You watch what I tell you. They're going to change it."

"Been like this all these years, ain't nothing a bunch of hungry soldiers can do about it."

"Don't tell me, man. I know. I was in the last war."

"What's that got to do with it? What did you change when you come back? They're going to come back with their bellies full of gas and starve just like they done before——"

"They ain't using gas in this war. That's where you're wrong. They ain't using gas——"

Bub opened the door of the hall and slipped inside. The hall was quiet and dark. He listened for footsteps. There was no sound at all. He made no effort to open the mail boxes, but peered inside them. The first three were empty. The next two contained letters—he could see the slim edges showing up white in the dark interior of the boxes.

Slow footsteps started on the stairs and he examined the hall with care. There was no place to hide. He didn't want to appear suddenly on the steps outside, for the two men would notice him and wonder what he had been doing.

He sat down on the bottom step of the stairs and bent over, pretending to tie his shoelace. Then he untied it, waited until he heard the footsteps reach the landing above him and started shoving the lacers through the eyelets of his shoe.

The footsteps came closer and he bent over further. He looked toward the sound. A skirt was going past him—an old lady's skirt because it was long; there were black stockings below the skirt and shapeless, flat-heeled shoes.

"Having trouble with your shoelace, son?"

"Yes'm." He refused to look up, thinking that she would go away if he kept his head down.

"You want me to tie it?"

"No'm." He lifted his head and smiled at her. She was a nice old lady with white hair and soft, dark brown skin.

"You live in this house, son?"

"Yes'm." Her old eyes were sharp, keen. He hoped she couldn't tell by looking at him that he was doing something not quite right. It wasn't really wrong because he was helping the police, but he hadn't yet been able to get over the feeling that the letters that weren't the right ones ought to be put back in the boxes. He would talk to Supe about it when he went home. Meantime, he grinned up at her because he liked her.

"You're a nice boy," she said. "What's your name?"

"Bub Johnson."

"Johnson. Johnson. Which floor you live on, son?"

"The top one."

"Why, you must be Mis' Johnson's grandson. You sure are a nice boy, son," she said.

She went out the door, murmuring, "Mis' Johnson's grandson. Now that's real nice he's here with her."

Bub remained on the bottom step. He had told two lies in succession. They came out so easily he was appalled, for he hadn't even hesitated when he said he lived here in this house and then that he lived on the top floor. That made two separate, distinct ones. What would Mom think of him? Perhaps he oughtn't to do this for Supe any more. He was certain Mom would object.

But he earned three whole dollars last week. Three whole dollars all at one time, and Mom ought to be pleased by that. When he had a lot more, he'd tell her about it, and they would laugh and joke and have a good time together the way they used to before she changed so. He tried to think of a word that would describe the way she had been lately—mad, he guessed. Well, anyway, different because she was so worried about their not having any money.

He opened three mail boxes in succession. The key stuck a little, but by easing it he made it work. He stuffed the letters in the big pockets of his short wool jacket.

The street door opened smoothly. He slipped quietly outside to the stoop. The men were still talking. They didn't turn their heads. He stood motionless in back of them.

"The trouble with colored folks is they ain't got no gumption. They ought to let white folks know they ain't going to keep on putting up with their nonsense."

"How they going to do that? You keep saying that, and I

keep telling you you don't know what you're talking about. A man can't have no gumption when he ain't got nothing to have it with. Why, don't you know they could clean this whole place out easy if colored folks started to acting up. What else they going to do but——"

Bub walked past them, hands in his pockets; paused for a moment right in front of them to look up and down the street as though deciding in an aimless kind of fashion which way he'd go and how he'd spend the afternoon.

And standing there with people going past him, the two men behind him arguing interminably, aimlessly, a sudden, hot excitement stirred in him. It was a pleasant tingling similar to the feeling he got at gangster movies. These men behind him, these people passing by, didn't know who he was or what he was doing. It could be they were the very men he was trying to catch; it could be the evidence to trap them was at that very moment reposing in the pockets of his jacket.

This was more wonderful, more thrilling, than anything he had ever done, any experience he had ever known. It wasn't make-believe like the movies. It was real, and he was playing the most important part.

He walked slowly down the street, his hands in his pockets, savoring his own importance. He paused in the middle of the block where he lived to watch a crap game that was going on. A big man leaning against an automobile pulled into the curb, held the stakes in his hands—fistfuls of money, Bub thought, looking at the ends of the dollar bills. Boy, but he's big all over —big arms, big shoulders, big hands, big feet. The other men formed a small circle around him, squatting down when they rolled the dice, standing up to watch whoever was shooting.

A thin, tall boy breathed softly on the dice cupped tight in his hand. "Work for poppa. Come for poppa. Act right for poppa. Hear what poppa say." His body rocked back and forth as he talked to the dice, oblivious of everything, the street, the big man, the impatient little circle around him.

"Come on, roll 'em! What the hell!"

"Christ, you going to kiss them dice all day?"

"Roll 'em, boy! Roll 'em!"

The boy ignored them, went on talking softly, sweetly to the dice. "Do it for poppa. Show your love for poppa. Come for poppa."

The big man kept turning his head, taking quick looks first up and then down the street. Bub looked, too, to see what it was he was seeking. A mounted cop turned into the block from Seventh Avenue. The horse picked up his feet delicately, gaily, as he came side-stepping and cavorting toward them. The sun glinted on the bits of metal on his harness, enriched the chestnut brown of his hide. Bub stared at the approaching pair completely entranced, for the street stretched away and away in back of them and the horse and the man glowed in the sunlight.

"Blow it," the big man said out of the side of his mouth.

Bub didn't move. He edged closer to the thin boy and stared at the boy's hand closed so tightly over the dice as he waited to hear again the rhythm of the boy's soft talking.

"Scram, kid," the big man said.

Bub moved a little nearer to the thin boy in the hope that if he stayed long enough he might be able to get his hands on the dice and talk to them himself.

"Get the hell out of here," the man growled, pushing him violently away.

Bub trotted off down the street. The big palooka, who does he think he is? The big palooka! He liked the sound of the words, and he said them over and over to himself as he walked along—the big palooka, the big palooka.

The key in his pants pocket made a pleasant jingling as he walked, because it clinked against his doorkey. He skipped along to make it louder. Then he ran a little way, but the sound seemed to disappear, so he slowed down, and began to imitate the dancing, cavorting horse that he had seen picking his way along the street with the sun shining on him.

"The big palooka," he said softly. He stopped trotting like the horse and the key jingled in his pocket. The sound reminded him that he hadn't done any work in his own street that afternoon.

Before he headed for home, he had stopped in three apartment houses. The letters he obtained formed lumps in his pockets. Going in and out of the doorways, pausing to listen

for footsteps in the halls, walking stealthily up to the mail
boxes, sitting down on a bottom step to tie his shoe whenever
someone came in or went out, tiptoeing out of the buildings,
quickened the excitement in him. People in the houses were
completely and stupidly unaware of his presence; their voices
coming from behind the closed doors of the apartments added
to his sense of daring.

He wished he could share the wonder of it with someone.
Supe was too matter-of-fact and never took any interest in the
details. His excitement and his pleasure in this thing he was
doing enchanted him so that he walked straight into the middle of the gang of boys who had chased him earlier in the
afternoon.

They were standing under Mrs. Hedges' window, talking.

"Aw, you can't go down there. Them white cops are mean
as hell——"

"You're afraid of 'em," Gray Cap said. There was a sneer on
his lean, black face. The light-colored gray cap that gave him
his name was far back on his head; the front turned toward the
back so that his face was framed against the pale fuzzy wool.

"Who's afraid of 'em?"

"You are."

"I ain't."

"You are, too."

It might have ended in a fight except that Gray Cap spied
Bub approaching. He was coming toward them, so wrapped in
thought, so unaware, so full of whatever dream was foremost
in his mind, that they nudged each other with delight. They
spread out a little so they could encircle him.

"You start it," one of them whispered.

Gray Cap nodded. He was standing feet wide apart, hands
on hips, dead center in Bub's path, grinning. It always worked,
he thought. Start a fight and then take the kid's money and
anything else he had on him. You could rob anybody that way
in broad daylight. The gang simply closed in once the fight
got started.

He waited, watching Bub's slow approach, savoring the moment when he would look up and see that he was trapped.
Three boys had moved slowly, carefully, so that they were in

back of Bub. There. They had him. Gray Cap moved forward a little, to hasten the entry of the bird into the trap. Perfect.

"Hi," he said, and grinned.

Bub looked up, surprised. He turned his head slowly, knowing beforehand what he would find. Yes, there was one on each side of him; two, no, three, in back of him. He kept on walking, thinking that he would walk right up to Gray Cap, and then suddenly swerve past him and run for the door.

Gray Cap's hand shot out, grabbed the collar of Bub's jacket.

"Take your hands off my clothes," Bub said feebly.

"Who's going to make?" Bub didn't answer. "Who's going to make?" Gray Cap repeated. Bub still didn't answer. Gray Cap's eyes narrowed. "Your mother's a whore," he said suddenly.

Bub was startled. "What's that?"

"He says he don't know what it is. Look at him." Gray Cap grinned at his henchmen. "He don't know what his mother is."

"She is not," Bub said defensively, impelled to deny whatever it was that had set Gray Cap to grinning and winking.

"What you mean she ain't? You just said you don't know what it is. Look at him. He don't know what it is and he says she ain't. Look at him."

Bub didn't answer.

"His mother's a whore," Gray Cap repeated. "Does nasty things with men," he elaborated.

"She don't either," Bub said indignantly. "And you stop talking about her."

"Yah! Who's going to make? Your mother's a whore. Your mother's a whore."

Bub doubled up his fist and reached for and found the boy's nose.

"Why, you——" The boy aimed a blow at Bub—a blow that slanted off as Bub ducked. Gray Cap pushed close against him, then knocked him off balance so that he went sprawling backward on the pavement. Bub got up and the boy hit him squarely on the nose. His nose started to bleed.

The others closed in, forming a tight knot around him, their hands reaching, ready to explore his pockets. Gray Cap spied Mrs. Hedges sitting in the window imperturbably watching the proceedings. He was so delighted with the thought of this young and tender victim ready for the plucking that he yelled out, "Yah! You're a whore, too!"

"You, Charlie Moore"—Mrs. Hedges leaned out of her window. "Leave that boy alone."

Their faces turned toward the window—sullen, secret, hating. Their hands were still extended toward Bub, reaching for him.

Gray Cap glared at her without replying.

None of them moved. "You heard me, you little bastards," she said in her rich, pleasant voice. "You leave that boy alone. Or I'll come out there and make you."

"Aw, nuts." Gray Cap's hands went down to his sides. The boys backed off slowly, turned toward the street, staying close together as they went.

Gray Cap was the last to leave. He turned to Bub. "Get other people to fight for you, huh? I'll fix you. I'll catch you coming home from school and I'll fix you good."

"No, you won't neither, Charlie Moore. That boy come home all messed up and I'll know you done it. Don't you fool with me."

He backed away from her hard eyes. "Aw, his mother's a whore and so are you," he muttered. It was a mere shred of defiance, and he didn't say it very loudly, but he had to say it because the gang was standing at the curb. Their hands were in their pockets as they stared up the street in apparent indifference, but he knew they were listening, because it showed up in every line of their lounging bodies.

"You go on outta this block, Charlie Moore." Mrs. Hedges' rich, pleasant voice carried well beyond the curb. "And don't you walk through here no more'n you have to."

Mrs. Hedges remained at the window, her arms folded on the sill. She and Bub looked at each other for a long moment. They appeared to be holding a silent conversation—acknowledging their pain, commiserating with each other, and then agreeing to dismiss the incident from their minds, to forget it as though it had never occurred. The boy looked very small in contrast to the woman's enormous bulk. His nose was dripping blood —scarlet against the dark brown of his skin. He was shivering as though he was cold.

Finally their eyes shifted as though some common impulse

prompted them to call a halt to this strange communion. Mrs. Hedges concentrated on the street. Bub went into the apartment house, his nose blowing bubbles of blood.

He was afraid. He examined his fear, standing in the hall. It was as though something had hold of him and refused to let go; and whatever it was set him to trembling. He decided it was because he had been lying and fighting all in one day. Yet he couldn't have avoided the fight. He couldn't let anyone talk about his mother like that.

He rapped on the cellar door under the stairs. He was still shaking with fear and excitement. The slow, heavy tread of the Super coming up the stairs sounded far away—menacing, frightening. When the Super opened the door, he followed him down the steep, old stairs to the basement in silence.

When they reached the bottom step, he began to feel better. He always delivered the letters to Supe down here. The fire was friendly, warm. The pipes that ran overhead with their accumulation of grime, the light bulbs in metal cages, the piles of coal—shiny black in the dim light—even the dusty smell of the basement, turned it into a kind of robbers' den.

It was a mysterious place and yet somehow friendly. The shadowed corners, the rows of garbage cans near the door that led to the areaway gaping wide and empty, the thick hempen ropes of the dumb-waiter, helped make it strange, secret, exciting. Those long brown ropes that held the dumb-waiter offered a way of escape if sudden flight became necessary. He could almost see himself going up, hand over hand, up and up, the stout ropes.

There was so much space down here, too. As he looked at the small dusty windows just visible in the concrete walls, at the big pillars that held the house up, he forgot about his bloody nose. The sudden sharp pain of hearing his mother talked about while the other boys laughed slowly left him. Only the memory of the horrid-sounding words that had come from Gray Cap's hard, wide mouth stayed with him.

This was real. The other was a bad dream. Going upstairs after school to a silent, empty house wasn't real either. This was the reality. This great, warm, open space was where he really belonged. Supe was captain of the detectives and he, Bub, was his most valued henchman. At the thought, the memory of

Gray Cap's jeering eyes and of the hard, young bodies pressed suffocatingly close to his slipped entirely away.

He lifted his hand to his forehead in salute. "Here you are, Captain." He pulled the wadded-up letters from his pockets.

The Super held them lightly in his great, work-worn hands. "I'll turn 'em over to the 'thorities tomorrow." He looked at Bub curiously. "You been in a fight?" he asked.

Bub wiped his nose on his jacket sleeve. "Sure," he said. "But I won. The other guy was all messed up. Two black eyes. And he lost a tooth. Right in the front."

"Good," Jones said. And thought they oughtta killed the little bastard.

"Supe," Bub said, "oughtn't those letters that ain't the right ones—oughtn't those others be put back?"

"Yeah," Jones nodded in agreement. "The other fellows put 'em back."

"Oh," he said, relief in his voice. And then eagerly, "Have they caught any of the crooks yet?"

"No. But they will. It takes a little time. But don't you worry none about it. They'll catch 'em all right."

"I guess I'll do a little more work, Captain," he said. Mom wouldn't be home for a long time yet. The street was better than that clammy silence upstairs. And this time he would keep a sharp eye out for Gray Cap and his gang. He wouldn't walk right into the middle of them like he did just now.

"That's good," Jones said. "The more you work, the sooner the cops'll catch the crooks."

Chapter 15

M IN CAME OUT of the apartment house with a brown-paper bag hugged tight under her arm. It contained her work clothes—a faded house dress and a pair of old shoes, the leather worn and soft and shaped to her bunions. She paused before she reached the street to look up at the sky. It was the color of lead—gray, sullen, lowering. Wind clouds of a darker gray scudded across it. She frowned. It was going to rain or snow; probably snow, because the air was cold and the wind blowing through the street smelt of snow.

The street was wrapped in silence. It was dark. The houses across the way were barely visible. Even the concrete sidewalk under her feet was recognizable as such only there where she was standing. By now she ought to be used to this early morning darkness, only she wasn't. It made her uneasy inside, and she kept turning her head, listening for sounds and peering across at the silent houses while she shifted the brown-paper bag from one arm to the other. It was the overcast sky and the threat of snow in the air that made her feel so queer.

Last winter there had been more mornings when the sky was a clear, deep blue and the sun spread a pink glow over the street. She had been filled with content then because she was free from the burden of having to pay rent and she was saving money to get her false teeth and getting little things to make Jones' apartment cozier and more homey.

She looked at the gloomy gray of the sky, at the dark bulge of the buildings, at the strip of sidewalk in front of her, and she saw the whole relentless succession of bitter days that had made this the longest, dreariest winter she had ever known. And Jones was the cause of it. She was used to going to work in the early morning dark, to coming home in the black of winter evenings; used to getting only brief and occasional glimpses of the sun when she made hurried purchases for Mis' Crane, and she had never minded it or thought very much about it until Jones changed so.

The change in him had transformed the apartment into a grim, unpleasant place. His constant anger, his sullen silence,

filled the small rooms until they were like the inside of an oven
—a small completely enclosed place where no light ever pene-
trated. It had been like that for weeks now, and she didn't think
she could bear it much longer.

Things had only been nice that time he had the headache.
He had talked to her all evening and come to stand close to
her while she washed the dishes and he wiped them, and then
later on for the first time he asked her to do something for him.

When she went to get the key made for him, a happy feeling
kept bubbling up inside her. She waited impatiently while the
man fiddled with the metal that would eventually come out of
his machine as a key, for she had been certain that Jones would
move back to the bedroom that same night, would once again
sleep beside her.

That was another thing. Though the apartment had grown
smaller, the bed had grown larger; night after night it increased
in size while she lay in the middle of it—alone. It wasn't right
for a woman to be sleeping by herself night after night like that;
it wasn't natural for a bed to stretch vast and empty around all
sides of her.

But when she came back with the key, he said his headache
was too bad, that he'd stay outside in the living room. The next
evening she had hurried home from work, looking forward to
a repetition of the pleasant evening they spent together the
night before, and he had acted so crazy mad that she stayed
in the bedroom with the door closed, so she wouldn't see him
and wouldn't hear him. But the hoarse wildness of his voice
came through the closed door in a furious, awful cursing that
went on and on.

The sound of his own voice seemed to increase his fury, and
as the minutes dragged by, his raging grew until she thought
he would explode with it. She sat down on the bed close under
the cross and put her hand in the pocket where she kept the
protection powder the Prophet gave her.

Maybe she should go see the Prophet again. No. He had
done all he could. He kept her from being put out, and Jones
still wouldn't try to put her out, but she didn't want to stay
any more.

Her eyes blinked at the thought. Her mind backed away
from it and then approached it again—slowly. Yes, that was

right. She didn't want to stay with him any more. Strange as it seemed, it was true. And it just went to show how a good-looking woman could upset and change the lives of people she didn't even know. Because if Jones hadn't seen that Mis' Johnson, she, Min, would have been content to stay here forever. As it was—and this time she acknowledged the thought, explored it boldly—as it was, she was going somewhere else to live.

Jones had never been the same after Mis' Johnson moved in, and he got worse after that night he tried to pull her down in the cellar; got so bad, in fact, that living with him was like being shut up with an animal—a sick, crazy animal.

Worst of all, he never looked at her any more. She could have stood his silence because she was used to it; could even perhaps have grown more or less accustomed to the rage that forever burned inside him, but his refusal ever to look in her direction stabbed at her pride and filled her with shame. It was as though he was forever telling her that she was so hideous, so ugly, that he couldn't bear to let his eyes fall upon her, so they slid past her, around her, never pausing really to see her. It was more than a body could be expected to stand.

Yes, she would move somewhere else. It wouldn't be on this street and she wasn't going to tell him that she was going. She took a final look at the sky. She would try to get her things under cover in some other part of town before the snow started. Mis' Hedges would get a pushcart man for her. She glanced at the street. It wasn't somehow a very good place to live, for the women had too much trouble, almost as though the street itself bred the trouble. She went to stand under Mrs. Hedges' window.

The window was open, and though she couldn't see her, she knew she must be close by, probably drinking her morning coffee. "Mis' Hedges," she called.

"You on your way to work, dearie?" Mrs. Hedges' bandanna appeared at the window suddenly.

"Well, not exactly" Min hesitated. She didn't want Mis' Hedges to know she was moving until she was all packed up and ready to go. "I ain't feeling so well today and I thought I'd stay in and do a little work 'round the house. I was wondering if you saw a pushcart moving man go past if you'd stop him and send him in to me."

"You movin', dearie?"

"Well, yes and no. I got some things I want moved some-where else, but I haven't got my mind full made up yet about me actually moving."

Mrs. Hedges nodded. "'Bout what time you want him, dearie?"

Jones had gone out of the apartment wearing his paint-splashed overalls early this morning, so he was probably paint-ing upstairs somewhere and wouldn't come back down until around twelve o'clock or so, and the man could load her things on the cart in a few minutes. It wouldn't take her very long to get them together, so by nine o'clock she should be gone.

"Tell him 'bout eleven," she said, and was startled because her mouth seemed to know what she should do before her mind knew. She hadn't thought about it before, but she needed to sit down in the apartment and really decide that she was going to get out, for it never paid to do things in a hurry. At the end of an hour or two, she would have her mind full made up, and she'd never regret leaving, because she would know it was the only thing she could have done under the circumstances. Queer how her mouth had known this without any prompting from her mind.

"'Bout eleven," she repeated.

"Okay, dearie."

When she opened the door of the apartment and walked into the living room, she saw that Jones was standing by the desk. He was tearing some letters into tiny pieces. The small bits of paper were falling into the wastebasket, swiftly and qui-etly like snow.

He didn't hear her come in, and when he became aware of her he turned on her with such suddenness, with such a snarling "What you doin' in here?" that she backed toward the door, one hand reaching up toward her chest in an instinctive gesture aimed to quiet the fear-sudden hurrying of her heart.

"What you doin' here?" he repeated. "What you doin' spyin' on me?"

The fact that she moved away from him seemed to enrage him, and he started toward her. His eyes were inflamed, red. His face was contorted with hate. She thrust her hand in her coat pocket, groping for the small box of powder, reached in further, more frantically. It wasn't there. She explored the other pocket. It, too, was empty.

As he approached her, she shrank away from him, half-closing her eyes so that she shut out his face and saw only his overalls—the faded blue material splashed with thick blobs of tan-colored paint and brown varnish; the shiny buckles on the straps and the rust marks under the buckles.

He would probably kill her, she thought, and she waited for the feel of his heavy hands around her neck, for the violence of his foot, for he would kick her after he knocked her down. She knew how it would go, for her other husbands had taught her: first, the grip around the neck that pressed the windpipe out of position, so that screams were choked off and no sound could emerge from her throat; and then a whole series of blows, and after that, after falling to the ground under the weight of the blows, the most painful part would come—the heavy work shoes landing with force, sinking deep into the soft, fleshy parts of her body, her stomach, her behind.

As she waited, she wondered where she had put the powder. She'd had it only yesterday in her coat pocket and last night she'd put it in the pocket of her house dress. That's where it was now, in the pocket of the dress hanging in the closet—the dress with the purple flowers on it that she'd bought in that nice little store on the corner where the lady was so pleasant, only the dress had run when she washed it and the purple flowers had spread their color all over the white background, muddying the green of the small leaves that were attached to the flowers.

He had lifted his hand. So it would be the face first and the neck afterward. She closed her eyes, so that she wouldn't see his great, heavy hand coming at her face, and thus she shut out the overalls and the paint on them and the rusting buckles that fastened the straps.

Nothing but trouble, always trouble, when there was a woman as good-looking as that young Mis' Johnson in a house. She wondered if white women, good-looking ones, brought as much of trouble with them, and then she thought of the Prophet David with warmth and affection. He had done the best he could for her. This that was going to happen wouldn't have come about if she had followed his instructions. It was a pity she had been so careless and left the protection powder in the pocket of that other dress.

And then the big, golden cross came to her mind. Nights alone in the bedroom she had sometimes sat up and turned on the light and looked up at it hanging over her head and been comforted by it. And it wasn't just because of the protection it offered either. There was something very friendly about it and just looking at it never failed to remind her of the Prophet and the quiet way he had listened to her talk.

She took her hand out of her pocket and without opening her eyes, and only half-realizing what she was doing, she made the sign of the cross over her body—a long gesture downward and then a wide, sweeping crosswise movement.

Jones' breath came out with a sharp, hissing sound.

She was so startled that she opened her eyes, for it was the same sound that she had heard snakes make, and it sent an old and horrid fear through her. For a moment she thought she was back in Georgia in a swampy, sedgy place, standing mesmerized with fear because she had nearly stepped on a snake that was coiled in front of her and she half-expected to see its threadlike tongue licking in and out.

"You god damn conjurin' whore!" Jones said.

His voice was thick with violence and with something else— almost like a sob had risen in his throat and got mixed up with the words. She stared at him, bewildered, reassuring herself that it was he who had made the hissing sound, that she was not back in the country, but instead was facing Jones in this small, dark room.

She was surprised to see that he had backed away from her. There was half the distance of the room between them. He was over by the desk, and his hands were no longer lifted in a threatening gesture; they were flat against his face. The sight held her motionless, unable to deny or affirm his charge of conjuring.

He walked out of the room without looking at her. She ought to explain why she had come back so unexpectedly, but he had reached the foyer before she could get the words out.

"My heart was botherin' me," she said in her whispering voice. He made no reply, and she wasn't certain whether he had heard her. The door slammed with a bang, and then he was going up the stairs—walking slowly as though he was having trouble with his legs.

She cocked her head on one side listening, because the room was filled with whispers, and it was her own voice saying over and over again, "My heart was botherin' me," "My heart was botherin' me." It had a gasping, faintly surprised quality, and she realized with dismay that she was saying the words aloud over and over again and that her heart was making a sound like thunder inside her chest.

Her legs were shaking so badly that she walked over to the sofa and sat down. This was where he slept when she was in the bedroom alone. It was a long sofa, very long, and yet tall as he was, when he was stretched out on it, his head would be about where she was sitting and his feet would have touched the arm at the other end. She wondered if he had been comfortable or had he twisted and turned unable to sleep because he didn't have room enough. She punched the seat with her fist. It didn't have much give to it.

What would he have done if she had come and lain down beside him on this sofa on one of those nights when she couldn't sleep? Only, of course, her pride wouldn't have permitted it —especially after that experience with the nightgown. She squirmed as she thought of its bright pinkness, its low cut, and of the vivid yellow lace that edged the neck and the armholes.

She had looked at it a long time in the store before she finally bought it. It was the same store where she'd got that nice flowered dress, only this time the lady wasn't there, and the white girl who waited on her got a little impatient with her, but she had a hard time making up her mind because she'd never worn anything like it before and it didn't look decent.

"But it's so beautiful, honey," the girl urged. Her long red fingernails had picked up a bit of the lace edging.

"I dunno," Min had said doubtfully.

"And it's glamorous. See?" The girl held it up in front of herself, catching it in tight at her waist and holding the neck up with her other hand, so that her breasts were suddenly accentuated, seemed to be pushing right out of the bright pink material.

Min looked away, embarrassed. "I ain't never wore one of them kind."

"Why, honey, you've missed half of life." The girl moved her shoulders slightly to attract Min's glance. Min's eyes stayed focused on the front of the store and the girl stretched the nightgown out on the counter, started putting it back into its crisp folds, and said impatiently, "Well, honey?"

"I still dunno." The shiny pink material, the yellow lace, the gathers at the bosom, were startling even spread out flat on the counter.

The girl sought desperately for some way to close the sale. "Why—why——" she fumbled, then, "Why, any man who sees you in this would get all excited right away."

Two-ninety-eight it had cost, and she remembered with a pang of regret how that night after she bought it she had put it on. It was a little too long and she had to walk carefully to keep from tripping, but she made several totally unnecessary trips back and forth through the living room, walking as close as possible to the sofa where Jones was sitting. He was so absorbed in some gloomy chain of thought that he didn't pay any attention until she stumbled over the hem and nearly fell.

"Jesus God!" he said, staring.

But after that first look, he had kept his eyes on the floor, head down, unseeing, apparently indifferent. The only indication that he wasn't wholly unconcerned showed in the way he started cracking his knuckles, pulling his fingers so that the joints made a sharp, angry sound.

No, she could never have brought herself to lie down on this couch with him, and anyway she ought to start packing. Her house dresses and the pink nightgown and the other ordinary nightgowns could go in a paper bundle along with her shoes and slippers and spring coat and what else—oh, yes, the Epsom salts for her feet. The comb and brush and hand mirror could go in the same package. That was about all except for the cross and the table and the canary cage. She wouldn't really need the medicine dropper and that red don't-love medicine the Prophet gave her, but she'd take them, because she might run across some friend with husband trouble who could use them.

Funny how she got to believe that not having to pay rent was so important, and it really wasn't. Having room to breathe in meant much more. Lately she couldn't get any air here. All the time she felt like she'd been running, running, running, and hadn't been able to stop long enough to get a nose full of air. It was because of the evilness in Jones. She could feel the weight of it like some monstrous growth crowding against her. He had made the whole apartment grow smaller and darker; living room, bedroom, kitchen—all of them shrinking, their walls tightening about her.

Like just now when he came at her with his hand upraised to strike; he had swallowed the room up until she could see nothing but him—all the detail of the overalls and none of the room, just as though he had become a giant and blotted out everything else.

These past few weeks she had become so acutely aware of his presence that his every movement made her heart jump, whether she was in the bedroom or the kitchen. Every sound he made was magnified. His muttering to himself was like thunder, and his restless walking up and down, up and down, in the living room seemed to go on inside her in a regular rhythm that set her eyes to blinking so that she couldn't stop them. When he beat the dog, it made her sick at her stomach, because as each blow fell the dog cried out sharply and her stomach would suck in against itself.

But when he had been quiet and no sound came from him, she felt impelled to locate him. The absence of sound was deeply disturbing, for there was no telling what awful thing he might be doing.

If she was in the kitchen, she would keep turning her head, listening, while she scrubbed the floor or cleaned the stove, until, unable to endure not knowing where he was or what he was doing, she would finally tiptoe to the living-room door only to find that he was sitting here on this sofa, biting his lips, glaring at her with eyes so bloodshot, so filled with hate, that she would turn and scuttle hastily back to the kitchen. Or if she was in the bedroom she would sit on the edge of the bed, watching the doorway, half-expecting to see him appear there suddenly, and then the silence from the living room would force her to get up and look at him only to find his hate-filled eyes focused straight at her.

She got up from the sofa, satisfied. She had full made up her mind now and she would never regret going, for there wasn't anything else for her to do. He was more than flesh and blood could bear.

She carefully inspected the kitchen to make certain none of her belongings were there and then entered the bathroom where she took a five-pound package of Epsom salts from under the sink. There was nothing of hers in the living room but the table and the canary's cage.

On her way into the bedroom, she glanced at the top of Jones' desk. He hadn't finished tearing up the letters and she looked at them curiously. He never got any mail that she knew of and these weren't advertising letters, they were regular ones with handwritten addresses.

She picked up two of the envelopes. The names had been partly torn off, and she traced what remained of the writing with her finger, spelling each letter out separately. None of them were for Jones. One envelope was almost intact, and she saw with surprise that it wasn't intended for this house. It belonged in a house across the street near the corner, that house where there were so many children and dogs that they overran the sidewalk and every time she went past it, whether it was morning or night, she had to pick her way along to keep from bumping into them.

But if it belonged across the street, what was it doing on Jones' desk? Perhaps the people were friends of his or maybe they were going to rent an apartment here and had dropped the letters when they came to pay a deposit or perhaps Jones had stolen them from a mail box.

And at the thought the envelopes slid out of her hands, landing on the floor. She was too frightened to pick them up. And what was it he had said when she came in and found him tearing them into little pieces? What was it—"What you doin' spyin' on me?"

Jones was doing something crooked. He was up to something that was bad. He had been ready to kill her just now because he thought she had found him out. If there had been any part of her that felt a reluctance about leaving the security that his apartment had offered, it disappeared entirely now, for she knew she would never be safe here again.

She walked carefully around the envelopes, entered the bedroom. There was the packing to be done and she would do it swiftly, so that she could be gone. She knelt on the bed and lifted the cross down, dusting it carefully with her hand. It should be wrapped in something soft to keep it safe. The pink nightgown, of course. It was new and silky and highly suitable. And she would wrap her house dresses and underwear and shoes and the slippers in with it. She would wear her galoshes because it was going to snow.

She transferred the protection powder from the pocket of her house dress to her coat pocket and then put the comb and brush, a hand mirror, and a towel on the bed near the cross. Mis' Crane would probably be mad because she hadn't come to work today. She got mad easy. Well, she'd tell her there was sickness in the family. It was true, too. Jones was sick; at least he certainly wasn't what you'd call well and healthy, so he must be sick.

She added her spring coat, a straw hat, and a felt hat to the pile of items on the bed. She brought newspapers from the kitchen to wrap them in. It was going to be a pretty large bundle, and she decided to make two separate packages and wrap the cross and the house dresses by themselves. She would carry that package, because these pushcart men were very careless and sometimes let things slip off the back of their carts.

The closet floor was dusty. She wiped it up with a damp rag and then scrubbed it with scouring powder until the boards had a bleached, new look that pleased her. When she straightened up, she started to wipe her hands on the sides of her dress and halted the motion abruptly. She was still wearing her coat, had the woolen scarf tied over her head.

"I musta known all along I was going," she said, aloud. "Never even took my hat and coat off."

The doorbell rang with a sudden loud shrilling that stabbed through her. She jumped and gave a frightened exclamation. Immediately she thought of Jones and her breathing quickened until she was gasping. Then the fear in her died. He never rang the bell. It must be the moving man that Mis' Hedges had sent.

She went to the door. "Who is it?" she said. He must be a heavy-handed man, a strong man from the vigorous way he'd pushed the bell.

"Pushcart man," the voice was deep, impatient, almost a growl.

She opened the door. "Come in," she said, and led him

toward the living room, talking to him over her shoulder. "It's the big table, the canary cage, and a bundle. I'll go get the bundle. The little one I'll carry myself, and how much will it be?"

She brought the big bundle out and put it on top of Jones' desk.

"This all?"

"Yes," she said, and looked him over carefully. He had wide strong shoulders, though he wasn't very tall. His skin was weather-beaten, so that the dark brown of it had a reddish cast as though he had plenty of sun on him. "Only the table is heavy. The other things is light," she said.

"How far they go?"

She wasn't going to live on this street or very close to it and she searched her memory of other near-by streets. A couple of blocks up near Seventh Avenue she had seen signs in the windows, "Lady Boarder Wanted"—she'd try there first.

"'Bout two blocks."

"Three dollars," he said. And then, as though he felt impelled to justify the price, "That there table weighs more than most folks' furniture put together."

"All right."

She held the door open while he struggled through it with the big table on his back. He went very slowly, so slowly that she grew impatient and kept looking up the stairs, afraid that Jones might have finished painting and would come down them before she got moved good. Then the pushcart man got the table out to the street and came back and picked up the big bundle and the canary cage.

"I'll be right out," she said. "You wait, because I'll be going along with the things."

He went out the door and she walked over to Jones' desk and laid the doorkey in the middle of it, where he couldn't possibly miss it when he sat down there. She stared at the key. She had held it in her hand when she left for work in the morning, because the last thing she did before she went out was to make sure she had it with her; and at night, too, she'd clutched it tight in her hand when she approached the door on her return. Leaving it here like this meant that she was saying good-bye to the security she had known; meant, too, that she couldn't come back, never intended coming back, no matter what the future held for her.

She ought to be going. What was it that held her here staring at this key? It was only a doorkey. She had her mind full made up to go. It wasn't safe here any more, she couldn't stand Jones any more. She looked around the room impatiently, seeking what it was that held her here while the pushcart man waited outside, while the danger of Jones coming into the apartment increased with every passing moment.

The trouble was she didn't know why she was going. Why was it? There was something that she hadn't satisfactorily figured out, some final conclusion that she hadn't reached. Ah, yes, and as this last full meaning dawned on her, she sighed. It was because if she stayed here she would die—not necessarily that Jones would kill her, not because it was no longer safe here, but because being shut up with the fury of him in this small space would eventually kill her.

"And a body's got the right to live," she said softly.

When she walked away from the desk, she didn't look back at the key. But she paused in the doorway filled with a faint regret that there wasn't anyone for her to say good-bye to, because a leave-taking somehow wasn't complete without a friend to say farewell, and in all this house she didn't know a soul well enough to say an official good-bye to them.

But there was Mis' Hedges. She walked briskly out of the door at the thought. Once outside, she verified the safety of the big varnish-shiny table. The pushcart was drawn up close to the curb and the table was slung atop of it. The ornate carved feet were up in the air. She saw with satisfaction that practically every woman who walked past paused to admire it; their eyes lingered on the carving, then they drew closer as they enviously estimated its length.

If she hadn't put a dark cover over Dickie-Boy's cage, everyone passing could have seen that, too, and their mouths would have watered. Too bad she had covered it, but if she hadn't he would have been excited by his strange surroundings and probably stopped singing for a week or more.

She turned toward Mrs. Hedges. "I come to say good-bye," she said.

"You goin', dearie?" Mrs. Hedges looked at the large newspaper-wrapped bundle under Min's arm.

Min nodded. "Prophet kept me from being put out, but I don't want to stay no more." Then her voice dropped so low that Mrs. Hedges had to strain to hear what she was saying. "Jones really ain't bearable no more," she said apologetically. She paused, and when she spoke again her voice was louder. "Well, good-bye now," she said, and smiled widely so that her toothless gums were revealed.

"Jones know you're leavin'?"

"No. I didn't see no point in telling him."

"Well, good-bye, dearie."

"See you," Min said. And then loudly, clearly, very distinctly she said again, "Well, good-bye now."

She walked near the curb, following the table's slow progress up the street. The table was heavy and the man had to lean all his weight on the handles of the cart in order to push it. With his legs braced like that, he looked like a horse pulling a heavy load. Well, he wouldn't have far to go, just a couple of blocks or so.

As she trudged along beside the cart, her thoughts turned to Jones; maybe if he'd had more sun on him he would have been different. After that time he'd tried to pull Mis' Johnson down in the cellar, he just got worse and worse. That was a terrible night, what with Mis' Johnson screaming and that long skirt all twisted around her and so dark near the cellar door that the two of them looked like something in a bad dream the way you'd remember it the next morning when you woke up.

Actually today was the first time Jones had gone for her since she went to the Prophet, because of course with the kind of protection she had it was only natural that he wouldn't try to put his hands on her. She gripped the bundle more tightly, searching for the shape of the cross through the softness of the dresses, felt for the protection powder in her coat pocket.

She looked at the pushcart man again. A woman living alone didn't stand much chance. Now this was a strong man and about her age from the wiry gray hair near his temples; willing to work, too, for this work he was doing was hard.

No, a woman living alone really didn't stand much chance.

Landlords took advantage and wouldn't fix things and land-ladies became demanding about the rent, waxing sarcastic if it was even so much as a day behind time. With a man around, there was a big difference in their attitude. If he was a strong man like this one, they were afraid to talk roughly.

Besides, when there were two working if one got sick the other one could carry on and there'd still be food and the rent would be paid. It was possible to have a home that way, too—an apartment instead of just one hall room and with the table her money would always be safe.

This was a very strong man. His back muscles bulged as he pushed the cart. She moved closer to him.

"Say," she said, and there was a soft insinuation in her voice, "you know anywhere a single lady could get a room?" Then she added hastily, "But not on this street."

Chapter 16

JONES LAID the big calcimine brush down on top of the ladder, pulled his watch out of the pocket of his overalls. It was two-thirty, way past the time when he usually ate. He climbed slowly down the ladder, feeling for each step. He was so damn tired that even his feet hurt.

He'd gone up and down the stairs until he'd lost track of how many times it was and all because he'd been fool enough to stick a note in the bell "Super Painting in 41," and it looked like everybody in the house had immediately discovered something wrong that had to be fixed right away—sinks and faucets on the third floor, a stopped-up tub on the second floor. He mimicked the old woman who lived on the second floor, "Clothes in the tub soakin', soakin', soakin', and the water ain't runnin' out, and what am I goin' to do with them wet pieces that need rinsin'?" On top of that, he'd gone down in the basement to fire the furnace.

He slammed the door of the apartment behind him, then turned and locked it. He'd better catch a breath of air before he fixed himself something to eat, because the smell of the paint was in his nose, looked like it had even got in his skin.

Min was home today. She was in the apartment right now. His steps slowed on the stairs as he remembered how he'd almost got his hands on her this morning. Had she made the sign of the cross or had he imagined it? Even now he didn't really know. There must be some way he could get over his fear of that cross just long enough to choke her good; and she'd leave so fast it wouldn't be funny. And she had to get out, because even without the cross being involved, he couldn't bear to look at her any more. Much as he hated Lutie Johnson, every time he looked at Min he thought of Lutie.

Once in the hall downstairs he walked swiftly past the door of his apartment, forcing his thoughts away from Min and Lutie, concentrating on how good the air would feel once he was out on the street.

The first thing he noticed when he got outside was that the sun had come out. He leaned against the building, breathing deeply, watching the people who walked past. He sniffed the air appreciatively. It was cold, but it smelt fresh and clean after the paint smell. Not much warmth in the sun, though, and the sky was grayish as though there was snow building up in it. Yes, it would snow tonight or tomorrow.

"Min's gone," Mrs. Hedges said blandly.

He clenched his fists as he turned toward her window. She was always interfering with him. He had been quietly studying the sky and enjoying the clear, cold air, and then that voice of hers had to interrupt him. He took another step toward the window and stood still, remembering the white man Junto who protected her, the white man who had a drag with the police and who had taken Lutie Johnson away from him. Some day he would get so mad he would forget that she had protection and he would pull her over that window sill and big as she was, he would beat her and go on beating her until she was all pulp and screams and then—— His mind echoed her words. She had said something about Min.

He looked directly at her. "What?" he said.

"Min's gone, dearie," Mrs. Hedges repeated.

"Gone?" He walked closer to the window, not understanding. "What you mean she's gone? Gone where?"

"She's moved out. Took her table and the canary and left about eleven o'clock."

"That's fine," he said. "I hope she don't come back. If she tried to come back I'd—I'd——" The words twisted in his throat and he stopped talking.

"She won't be back, dearie." Mrs. Hedges' voice was calm, placid. "She's gone for keeps." She leaned toward him, established her elbows in a comfortable position on the window ledge. "Now what was it you said you was going to do if she tried to come back?"

He turned away without answering her and went inside the house. It could be that she was lying, had made the whole thing up to see what he was going to say. It was probably a trap, some kind of trap, and the quicker he found out what it was all about the better.

The instant he opened the door, he knew that Mrs. Hedges had told the truth. Min had gone. The living room was deserted, empty. She was never home at this time of day, and he looked around him wondering what it was that made him so sharply aware that she had gone; trying to determine what the difference was in the room.

The wall in front of him was bare, blank. That was it—that long empty space was where the table used to stand. He pushed the easy-chair over against the wall and stared at it, dissatisfied. It couldn't begin to take the place of the table; instead it emphasized the absence of the gleam and shine of the table's length; made him remember how majestic the claw feet had looked down near the floor. He hadn't realized how familiar he had become with all the detail of that table until it was gone. It was only natural he should miss it, because he had stared at it for hours on end when he sat there on the sofa.

He would put his desk there instead. That's where it was before Min moved in. Immediately he began pushing and pulling the desk across the room, and while he struggled with it he wondered why he bothered, tired as he was.

The room still didn't look right. The wood of the desk was dull oak. It was grimy. It had no shine to it. He shrugged his shoulders. In a coupla hours or so he would be used to it. Meanwhile, he'd go into the bedroom and see if she took anything that didn't belong to her.

He was turning away when his eyes fell on the torn envelopes on top of the desk. How could he have moved the desk and not noticed them? Where had they come from? He brushed his hand across his face in an effort to clear his mind because it was as cloudy as though it were full of cobwebs. He picked the letters up and looked at them. They were the same ones he was tearing up this morning when Min came back into the house, the letters that thieving little kid had brought to him last night. He'd stuck them in his pocket and forgotten about them until this morning.

Min had seen them, seen him tearing them, probably examined them after he went out of the house. And he didn't know where she'd gone, and as long as she was alive, he wasn't safe, because she undoubtedly thought he'd stolen them and she'd tell on him.

He should have killed her this morning, only he couldn't because of that cross, and he didn't know whether she'd really made the outline of it over her body or whether his eyes had been playing tricks on him again. He ought to get out of here in a hurry, go somewhere else where the police couldn't find him.

There were parts of an envelope over near the bedroom door, too. Or was it his imagination? No, they were partly torn and they were real. Two of them. Had they fallen off the desk when he was moving it or had Min dropped them and left them there, so he would know that she had seen them?

He walked up and down the room. There must be some way he could figure this thing out. This way he was left holding the bag and the kid would go free, and Lutie Johnson would go on sleeping with that white bastard. Only he mustn't think about that, he got all confused whenever he did, got so he couldn't do anything, couldn't even move, just like he was paralyzed.

After all, it was only Min's word against his. She was the one who got the key made and there couldn't be much longer to wait before the kid got caught. All he had to do was bide his time, and if Min said anything, why, he would say that she was the one who'd done the stealing.

That was it. He could see himself now in front of the Judge. "I tell you that woman hated me." He'd point right at her. He could see her eyes blink and she would crouch away from him all down in a heap, so that she looked like a bag of old clothes. "Yes, sir, she hated me. And so she moved out and tried to get me in trouble. She was the one who done the stealin' and she done it because she was dead set on gettin' even with me. All she ever caused me was trouble. Used to take my money every time I turned around. I saw them letters for the first time when she left."

That would be his story, and it was a good one. There wasn't any point in his getting himself all worked up. He was still safe, and there wasn't a thing she could do that would really harm him, and if she actually did start any trouble, why, his story would land her behind jail bars. He'd leave those torn letters right there where they were. They would show he was innocent, because if he'd been guilty, why, the first thing he would have done would have been to burn them up.

Now that was settled, he'd look in the bedroom and see how she left things. With a woman like her there was no telling what she'd take that wasn't hers.

He glanced around the room, carefully avoiding the place where the cross had hung over the bed. The furniture was all here. He looked in the closet. It was empty. There was nothing —no bit of dust, no worn-out shoe or old discarded hat— nothing to indicate that Min had ever used it. The floor boards were scrubbed so clean and white they re-emphasized the closet's emptiness. The coat hangers dangling from the hooks in the back of the closet had been dusted. They looked as though they had never been used.

"I oughtta put some clothes on 'em," he said, aloud.

He turned away from the closet. The dresser was bare and clean, too. Min's worn hairbrush and toothless piece of comb had always been on the right-hand side; and a long-handled celluloid mirror used to be on the opposite cover. They were gone, and so was the towel she kept on top of the dresser. The bare, ugly wood was exposed.

He looked at himself in the mirror and then, with no intention, no conscious effort, his eyes went toward the bed, hunted for the cross. He gave a start. She had left it behind.

"God damn her," he said. "She left it here to haunt me."

He looked again. No. The cross was gone, but while it hung there the walls had darkened with grime and dust, so when it was removed its outline was left clear and sharp on the wall— an outline the exact size and shape of the cross itself.

It was everywhere in the room. He saw it again and again plain before his eyes. She had conjured him with it—conjured him and the apartment and gone. He left the room hastily and slammed the door shut behind him.

He walked restlessly through the living room, the kitchen, in and out of the bathroom, listening to the empty echo of his own footsteps. He could see the cross on the floor in front of his feet; it appeared suddenly over the kitchen stove; he had to look twice before he saw that it wasn't actually suspended from the center of the ceiling in the narrow confine of the bathroom.

Min had done this to him. And if he went on like this, seeing crosses all about him and never being certain whether they were real or figments of his imagination, he would go to pieces. But he didn't have to stay here. He paused in the middle of the living room to enumerate all the reasons why he should live somewhere else. He'd be away from the constant, malicious surveillance of Mrs. Hedges. He wouldn't have to see Lutie Johnson going back and forth to work with her head up in the air, never glancing in his direction, looking straight ahead as though he were a piece of dirt that would soil her eyes.

Nobody liked him much here, either. The folks weren't friendly. Well, when the white agent came around next week, he'd tell him he was quitting. The thought of leaving made him feel free. He could still have his revenge, too. Because wherever he went he'd make it a point to keep in with Bub and eventually the little bastard would get caught.

This place was too small, anyway. He'd find a house where the Super's apartment looked out on the street, a place that had a front window where he could sit down when he had any spare time and see what was going on outside.

The thought of a front window made him suddenly hungry for the sight of people, eager to watch their movements. He would go outside and stand awhile. And he'd get well out of sight of Mrs. Hedges' window, around near the front of the building where she couldn't look at him.

It was mighty cold standing outside. The people who went by moved along at a brisk pace. He picked out young women and watched them closely, thinking that now that he was free, now that Min was gone, he could get himself any one of these girls who swung past. It was too bad it was winter and they had on thick concealing coats, because it was difficult to get an accurate picture of just what they looked like.

They moved past without glancing at him or, if they did glance at him, they looked away before he could catch their eyes. He shifted his attention across the street where a group of men talked and laughed together in the thin sunlight.

If he should join them, try to get into the conversation, they would stop talking. He'd never acquired the knack of small talk and after a while his silence would weigh on them so heavily that the conversation would slow up, grow halting, and then die completely. The men would drift away. It always happened.

Maybe if he could think of a story, something to hold their attention, they would stay put. It was a jolly little group. He could catch phrases here and there. "Man, you ain't heard nothin' yet," and then the voice of the man who spoke would grow fainter and the little group draw closer to the one who talked.

He started talking to himself, softly, under his breath, rehearsing what he would say. "Man, you ain't heard nothin' yet," he said.

It sounded so good that he repeated it. "Man, you ain't heard nothin' yet. You oughtta work in one of them houses"—he'd gesture toward this house. "You don't never know what a fool woman is goin' to think of next. Why, one time one of 'em come runnin' down the stairs, hollerin' there was a mouse in the dumb-waiter and what was I goin' to do about it. Well, man, I told her——"

He was so intent on the slow unfolding of his story that he was completely unaware of the two white men who had stopped in front of him until the shorter of the two spoke.

"You the Super in this building?"

"What's it to you?" He hadn't had time to look them over and he was instantly on the defensive because they had caught him off guard.

"Post-office investigators." The pale sunlight glinted on a badge.

This was what he'd been waiting for. His eyes followed the badge until it disappeared inside the man's coat pocket. "Yeah," he said. His voice was thick, not quite intelligible, because there was a beating inside his head from the blood pounding there and the same beating was inside his throat, blurring his voice. "Yeah," he repeated, "I'm the Super."

"Any of the tenants complain about letters being stolen?"

"Nope." He had to be careful what he said. He had to go slow. Take it easy. "I'm around too much for anybody to do any stealin'."

"That's funny. There've been complaints from almost every house in the block except this one." They were turning away.

"Say, listen," he said. He talked slowly as though the idea had just come to him, and he was feeling it out in his mind. "There's a kid lives in this house"—he indicated the building in back of him with a motion of his head. "He's always runnin' in and out of the hallways up and down the street. I seen him every afternoon after school and wondered what he was doin'. Could be him."

The men exchanged dubious glances. "Might as well hang around. If you see him go past, call him over to you and put your hand on his shoulder."

"Okay."

Jones waited impatiently as he watched the kids swarming into the street. School was out and Bub ought to be coming along. Maybe he wouldn't come. Just when everything was fixed, he probably wouldn't come, just to spite him. That was the way everything turned out.

Then Bub came running through the crowded street. His school books were swinging from a strap. He ducked and dodged through the crowd, never allowing anyone to impede his progress, never slackening his pace, twisting, turning, coming swiftly.

"Hi, Bub," Jones called.

The boy stopped, looked around, saw the Super. "Hi, Supe," he said eagerly. He walked over to him. "How come you're out on this side today?"

"Air's better over here," Jones said. Bub grinned appreciatively. Jones placed a heavy hand on the boy's shoulder, kept it there. Yes. The men were watching. They were standing a little way off, near the curb. "You oughtta start work right now," he said.

"Okay, Captain." Bub lifted his hand in salute.

He darted across the street, lingered on the sidewalk for a moment, and then disappeared through the doorway of an apartment house.

The white men followed him. "Listen," the shorter one said. "If we catch this kid, we got to get him in the car fast. These streets aren't safe."

The other man nodded. They, too, disappeared into the building. Jones, watching from across the street, licked his lips while he waited. A few minutes later, he saw the men come out of the house with Bub between them. One of them held a letter in his hand. The white envelope showed up clearly. The boy was crying, trying to pull away from them.

There was a short, sharp struggle when they reached the

sidewalk. Bub wriggled out of their hands and for a fraction of a second it looked as though he would get away.

The people passing stopped to stare. The men lounging against the side of the building straightened up. Their faces were alert, protesting, angry.

"Hey, look. They got a colored kid with them."

The sight of the people edging toward the car parked at the curb set the two men to moving with speed, with haste, with a dispatch that landed Bub on the seat between them, closed the car door. Then the car was off up the street.

"What happened?"

"What'd he do?"

"I dunno."

"Who were they?"

"I dunno. Two strange white men."

The car disappeared swiftly, not pausing for the red light at the corner. The people stared after it. The men who had been leaning against the building walked back to the building slowly, but they didn't resume their lounging positions. They stood up straight, silent, motionless, looking in the direction the car had taken.

Slowly, reluctantly, the people moved off. Finally the men leaned their weight against the building; other men resumed their lounging on the stoops. And each one was left with an uneasy sense of loss, of defeat. It made them break off suddenly in the midst of a sentence to look in the direction the car had taken. Even after it was dark, they kept staring up the street, disturbed by the memory of the boy between the two white men.

Long after the car had gone, Jones stayed in front of the building. That was that. Even Junto couldn't get him out of it. They had caught him red-handed and there wasn't any way of fixing such cases. The little bastard would do time in reform school sure as he was standing there. He'd fixed her good. He'd fixed her plenty good.

He couldn't move away from here now. He had to stay and watch her and laugh at her efforts to get Bub out of it. Maybe there was some way of letting her know he had a hand in it. The more he thought about it, the more excited he became. He'd stay on here and one of these days she'd ring his bell and say, "I come down to call on you, Mr. Jones. It's kind of lonesome upstairs with the boy gone and everything." And he'd slam the door shut in her face, but first he'd tell her what he thought of her and how he'd had a hand in fixing her.

"You—you——" he began, but the rest of the words, the words saying exactly what he thought of her, refused to come out. He might as well go inside. His feet were tired. He felt tired all over from the excitement, from the satisfaction of having her where he wanted her. His head ached a little, too, because of the way the blood had pounded through it.

"Bub's kind of late today, ain't he?" Mrs. Hedges hailed him as he went past her window.

"I dunno," he said gruffly. She couldn't know anything. He'd never talked to Bub out here on the street. And just now, when he talked with the white men, he had been well out of earshot. It was impossible for her to know what he had done.

Perhaps he had been right in the beginning and she could really read his mind. The thought frightened him so that he stumbled in his haste to get inside, away from that queer speculative look in her eyes. No matter what she knew, he couldn't leave here until he saw Lutie Johnson all broken up by what had happened to her kid. He just wouldn't stand outside on the street any more. That way he'd be safe, because it was a sure thing Mrs. Hedges couldn't read his mind through the walls of the house.

Mrs. Hedges stopped Lutie as she came home from work. "Dearie," she said, "they're waitin' for you."

"Who?" Lutie said.

"Detectives. Two of 'em. Upstairs."

"What do they want?" she asked.

"It's about Bub, dearie."

"What about him?" she said sharply. "What about him?"

"Seems he's been taking letters from mail boxes. They caught him at it this afternoon, dearie."

"Oh, my God!" she said.

And then she was running up the stairs, going up flight after flight, not pausing to catch her breath, not stopping on the landings, but running, running, running, without thought, senselessly, up and up the stairs, with her heart pounding as she forced herself to go faster and faster, pounding until there was a sharp pain in her chest. She didn't think as she ran, but she kept saying, Oh, my God! Oh, my God! Oh, my God! over and over in her mind.

The two men standing outside the door of her apartment talked as they waited.

"Every time I come in one of these dumps, I can't help thinking they're not fit for pigs to live in, let alone people."

The other shrugged. "So what?" They were both silent, and the one who had shrugged his shoulders continued, "Mebbe you don't know that a white man ain't safe in one of these hallways by himself."

"What's that got to do with it?"

"I dunno."

They were silent again. And then one of them said, "Wonder what the mother looks like," idly, aimlessly, passing the time.

"Probably some drunken bitch. They usually are."

"Hope she doesn't start screaming and bring the whole joint down on our ears." He looked uneasily at the battered wood of the closed doors that lined the hall.

When Lutie reached the top floor, she was panting so that for a moment she couldn't talk. "Where is he?" she demanded. She looked around the hall. "Where is he? Where is he?" she asked hysterically.

"Take it easy, lady. Take it easy," one of them said.

"Don't get excited. He's down at the Children's Shelter. You can see him tomorrow," said the other, as he extended a long, white paper. It crackled as he placed it in her hand.

Then they left, jostling against each other in their haste to get down the stairs.

She tried to read what it said on the paper and the print wavered and changed shape, grew larger and then smaller. The stiff paper refused to stay still because her hands were shaking. She flattened it against the wall, and looked at it until she saw that it said something about a hearing at Children's Court.

Children's Court. Court. Court. Court meant lawyer. She had to get a lawyer. She started down the stairs, walking slowly, stiffly. Her knees refused to bend, her legs refused to go fast.

Her legs felt brittle. As though whatever had made them work before had suddenly disappeared, and because it was gone they would break easily, just snap in two if she forced them to go quickly.

She had thought Bub would be waiting there at the top of the stairs. But he was in the Children's Shelter. She tried to visualize what kind of place it could be and gave up the effort.

Bub would go to reform school. She stopped on the fourth-floor landing to look at the thought, to examine it, to get used to it. Bub would go to reform school. And she reached out and touched the wall with her hand, then leaned the weight of her body against it because her legs were trembling, the muscles quivering, knees buckling.

Her thoughts were like a chorus chanting inside her head. The men stood around and the women worked. The men left the women and the women went on working and the kids were left alone. The kids burned lights all night because they were alone in small, dark rooms and they were afraid. Alone. Always alone. They wouldn't stay in the house after school because they were afraid in the empty, silent, dark rooms. And they should have been playing in wide stretches of green park and instead they were in the street. And the street reached out and sucked them up.

Yes. The women work and the kids go to reform school. Why do the women work? It's such a simple, reasonable reason. And just thinking about it will make your legs stop trembling like the legs of a winded, blown, spent horse.

The women work because the white folks give them jobs —washing dishes and clothes and floors and windows. The women work because for years now the white folks haven't liked to give black men jobs that paid enough for them to support their families. And finally it gets to be too late for some of them. Even wars don't change it. The men get out of the habit of working and the houses are old and gloomy and the walls press in. And the men go off, move on, slip away, find new women. Find younger women.

And what did it add up to? She pressed closer to the wall, ignoring the gray dust, the fringes of cobwebs heavy with grime and soot. Add it up. Bub, your kid—flashing smile, strong, straight back, sturdy legs, even white teeth, young, round face, smooth skin—he ends up in reform school because the women work.

Go on, she urged. Go all the way. Finish it. And the little Henry Chandlers go to YalePrincetonHarvard and the Bub Johnsons graduate from reform school into DannemoraSingSing.

And you helped push him because you talked to him about money. All the time money. And you wanted it because you wanted to move from this street, but in the beginning it was because you heard the rich white Chandlers talk about it. "Filthy rich." "Richest country in the world." "Make it while you're young."

Only you forgot. You forgot you were black and you under-estimated the street outside here. And it never occurred to you that Bub might find those small dark rooms just as depressing as you did. And then, of course, there wasn't any other place for you to live except in a house like this one.

Then she was shouting, leaning against the wall, beating against it with her fists, and shouting, "Damn it! Damn it!"

She leaned further against the wall, seemed almost to sink into it, and started to cry. The hall was full of the sound. The thin walls echoed and re-echoed with it two, three floors below and one floor above.

People coming home from work heard the sound when they started up the first flight of stairs. Their footsteps on the stairs, slowed down, hesitated, came to a full stop, for they were re-luctant to meet such sorrow head-on. By the time they reached the fourth floor and actually saw her, their faces were filled with dread, for she was pounding against the wall with her fists—a soft, muted, dreadful sound. Her sobbing heard close to made them catch their breaths. She held the crisp, crackling white paper in her hand. And they recognized it for what it was—a symbol of doom—for the law and bad trouble were in the long white paper. They knew, for they had seen such papers before.

They turned their faces away from the sight of her, walked faster to get away from the sound of her. They hurried to close the doors of their apartments, but her crying came through the flimsy walls, followed them through the tight-shut doors.

All through the house radios went on full blast in order to drown out this familiar, frightening, unbearable sound. But even under the radios they could hear it, for they had started crying with her when the sound first assailed their ears. And now it had become a perpetual weeping that flowed through them, carrying pain and a shrinking from pain, so that the music and the voices coming from the radios couldn't possibly shut it out, for it was inside them.

The thin walls shivered and trembled with the music. Upstairs, downstairs, all through the house, there was music, any kind of music, tuned up full and loud—jazz, blues, swing, symphony, surged through the house.

When Lutie finally stopped crying, her eyes were bloodshot, the lids swollen, sore to the touch. She drew away from the wall. She had to get a lawyer. He would be able to tell her what to do. There was one on Seventh Avenue, not far from the corner. She remembered seeing the sign.

The lawyer was reading an evening paper when Lutie entered his office. He stared at her, trying to estimate the fee he could charge, trying to guess her reason for coming. A divorce, he decided. All good-looking women invariably wanted divorces.

He was a little chagrined when he discovered he was wrong. He listened to her attentively, and all the time he was trying to figure out how much she would be able to pay. She had such a good figure it was difficult to tell whether her clothes were cheap ones or expensive ones. And then, as the case unfolded, he began to wonder why she didn't know that she didn't need a lawyer for a case like this one. He went on scribbling notes on a pad.

"Do you think you can do anything for him?" she asked.

"Sure"—he was still writing. "It'll be simple. I'll paint a picture of you working hard, the kid left alone. He's only eight. Too young to have any moral sense. And then, of course, the street."

"What do you mean?" she asked. "What street?"

"Any street"—he waved his hand toward the window in an all-inclusive gesture. "Any place where there's slums and dirt and poverty you find crime. So if the Judge is sympathetic, the kid'll go free. Maybe get a suspended sentence and be paroled in your care." There was sudden hope in her face. "My fee'll be two hundred dollars." He saw anxiety, defeat, replace the hope, and added quickly, "I can practically guarantee getting him off."

"When do you have to have the money?"

"Three days from now at the latest."

He escorted her to the door, and stood watching her walk down the street. Now why in hell doesn't she know she doesn't need a lawyer? He shrugged his shoulders. It was like picking two hundred bucks up in the street.

"And who am I to leave it there kicking around?" he said, aloud. He picked up the notes he had made, inserted them in an envelope which he placed in an inside pocket, and went back to reading the paper.

Chapter 17

"TWO HUNDRED DOLLARS. Two hundred dollars. Two hundred dollars." Lutie repeated the words softly under her breath as she left the lawyer's office.

If it were in dollar bills and stacked up neatly, it would make a high mound of green-and-white paper. A bundle that size could buy divorces, beds with good springs and mattresses, warm coats, and pair after pair of the kind of shoes that wouldn't wear out in a hurry. It could send a kid to camp for a couple of summers. And she had to find a stack of bills like that to keep Bub out of reform school.

She had never known anyone who had that much money at one time. The people that she knew got money in driblets, driblets that barely covered rent and food and shoes and subway fare, but it never added up to two hundred dollars all at once and piled up in your hand.

Pop wouldn't have it. His only assets were an apartment filled with seedy roomers and shabby furniture and the rank smell of corn liquor. The corn liquor brought in occasional limp dollar bills. None of it added up to a pile of green-and-white paper that high. He wouldn't even know where or how to get it if she should ask him for it.

Neither would Lil. She had never seen a mound of money like that, never needed it because nickels and dimes for beer took care of all her wants, and she had always been able to find someone like Pop to provide her with a place to sleep and eat and keep her supplied with too tight housecoats.

She walked toward the small open space where St. Nicholas Avenue and Seventh Avenue ran together, forming a triangle which was flanked with benches. She sat on one of the benches and watched pieces of newspaper that were being blown by the wind. The ground under the benches was packed firm and hard and the newspapers skimmed over it, twisting against the trunks of the few trees, getting entangled with the legs of the benches. A large woman waddled past with a dog on a leash. Two children banged on the sides of a garbage can with a heavy stick. Otherwise the streets on both sides of the square were deserted.

The wind made her turn her coat collar up close around her throat. Even though it was cold, she could think better out here in the open. She didn't own anything that was worth two hundred dollars. A second-hand furniture dealer might offer ten dollars for the entire contents of her apartment lumped together. But she ought to make certain. Just around the corner on 116th Street there was a group of second-hand stores; their wares edging out to the sidewalk. She could at least inquire as to the price they were asking for things.

It would be a waste of time. All of it put together—battered studio couch, rungless chairs, wobbly kitchen table, small scarred radio—wouldn't bring a cent more than ten dollars.

She thought of the girls who worked in the office with her. She didn't know any of them intimately. She didn't really have time to get to know them well, because she went right home after work and there was only a forty-five-minute lunch period. She always took a sandwich along for lunch, and when the weather was good she ate it on a park bench, and when it was rainy or snowing she stayed inside, eating in the rest room and there were confused and incomplete snatches of conversation and that was all.

None of them would have two hundred dollars even if she knew them well enough to ask them. By the time the income-tax deductions and the war-bond deductions were taken out, there wasn't much left to take home. Most of them cashed the bonds as soon as they got them just like she did, because it was the only way they could manage on the small pay.

Remembering bits of the conversation she had heard in the rest room, she knew they had husbands and children and sick mothers and unemployed fathers and young sisters and brothers, so that going to an occasional movie was the only entertainment they could afford. They went home and listened to the radio and read part of a newspaper, mostly the funnies and the latest murders; and then they cleaned their apartments and washed clothes and cooked food, and then it was time to go to bed because they had to get up early the next morning.

There ought to be more than that to living, she thought, resentfully. Perhaps living in a city the size of New York wasn't good for people, because you had to spend all your time work-ing to pay for the place where you lived and it took all the rest of the hours in the day to keep the place clean and fix food, and there was never any money left over. Certainly it wasn't a good place for children.

If she had been able to get that job singing at the Casino, this wouldn't have happened. And for the first time in weeks she thought of Boots Smith. He would have two hundred dol-lars or would know where to get it. She started to get up from the bench and sat back down again. She didn't have any reason to believe he would lend it to her just because she needed it. It would take her a long time to pay him back and certainly she wasn't a very good risk.

Half-angrily she decided he would lend it to her because she would make him. It didn't matter that she had neither seen nor heard from him since the night he had told her she wouldn't be paid for singing. It didn't matter at all. He was going to lend her two hundred dollars because it was the only way to keep Bub from going to reform school and he was the only person she knew who could lay hands on that much money at one time.

She went into the cigar store across the street, thumbed through the phone book, half-fearful that he wouldn't have a telephone, or if he had one that it wouldn't be listed. There it was. He lived on Edgecombe Avenue. She memorized the ad-dress, thinking that she would call him and then go up there now, tonight, because she didn't want to tell him what she wanted over the phone. It was best to go and see him and if he looked as though he were going to refuse, she could talk faster and harder.

She dialed the number and no one answered. There was only the continual insistent ringing of the phone. He had to be home. She simply would not hang up. The phone rang and rang and rang.

"Yeah?" a voice said suddenly; and for a moment she was too startled to reply.

The voice repeated, "Yeah?" impatiently.

"This is Lutie Johnson," she said.

"Who?" His voice was flat, indifferent, sleepy.

"Lutie Johnson," she repeated. And his voice came alive, "Oh, hello, baby. Christ! where you been?"

He didn't understand what she was saying and she had to begin all over again, going slowly, so slowly that she thought she sounded like a record that had got stuck on a victrola. She said she had to see him. It was very important. She had to see him right away. Because it was very important. And instantly he said, "Sure, baby. I been wanting to talk to you. Come on up. It's apartment 3 J."

"I'll be right there. I'll take the bus," she said. And thought again that she sounded like a victrola, but not one that had got stuck, like one that had run down, that needed winding.

"Where are you now?"

"116th Street and Seventh Avenue."

"Okay, baby. I'll be waitin' for you."

It took her a few minutes to get the receiver back on the hook. She made futile, fumbling dabs at it, missing it because her hands were taut and tense and unmanageable.

She waited impatiently for the bus and when it came and she got on it, it seemed to her it crawled up Seventh Avenue; and each time it halted for a red light, she could feel her muscles tighten up. She tried to erase the hopes and fears that kept creeping into her mind and couldn't. Finally the bus turned and crossed the bridge, and she remembered that it didn't stop at Edgecombe Avenue. If she wasn't careful, she'd ride beyond it and have to walk back a long way.

But there was no mistaking the apartment house where Boots lived. It loomed high above all the other buildings and could be seen for a long distance. She pulled the stopcord hastily and got off the bus.

As she walked toward the awninged entrance, she recalled the stories she'd heard about the fabulous rents paid by the people who lived here. She remembered when Negroes had first moved into this building and how Pop had rattled the pages of the paper he was reading and muttered, "Must have gold toilet seats to charge that much money."

Her only reaction to the sight of the potted shrubs in the doorway and to the uniformed doorman was that if Boots could afford to live here, then lending her two hundred dollars would present no problem to him.

Inside there was a wide, high-ceilinged hall. An elevator with gleaming red doors opened into it. The elevator boy took her up to the third floor, and in answer to her inquiry said, "It's the fourth door down the hall," before he closed the elevator doors.

She pressed the bell harder than she'd intended and drew her hand away quickly, expecting to hear the loud shrilling of a bell. Instead there was the soft sound of chimes and Boots opened the door. His shirt was open at the throat, the sleeves rolled up.

"Sure is good to see you, baby," he said. "Come on in."

"Hello," she said, and walked past him into a small foyer. The rug on the floor was thick. It swallowed up the sound of her footsteps.

The living room was a maze of floor lamps and overstuffed chairs. The same kind of thick, engulfing carpet covered the floor. Logs in an imitation fireplace at the far end of the room gave off an orange-red glow from a concealed electric light. The winking light from the logs was like an evil eye and she looked away from it. Ponderously carved iron candlesticks flanked the mantel.

She couldn't go on standing here, taking an inventory of the room. She had to tell him what she wanted. Now that she was here, it was difficult to get started. There was nothing encouraging about his appearance and she had forgotten how tough and unscrupulous his face was.

"Let me take your coat," he said.

"Oh, no. I'm not going to stay that long. I can't."

"Well, sit down anyway." He sat on the arm of the sofa, one leg dangling, his arms folded across his chest, his face completely expressionless. "Christ!" he said. "I almost forgot what a warm-looking babe you are."

She sat down at the far end of the sofa, trying to think of a way to start.

"What's on your mind, baby?" he said.

"It's about my son—Bub——"

"You got a kid?" he interrupted.

"Yes. He's eight years old." She talked swiftly, afraid that if she stopped, if he interrupted her again, she wouldn't be able to finish. She didn't look at him while she told him about the letters Bub had stolen and the lawyer and the two hundred dollars.

"Go on, baby," he said impatiently when she paused.

His face had changed while she talked to him. Ordinarily his expression was unreadable; now he looked as though he had suddenly seen something he had been waiting for, seen it spread right out in front of him, and it was something that he wanted badly. She puzzled over it while she repeated what the lawyer had said and then decided the expression on his face was due to surprise. He hadn't known about Bub. She had forgotten that she hadn't told him she had a child.

"Can you let me have it? The two hundred dollars?" she asked.

"Why, sure, baby," he said easily. "I haven't got that much on me right now. But if you come by here tomorrow night about this same time I'll have it for you. Make it a little later than this. About nine."

"I can't ever thank you," she said, standing up. "And I'll pay you back. It'll take a little while, but you'll get every cent of it back."

"That's all right. Glad to do it." He stayed on the arm of the sofa. "You ain't going so soon, are you?"

"Yes. I have to."

"How about a drink?"

"No, thanks. I've got to go."

He walked to the door with her, held it open for her. "See you tomorrow night, baby," he said, and closed the door gently.

The thought that it had been very easy stayed with her all the way home. It wasn't until she opened the door of her apartment and was groping for the light in the hall that it occurred to her it had been too easy, much too easy.

She turned on all the lights in the house—the ceiling lights in the bedroom and the bathroom, the lamp in the living room. The flood of light helped thrust away the doubts that assailed her, but it did nothing to relieve the emptiness in the rooms. Because Bub wasn't sprawled in the middle of the studio couch, all the furniture had diminished in size, shrinking against the wall—the couch, the big chair, the card table.

The lights made no impression on the quiet in the apartment either and she switched on the radio. Bub usually listened to one of those interminable spy hunts or cowboy stories, and at night the living room was filled with the tumult of a chase, loud music and sudden shouts. And Bub would yell, "Look out! He's in back of you."

This lavish use of light is senseless, she thought. You used to lecture him about leaving lights on at night because the bill would be so big you couldn't pay it. He left them burning because he was frightened, just like you are now. And she wondered if he was afraid now in that strange place—the Children's Shelter—and hoped there were lights that burned all night, so that if he woke up he could see where he was. It was easy to picture him waking in the dark, discovering that he wasn't here where he belonged, and then feeling as though he had lost himself or that the room he knew so well had changed about him while he slept.

She sat down near the radio, tried to listen to a news broadcast, but her thoughts kept twisting and turning about Bub. What would happen to him after this was over? The lawyer had assured her he could get him paroled in her care. But he would have a police record, and if he played hookey from school two or three times and broke a window with a ball and got into a fight, he would end up in reform school, anyway.

Even his teachers at school would have a faint but unmistakable prejudice against him as a juvenile delinquent and they would refuse to overlook any slight infraction of the rules because he had established himself in their minds as a potential criminal. And in a sense they were right, because he didn't have much chance before living in this street so crowded with people and children. He had even less now.

They would have to move away from here. She would get a job cooking for a family that lived in the country. Unfortunately, the idea didn't appeal to her. She knew what it would be like. He would become "the cook's little boy," and expected to meet some fantastic standard of behavior. He would have to be silent when he was bursting to talk and to make noise. "Because Mrs. Brentford or Mrs. Gaines or Mrs. Somebody Else has guests for dinner."

She didn't want him to grow up like that—eating hurried meals at a kitchen table while he listened to "the family" enjoying a leisurely meal in a near-by dining room; learning young the unmistakable difference between front-door and back-door and all that the words implied; being constantly pushed aside because when he came home from school running over with energy, she would be fixing salads and desserts for dinner and only have time to say, "Get a glass of milk out of the icebox and go outside and play and be quiet."

It was quite possible that he wouldn't have much opportunity for playing. Lil had painted a grim picture of what it could be like, based on the experience of one of her friends. "That poor Myrtle said they counted practically every mouthful that poor boy child of hers ate. And wanted him to work, besides. Little light tasses the madam said like cleaning the car and mowing the lawn." Lil had taken a big swallow of beer before continuing, "And Myrtle and that poor child of hers had to sleep together because the madam said, well, of course, you all wouldn't expect me to buy another bed and he's small and don't take up much room."

The pay would be miserable because of Bub, and the people she worked for would subtly or pointedly, depending on what kind of folks they were, demand more work from her because they would feel they were conferring a special favor by permitting his presence in their home.

Perhaps it wouldn't be like that. Even if it was, it was the best she could do for him. Somebody else's kitchen was a painfully circumscribed area for a kid to grow up in, but at least it would be safe. She would be with him all the time. He wouldn't come home to a silent, empty house.

She switched off the radio, put out all the lights except the one in the bedroom, thinking that tomorrow she wouldn't go to work. Instead, she would go to the Children's Shelter and see Bub.

While she undressed, she tried to remember if she had been afraid of the dark when she was Bub's age. No, because Granny had always been there, her rocking chair part of the shadow, part of the darkness, making it known and familiar. She was always humming. It was a faint sound, part and parcel of the darkness. Going to sleep with that warm sound clinging to your ears made fear impossible. You simply drifted off to the accompaniment of a murmured "Sleepin', Sleepin', Sleepin' in the arms of the Lord." And then the gentle creak of the rocking chair.

She had never been alone in the house after school. Granny

was always home. No matter what time she reached the house, she knew in the back of her mind that Granny was there and it gave her a sense of security that Bub had never known.

When there was no one in a house with you, it took on a strange emptiness. This bedroom, for instance, was strangely empty. The furniture took up the same amount of room, for she bumped her knee against the corner of the bed. But the light in the ceiling reached only a little way into the living room. She stared at the shadows beyond the brief expanse of light. She knew the exact size of that room, knew the position of every piece of furniture, yet it would be easy to believe that beyond the door, just beyond that oblong of light, there stretched a vast expanse of space—unknown and therefore dangerous.

After she turned out the light and got into bed, she kept listening for sounds, waiting to hear the stir of some movement from the shadows that enveloped the bed and turning her head from side to side in an effort to make out the familiar outline of the furniture.

When people are alone, they are always afraid of the dark, she thought. They keep trying to see where they are and the blackness around them keeps them from seeing. It was like trying to look into the future. There was no way of knowing what threat lurked just beyond tomorrow or the next day, and the not knowing is what makes everyone afraid.

She woke up at seven o'clock and jumped out of bed, reaching for her dressing-gown and thinking that today they had assembly at school and she had forgotten to iron a white shirt for Bub and she would have to hurry so he wouldn't be late.

Then she remembered that Bub was at the Children's Shelter. She wasn't going to work today. She was going to see him.

It was her fault he'd got into this trouble. No matter how she looked at it, it was still her fault. It was always the mother's fault when a kid got into trouble, because it meant she'd failed the kid somewhere. She had wanted him to grow up fine and strong and she'd failed him all the way along the line. She had been trying to get enough money so that she could have a good place for him to live, and in trying she'd put so much stress on money that he'd felt impelled to help her and started stealing letters out of mail boxes.

Lately she had been so filled with anger and resentment and

hate that she had pushed him farther and farther away from her. He didn't have any business in the Children's Shelter. He didn't have any business going to court. She was the one they ought to have arrested and taken to court.

Pulling the cord of the robe tight around her waist with an angry jerk, she went into the kitchen where she put coffee into an enamel pot on the stove. While she waited for it to boil, she raised the window shade and looked out. It was a dark, grim morning. The blackness outside pressed against the panes of glass, and she drew the shade hastily.

She scrambled eggs and made toast, but once she was seated at the kitchen table she thrust the food away from her. The very sight and smell of it was unpleasant. The coffee didn't go down her throat easily; it kept sticking as though an ever-tightening band were wrapped around her neck, constricting her throat.

Getting dressed for the trip to the Center was a slow process, for she found herself pausing frequently to examine all kinds of unrelated ideas and thoughts that kept bobbing up in her mind. Pop had never got anywhere in life and certainly Lil hadn't ever achieved anything, but neither one of them had ever been in jail. Perhaps it was better to take things as they were and not try to change them. But who wouldn't have wanted to live in a better house than this one and who wouldn't have struggled to get out of it?—and the only way that presented itself was to save money. So it was a circle, and she could keep on going around it forever and keep on ending up in the same place, because if you were black and you lived in New York and you could only pay so much rent, why, you had to live in a house like this one.

And while you were out working to pay the rent on this stinking, rotten place, why, the street outside played nursemaid to your kid. The street did more than that. It became both mother and father and trained your kid for you, and it was an evil father and a vicious mother, and, of course, you helped the street along by talking to him about money.

The last thing she did before she left the apartment was to put the stiff, white paper in her pocketbook. And on the subway she was so aware of its presence that she felt she could see its outline through the imitation leather of the bag.

It was just nine o'clock when she got off the subway. She asked the man in the change booth which exit was nearest the Shelter.

"You shoulda took another line," he said. "Walk five blocks that way"—he pointed to the right-hand exit. "And then two down."

The crosstown blocks were long. She started walking rapidly and then, tired by the effort, she slowed down. She had never been in this section of the city before. The streets were clean and well-swept, and the houses and stores she passed had a shine and a polish on them. Immediately she thought of Bub leaning out of the kitchen window playing a game that involved the inert dogs sleeping amidst the rubbish in the yard below.

This was, by comparison, a safe, secure, clean world. And looking at it, she thought it must be rather pleasant to be able to live anywhere you wanted to, just so you could pay the rent, instead of having to find out first whether it was a place where colored people were permitted to live.

The Children's Shelter was housed in a tall brick building. And as she approached it, she kept thinking, But it can't be full of children. She walked up the steps, conscious of a hollow, empty feeling in the pit of her stomach. A uniformed guard stopped her just inside the door.

"I came to see my son," she said. She drew the stiff white paper from her pocketbook. "He was brought here yesterday."

He gestured toward a waiting room just off the hall. It was a large room filled with people, and the instant she entered it she was assailed by the stillness in the room.

The gray-haired woman behind a desk marked "Information" asked for her name and address, riffled through a thick card file.

"His case comes up Friday," the woman said. "If you care to wait, you can see him for a few minutes this morning."

Lutie sat down near the back of the room. It was filled with colored women, sitting in huddled-over positions. They sat quietly, not moving. Their patient silence filled the room, made her uneasy. Why were all of them colored? Was it because the mothers of white children had safe places for them to play in, because the mothers of white children didn't have to work?

She had been wrong. There were some white mothers, too —three foreign-looking women near the door; a gray-haired woman just two seats ahead, her hair hanging in a lank curtain about the sides of her face; a tall, bony woman up near the front who kept clutching at the arms of her fur coat, a coat shiny from wear; and over on the side a young, too thin blond girl holding a small baby in her arms.

They were sitting in the same shrinking, huddled positions. Perhaps, she thought, we're all here because we're all poor. Maybe it doesn't have anything to do with color.

Lutie folded her hands in her lap. Fifteen minutes went by. Suddenly she straightened her shoulders. She had been huddled over like all these other waiting women. And she knew now why they sat like that. Because we're like animals trying to pull all the soft, quivering tissue deep inside of us away from the danger that lurks in a room like this, and the silence helps build up the threat of danger.

The room absorbed sound. She couldn't hear even a faint murmur of traffic or of voices from the street outside. As she waited in the silent room, she felt as though she were bearing the uneasy burden of the sum total of all the troubles these women had brought with them. All of us started with a little piece of trouble, she thought, and then bit by bit more was added until finally it grew so great it pushed us into this room.

When the guard finally escorted her to the small room where Bub waited, she had begun to believe the silence and the troubled waiting that permeated the room had a smell—a distinct odor that filled her nose until it was difficult for her to breathe.

Bub had grown smaller. He was so little, so forlorn, so obviously frightened, that she got down on her knees and pulled him close to her.

"Darling," she said softly. "Oh, darling."

"Mom, I thought you'd never come," he said.

"You didn't think any such thing," she said, patting the side of his face. "You know you didn't really think that."

"No," he said slowly. "I guess I really didn't. I guess I knew you'd come as soon as you could. Only it seemed like an awful long time. Can we go home now?"

"No. Not yet. You have to stay here until Friday."

"That's so long," he wailed.

"No, it isn't. I'll be back tomorrow. And the next day. And the next day. And then it'll be Friday."

Then the guard was back, and she was going out of the building. She hadn't asked Bub anything about the letters or if he'd been frightened. There were so many things she hadn't said to him. Perhaps it was just as well, because the most important thing was for him to know that she loved him and that she would be coming to see him.

There was a whole day to be got through. And once she was back in the apartment, time seemed to stretch out endlessly in front of her. She scrubbed the kitchen floor and cleaned out the cupboards over the sink. While she was working, she kept thinking of all the reasons why Boots might not have the money for her tonight.

She started to wash the windows in the living room. She sat on the window sill, her long legs inside the room, the upper part of her body outside. At first she rubbed the panes briskly and then stopped.

It was so deadly quiet. She kept listening to the silence, hoping to hear some sound that would destroy it. It was the same kind of stillness that had been in the waiting room at the Shelter.

She polished one pane of glass over and over. The soft sound of the cloth did nothing to disturb the pool of silence that filled the apartment. She turned to look at the blank windows of the apartment houses that faced her windows. They revealed no sign of life. In the distance she could hear the faint, tinny sound of a radio. The sky overhead was dark gray. A damp cold wind rattled the windows, tugged at the sleeves of the cotton dress she was wearing.

Suppose that for some reason Boots didn't have the money for her tonight? Doubt grew and spread in her, alarming her so that she stopped washing the windows, went inside the room. She collected the window-washing equipment, poured the water out of the enamel pan she had been using, and stood watching it go down the sink drain. It was black and syrupy, thick with the grime and dirt from the windows. She put the window cloths to soak in the set tub.

He would either give her the money or he wouldn't. If he didn't, she would have to figure out some other way of getting it. There was no point in her worrying about it. And as long as she stayed alone in these small rooms, she would worry and wonder and the knot of tension inside her would keep growing and her throat would keep constricting like it was doing now. She swallowed hard. Her throat felt as though the opening were growing smaller all the time. It was smaller now than it had been this morning when she tried to drink the coffee.

If she went to the movies, it would take her mind away from these fears that kept closing in on her. But once inside the theater, she was abruptly dismayed. As her eyes became adjusted to the dimness, she saw that there were only a few seats occupied. She deliberately sat down near a little group of people—a protective little group in back of her and in front of her.

And the picture didn't make sense. It concerned a technicolor world of bright lights and vast beautiful rooms; a world where the only worry was whether the heroine in a sequined evening gown would eventually get the hero in a top hat and tails out of the clutches of a red-headed female spy who lolled on wide divans dressed in white velvet dinner suits.

The glitter on the screen did nothing to dispel her sense of panic. She kept thinking it had nothing to do with her, because there were no dirty little rooms, no narrow, crowded streets, no children with police records, no worries about rent and gas bills. And she had brought that awful creeping silence in here with her. It crouched along the aisles, dragged itself across the rows of empty seats. She began to think of it as something that was coming at her softly on its hands and knees, coming nearer and nearer to her aisle by aisle.

She left in the middle of the picture. Outside the theater she paused, filled with a vast uneasiness, a restlessness that made going home out of the question. There was a beauty parlor at the corner. She would get a shampoo that she couldn't afford, but she would have people around her and it would use up a lot of time.

Walking toward the shop, she tried to figure out what was the matter with her. She was afraid of something. What was it? She didn't know. It wasn't just fear of what would happen to Bub. It was something else. She was smelling out evil as Granny said. An old, old habit. Old as time itself.

It was quiet in the beauty shop except for the noise that the manicurist made. She was sitting in the front window, chewing gum, and the gum made a sharp, cracking sound. It was the only sound in the place.

The hairdresser, normally talkative, was for some reason in an uncommunicative mood. She rotated Lutie's scalp with strong fingers and said nothing. It was so quiet that the awful stillness Lutie had found in the Shelter settled in the shop. It had followed her in here from the movies and it was sitting down in the booth next to her. She shivered.

"Somep'n must have walked over your grave"—the hairdresser looked at her in the mirror as she spoke.

And even under the words Lutie heard the stillness. It was crouched down in the next booth. It was waiting for her to leave. It would walk down the street with her and into the apartment. Or it might leave the shop when she did, but not go down the street at all, but somehow seep into the apartment before she got there, so that when she opened the door it would be there. Formless. Shapeless. Waiting. Waiting.

Chapter 18

IT WAS BEGINNING TO SNOW when Lutie left the beauty parlor. The flakes were fine, small; barely recognizable as snow. More like rain, she thought, except that rain didn't sting one's face like these sharp fragments.

In a few more minutes it would be dark. The outlines of the buildings were blurred by long shadows. Lights in the houses and at the street corners were yellow blobs that made no impression on the ever-lengthening shadows. The small, fine snow swirled past the yellow lights in a never-ending rapid dancing that was impossible to follow and the effort made her dizzy.

The noise and confusion in the street were pleasant after the stillness that hung about the curtained booths of the beauty shop. Buses and trucks roared to a stop at the corners. People coming home from work jostled against her. There was the ebb and flow of talk and laughter; punctuated now and then by the sharp scream of brakes.

The children swarming past her added to the noise and the confusion. They were everywhere—rocking back and forth on the traffic stanchions in front of the post-office, stealing rides on the backs of the crosstown buses, drumming on the sides of ash cans with broomsticks, sitting in small groups in doorways, playing on the steps of the houses, writing on the sidewalk with colored chalk, bouncing balls against the sides of the buildings. They turned a deaf ear to the commands shrilling from the windows all up and down the street, "You Tommie, Jimmie, Billie, can't you see it's snowin'? Come in out the street."

The street was so crowded that she paused frequently in order not to collide with a group of children, and she wondered if these were the things that Bub had done after school. She tried to see the street with his eyes and couldn't because the crap game in progress in the middle of the block, the scraps of obscene talk she heard as she passed the poolroom, the tough young boys with their caps on backward who swaggered by, were things that she saw with the eyes of an adult and reacted to from an adult's point of view. It was impossible to know

290

how this street looked to eight-year-old Bub. It may have appealed to him or it may have frightened him.

There was a desperate battle going on in front of the house where she lived. Kids were using bags of garbage from the cans lined up along the curb as ammunition. The bags had broken open, covering the sidewalk with litter, filling the air with a strong, rancid smell.

Lutie picked her way through orange skins, coffee grounds, chicken bones, fish bones, toilet paper, potato peelings, wilted kale, skins of baked sweet potatoes, pieces of newspaper, broken gin bottles, broken whiskey bottles, a man's discarded felt hat, an old pair of pants. Perhaps Bub had taken part in this kind of warfare, she thought, even as she frowned at the rubbish under her feet; possibly a battle would have appealed to some unsatisfied spirit of adventure in him, so that he would have joined these kids, overlooking the stink of the garbage in his joy in the conflict just as they were doing.

Mrs. Hedges was leaning far out of her window, urging the contestants on.

"That's right, Jimmie," Mrs. Hedges cried. "Hit him on the head." And then as the bag went past its mark, "Aw, shucks, boy, what's the matter with your aim?"

She caught sight of Lutie and knowing that she was home earlier than when she went to work, immediately deduced that she had been somewhere to see Bub or see about him. "Did you see Bub?" she asked.

"Yes. For a little while."

"Been to the beauty parlor, ain't you?" Mrs. Hedges studied the black curls shining under the skull cap on Lutie's head. "Looks right nice," she said.

She leaned a little farther out of the window. "Bub being in trouble you probably need some money. A friend of mine, a Mr. Junto— a very nice white gentleman, dearie———"

Her voice trailed off because Lutie turned away abruptly and disappeared through the apartment house door. Mrs. Hedges scowled after her. After all, if you needed money you needed money and why anyone would act like that when it was offered to them she couldn't imagine. She shrugged her shoulders and turned her attention back to the battle going on under her window.

As Lutie climbed the stairs, she deliberately accentuated the clicking of the heels of her shoes on the treads because the sharp sound helped relieve the hard resentment she felt; it gave expression to the anger flooding through her.

At first, she merely fumed at the top of her mind about a white gentleman wanting to sleep with a colored girl. A nice white gentleman who's a little cold around the edges wants to sleep with a nice warm colored girl. All of it nice—nice gentleman, nice girl; one's colored and the other's white, so it's a colored girl and a white gentleman.

Then she began thinking about Junto—specifically about Junto. Junto hadn't wanted her paid for singing. Mrs. Hedges knew Junto. Boots Smith worked for Junto. Junto's squat-bodied figure, as she had seen it reflected in the sparkling mirror in his Bar and Grill, established itself in her mind; and the anger in her grew and spread directing itself first against Junto and Mrs. Hedges and then against the street that had reached out and taken Bub and then against herself for having been partly responsible for Bub's stealing.

Inside her apartment she stood motionless, assailed by the deep, uncanny silence that filled it. It was a too sharp contrast to the noise in the street. She turned on the radio and then turned it off again, because she kept listening, straining to hear something under the sound of the music.

The creeping, silent thing that she had sensed in the theater, in the beauty parlor, was here in her living room. It was sitting on the lumpy studio couch.

Before it had been formless, shapeless, a fluid moving mass —something disembodied that she couldn't see, could only sense. Now, as she stared at the couch, the thing took on form, substance. She could see what it was.

It was Junto. Gray hair, gray skin, short body, thick shoulders. He was sitting on the studio couch. The blue-glass coffee table was right in front of him. His feet were resting, squarely, firmly, on the congoleum rug.

If she wasn't careful she would scream. She would start screaming and never be able to stop, because there wasn't anyone there. Yet she could see him and when she didn't see him she could feel his presence. She looked away and then looked back again. Sometimes he was there when she looked and sometimes he wasn't.

She stared at the studio couch until she convinced herself there had never been anyone there. Her eyes were playing tricks on her because she was upset, nervous. She decided that a warm bath would make her relax.

But in the tub she started trembling so that the water was agitated. Perhaps she ought to phone Boots and tell him that she wouldn't come tonight. Perhaps by tomorrow she would be free of this mounting, steadily increasing anger and this hysterical fear that made her see things that didn't exist, made her feel things that weren't there.

Yet less than half an hour later she was dressing, putting on the short, flared black coat; pulling on a pair of white gloves. As she thrust her hands into the gloves, she wondered when she had made the decision to go anyway; what part of her mind had already picked out the clothes she would wear, even to these white gloves, without her ever thinking about it consciously. Because, of course, if she didn't go tonight, Boots might change his mind.

When she rang the bell of Boots' apartment, he opened the door instantly as though he had been waiting for her.

"Hello, baby," he said, grinning. "Sure glad you got here. I got a friend I want you to meet."

Only two of the lamps in the living room were lit. They were the tall ones on each side of the davenport. They threw a brilliant light on the squat white man sitting there. He got up when he saw Lutie and stood in front of the imitation fireplace, leaning his elbow on the mantel.

Lutie stared at him, not certain whether this was Junto in the flesh or the imaginary one that had been on the studio couch in her apartment. She closed her eyes and then opened them and he was still there, standing by the fireplace. His squat figure partly blocked out the orange-red glow from the electric logs. She turned her head away and then looked toward him. He was still there, standing by the fireplace.

Boots established him as Junto in the flesh. "Mr. Junto, meet Mrs. Johnson. Lutie Johnson."

Lutie nodded her head. A figure in a mirror turned thumbs down and as he gestured the playground for Bub vanished, the nice new furniture disappeared along with the big airy rooms. "A nice white gentleman." "Need any extra money." She looked away from him, not saying anything.

"I want to talk to you, baby," Boots said. "Come on into the bedroom"—he pointed toward a door, started toward it, turned back and said, "We'll be with you in a minute, Junto."

Boots closed the bedroom door, sat down on the edge of the bed, leaning his head against the headboard.

"If you'll give me the money now, I'll be able to get it to the lawyer before he closes his office tonight," she said abruptly. This room was like the living room, it had too many lamps in it, and in addition there were too many mirrors so that she saw him reflected on each of the walls—his legs stretched out, his expression completely indifferent. There was the same soft, sound-absorbing carpet on the floor.

"Take your coat off and sit down, baby," he said lazily.

She shook her head. She didn't move any farther into the room, but stood with her back against the door, aware that there was no sound from the living room where Junto waited. She had brought that awful silence in here with her.

"I can't stay," she said sharply. "I only came to get the money."

"Oh, yes—the money," he said. He sounded as though he had just remembered it. "You can get the money easy, baby. I figured it out." He half-closed his eyes. "Junto's the answer. He'll give it to you. Just like that"—he snapped his fingers.

He paused for a moment as though he were waiting for her to say something, and when she made no comment he continued: "All you got to do is be nice to him. Just be nice to him as long as he wants and the two hundred bucks is yours. And bein' nice to Junto pays off better than anything else I know."

She heard what he said, knew exactly what he meant, and her mind skipped over his words and substituted other words. She was back in the big shabby ballroom at the Casino, straining to hear a thin thread of music that kept getting lost in the babble of voices, in the clink of glasses, in the bursts of laughter, so that she wasn't certain the music was real. Sometimes it was there and then again it was drowned out by the other sounds.

The faint, drifting melody went around and under the sound of Boots' voice and the words that he had spoken then blotted out what he had just said.

"Baby, this is just experience. Be months before you can earn money at it."

"Nothing happened, baby. What makes you think something happened?"

"I don't have all the say-so. The guy who owns the Casino —guy named Junto—says you ain't ready yet."

"Christ! he owns the joint."

The guy named Junto owned the Bar and Grill, too. Evidently his decision that she wasn't to be paid for singing had been based on his desire to sleep with her; and he had concluded that, if she had to continue living in that house where his friend Mrs. Hedges lived or in one just like it, she would be a pushover.

And now the same guy, named Junto, was sitting outside on a sofa, just a few feet away from this door, and she thought, I would like to kill him. Not just because he happens to be named Junto, but because I can't even think straight about him or anybody else any more. It is as though he were a piece of that dirty street itself, tangible, close at hand, within reach.

She could still hear that floating, drifting tune. It was inside her head and she couldn't get it out. Boots was staring at her, waiting for her to say something, waiting for her answer. He and Junto thought they knew what she would say. If she hummed that fragment of melody aloud, she would get rid of it. It was the only way to make it disappear; otherwise it would keep going around and around in her head. And she thought, I must be losing my mind, wanting to hum a tune and at the same time thinking about killing that man who is sitting, waiting, outside.

Boots said, "Junto's a good guy. You'll be surprised how much you'll take to him."

The sound of her own voice startled her. It was hoarse, loud, furious. It contained the accumulated hate and the accumulated anger from all the years of seeing the things she wanted slip past her without her ever having touched them.

She shouted, "Get him out of here! Get him out of here! Get him out of here quick!"

And all the time she was thinking, Junto has a brick in his hand. Just one brick. The final one needed to complete the wall that had been building up around her for years, and when that one last brick was shoved in place, she would be completely walled in.

"All right. All right. Don't get excited." Boots got up from the bed, pushed her away from the door and went out, slamming it behind him.

"Sorry, Junto," Boots said. "She's mad as hell. No use your waiting."

"I heard her," Junto said sourly. "And if this is something you planned, you'd better unplan it."

"You heard her, didnya?"

"Yes. But you still could have planned it," Junto said. He walked toward the foyer. At the door he turned to Boots. "Well?" he said.

"Don't worry, Mack," Boots said coldly. "She'll come around. Come back about ten o'clock."

He closed the door quietly behind Junto. He hadn't intended to in the beginning, but he was going to trick him and Junto would never know the difference. Sure, Lutie would sleep with Junto, but he was going to have her first. He thought of the thin curtains blowing in the wind. Yeah, he can have the leavings. After all, he's white and this time a white man can have a black man's leavings.

Junto had pushed him hard, threatened him, nagged him about Lutie Johnson. This would be his revenge. He locked the door leading to the foyer and put the key in his pocket. Then he headed toward the kitchenette in the back of the apartment. He'd fix a drink for Lutie and one for himself.

The murmur of their voices came to Lutie in the bedroom. She couldn't hear what they said and she waited standing in front of the door, listening for some indication that Junto had gone.

As soon as Junto left, she would go home. But she had to make certain he had gone, because if she walked outside there and saw him she would try to kill him. The thought frightened her. This was no time to get excited or to get angry. She had to be calm and concentrate on how to keep Bub from going to reform school.

She'd been so angry just now she had forgotten that she still had to get two hundred dollars to take to the lawyer. Pop might have some ideas. Yes, he'd have ideas. He always had them. But she was only kidding herself if she thought any of them would yield two hundred dollars.

There was the sound of a door closing, and then silence. She looked out into the living room. It was empty. She could hear the clinking sound of glasses from somewhere in the back of the apartment.

And then Boots entered the room carrying a tray. Ice tinkled in tall glasses. A bottle of soda and a bottle of whiskey teetered precariously on the tray as he walked toward her.

"Here, baby," he said. "Have a drink and get yourself together."

She stood in front of the fireplace, holding the glass in her hand, not drinking it, just holding it. She could feel its coldness through her glove. She would go and talk to Pop. He'd lived three steps in front of the law for so long, he just might have a friend who was a lawyer and if Pop had ever done the friend any favors he might take Bub's case on the promise of weekly payments from her.

And she ought to go now. Why was she standing here holding this glass of liquor that she didn't want and had no intention of drinking? Because you're still angry, she thought, and you haven't anyone to vent your anger on and you're halfway hoping Boots will say something or do something that will give you an excuse to blow up in a thousand pieces.

"Whyn't you sit down?" Boots said.

"I've got to go." And yet she didn't move. She stayed in front of the fireplace watching him as he sat on the sofa, sipping his drink.

Occasionally he glanced up at her and she saw the scar on his cheek as a long thin line that looked darker than she had remembered it. And she thought he's like these streets that trap all of us—vicious, dangerous.

Finally he said, "Lissen, you want to get the little bastard out of jail, don't yah? What you being so fussy about?"

She put the glass down on a table. Some of the liquor slopped over, oozing down the sides of the glass, and as she looked at it, it seemed as though something had slopped over inside her head in the same fashion, was oozing through her so that she couldn't think.

"Skip it," she said.

Her voice was loud in the room. That's right, she thought, skip it. Let's all skip together, children. All skip together. Up the golden stairs. Skipping hand in hand up the golden stairs.

"Just skip it," she repeated.

She had to get out of here, now, and quickly. She mustn't stand here any longer looking down at him like this, because she kept thinking that he represented everything she had fought against. Yet she couldn't take her eyes away from the ever-darkening scar that marred the side of his face; and as she stared at him, she felt she was gazing straight at the street with its rows of old houses, its piles of garbage, its swarms of children.

"Junto's rich as hell," Boots said. "What you got to be so particular about? There ain't a dame in town who wouldn't give everything they got for a chance at him." And he thought, Naw, she ain't acting right. And she was all that stood between him and going back to portering or some other lousy, stinking job where he would carry his hat in his hand all day and walk on his head, saying "Yessir, yessir, yessir."

She moved away from the fireplace. There wasn't any point in answering him. Right now she couldn't even think straight, couldn't even see straight. She kept thinking about the street, kept seeing it.

All those years, going to grammar school, going to high school, getting married, having a baby, going to work for the Chandlers, leaving Jim because he got himself another woman —all those years she'd been heading straight as an arrow for that street or some other street just like it. Step by step she'd come, growing up, working, saving, and finally getting an apartment on a street that nobody could have beaten. Even if she hadn't talked to Bub about money all the time, he would have got into trouble sooner or later, because the street looked after him when she wasn't around.

"Aw, what the hell!" Boots muttered. He put his glass down on the table in front of the sofa, got up and by moving swiftly blocked her progress to the door.

"Let's talk it over," he said. "Maybe we can work out something."

She hesitated. There wasn't anything to work out or talk over unless he meant he would lend her the money with no strings attached. And if he was willing to do that, she would be a fool not to accept it. Pop was a pretty feeble last resort.

"Come on, baby," he said. "Ten minutes' talk will straighten it out." And she went back to stand in front of the fireplace.

"Ain't no point in your getting mad, baby. We can still be friends," he said softly, and put his arm around her waist.

He was standing close to her. She smelt faintly sweet and he pulled her closer. She tried to back away from him and he forced her still closer, held her hands behind her back, pulling her ever closer and closer.

As he kissed her, he felt a hot excitement well up in him that made him forget all the logical, reasoned things he had meant to say; for her skin was soft under his mouth and warm. He fumbled with the fastenings of her coat, his hand groping toward her breasts.

"Aw, Christ, baby," he whispered. "Junto can get his afterward." And the rhythm of the words sank into him, seemed to correspond with the rhythm of his desire for her so that he had to say them again. "Let him get his afterward. I'll have mine first."

She twisted out of his arms with a sudden, violent motion that nearly sent him off balance. The anger surging through her wasn't directed solely at him. He was there at hand; he had tricked her into staying an extra few minutes in this room with him, because she thought he was going to lend her the money she so urgently needed; and she was angry with him for that and for being a procurer for Junto and for assuming that she would snatch at an opportunity to sleep with either or both of them. This quick surface anger helped to swell and became a part of the deepening stream of rage that had fed on the hate, the frustration, the resentment she had toward the pattern her life had followed.

So she couldn't stop shouting, and shouting wasn't enough. She wanted to hit out at him, to reduce him to a speechless mass of flesh, to destroy him completely, because he was there in front of her and she could get at him and in getting at him she would find violent outlet for the full sweep of her wrath.

Words tumbled from her throat. "You no good bastard!" she shouted. "You can tell Junto I said if he wants a whore to

get one from Mrs. Hedges. And the same thing goes for you.
Because I'd just as soon get in bed with a rattlesnake—I'd just
as soon——"

And he reached out and slapped her across the face. And as
she stood there in front of him, trembling with anger, her face
smarting, he slapped her again.

"I don't take that kind of talk from dames," he said. "Not
even good-looking ones like you. Maybe after I beat the hell
out of you a coupla times, you'll begin to like the idea of sleeping with me and with Junto."

The blood pounding in her head blurred her vision so that
she saw not one Boots Smith but three of him; and behind
these three figures the room was swaying, shifting, and changing with a wavering motion. She tried to separate the three
blurred figures and it was like trying to follow the course of
heat waves as they rose from a sidewalk on a hot day in August.

Despite this unstable triple vision of him, she was scarcely
aware of him as an individual. His name might have been
Brown or Smith or Wilson. She might never have seen him
before, might have known nothing about him. He happened
to be within easy range at the moment he set off the dangerous accumulation of rage that had been building in her for
months.

When she remembered there was a heavy iron candlestick on
the mantelpiece just behind her, her vision cleared; the room
stopped revolving and Boots Smith became one person, not
three. He was the person who had struck her, her face still hurt
from the blow; he had threatened her with violence and with a
forced relationship with Junto and with himself. These things
set off her anger, but as she gripped the iron candlestick and
brought it forward in a swift motion aimed at his head, she
was striking, not at Boots Smith, but at a handy, anonymous
figure—a figure which her angry resentment transformed into
everything she had hated, everything she had fought against,
everything that had served to frustrate her.

He was so close to her that she struck him on the side of the
head before he saw the blow coming. The first blow stunned
him. And she struck him again and again, using the candlestick
as though it were a club. He tried to back away from her and
stumbled over the sofa and sprawled there.

A lifetime of pent-up resentment went into the blows. Even after he lay motionless, she kept striking him, not thinking about him, not even seeing him. First she was venting her rage against the dirty, crowded street. She saw the rows of dilapidated old houses; the small dark rooms; the long steep flights of stairs; the narrow dingy hallways; the little lost girls in Mrs. Hedges' apartment; the smashed homes where the women did drudgery because their men had deserted them. She saw all of these things and struck at them.

Then the limp figure on the sofa became, in turn, Jim and the slender girl she'd found him with; became the insult in the moist-eyed glances of white men on the subway; became the unconcealed hostility in the eyes of white women; became the greasy, lecherous man at the Crosse School for Singers; became the gaunt Super pulling her down, down into the basement.

Finally, and the blows were heavier, faster, now, she was striking at the white world which thrust black people into a walled enclosure from which there was no escape; and at the turn-of-events which had forced her to leave Bub alone while she was working so that he now faced reform school, now had a police record.

She saw the face and head of the man on the sofa through waves of anger in which he represented all these things and she was destroying them.

She grew angrier as she struck him, because he seemed to be eluding her behind a red haze that obscured his face. Then the haze of red blocked his face out completely. She lowered her arm, peering at him, trying to locate his face through the redness that concealed it.

The room was perfectly still. There was no sound in it except her own hoarse breathing. She let the candlestick fall out of her hand. It landed on the thick rug with a soft clump and she started to shiver.

He was dead. There was no question about it. No one could live with a head battered in like that. And it wasn't a red haze that had veiled his face. It was blood.

She backed away from the sight of him, thinking that if she took one slow step at a time, just one slow step at a time, she could get out of here, walking backward, step by step. She was afraid to turn her back on that still figure on the sofa. It had become a thing. It was no longer Boots Smith, but a thing on a sofa.

She stumbled against a chair and sat down in it, shivering. She would never get out of this room. She would never, never get out of here. For the rest of her life she would be here with this awful faceless thing on the sofa. Then she forced herself to get up, to start walking backward again.

The foyer door was closed because she backed right into it. Just a few more steps and she would be out. She fumbled for the knob. The door was locked. She didn't believe it and rattled it. She felt for a key. There was none. It would, she was certain, be in Boots Smith's pocket and she felt a faint stirring of anger against him. He had deliberately locked the door because he hadn't intended to let her out of here.

The anger went as quickly as it came. She had to go back to that motionless, bloody figure on the sofa. The stillness in the room made her feel as though she was wading through water, wading waist-deep toward the couch, and the water swallowed up all sound. It tugged against her, tried to pull her back.

The key was in his pocket. In her haste she pulled all the things out of his pocket—a handkerchief, a wallet, book matches, and the key. She held on to the key, but the other things went out of her hand because as she drew away from him she thought he moved. And all the stories she had ever heard about the dead coming back to life, about the dead talking, about the dead walking, went through her mind; making her hands shake so that she couldn't control them.

As she moved hurriedly away from the couch, she almost stepped on the wallet. She picked it up and looked inside. It bulged with money. He could have given her two hundred dollars and never missed it.

The two hundred dollars she needed was right there in her hand. She could take it to the lawyer tonight. Or could she?

For the first time the full implication of what she had done swept over her. She was a murderer. And the smartest lawyer in the world couldn't do anything for Bub, not now, not when his mother had killed a man. A kid whose mother was a murderer didn't stand any chance at all. Everyone he came in contact with would believe that sooner or later he, too, would turn criminal. The Court wouldn't parole him in her care either, because she was no longer a fit person to bring him up.

She couldn't stop the quivering that started in her stomach, that set up a spasmodic contracting of her throat so that she felt as though her breath had been cut off. The only thing she could do was to go away and never come back, because the best thing that could happen to Bub would be for him never to know that his mother was a murderer. She took half the bills out of the wallet, wadded them into her purse, left the wallet on the sofa.

Getting back to the foyer door was worse this time. The four corners of the room were alive with silence—deepening pools of an ominous silence. She kept turning her head in an effort to see all of the room at once; kept fighting against a desire to scream. Hysteria mounted in her because she began to believe that at any moment the figure on the sofa might disappear into one of these pools of silence and then emerge from almost any part of the room, to bar her exit.

When she finally turned the key in the door, crossed the small foyer, and reached the outside hall, she had to lean against the wall for a long moment before she could control the shaking of her legs, but the contracting of her throat was getting worse.

She saw that the white gloves she was wearing were streaked with dust from the candlestick. There was a smear of blood on one of them. She ripped them off and put them in her coat pocket, and as she did it she thought she was acting as though murder was something with which she was familiar. She walked down the stairs instead of taking the elevator, and the thought recurred.

When she left the building, it was snowing hard. The wind blew the snow against her face, making her walk faster as she approached the entrance to the Eighth Avenue subway.

She thought confusedly of the best place for her to go. It had to be a big city. She decided that Chicago was not too far away and it was big. It would swallow her up. She would go there.

On the subway she started shivering again. Had she killed Boots by accident? The awful part of it was she hadn't even seen him when she was hitting him like that. The first blow was deliberate and provoked, but all those other blows weren't provoked. There wasn't any excuse for her. It hadn't even been self-defense. This impulse to violence had been in her for a long time, growing, feeding, until finally she had blown up in a thousand pieces. Bub must never know what she had done.

In Pennsylvania Station she bought a ticket for Chicago. "One way?" the ticket man asked.

"One way," she echoed. Yes, a one-way ticket, she thought. I've had one since the day I was born.

The train was on the track. People flowed and spilled through the gates like water running over a dam. She walked in the middle of the crowd.

The coaches filled up rapidly. People with bags and hatboxes and bundles and children moved hastily down the aisles, almost falling into the seats in their haste to secure a place to sit.

Lutie found a seat midway in the coach. She sat down near the window. Bub would never understand why she had disappeared. He was expecting to see her tomorrow. She had promised him she would come. He would never know why she had deserted him and he would be bewildered and lost without her.

Would he remember that she loved him? She hoped so, but she knew that for a long time he would have that half-frightened, worried look she had seen on his face the night he was waiting for her at the subway.

He would probably go to reform school. She looked out of the train window, not seeing the last-minute passengers hurrying down the ramp. The constricton of her throat increased. So he will go to reform school, she repeated. He'll be better off there. He'll be better off without you. That way he may have some kind of chance. He didn't have the ghost of a chance on that street. The best you could give him wasn't good enough.

As the train started to move, she began to trace a design on the window. It was a series of circles that flowed into each other. She remembered that when she was in grammar school the children were taught to get the proper slant to their writing, to get the feel of a pen in their hands, by making these same circles.

Once again she could hear the flat, exasperated voice of the teacher as she looked at the circles Lutie had produced. "Really," she said, "I don't know why they have us bother to teach your people to write."

Her finger moved over the glass, around and around. The circles showed up plainly on the dusty surface. The woman's statement was correct, she thought. What possible good has it done to teach people like me to write?

The train crept out of the tunnel, gathered speed as it left the city behind. Snow whispered against the windows. And as the train roared into the darkness, Lutie tried to figure out by what twists and turns of fate she had landed on this train. Her mind balked at the task. All she could think was, It was that street. It was that god-damned street.

The snow fell softly on the street. It muffled sound. It sent people scurrying homeward, so that the street was soon deserted, empty, quiet. And it could have been any street in the city, for the snow laid a delicate film over the sidewalk, over the brick of the tired, old buildings; gently obscuring the grime and the garbage and the ugliness.

THE NARROWS

This book is for
Mabel Louise Robinson

. . . *I tell you, captain, if you look in the maps of the 'orld, I warrant you sall find, in the comparisons between Macedon and Monmouth, that the situations, look you, is both alike. There is a river in Macedon; and there is also moreover a river at Monmouth: it is called Wye at Monmouth; but it is out of my prains what is the name of the other river; but 'tis all one, 'tis alike as my fingers is to my fingers, and there is salmons in both.*

FLUELLEN,
King Henry V, Act IV, vii.

I

ABBIE CRUNCH began to walk slowly as she turned into Dumble Street, market basket over her arm, trying not to look at the river; because she knew that once she saw it with the sun shining on it she would begin to think about Link, to worry about Link, to remember Link as a little boy. A little boy? Yes, a little boy. Eight years old. Diving from the dock. Swimming in the river.

She could hear the lapping of the water against the piling close at hand; and faint, far off, borne inshore on the wind, the crying of the gulls, the hoot of a tugboat; and she could smell the old familiar dampness from the river. And so, as usual on a sunny morning, she could see herself and Frances Jackson standing on Dock Street, a pushcart at the curb half concealing them, so they were peering over mounds of potatoes and kale and bunches of carrots and countless round heads of cabbage. She was short and fat, no, plump. Frances was tall and thin and bony.

Frances was saying, "Look! Look over there!" and pointing, forcing her to look.

She remembered how she had resented that dark brown forefinger, long, supple, seemingly jointless, which directed her glance, commanding her to look, and she not wanting to look, but her eyes following the stretched-out arm and the commanding forefinger.

She saw Bill Hod standing on the dock, wearing dark trunks, short dark swimming trunks and nothing else. His chest, shoulders, arms, white by contrast with the trunks, shockingly naked because of the trunks. His straight black hair was wet, and he was running his hands through it, flattening it, making it smooth, sleek. She remembered too how she had thought, I have lost my mind, lost it, no control over it any more. Because she was genuinely surprised that his hair should lie so flat— she had somehow convinced herself that there would be horns on his head—something, anyway, that would show, would indicate— She closed her eyes. The sunlight was unbearable.

She was accustomed to darkness, window shades always pulled
down in the house, draperies drawn, no lights turned on at
night because she preferred darkness.

Frances Jackson seemed all elbow that morning, tall, elbows
everywhere. She poked at her, "Open your eyes. Abbie, Abbie,
Abbie—"

Sunlight on the river, sunlight on Bill Hod, sunlight on her
own face, or so she thought, hurting her eyes, hurting her face,
so she kept her eyes closed. She heard Link's voice, a child's
voice, light, high in pitch, excitement in his voice and something else—affection.

She opened her eyes and saw Link dive from the dock, dive
down into the river. She wanted to stop him. It wasn't safe. He
didn't know how to swim. She couldn't stand any more sudden
shocks. He was so little. The river was so wide and so deep, so
treacherous. Then he was swimming, going farther and farther
away, his head like the head of a small dog, head held up out
of the water, moving farther and farther away. She said, "No!"

Bill Hod yelled, "Hey—you—come on back—" Bass voice,
arrogant, domineering voice, the tone of his voice, just the
tone, was an insult, voice that she could never forget, could
hear, even in her sleep—

The head, the small head kept moving away, always moving
away, farther and farther out toward the middle of the river,
growing smaller, like the head of a newborn puppy now. Then
out of sight. No, still there, but still moving away.

Bill Hod shouted, wind carrying the voice back toward the
pushcart, back toward Frances Jackson and Abigail Crunch,
rage in the voice, "If I—have to—haul you—out of there—
come back—"

Was that small head still there? Yes, coming back now, but so
slowly. She thought he'd never—why didn't that man—

Then, finally, Bill Hod reached down and pulled Link up
on the dock. Bill Hod slapped him across the face. She could
hear the sound of the blow, slapped him again, again, said, "If
you ever"—slap—"do that again"—slap—"I'll fix you"—slap
—"for keeps"—slap.

No one had ever struck Link. Neither she nor the Major.
She started to cross the street, thinking, By what right, that
man, face of a hangman. Frances Jackson's hand held her back,

strength in the bony thin hand, determination in the hand holding her there behind the pushcart, behind the potatoes and the cabbages and the kale.

Frances said, "Abbie—don't. You've lost the right to interfere. Link's been living in that saloon for three months—for three months. Abbie, listen to me—"

That afternoon when they went in The Last Chance to get Link, he ran and hid under the bar, crying, "I won't go back there. I won't go back there."

She could see herself and Frances Jackson down on their hands and knees, pleading with Link, trying to pull him out from under the bar in The Last Chance. And Bill Hod stood watching them, saying nothing, watching, his hands on his hips. His face? She couldn't look at his face. How then did she know that he was laughing inside, why was she so certain that he was thinking, The old maid undertaker and the widow are here in my saloon. She supposed it was the way he leaned against the bar watching them. He made her conscious of the ridiculous picture they must have made: a short plump woman and a tall thin one trying to pull an eight-year-old boy out from under a bar when they couldn't reach any part of him; down on their hands and knees, reaching, reaching, trying to grab anything—pants, legs, sneakers, shirt; and he kept scrambling back away from them.

It was Frances who gave the whole thing up as impossible. She stood up, brushed off her hands, said, "Mr. Hod, I want to talk to you."

Frances was in the habit of giving orders, in the habit of dealing with the bereaved and the sorrowful, with the hysterical and the frightened; and so she knew better than Abbie when to retreat and when to advance and could do either with dignity. But when Frances stood up she looked down at her skirt, surprised. Abbie knew why. There was no dirt, no dust on the dark skirt. The floor behind the bar in The Last Chance was dustfree, dirtfree.

Link was eight years old then. He was twenty-six now and he worked in The Last Chance. Behind the bar. Bill Hod had won—effortlessly, easily.

Whenever she turned into Dumble Street, she always asked herself the same question, If Link had been her own child instead of an adopted child, would she, could she, have forgotten about him for three months, three whole months?

Sometimes she tried to blame this street which, now, in the mellowness of an October morning, looked to be all sunlight and shadow—intricately patterned shadow from the young elm trees, denser shadow and a simpler pattern where the old maple stood near the end of the block; shadow softening the harsh outlines of the brick buildings, concealing the bleakness of the two-story frame houses; sunlight intensifying the yellowgreen of the elms, the redorange of the maple, adding a sheen to the soft gray of the dock. No, she thought, not this street. It was the fault of Abbie Crunch. If she hadn't said to herself, Murderer, murderer; if she hadn't been chief witness against herself, condemning herself to death, willing her own death, so that she forgot Link, forgot about him as though he had never existed, she wouldn't have lost him.

She hadn't meant to look at the river but she had glanced at the dock and so her eyes moved on to the river. She stood still looking at it. In the sunlight, the River Wye was the blue of bachelor buttons, of delphinium; small frothy waves, edged with white, kept appearing and disappearing on the blue surface—a sparkling blue river just at the foot of the street, a beautiful river.

Even the street was beautiful. It sloped gently down toward the river. But the signs on the buildings dispelled the illusion of beauty. The red neon sign in front of The Last Chance was a horrible color in the sunlight—Link already there at work. Then there were all the other signs: Room For Rent, Lady Tenant Wanted, Poro Method Used, Get Your Kool-Aid Free, Tenant Provide Own Heat, Rooms Dollar and Half A Night. Rooms. Rooms.

She could remember when Mrs. Sweeney changed the sign in her window from Room To Let to Rooms For White, explaining, apologetically, that so many of the colored stopped to ask about rooms that she couldn't get her work done for answering the bell. "It's just to save time," she had said, "my time and theirs."

Mrs. Sweeney's sign had long since been replaced by a much larger and very different sign: "Masters University—Church of Metaphysics and Spiritual Sciences—Revealing the Strange

Secrets of the Unseen Forces of Life Time and Nature. Divine Blessings—Healings of Mind and Body. I Am the Way, the Truth, and the Life; no man cometh unto the Father, but by Me. Hear the Voice of the Master: Dr. H. H. Franklin Longworth, F.M.B. Minister, Psychologist, Metaphysician. Everyone Is Welcome."

Yes, she thought, Dumble Street has changed. The signs tell the story of the change. It was now, despite its spurious early-morning beauty, a street so famous, or so infamous, that the people who lived in Monmouth rarely ever referred to it, or the streets near it, by name; it had become an area, a section, known variously as The Narrows, Eye of the Needle, The Bottom, Little Harlem, Dark Town, Niggertown—because Negroes had replaced those other earlier immigrants, the Irish, the Italians and the Poles.

Fortunately, the river hadn't changed. Nor had the big maple tree. But she, Abbie Crunch, had changed because for the last few years she had been calling the tree The Hangman just like everyone else who lived in The Narrows. It was, she supposed, inevitable. People talked about the tree as though it were a person: "The Hangman's losin' his leaves, winter's goin' to set in early"; "Spring's here, The Hangman's full of buds." When it was cold, bone-biting cold, wind blowing straight from the river, the sidewalks grown narrower, reduced almost to cowpaths because of the snow piled up at the sides, a coating of ice making walking hazardous, the great branches of the tree swayed back and forth, making a cracking sound. Then passers-by said: "Lissen. The Hangman's creakin'. Hear him?" or "The Hangman's talkin'. Hangman's groanin' in his sleep," and shivered as they moved away.

She had tried, years ago, to find out why the tree was called The Hangman and couldn't. There would always be something of the schoolteacher's tiresome insistence on accuracy left in her, so she had searched through all the books on horticulture in the Monmouth Library but she could not find any mention of a hangman's maple. She decided that some one may once have said that the big maple was the kind of tree a hangman would choose to swing his victim from—tall, straight, with mighty branches; that whoever heard this statement changed it when he repeated it and called the tree a hangman's maple;

that, finally, some imaginative Negro, probably from South Carolina, gave the tree its name. These days she, too, called the maple The Hangman, as easily, and as inaccurately, as the rest of The Narrows.

This morning The Hangman was like a picture of a tree—a picture on a calendar, the orange-red of the leaves not really believable. Sometimes she wished she had not insisted on buying that old brick house which was Number Six Dumble Street. But not now. Who could regret the purchase of a fine old house when the tree that stood in its dooryard was like a great hymn sung by a choir of matched voices?

The Hangman had, of course, been the source of many small annoyances, and, possibly, the cause, though indirectly, of one major disaster. The neighborhood dogs were always in the yard, sniffing around the tree, lifting a leg, digging up the lawn with vigor afterwards. During the day lean cats napped in the dense shade made by its branches and at midnight carried on a yowling courtship. On warm summer nights, drunks sprawled under the tree, in a sleep that was more torpor than sleep. She kept a bucket filled with water on the back steps, and, early in the morning, fear making her heart beat faster, fear urging her back toward the house, she would approach the sleeping man, dump the pail of water over him, recoiling from the smell of him, the awful loosejointed look of him, even as she said, "Get out of here. Get out of here or I'll call a policeman—" There was always the shudder, the stumbling gait, the muttered curses in the thickened speech that came to mean drunkenness, and only drunkenness, as the man lurched to his feet. They always went toward The Last Chance, the saloon across the street, as though by instinct.

Yes, she thought, everything changes, and not always for the best, her mind moving away from the subject of intoxication as she had trained it to do. But her house had changed for the best. Number Six Dumble Street had a very definite air about it—an air of aristocracy. The brass knocker on the front door gleamed, the white paint on the sash of the smallpaned windows, and on the front door, was very white. In this early morning light, the brick of the house was not red but rose colored—the soft pinkish red found in old Persian carpets. The wrought iron railing on each side of the front steps was so intricately and delicately worked that it resembled filet crochet, incredible that a heavy metal like iron could be twisted and turned and bent until it looked like lace.

She gave a little jump, startled, because she heard footsteps close behind her. She turned to see who it was and a man passed her, walking briskly. A colored man. His skin was just a shade darker than her own. Yet he was dressed with a meticulousness one rarely ever saw these days—creased trousers, highly polished shoes, because the back of the shoes gleamed, a dark gray felt hat on his head, the shape perfect.

What could he have thought when he saw her standing still in the middle of the sidewalk? From the back, seen from the back, glanced at quickly from the side, how had she looked to him? Shabby? Old? Like the toothless old women who sat hunched over, mumbling to themselves, in the doorways, on the doorsteps of the houses in The Narrows? The curve of their backs, the dark wrinkled skins, the black glitter of their eyes, the long frowsy skirts always made her think of crones and witches, of necromancy.

Feeling embarrassed, she moved on, walking fast, feeling impelled to take a mental inventory of her appearance. The market basket? It was made by hand by Willow Smith, the old basket-maker. A lost art. Women these days carried brown paper shopping bags, impermanent, flimsy, often replaced. The string handles cut their fingers. She'd had this basket almost forty years. It was sturdy but light in weight; and it was as much a part of her Saturday morning shopping costume as the polished oxfords on her feet, and the lisle stockings on her legs. The shoes had been resoled many times, but the uppers were as good as new. She glanced at her hands—the beige-colored gloves were immaculate; true, they'd been darned, but she doubted that anyone would know it, certainly not a casual passer-by.

She wasn't bent over, she knew that. She had always prided herself on the erectness of her figure; and now, watching the brisk progress of the man walking ahead of her, she straightened up even more. She couldn't have looked too queer to him. The plain black wool coat had been brushed before she left the house as had the plain black felt hat—a hat chosen because it would never really go out of style and yet it would never attract attention. She wore it straight on her head, pulled down, but not so far down that it covered her hair—white silky hair. Proud of her hair. Two or three tendrils always managed to escape from the hairpins, and, shifting the market basket to the other arm, she reached up and patted the back of her head, still neat, as far as she could tell with gloves on.

What made me do that, she thought. I know how I look. But all my life I've been saying to myself, What will people think? And at seventy I wouldn't be apt to stop doing it. So a short briskwalking man passes me on the street at a moment when I am standing still and I immediately start checking my appearance. Possibly he didn't wonder about me. But he looked at me, sideways, quickly, and then away. He isn't much taller than I am, she thought, still watching him. But he weighs less. Not that I'm fat but I've got flesh on my bones—small bones—so I look plump.

To her very great surprise, this man, this welldressed little man, turned in at Number Six, walked up the steps, and lifted the brass knocker, letting it fall gently against the door, repeating the motion so that she heard a rat-tat-tat-tat, gentle, but insistent. That surprised her, too, for very few people knew how a knocker resounded through a house and thus she was always being startled by salesmen or itinerant peddlers who set up a great banging at her front door, enough to wake the dead.

Now that she was so close to him she saw that his dark suit fitted him as though it had been made for him. His posture was superb, head up, shoulders back. He turned toward her just as she started up the steps and she noticed that he wore black shoes—highly polished. Link always wore brown shoes, most of the young men seemed to these days though she didn't know why. A brown shoe never looked as dressy as a black shoe.

Then the stranger standing on her front steps took off his gray felt hat and bowed and said, "Good morning."

It was done with an elegance that she hadn't seen in years. It reminded her of the Governor, of the Major, both of whom managed, just by lifting their hats and bowing, to make her feel as though they had said: Madam—Queen of England—Empress of India.

"Mrs. Crunch?"

"Yes," she said.

"My name is Malcolm Powther. I've taken the liberty of coming to inquire about the apartment that you have for rent."

"Oh," she said, startled. The Allens hadn't even moved yet.

"I am the butler at Treadway Hall. I have been with Mrs. Treadway for nine years," he said. "I thought I should tell you this so you would know that I can give you references. And also so that you would understand why I came so early in the morning."

Treadway Hall, she thought. Why that's the mansion that belongs to the Treadway Gun people. It sat on the outskirts of Monmouth. You could see the red tile roof from far off. The tile had been imported from Holland and installed by foreign workmen, some of whom still lived in the city. Every Fourth of July, Mrs. Treadway invited all the workers from the plant to a picnic. It was written up in the *Chronicle*. There was always a whole page of pictures of the house, of the park, and the deer in the park, of the lake and the swans on the lake. The driveway that led to the house was said to be a mile long.

She looked at Mr. Powther with something like awe. No wonder he had such an air of dignity. No wonder he was so carefully dressed. Everything about him suggested that his entire life had been spent in close association with the very wealthy. His skin was medium brown, not that she had any prejudice against very dark colored people, but she had never had any tenants who looked as though they were descended in a straight line from old Aunt Grinny Granny. He had a nose as straight as her own. But how had he known that the apartment would soon be vacant? The Allens had lived upstairs for six years and they were moving but not until next week. How had word about this expected vacancy on Dumble Street seeped through the stone walls of that great mansion where he worked?

"How did you know that the apartment would be for rent?" she asked.

His appearance changed in the most peculiar way. At one moment he was a little man with tremendous dignity, his back straight, his shoulders squared, his chin in, head up. And at the next moment all of him seemed to bend and sag and sway, even his expression changed. He flinched as though from an expected blow.

Why whatever is the matter with him, she thought. Perhaps he has gas in his stomach or he's trying not to sneeze or holding back a cough. Then almost immediately he was all right, he had controlled whatever tremor had passed through him.

"My wife's cousin told me," he said, and then after a barely perceptible pause, he went on, "We have to move right away. The city is tearing down a whole block of buildings to make way for one of those new housing projects. We're living right at the corner of the first block to be condemned."

"The Allens haven't moved yet," Mrs. Crunch said. "But I don't suppose Mrs. Allen would mind if you looked at the apartment. She's home this morning. Won't you come in and I'll go and ask her."

She ushered Mr. Powther into the sitting room and indicated a chair near the bay window. Again she thought how very polished he looked, shoes gleaming, the crease in his trousers so perfect. He didn't sit down until she had turned to leave the room, but out of the corner of her eyes she saw him hike up his trousers with a gesture that was barely noticeable.

He said, "Oh, Mrs. Crunch," and stood up. "It's only fair to tell you that we have three children. It's not easy to find a place to live at best and with three youngsters—well, it's almost hopeless. Do you—perhaps you object to children?"

"Oh, no," she said. "I'm very fond of them." She paused, and then said quickly, "Of course I would have to get ten dollars more a month for rent. That's a rather large family—five people. And there'd be more wear and tear on the house. I'd have to get seventy dollars a month."

There was a flicker of something like amusement that showed briefly in his eyes. She felt she ought to justify the extra ten dollars. "I've always had middle-aged childless couples living upstairs. With five in the family instead of two I'd have to paint oftener, allow more for repairs to the walls and floors."

"You're quite right," he said.

"I'll go up now and see if Mrs. Allen will let you look around."

She went up the front stairs, slowly—she had to because of what she called her "bad" knees, and cool weather always made the ache in them worse—trying to find a word to rhyme with Powther, not wanting to, but not being able to help herself. She had the kind of mind that liked jingles, so she was forever matching words as she called it, lip-sip, tap-nap, cat-mat, long-song, tea-me, love-dove. Powther? Powther? She gave up and made up a word, then made up a line, Malcolm Powther Sat on a Sowther.

Powther was as difficult a word to rhyme with as Major. After she and the Major were married she spent months trying to find a proper rhyme and never got any farther than:

> Along came the Major
> He said he would page her.

Even now, eighteen years after his death, there were times when the memory of him assailed her with such force that she could almost see him, hear him—a big man with a big booming laugh that made echoes even in a room filled with furniture and hung with draperies. A man so brimming with life, so full of energy that it would be easy to believe that he'd be coming in the kitchen pretty soon, humming, that she'd hear him shouting, "Hey, Abbie, you got some food for a starving Abyssinian?"

She stopped halfway up the stairs, wondering why she had been so suddenly overwhelmed by this vivid picture of the Major. It was because of that polite, precisely dressed, little man, waiting downstairs in her sitting room. A matter of sheer contrast. The Major had been such a big Teddy bear of a man that even in the last years of his life, when they could afford to have his suits made for him, he always had a rumpled slept-in-his-clothes look. If he sat down for as much as two minutes his trousers wrinkled at the knees, at the crotch, his coat developed creases across the middle of the back, and a fold of material popped up from somewhere around the collar region to give him a hunched-up look. Little Mr. Powther could sit indefinitely and when he stood up his suit would still look as though it had just been pressed.

Once she got after the tailor about the Major's suits. The tailor, a Mr. Quagliamatti, said, "Mrs. Crunch, it's not the fault of my suit. It's the Major. It's the way he sits, all to pieces, in a chair. I can't make an elastic suit and that's what he'd have to have. He sits in heaps and mounds. You make him sit up, make him lift his trousers. He sits every which way and the material is only goods, yard goods, not elastic—"

She was still thinking about the Major when she told Mrs. Allen that some one wanted to look at the apartment. The Major always had a slightly rumpled look but somehow men never looked as—well, as unattractive as women, especially the first thing in the morning. She tried not to stare at the white cloth wound around Mrs. Allen's head, at the faded house dress with some important buttons missing in the middle so that the dress gaped open over her fat little stomach; couldn't help glancing down, quickly, of course, to see what she had on her feet. She was wearing sneakers, the laces not tied, and she didn't have any stockings on. Her bare legs were a grayish brown.

Mrs. Allen said, voice pitched high, "Let somebody see the apartment? At this hour in the morning? Really, Mrs. Crunch —"

"It's Mr. Malcolm Powther who wants to see the apartment. He's the Treadway butler."

"I'm not going to—" Mrs. Allen's voice went up, way up, high. "The Treadway butler!" she said, her eyes widening. She took a deep breath. "I can't—wait—you give me ten minutes, Mrs. Crunch. Just ten minutes and I'll be ready for him. You bring him right up in ten minutes."

In the sitting room, she kept thinking that Mrs. Allen had the most unpleasant way of squealing when she got excited. She'd be glad when Mrs. Allen moved. It would be a pleasure to have this quiet little man and his family occupying the top floor. She told Mr. Powther that they would go upstairs in a few minutes, meantime she wanted him to notice how very well her white geraniums were doing, all of them in bloom; told him that Pretty Boy, the battle-scarred tomcat dozing in the Boston rocker, was getting old and he wasn't as lively as he once was; spoke briefly of the way Dumble Street had changed, adding almost immediately that it was a convenient place to live because Franklin Avenue where the trolleys ran was just one block away.

"I think we can go up now," she said.

This time when Mrs. Allen opened the door of her apartment she almost curtsied. She had fixed her hair and bangs now formed a curly frieze across her forehead. She was wearing a print dress, and highheeled patent leather pumps. There was rouge on her round brown cheeks.

Rather too much rouge, Abbie thought as she introduced Mr. Powther and then stood just inside Mrs. Allen's living room, listening to the bill and coo of Mrs. Allen's voice which now sounded as though all her life she had been perfecting the sounds of the dove. She was smiling and nodding and saying, "Don't you think so, Mr. Powther? You know what I mean, Mr. Powther."

"I'll wait for you downstairs, Mr. Powther," Abbie said. This would give Mrs. Allen a chance to display all her middle-aged coyness, to titter behind her hand, to arch her thin bosom, without the inhibiting presence of one Abigail Crunch.

In the sitting room downstairs, she tried again to find a word to rhyme with Powther, and ended just where she started:

> Little Mister Powther
> Sat on a sowther.

Whenever she was at peace with the world, and sometimes when she wasn't, she made up jingling little rhymes, not wanting to, but she couldn't seem to help it. She jotted them down on the backs of envelopes, on the brown paper bags that came from the grocery store, on the pads of Dexter Linen that she used for letter paper. Having written them down, she couldn't bear to throw them away; and so she hid them, in bureau drawers, behind the sheets in the linen closet.

She heard Mr. Powther coming down the front stairs, his step light and quick. Little Mister Powther—Sat on a Sowther —she thought.

Mr. Powther said, "It's a pleasant apartment, Mrs. Crunch. I'll leave a deposit on it, subject, of course, to Mrs. Powther's approving the place. Though I am certain she will like it."

"A deposit isn't necessary," Abbie said.

"Thank you so much," he said. "I wonder if we can move in as soon as Mrs. Allen goes. That is, if Mrs. Powther likes the rooms. We're in rather of a hurry because the six months' notice we received expires this coming week."

It doesn't need much of anything done to it, Abbie thought. Mrs. Allen was one of those fussbudget housekeepers, who always had a scrub brush or a vacuum cleaner or a dustcloth in her hand. Poor Mr. Allen was kept busy, too. He was always painting or waxing floors or washing windows.

She said, "The Allens move out a week from today. We will need at least three days in which to freshen up the kitchen and bathroom. Will the thirtieth be all right?"

"Thank you so much," he said. At the door he bowed again.

She watched him go down the steps. He paused for a moment on the sidewalk and looked up at the branches of The Hangman, and then he was gone.

She supposed the young colored men of Link's generation couldn't have manners like Mr. Powther's, though she didn't know why. Wars and atom bombs and the fact that there was so much hate in the world might have something to do with it. There were times when she had thought that rudeness was a characteristic of Link's; that other young men had a natural courtesy he would never have. Then she would see or hear something in The Narrows that suggested all these young men were alike—something had brutalized them. But what?

In Link's case—well, if they hadn't lived on Dumble Street, if the Major had lived longer, if Link had been their own child instead of an adopted child, if she hadn't forgotten about him when he was eight, simply forgotten his existence, if she hadn't had to figure so closely with the little money that she had— rent from the apartment, pension from the Governor (the Major's pension)—and eke it out with the small sums she earned by sewing, embroidering, making jelly. If. But she had managed to keep the house, to feed and clothe herself and Link. It meant that she didn't have much time to devote to him. There was The Last Chance across the street, there was Bill Hod who owned it. He had plenty of money. Sometimes she had believed he was playing cat-and-mouse with her deliberately, cruelly, no—brutally. And she was helpless, unable to compete with him for Link's devotion.

At supper that night when she told Link about the new tenant, she carefully avoided any mention of Mr. Powther's beautiful manners; but she couldn't conceal the pleasure she felt about having him in the house; and she kept talking about the neatness of his appearance.

Link grinned. "You mean you're taking him in just like that? Without having seen his wife and his kids?"

"After all, he's the Treadway butler," she said. "If you had seen what a polishedlooking person he was you wouldn't need to see his family either."

"Miss Abbie, a man hasn't got a corner on virtue just because his shoes are shined. You'd better get a look at his family in spite of the pretty creases in his pants."

"You sound just like Frances," she said, annoyed because he had called her Miss Abbie.

"Well, of course, honey. A man can't have two women in his hair practically from birth without ending up sounding like one or both of them."

"Frances didn't live here with us," she said.

"She might just as well have. She might just as well have. She was here so often that I used to think she was my father and you were my mother."

"She's been awfully good to me," Abbie said, remembering.

"Yeah. I don't doubt that. But F. K. Jackson is right at least ninety-nine point nine times out of a hundred. It's very difficult for us average humans to love a female with a batting average like that. If she'd been a gambler she could have made a fortune."

"A gambler? She doesn't play cards—"

"No," he said, and he half closed his eyes, as though he were looking at a picture that pleased him, half closed his eyes and threw his head back. Abbie looked at the line of his throat, at the slight forward thrust of his chin, at the smoothness of his skin, the perfection of his nose and mouth, the straightness of his hair, and thought, Sometimes, just sometimes, I wish he wasn't so very goodlooking; or rather, I wish that the rest of him matched his good looks. He simply does not care about the right things. How can he go on working behind that bar? What was the point of his going to college if he was going to end up working in a bar?

Was it my fault? Yes. I forgot about him when he was eight. When he was sixteen I had the chance to win him back and somehow muffed it. And now it's too late. Now I do not dare say what I think about his working in that saloon for fear he will leave me and never come back.

"No," Link said, voice dreamy now. "But I wish she did. I wish she played poker. I'd like to see her in a game with Bill Hod. I would pay out folding money to get F. K. Jackson and Mr. B. Hod in a poker game."

Abbie made no comment on this statement. When Link finished college he had said he was going to write history books. Shortly after that he went into the Navy and was gone four years, and when he came home it was to work in a bar on Dumble Street. On Saturdays he played poker until four and five o'clock in the morning, played with his friends: a white man, a photographer, who had the unlikely name of Jubine and the unkempt look of a Bolshevist; a colored man named Weak Knees, who walked as though he were drunk, and did the cooking in The Last Chance; and Bill Hod, who owned The Last Chance and controlled or operated every illegal, immoral, illicit enterprise in The Narrows—though nobody could prove it—and who had the face of a hangman, face of a murderer. Colored, too.

Now Link was imitating Frances, clipping his words off the way she did, pursing his lips, lifting his eyebrows, pretending to remove a pair of pince-nez glasses.

He was saying, "Do you remember the time that F. K. Jackson said: 'Abbie, never never rent out any part of the premises without first seeing *all* the members of the family. Males have been known to marry females who bear a strong resemblance to the female fruit fly; and females have been known to marry males that are first cousin to the tomato worm. On the other hand, perfectly respectable couples have been known to produce children who have all the unpleasant qualities of the Japanese beetle!'"

Abbie listened to him, thinking, His voice doesn't match the rest of him either. It is a deep, resonant, musical voice. A perfect speaking voice. And—somebody has to go through that apartment upstairs to find out what needs to be done to it before the Powthers move in. If Link went up there now, Mrs. Allen wouldn't care if it was suppertime. She'd look at the breadth of his shoulders, listen to the music in his voice, and immediately start making the sounds of the dove and even show him the inside of the closets.

"Link," she said, "will you go upstairs and ask Mrs. Allen to let you go through the apartment so you can see if anything needs to be done to it before the Powthers move in?"

"Right now?"

"Of course not. After you finish your supper."

"Sure, Miss Abbie, sure. I didn't know. I thought you meant with knife and fork in hand and napkin tied tight under chin. I am, after all, only mortal man and mortal man is so conditioned to attack from immortal female that he—well, he never really knows."

The week slipped by. The Allens moved out. Abbie began to worry about Mrs. Powther. Why hadn't she been to see the place?

On Thursday, toward dusk, Mr. Powther stopped at the door. He wouldn't come in. He was in a hurry. He paid a month's rent in advance, seventy dollars in crisp new bills.

He said, "Mrs. Powther is busy with the packing and the children. She's perfectly willing to take the apartment on my say-so."

After he left, Abbie fingered the bills, wondering for the first time why he and his wife and the children didn't live at Treadway Hall, thinking almost at the same time that one never saw crisp new money like this in The Narrows. These bills looked as though they had gone straight from the mint into Treadway Hall, where they had been handed to Mr. Powther, who in turn handed them to Abbie Crunch. She hoped he was right about his wife's willingness to live on Dumble Street.

She was still thinking about Mrs. Powther, the next afternoon, when the knocker sounded. There was a repeated banging, a thundering on the door, that echoed and re-echoed through the house from cellar to attic, startling her so that she dropped the handle of the carpet sweeper she was using on the stairs. Who on earth would bang on a door like that? She kicked the carpet sweeper out of the way, thinking, I ought to pick it up and take it to the door with me and use it on his head. Anyone would think that he, whoever he is, was summoning a charwoman, and a deaf charwoman at that.

Usually she stood back from the smallpaned windows at the side of the door so that she could not be seen when she looked out. But this time she wanted to be seen, she glared out of the little windows and then frowned. There was a woman standing on the steps. A stranger. Or at least her face was unfamiliar. She'd seen the type before though: young, but too much fat around the waist, a soft, fleshy, quite prominent bosom, too much lipstick, a pink beflowered hat, set on top of straightened hair; the hair worn in what they called a pageboy bob, hanging loose, almost to the shoulders. She had on a light tan coat, very full, very long. Under one arm she carried a big loosely wrapped package which was held together by red and green string, carelessly tied. The package looked as though one good jounce would make the whole thing open up all at once.

The woman lifted her hand and banged the knocker against the door again, a peremptory, commanding knock. Abbie wouldn't have opened the door, but the woman had a little boy by the hand—a bulletheaded, bigheaded little boy. Bulletheaded. Bigheaded. The Major's expressions. They were always cropping up in her thoughts. He loved to describe children in that fashion; he took a special delight in pointing out small dark specimens that she had to agree, reluctantly, really fitted the words. And this child standing on her doorstep was both bulletheaded and bigheaded.

Because of the child she decided the woman might well be someone who had come to see the Allens and didn't know they'd moved. She was certain she'd seen the little boy somewhere. She opened the door, not too wide, just wide enough to be able to shut it quickly if she had to. After all, she was alone in the house.

"How do you do?" she said. She made it sound like a question.

"Afternoon. Are you Missus Crunch?"

Abbie nodded, staring, now.

The woman smiled, the thick coating of dark red lipstick on her mouth made her teeth look very white. They were good teeth, even, strong.

"I'm Mamie," she said.

Abbie said, "Yes?" There was music in the woman's voice, a careless, easy kind of music.

"I'm Mamie Powther."

"Mamie Powther? Mamie Powther? Oh—I—oh, of course. Come in, Mrs. Powther."

There was an awkward moment during which they stood in the hall looking at each other, Mrs. Powther smiling and showing her strong white teeth and Abbie trying to maintain an expression of cordiality and welcome. She didn't know when she'd ever felt quite so at a disadvantage. What had she expected Mrs. Powther to look like? She didn't know exactly. Certainly not like this woman. She supposed she had expected a sort of female edition of Mr. Powther, small, neat, precise of speech, businesslike in manner. She remembered Mr. Powther's highly polished shoes and without really meaning to, glanced down at Mrs. Powther's feet. She had on black suede shoes, scuffed at the toe, a kind of ballet-type shoe that bore a most unfortunate resemblance to a house slipper, and there was a bulge on each shoe, a kind of little hump, that only came from bunions.

"This here is J.C." Mrs. Powther said, still smiling.

At the mention of his name, the bulletheaded little boy retreated behind Mrs. Powther's tan coat, clutching at the folds.

"You stop that, you J.C.," Mrs. Powther said sharply. "Come out here where Missus Crunch can see you."

J.C.'s response to this command was to wrap the long full skirt of the coat more tightly around him, disappearing from view entirely except for one scuffed brown shoe and a dirty blue sock.

"He's shy," Mrs. Powther said benevolently.

"What is his name?" Abbie asked.

"J.C."

"But—" Abbie tried again. "What do the initials stand for?"

"Oh, they don't stand for nothing. It's just initials. I thought it was kind of a nice thing to do for him. When he gets old enough he can pick a name for himself, to match up with the initials. This way he won't be worried with no name he don't like for the rest of his life."

"Why I never heard of such a thing."

"No'm. Most folks haven't."

"Aw, Mamie," J.C. said suddenly, his voice muffled. "Come on and look at the place."

"He don't really want to move here," Mamie Powther said. She made no effort to disentangle J.C. from her coat. "He's got a lot of friends over where we been livin'. All 'bout his own age. And he's head man, ain't you, honey?"

Abbie wanted to end the conversation. She needed to think, to sit down alone and think, she'd heard of all kinds of names for children, but initials—what about the other children?

"Mr. Powther said there were three children. Are they—do the others have initials, too, instead of names?"

"No, ma'am. I didn't think of it until J.C. come along," she paused, as though in recollection, smiled. "There's just the twins. They're seven. Named Kelly and Shapiro. It'll take you awhile to tell 'em apart, but Kelly is the quiet one and Shapiro is the loud-mouthed one."

"I see," Mrs. Crunch said. Then she added hastily, because Mamie Powther had opened her mouth as though to continue and she looked like the kind of woman who enjoyed giving all the details of her last confinement, "You go right up and look at the rooms. My knees aren't what they used to be so if you don't mind, I'll stay down here."

She had planned to escort Mrs. Powther through the rooms, answering questions, explaining about the position of the sun in the afternoon, showing off the view of the river that one got from the living room windows. But this Mrs. Powther wasn't the one she had expected. She didn't want to watch this Mrs. Powther's bosom quiver as she walked through the bedroom that she, Abbie, had once shared with the Major.

"You can go right up. The doors are all open. You don't need a key."

"That's fine," Mrs. Powther's voice was cordial. "Come on, J.C."

Abbie sat down heavily in the Boston rocker in the dining room—she still referred to it like that when she got upset, though it had long since been converted into a sitting room. Twins, she thought. Kelly and Shapiro. Why it was fantastic. Incredible. She couldn't very well *not* rent the apartment to the Powthers. She'd taken Mr. Powther's money, promised it to him, and she'd always been a woman of her word. Perhaps Mrs. Powther wouldn't like the place. Nonsense. Mamie Powther would love Dumble Street. Besides there weren't any places for rent in Monmouth. Or perhaps that horrible little boy, J.C., whoever heard of such nonsense, initials for a name, perhaps he wouldn't like it, because it wouldn't offer sufficient opportunity for him to be head man. Oh, they'd take it. J.C. and Mamie. He didn't even call her Mother. How on earth had that polished little Mr. Powther managed to acquire a bigbosomed creature like this one, painted fingernails, some of the paint peeling off, jingly earrings in her ears, smelling of bergamot or something equally as sickeningly sweet, and the little boy with a distinct smell of urine about him.

Hearing Mrs. Powther's footsteps, soft, heavy, on the front stairs, muted by the carpet, she got up and met her in the hall.

"Well?" she said.

Mamie Powther started drawing a pair of soiled white gloves over her hands, covering the scarlet fingernails. "It's a lovely place, Missus Crunch," she beamed. "A lovely place. Actually I wouldn't have come to look at it, I would have moved right in on the strength of Powther's say-so. He knows an awful lot about houses. But J.C. he wouldn't let me be until I brought him over. Just kept on sayin', Mamie I'm not a-goin' to move until I see where I'm goin'."

"And did you like the apartment, J.C.?" Abbie asked, being deliberately sarcastic.

J.C. disappeared in the folds of Mrs. Powther's coat again.

"He liked it fine. He liked it so much he already moved in, Missus Crunch. His things is up there now."

What in the world is she talking about? Abbie wondered.

"He left his comic books up there. That's what was in that big bundle. He said, 'Mamie if I like it I'm a-goin' to be the first to move in.' It suits us as though we thought it up ourselves, don't it, J.C.?" She paused but J.C. did not answer. "And it's so nice that there's a back stairs, a outside back stairs."

Abbie Crunch thought there was a kind of anticipatory gleam in Mamie Powther's eyes that the existence of an outside back stairs hardly seemed to justify. Certainly there was an extra gaiety in her manner.

"Back stairs do save so much wear and tear on a front stair carpet," Mamie Powther explained. "Children is always runnin' up and down and in and out you know."

Abbie watched them cross the street. Mamie Powther was

moving swiftly and J.C. was trotting to keep up with her. Wind from the river rippled the pages of the comic book he held in his hand, toyed with the full skirt of Mrs. Powther's coat.

Bill Hod was standing in front of The Last Chance. He lifted his hat as they passed. Mrs. Powther nodded, lifting one gloved hand in a gesture that was part salute, part wave. Abbie wondered if he knew her or if he was merely paying tribute to her quivery bosom. The ballet slippers gave her a flatfooted appearance. As they disappeared from sight, Abbie decided they looked like figures out of the old Mother Goose books, the proportions all wrong, highly exaggerated. And almost immediately she was rhyming again:

> Mister Powther Sat on a sowther
> Eating his curds and whey.
> Along came a Mamie
> And said, You must pay me.
> And so he did pay, did pay.

How old was Mamie Powther? In her early thirties? Mr. Powther was a lot older, closer to fifty, at least. Link would laugh. Female fruit fly? Japanese beetle? Tomato worm? Not Mamie Powther. Mamie Powther was Dumble Street.

The Major had been dead set against this street. "Fine old brick house, yes. But Dumble Street—Dumble Street—that's not a good place to live." Then he had startled her by saying, "It ought to be called Fumble Street. That's what it is."

She had glanced at him sharply, wondering if he, too, was a victim of rhyming, and that she'd never known it. No. Because he snorted his contempt, his disgust, for the street, unconscious of the endless possibilities for rhymes: dumble, fumble, stumble, tumble, mumble. It had proved itself to be all of those things. The people who lived here near the waterfront fumbled and they mumbled and they stumbled and they tumbled, ah, yes, make up a word—dumbled.

> Got no roof over my head
> Slats keep fallin' out of my bed
> And I'm lonesome—lonesome.
>
> Rent money's so long overdue
> Landlord says he's goin' to sue
> And I'm lonesome—lonesome.

The words were clear but the voice seemed far away. It came nearer, slowly, slowly, increasing in volume, until it seemed to be right there in the kitchen. "And I'm lonesome." A big warm voice with a lilt in it, and something else, some extra, indefinable quality which made Abbie listen, made her want to hear more, and more; as though the singer leaned over, close, to say, I'm talking to you, listen to me, I made up this song for you and I've got wonderful things to tell you and to show you, listen to me.

Abbie looked across the breakfast table at Link. The people next door played records morning, noon, and night. He might think this was a record. He was buttering a piece of toast and he didn't seem to hear that big clear attention-getting voice that was filling the kitchen with song. It isn't a soprano, she thought, it goes down too far, too easily for a soprano, lonesome was sung way down, almost down to a tenor's middle range, but head and bed, sue and due were way up high.

Link looked toward the screen door. "Is that a record?"

Abbie hesitated, wishing she could bring herself to say, Yes, it's a record, a blues or a boogiewoogie or a jazz record or whatever they called the bleating that issued from all the gramophones and radios these days, all of it sounding alike, too loud, too harsh, no sweetness, no tune, simply a reiterated bleating about rent money and men who had gone off with other women, and numbers that didn't come out. It was perfectly ridiculous, she knew it, admitted it, but she did not want Link to see Mamie Powther. Sooner or later he was bound to. The Powthers had been living upstairs for two days now but it was usually noon before her voice came drifting down from an upstairs window.

"No," she said reluctantly. "That's not a record. That's Mrs. Powther, the new tenant."

He went to the back door and stood there so long, motionless, watching something, that Abbie got up from the table to look, too.

Mamie Powther was hanging up clothes in the backyard. Abbie frowned. She'll have to get her own line or I won't have any place to hang my things. She must have got up very early to turn out such a tremendous wash. Very clean clothes they were, too. A big clothes basket heaped to the top stood on the grass under the line. There was an almost hypnotic rhythm about her movements, Abbie found that she, too, couldn't look away. Bend over and pick up shirt, straighten up, and shake it out, reach for clothespins, straighten up, pin shirt on line, bend over.

> Big John's got a brandnew gal
> High yaller wench name of Sal
> And I'm lonesome—lonesome.

She keeps changing the words, Abbie thought, listening, and watching. Wind whipped the clothes back and forth, lifting the hem of Mamie Powther's short cotton dress as though it peered underneath and liked what it saw and so returned again and again for another look. What a vulgar idea. I never think things like that. It's that getup she has on. A sleeveless dress, printed material, white background with big red poppies all over it. A bright red scarf wound around her head. And there among the sheets, the pillowcases, the towels, the children's socks and underwear and overalls, her figure stood out—a gaudy, bigbosomed young woman with sturdy arms, dimpled at the elbows. When she bent over you could see that she had no stockings on, you could see the back of her thighs, more than halfway up, just as though she were leaning over in a bathing suit. The bending over effortless, the straightening up, all in one smooth unbroken motion, the wind whipping the clothes, lifting them, returning them to her, and she singing in time to all this movement:

> Trouble sits at my front door
> Can't shut him out any more
> And I'm lonesome—lonesome.

Watching her, you could almost believe it was a dance of some kind, the dance of the clothes, the wetwash dance. I don't dance. I never could, Abbie thought. I haven't any sense of rhythm and yet she hangs clothes and I think about dancing. I don't believe she's got a thing on under that dress.

When Link turned away from the door, Abbie waited for him to say something funny about the red poppies on the dress, or about the soft brown flesh so very exposed to view.

But all he said was, "My! my! my! So that's Mrs. Powther."

He drank the rest of his coffee standing up, then he leaned down, patted Abbie's cheek and kissed her, straightened up, said softly, "The female fruit fly," and laughed.

For a barely perceptible second there was a break in the rhythm of Mamie Powther's song and Abbie knew that she'd heard that powerful male laughter coming from the first floor. Heard it and probably made a note of it for future reference.

Then he was gone. Whistling. Whistling the tailend of the same tune: I'm lonesome—lonesome.

Somehow she would have to get rid of that big young woman, still hanging up clothes, pausing now and then to look straight up at the sky. Blowzy. No. Gaudy. Well, yes. She simply did not belong in that neat backyard with its carefully tended lawn and its white fences. The brilliant red of the poppies on her dress made the red of the dogwood leaves look faded, washed out. She did not match the yard or the kind of morning that it was. Sunny. Fairly warm. Winter still far away but coming, the potential there, in the east wind, but the grass still green. She dominated the morning so that you saw nothing but Mamie, heard nothing but Mamie, and with a little concentration, it was possible to believe that you could smell nothing but Mamie—that sweet heavy perfume was definitely in the air. Brassy. That was the word. Mamie Powther was like a trumpet call sent out over the delicate nuances and shadings of stringed instruments played softly, making you jump, startled, because it didn't belong there.

"I'm lonesome—lonesome—"

Mamie Powther. Why not Mrs. Powther. Somehow natural to eliminate Mrs. Not a man's wife, permanently attached, but an unattached unwifely female. She didn't belong in the backyard any more than her furniture belonged in Number Six Dumble Street. Such furniture! Lamps with pink rayon shades, and a bed with the headboard and footboard covered with cupids and grapes and grape leaves, a big chest of drawers almost like a highboy, with the same appalling cupids on the handles of the drawers. The packing hadn't been done properly, or rather, Mamie Powther hadn't made any effort to pack at all. There were a thousand-and-one loose items that had to be carried upstairs in piles. Clothing and pots and pans and nursing bottles. There was a battered highchair with food particles stuck on it and a child's pot made of pink plastic. That, too, somehow characteristic of the woman. And toys, she hadn't even tried to get hold of any cartons—legless dolls and broken fire engines and trucks without wheels, and scooters without steering gear were carried up in piles—and she wasn't certain but there seemed to be a great wudge of what looked like soiled diapers, but surely none of those children could be still wearing diapers.

There were two moving-men on the truck—one was big and one was little but their voices were the same size. It took both of them to get some of the furniture up the stairs. The house was filled with their shouts, "On me!" "On you!" Only they made it sound like "Awn me!" "Awn you!" To see what they were doing Abbie had gone to the front of the house. The little one stepped back bracing his body for the weight of a tremendous sofa upholstered in pale blue brocade, shouting "Awn me!" Though the other man was not two feet away from him, he shouted back, "Awn you!" Then when they reached the landing, the big man braced himself shouting "Awn me!" "Awn me!" "Awn you!" and then the children took it up, loving the sound of it, and she could detect no difference in the loudness of Shapiro's voice or Kelly's voice.

As soon as she finished doing the breakfast dishes she would tell Mrs. Powther about the clothesline. She heard a soft drumming sound that came from the front of the house. She listened. What could that be? A muffled drumming, not a banging but a drumming sound.

As she went toward the hall, walking briskly, she thought, I've been afraid of everything, ever since the Major died. No one has ever known how afraid I've been. Any unexpected sound makes my heart beat faster, makes me catch my breath.

J.C. was sitting on the stairs, two steps up, drumming his

heels against the riser of the lower step. The sound of his heels striking against the stair carpet made a soft, regular rhythmic sound. Inherited sense of rhythm, she thought. Inherited from Mamie. It didn't seem possible but he was drinking from a nursing bottle. As she approached he took his hands away from the bottle, holding it in his mouth with his teeth, so that it swung back and forth, and he began to rock his body back and forth too. He was staring at the Major's silk hat and at the goldheaded cane—the hat still on the coatrack in the hall, the cane hanging there beside it.

He looked at Abbie briefly, and then his gaze returned to the hat. Again she got the feeling that she'd seen him somewhere before.

He transferred his hands to the bottle, drank from it, gave a little wiggle of pleasure, then, twisting one arm through the balustrades, he half lay down on the stairs. He placed the bottle on the step beside him.

"Crunch," he said, "what's that?" He lisped and it sounded as though he said, "Crunth—whathethat?"

It was perfectly obvious that he was talking about the Major's hat and the cane, because he kept his unwinking gaze focused on them.

"You call me Mrs. Crunch, young man."

"Missus Crunch," he said, giving her a look so adult and so malevolent that she wanted to shake him. "What's that?"

"A silk hat and a goldheaded cane."

"What's a goldheaded cane?"

This could go on forever. If she answered him or tried to, he'd think up a hundred other questions on the basis of her reply.

"You ask your mother and she'll tell you."

"What's a goldheaded cane?" he repeated.

"You ask your mother and she'll tell you," she said again as imperturbably as though he had asked the question for the first time. Then she said abruptly, "What's a big boy like you doing drinking out of a bottle?"

"Drinking milk."

She glanced at him sharply. He hardly seemed old enough for such expert evasion. Four-year-olds didn't usually—Or was he?

"How old are you?"

"Three and a half." He didn't look at her, he was staring up at the hat, at the cane.

"Well, you're old enough to be drinking milk from a glass."

"Me don't like it that way."

"Say I don't like it that way. Not 'me.'"

"I don't like it that way," he said obediently, still not looking at her.

That was fairly simple, she thought. It's just a matter of being firm with them. He had a comic book thrust in the front of his shirt and she started to ask him about it, he certainly couldn't read and she didn't see why he should be so fond of comic books, some one must have spoiled his taste already, and perhaps— But she never got around to the comic book because she heard a faint hissing noise, a kind of *h-stt*. J.C. was looking at her very gravely and she turned away. Something must have gone wrong with the radiator in Link's room. As she turned she glanced down at the floor, at the polished parquet floor. Those beautiful floors were partly responsible for her insistence on buying this house even though the Major disapproved. There was a little puddle of water there and as she looked it grew larger. She stared at the little boy sprawled there on the stairs, dismayed. Why he isn't trained yet, three and a half years old and he isn't trained. My stair carpet, my floor, and there will be a smell of urine in the front hall just like in the tenements—

"You listen to me," she said angrily. "There are some things I simply will not put up with. And this is one of them. You can tell that mother of yours that I said so."

He didn't reply, just looked at her with that same grave air. "Did you hear what I said?" She laid her hand on his arm.

He flung the hand away, got up, and scuttled up the stairs. When he reached the landing he stopped, peered down at her, shouted, "Jaybird, jaybird, sittin' in the grath, draw back, draw back, shoot him in the—YAH! Crunth—Crunth—Crunth!"

She made a motion as though she were going to pursue him and he stuck his tongue out and then scrambled up the stairs, moving fast, his feet thumping on the steps.

Mopping up the puddle he'd made, she kept thinking, Maybe he isn't quite bright, three and a half years old and he was still using a nursing bottle, still wetting himself, but his eyes were highly intelligent, almost too much so, and he was inquisitive, always asking questions, just as any normal child should. He'd left the bottle of milk on the stairs. Well, she'd put it in the garbage can and then she'd tell Mamie Powther about the clothesline and tell her, also, to keep J.C. off the front stairs.

Outside in the backyard she walked toward Mamie Powther's bentover figure, thinking, I'll start off by saying, "About the clothesline—"

But she didn't say anything because she heard a man's voice saying, "Hi, Mamie, what's the pitch?"

There, on the other side of the clothesline stood Bill Hod.

Mamie Powther said, "Lord, babe, you sure gave me a turn. I didn't hear you come in the yard. How are you anyway?" She laughed. It was a warm joyous sound. "Come on up and see the place. It's a mess but I can give you a cup of coffee."

I won't have it, Abbie thought. I won't have him in my yard.

Mamie turned toward the house, "Oh! Good mornin', Missus Crunch. I didn't see you," she said, smiling, showing her white, strong teeth. "Meet my cousin, Mr. Bill Hod."

In the kitchen, Abbie sat down heavily on the nearest chair, sat there shaking as though she'd had a chill, thinking, The house, the Major, Dumble Street. In that order. He had disapproved of her choice of a house, not so much the house, though it was big, neglected, had been vacant for years and so repairs would be expensive, not the house, but its location. Near the river. Near the dock. He said rivers and waterfronts were not good places to live. But it was a brick house and Abbie had always wanted a brick house and the price was very low so they bought it.

It was almost twenty years ago that it happened. All of that. Yet the sight of Bill Hod in my yard makes me keep shivering as though it were yesterday. It was on a Saturday afternoon in August. The Hangman was in full leaf. She had gone out to select a handful of especially beautiful leaves to show to her Sunday School class in the morning. She happened to look down the street, down toward Franklin Avenue, and she saw the Major, lurching along, leaning on Bill Hod. Sometimes he stopped and waved both arms in the air, and then gestured vaguely, using the goldheaded cane to accent his gestures, sometimes he dragged it along the sidewalk, then held it straight up in the air.

Inside the house, she waited for them, watching from the window. As they approached the steps, she opened the front door.

"He's sick," Bill Hod said.

She'd seen them before, these "sick" men, pushed and pulled toward home by loyal embarrassed friends. Mrs. O'Leary's husband was always "sick" on Saturday nights and all day Sunday —or so the children said.

"I can see that," she said coldly. She'd seen the stumbling, uncertain gait, the unfocused bleary eyes of the drunken bums who slept in doorways, lurched across the dock, stumbled out from under the sheltering branches of The Hangman, too often not to recognize this type of sickness. The Major smelt of whiskey, not just smelt of it, it was all about him, as though he had taken a bath in it.

"Put him in a chair—" She pointed toward the door of the parlor, hurriedly spread newspapers all around the chair, thinking, My carpet, my beautiful new carpet—

"He should be in bed—"

The Major said something or tried to. It was only a blurred muttering in his throat, a horrible drunken sound, suggesting that even the muscles of his throat were drunk.

She turned on Bill Hod. Oh, she knew him. She had tried to prevent his getting a liquor license for that place he ran right across the street.

"Get out of my house—"

Bill Hod said, "He's a sick man. You better get a doctor."

The Major made that horrible drunken muttering in his throat again and the smell of what she always called cheap whiskey seemed to be everywhere in the room. She thought, I can't stand that smell; if I don't get out of here quickly, I will be sick. Bill Hod hadn't moved; he was looking at her, staring at her, defying her.

She picked up a poker from the fireplace, a very old handwrought poker, black, crudelooking, handed down in her family from one generation to the next, and even as she picked it up, felt the coldness of the metal, the roughness of it, the weight of it, she thought, Has it ever been used as a weapon before?

She said, "*Will* you get out of here or will I have to call a policeman?"

The poker slid out of her hand, clattered on the hearth. She thought Bill Hod was going to strike her, no, not strike her, his eyes, his voice, she'd never heard such fury in a human voice, she thought he was going to kill her. Strangle her with his hands. He took a step forward, and his eyes were cold, absolutely inhuman. The eyes of a hangman. Face of a hangman.

He said, "You fool—you goddamn fool—get a doctor—" And he was gone.

She went into the kitchen, sat down at the table. She couldn't seem to think straight. She would have Hod arrested. She kept hearing the Major's breathing, labored, stentorian, like a snore. Drunk. Drunk as a lord. What could have come over him? People would laugh at her. President of the local WCTU and her husband so drunk he couldn't stand up. Ha-ha, ha-ha, ha-ha. The colored president of the white WCTU. A drunken husband. Well, he's colored. Ha-ha, ha-ha, ha-ha.

Six o'clock. Suppertime. And he still sounded exactly the same. Link kept tiptoeing in to look at him, coming back to the kitchen, face frightened, eyes frightened, but too fascinated to pay any attention to her repeated warnings to stay out of the parlor.

She had forgotten that she had invited Frances to have supper with them. Link must have been waiting in the hall, waiting for the sound of the knocker, so that he could get to the door first and let Frances in. Frances came straight back to the kitchen and before she could get her hat off, Link said, "Uncle Theodore's sick. He's in the parlor and he's got newspapers all around him on the floor."

So, of course, Frances went into the parlor to find out how he was, and Abbie went, too. Frances listened to his breathing, stopped just inside the door to listen, and then crossed the room quickly, bent over him, frowning, feeling his pulse, forcing his eyelids open, and the newspapers made a rustling sound under her feet as she moved around him.

When Frances spoke her voice was brusquer than Abbie had

ever heard it, and her eyeglasses seemed to have an added glitter. She said, "He's seriously ill, Abbie. Mortally ill. I think he's
had a stroke. I'll get a doctor—"

She still didn't believe that he was sick. He was a big man,
six feet tall, weighing two hundred pounds, and he looked
even bigger than usual, mountainous. Perhaps it was the way
his body sagged in the chair. His head lolled on his shoulder,
as though it had no connection with his neck, his spine. His
mouth was open and a little trickle of saliva was running out
of his mouth, down the side of his cheek. His arms were hanging down, dangling, the hands open, limp, dangling too. The
drunks who slept under The Hangman in the summer looked
just like this, smelt just like this, sounded just like this, the
same queer snoring issued from their throats. The only thing
—his hands—. She touched both of them. They were cold. His
hands were always warm, great big warm hands.

Then Frances was bringing the new doctor into the parlor. Dr. Easter. A black man, young, she supposed, but with
a manner so pompous, so dignified, that he might have been
seventy-odd. He didn't even open his bag, he felt for the
Major's pulse, he leaned over and apparently listened to his
breathing, just with his ear, and then straightened up and said,
"We must get him in bed. At once."

Why he's a West Indian, Abbie thought. She said, "Is he—"

He interrupted her, "I do not know, madam. He is very ill. I
cannot discuss the case now. There is no time. Miss Jackson, I
will need help. We must get him in bed. At once."

He made her feel in the way. So did Frances. Frances was
at the telephone again. And almost immediately, there were
two men at the front door, and then they were in the parlor.
Perhaps it wasn't that fast. But it seemed so. When, finally, she
went upstairs into the bedroom, they had undressed the Major, put him to bed. The smell of whiskey was gone. She could
see now that they were right, he was terribly, terribly sick. It
was incredible. He had never been sick in all the years they
had been married. The color of his skin had changed. It was
gray. Skin gray. He lay motionless under the sheets, under the
soft rose-colored blanket, the magnificent head perfectly still
on the pillows, the bigboned hands still too, the hands open,
fingers straight out, all of them, on the rose-colored blanket.

He never lay still when he was in bed. He turned and twisted in his sleep as though sleep were an enemy and he determined to destroy it, to fight the sheets and the blankets and the pillows which were the enemy's first line of defense. In the morning, in the winter, he was always lying on his side, the covers pulled over his big shoulders, so that when she first woke up she always thought she had been sleeping in a tent, the covers were tent-like, lifted up by the Major's shoulders, and drafts played around her neck and back, down the tunnel that the covers formed. When the Major got out of a bed it looked like a battleground, all furrowed and riddled, the sheets rumpled, the blankets on the floor. She used to wonder if this bed-mauling was a family trait, just as some families run to cleft palates and buck teeth and rheumatism, so perhaps the Crunches for generations back had been bed-maulers, unable to lie still in a bed, congenitally forced to twist and turn, and pull the sheets and push the blankets and punch the pillows, warring against sleep. She would cast one last disgusted look at him, and then go quietly down the stairs to make the morning coffee.

About seven o'clock she would hear his footsteps on the stairs, heavy and yet quick. He came down the stairs singing in that sweet pure tenor voice, a voice utterly incongruous in so big a man, "You must wake and call me early, call me early, Mother dear," and she supposed he timed it because when he reached the kitchen door he let his voice out, "For I'm to be Queen o' the May, Mother, I'm to be Queen o' the May." Then he kissed her and patted her hand, saying, "Well, Abbie, another day—more dough—as the baker said to the bread mixer," and let out a roar of laughter, so loud and with so much lung power behind it, or perhaps it was the pitch, anyway his laughter made the plates, the cups, and saucers on the table rattle.

She sat there by his bedside all night. There had been something else that would have told her how dreadfully sick he was, something more than his lying so still. When she first came into the room Frances and Dr. Easter had been leaning over him, and when they saw her, they straightened up and stood aside, drawing back, away from the bed, no expression on their faces. It was that standing aside that told her he might not survive. People stood aside like that, not saying anything, when the chief mourner came into the room to view the body for the first time.

Sometimes she held his hand, that big powerful hand—a hand that was all compassion and tenderness, and that might somewhere else and under a different set of circumstances have been the hand of a surgeon because the fingers were enormously sensitive, controlled, skilful. Sometimes she prayed, kneeling by the side of the bed, burying her face in her hands, aware that the sheets smelt ever so faintly of lavender. Pride once in the fine sheets, in the box springs, the hair mattress, the soft blankets, pride in anything now worthless, meaningless. Don't let him die. Her fault. She should have known that he wasn't drunk. He was sick. Dear God, don't let him die. I can't live without him. I wouldn't want to.

At intervals during the night Dr. Easter came into the room. She knew he was doing everything he could for the Major. But his breathing didn't change, except that the sound, and maybe it was her imagination, perhaps she had grown accustomed to it, but it wasn't as loud. Frances was, she thought, always somewhere in the room.

Toward morning Frances said, "Go downstairs, Abbie. Go outside and get some air. I'll be right here. I'll call you if I need you."

She went reluctantly. If he died it would be her fault. It would be murder really. She should have known. She should have called the doctor the moment the Major came in the house. She let him sit there. "He's got newspapers all around him." Link's young voice. Reproach, wasn't it? The new carpet. Newspapers. The *Monmouth Chronicle*. Yesterday's. Spread out on the floor.

She stood outside on the front steps. It was beginning to get light. There were a few stars still in the sky. Or was that just the tears in her eyes? Tears. Not stars. It was daylight. The Hangman bulked large and dark off to the right. Dear God, don't let him die. She looked down at the sidewalk. There was something written there. Right in front of the house. She went down the steps, not wanting to read whatever it was, afraid not to, remembering the stories about the prophetic power of Cesar the Writing Man who went all over Monmouth writing verses from the Bible on the sidewalks. Always writing on Dumble Street.

At first she couldn't make it out. There were so many scrolls and flourishes and curlicues and small adorning parts, in pink, red, blue, and yellow chalk, that it seemed to be just a pattern, intricate in design, drawn on the sidewalk. Her eyes kept filling up with tears, they welled up, again and again, so that she could not see clearly. She kept wiping them away with the back of her hand. Don't cry. Don't cry. Dear God, don't let him die. Don't let him die. I mustn't cry. I mustn't cry.

She made herself stop crying so that she could see what Cesar had written on the sidewalk in front of her house. Having read it, she was assailed by fear, by horror, so that she trembled and cried out, in refutation, "NO! NO! NO!" And the morning was suddenly unbearable, the sun coming out, the air filled with the smell of the river, fog blowing in from the river, damp and cold on her face. She leaned over and read it again: "At her feet he bowed, he fell, he lay down: at her feet he bowed, he fell: where he bowed, there he fell down dead."

She turned and went back in the house, aware of a dreadful giddiness that made her want to pitch forward on her face, fall forward and never get up, went up the stairs, swiftly, listening, listening, listening now for the same sound that had made her so angry when she first heard it, wanting to hear it now, praying that she would still hear it. She stopped in the doorway of the bedroom and heard the peculiar snorelike breathing of the Major, definitely not as loud, not even as loud as when she left the room.

His hands were still cold but they responded to her touch. He knew her. Apparently he could only convey his recognition of her by a slight sustained pressure of his hand.

That night he died. Just before he died he tried to sit up, seemed to bow, and he said, "The house—Abbie—the house—" She couldn't understand the rest of it, the rest of it was just a muttering in his throat, and then he pitched forward and she caught him in her arms.

Blank space. Just weeping. And then the funeral. I will not cry. Where did all these people come from? I will not cry. I will not make a sound. And all the flowers. So many flowers. The whole front of the colored Congregational Church covered with flowers. When they were first married she had suggested that they attend the white Congregational Church and he had said, "I'd never get to be a deacon in the white church. And that's all right. I want to be a deacon so I'm going to belong to the colored church." I will not make a sound. So many people. So many flowers. Old men with bleary eyes. He bought snuff for them, and chewing tobacco. Colored ones and white ones. The Governor was crying. So was his wife. Right across the aisle. And children. How strange. But he always had lollipops in his pocket. Young men, too. Colored ones and white ones. He always had a good story to tell. Born storyteller.

I will not cry. So many people. All those women from Dumble Street who went to work in the morning with little paper bags under their arms. All here. And the tailor and the man from the bakery, and the man who had the grocery. Rich people. Poor people. Young people. Old people. I will not cry. Even the Dumble Street sporting women. Legs and bosoms, always on the verge of complete exposure, all laughter or all tears, all singing or all cursing. He lifted his hat to them as though he were bowing to the Queen of England. Empress of India. The Governor, whitehaired, leaning on a cane, a goldheaded cane exactly like the one he gave the Major. I will not cry. The Governor with tears running down his cheeks. His wife, too.

Look straight ahead. Look at the flowers. Hold everything still inside of you. Frances keeps her hand on mine. Don't let it go. Keep it there. All right so far. Past the prayers. Past the reading from the Scriptures. Past "Lead, Kindly Light." I am the resurrection and the life: he that believeth in me. How will I walk down this aisle. Not cry.

She was not prepared for—oh, who could have. Who planned this? Not that woman. She was standing up. So she was going to sing. Now the organ. The Governor she supposed. A white organist she had never seen. The Major used to sing in the choir. Sing solos. Only three times a year. He said, "You play the organ there, Abbie. If I were to sing solos every Sunday it wouldn't look right. People would think we'd taken over the church." Christmas. Easter. Children's Sunday. He sang solos

then. He is risen. Hallelujah. Silent night, Holy night. Voice
sweet. Sweet tenor voice. Always humming and whistling and
singing.

The strange organist was playing "Goin' Home." That
woman was going to sing it. A big woman. Light brown.
Freckles on her face. A soprano. From the Baptist Church. She
had a voice like a cry from the grave. Sadness. Sorrow. Regret.
Reproach—no other voice like it. The high notes a little off
pitch, deliberately off pitch, so that it was no longer singing, it
was a wail, echoing in the blood, in the bones.

At the first sound of that voice, lifted now, unearthly, terrible
in its sorrow, she told herself, Think of something about him
that you did not like. If you don't you'll faint. There is a moaning in your throat and it will come out. Think fast.

There were the stories. The stories about his family. She'd
never liked those stories. He told them with gusto. He said
his people were swamp niggers and laughed. There was Uncle Zeke, his great-great-uncle, who had red eyes and carried
toads and roots in his pockets and could conjure. "Don't say
goodbye to me." Told them that at a railroad station. Were
the stories true? Did they have railroad stations in those days?
When they got off the train, Uncle Zeke was standing on the
station platform waiting for them. Uncle Zeke could rise up off
his bed, in a prone position, and go around in circles, three feet
up from the bed, in a prone position, around and around, bony
legs thrust out straight from a white nightshirt, lids closed over
the red eyes, and he always said the same thing, as he floated
around circling over his bed, "Watch that straight coattail,
Sam, watch that straight coattail." Nobody had ever known
what he meant by it.

Had the Major made them up? Made up all the stories about
those other long since dead members of the Crunch family.
But the details were so vivid. The stories obviously handed
down, handed down, always told the same way, so that they
sounded true. She even knew what Uncle Zeke looked like,
a small dark man who walked with a limp and his hands were
unpleasant to the touch, damp and cold. Whenever anybody
got sick they sent for Uncle Zeke. She even knew how his voice
had sounded, a highpitched cackling, almost feminine, voice,
"Zeke'll ponder it. Zeke'll squat down by the fire. And Zeke'll

ponder it. Hush, hush, hush. Zeke is ponderin' it." And wind
howled down the chimney.

Shut out the sound of that wail. Keep remembering. You
didn't like the stories. He made those people live again. They
were an emotional primitive people, whose existence even in
the past seemed somehow to be an affront to the things you
believed in, and stood for. His great-grandfather, Theodore
Crunch, bit an Irishman's ear off in a fight in the dooryard of
an inn. And another one of the male Crunches, after the Emancipation, used to glance around his dooryard and then gather
up all the little pickaninnies, as he called them, and sell them
off for ten dollars apiece, to anyone who would buy them, saying that he was tired of looking at them. Then the rest of the
family would have to go scurrying around the countryside to
get the children back.

There was Aunt Hal, who wore men's shoes, and who could
conjure, and who had her conjure books buried with her, and
the story was that a white man offered a thousand dollars for
the conjure books but the surviving Crunches did not dare sell
them, because Aunt Hal had warned them, on her deathbed,
"Them books goes in the casket with me. Anybody takes 'em
out, I'll be back. If I has to come back, I'll take every one of
you niggers over Jordan with me."

Aunt Hal stood six foot in her stocking feet, Aunt Hal wore
long black skirts, Aunt Hal had a deep voice, bass, like a man's
voice. Her eyes were the black unfathomable eyes of a witch, a
gypsy. When one of the early Crunches died, Aunt Hal wasn't
invited to the funeral. But when the funeral procession got
under way, there was Aunt Hal perched on the back of the
hearse, riding in the procession, leading the way, holding on
with one hand, and with the other hand thumbing her nose at
the mourners in the carriages following the hearse. Somebody
shouted, "Whip up them horses! Whip 'em up!" And the hearse
started going faster and faster, Aunt Hal, holding on, jounc-
ing up and down, faster, faster, and the dead Crunch in the
casket completely forgotten. The living Crunches thrust their
heads out of the windows of the carriages following the hearse,
shouting, "Whip 'em up! Whip them horses! When Hal falls off
ride her down! Ride Hal down!" An ungodly crew. None of
the stories were ever about goodness and mercy, always death

and cruelty. People stopped and stared and wondered at the
sight, horses stretched out straight, hoofbeats, fast, furious, the
carriages swaying, Hal clutching the sides of the hearse, refusing to be jolted off, and finally, at the cemetery, as the casket
was being lowered into the grave, she spat at them, spat at all
those darkskinned Crunches who stood glaring at her across
the open grave, and said, "Well! I come to the funeralizin' anyway. Didn' I?" Deep bass voice. Man's voice.

The story about Hal, the remembered story, took her down
the aisle of the church, following behind the body of the last
of the Crunches, the last Theodore Crunch. Home to his fathers. Gone to his long home. Crunches waiting for him. This
one, the last of them, never had the son he wanted. Never had
any children. A man who loved boys and gardens and horses.
Loved boys. So they adopted Link. At the Major's insistence.
Where was Link? He wasn't at the service. She thought about
him that one time, coming out of the church. Then not again.
Forgetting him as though he had never existed. Because she
believed that it was her fault that the Major died.

All those years ago, and she remembered it as though it had
happened yesterday. Had never really gotten over it. Because
there was always the feeling that it was her fault that the Major
died. But there had been the smell of whiskey and because of it
she hadn't really looked at him, wouldn't look at him. Bill Hod
brought him home and there was the smell of whiskey.

As she sat there in the kitchen she heard somebody whistling. Then Bill Hod went past the back door. Why, he's been
up there all this time. She hadn't heard his footsteps coming
down the stairs. He had made no sound at all. There was just
the whistled tune, seemingly descending the outside back
stairs, coming down, by itself, nearer and nearer. A tune she'd
heard before. Where? Of course. The tune that Link had
been whistling when he left the house, the tune that Mamie
Powther had been singing while she hung clothes on the line:
"I'm lonesome—lonesome."

I don't know what to do, she thought. Then she straightened up. She would make some tea and then she would go
and ask Frances to help her figure out some way, some polite
way, of course, by which she could get rid of the Powthers
quickly.

The twelve o'clock whistle sounded at the Treadway Munitions Company. Tea for lunch? No. She heated soup and rolls and fixed a salad. Then set the table as carefully as though she were expecting a guest, thinking, I've always been the Englishman dressing for dinner even in the jungle. Then she sat down at the table and bowed her head as she said the blessing.

"What you doin'?"

She gave a little jump. J.C. was standing in the kitchen, right near the table. His expression was exactly like that she had seen on the faces of a group of people over on Franklin Avenue who were standing in a semicircle looking down at something —a mixture of puzzlement and awe and fear. Ordinarily she avoided crowds that collected on the street, but there was something so extraordinary in the faces of these people that she had stopped to find out why. There on the sidewalk, motionless, oblivious to the crowd standing back at a respectful distance, was a praying mantis. Now she thought, wanting to laugh, I must have looked exactly like that mantis to this dirty little boy; and he was dirty—his face, his hands, his clothes.

"What was you doin'?" he said. Awe still on his face.

"I was saying grace." He moves like a mouse, she thought. I didn't hear him come in here. "I was saying a blessing." No response. "Before people eat," she said slowly, "they bless the food." She thought he would ask why, but he didn't.

"Where to sit?" he demanded. He had moved closer to her, if he came any closer his nose would be in her soup.

Oh, she thought, as she got up from the table, this one time won't do any harm. "Sit there." She pointed to the place where Link always sat. "But wait a minute." She washed his hands and his face. He made no comment. "Now," she said, "you can sit down at the table."

She set a place for him and filled a glass with milk and handed it to him because this was as good a time as any to get him to drink milk from a glass rather than from a nursing bottle. He ate steadily, not talking, but making a rather musical murmuring as he ate, umh, umh, umh, umh. He gulped the milk down, polished off a big bowl of applesauce, grabbed three cookies, said, "Me gotta go now," and went out the back door, fast.

"Well!" she said aloud.

3

SATURDAY AFTERNOON and Jubine, the photographer, leaned way over the desk, bar, barrier, table, whatever it was that separated the girl behind the switchboard in the office of the *Monmouth Chronicle* from bringers-in of items about weddings and funerals, births and christenings, and complainers about misspelled names.

Jubine leaned way over and whispered in the girl's ear, "'How beautiful are thy feet with shoes, O prince's daughter—'"

The girl turned and smiled at him, thus she brought her face quite close to his and did not immediately move it away.

"Jubie!" she said. "I knew that was you before I looked."

"You mean the *Chronicle*'s bright young men no longer speak English? Is it that they speak in unknown tongues? I forgot. They all talk Bullockese—a fiery wrathful blasphemous language. Thus if Jubine even so much as whispers he is immediately recognized." He worked a cigar around in his mouth.

"Where've you been?" the girl asked.

"Oh, around and around and around. In circles. Back and forth and around."

"How come we haven't seen you?"

"We? We? You mean you, don't you? Miss me?"

"Of course."

"Why'n't you call me up?" He didn't wait for an answer. "Too busy? No telephones? No nickels to put in telephones? Or does the telephone company annoy you so you boycott telephones? How about dinner? Tonight?"

"Jubie, I think you're sweet. But I don't want to eat a sandwich at a wake. With or without you. Or on the dock. Or on the back of your motorcycle."

"Breakfast. How about breakfast? Sunday morning. Any place you say."

"Not me. I tried it once. Never again."

He sighed. "Can I help it if I keep believing that one of these days I will come across a small and lovely one with curly black hair, like yours, and dimples in the cheeks, like yours, and a mouth that suggests honey, like yours. But she will not

want Simmons mattresses and Toastmaster toasters and Can-
non sheets and Gunther coats and De Beers Limited will not
rate with her. She will want me. That's all. She will share my
pumpernickel and my pail of beer and because she can hold
my hand she will not want anything else. And she will look just
like you."

"What's De Beers?"

"Little one, you mean you haven't got that far yet? I forgot.
You're only twenty-one. But you'll find out. They all do."

"Jubie, you don't want a wife. You don't want a girl. All you
need for the rest of your life is a camera. And you know it. You
can't kid me."

"I thought perhaps you'd changed your mind."

"Nope." She worked the switchboard, fast, said, Yes, No,
Hold on please, ah, shut up you dope, no, fathead, Yes, sir, No,
sir. "Did you want something, Jubie? Other than to look at me
and practise using words?"

"Is the owner in?" he asked humbly.

"I'll see."

"You don't have to use the technique on me, sweetie. A man
that size wearing a camel-hair coat that color could not possibly go out without you seeing him. Besides the Bullock stamps
his hoofs as he walks and he exhales smoke and fire through
his nostrils. Or does he have a private staircase for emergency
use, just in case his past should catch up with him? Besides that
five-thousand-dollar-fob Detroit job is right out there at the
curb. Dead center in front of the door."

The girl giggled. "If he's in shall I say that you have some
pictures for him?"

"I am not here to sell him any pictures unless I feel a sudden
wave of pity for him. Which I doubt. You tell the Keeper of
the Gate that Jubine is here because Bullock sent for Jubine.
Jubine always comes on horseback whenever his friend the editor, owner, and publisher of the *Monmouth Chronicle* gets into
trouble and sends for him."

"Trouble? Trouble? What kind of trouble is he in, Jubie?"

"Maybe he's pregnant. That's why I came so fast. I want to
know, too."

The girl said, "Mr. Jubine to see Mr. Bullock," into the
mouthpiece and waited about five minutes, then she said, "All
right."

"You can go right in. But don't bait him, Jubie. He's not feeling so good today."

"Tch! Tch! He should live so. A big strong young man in a camel-hair coat, not feeling so good today. Now remember I had a head, two arms, two legs, and a torso, all intact when last you saw me go through yonder door. Grrrrrrrrr!" he growled, and blew her a kiss.

Peter Bullock looked at Jubine and thought, I don't know why I was weak enough to send for him, except that I've had to buy too goddamn many of his pictures lately, sometimes even had to call him up and ask him if he had what I wanted. Just that morning he'd been raving at the halfwits in the photo department, "What's the matter with you? That damn Jubine gets pictures. Why can't you?"

Even while he said it he was thinking, You can't pay a man to do what Jubine does, sleep in snatches, half awake even when asleep, eat where and when he can, ear always cocked to police calls, camera always close by, camera to be woman, children, home, life, sleep, everything. Had thought that and then decided, I'll offer him a job. And so sent for him. And here he was. So he offered him the job—head of the photo department.

Jubine laughed. He took the cigar out of his mouth to laugh, and then put it back in his mouth, lit it. Bullock had never seen him light it before, had figured that the one cigar lasted him a year or so, all he ever did was hold it in his mouth, not even chewing on it, just working it around.

He blew out a great cloud of bluegray smoke. "You know what I make a year, Bullock?"

Bullock shook his head.

"You guess. Sometimes for just one shot, I get more than you could afford to pay me for four months' work."

"I don't believe you. Whyn't you buy some decent clothes and a car? And live in a decent house." Jubine lived in a loft, wore GI pants and shoes, rode on a motorcycle.

"For what? My clothes keep me warm. My loft keeps the rain and the wind away from my person. And I am free. But you, my dear Bullock, you are a slave, to custom, to a house, to a car. You have given yourself little raw places in your stomach, little sore burning places, so that you cannot eat what you want and you cannot sleep at night, because you have turned so many handsprings to pay for that long shiny car, and you've got to keep on turning them so that you can buy expensive tires for it, so that you can buy the expensive gas that goes in its belly. It's a slave ship. Think of it—a slave ship right here in this beautiful little New England city called Monmouth—"

"Oh, for God's sake," he said impatiently. "Go on home and eat roots and herbs from the meadows, go on home and live naked in a cave, I wish to God I'd never—"

"I know, Bullock, I know," voice tender, voice all compassion. "I like you, that's why I enjoy talking to you. You see your newspaper could be so good but you can't afford to fool around with it because it would frighten the readers and they would cancel their subscriptions and the advertisers would get angry and withdraw their advertising and—"

"The advertisers don't run the paper."

"I didn't say they did. But they'd be fools if they didn't let you know when they were displeased, because of a story or an editorial."

"Bosh."

"No advertiser ever tried to keep a story out of the *Chronicle*?"

"You've been reading *Pravda*."

Jubine shook his head. "You mean to tell me that there is not left in your newspaper or in you even so much as a spark, just the faintest suggestion of a spark of life, that would disturb an advertiser? Not even an editorial that makes an advertiser register a complaint over the telephone?" He paused, eyed Bullock, said, "Do you know what history will record about you and your newspaper?"

Bullock didn't answer.

"Nothing. Absolutely nothing. Neither will history mention the city of Monmouth, as a place of interest. It will be mentioned only as the birthplace of Jubine, the man who spent a lifetime photographing a river, and thus recorded the life of man in the twentieth century. For the first time."

"In that case," Bullock made his voice dry, deliberate, "why do you waste your valuable time talking to me? Why don't you—"

"Because, my dear Bullock, I am trying to save you."

He walked straight into it. "Save me? Save me from what?"

"From ulcers and the fate of ulcer victims, from slavery and the fate of slaves, from whoredom and the fate of whores—"

"Get out," Bullock roared. "Go on, get out, and don't ever come back—"

"Wait. I have brought your Christmas pictures." He opened his shabby briefcase, extracted a large blownup photograph, blew on it, kissed his hand to it. "Look—"

Bullock held the picture a long time. He had seen the church all his life, but never quite like this. Snow on the ground, and in the background the river, the melted snow had increased its size, widening it, or else it was the angle of the camera, the wind must have been blowing because there were little rippling waves in the water, motion in the water, and the church was all slender steeple, going up, up, toward the sky. And a cloud, just one cloud far up. Church, river, sky, cloud, all of it timeless, ageless. Hope in it, in the sun sparkling on the river, on the snow, on that fragilelooking steeple that lifted itself up, and up, up.

"That's beautiful," he said, and sighed.

"Why did you sigh?"

"Don't start talking. Just let me buy the picture and then run along and save somebody else's soul. How much do you want for it?"

"Wait. I have something else to show you. Here. This goes with the picture of the church. You have just seen religion on the River Wye, man's aspiration, his hope, his faith, part of his dreams. But the river reveals many things about men. Here is despair written almost on the face of the river."

He shook his head as he looked at the next photograph. The river was in the background of this one, too, but it must have been taken on a cold night, and the river was black, ugly. It seemed to resent the dock for the dock was in the foreground, snowcovered, and the river had thrown a border of frozen spray along the edge of the dock, as though it had been spitting at it. There were footprints, a man's prints, and off to one side was the body of a man, flat on his belly, snow on him, too. His footprints were black in the white snow, water in the heel prints.

He handed the picture back, said nothing.

Jubine reached in the briefcase again. "I went back in an hour—and this is what I got."

You could see where the man had been lying, the imprint of his body. You could see, in the snow, how he had struggled, clawing at the snow to get on his feet, and then his footprints. He dragged his feet when he walked, the dragging unsteady feet had gone in a zigzag line to the edge of the dock, ended there. There were no footprints coming back.

"You mean—why didn't you stop him?"

"Stop him? I didn't see him do this."

"But when you saw him lying there in the snow, why didn't you find out what he was doing there? You must have known he was heading for the river."

"Me?" Jubine's popeyes widened. He worked his cigar from the right-hand corner of his mouth to dead center, worked it back to its first position. "Me? Am I the hand of God, Bullock? Should I interfere with the inevitable, the foreordained? Interfere with the doomed and the damned?" He made a gesture with his hand, as though he were rejecting the idea, pushing it away. "Not Jubine. Jubine watches. Jubine waits. Jubine records but Jubine never, never interferes—"

"I always knew you set these things up," Bullock said furiously. "Anything for a picture—even a man's life." Jubine reached over, took the picture of the church, and put it back in the briefcase. "Hold on. I want that one."

"All or none. These three pictures belong together. They must be printed together. You cannot use the church by itself. You see, I am interested in the immortal souls of your readers as well as yours. They are poor peons, too. And so on Christmas morning—"

"You couldn't pay me to put those other two pictures in the paper on Christmas Day."

"I was afraid you'd feel like that. Some day I shall become discouraged and I will stop offering you immortality. You are a stupid man, Bullock. These pictures will be reprinted, together, not just one of them, as long as there is any paper left in the world. They will become better known than the Mona Lisa, than a Raphael Madonna, and when I think that they might first have appeared in the *Monmouth Chronicle*, why I weep for you, Bullock. I weep for you."

He supposed it was childish, but as Jubine went out the door he followed him, and when he reached the little anteroom where his secretary sat, he said, loud enough for Jubine to hear, "Don't let him in here again. I don't want any more of his pictures. I don't want to talk to him on the telephone. Tell that cutie on the switchboard the same thing."

The irritation that Jubine had set up in him, hung around him like a cloak; it seemed to increase in size, until when he finally got home even the sight of his own home infuriated him. Lola sensed his mood, the instant he entered the house, and she practically tiptoed around him, and that made him angrier.

We live like millionaires, he thought, got to have a maid and a cook and a cleaning woman and God knows what else. The dinner table set up like it was for a banquet, lighted candles and flowers on the table. Good food, he supposed, and he had mashed potatoes and cream.

"Had a hard day, Pete?"

"Mmmmmm."

That took care of the conversation during dinner. Afterwards they went into the living room, and he thought, Rose-colored curtains drawn across the picture window, glass house, never throw stones when you live in a glass house. Cozy. Almost winter. Stage all set for it. The wife in black velvet, ankle length, fullskirted, gold something or other around the waist, the husband in tweed jacket, pants didn't match, pipe in hand, leaning against the fireplace, fire flickering in the fireplace, fireplace built practically in the middle of the living room, chimney part of the decorative value of the room, according to the pansy who selected the furnishings. Logs of applewood being burned, sold practically by weight, he ought to know, he paid the bill for the goddamn wood and wondered what the hell kind of world this was where you bought wood for a fireplace, when you burned oil to heat the joint with, but then you had a fireplace and you lived in a city so you had to buy wood by the piece from a farmer who insulted you even as he pocketed your money, and then pay a fortune to have it hauled here, and then you burned the stuff not to keep warm but to— Decorative effect. Hearth. Home. Siamese cat part of it. No children. Siamese cat took their place. Sat in front of the fire warming its behind and sneered. Lola's cat.

Lola was reading a magazine. He thought, I don't hate her. I think I do sometimes. But I don't. I couldn't. It's just the old war between the male and the female. Never resolved and never will be. I couldn't hate her. She's beautiful. A redhead. How the hell did we get here anyway? Why do I get so mad at her, at myself, at the goddamn newspaper, this house, even the wood, burning in the fireplace. It cost a couple of arteries but it burns smoothly, evenly, throws no sparks, stays lighted.

He sighed. Lola looked up, and he thought, she knows me so well that she knows it is now safe to talk to me, that I am now a human being again and not an animal holed up somewhere with a front paw caught in a trap, paw swelling, pain in it, animal crazy with pain, would bite off the hand of a would-be rescuer. Lola. In this light—red hair—

"What're you readin'?"

"*Vogue*. New issue. It's got the most marvelous photograph. Look."

She came across the room with it, stood beside him, magazine held open. He might have known. One of Jubine's shots. Old colored washerwoman. Taken, he was certain, right here in Monmouth. Looked though as if it had been taken in Charleston. Woman sitting on a stoop. Face like—he didn't believe any such face existed—face like a painting by an old master, master hand, a strong old face, tough, not tough in the modern sense, tough like leather, indestructible, would wear forever, a face that had seen all kinds of things, a face that had survived everything, a face suggesting what—compassion. He had the feeling that if this old woman looked at him, Bullock, she would feel sorry for him. And he thought, That's the thing about Jubine that infuriates me. It's not that rot he talks, it's not that he talks all the time like it was a compulsion, speech eases him, so he has to talk and talk and talk and talk; it's that he actually feels sorry for me. Why did I know instantly that this was a washerwoman, yes, sign right by the door, said Han Launderey, beautifully misspelled, and the old hands were out of shape at the knuckles and joints.

He handed the magazine back to Lola. "He's a goddamn Communist."

"Who?" she said, startled.

"Jubine. The world's greatest photographer. The crackpot who took that picture."

"Why do you say he's a Communist?"

"Because he's against wealth. Every time he gets a chance he takes a potshot at the wealthy."

"Well," she said hesitantly, obviously not wanting to get in an argument with him, and yet determined to show that he was wrong, "I haven't seen all of his pictures. But I can remember two of them that were anything but potshots at the wealthy. Those photomurals of the river in Treadway Hall, in the entrance hall, are just beautiful pictures of a river and that's all. And I remember that shot he took of the Treadway girl's wedding, the wedding party coming out of the church. It was in *Vogue* four or five years ago. And it was a honey."

"Yeah. He sold the honey to *Vogue*. Did you see what he brought me? He brought me the one with what he calls the peons flowing into and around the picture. He never says the people and he doesn't use the word peasants, no, he says peons, so you'll get a picture of enslavement, ignorance, racial mixture. And people don't know whether they ought to laugh or get mad. Yeah, he took the honey to *Vogue*, all light and shadow, the Treadway girl and that man she married, whoever he was, perfect down to the last jewel, the last cufflink, and stretching behind them the aisle of the church, partial view of the altar. I Thee Do Wed, so that even the impure and the dissolute will wipe away a tear when they look at it.

"But he brought me the shot with the peons crowding into the picture, one with no legs practically sitting in the bride's dress, squatting in the folds of the wedding gown, and the damn fool who does the society page fell for that torrent of talk that comes out of his mouth, 'Look at the light, the shadows, the tree branches forming a pattern, look at the contrast, the adoration on the face of the legless man, adoration, same expression on the face of the young groom—but expectancy on the face of the young bride—'"

"It was true," Lola said thoughtfully. "I remember it now. It was one of the pictures of the year."

"You mean you didn't see what he'd done?" He snorted in disgust. "Where'd the Treadway money come from? Munitions, guns, explosives. How'd the man lose his legs? Shot off in the First World War. Jubine wouldn't miss a bet like that. Contrasts all right but not in light and shadow. He probably paid that legless man to sit outside the church."

She said, softly, "I suppose it's all in the way you look at a thing."

"It is not. It's the way he arranges things, or waits for hours until they arrange themselves, to fit the pattern of his thinking. Why do you think he leaves Monmouth and his precious river every year to attend the opening of the Met? Because he likes music? Hell, no, because he knows he'll get pictures of the rich making fools of themselves, riding horses up the steps, taking their clothes off, or of be-diamonded horriblelooking old women with their skirts lifted, their lean shanks exposed, because they've got their old legs up on tables. He gets quotes, too, like the time that woman lost her tiara, he had her saying, 'I'm cold without it.' You notice none of his poor people, his peons, ever have their mouths open or their tongues stuck out or their behinds bare."

"But he does show them that way. He takes drunks and prostitutes and murderers and you look at the picture and you know what they are—"

"Oh, sure. But he always gives them dignity, even lying in the gutter. That woman who shot her husband, last year, looked like an avenger, a fury, not ridiculous or silly or simpleminded."

"Perhaps the poor have dignity because—"

"That's communism. That's what he's saying in his pictures."

"Wait a minute, Pete. I didn't say the rich were undignified because they were rich."

"No. But you were going to say poor people have dignity because they're poor. Jubine says that all the time in his pictures. And the rich sucker peons eat it up and pay him a fortune for it."

Rich sucker peons. "I always hope that some day you will realize that you are a poor peon like the rest of us. Then you will be a free man." Jubine said that when he brought him the shot of the old governor's funeral cortege. Oh, sure, the *Chronicle*'s flashbulb boys had pictures, but not like that one of Jubine's—death in his picture, grandeur in it, and something else that after one hasty glance made you think that you had been an eyewitness to the passing of the last of the aristocrats in government and you were left the poorer because of it.

He said, "I won't buy any more of his goddamn communist pictures."

And then changed the subject because with the female to whom you were legally wed you had to be very careful to avoid an argument, otherwise on a Saturday night you would find yourself sleeping alone in the less comfortable of the two guest rooms.

"What have you been doing all day, beautiful?" He ran his hand through her hair—soft, silky, fragrant. The cat looked up and blinked its eyes and he thought, It's a good house, it's a good room, it's a good fire. The cat? Ah, well, as a cat it is a good cat, as a substitute for male and female children it is a hell of a lousy thing. But as a cat it belongs in this room, like the fireplace, and Lola's hair.

"Love me?" she said.

"I love you. All my life I've loved you. And always will." He put his arm around her waist. "Leave us talk about you." He thought, Jubine's face suggests laughter, yet he doesn't laugh often. Why then? Because it is basically the face of a clown, with a few added touches it would be a clown's face; the potential was there, the mouth a little too large, the nose too prominent, the eyes bulged, the ears stood out, too big. Clown's face.

"Let's go up early," he said, putting his cheek down close to hers. "Gosh, you smell good."

When he turned out the light in their bedroom, he thought, Well, at least that pansy who picked out the furniture knew what he was doing when he put a kingsize bed in here, or maybe it was Lola's idea. And asked her, and she giggled, leaned close to him, then whispered, her mouth in the hollow of his neck, her mouth tickling him as it moved, soft, warm against the hollow of his neck, "Stalin thought it up—part of the Communist plot to hasten the downfall of the capitalist class."

4

AT MIDNIGHT, on the same Saturday night, Link Williams stood on the dock, leaning against the railing, waiting for Jubine. Fog was blowing in from the river, soft, wet, clinging, all-enveloping fog. He listened to the water lap against the piling. There was a southwest wind and it lifted the fog now and then, blew it back, lifted it, so that he caught an occasional glimpse of the river, of light reflected in it, could see stretches of the dock itself, then the fog would blow in again, thicker than before, billowing in from the river. When he turned and looked in the direction of Dumble Street, it was as though a cloud, a cumulus, was moving in on Dumble Street.

Fog over the river, fog over Dock Street, the street that ran alongside the river. He heard the chug-chug of Jubine's motorcycle, way down on Franklin Avenue, going slowly, visualized him, head bent forward, peering, trying to see both sides of the street at once for fear he'd miss something, miss the chance to photograph someone coming into the world, or just leaving it.

As he stood there waiting for Jubine he grinned, thinking about Abbie. She had been all upset at supper because she had found out that Mamie Powther, Mrs. Mamie Powther, was Bill Hod's cousin. Mr. B. Hod's cousin. He had been kind of jolted himself. But for different reasons. Cousin, he thought. Yah!

Abbie had been so upset he had felt a little sorry for her. But being upset did not prevent her from reciting her regular Saturday night lines. He knew his by heart too. So the whole thing went off smoothly. They'd been doing it for about two years now, ever since he had come back from the Navy, so that it was never necessary for one to prompt the other. His lines, her lines, unchanged, unchanging. The only variation occurred in the comments on the weather. In the summer Abbie said, "This heat"; in winter she said, "This cold"; fall and spring, "This wind"; and, of course, rain, snow, fog, hail, whatever form of precipitation fell from the heavens above:

"Those poker games—that man—you get in so late—"

"It's the shank of the evening—"

"Alone in the house—every Saturday night—hear noises—"

"Noises from the street—"

"Someone walks through the backyard—"

"Probably a dog—"

"Knocks over the ashcan—"

"Probably a dog—"

"You ought to wear a coat—this dampness—"

"Don't need one"—whistle, hum, sing "I got my love to keep me warm."

"Those poker games—that man—Saturday night—Dumble Street—the fog—"

He always let that one go without answering it.

"Dumble Street—not safe—people knifed—held up—robbed —this fog—"

"Unlikely—know everybody—for blocks around—safe in Dumble Street—safe as a church—my end of town—"

Why as a church? Why did he always say, safe as a church? Who was safe in a church? Safe from what?

"You don't go to church any more—you ought to go to church—I don't understand why—that man—"

He'd gone plenty when he was a kid, enough to last him the rest of his life. He could remember how church ate the heart, the life out of Sundays. He could see himself, washed and scrubbed and carrying a Bible, walking always within hand's reach of the white gloves Abbie wore. She carried a Bible too. They walked side by side, the straightbacked, small-boned woman and the reluctant boy, the carriers of Bibles. And down at the other end of Dumble Street, in the opposite direction, was the river. Every kid he knew was on the dock, near the dock, around the dock, drying off, sunning himself, diving in, swimming, loafing. And he, in Sunday School, and then in church, and the new minister's prayers were so long, so long, he closed his eyes and tried not to think, to go to sleep, and the voice went on and on, "Look down on us poor sinners, help us, oh, Lord—"

He opened his eyes and counted the panes in the nearest of the stained-glass windows. He stared up at the ceiling and counted the light bulbs in the chandelier, wishing that he could sit in some other part of the church besides the choir loft. Abbie sat in the choir loft because she played the organ

so he had to sit there, too, so he wouldn't "get into mischief."
He dropped the hymnbook just for the exquisite pleasure of
hearing the explosive sound it made, pulled his ear, wriggled in
his chair, and then slid way down in it until he was half reclin-
ing, then, remembering that Abbie could see him in the little
mirror with the oak frame that was right above the organ, he
would straighten up.

Sometimes he amused himself by wondering what would happen if he stood up quickly and dropped a hymnbook squarely
on top of old Mrs. Brown's head; she wore a squashed-down
black felt hat and it would be fun to flatten it a little more.
But he never did. It was fidget and twist and turn, put his feet
squarely in front of him, turn his ankles in, then out, crack
his knuckles, while he contemplated the long expanse of time,
limitless, never ending, and he in the middle of it, forced to sit
still, when he wanted to run and jump and whoop and holler
and land in the river, yelling, "Last one in is a horse's tail."

He tried to figure out ways of waging warfare, open warfare,
jungle warfare, leap from ambush, guerilla warfare. He would
declare war with a shout, declare war on Abbie, the minister,
the old ladies dozing in the front pews, the old men who sat
in the back pews leaning on their canes, the choir. He would
shoot the soprano just at dawn, she had a quaver in her voice
and buck teeth, and was always poking at him with her foot.
Then he was God and all the angels, he was Gabriel blowing
on a horn, blowing for the Judgment, and he was Ezekiel and
he saw a wheel and a wheel and wheels, he was Moses leading
his people to the Promised Land, booting his people to the
Promised Land.

He was never ten-year-old Link Williams trapped in the choir
loft on a morning when there was no school, when the sun was
shining and the air was hot and the river ran practically in his
front yard. So he lifted the hymnbook and sighted down the
length of it, then put it to his lips, getting ready to blow that
great big final blast for the Judgment, and then would drop it,
bang, just to break the monotony.

Every Sunday, after church, Abbie said, "For heaven's sake,
Link, why do you keep dropping your hymnbook? Sometimes
I think you do it on purpose."

The afternoons weren't much better. He was caged under

The Hangman, still within arm's reach of Abbie. She read the Sunday edition of the *Chronicle*, all afternoon, and he mostly sat around, restless, at a loss, until six o'clock. Right after supper he was on his own for an hour or so and as he took off his Sunday clothes, exchanging them for an old pair of pants and a jersey, he began to feel free. He went straight across the street, around to the back door of The Last Chance and into the big kitchen, knowing that he was just in time to eat with Weak Knees and Bill. Bill said, "Your aunt must have Jew blood. Sundown and the religion is put away for the night."

Weak Knees said, "Pull up a chair, Sonny, and start layin' your lip over this here fried chicken. I know you ain't had a goddamn thing to eat all day."

The putt-putt of Jubine's motorcycle had stopped, he hadn't heard it for quite a while. He must have found his picture though, because it began again, a staccato sound, immediately recognizable, despite the sound of busses starting and stopping, the clang-clang of the Franklin Avenue trolley.

The fog kept lifting and closing in, and he thought that the bleat of the foghorn kept changing with the rolling in of the fog, perhaps it was a change in pitch or in volume due to the shifting of the wind, first it was like a groan, on one note, and then it had two notes, now up, now down, Groan-sigh, groan-sigh, groan-sigh.

He could tell from the sounds that Dumble Street was all set now for Saturday night. It had passed the yawning, stretching stage, was now out of the house, wearing its best pants, razor-edge crease in the pants, clean shirt on its back, had long since patted its hip pocket to make sure the wallet was there, had adjusted its hat brim on its wellgreased hair, run its fingers over its just-shaved jowls, fingertips smelling of carnation talc and lilac aftershave for a good half-hour after contact with the jowls. It had long since taken stock of the potentialities, the possibilities, offered by this stretch of time, payday time, no-work-in-the-morning time, money-and-plenty-of-places-to-spend-it-in time, stay-up-all-night time and lie in bed half the next day, luxuriating in the memory of the conquests of the night before. Dance in the Dance Hall. Yes. Those that didn't want to dance were standing hipdeep in The Last Chance, just drinking and talking. He'd have to duck back in there pretty soon and check the cash register again. The Moonbeam would be packed right straight back to the door. There was, if you listened for it, a kind of hum and buzz in Dumble Street, later there would be fights and holdups and violence—largely unpremeditated.

Whenever the fog lifted he caught glimpses of the street, the harsh redorange neon sign of The Last Chance, the frame houses, the no longer used trolley track, could even see where the sidewalks were broken, broken by coal trucks and moving vans. He turned his back on the river, fog over it, so thick you couldn't see anything, wouldn't know it was there.

He heard the roar, the staccato beat, the putt-putt of a motorcycle. Jubine was getting near the dock; recording angel on a motorcycle, on the prowl, at night, hunting for death, the ones dead by their own hands, the ones dead by knife or gun in some one else's hand. Then motor cut off. Headlight cut off. Silence. He heard him walk across the dock, knew that he was standing still, trying to see the river.

"You're late, Jubie," he said.

"Link?"

"Yeah."

"Jesus, you must be wearing sneakers. You practising cops and robbers or somep'n?"

"The fog deadens sound. But it's a good night for it."

"A lovely night. Night for murder. Night for rape. Night for sabotage. Night for all the poor peons to cry, to wail, to gnash their teeth. The poor peons. It's the nights that get them." His voice soft, compassionate.

Fog all around them, lifting, swirling, now concealing, now revealing, drifting, intangible, wet, there, not there, touching their faces, touching their hands, cold and wet, warm and wet, soft and wet.

Jubine lit his cigar and the sudden spurt splash flare of light, brief, gone suddenly, illumined his face, revealed the popeyes which seemed to be staring at the match, cataloguing it, prying into it. Link thought, It's the face of a born snoop—got to know, want to know, got to see, want to see, ears that are big and out of shape, the mouth, well, the lips full, got to talk, see all hear all, talk about himself, the nose, a flare at the nostrils, as though the nose must smell all, too, and the hands big, capable, black hair on the backs, hands feel all. But the eyes were what held you, embarrassed you, bold bulging eyes that made no pretense of not looking, that couldn't get enough of looking. It was not the childlike concentrated gaze that stared without comprehension; it was the child's unwinking gaze with a lively intelligence added. His voice always came as a shock, it should have been a hoarse tough voice, instead it was soft cajoling—voice of a mother comforting a child, You're all right, I'll put cold water on your knee, and a bandage. See? It's all right now. Tender, compassionate voice, and so people turned toward him and he got his picture.

The fog lifted and Link saw him look toward Dumble Street, turn that inquisitive roving gaze of his down the length of the street.

"Don't you ever stop hunting angles, judging distances, measuring light?"

He shook his head. "You wait, you watch, you listen, and on a Saturday night in Dumble Street, you can catch 'em coming into the world, Sonny, and you can catch 'em going out."

They both heard the whine of a siren at the same time. Jubine said, "Ambulance. Franklin Avenue. See you later."

And was gone again. Link was fairly certain that the poker game was shot to hell and back but he'd wait a half-hour, and if Jubine didn't show up he'd go chew the fat with Weak Knees in the kitchen.

Standing there, leaning against the piling, fog all around him, river lapping under the piling, he could have sworn that the fog touched his face, his hands. He thought about Mamie Powther, hanging up clothes, reaching, bending, a younger shapelier browner edition of China—within hand's reach. Except, this time, too, except for Bill Hod. He was sixteen when he went in China's place for the first time. China. Yellow flesh, warm yellow flesh. "You wait," and he, believing, waited in the hallway.

China had been pale yellow and fat; her face, and he could see it again, clearly, would never forget it, the mouth and the nose pushed in, somehow flattened, even the eyes flat against the face and the whole face not wrinkled or lined yet giving the impression of great age, an old face, due to the thick quality of the skin itself, a tiredness in the eyes that made the face old.

Mamie Powther's face had a kind of energy about it, due to the firmness of the flesh, a decisiveness that touched all the features, the nose, the mouth, the eyes, the mouth was really lovely, the lips—well, you knew there were lip muscles there, it was a singer's mouth. The fog lifted, closed in, lifted, closed in. Fog. China and Bill Hod. China said, "You wait right here in the hall." And he waited there in the hallway, and he, believing, waited there in the hallway. Why did he remember it now? It was the fog, he was enclosed by it, and in that hallway he had suddenly got the same feeling of being enclosed.

The fog lifted, closed in, lifted, closed in, so thick now it was like smoke from a fire that had had water poured on it, clouds of it, white, thick, visibility zero, ceiling zero.

He turned and listened. Someone was coming down the dock, running down the dock, running at a headlong reckless pace. There was another sound too, a sound he could not identify, it seemed to accompany, to follow after, the running feet. The footsteps came nearer and nearer, a woman's footsteps, light, fast on her feet. And then the fog lifted a little and he saw a girl running toward him, a girl in a long full coat, running with a kind of frenzy that suggested she was literally running for her life.

He still could not identify the other sound, and he could not see what she was running from. She was visible and then invisible. He caught glimpses of her at intervals but he still could not see what was pursuing her.

As she drew nearer, he could hear the sound of wheels, small wheels moving along the planking of the dock. It meant only one thing. Cat Jimmie—that obscene remnant of a man was chasing a woman under cover of the fog. He wondered how he could follow the girl so closely, guide that flat board on its little wheels with such uncanny accuracy that he never once lost her; true, he knew the dock, he was always hanging around it, but there was always the chance he'd go straight into the road, because he used his arms, the stumps that were left, as though they were oars to propel the wagon. Nobody could see anything in this fog.

Now that he knew he was to look down, he caught a glimpse of him, the worn leather jacket, the stumps of legs, even the fierce gleam of his eyes. The girl still running, running, apparently so frightened that she could not scream. She was so close that he could hear her breathing, a quick gasping, painful to listen to, obviously too frightened, too exhausted to scream. How long had the damn fool been chasing her? He could hear the grunting sound Cat Jimmie made when he was excited.

"Hey!" Link shouted. "This way. This way!" The girl could not see him because of the fog but she headed straight toward the sound of his voice, reaching for him, close now, grabbing at him, holding on to him, clutching at his hand, his arm, her hand with a tremor in it, tremor all over her.

Cat Jimmie stopped right in front of them.

Link leaned down, said, "Get off the dock before I kick your face in," and thought, Even now, not seeing him, I'd know he was there, know exactly where he was, because of that grunting sound, fierce, excited, like his eyes, and because of the stink he gives off.

Cat Jimmie made a threatening sound in his throat.

Link said, "You goddamn bastard," and kicked at the wagon, aiming low, but not too low, thinking, I hope it's his face, and heard the wheels move away, perhaps a foot away, along the dock, and then stop.

"It's Link, ain't it?" voice hoarse, deep in his throat, then without waiting for an answer, he said, "It's Link. Thought it was."

There was the wheeling sound of the flat little cart crossing the street, and then it was gone. Link thought, Probably the only emotion that Abbie and I share, have ever shared, is complete and absolute revulsion at the sight of Cat Jimmie. I should have kicked his face in.

The girl was still gasping for breath. He turned toward the sound, impossible to see what she looked like, she could have been a wraith, a figure created by the fog and the river, insubstantial. He was fairly certain she was one of the clinker tops from China's Place. It's a strange thing, he thought, but that fat woman with the yellow skin managed to leave such a mark on her profession that all the houses run by all her successors, no matter what their names or what they call themselves, are known as China's Place, and the girls as China's girls.

He said irritably, "For Christ's sake, haven't you any sense at all? The dock isn't any place to be looking for business at this hour in the morning."

"I—" she said. "I—"

"I'm not buying any tonight."

She didn't answer, didn't move, stood there leaning against the railing, gasping. Her hand still clutched at his arm. The fog lifted and he got a none-too-good look at her, saw that her hair was either bleached or dyed a pale yellow, that it curled about her face. She must be new at China's. What the hell was a piece of crow bait like this one doing hustling on the dock on a Saturday night.

"Go on, honey," he said and moved his arm, not gently, pulling it away from her hand. "Beat it."

"I—" she said. "I'm afraid to."

"Ah—go on. Beat it!"

He edged away from her, moving quietly, thinking, This little lonesome gasping female can spread her loneliness around for some other son of a bitch to appraise and decide whether he'd buy and at what price. The girl followed him, not really followed him, followed the edging movement, her hand found his arm, stayed on his arm, clutched at his arm. And he stood still.

"Look, honey," he said. "Don't follow me. There's nothing that irritates a man faster than to be followed around by a little lonesome female wagging her tail, especially when said tail has a price tag affixed to it." She didn't move. "This dock belongs to me," he went on, "I laid down a claim to it, staked it out, and nailed it down a long time ago. You get off the reservation, honey." Maybe she didn't understand English. "There'll be no strike today." He took her by the arm and gave her a none-too-gentle push toward Dumble Street. "Back to the mines, honey. Back to those bottomless mines that China owns. When you get there you tell China I said I can still make up my own mind as to when I want it. I'm a big boy now. I can walk right in there all by myself. I don't need a convoy or a note from teacher."

"Don't—" she said. "Please. I'm afraid. I left my car two blocks away."

She was still gasping for breath, and he thought, Oh, what

the hell. I can always get her under an electric light, get a good look at her, and then take her by the nape of the neck and drop her in the river. "Okay, okay. Where'd you leave this car?"

They walked in the direction in which she pointed. He walked fast, purposely. Her footsteps, light, quick, kept pace with his though she almost ran to keep up with him, and she was still breathing too fast. She kept looking over her shoulder, peering into the fog. They walked about a block and a half and she said, "Here it is."

There actually was a car, parked under the street light on the corner. A long red convertible with New York markers. She quickened her pace as they approached it, and then fumbled with the handle of the door until he opened it for her. He felt the smooth coldness of the upholstery on the inside of the door, and thought, Ha, leather, and a special job, a newer model than the one Bill used to drive. I damn near wrecked his car one night when I was very young. That was the night he used his belt on me while he delivered the Irish cop lecture. Mr. B. Hod on Irish cops. It ought to be on a record.

She fished the keys out of her pocket, and then couldn't find the ignition switch, and kept fumbling for it. So he opened the door on the other side, got in, took the keys away from her, shoved the key in place.

"Can you start it now?"

"I guess so."

"Suppose you wait a minute. Here—smoke a cigarette." Let's know the worst before we get down to first names. He struck a match and held it after he'd lighted her cigarette, and kept on holding it, staring, thinking, What the hell kind of game is this, what is a younger fairerskinned thinner more beautifully put together edition of Mamie Powther doing on the loose on Dumble Street, at this hour. Her hair was pale yellow, soft, silky, curling about her face. Mother of God, he thought, what a lovely lovely face, a lovely frightened face.

"What brought you to this end of town at this hour?"

"I was driving past and I thought I'd see what it was like down here. I'd been reading about it."

"Well, you did," he said dryly.

"Not really. Nothing happened until—"

"Until you started running for your life."

"I thought I was. It was horrible. I couldn't see because of the fog but I kept hearing something moving behind me. It kept getting closer and I started to run, and the fog lifted and I looked back and I saw that cart, and it looked like an animal and I could hear it breathing and grunting and—"

"You need a drink," he said. "Come on." And got out of the car. Any woman who thought about Cat Jimmie long enough would end up with hysterics, and this girl was much too pretty to slap. Even Abbie, who usually managed to retain her composure, lost it completely when she saw Cat Jimmie wheeling himself along the street. He knew better than Abbie what probably went on inside Cat Jimmie's mind, could realize more fully the horror of being a fullgrown male, with all the instincts and urges of the male left, and no way in the world of satisfying them. Besides, he saw him oftener than Abbie did, saw him days and nights too, lurking on the sidewalk, near the bottom of the high-stooped houses, near doorways, at curbs and street crossings, had seen him lie flat on his homemade cart and moan like an animal as he looked up under a woman's skirts, had seen women turn away and cross over on the other side of the street when they saw him sitting on the cart, his back against the wall of a building. Everything about him was repulsive—the flesh on the stumps that once had been arms was red, angry, covered with scar tissue, purposely revealed, because he covered them with leather pads when he propelled himself along on his homemade cart; his shoulders were tremendous, overdeveloped. He was legless from the thighs down, and the same rawlooking angrylooking flesh was exposed to view on the stumps that were his legs. This red rawlooking flesh of the arms and legs formed a shocking contrast to the dark brown skin of his face and neck. His eyes were straight out of a nightmare—there was a red glare in them, there was excitement in them, and hate. Women who caught him in the act of looking under their skirts, moved away from him, horror on their faces, as though they had been violated, just by his eyes.

He could understand why this girl, walking beside him, through Dumble Street, past The Last Chance, still had a catch in her breath. The redorange neon sign was still on. It would be a couple of hours before Weak Knees put it out. He seemed to get a special satisfaction from turning out that sign, as though in doing it he extinguished the public side of the building and turned it into a home, private, comfortable, completely his.

They passed Abbie's house. He turned and looked back through The Hangman's branches, peering through the fog, and thought, No lights. Yes, there was. A pinkish light, dim, upstairs, in the back. He wondered if Mr. B. Hod was paying a cousinly visit on Mamie Powther, wondered how Bill and Mamie placated Powther, that neat precise little man. Maybe they didn't bother. Perhaps Bill stalked into Number Six, jerking the door of Powther's apartment open with that explosive suddenness that suggested a physical attack on the door, tied Powther in a chair, and then paid his respects to Mamie. He grinned at the thought of Powther in his neat black clothes, so decent and so proper, being forced to witness a scene that would be indecent and improper. Something about the size or the shape or the maliciousness of the grin must have reached through to the girl, disturbing her, because she said, "Did you say something?"

"No. I was thinking about a friend of mine who has a macabre sense of humor." A macabre sense of humor and no moral scruples. No scruples, moral or otherwise. No scruples and a strong right arm.

"What had you been reading about the dock that made you want to see it?"

"It wasn't just the dock. It was this whole section."

"The Narrows. The Bottom. Little Harlem. The Hollow. Eye of the Needle. Sometimes they just say Dumble Street. It all means the same thing. Where were you reading about it?"

"In the *Chronicle*. They've been running a series of articles on the relationship between bad housing and crime in this section. They used some wonderful pictures—"

Jubine's pictures. Cesar the Writing Man. Old Man John the Barber. The river. Franklin Avenue. Ah, well, he thought, it was nice to have known you and your yellow hair and your light sweet-sounding voice for these few minutes. But a female who talks about the relationship between bad housing and crime ain't for me. Abigail Crunch and F. K. Jackson have, for the last two years, been trying to tie me in the same room with one of those Vassar-Wellesley housing-crime experts. Most of them were put together all right but they talked and talked and talked about housing and crime, about Stalin and Churchill and Roosevelt and housing and crime and Churchill and Roosevelt and Stalin. And they all had names like Betty and Karen.

He had at various times lolled in F. K. Jackson's living room, upstairs over the funeral chapel, and said, Ah, yes, politely, or You don't say, No, I didn't know that, and he could tell by the expression on F. K. Jackson's face that she would like to kick him in the behind and couldn't and therefore her face kept freezing up and she kept thrusting out her jaw, and kept trying to lead the conversation around to dancing or Canasta and the little item from Vassar-Wellesley would keep right on talking about housing and crime.

There had been one who went to Bennington, too. The one from Bennington was a doctor's daughter from Washington, D.C., who most mysteriously and most illogically came to spend the weekend with F. K. Jackson. The doctor's daughter was one of those young brown editions of Marlene, the brown making for a little more voluptuousness, brown skin, smooth skin, lovely skin, and the doctor's daughter had long lovely legs, they undoubtedly started feeding her orange juice and Vitamin D at the proper age of six weeks, long lovely legs and a sweet little behind and we went swimming in the river, diving off the dock, and she could swim and dive and dance and sing and had a face like an angel. She was going to be a dancer, so she talked about the Czar and the Russian Ballet, about Stalin and the Russian Ballet and the Sadler's Wells and Bach and Beethoven. Dedicated. All of them were dedicated. They were so goddam grim about it he could only sit back and try to kid their pants off. The ballet one, when he kissed her, merely shook her head, and said, "I haven't got time for that sort of thing, Link," and she sounded just like a schoolteacher, gentle reprobation in her voice.

The most beautiful one of all was going to be an engineer. Why would the good God take the time and the trouble to put together a female in such a careful beautiful lovely way and then give her the idea of being an engineer? This one walking through Dumble Street with him, this one walking beside him, the one with the silky hair, was probably going to be a doctor or a dentist, maybe a veterinarian. A dentist with that hair would be something extra, "Hey, Doc, move your head, your hair's fallin' in my face."

This one was probably a doctor's daughter, too. The new aristocracy, the new black aristocracy, had been spawned by medical schools. "My father is a doctor," they loved to say it. Ha! Some day he would stare at one of the prideful little females who said that, and ask if her daddy made his pile peddling dope or peddling abortions.

"Do you go there very often? Down on the dock?" the girl asked.

"Yeah."

Silence again. Then she said, "It's foggy, isn't it?"

"It is foggy," he said solemnly. And now I will pay you back, you littlelonesome female stranger, I will pay you back for being interested in bad housing and crime—what was it you said—the relationship between bad housing and crime. Good God. "Yeah, it's foggy. It's a night for murder, a night for rape, or any other dark midnight deed that needs concealment."

Then he said politely, "Do you live around here?"

"No, I don't. I live at the other end of the city. I came down here to look at the river."

Down? he thought. This is up from the other end of town. Don't you know that uptown means us dark folks? That's the second time you've said that. And you don't belong around here, honey, or you'd know that simple fact, that difference. Furthermore, if you really lived in Monmouth you wouldn't be looking at the Dumble Street end of the river at two o'clock in the morning. You'd know better. If your daddy was a doctor, as I suspect he was, he would have taught you better. To the tune of the hickory stick. That's how they always teach the very young. Besides you lie in your teeth. You don't live in Connecticut. You've got New York markers on your car. Maybe you stole it.

They turned into Franklin Avenue. He said, "We can get a drink in here," and guided her toward the door of The Moonbeam.

THE MOONBEAM was crowded all the way back to the door. Standing in the doorway, he kept his hand on the girl's arm, as he looked around to see if there was even so much as an inch of unoccupied space. Yes, he thought, filled with people, filled with noise, blast from the jukebox, rattle of dishes, clink of silver, roar of voices; filled with smells, too, beer, cigarette smoke, cheap perfume, and smells from the kitchen, greasy dish water, unwashed icebox, strong yellow soap. Quite a mixture. Not too much light in the place, bluish pinkish light from the wall lamps, so dim it barely illuminated the big room, gave it the effect of a cave. Waiters hurried through the cave, bumping into the chairs, the tables, the customers, beer slopping over on the trays, the tables. They all drank beer because it was cheap and if you drank enough of it, you could get a slight jag on and if you got a slight jag on, the little floosey you'd picked up over on Franklin began to look like Marlene, and the thin straight legs began to look like Marlene's legs, and the toobig stuckout can began to look like Marlene's. Roar of voices again. People had to talk too loud, to shout, to make themselves heard over the racket made by the fans. They kept the fans going all the time, winter and summer, had to or the customers would suffocate from the smell, smells they brought in with them, smells indigenous to the place. Noisy fans. Noisy exhaust in the dirty kitchen.

It was a little too early for a fight to start, the boys really hadn't got enough beer under their belts. After you drank enough beer you would get a jag on and if you got a jag on you could convince yourself you packed a punch like Old Man Louis had when he was young and you said Joe and people knew who you were talking about. But Old One-One ran The Moonbeam and he could stop a fight before it really got started. He had been a wrestler and a stevedore and a weightlifter, or so people said, anyway he looked like Gargantua and he got his name from the fact that he had never been seen anywhere, any time, any place, with a woman. One of the Geechie boys from South Carolina named him Old One-One explaining that where he came from that's what they called the red-wing blackbird—the males and females gathered in separate flocks in the fall and winter, so that the male was always found without a female, only he was strictly obscene about it.

Old One-One was a dirty fighter so that even with a jag on, even having convinced yourself that you were Old Man Louis, but young and fast, a part of your mind would tick off a warning, reminding you of the stories about Old One-One, how he'd grab a bottle and smash it on the bar and go for you with the jagged end, or get out his blackjack, or trip you and once you were down, do his damndest to kick your teeth down your throat, so that even though you were fogged up with beer, once you saw Old One-One plowing toward you through the crowded noisy Moonbeam, you quit believing you were Old Man Louis and left by a side door, because part of your mind remembered all the business about smashed skulls and ruptured kidneys and ruined testicles.

The Moonbeam Café. It belonged to Bill Hod, like a lot of other places, though Link hadn't known it in the days when he was what the law calls a minor, and had sneaked in for a glass of beer, thinking Bill would never know about it. Old One-One belonged to Mr. B. Hod, too, like a lot of other people.

Link suddenly thrust out an arm, stopping one of the hurrying waiters, "Hey, Bug Eyes," he said. "Where can I find a place to sit?"

"In the back, Sonny. Go all the way in the back. All the way in the back. I'll squush some of 'em out of the way with a table."

Bug Eyes moved off, having barely looked up, balancing his tray, high up, arm bent stiff, hurrying toward the back of the Moonbeam, toward the bar. By the time Link and the girl squeezed through the crowd, avoiding tables, stepping over legs, Bug Eyes had a table in place, and two chairs, close to each other. "What'll you have, Sonny? What'll you have?"

"Well?" Link looked at the girl.

"Rye. With soda."

"Okay, Bug. Two. Double rye. Soda."

"Gotcha, gotcha." Bug Eyes was already hurrying away as he said it.

"What's your name?" the girl asked. She had been looking

around, at the people sitting close by, now she looked at Link and her expression changed.

"Link Williams." What's the matter with her now? She looks scared out of her wits. If she's got the nerve to wander around on the dock at two in the morning what the hell is there in The Moonbeam to scare her. All good sociologists study the critters at first hand, and true the place is noisy, and true the stink in here is terrific—but these are The People.

"Link?" she said it with an obvious effort. "Is that a nickname?"

"Yeah. A contraction of Lincoln." The Emancipator with the big toobig bony hands, the sad deepset eyes, the big bony hands almost always resting on the outsize knees, an outsize man with outsize ideas. Man of the people. Something wrong with his glands. Overdeveloped? Underdeveloped? All men free and equal pursuit of happiness—words on paper and he believed them. Emancipation Proclamation Williams. Named after him. Why? The women name the children, reward for services rendered, award for valor, for the act of birth, the act of creation. So the creator names the child. What did my mother mean? What was it? Act of gratitude? A way of saying thankyou? Or perhaps some of the males in her own family had been named Lincoln and so she, without thought, without real purpose, simply gave the name to her male child. Lincoln Williams. The name handed on without the trace of a recollection of who or what or how or why, no special meaning, forgotten, long since. Perhaps never known?

He was about to ask her what her name was, though he would have been quite willing to go on calling her Honey, but sometimes the female preferred, or at least pretended to prefer, to retain some trace of the amenities by saying I'm so-and-so, who are you, though what the hell difference it made, only a female would know. But Bug Eyes came toward them just then, moving slowly. He always ran. Link forgot all about the girl's name, wondering what had slowed Bug Eyes down.

It was the girl, the girl with the silky pale yellow hair. Bug was looking at her, looking at her in the most curious fashion, a covert, all-embracing, analytical stare that transferred itself elsewhere so quickly that Link would have been unaware of this swift appraisal if he hadn't been watching him. Almost immediately his eyes went blank, curtained, but something very like hostility showed in his face.

Link looked at the girl too, critically, analytically, and saw then what Bug had seen and wondered why Bug had seen it so quickly and he hadn't. He had talked to her, walked at least two blocks with her, entered The Moonbeam with her, consulted her about her choice of drinks, without seeing what Bug had seen in one swift glance. He studied her face. If it hadn't been for that wary immediate knowledge in Bug's eyes, there one minute and blanked out the next, would he, Link, have known that she was white? No. Why did the knowledge come to Bug at first glance and to him only now at second hand? Bug hadn't looked at the girl when they came in the place, or when they sat down. Bug was older, more experienced. Nuts. Because? Well, Bug had been born in the South, had lived in the South where his wellbeing, yea, verily, his life would depend on his ability to recognize a white woman when he saw one.

But how could he or Bug or anybody else be certain? He'd seen colored girls with hair as blond and silky, with eyes as blue and skin as white, as this girl's. The colored ones, the Vassar-Wellesley-Bennington colored ones talked just as glibly about crime and bad housing as this little female he had taken in tow.

Take Mamaluke Hill's mother, that is if you wanted to take something for some reason, she was just as blond and blue-eyed as the girl sitting beside him in The Moonbeam. She was the wife of the Franklin Avenue Baptist minister. When the Hills first came to Monmouth, first took over the Franklin Avenue Baptist Church, there was enough energy used up in head shaking and eyebrow raising to run a Diesel motor as people asked: Is she or isn't she? Mamaluke was a skinny brown boy and when Mamaluke's blue-eyed mother showed up at the grammar school on Parents' Visiting Day, the entire school was thrown into shock, because it didn't seem possible or reasonable or logical that she could be the mother of Matthew Mark Luke John Acts-of-the-Apostles Son-of-Zebedee Garden-of-Gethsemane Hill, known as Mamaluke Hill. For short. Mamaluke's pappy was a big black man who sweated easily, and shouted easily, too, you could hear him all up and down Franklin Avenue, every Sunday morning, shouting in a voice like thunder, about hell fire and damnation and the Blood of the Lamb, getting louder and louder as he worked up to a climax, and just before he got there, he took his coat off, stopping right in the middle of the preaching to take his coat off, telling the sisters and the brothers that he had just broken out all over in a good Baptist sweat. Hallelujah!

Mrs. Ananias Hill was colored but her skin was as white as the skin of this little frightened one staring at the glass of whiskey on the table in front of her. He thought, What in hell does she see in here that makes her look as though she were drowned in fear? She was staring at the people who were packed in around the bar and he looked too. Nothing to see but a lot of young men and young women draining beer glasses.

"What's the matter?" he asked. Because she was now staring at him in the same way. If she'd been under water for a long time, a month or so, and then slowly floated to the surface, she couldn't look more drowned than she does at this moment. "Are you all right?"

She nodded, apparently unable to speak, and he frowned. What the hell will I do with her if she passes out in here? Where can I take her? How explain her? And then—Is she or isn't she? How can I decide? How know? Mrs. Hill? Dumble Street said that Old Hell and Damnation Hill didn't know himself whether his wife was white or colored and snickered, playing endless variations on a theme—she was white as the Lamb and the Reverend Ananias was black as the pit itself. Abbie made up her mind about Mrs. Hill when Mamaluke was christened. F. K. Jackson went to the christening and came back and told Abbie about it.

F. K. Jackson: They christened him Matthew Mark Luke John Acts-of-the-Apostles Son-of-Zebedel Garden-of-Gethsemane Hill.

Abbie (long silence): No question about it. She's colored. (another long silence) What will they call him for—well, for everyday use?

F. K. Jackson: His basket name is Mamaluke.

Abbie (absolute outrage in voice): Basket name? What's that?

F. K. Jackson: A kind of pet name that they give an infant until such time as he's baptized and his christened name is officially fastened to him. They use the pet name lest an evil spirit learn his real name and turn him into a changeling.

He studied the girl again. White? Colored? Her hair had a wonderful shimmer but—so did Abbie's. He wondered what that pale yellow hair would feel like to touch. Was she or wasn't she? She had slipped off her coat and the dress she wore was made of some kind of dark velvetylooking stuff. She had a long thin senseless scarf about her shoulders, pale green in color, shot through with metal threads that glinted in the dim light. He wondered whom she belonged to and where she had been going in the longskirted coat, with that thin flimsy scarf around her shoulders. So he asked her.

"I was going to a dinner party and I changed my mind. I drove all the way to New York and then I changed my mind."

"Oh." Her voice, on the dock, had been frightened, her breathing a kind of gasping, but now, she was panic-stricken, there was a frantic hurried note in her voice, she kept repeating words and phrases, didn't seem to be able to stop talking.

"When I got in Monmouth I kept driving thinking I would find some place—where I could see the river—and then the fog kept getting thicker—the fog—thicker and thicker—I got out of the car at the dock and walked through some of the streets—and I read the street signs and I decided to look around—look around—but I didn't see anything much—the streets looked like the streets in any other city—then I came back to the dock and the fog was so thick I couldn't see—but I kept hearing—kept hearing—that funny noise—and it kept getting closer and closer—and—" Her voice broke, as though she were about to cry.

"Cut it out. Here, finish your drink and let's get out of here."

She picked up the whiskey and soda and her hand was trembling, and she tried to steady it and spilled part of the drink on the table, and then drank quickly, obviously not liking it, because she made an involuntary face, as though her throat rejected the taste of the stuff. And he, watching her, wondering about her, said, "Shall we go now?"

Outside, on the sidewalk, she said, "Oh!—the fog. It's still foggy," and the gasp was back in her voice. "Which way—I can't even tell which way we came—"

"I could walk it blindfold. Put your hand on my arm." He guided her through the fog, and he thought, She could be purple or blue in this fog, in this can't-see-your-hand-before-your-face fog. All cats are gray in the dark. B. Franklin. The cat would eate fish but would not wet her feete. When all candles bee out, all cats bee gray. John Heywood. White women is all froze up. Weak Knees. Quote from L. Williams? No comment. No quotes. L. Williams shared J. Heywood's opinion: When all candles bee out—

He said, "We turn here. This is Dumble Street."

"I thought it would lift, that the fog would lift, while we were inside. It's even thicker—what's that?" She jumped and looked back over her shoulder.

"Nothing but the foghorn. Car on Franklin Avenue."

She kept looking back as though she expected to see Cat Jimmie behind her, not see him but hear him. How the hell was she going to drive, drive through this damn fog, shivering and shaking? I can't go off and leave her sitting in that car on Dock Street, she'd be dead of hysterics by morning.

She said, "The fog—" And stopped.

He thought, the fog, the fog, the fog. She sounds like a record that's stuck. "Listen," he said. "It's even more upsetting when the weather or the degree of light changes while you're inside a place." That's fine, my boy, keep talking, talk fast, before she starts screaming her lovely little head off. "I remember going to a movie when I was a kid. I'd never been to one before. When I went inside the theater it was daylight and when I came out it was dark. It seemed all wrong. I thought time should have stopped while I watched the movie. But it hadn't. It got dark just as it always does."

When he opened the door of her car, she made no effort to get in. She said, "Would you—would you—like to go for a ride?"

"Not especially."

"I can't drive through this horrible fog—alone. I keep seeing that thing on the little cart, keep hearing its breathing, keep wondering if I'll be able to run any more—"

"All right." She started to get in the car, behind the steering wheel and he put his hand on her arm, thrusting her aside, suddenly bored with the whole thing, the girl, the car, the fog, the hysterics, Cat Jimmie, Dumble Street. "I'll drive."

He let her get in by herself, let her close the door on the other side by herself. Then he turned the car around, went through Dumble Street, past The Last Chance, dark now, turned into Franklin Avenue, went past The Moonbeam, still lighted.

"You've driven one of these before."

"Yeah." One of these, nice way to put it. Oh, you've held a tennis racket before, oh, you've worn shoes before, oh, you've used a toothbrush before. Bug Eyes is a weisenheimer but he was right. The lady is white. That surprised condescension in the voice is an unmistakable characteristic of the Caucasian, a special characteristic of the female Caucasian. The funny thing is they don't even know they do it.

Yeah, he'd driven one of these before and damn near smashed it up. When he was sixteen. That one belonged to Mr. B. Hod. Then when he finished college, Abbie gave him the Major's solid gold watch and the Major's diamond stickpin, reward for finishing, reward for the Phi Beta Kappa key that he had never worn; and Mr. B. Hod presented him with a brandnew shiny Cadillac convertible. Special Job. Bill said, "I didn't think you'd make it. Mark of respect, Sonny."

Abbie stood on the front steps and frowned at the car when she saw it, obviously not liking its size, its shape, its color, its make. Sun shining on the car, making the dark red finish glisten. "It looks like a gambler's car," she said.

"It is," F. K. Jackson said and sniffed, snorted, and the thick-lensed glasses glinted in the sunlight.

And now here with him, beside him, in the same make car, a female smelling of something exquisite. Flowers. Which flowers? The nightblooming stock that Abbie grew in her garden. At dusk the backyard was—well, not filled with the scent because there was always the smell of the river, but if you walked close to the flower border on a hot night in August the smell arrested you, challenged you, made you stand motionless, sniffing the air in disbelief. Your heart beat a little faster. Your breath came a little faster. Because you evoked images in your mind, of women, not short, not plump, not tall, not bony, but the height just right, the bone structure perfect, the amount of flesh covering the bones absolutely right, absolutely perfect. And for a moment, only for a moment, and it was, of course, an illusion, an illusion wrought of the moonlight, the white light, curious, unreal, mysterious light of the moon and the sweet thick incredible smell of the stock, you believed that if you reached out your hand you would touch a woman, not short and plump and erect and full of pride and untouchable because of morals and religion and impossible standards of cleanliness and righteousness and not tall and bony and nervous and too astute and alert, too logical and too masculine, but a just right, soft to the touch, sweetsmelling, beautifully put together female, with all the parts in the right place, never the look as though if touched, the bone that lay just beneath the skin would reject the hand because of the unyielding quality of the bone or that the flesh would reject the hand because of the righteousness, the pridefulness of the flesh.

The girl sitting beside him was silent. He glanced at her and her eyes were on the road, or what could be seen of the road, the fog so thick the headlights of the car couldn't cut through the white vapor. She was sitting with her legs crossed and he could see the sheer sheer stockings over the lovely ankles, the skirt flaring over the calves of the lovely legs. And he thought he had never seen one quite so beautifully put together—like a swimmer or a racehorse or an airplane, all the essential parts in the exact right place. Lovely.

The car had veered to the right, even in that brief moment in which he took his eyes off the road to look at her. It was a damn fool business to be driving on a night like this anyway, watching or trying to watch what he could see of the black line that was the center of the road, maintaining a thirty-mile-an-hour pace; he stepped it up to thirty-five. Not safe. Slowed down to thirty, slow steady pace. He became aware of the sound of the motor, hum, hum, hum, on and on, eyes on the black line dividing the road. Occasionally he glanced off to the right, toward the shoulder of the road, and when he looked that way the car went off to the right, seemingly of its own volition. Hum of motor, slow steady motion, slow steady pace, slow steady motion, slow, steady, thin black line in the center of the road, graywhite of the concrete barely visible, headlights not strong enough to cut through the fog, fog swallowing the lights. He shifted the wheel sharply to the left because for a fraction of a second he had gone to sleep, dozed off, watching that black line.

I've got to change this pace, he thought, go faster or go slower, sing or whistle or talk, or I'll go to sleep, hypnotized watching that black line. Go to sleep and drive smack into the side of somebody's house, drive right into the front porch, the sunporch, over the straw-matting rug they put on sunporches, right into the glider they put on sunporches, knock over the plants, crashbang as the plants go over, always have plants on sunporches. It's a little early for breakfast though. Wonder what the farmer in the dell would say if a gentleman of color accompanied by a lady not of color should arrive suddenly on the sunporch, driving right up into the sunporch.

Good morning. We came for breakfast.

Ah, but your colors don't match. We will not serve breakfast to a lady and a gentleman who are of a color, who have colors, one of whom is colored, and one of whom is not. Don't match.

They may all look alike in the fog, brother, but not under electric light.

Besides it wouldn't be the farmer in the dell who would give expression to his outrage at the sight of the unmatched colors of the male and the female encased in the red convertible. The farmer takes a wife. It would be the farmer's wife who would shriek and scream at the sight of them.

Scarlet woman! Whore of Babylon!

Say not so, farmer's wife, wife of the farmer in the dell. I found her on the dock. She was a lost and lonely one, a little running lonely little lost one on the loose on the dock in Niggertown. I am here by her invitation. It was not of my making nor of hers, farmer's wife. It was the hand of Fate. It was an Act of God.

I have not laid even so much as the finger of my left hand upon the finger of her left hand. It was, in fact, the other way around. It was she who held on to me, who clutched me to her bosom. She has a lovely lovely bosom. Has she not, farmer's wife? She would not let me go. It was not of my doing at all at all. I was merely the instrument, the vessel, the clay in the potter's hand and the potter turned the wheel, the little wheel run by Fate and the big wheel run by the grace of God. I saved her from a fate worse than death. Actually he only wanted to look. He could not walk, has not walked for years. But she did not know that.

You see? You see how it was, wife of the farmer in the dell? You ask the farmer. He knows about such matters. He will tell you. The old Adam left in him will immediately recognize the situation and he will nod his head and he will tell you, It was the woman.

He dozed off again, and the car went imperceptibly toward the right, way over toward the right-hand side of the road. He jerked himself awake. Jesus, he thought, I've got to talk or I'll be in a firstclass position to find out whether Old Hell and Damnation Hill was right about the blackness of the Pit. He glanced at the girl again, and then back at the black line in the center of the road. She had the concentrated look of someone contemplating the past or the future. It won't make any difference what I talk about. She won't hear me. She's looking into her own personal crystal ball. Well, honey, I'll take mine out, too.

He said, "I started to tell you about the time I saw my first movie." He paused. She didn't even turn her head, and that was okay, because he wouldn't have to worry about making sense. He could just talk. "I never quite got over it." Weak Knees was shocked when he found out Link had never been to a movie, "Name-a-God, Sonny, here's a buck, you go this afternoon, down to the Emporium. And buy yourself some chocolit to eat. Name-a-God, Sonny, a kid your age ain't never seen a movie."

He went to the matinee. Saturday afternoon. He couldn't remember much about the picture but there had lingered in him down through the years a faint echo of the excitement, the amazement that had grown in him as he stared at the screen.

"It was broad daylight when I went into the Emporium. I was only a kid. And I remember that I stopped and looked at the sunlight on the pillars in front of the place."

He had paused to look at the flickering, moving sunlight on the big white pillars. It filtered through the leaves and branches of the elm trees and because the leaves kept moving, the sunlight moved or seemed to. If he stared hard enough and long

enough he could convince himself that it wasn't the sunlight
or the leaves that moved but the pillars themselves, moving in
small irregular places.

It had occurred to him that the pillars might actually be disintegrating, breaking up into leaf-shaped bits, branch-shaped
sections. He thought about Samson pulling down the pillars to
which he'd been chained. He touched one of the big columns
with his hands to reassure himself. When those other pillars
came down, the ones Samson had been so tightly chained to,
they probably broke up into bits and separate parts like these
sunlit, moving pillars seemed to be doing.

"I touched one of the pillars. Because the sun made them
look as though they were moving. It was made of wood. The
pillar. It was an awful shock. I almost forgot that I was going
to my first movie. I thought those pillars were marble, stone,
that they would be cold to the touch. Instead they were wood.
Warm, almost yielding when compared to the feel of stone."

He had stared up at the column in utter disbelief. It mounted
straight up to the roof of the building. There were nine others,
spaced along the front at intervals. He couldn't help himself,
he had to touch each one of them. They were all made of
wood. He felt cheated, defrauded, and angry, too.

"I began to wonder if there were other things I hadn't
known about, other things that weren't what they seemed to
be. People kept going past me, in through the big doors while
I stood staring up at those columns, trying to figure out what
other things there were that were something else. It made me
furious to find out that a thing could look like something else,
not be the thing I had always believed it to be."

Freckled Willie Pratt came bursting out through the door
and grabbed him by the arm and said, "Hey, Link, come on
in. The pitcher's goin' to start. Mis' Bushnell just set down to
the organ with her music and me and Johnnie been spreadin'
across three seats in the front row tryin' to save one for you.
Come on because he can't keep spreadin' over three seats by
himself and somebody's goin' to grab one of them front seats
sure. Come on."

When he got inside the music was loud and strong, and everybody got quiet, and he began to get a prickly feeling all over
down his back. Then he forgot about the music. Because the

picture started and he was gazing into a new and wonderful
world, looking straight into it, and as he looked he became a
part of it. It was the kind of world that he had suspected must
exist somewhere, but here was the proof. The sight of it pulled
him forward until he was sitting on the very edge of the hard
wooden chair. He held tight to the sides of the chair because
he was afraid that if he didn't he would float off around the
ceiling, he had grown so light and buoyant. He had left everything solid and commonplace and ordinary that composed his
everyday world far behind him.

When the picture ended, the lights came on in the hall. Mrs.
Bushnell played some fast, lively march music on the organ, so
fast and so lively that the kids got out of their seats, fast, like
the music. There was a stir around him, feet scraping on the
floor, giggles, talk, scrambling for position, and then the kids
were plunging into the aisles. He was pushed out of his seat,
caught up, carried along, by the general movement toward the
door. He wasn't aware that he was walking or moving his feet
and legs, he did it automatically, without thought, really not of
his own volition at all. It was like sleepwalking, a trance.

"I went in the Emporium and it was daylight when I went
in. When I came out it was dark. It confused me because I
thought time should have come to a stop while the movie was
being shown. I kept thinking that somehow I had been leading a double life, my own life as the boy Link Williams, and
another far more exciting life. The fact that it got dark while
I was in the world that was the movie made the whole thing
very strange."

Afterwards he stood on the steps of the Emporium, shaking
with excitement.

He heard a woman say, "Good picture, wasn't it?"

A man said, "Sure was. The feller who climbed up to the top
of the ship was okay."

That was all they said about the picture. Someone else said,
"Think it's goin' to rain?"

They all looked up at the sky. Even the kids. He realized
then that for them the picture was over and done with. No part
of its glory lingered in their minds. But because all of them
were looking up, he did too. Far off at the edge of the sky, but

faintly, because of the big bright lights outside the Emporium, he could see the evening star.

It looked very small and faint and faraway in the dark sky. Yet the sight of it reassured him. That star could be seen in distant places. Someday, he didn't know when it would be, but someday he would see those places, those big cities with their easily found adventures. As he waited his turn to go down the steps, he tried to find appropriate words to express the feeling that had enveloped him while he was looking at the picture.

The only words that seemed to fit, that were fine words with a special high sound to them were "the power and the glory." He was shocked when he remembered that these words came from the Lord's Prayer. He couldn't quite place them at first and when he did he debated with himself as to whether it was proper to use them ordinary like that in reference to something that had nothing to do with God or the church or Sunday School.

He never did decide about the right or wrong of it. He had to use those words because they summed up how he felt about the new, fabulous, exciting world he'd just looked at, been a part of, could almost touch. A world of buildings, high up, with thousands of people moving around, of traffic so heavy it snarled up constantly, shifting, moving, getting hopelessly entangled and then moving on again. Ships pulled into a dock the like of which he hadn't dreamed existed and the city itself stretched out behind the dock for miles, with its buildings pushing up against the very sky itself.

"I never quite got over it," he said. "I made up my mind then that someday I would conquer the world—don't ask me what world. I believed that the only thing that would ever stop me would be the fact that some other guys got there first. I didn't believe that was possible. I didn't believe there was anybody as smart and as tough as I was anywhere, any time, any place. Or ever would be. So I would get there first. I would conquer the world."

"Don't you believe it any more?"

Her voice startled him. Oh, he thought, so you were listening all the time. I thought I was talking to myself. "Honey," he said, "I'm the day man behind the bar in The Last Chance. And

I'm perfectly content to be just that and nothing more. Any itch I ever had in my soul, any run-around I ever had in my heel, I lost when I grew up. You only get those world-conqueror ideas when you're eight years old. After that—uh-uh."

"Why did you feel as though you could conquer the world?"

"I don't know exactly. That was a long time ago and I was just a kid. All I remember is that I had seen a new world, found a new world, a new continent, and like all discoverers I decided to conquer it, make it mine. That's all. Kind of feeble. But that's the way it was."

"What was the name of the movie?"

The fog had begun to lift, he could see both sides of the road and he increased the speed of the car.

"That's gone, too, vanished down the long corridor of time. Like a lot of other things."

He stopped talking, aware that she was looking at him, straight at him, staring, really. Probably trying to make sense out of what he'd said.

She said, "I'm all right now. This is far enough. Turn around and go back."

He went on driving as though he hadn't heard her, driving faster and faster, thinking, She sounded exactly as though she were talking to a chauffeur. Home, James. Well, James had taken off his uniform and cap, James was now wearing flannel pants and a striped T-shirt and James was all set to drive to hell and back and had every intention of taking the madam with him because he wasn't working there any more. He had quit and the madam was—well—when all candles bee out all cats bee gray. Under electric light? No. Strong hot light of the sun? No. But in the dark, in the dark—

She said, sharpness in her voice, arrogance in her voice, something else he couldn't quite give a name to, not as uncontrolled as rage, but controlled rage, rage because the chauffeur was late, the chauffeur talked back, was impudent, impertinent, had to be put in his place, "I want to go back. Stop and turn the car around."

"This ride wasn't my idea, honey," he said softly. "But I'm beginning to enjoy it. So I plan to ride a long while yet. I'm afraid there isn't a damn thing you can do about it except go along, too."

It was so late that there were no other cars on the highway. On the straight stretches he shoved the speedometer up to eighty. He waited for her to protest but she didn't. Her hands were clenched into fists, and her body was braced, stiffened, against the seat as though against an expected attack. He kept following the river. He would drive forty more miles before he turned back. The girl still said nothing.

She's scared, he thought. She's scared deaf, dumb, and blind. She thinks I'm going to rape her. I'm due to rape her, or try to, because I'm colored and it's written in the cards that colored men live for the sole purpose of raping white women, especially young beautiful white women who are on the loose. How do I know she's on the loose? Well, what the hell was she doing at the dock? She'd scream for help if there was anybody to hear her, and there isn't, so she's braced herself, waiting.

He turned down a side road, parked the car, cut the motor off. The soft hum of the motor had been like a not-listened-to conversation, like a radio tuned low, you didn't pay attention to it until it stopped, and then you wanted to turn it on again, wanted the conversation you hadn't been listening to to continue because the stillness was disturbing. He heard the girl sigh, well, not sigh, but as she exhaled she made a small sound, anxious, afraid.

They sat in the car, silent, both of them, for perhaps five minutes. He was grinning, though the girl could not see the grin. She had moved so far away from him, must have moved away, slowly, imperceptibly, for he had been unaware of any movement, that she was jammed up against the door, had one hand on the door.

Then he stopped grinning because for one moment, one long incredible moment he wanted to, he wanted to— Heat behind his eyes, thick hot feeling in his throat, blood pounding in his ears. He leaned toward the girl, the perfume that was like the smell of stock drawing him toward her, the impulse absolutely uncontrollable now, like standing waiting, years ago, in the hallway at China's Place, waiting, and not thinking, not able to think. He watched her fumble with the handle of the door. Ah, the hell with it, he thought, and started the car —viciously.

He did not speak again until they were back in Monmouth, back at the corner of Franklin Avenue and Dumble Street. He said, "I wouldn't go sightseeing on the Dumble Street dock any more if I were you."

Then he got out of the car, slammed the door, hard, as though he hoped the hinges would tear loose, said, in a matter-of-fact voice, "Thanks for the buggy ride."

6

LINK WILLIAMS was standing on the dock again, his coat collar turned up, leaning against the piling. He had turned the collar of his coat up about an hour before, and even as he did it thought that no cloth had ever been woven that could deflect the icy wind blowing in from the river. Jubine, the photographer, stood beside him, facing the river, waiting for something extraordinary to happen, just as he did every night.

Link was waiting for something extraordinary to happen, too. He was waiting for the girl to come back, had been waiting, night after night, for two weeks, in spite of fog and rain and cold winds. He kept telling himself that it was illogical, it was against all reason, because no one would return to a place like this, a place where the night spewed forth creatures like Cat Jimmie.

Jubine knew that he was waiting for someone, looking for someone, because each night after he got on his motorcycle and adjusted his goggles, he always said the same thing: "Not tonight, eh, hombre? Ah, well, perhaps another night." And then was gone, putt-putting down Dock Street, going faster and faster, the motor making a sound like a series of gun shots.

At the end of two weeks, having stared at the river, having been stared at by Jubine, having listened to the foghorn and the hoarse hoot of the barges, having listened to the sound of the river like a mouth sucking against the wood of the pilings, having watched the big door of The Last Chance swing open, swing shut, having been wet, having been cold, he gave it up. On a Saturday night. Late.

He crossed Dock Street, heading toward the poker game at The Last Chance. At the door he turned, why he did not know, perhaps just habit, perhaps he turned and looked toward the dock whenever he was on Dumble Street, perhaps some sixth sense told him he would see what he had been waiting to see. Her car was parked near the dock. He looked once, made certain that it was the same car, and shoved the door open and went inside.

Mr. B. Hod and Mr. Weak Knees were getting ready to close up for the night. Jubine was standing at the bar, studying Old Man John the Barber. Bill had evidently booted everybody else home. Old Man John the Barber was nursing a beer, and watching Bill's every move, his lower lip thrust out, his eyes fierce under the shaggy eyebrows, one foot rested on the polished brass rail, the shoes discolored, worn, dusty. His suit coat, once black, was now gray in color, the back hiked up, the sleeves the exact shape of his arms, especially at the elbows.

Link said, "Is it safe to come in here?"

Bill ignored him, ignored Jubine's delighted grin.

Jubine said, "Sure. Safe as a convent. The boss threw a big peon out on his can about an hour ago and damn near broke his neck. A big Swede peon. And his neck made a lovely grinding sound as it very nearly separated in two straight clean pieces. So everything's fine now. Cozy. Homelike."

When Bill opened the door, opening it the way he always opened doors, as though he were attacking it, the clock over the bar said ten minutes to two.

"What you closin' up so early for, Bill? It ain't closin' time," Old Man John the Barber protested. "I ain't got a God's place else to go but here." He hunched over a little farther, blinking his eyes as he looked out at the dark cold windswept street.

Bill kept turning out lights. "Okay, Barber," he said. "You can stay in any of those Saturday night jump joints over on Franklin until three or four o'clock. By that time your wife'll be asleep and you'll have some place to go. You can go home. Okay, Barber, out you go."

In the kitchen, they waited for Weak Knees to brew the coffee. Bill Hod sat down at the kitchen table, shuffling a deck of cards, brandnew deck. Link and Jubine stayed near the stove, watching Weak Knees. He moved quickly despite his shambling gait. Link thought, They're all at their favorite occupations. Jubine is measuring the light in here, measuring it with his eyes, eyes half closed as he studies Weak Knees. Mr. W. Knees has the dedicated look of a high priest, performing his rites, stove serves as altar, big copper hood over the stove, gives it the gleam and the apartness of an altar. Mr. B. Hod is listening to the music of the cards, swish-slish, swish-slish, fast motion, too fast, eye cannot follow but ear can hear.

Kitchen now filled with the fragrance of fresh-brewed coffee. Funny thing, both gentlemen tried hard, did their damndest, to hand their heart's true love on to me—but I wasn't built for it. I still can't make a deck of cards swish-slish like that. And I can't cook. They worked at it though. I used to polish that copper hood when I was a kid, stand on top of the stove, fire out, pink outside sheets of a tabloid newspaper on the stove for me to stand on, so that I always had pictures of bigbosomed cuties under my feet as I rubbed and rubbed the copper. Had to put a chair on top of the stove to reach the top of the hood. L. Williams, the acrobat-acolyte. Liked the job, too, liked the glow and the gleam of the copper, stood on the chair, way up high, and turned to look down at the pots and pans hanging on the wall, liked the glow of them, too, the glow and the gleam. Acrobat-acolyte standing on a chair polishing the copper hood. But Mr. W. Knees said I'd never make a chef-cook. And I didn't. Heart not in it. Swish-slish of the new deck. Heart not in that either. Girl with pale blond hair looking for the acolyte at the dock. He grinned. Heart in that though.

Jubine said, "Now what canary have you just eaten, Sonny?"

He grinned again because he couldn't help it. "I haven't yet. But I will, Bud. I have only just got the lovely creature within gunsight."

"Come on, let's get the game started," Bill said. "You guys mess around too much. We haven't had a decent game for two weeks. Sonny's got to watch the river, hunting canaries. Jubine's got to run to a fire or a wake or a suicide."

"I'm always right here, Boss. Ready, willin' and able," Weak Knees said. "I ain't never cut the heart outta the game by not showin' up."

Bill said, "Yeah, you're here when you're not cuttin' the heart out of the game by trying out a new kind of spaghetti."

"That last one was good," Weak Knees' voice, normally high-pitched, dropped a whole register, it had a note of reverence in it. "Best spaghetti I ever laid my lip over. Had salt pork and mushrooms in it. I never done it like that before. And about a peck of parsley. Some American white lady brought that receipt over from Brussels. She got it from a Eyetalian chef-cook. Say, where is Brussels?"

"In Belgium," Jubine said. "When you going to make it again?"

"If I'da been that Eyetalian chef-cook I never woulda give that receipt away. Never tasted nothing like it before. Make it again? Let's see. I'll be makin' that Belgium Eyetalian spaghetti again on Saturday. This Saturday comin' up. I'll make it for after the poker game. Sonny, you goin' to be here for the game or are you goin' to be chasin' canaries around on the dock?"

Link said, "I'll let you know."

Weak Knees frowned. "I never knew they had no canaries around the dock. I ain't never seen none."

Jubine laughed. "You're too old to see 'em. You got to be about twenty-six, like Link. You got to have a build straight from the Greek, like Link. And you got to have one of those Pied Piper speaking voices, like Link. Even at that he only sees 'em when there's one of those London fogs blowing in from the river." He laid his hand on Weak Knees' arm. "Listen, Weak Knees," he said, "make the spaghetti this coming Saturday. Game or no game. And save some for me. I'll stop by for it."

"Okay, Jubie. I'll save half the pot for you. I don't know how that Eyetalian could have give that receipt away."

"If he hadn't given it away you wouldn't know about it," Jubine said.

"Yah-yah—yah. I know that. But he coulda made himself a multonmillionaire just with that one receipt."

Jubine made a sound of derision, "Then he'd of had to come to the United States, that is if he was going to be a spaghetti millionaire. And he'd of spent so much time worrying about his income tax, and his labor problems, and the shortage of salt pork and the shortage of mushrooms and the high cost of everything that he wouldn't be able to sleep at night for worrying. And all that worry would give him little sore places in his stomach and he wouldn't even be able to eat his own spaghetti any more. But he passes the receipt along and a lot of people eat his good spaghetti and they're grateful to him and he can eat anything he wants to, and he gets in his big soft bed every night and goes straight to sleep, because there's nothing in his life to give him nightmares—no CIO, no shortages—"

Weak Knees said stubbornly, "There ain't no shortage of salt pork. There never is because most chef-cooks don't know nothin' about usin' it."

Jubine said, "Sure, sure. But if some scientist should find out it's got some big important vitamin in it like in liver then everybody in America would start using it and then there'd be a shortage. Besides if everybody in this country started buyin' this new spaghetti dish made with salt pork in it why then there'd surely be a shortage—"

Bill said, "For the love of God, will you guys stop that yak-yak and cut for the deal?"

He waited on the dock again Monday night. The air was crisp, cool, clear. He could see the whole length of Dumble Street, and he looked at it and found it good, thinking of it as the street in which he grew up, the street in which he had gone through the seesaw process of reaching manhood, let go of something, hold on to something else, learning, growing, until finally he grew all the way up. Or had he? Or did anybody? Ever?

It was midnight when he saw her car, coming slowly along Dock Street. He watched her as she got out of the car and crossed the road. She walked as though she had always owned the world, and always would own it and knew it. This time she was wearing a suit, a gray flannel suit. She had a striped scarf, vivid green stripes, knotted around her throat. Her footsteps were quick, light. Brown shoes on her feet. And the legs—legs like Dietrich, only better. Actually.

"Hello," she said. There was a sparkle in her eyes, animation in her face, in her voice, a smile kept coming and going around her mouth.

Well, he thought, this is what you wanted to know. This is what she looks like when she's not been frightened half to death.

"Hello, yourself," he said.

"I've been looking for you."

She was standing quite close to him now. He thought, again, the perfume she uses smells like stock on a hot night in August, when there's a full moon—only not as direct and uncomplicated as stock, sweet, yes, but more elusive so that you want to get closer and closer, so that you can keep on smelling it.

"Yeah, I know. I saw you."

"You saw me? You—well—why didn't you let me know that you saw me?"

"Because every night for the last two weeks I waited for you. Right here. On the dock. And some nights it rained, and some nights there was fog, and some nights it was cold enough to freeze the tail off a brass monkey. So—" he patted her arm, "I decided it was your turn to wait."

"Oh."

She was almost pouting, the way a spoiled and arrogant child pouts when you tell him he can't have the fifteenth lollipop. He wondered how she would express her displeasure.

To his surprise she said, "Would you like to go for a ride?"

"No." Pause. "Thank you."

"Well, is there some place where we can go and talk? Perhaps that place where we went before?"

"The Moonbeam?"

"Is that what it's called? It doesn't exactly suit it, does it?"

He let that one go. The Moonbeam Café. Where else would he take a white girl, in Monmouth, at midnight? They would not be stared at, but looked over, carefully, covertly, in The Moonbeam. He took her there before. But he had taken it for granted that she was a high yaller. He couldn't half see in the fog, couldn't half see in The Moonbeam. It wouldn't have occurred to him that the girl was white, not then, anyway, if it hadn't been for the way Bug Eyes looked at her. If he had known she was white, would he have taken her there, anyway? Where else? What kind of race discrimination was he practising here in his thinking? Why was he reluctant to take her there now? He would be reluctant to take any girl there, white or colored, if he wanted to talk to her, to listen to her talk, wanted to go dancing with her, to— He simply did not want to sit in the smoky cave-like interior of The Moonbeam, to try to talk over or under the noise, to be surrounded by a lot of people, all talking, all looking at them, all conjecturing about them, while the jukebox bleated out a song about old lost loves and undying hates and my man gone.

"All right," he said. "We'll go to The Moonbeam and drink beer. If we drink enough of it we'll begin to believe we're somewhere else."

"Wait," she said. "I want to tell you something."

"Well?" She didn't say anything, and he said, "Go on. What is it?"

"That night," she started and then stopped, began again. "That night when I was on the dock, well, I couldn't see anything because of the fog. But once, when it lifted, I caught a glimpse of that creature propelling himself along on that little wagon. I thought I'd never get my breath back. I ran and ran and ran and the thing on the wagon kept getting nearer and there was a smell, an odor, like in the zoo. Or at the circus. And I knew it came from that thing chasing me—on the cart—"

"Wait a minute. What're you going all over this for?"

"I have to. I have to explain something to you."

"You sound as though you were getting ready to explain yourself into a fancy case of hysterics. Or do you enjoy scaring yourself?"

"I'm not scared any more. I have to tell you this. Keep quiet and listen until I've finished."

He lifted an eyebrow and whistled. Then he said, softly, in a singsong voice:

> Come when you're called
> Do as you're bid
> Close the door gently
> Never be chid.

"I'm sorry," she said quickly. "I didn't mean that the way it sounded. But if you keep interrupting, I'll never finish. And I have to tell it this way or you won't understand."

"All right. Go ahead."

"I—I couldn't see where I was going. Not in the fog. It was like a nightmare, trying to run away from something horrible, having to run, knowing that unless I ran and kept running that evilsmelling thing would finally overtake me. It was like running blindfolded, run and run, and not be able to see where you're going—"

"So you ran," he said dryly.

"Yes!" she said, anger in her voice. "I ran. You don't know what it was like so you can stand there safe and superior because you've never been afraid of anything in your life."

"Afraid of anything? Never been afraid of anything? But of

course I have. Go on. I won't say anything until you've finished." She was silent and he prompted her. "You ran and then what?"

"Then you said, 'Hey!' I ran toward you, head on at you, not you, but your voice. I knew if I could reach the spot where your voice came from I'd be safe. The fog lifted a little and I could see that you were big enough and strong enough and young enough to fight off that thing, whatever it was, on the cart."

Then she said, her voice slowing, "I couldn't see very well because I was so frightened and because of the fog. I wanted to keep holding on to your hand and your arm, stay within hearing of your voice, and there was a clean good smell about you. I knew that you were trying to make me go away from you. I don't know what you said. It didn't make sense. But I knew, no matter what you said to me, that I wasn't going to walk through that fog, alone, to reach my car. The foghorn kept blowing, blowing. For all I knew that thing on the cart might be waiting for me, waiting in the fog. The foghorn said so, the river said so, over and over, 'Get you, get you, get you.' It wasn't until I sat down in that place, in The Moonbeam—" She stopped, started again. "You see, I didn't know you were colored. When we got inside The Moonbeam, when we sat down and I looked around and saw all those colored people I was—I began to get frightened, all over again. Then I saw that you were colored too. I couldn't get the confusion out of my mind. I don't know what I thought—"

"But you came back here, anyway?"

"Wait," she said. "You asked me again, there in that place, how I came to be on the dock, and it was the same voice. The voice that I had refused to leave, couldn't have been pried loose from there on the dock. And I kept telling myself, You didn't know he was a Negro and you clung to him, clung to him, because his voice said, You're safe with me, safe, safe, safe, safe. Not in words. You didn't put it in words. I couldn't understand what you were talking about, something about China, but I could understand the clean clear enunciation, the resonance, the timbre— It was a perfectly beautiful speaking voice and it belonged to a colored man. I had to try to match that voice that meant safety with your being colored and I couldn't. In the fog, when I couldn't see, I clutched at you, because all I had to go on was the sound of your voice and the feel of your arm, the long smooth muscle in the forearm, a man's arm, hardfleshed, a man's hand, strong, warm, the skin smooth. Yet the hand and arm belonged to a colored man.

"Then the waiter, the one you called Bug Eyes, stared at me, a long hard stare. His face had been friendly, laughing, a simple peasant face, when you spoke to him about finding us a place to sit. I thought he looked like a South European peasant except that his skin was so dark. When we were sitting at that little table he looked at me and his face changed right before my eyes. It became a closed hostile face, complex and dangerous. I looked around and all of them were staring at me, all their faces were like the waiter's face, closed, hostile.

"I tried to get up, to get out of there, and I couldn't move. My knees wouldn't work, my legs wouldn't function. I knew that even had I been able to stand up I couldn't have walked through that noisy smoke-filled room. And your face had changed, too. It wasn't hostile, but there was something there, something that hadn't been there before, a kind of disdain and a puzzlement.

"When we left there was the fog outside, waiting. It was worse than before. I knew I couldn't drive alone through that fog because I would imagine that wagon was just behind me, always getting a little nearer. I thought that if you got in the car with me, rode around with me for half an hour or so I'd be able to get myself back together. Yes, you were colored but you were the only normal, clean, known creature anywhere in that fog—and you see—you cling to, hang on to, whatever represents safety—security—and—"

She seemed to be waiting for him to say something but he couldn't. He felt a curious kind of anger. He wanted to say, Well, what did you come back for? Do you know what you have just said, what you really said—

The girl said, "When I told you to turn around and you kept on driving I thought, What'll I do, what'll I do. When you finally stopped and parked the car, I thought the same thing, What'll I do, what'll I do? I can't run any more. I can't scream, there's nothing left in me to scream with, there's nothing left to fight him off with. I thought, No, impossible, a man with a voice like that couldn't— Then when you drove the car back to Monmouth and got out, I felt relieved.

"Afterwards I began to be ashamed of myself, ashamed that I had thought, Yes, he's a Negro but there isn't anyone else to protect you and therefore he is good enough for that, ashamed of the whole thing. So I came back."

"Because?"

"Because I wanted to thank you and I felt I owed you an explanation, an apology. And I wanted to know you better."

"Know me better?"

"I thought we could be friends," she said timidly.

"You came back here, to the dock, where you had been so badly frightened?"

"Of course I came back. I planned to keep on coming back until I found you here again. It was the fog that terrified me. I couldn't see anything, couldn't see where I was going. There's nothing here to frighten anyone on a clear night like this."

You're wrong there, honey, he thought, and this is a damn queer way to start a friendship. Friends. Ha!

"Friends, it is," he said. "Shall we go drink beer in The Moonbeam to celebrate the Emancipation? Even though the sight of all those colored people left you limp?"

She looked so completely bewildered that he laughed and said, "Don't try to figure it out. You're much too beautiful to think. Leave us go wet our whistles."

So once again they walked through Dumble Street, quiet now, Monday night quiet, wind from the river, smell of the river, clang-clang of trolley car in the distance, whine of siren somewhere, far off, faint, in the heart of the city, rumble of a truck on Franklin Avenue, lights still on in The Last Chance, the harsh redorange of the neon sign turning a patch of the sidewalk a paler redorange. He looked back at Number Six and saw a pink light upstairs where the Powthers lived, dimly, through the branches of The Hangman. No light downstairs where he and Abbie lived and had their being.

They turned into Franklin Avenue. "Say," he said. "What's your name?"

"Camilo Williams."

"Williams?" he said startled.

"Williams."

That, he thought, I don't believe. Camilo? Yes. Because it's somehow right. Williams? No. You had it all made up, ready to hand, no, you didn't, you handed it out quickly because you weren't ready for that particular question at that particular moment, but you had to have a last name, at least folks do in most circles, so you grabbed at that one. You've probably forgotten that it's my last name, too. For some reason your own last name, your real name, whatever it is, won't do.

They were in front of The Moonbeam when she said, "Oh, look!" and pointed at a man who was kneeling on the sidewalk.

If the girl had not stopped to watch Cesar the Writing Man, Link would have walked past him, because he had seen him so many times, watched him so many times, that he knew his every motion, every change of expression. Cesar always bowed toward the East, making an obeisance that should have been ridiculous and wasn't, then opened the cigar box, put on his glasses, and began writing on the sidewalk. He wrote with a kind of fury, pausing now and then to select a piece of colored chalk from the cigar box, adding the curlicues, the decorations, the little adornments to the capital letters as he went along.

And now Cesar glanced at them, glanced away, made his obeisance, and started writing on the sidewalk. Link wondered how he managed to look so clean when he always wore the same clothes—a heavy brown sweater, gray tweed knickers, dark gray golf hose. The bulk of the sweater, the blouse of the knickers suited his lean wiry build.

The girl stood back a little, as though she were watching an artist at work in oil or watercolor, and was respecting his right to the privacy necessary for the act of creation. She made no effort to read what he was writing until he had finished.

After Cesar removed his glasses, he arranged the blue and red and green chalk in the cigar box, closed the cover. He made another obeisance toward the East and somehow managed to look like a Mohammedan bowing toward Mecca. Then he was gone, walking down Franklin Avenue, with his lithe quick gait, the cigar box under his arm.

The girl leaned over and read what he had written on the sidewalk, reading it aloud: "Is there anything whereof it may be said, See, this is new? It hath been already of old time, which was before us. Ecclesiastes I:10." She leaned over a little farther, studying the curlicues, the flourishes, and decorative lines that adorned the writing.

"What does it mean?" she asked. "Why did he write it?"

"Mean?" Link repeated. "Why I suppose it's a kind of admonishment, a small sermon written on the sidewalk, for the benefit of anyone who stops to read it. He could have been describing The Moonbeam, saying that there have always been places like it and that there always will be. Or he may have been telling you or anyone else that no matter what your troubles or your worries or your pleasures or your delights may be, other people have experienced the same thing before and will again. As to why he wrote it—who knows? He's been writing verses on the streets and sidewalks of Monmouth for years—Eastside, Westside, Uptown, Downtown. He calls himself Cesar the Writing Man."

She said, softly, as though to herself, "It hath been already of old time, which was before us."

Then they were standing inside the door of The Moonbeam. It was filled, even now, on a Monday night, with a goodsized crowd, filled as usual, every night, with the oversize bleat of the jukebox. In all these places, Link thought, they play the same song, a different record, and a different singer, and perhaps a different tune, but the same song about lost loves and old hates, violent love, blue violent love, the man gone, gone, gone, sung in a blurred fuzzy voice, not sung but moaned, pain in it, regret in it, a wail in it. The young men and the young women sitting at the tables, leaning against the long bar, looked as though they had been thinking about the man gone, the woman lost, remembering the old loves, the old hates, for the last hundred years.

While he stood there looking down the length of the big dimly lit room, he began to think about China and the smell of incense, about Bill Hod and China, about Bill Hod and Mamie Powther.

Bug Eyes approached them, hurrying, tray balanced on the palm of his hand, tray held high. He smiled at them, said, spontaneously, "I gotcha a nice table, this time, 'bout midway. Gotcha a nice table."

It was, Link supposed, a nice table. The nearest arms and legs and ears were about three feet away. So they could talk, if they wanted to, without including six or seven others in the conversation. Whenever he looked at the girl, at the passionate lovely mouth, the deepset blue eyes, the arched eyebrows, the pale yellow hair that had a silky shimmer even in the dimly lit interior of The Moonbeam Café on Franklin Avenue, he was aware of a thickness in his throat that would have interfered with any words he might have said. What, he thought, does one say to a white female who has expressed horror at the thought of having laid her hand on the arm of a Negro? Her reaction to him, Link Williams, and "to all those colored people" had been exactly the same as her reaction to the repulsive creature who had chased her through the fog. Cat Jimmie on a cart equals terror, equals drowned-in-fear. All those colored people in a beer garden equals terror, equals drowned-in-fear. Link Williams, once one knows he is colored, also equals terror, equals drowned-in-fear. Equals friendship? Highly implausible. Come to think of it, what in hell had she expected to find on the Dumble Street Dock, in a beer garden on Franklin Avenue? Polar bears, maybe? You see some of Jubine's pictures somewhere, so you think you'll find Old Man John the Barber and he will not look like a Negro, he will look like an etching by Rembrandt, and therefore all the colored people who live in this area will look like etchings by Rembrandt, only they don't, they look like a whole mess of colored people, and they talk with their mouths, and they pour beer down their throats, and they move around, and their clothes look all wrong to you, and their voices sound all wrong to you and my voice was okay until you saw the color of the skin on my face, color of the skin on the outside of the throat from which the voice issued. Ha!

He ordered beer. She didn't drink it. She looked at the glass that Bug Eyes placed in front of her, and then sat forward, leaning her elbows on the table.

She said, "Tell me what you do, where you've lived, and how. I want to know everything about you. Were you in the war?"

"In the Navy. Censor. Navy installation. Hawaii. I read all the guys' letters. Read I love you, misspelled in all the known ways and some new and unknown ways, read I love you, figuratively blotted with tears, figuratively sticky with heart's blood, literally stained with sweat. I read I can't live without you, written the same way, and then—I love you, over and over again."

She took her elbows off the table and sat up very straight.

"Did you like it?" she asked, voice even, voice a little constrained.

"You mean the Navy? Or the reading of another guy's sweat and blood and tears spelled out in one-syllable words?"

"I mean the Navy."

"Not especially. Good? Bad? It isn't that simple. I know that for four years I sat on that damn island reading I love you, I love only you, I love you only, I will always love you. I don't know whether I felt any way about it at all except that I hoped to hell we wouldn't get blown to kingdom come early some morning. Sometimes I hoped that we'd get blown up just a little bit, to change the pace." He grinned at her because each time he had said I love you, her back had got straighter until now she was sitting up just like Abbie or Queen Victoria.

"Do you like living in Monmouth?" she asked.

"Sure. I grew up here. I doubt that it would be possible to really and truly hate the place where you grew up unless something happened to you that destroyed your belief in yourself. And nothing much happened to me—I just grew up—pretty much like anybody else. With a couple of exceptions that may or may not have been average."

He thought, All life goes in a circle, around and around, you started at one place, and then came right back to it again. "It hath been already of old time, which was before us." In a way, his life had really started inside The Last Chance. So he was back there again, working as day man behind the bar, ten in the morning until six at night, right back where he started. And the girl? This girl, who at the sound of the words "I love you" repeated, and he had been repeating them purposely, had withdrawn, moved away, is she someone you have known before? No. He had never known anyone with quite so easy and natural a manner. There was something gay about her and something quite imperious. When he had wrung changes on all those different ways of saying I love you, her back had stiffened. Did he still believe that all cats bee gray? Well, yes. Well, no. This little one with her head lifted, chin up in the air, revealing the flawless throat, the long neck, ballerina's neck, small hollow place at the base made for kissing, had revolt, refusal to submit, written in every line of her tautly held body. She was like a thoroughbred racehorse balking at the barrier. All cats bee gray? No.

"What do you do?" he asked.

"Do?"

"Do for a living."

"Oh. I write about fashions. I go to all the openings and look at the new clothes. And write about them. I fly to Dallas and Chicago, to Paris and to London, and back to New York to look at all the new glitter that the fashion designers dream up."

"Where do you live?"

"In New York most of the time. Sometimes in Chicago, sometimes in Montreal. Sometimes in London and in Paris and in Monmouth."

New International Set, he thought. Pictures in *Life* magazine. French Riviera, Eden Roc, Hôtel du Cap, Ali Khan, Shah of Persia, Argentina millionaires. Maybe she's an international tramp. He studied her face, No, impossible, even in this dim inadequate light, the eyes are too beautiful, too honest, the whole face too young, too pure, an absolutely vulnerable face, an expectant face. There's something she isn't telling and it's making her uncomfortable but international tramps, no matter how beautiful they are, do not have this look of wonder, of expectancy, this eagerness in the eyes, in the mouth.

"Where were you born?"

"In Monmouth."

"But you—did you grow up here?" Do you mean, he thought, that we've walked the same streets? You and I? Impossible. I would have seen you somewhere. If I had seen you only once, watched you cross a street only once, and never seen you again, I would have remembered it.

"Off and on—mostly off—"

He tried to picture her living in Monmouth, going to high school here, growing up in this small bustling city, and couldn't. Perhaps Monmouth turned them out like this, but he didn't believe it. Now as he looked at her, he thought that she might have been sitting in a drawing room, drinking tea, visiting over the teacups, she seemed so unaware of the noise, the blare of the jukebox, the smoke, the dim light, the people. He supposed it was the way she sat, her back so very straight, her head lifted, that made him think of Abbie.

He had seen Abbie sitting midway in a crowded trolley car, talking to F. K. Jackson, and Abbie, too, gave the impression that she was in her own living room serving tea. Up until now he had thought this air of quiet elegance was an attribute of a handful of aristocratic old colored women and a handful of aristocratic old white women, thought too that it came only with age. Yet here was this girl with the same quality. It surprised him and puzzled him. And strangely enough, he found it delightful.

"Did you go to college?" he asked.

"Of course. I went to Barnard and loved it. I was good at it. So good at it that I was offered an instructorship in English once I got an M.A., preferably at Columbia."

"Professor Williams," he said and laughed. "That I can't picture. I'm trying to picture the rest of it—but that—that's funny."

"No it isn't," she said sharply. "It was something that I did by myself with my own brain. Don't laugh at me. I would have been good at it. I would have been somebody in my own right and instead—instead—"

"Instead?" he prompted.

She pushed the beer glass away from her as though she were not only rejecting beer but a whole way of life. "Well, I traipse around Paris twice a year thinking up new ways of saying that the skirts are longer or the skirts are shorter. The waistline is up or the waistline is down." Then she stood up, and said, "I'm driving to New York tonight so I'll have to get started."

When he held the door of the car open for her he was still wondering what really came after the "instead"— Instead what? Obviously something more than fashion reporting had interfered with her being somebody in her own right.

He said, "When will I see you again?"

"Saturday? Here? Is that all right?"

"Not Saturday. Sunday. Late in the afternoon."

"Fine," she said.

"About five-thirty?"

"Fine, again." She shook hands with him before she got in the car, and said, "I enjoyed myself." And smiled. Then, for no reason at all that he could determine, she laughed—a bubbling joyous sound.

He watched her drive off, and frowned, thinking, She drives too fast. She zooms past those side streets as though she had a police escort in front of her, clearing the way. Then he stopped frowning, remembering what her face was like when she laughed, the mouth curving with laughter, the eyes lighted, head thrown back, showing the long line of the throat. It's not possible, not possible, but inevitable, he thought. There is nothing I can do to stop the process. I am falling in love with her. Not falling in love with her. I am in love with her. I have already, at the sight of that beautiful laughing face, once again, placed my trust, my belief, placed it irrevocably, in the hands of another human being. Hopelessly, inextricably involved. Again. For the third time. First there had been Abbie Crunch, and then Bill Hod, and now—a girl.

This time? This time? Would this girl with the laughing beautiful face, the long neck, the deepset eyes, would she, too, play some fantastic trick on him? "Such fantastic tricks as make the angels weep."

He went in The Last Chance. Bill Hod was behind the bar. Alone.

"Friend," Link said, "let us drink to the night."

Bill stared at him, face expressionless, black obsidian eyes expressionless. He said slowly, "Sometimes I think you smoke reefers."

"Even so, Comrade. Even so. Have a drink with me, anyway."

"Okay. What'll it be?"

"Whiskey and soda."

Bill mixed the drinks quickly. Link watched his hands, deft hands, clean hands, hands with the nails carefully filed, hands that could hold a gun or a knife or a blackjack, hold anything, use anything, quickly, deftly. I bet when he's a hundred and two he'll look exactly the same, sound exactly the same, use his hands exactly the same. Indestructible.

Bill said, "What're we supposed to be drinking to?"

Link said, "We will drink first to Bill Hod, then to Bill Shakespeare. The immortals." He leaned against the bar. Bill obviously thought he was high as a Georgia pine, there was no reason why he should hesitate to present him with further evidence of the advanced state of intoxication he was supposed to be enjoying. He said, "'How many goodly creatures are there

here! How beauteous mankind is! O brave new world, That
has such people in't.' Bill Hod, who stands behind the bar and
Bill Shakespeare who forever sits on my shoulder." He paused,
eyed Bill, repeated, "'O brave new world, That has such people
in't!'" Then he drained the glass, quickly. "Bill," he said, "just
between friends, and confidentially, of course, absolutely confidentially, have you ever been in love?"

"Whyn't you go across the street and get in bed before you
reach the cryin' stage?"

"What kind of answer is that? Here, Mr. Boss, give me another one of these."

"No," Bill said flatly. "You're drunk now."

"Be damned if I am. One whiskey and soda. That's all I've
had. Right here before your eyes. No reefers. I have never
smoked a reefer in my whole life long, chum. They stink too
bad. Friend of mine took me in one of those joints once. In
Harlem. Dark blue lights inside, hellish light. And the cullud folks were all mixed up with the white folks, all groaning
and moaning, legs and arms and torsos all mixed up on sofas
and on rugs, too. I got one whiff of the interior and I said to
my friend: My dearly beloved friend, I promised my dear old
whitehaired mother, when I was in knee pants, that if I ever
hit a joint that had a stink in it like this one, a stench, a stank,
an offense to the nostrils of this kind and nature, I would leave
at once and get some clean fresh air. I said: I have a bottle of
clean fresh air in my pocket, and I am now leaving, and when
I get outside will take said bottle out of my pants pocket, and
breathe that clean fresh air until my nose begins to forget the
offense, the insult, that has damned near made it stop func-
tioning. I must go immediately for if I linger in this—er, odor,
this—er, smell, this—er pollution and corruption one moment
longer, I will—er regurgitate—" He smiled sweetly at Bill. "I
have not been smoking reefers, old man."

"What in hell's the matter with you then?"

"If you will be kind enough to refill this tall tall glass, I will
tell you. Come, come, señor. No drinkee. No tellee."

Bill filled the glass. "Here," he said. "If this is the only way
to get you out of here, for Christ's sake drink it up fast and get
out."

Link drank it slowly, sipping it delicately. "Stuff tastes like hell. Not fit for human consumption. Oh, it's good liquor, Boss Man, but this one followed the first one too fast. I have a delicate stomach, a nervous stomach, Father Hod. My stomach does not like the way this stuff tastes. Neither does my throat. Say," he said, using the conversational tone that a man uses when he plans to talk a long time, "did you know that F. K. Jackson has a nervous stomach? Imagine an undertaker with a nervous stomach. Partner, can you picture how her stomach must jump when she lays the boys out on the cooling board? Come to think of it, they call themselves morticians, don't they?" He paused just a little too long, he gave Bill a chance to say something.

Bill said, "Well?"

"Well, what?"

"If you're not drunk, what's the matter with you?"

Link grinned at him. "That's right, we made a pact, didn't we?" He started walking toward the door, turned, said "Shhh! Don't tell anybody, friend, but—I'm in love." He opened the door wide, stepped over the threshold, leaned inside, and let out a rebel yell—long, high in pitch, wild, repeated it until the wild highpitched yelling made the glasses tinkle on the shelves.

The sound brought Weak Knees running from the kitchen, falling over his feet. Link heard him shout, "Whassamatter, Boss? Who did that in here? Who did that in here? I'll kill the bastard—"

Link let the door swing shut, stood outside, on the street, looking up at the sign. The Last Chance. Redorange, harsh redorange, see-it-for-a-block neon sign. And laughed. Because once again he felt as though he could conquer the world. The Last Chance. The Last Chance.

7

LINK HAD FINISHED EATING his breakfast.

Abbie Crunch said, "I wish you'd—" stopped, said, "I—" and never finished what she was going to say.

They both heard the screams that came from upstairs. Link knew by the volume, by the pitch, that these hair-stand-on-end screams, these curdle-the-blood screams could only have issued from the throat of Mrs. Mamie Powther; thinking how aware of her he had become, how familiar with the sound of her voice, that he should recognize it even when lifted in distress.

Abbie said, "Why—what—" shuddered, took a deep breath and said, "Link—go and see what—"

He ran up the outside back stairs, ran up them, thinking, Well, perhaps Powther had come hurrying home, in his dark suit, razor crease in the pants, in his black shoes with the mirror shine, had come home, and found Mr. B. Hod in his bed, and had murdered Mr. Hod, and was now murdering Mrs. Powther.

In the kitchen, upstairs, Mamie Powther was standing on a chair, skirts wrapped around her, held high, wrapped tight around her, so that knees, leg, thighs were exposed. She had red sandals on her feet. No stockings. One hand over her eyes, the other hand holding up the skirts. He thought of a girl wading, a girl with her skirts wrapped around her, skirts lifted, wading. Not good enough, what then? Venus. Why Venus? Goddess. It was the shape of the calf, the swelling of the thigh. Only the Greeks reproduced it like that. Goddess. Hardly. Well, a profane goddess then. Lead us not into temptation. But who would not follow where Mrs. M. Powther's softfleshed thighs—

He glanced around the kitchen, looking for an intruder, a robber, an outraged husband. Nothing. Nobody. Dishes piled in the sink. Coffee cup on table.

He said, "What—"

"That way—" she didn't point, she just said, "That way. Oh, get him, get him, get him—" One hand clutched at the skirts, the other covered her eyes.

He went all through the apartment. Nothing. He stayed longest in the Powthers' bedroom, recognizing it immediately because of the cupids that adorned the bed. He grinned at the cupids, saluted them, thinking, Friends, Fellow Travelers, Eyewitnesses, Comrades-in-Arms. Hail, Cupids!

He returned to the kitchen. "What was it?" he asked.

She took her hand away from her eyes. "Oh, it's you—"

"Yeah," he said. "Who went—er—that way?"

"Mouse."

He looked at her for a long moment, skirts still held up, wadded up, had she forgotten them or—

"You mean a small four-legged gray creature, relative of the rat?" Sometimes Dumble Streeters gave choice, highly appropriate names to friends and enemies. "Mouse" could be a second-story man.

"A mouse," she said, dropping the skirts.

So she really did forget about them. I wish you hadn't though, Mamie Powther, after all a man can dream, he thought, and said, "Well—uh—no mouse—anywhere. He was probably as scared as you were."

He held out his hand, intending to help her down from the chair. She got down by herself, gave her skirts a shake, patted them in place.

She smiled at him, a great big flashing heartwarming smile, and said, "Thanks. I'm all right now. Only thing I'm scared of is mice. I been tellin' Powther to set a trap—"

The instant he re-entered Abbie's kitchen she said, "What—"

"Mice," he said. "A mouse ran across the kitchen floor. She's afraid of 'em." Not men. Mice. Not afraid of men because if he had stayed up there another five minutes, he and the cupids on the headboard of the bed would have been better acquainted. He would have been able to study the cupids, just lift his eyes and study them—wings, behinds, grapes, et al. Invitation in Mrs. M. Powther's eyes, in the curve of her mouth, invitation cordially, consciously, graciously extended.

Abbie said, "You mean to tell me that that woman, a big woman like that, is afraid of mice?"

"Yeah. She was standing on a kitchen chair, her hand over her eyes, screaming her head off. Because she's afraid of mice."

"How perfectly ridiculous," Abbie said, anger in her voice.

"One man's meat, Miss Abbie," he said lightly and went on across the street to open up the bar for the day, thinking that Abbie's voice when she said "that woman" had the same tone as when she referred to Bill Hod as "that man."

He wedged the door so that it would stay open. It would be two hours before Old Man John the Barber stalked in for his morning beer. By that time the place would be aired out, cleaned up, slicked up.

While he worked, opening cases of liquor, cleaning out the beer pumps, polishing the bar, he thought, not about the girl, the girl who called herself Camilo Williams, not about Mamie Powther, not about China, but about The Last Chance.

When he was eight years old, and he always went back in his thoughts to the time when he was eight, The Last Chance fascinated him, with the special fascination of something evil, forbidden, mysterious. He tried to imagine what it looked like inside and couldn't. Would there be vats of beer and strong drink? When men drowned in the strong drink and the beer, did they wade in by themselves, or did other men put them in the vats and hold them there until they drowned? He couldn't picture it in his mind, though Abbie was always talking about the place, using the phrase "drowned in drink."

Eight years old. And when he and Abbie set out for church on Sunday mornings, Bill Hod, who owned this mysterious place, was always standing across the street, sleeves of his white shirt rolled up, a white bulldog lolling on the sidewalk beside him. The kids on the block said the dog had a gold tooth. Link didn't quite believe this. He wanted to. But it sounded like the kind of stuff kids told you just to see if you were fool enough to fall for it. He didn't ask Hod about the dog's gold tooth because he knew that Abbie wouldn't like it if he talked to Hod. Though as far as Link could see, there was nothing about Hod's appearance that suggested he drowned his customers as part of the day's work.

The other man who lived at The Last Chance was quite extraordinary. He was a short darkbrownskinned man and he walked with a shambling, shuffling, unsteady gait, like the off-balance walk of a drunk. He wore white cotton pants and a dark brown sweater buttoned all the way up to the neck, and a dusty out-of-shape felt hat jammed on his head, not tilted, but set square on his head and pulled down. The only change he made in this outfit was in winter when he added an overcoat to it; and he didn't button the coat so when the wind blew, as it often did, straight from the river, the coat ballooned away from his body, and Link could see the brown sweater buttoned up to the neck just as it was on a hot day in August.

He saw the man with the funny walk every Saturday when he went to market with Abbie. Those trips to the stores, especially to Davioli's fruit and vegetable store, were deeply satisfying. He was in love with Abbie in those days, he wanted to be with her all the time, and though he called her Aunt Abbie when he spoke to her, he called her Abbie in his mind because he thought it a beautiful name and liked to say it. Eight years old. So he was going to marry her when he grew up, though he did not know exactly how this would be accomplished, in view of the fact that she was already married. Anyway he was always going to live with her.

When they went shopping, he carried the market basket, swinging it back and forth, delighting in the quietness of the street, in the quick brisk way Abbie walked, in the sound of her voice, in the fact that she called Mr. Davioli "Davioli," leaving off the Mister, clearly establishing the social difference between them. She referred to Davioli's store as the greengrocer's, putting together two words that didn't belong together, that no one else used, and yet when he thought about it, the words belonged together even though they sounded strange.

They always saw the same people, saw them almost always in the same places, on those Saturday morning trips. Abbie said that even though they didn't know each other, the fact that they were all of them dressed, heads combed, teeth brushed, had had breakfast, and were out on the street, at eight o'clock when the rest of Dumble Street still lay abed, faces sticky with sleep, heads tousled, there was always the possibility of their becoming acquainted, because this business of early rising was something they all had in common.

Sometimes they met the man with the funny walk when he was coming away from Davioli's, carrying two big brown paper bags, celery always sticking out of the top of one of them. He carried the bags in front of him, close to his chest, his arms around them, and the dark green leaves of the celery came right under his nose. By half closing one eye Link could almost convince himself that this was a horse or a cow coming down the street, head deep in meadow grass, and not a man. It was the kind of celery that Abbie didn't like and whenever Davioli tried to sell it to her, she shook her head, saying, "It's too coarse, Davioli."

One morning he and Abbie reached Davioli's store earlier than usual or else the dark brown man was late. Anyway, Abbie was selecting oranges and Link was wandering around enjoying the fruity smell, thinking what a pleasant place this store was. There was a small stove in the middle of the floor that gave off just enough heat to keep the vegetables from freezing and made for comfort on a cold windy morning. There were chairs where you could sit down and look out on Franklin Avenue and the radio was always playing good and loud and there was the smell of Davioli's coffee—all of which made the store like the inside of a house. Davioli kept a big white enamel coffee pot on the stove, and while he waited for the customers to make up their minds, he drank coffee from a thick brown mug and took big bites out of a doughnut.

Davioli handed him the bag of doughnuts every Saturday and said, "It's okay, Mis' Crunch. Boys is always hungry. I know everything about the young fellers. The old woman and me made four boys. Now you just eat up, young feller."

Link was munching on a doughnut, hoping that this morning Davioli's nephew, the one he called the Idiot, would come in the store before he and Abbie left. Abbie said he really wasn't an idiot, just a trifle slow mentally, and that Davioli was such a quick-moving, fast-talking little man that the slow speech, the slow movement, of his big fourteen-year-old nephew irritated him. Link had never seen the Idiot close to but he always hoped that he would. Sometimes they met him peddling his bike slow, slow, up Franklin Avenue, his mouth open, looking as though he were asleep on the bike.

He was thinking about the Idiot when he heard Davioli say, "Excuse me a minute, Mis' Crunch. I gotta get some vegetables outta the back for Weak Knees."

He turned and saw Davioli and the man with the shambling funny walk go toward the back room of the store. He thought,

Weak Knees, Weak Knees, that's his name and it suits him; it matches the way he walks. Weak Knees.

Davioli said, "Here's your mushrooms and I got ye some pink grapefruit and a basket of them Cortlands. I'll send them apples over by the Idiot if he ever gets his big can outta bed and here's a coupla bunches of pasqualey and there's kale and some of them oranges ye wanted, and the mother finocchio."

Weak Knees said, "Check," and came out of the back room carrying two big bags. He put the bags down on a chair. "I forgot the garlic. Davie, you got fresh garlic?" fingered through the garlic on the stand, said, "These are as dried up as my—" stopped abruptly and tipped the shapeless dusty felt hat, saying, "Good morning, ma'am, didn't see you," to Abbie. Then, "How're they runnin' this mornin', young feller? How're they runnin'? Yours out in front?" to Link.

He had a funny highpitched voice but Link found the tone of it pleasing. He had sounded exactly as though he were talking to someone his own age. He said, "Fine, sir," and wondered what Weak Knees was talking about. He noticed that Abbie didn't say good morning, she looked away, and nodded, well, half nodded, half bowed, in the general direction of a big mound of potatoes, and started picking out some small ones though they had enough potatoes at home to last at least another week.

When they left the store, Weak Knees was just ahead of them. Link remembered thinking, The trouble is his legs are crooked and they're getting more and more crooked as he goes along. One leg suddenly gave way. It just doubled up and Weak Knees almost fell. He was way off balance and as he strove desperately to straighten up, he seemed to have fifty legs, all of them completely out of control, his weight first on one and then the other, the leg he tried to stand on buckling and as that leg straightened itself out, the other leg went under. It was like a dance, a crazy kind of dance. Link stood still, watching him. Weak Knees made a final dreadful effort to stand erect and both bags went out of his arms, fell on the sidewalk, split, broke open, oranges, grapefruit, kale, celery, mushrooms, lettuce rolled in every direction.

Weak Knees said, "Oh, God damn that crocus sack anyway. God damn—" He looked back over his shoulder, brushed at something that Link couldn't see, muttering, "Get away! Get away, Eddie!"

He turned and looked, too, saw no one. Looked for a wasp, a bee, a mosquito, decided that it must be a person, because there weren't any insects anywhere nearby, besides no one would try to nudge a mosquito away, and Weak Knees was now making a nudging motion with his elbow, saying, "God damn it, Eddie, get away. Get away."

Abbie said, "Come along, Link."

He didn't move. He said, "Let go my hand, Aunt Abbie. I want to help him pick his stuff up."

Abbie tightened her grip on his hand and because he loved her, though it often meant leaving something exciting and new and very puzzling, like this man—this Weak Knees who was still muttering, talking to some unseen person, poking at the person with his elbow—he followed the tug and pull of her hand, even matched his gait to hers, so that they moved away from Weak Knees and the scattered fruit and vegetables, quickly.

When they got home, he said, "Aunt Abbie, who was Mr. Weak Knees talking to?"

"I don't know."

"Well, what did he mean when he said, 'Get away Eddie'?"

"I don't know. I don't know anything about him. He's not the kind of person I'd be apt to know."

That night, at supper (Saturday night—so it was baked beans and brown bread, homemade pickles and coleslaw, gingerbread and applesauce, hearty, and filling, and cheap, according to Abbie) he patiently waited for a moment when Abbie and the Major weren't talking, so that his question wouldn't be lost by Abbie's saying, "You mustn't interrupt, dear."

The Major took the cover off the big earthenware bean pot, leaned over and sniffed the fragrant steam that issued from it. He served all the plates and while he sliced the brown bread with a string, Abbie put coleslaw on the plates, both of them talking because they hadn't seen each other all day. He thought they'd never be done with talking, then the Major said the blessing, and there was a little pause.

Link said, "Uncle Theodore, what's it mean when somebody asks you how they're runnin'?"

The Major said, "Well, now let me see. Who asked you that and just how did they say it?"

"It was Mr. Weak Knees, the man with the funny walk. I saw him at the greengrocer's and he said, 'How they runnin' this mornin', young feller? Is yours out in front?' What's that mean?"

"He wanted to know if everything was all right with you," the Major said, and let out a great roar of laughter, laid his knife and fork down, leaned back in his chair, held on to the edge of the table, and seemed to laugh all over. Abbie smiled and then laughed. So did Link.

"That's what he meant," the Major said. "He must be a racetrack man. Probably loves horses. About the best thing that can happen to a man that's got a passion for racehorses is to have the pony he put his money on start running way out in front. The Governor's a great man for horses. That is," he said, glancing quickly at Abbie, and then away, "he was in his younger days. When his horse was so far out in front there was no question but what it would come in first, he'd jump up and down, hollering and shouting, just like a crazy man. There's something about a horse when he's running out in front, in a race, that—"

Link liked the Major's stories but he had to get back to Weak Knees. He said, "Is he crippled? I mean, Mr. Weak Knees."

"I suppose you could say he is. He's got something wrong with his legs."

"Well, who was he talking to when he said—"

"Why are you asking so many questions about him?" Aunt Abbie said.

"Let the boy talk, Abbie. He's got the right to an honest answer to an honest question. Go on, Link."

"Well, he dropped his groceries, I mean his vegetables, and the bag broke and he nearly fell down. He was all off balance and when he finally got his legs sort of straightened out he kept saying, 'Get away, Eddie, get away,' and he kept brushing at something, pushing something away from him. Who was he talking to? There wasn't anybody around but me and Aunt Abbie." He paused, remembering the early morning quiet of the street, and the small man in the dusty hat with the fruit and vegetables scattered all around him, saying, "Oh, God damn that crocus sack anyway." Then he said quickly, lest Abbie interrupt again, "I'd probably of found out if she'd let me pick his stuff up for him. I didn't see how he was going to get it up off the sidewalk with his legs going all to pieces like that.

And after I picked the stuff up I was going to ask him who he was talking to but she didn't give me a chance to. Who was he talking to, Uncle Theodore?"

Abbie said, "I'm sure if he couldn't pick the fruit up himself the other one would have seen to it that it was picked up."

"The other one?" Link said.

"The other man. That Mr. Hod who owns the saloon."

Link knew that if Abbie ever got started on The Last Chance and the vats of beer and the men who drowned in them, he would never find out what he wanted to know. He said, "Oh," to Abbie and then without pausing, said again, "Uncle Theodore, who was Mr. Weak Knees talking to?"

"Whenever he's upset he seems to think that an old friend of his is standing near him. So he nudges him and says, 'Get away, Eddie, get away.' Weak Knees believes he killed his friend. It happened years ago in Washington. They were wrestling with each other, just for the fun of it, and Eddie, who was Weak Knees' best friend, fell and struck his head, and died."

"Who told you that?" Abbie asked.

"Bill Hod. Sometimes he's standing across the street when I come home at night and I stop and pass the time of day with him. One night we got to talking about good cooking and good food. Hod told me that Weak Knees is probably the finest chef in this country but he's never had really firstclass jobs because of his legs. People always thought he was a drunk and wouldn't hire him. Right after that Hod told me the story about Eddie."

Abbie gave the Major a long level look, "Really, Dory," she said, "I should think it would be possible to find a—well, a better type of person to talk to."

Even now, almost twenty years afterwards, Link could remember the sound of the Major's voice when he answered Abbie. The Major loved to eat, eating steadily until he had finished, talking, but never really pausing in his eating. He stopped eating, put his fork down on his plate, voice heavy, the same heaviness in his face, voice slow, face somehow slow, too, though Link did not know why his face should look slow but it did, as he said, "Abbie, if you believe that the Lord watches over and cares about a sparrow, then you must also believe that He watches over and cares about Bill Hod."

Silence in the dining room. Link stared at the white place mats on the polished table, at the brown teapot, at the tea cozy that covered it, watched Abbie's hands, small plump hands, busy with the cups and saucers, with the teapot and sugar bowl and creamer, hands busy pouring tea, looked at the Major's hands, flat on the table, big dark brown hands flat on the table, not holding a fork or a spoon, not holding anything, just flat on the table. Then the Major picked up his fork and he and Abbie were talking and laughing again as they always did at supper.

That was on a Saturday. A week later, the Major was sick, taken suddenly sick, in the afternoon. The Major had a Saturday afternoon to himself every other week, he always spent it working in the yard or in the house, and Link came in the house looking for him and there was the Major sitting in what Abbie called the gentleman's chair, in the front parlor, head lolled over on his shoulder, head somehow loose, no longer connected to the rest of him, mouth open, and a little trickle of saliva coming out of the side of his mouth. He was snoring. He smelt of whiskey. There were newspapers spread on the floor under the chair, in front of the chair, under the Major's feet. Link stared at the newspapers, trying to figure out why they were there. Newspapers on the floor. Abbie put newspapers on the floor under the cat's box. Why under the Major? What did she expect the Major to do?

Despite Abbie's objections, he kept going in the parlor to look at the Major. Then F. K. Jackson came to have supper with them. F. K. Jackson sent for Dr. Easter. And Dr. Easter came and stayed and stayed and stayed.

He knew that Abbie was worried about the Major and he could understand why, yet he couldn't quite understand why she should forget about one Link Williams, forget to tell him to go to bed, forget to fix anything for him to eat, Saturday night and all day Sunday, and Sunday night, too.

She forgot all about him. Then the Major was dead.

Early Monday morning, F. K. Jackson came down the front stairs, quickly, quietly, and meeting Link in the hall said, not looking at him, not really talking to him, but talking apparently to the striped wallpaper, because she kept looking at it, "You must be very quiet. You must be very good. The Major is dead. You will have to look after your Aunt Abbie. You will have to take care of her now." She patted his shoulder with one of her thin, bony hands, and he drew away from her, drew away from the hand. Abbie's hands were soft, plump hands, small hands, quieting hands, and F. K. Jackson's hands were big, and bony, and nervous, and the touch of them made him tremble.

He sat in the kitchen, waiting for Abbie to come downstairs and tell him about the Major. He had seen a dead person close to, last summer. The Hangman was full of leaves. People were sitting on the front steps and in the small backyards. Only the children were running about, shouting. He was out on the sidewalk in front of Number Six, running and shouting, too. It was close to bedtime and so the shouting was louder and longer, wilder, more fun than usual, for all of them knew that in a few more minutes they would be herded into bathtubs, would be listening to all the threats, and the orders to hurry up, wash behind your ears, scrub your feet, hurry up, that accompanied the business of going to bed.

Suddenly they all ran toward the dock for no reason at all, one of the boys headed that way so they followed him. Once on the dock, they stood still because there was a woman there, lying flat on her back.

Link said, "It's Pearly Gates. Come on, we'll have some fun with her. Let's poke at her till she wakes up."

One of them leaned over and touched her hand, poked at her hand, and then straightened up, scared, strangeness in his voice, fear, puzzlement, "She's kind of cold. Here, Link, you feel her—"

He touched the hand and was revolted, absolutely revolted, by the coldness of it.

The other boy looked at him, frowned, said, "I think she's died—I think—she's so cold—she's died—I think—"

They turned tail and ran home, each one of them ran into his own house, up the front steps, hurrying to get inside a house. Because just that morning, Pearly Gates had been alive, they had all seen her in the morning, staggering down Dumble Street, mumbling to herself, black felt hat crooked on her head, black clothes all a which way, long black skirt trailing on the sidewalk, the edges graybrown from dirt and dust, smelling all over of whiskey. They had all seen her and run after her, yelled at her, and if this thing whatever it was could happen to her, it could happen to them, too.

Link went inside Number Six, and was sick, violently sick at his stomach, and Abbie said, "Link, what on earth have you been eating?"

He could only shake his head, he would never be able to tell her that he had touched death with his own hand, he would never be able to tell anyone and he would never be able to forget it.

Now this same thing had happened to the Major.

While he was sitting in the kitchen, he heard someone coming down the stairs, he thought it might be Abbie, and he went into the hall to meet her. Thus he saw three men bringing a heavy bag down the stairs. He did not want to believe that the Major was inside that canvas bag but he knew that he was—he could tell by the way the men looked at him, frowning, and flicking their eyes, and shaking their heads.

He went outside and sat down on the back steps, shivering, tasting the sour acid taste of the saliva that poured from the inside of his cheeks, feeling his stomach contract as though it were being squeezed by a big hand. Sparrows scratched in the loose dirt under the hedge, the high privet hedge that Abbie said was cheaper to keep up than a fence, fences had to be painted, and the posts replaced, but with a hedge you just kept it clipped; and the hedge cut off the view of the depraved goings-on of the Finns next door in summer, and served as a screen in winter, when it didn't really matter what the Finns did because with the doors and windows all closed you couldn't hear the Finns fall out of the windows, cursing each other in English, though when they were sober they spoke in Finnish. Every winter a drunken Finn fell out of the window. A bluejay was screaming like crazy in the pear tree, he watched it fly away, with a sudden upswoop, making a flash of blue, its harsh cry was like the sound of the Finns' cursing. The Finns cursed as they died.

Why had they dumped the Major in a sack like that? Why hadn't they had a funeral for him, like they did for other people. For the Finns?

Late in the afternoon, he went in the house to ask Abbie

about it. F. K. Jackson was in Abbie's room, and came and stood in the doorway, barring the way, whispering, "You mustn't bother her now. She's gone to sleep. You run along now, and get yourself something to eat. She'll be all right. You run along now."

He couldn't eat anything. He went to bed. When he finally went to sleep, he kept waking up, remembering.

The next day they brought the Major back. He didn't know when they brought him back. He was tiptoeing down the front stairs, and when he reached the hall, he stopped and took a cautious look into the parlor, stood on the threshold looking in and saw that they had brought the Major back. He was lying in an open coffin. The coffin was in front of the fireplace.

The parlor looked queer. Someone had taken down all the pictures, taken down the long goldleaf mirror that the Governor's wife had given to Abbie, taken out the plants, taken away the books and the magazines that stood on the marbletopped table near the fireplace, pulled down the window shades. There were white candles in a pair of three-branched candlesticks that he had never seen before. The candles were lighted and they kept flickering, as though a draft was blowing through the room. And there were flowers, all around the coffin, flowers, red, and white, and yellow flowers, he had never seen so many at one time, in one place.

He walked over to the coffin. The Major was dead, and he was wearing his best black broadcloth suit, and a striped necktie; and he did not look like anyone Link had ever known, bore absolutely no resemblance to the Major, lids closed down over his eyes, lids shut tight over his eyes; his face lopsided, thinner, even his hands, thinner, bonier; hands crossed, no, folded, and a Bible, with a worn leather binding, black but mottled with brown, in one hand, held loosely in one hand, not held, the hand placed over the small Bible, and a carnation, a white carnation in his buttonhole. All of him thinner, smaller. Link bent over the coffin and there was a queer, sweetish, sickening smell that made him gasp. He made himself touch the Major's hand, his face. The Major was dead. Dead meant cold. Dead meant not moving. Dead meant to feel like a stone. A cold stone picked up in the winter, fingers withdrawing from its coldness, its hardness. Pearly Gates. And now the Major. He stayed there by the coffin, too frightened to move away.

He turned around because he heard F. K. Jackson talking to someone in a soft voice. F. K. Jackson was leading Abbie into the parlor. Abbie didn't seem to see where she was going and she was saying, "Oh, Dory, Dory," over and over again.

"It's all right, Abbie. It's all right," F. K. Jackson said.

Abbie didn't answer. She walked straight to the coffin, and went down on her knees, weeping, saying, "Our Father—Our Father—Dory, Dory—"

F. K. Jackson said, "Link! I didn't know you were in here. You run along and play. Go outdoors and play, dear."

"I don't want to. I can't—"

"Run along now. I'll look after Aunt Abbie."

He sat on the dock and looked at the river, hunched over, his arms folded, sitting like an old man. He felt like crying, and didn't, couldn't. He stayed there until eight o'clock at night and then went home. No lights anywhere in the house. Total darkness. House cold. He turned the hall light on. Abbie was in the parlor, by the coffin, not kneeling, sitting in a chair, weeping. The sound of her weeping hurt him deep inside.

He said, "Aunt Abbie—"

She didn't even turn her head toward him, just sat there, weeping, weeping, weeping, not seeing him, not hearing him. He tiptoed out of the room, wondering if perhaps she thought he was, somehow, though he did not know how, somehow responsible for the cold stonelike unmoving condition of the Major.

He felt guilty and ashamed and afraid and so alone that he did not dare go to sleep. Finally, in that upstairs bedroom, across the hall from Abbie's and the Major's room, he collapsed into sleep, with all his clothes on, lying on top of the clean white bedspread.

Some time during the night, he made up his mind that he could not, would not, go to the Major's funeral. He wandered about the dock all day and toward dusk, hungry, cold, lonely, he went home. Abbie would be angry and scold him but he was glad because then he could explain everything to her, about the sack, about Pearly Gates, about being afraid.

He left the house almost as quickly as he had entered it. Abbie was in bed, flat on her back in the big mahogany four-poster bed, and the lamp by the bed had a tan-colored cloth draped over the shade, so that the light in the room was very dim. F. K. Jackson sat beside the bed, holding Abbie's hand, murmuring to her in a soothing voice that made him think of the cooing of pigeons. F. K. Jackson had a shawl around her shoulders, big, bulky, dark in color. It made her look fat and humped over and so different that he stared at her, not speaking, thinking that everything was changing, even Miss Jackson, referring to her like that in his mind, not as old Frances Jackson, or F. K. Jackson, but as Miss Jackson. She was sitting right near the bed, and the dimmed light from the lamp threw a shadow on the wall, Miss Jackson's shadow, huge, doubled up; and the shadow was the exact shape of the bag they had carried the Major away in.

He said, "No! No!"

Miss Jackson turned around, saw him, said, "Did you want something, Link?"

He wanted to talk to Abbie but he didn't say so. He walked over to the bed, and Miss Jackson moved closer to Abbie, as though she were using the dark bulk of the shawl to screen Abbie, block his view of her. He had to peer around Miss Jackson.

Abbie's eyes were closed. She looked smaller in bed. As he looked at the two women, the one lying flat on her back in bed, and the other biglooking, humped over, wrapped in a shawl, sitting by the bed, he began to shiver as though he had a chill. They hadn't even missed him. They didn't know he hadn't been at the Major's funeral. They had shut him out of their lives, cut him off from them. He didn't care about Miss Jackson and what she did or didn't do. But Abbie had been his whole existence, she had watched over him, listened to everything he said, told him what to wear, what to eat, when he should go to bed, had loved him. Now she had forgotten all about him. It was like being nowhere. Lost. Nowhere at all.

He made himself look at the ugly shadow on the wall, at Miss Jackson who was holding Abbie's hand, and had begun that soft lowpitched pigeon cooing in which he could not make out the words, could only hear sounds that must have been words, repeated, over and over again, as though she were saying, There, there, there, Yes, yes, yes, I know, I know, I know, I'm here, I'm here, I'm here.

He thought, Yes, the two of them together—but what about me?

Abbie sat up, reaching for Miss Jackson and Miss Jackson put her arms around Abbie, enveloping her in the big dark shawl. Abbie had on the gray bathrobe, dark gray, the one she called a fright and a horror because it was so big and shapeless, because of the color, a muddy gray; but it was warm and it was perfectly good, not a brack or a break in it, so she couldn't throw it away though it did make her look exactly like Aunt Mehalie.

The first time he had heard her say this, he had asked her who Aunt Mehalie was and Abbie had laughed, saying, "Nobody, really. It's just a very old and rather funny way of describing all slovenly black women. When a colored woman looks old and fat and rumpled and not too clean we say she looks like Aunt Mehalie. That's the way this bathrobe makes me look."

He thought, she sounds like Aunt Mehalie too—old and rumpled. She was saying, "Oh, Dory, Dory—" She wasn't crying but it sounded like crying and her voice was muffled by the shawl. They were both under the shawl now, wrapped up in it. He wanted to push Miss Jackson away, push her out of the house. He blamed her for the way Abbie looked, the way she sounded, the way she acted, the dreadful way she had changed.

He left the house quickly. He was cold. He was hungry. He was alone. He was afraid. Worst of all, he now distrusted Abbie. Though he did not know it, he was already seeking for something, or someone, to put in the place that Abbie had held in his heart.

Bill Hod was standing across the street in front of The Last Chance. It no longer mattered that Abbie had always referred to him as that other one, that Mr. Hod, that man, the tone of her voice saying, the horned one, the one with hoofs, the evil one, it didn't matter at all, because he was the only person in sight on Dumble Street. So he went and stood beside Bill Hod, not saying anything, just standing beside him, in the hope that being near a grownup would help some of the misery, some of the lonesomeness to leak out of him. This man would not say, "Oh, Dory, Dory"; neither would he say, "Run along and play."

Bill Hod said, "Hi, Sonny. How're they runnin'?" and put his hand on Link's shoulder.

It was a warm firm hand. Link said, in response to the touch of the hand, to its warmth, its firmness, hand that could grip, could move, you could feel life in it, not meaning to say it, "Mister, have you got anything I could eat?"

"Eat? Eat? Oh—sure. Come on in the kitchen."

So for the first time he went inside The Last Chance. He followed Bill Hod through the big swinging door, almost stepping on his heels, he walked so close to him. The strange yeasty smell, not unpleasant, that he caught a whiff of now and then in summer when he walked past the open door, was stronger inside. He cast a swift side glance at the dark polished wood of the bar, at the brass rail, at the bottles, row on row of them, on shelves on each side of the biggest mirror he had ever seen, looked longest at the man who stood behind the bar, wiping a glass, a man in a white coat. Except for the mirror and the bottles it seemed to Link a barelooking place, disappointing in its bareness. Abbie was wrong. There were no vats anywhere. On the other side of the room, across from the bar, there were chairs and tables. And not very many of them. That was all.

Then they were in the kitchen, a kitchen almost as big as the barroom, and filled with such delicious smells of food that he was afraid for a moment he would cry, smells like on Franklin Avenue over near the bakery on Saturday morning when they were baking bread, and just the smell of it made him hungry, and baking cakes, and he thought they smelt as though they ought to be a mile high, and covered thick with chocolate frosting; smells like on Sunday on Dumble Street, and he coming home from church with Abbie, getting hungrier and hungrier, one o'clock and he hadn't had anything to eat since seven-thirty, and his stomach sucking in on itself, and Dumble Street filled with the smell of fried chicken and baked yams, and kale cooked with ham fat, and Abbie going slower and slower, and he trying to hurry her along so he could get something to eat before he died of starvation, starving to death in a street filled with heavenly smells, that came at him out of every doorway and every window.

It was warm in this big kitchen. There was a lot of light. Weak Knees was standing by a tremendous stove, copper hood over the stove, tasting something, stirring something in a pot and tasting it, and he didn't turn around until Bill Hod said, "The kid's hungry."

Weak Knees looked at Link and his mouth opened slightly, as though he were surprised. He said, "Hiya, Sonny. Yours out in front?" and turned back to the stove. "Park it anywhere. Just park it anywhere. It'll be on the table by the time you get it parked."

And it was. Weak Knees filled the plates right at the stove. There wasn't any waiting to pass your plate, he filled them up and put them on the table, a round table, the wood white and smooth. There weren't any doilies or place mats or tablecloth. No napkins either. Link tried to eat slowly because both of them seemed to be watching him, but he was so hungry, so empty, his stomach felt as though it were empty all the way down to his heels, that he gulped down a plate of fried chicken and rice and gravy and kale and four biscuits and swallowed a glass of milk before the other two had really got started good. And even then didn't feel quite full.

Weak Knees said, "You want more cow, Sonny?"

"Cow, sir?"

"He means milk," said Bill Hod.

"Yes, sir."

Now that he was beginning to feel better, he looked around the kitchen. The wall nearest to the stove was almost covered with all sizes and shapes of pots and pans and frying pans, colanders and strainers, longhandled spoons and cake turners, all hung on the wall. Some of them were made of aluminum, some of copper, some were black iron, and they were arranged so that they looked like a design on the wall, a kind of decoration. Abbie kept all her pots and pans stuck away in cupboards and drawers where you couldn't see them, and he thought this was a much better way, handier, and betterlooking too.

He heard a sound that startled him, a kind of snoring that came from under the table. He looked a question at Bill Hod.

"That's Frankie," Hod said. "He's still young but he snores just like Yellow Man Johnson."

The white bulldog was on the floor, under the table, asleep.

He lifted his head, probably because he heard his name mentioned, got up, sniffed at Link's legs, wagged his tail, and settled back into sleep. Link drew his legs tight together, remembering Abbie's stories about strange dogs and how they might bite you, with no warning. The big white bulldog ignored him, went on snoring, and he relaxed a little. He wondered who Yellow Man Johnson was, and why he snored so loudly, and didn't ask because Abbie was always saying you mustn't ask questions when you were a guest in someone else's house.

Weak Knees put a piled-up plate down in front of him. He said, "There was just this one little lonely piece of chicken settin' there in the pan, a piece of leg meat, best part of the bird, breast meat's dry, leg meat's moist and sweet, breast meat's only good for samwiches and salat where you can wet it down. And there was this little forkful of rice that was setting there waitin' for a spoonful of gravy and the gravy was right there in the skillet waitin' to lay itself over the rice. So there you are, Sonny, there you are. Start layin' your lip over it." He said it all on one breath.

"How they comin' now?" Weak Knees asked.

"Fine, sir."

"I ain't no sir. You can just call me Weak Knees."

"He's just a plain man from plain people," Bill Hod said. "Call him Weak Knees and call me Bill."

Link nodded. It would be easy to say Weak Knees. Not so easy to say Bill. There was something about Mr. Hod that—well, he was quieter than anyone he'd ever been around. He didn't say much. He seemed to see everything, he had known Link was scared of the dog. Looking at him, close to, he couldn't understand why Abbie called him "that man," or "the other one," just as though she were saying that outcast, the leprous one. Bill Hod's hair was straight, absolutely straight, and Abbie thought it was wonderful when a colored person had straight hair. His skin was light, and Abbie thought that was good, too, in a colored person, even though she herself wasn't exactly light, and neither was the Major. Then he remembered that what Abbie thought, or said, no longer counted with him. He could no longer depend on her. So he would form his own opinion about Bill Hod.

Weak Knees said, "You got room for a small piece of cake?

A man ain't really full till he's put a sweet taste in his mouth —that's the finish line—and you ain't got there till you had some sweet—"

He had room for two pieces of chocolate cake. He was finishing the second piece when Bill Hod asked him if he liked to swim. He said that he didn't know how, that he'd never been swimming.

Bill said, "You come on down to the dock with me, next Sunday, and I'll teach you."

Link thanked him though he knew that it wasn't possible because he had to go to Sunday School, and to church, with Abbie because Abbie was superintendent of the Sunday School, and they had to set an example for the other colored people, so even if it rained or snowed, they went just the same.

But he wasn't going to live with her any more, he wasn't going back to that cold house across the street, house of weeping, house of darkness, in which for the last four days he had lived with fear, moving through the rooms as though he were a ghost, not even a ghost, for Abbie would have sensed the presence of a ghost, reacted to it in some way, at least turned the lights on. She walked slowly through the house, she who had always been so erect was now bent over like an old woman, she held one hand in front of her as she walked, feeling her way, like she was blind, didn't comb her hair, wore a nightgown and that Aunt Mehalie bathrobe all day, and either went barefooted or wore felt slippers. He couldn't go back to that house.

He had finished eating. So had Weak Knees. And Bill Hod. He had better tell them now. Tell them? Ask them. Explain.

It was warm in the kitchen, and there was so much light that there weren't any ugly shadows on the walls, there was no sound of weeping. The big teakettle boiling on the stove was making a hissing-bubbling sound, and the dog kept up his snorting-snoring, sometimes so loud that it sounded like coughing, sometimes he seemed to clear his throat, and grunt.

Bill Hod said, "Yellow Man Johnson is a lightweight compared with Frankie when it comes to snorin'. Hey, Frankie, cut out the racket, you'll put us all to sleep."

Weak Knees laughed. The highpitched cackling sound he made was so very different from the bass rumbling, the great roaring, that had been the Major's laughter, that Link stared at him, verifying the fact that this nervous cackling was really laughter. He decided he liked the sound.

"Could I live here?" he asked.

They both looked at him: Weak Knees with gravity, concern in his face, a frown wrinkling his forehead; Bill Hod with no change of expression at all. Neither of them said anything. Weak Knees moved his feet, shuffled them under the table. The dog stopped snoring.

"He died," Link explained. "And she cries all the time."

They still didn't say anything and he thought, If he could make them know what it was like, the dark cold house, the being afraid, the not being looked at, or listened to, or talked to, and ended up saying, "She don't see me and she don't even hear me when I talk. She don't seem to know it when I'm there."

Bill Hod shrugged, said, "So?" and then to Weak Knees, "He can sleep in the room in the back. Fix it up for him."

"Okay, Boss."

Weak Knees fixed the room for him by making the bed. Link went to sleep almost immediately. He didn't know how long he had been asleep, but he woke up, covered with sweat, sobbing, "I didn't do it. I didn't do it." At least that's what he was trying to say, though he didn't know why, but the words wouldn't come out, instead there issued from his throat a dreadful groaning, a sound so horrid that it terrified him. He had no control over it, couldn't stop it, and yet he knew that it was he who made it, and as he lay there groaning, aware of the darkness, aware that he was alone in a strange room in a strange bed, he told himself all over again that the Major was dead, remembered how he looked in the casket, remembered touching his hand, his face, and he began to cry.

Bill Hod's hand, firm, warm, patted his shoulder, touched his face, lightly, offering warmth, comfort. He recognized the feel of his hand in the dark.

"There, there, Sonny," he said. Then, his voice a little more insistent, "You're all right," the pressure of the hand stronger as he said, again, "You're all right."

He kept on shivering and sobbing. It wasn't just the Major. He had lost Abbie too, and so was lost himself.

Bill Hod said, "Come on. Get out of this." He pushed him into a sitting position, helped him walk across the bare unfamiliar room, across a hall, into Bill's room, into Bill's bed, where he fell asleep.

When he woke up the next morning, warm and relaxed, the room was full of sunlight. No curtains at the windows, no pictures on the walls, walls painted white, and so there was sunlight or reflected light everywhere. As he looked around, Bill Hod came into the room, naked, nothing on his feet. He stared at him, surprised, a little shocked, because he had never seen a grownup without any clothes on.

Once he'd seen the Major soaking his feet in a big foot tub in the kitchen. Abbie hadn't liked it because Link had squatted down, nose practically in the tub, staring, pointing at the bunions and the corns, asking the Major what they were, and how they got on his feet. Abbie had said, "Dory, I told you not to do that here in the kitchen. It's the kind of thing sharecroppers do."

He supposed he ought not to look at this man who was walking about the room barefooted. But he couldn't help it. He had no corns on his feet, no bunions. His stomach didn't stick out, it was flat, absolutely flat; his waist was narrow and his shoulders were wide. The skin on his body was almost white, the forearms, and his face, tan by contrast. He made no sound as he walked, and Link thought, He's air-borne, light as air.

The windows were wide open so that the room was not only full of sunlight but full of air—cold air; and he could see the branches of the trees outside. As long as he lived that picture of Bill Hod, naked, moving about as though he enjoyed having no clothes on, lingered in his memory, inextricably mixed up with sunlight, and fresh, cool air.

Bill Hod stopped collecting his clothes, and lit a cigarette. He glanced at the bed, saw that Link was looking at him, said, "Hungry?"

He said, "Yes—Bill."

It would have been impossible for him to describe the way he felt about Bill Hod at that moment. He had been living in dark, heavily curtained rooms, always within hearing of Abbie's weeping, and it had been like living alone, trying to live alone, deep down in the earth where no light could enter, with the sound of mourning always in his ears; this man, Bill Hod, had taken him out of the dark and put him in the sun. He had loved Abbie but in a different way, a quieter, less violent way. There was something of worship as well as passion in his feeling for Bill Hod.

That time he lived at The Last Chance for three months. For three solid months Abbie Crunch forgot that he existed.

He learned to swim, to cook, to hit a target with a rifle, to love a dog, a dog who really and truly had a gold tooth. He took showers instead of baths. He answered to the name of Sonny instead of Link.

And, on Saturdays they didn't have baked beans.

Early, on a Saturday afternoon, he went in the kitchen, and found Weak Knees stirring something in a tremendous frying pan, on the back of the stove. It smelled so good that he could have eaten some of it right then, even though he wasn't really hungry. He asked Weak Knees what he was making.

"Meat sauce for the spaghetti."

"Is it for tonight?" he asked.

"Sure thing."

"We always had baked beans on Saturday nights," he said, surprised. Eight years old, and he thought everybody ate baked beans on Saturdays.

"Baked beans? Saturday nights?" Weak Knees stopped stirring the sauce, turned away from the stove, and looked at him with something very like horror. "Name-a-God, Sonny, what kind of eatin' is that? Make a man fart all night."

When Old Man John the Barber stalked in through the open door, Link was putting on one of the starched white monkey jackets that the bartenders wore in The Last Chance; thinking, My idea, it pleases me that Mr. Hod's barkeep boys should be done up all proper and elegant.

Barber smacked a dollar bill down on the bar, said, "Beer," and glared at Link, glared at the monkey jacket, as usual.

Link drew a glass of beer, placed it on the bar in front of the old man, then put a copy of the *Chronicle* right beside the glass. "There," he said, "that should take care of you almost indefinitely. Now—if any gentlemen with unquenchable thirsts should enter through yonder door and should inquire as to the whereabouts of the bartender, will you be so kind as to tell them that he is in the kitchen laying his lip over a cup of honest-to-God coffee while he talks with his friend and mentor, Mr. Weak Knees. Kindly call me, Mr. Barber, if any customers should arrive."

Barber grunted by way of reply.

HE LAY FLAT on his back, eyes half closed; half awake, half asleep; he was aware of a sense of expectancy that was quickening the beat of his heart, causing a slow increase in the pressure of his blood; he deliberately prolonged this moment in which his conscious mind had not yet analyzed, explained, whatever it was that had not yet happened, but was about to happen. Wonderful whatever the thing was. Indefinably wonderful.

Then he remembered. This was Sunday. He had a date with Camilo Williams.

He took a shower in the expensive bathroom that Bill Hod had paid to have installed, in what had once been a big closet, in the front parlor, in Abbie's house. Same front parlor where the Major's coffin had stood all those years ago. After Abbie and F. K. Jackson got him out of The Last Chance, they turned the parlor into a bedroom for him; and it continued to look like a front parlor until Bill Hod paid an interior decorator to do the room over. It was still a good room. Though Abbie would never think so.

He had almost finished dressing when he heard a peculiar scrambling sound. It came from his bedroom. He frowned, listening. Oh, damn that cat, he thought. Anyone would think Abbie was an old maid all of whose latent passion, emotion, affection, suppressed sexual desires were hung around the neck of a tomcat—even to the name, Pretty Boy.

Taking his shoes in his hand, he opened the door that led into the bedroom. I'll brain him, he thought, flatten him out. He's having a wrestling match with the stuff I left strewn around on the top of the desk.

It wasn't the cat. It was J. C. Powther. He was not scrambling around in the stuff on top of the desk, he was going through the top drawer, methodically, and yet quickly, his round head almost inside the drawer, his small behind bobbing up and down in the most tempting fashion as he reached farther and farther inside the drawer.

Link said, "Hey! Get the hell out of there."

J.C. turned, looked at him doubtfully, obviously estimating the degree and the strength of Link's wrath but one hand stayed inside the drawer, feeling, clutching, and discarding, continuing the investigation, while the rest of his body drew itself together in preparation for flight or counterattack.

J.C. said, "You got a penny?"

Link handed him a nickel. "Here. Go buy yourself an ice cream cone. And choke on it while you're eating it."

J.C. gave him a black and venomous stare. He did not move away from the desk, simply reached for the nickel and knotted his fist around it, saying, "They costs six cents now." Having dismissed Link as a source of danger, he turned his attention back to the drawer.

"Here's a dime. It's blackmail but like all other victims of blackmailers I hope it's insurance. Anyway, you stay out of my room. If I catch you in here again I'll cut you up in little pieces and boil each piece separately in oil."

J.C. grabbed the dime and started backing toward the door. "I'm goin' get me some Kool-Aid."

Link glared at him. "You get yourself some arsenic, old man. You trot down to the candy store right now, six-fifteen in the ayem and you kick on the door until Mintz opens it at six-thirty and you say, 'Mintz, I want me a half-pound of arsenic.'"

"Mintz don't run the candy store."

"No?"

"Miss Dollie has the candy store. She don't open until near nine o'clock."

"Well, well, well. Is Miss Dollie colored or does she belong to the same race as the Great White Father?"

"She's cullud."

"Ah! That accounts for the late opening. In my day the candy store on the corner of Franklin and Dumble belonged to a gentleman named Mintz and a man could refresh himself with a soda pop or an ice cream cone at six-forty-five in the ayem if he were so minded. Mintz opened up early and closed up late. Your Miss Dollie'll never get to be a millionaire opening up at nine. Anyway when she does get the joint opened, you go right down there and order up a half pound of arsenic from her and you eat some every morning at this hour and—"

"Yah!" J.C. paused in the doorway. "You don't know your ass from your elbow," he shouted and ran up the front stairs, his feet making a soft thud on the carpeted stairs.

Link yelled after him, "I catch you in here again, you little bastard, and I'll guarantee you'll know yours because it'll be the part you can't sit on for a month."

Abbie came out in the hall. "What in the world—"

"Good morning," he said. "I was just telling my little friend to batten down his hatches. I trust I did not unduly disturb you with my bellowing. I hope I did not rudely thrust you forth from the arms of Morpheus—"

"Arms of—arms of—whose arms?" she asked. "Was he in your room? Link you confuse me so. You do it on purpose. Why don't you talk like other people? Was J.C. in your room?"

"Yes, ma'am. I ejected him. Verbally. Not forcibly. It was the threat of force that you heard."

"Arms of—whose arms—what were you talking about?"

"I meant that I hoped I didn't get you out of bed, Miss Abbie. But you were up, weren't you? Come on, I'll help you get breakfast. Sunday morning. Special breakfast."

He could tell by her eyes that she was surprised by this unexpected offer. Whatever she thought or felt was instantly revealed in her eyes—fine eyes; the expression, on the whole, one of valor. Yet she wasn't valorous. Or was she? She was afraid of everything under the sun, storms, strange dogs, tramps, drunks, any unexpected sound. Too much imagination, that was all. She could visualize disaster, see it, feel it; and had never liked it because he refused to share her fears. But she had survived a personal disaster, a big one; and that accounted for the valor in her eyes. He thought, as he looked down at her, smiling, We might have been friends, if you had had a slightly lower set of standards, if your judgments of people had been less unkind, less critical; if that outer layer of pride had not been so prickly, so impenetrable.

Abbie said, "Help me? Why, I suppose you could. But you —somehow you're different this morning. What's happened to you?"

"It's the time of year," he said solemnly. "I always act like this in the fall. I shed my hair and get a brandnew crop of hair, and it—well—it stimulates me. Preparation for winter. You know, like a cat or a dog or a woodchuck or a squirrel. Makes me brisk. Ho! Leave me make the coffee."

"Link! You're barefooted. Go put your shoes and your socks on."

"Not me, honey. That's due to the change in the seasons, too. My feet cry out for freedom at this time of year. That's the native African in me. Come on. Leave us brew up the coffee and fry up the bacon and scramble up the eggbeggs."

They had just started to eat, he and Abbie, when he heard Mamie Powther's voice, voice lifted in song, voice ascending and descending the outside back stairs, voice increasing in volume, voice diminishing, almost disappearing, so that he found himself listening, straining to hear as though something important depended on his not losing the sound. Then it slowly increased again, increasing, increasing, as she came down the stairs until finally it seemed to be right beside him, not just the voice but the woman, too. Sometimes at night he'd heard her singing, the voice sounding faint, faraway.

Abbie had opened the kitchen windows. No matter how cold the morning, she always aired the kitchen out, always said the same thing as she flung the windows up, "Colored people's houses always smell of food, ham and fried chicken and greasy greens. Sometimes I think they're all stomach and no mind." He was always tempted to say, "But Miss Abbie, that's not possible. Aren't you colored, too?" and never did.

With the windows open Mamie Powther might just as well have been standing right beside him, as she sang:

> Same train carry my mother;
> Same train be back tomorrer;
> Same train, same train.
> Same train blowin' at the station,
> Same train be back tomorrer;
> Same train, same train.

He supposed that it was a song about death and it might have been a spiritual originally though he'd never heard it before, but that smooth warm voice singing it now turned it into a song about life, about man and his first fall, about Eve and all the wonders of her flesh, about all the Eves for generations back and generations yet to come. She may have been singing about a female who rode on a train, a train that would come back again tomorrow, but the texture of the voice, the ripeness of it told you that there must have been a male aboard that train.

Abbie said, "She never remembers to bring down all the things she'll need. She keeps going up and down the stairs, to get clothespins, to bring down clothes that she's forgotten, and then goes back again after a clothesline. She always washes on Sunday just as though it were any other day in the week and then hangs the wash out. I asked her not to. There's something about clothes hanging on lines on Sundays that—well, it's slovenly and it's outrageous. But then she has children and I suppose—"

She got up and looked out the window. "I should think she'd be cold. Nothing on her head. Her arms practically bare—"

Link got up to pour himself another cup of coffee and glanced out of the window on his way back to the table, and stood, coffee cup in hand, watching Mamie Powther. A cold morning, early, so that the sunlight was thin, pale, and Mamie Powther wore a cotton dress, and a red sweater, the sweater accentuating the big breasts, the sleeves rolled up, revealing the forearms, dimples in the elbows. All of her vigorous, elemental —the arms, the breasts. Softfleshed. Smoothskinned. Brown.

Mamie Powther leaned way over, back toward the house, no stockings on, bare leg exposed, part of thigh exposed. High-heeled red shoes on her feet.

Abbie said again, "I should think she'd be cold. Her arms are practically bare."

"She's probably got her love to keep her warm," he said. Arms practically bare—ha—well, everything else was practically bare, too. Abbie could look smack at the woman's behind, and either not see it, refuse to see it, or see it, and something, some part of her mind, would not admit having seen it, so she spoke of the arms.

That's what's the matter with me, he thought, it's that woman out there bending over a clothes basket. Who the hell could live under the same roof with Venus Powther and not make a pass at the lady, especially when the lady practically waves it in your face, when the lady is built for it, when the lady knows, and I would take an oath on it, I would swear on the

Book that the lady knows that at this early morning hour I am always about to lay my lip over a cup of coffee.

That's what's the matter with me. I'm not in love. It's MamiePowtherChinaCamiloWilliams that has me by the throat. She is what all men chase and never capture, some one man finally touches her with the tips of his fingers and then spends the rest of his life with his hand outstretched, reaching for the warm soft flesh, and all the other women that he chases and finally captures are not what he really wants, he only pursues them because of some real or fancied resemblance to MamiePowtherChinaCamiloWilliams: tone of voice or turn of head, line of throat or—It's MamiePowtherChinaCamiloWilliams that has turned me into a mooncalf, aware of sunrises and sunsets, staring at the bare branches of The Hangman grayblack against the morning sky, staring in the same astonished fashion at the brass knocker on the front door of this house just last night before I put the key in the door, standing, arrested, looking at a knocker I have seen a thousand-and-one times, admiring its size and shape, thinking that it looked like pure gold gleaming in the light from the street lamp; looking back at Dumble Street, Dumble Street at night, lights in the houses, voices, sound of laughter, the tempo of the street increasing, night concealing the broken pavement, shadows softening the stark upanddown shape of the buildings, shadows lengthening the street, widening it, transforming it, no longer bleak, downattheheels, overcrowded, but all light and shadow, all murmur of voices and ripple of laughter.

By four o'clock he was at the dock. There was a pink-and-redorange glow across the western sky. The river was redgold along the edges, the windows of the buildings on Dock Street, and what could be seen, at an angle, of Dumble Street were redgold, too. He walked up and down, up and down, impatient, restless, thinking, All I need is a tight little bouquet of flowers, field flowers, daisies and buttercups, wudged together in my hot little hand, and a volume of poetry, limp leather binding, and inside the small book all the monologues and soliloquies about love: My dust would hear you and beat; come live with me and be my love; make me immortal with a kiss; it was the lark; her lips suck forth my soul; I will make thee beds of roses and a thousand fragrant posies. Frankie and Johnnie. He was dressed for the part too; he had shaved again; he had bathed again; he had changed all of his clothes again—clean from top to toe, head to foot. Did he believe that business—my dust, my soul, my love. No. And never would. Was absolutely incapable of the kind of total and complete immersion in another human being that was necessary before one could think in phrases like that. Yet he would never be able to quite forget this girl, this Camilo Williams, not the face, not the figure, but the impression she gave of absolute innocence, of laughing innocence.

He had been looking at the river, and he turned because he heard footsteps on the dock, the girl was walking toward him, smiling. He thought of Mamie Powther singing "Same Train," of China, leaning in the doorway of the hall in that house on Franklin Avenue, incredibly fat, no longer young, treacherous as a snake. Why did this girl in a black suit, white gloves on her hands, dark brown fur around her shoulders, fur reaching to the knees, girl with a walk like a ballerina's, with the straight back and the long neck of a ballerina, girl with a look of elegance, air of innocent gaiety, girl smelling of nightblooming stock under an August moon, why should she make him think of China, of Mamie Powther? There was absolutely no resemblance. They might have come, all three of them, from different planets, and yet—there must be something, an emanation, an aura, something that made him bunch them together. He decided it was the facial expression: part challenge, part expectancy, part invitation.

Camilo said, "Link! How wonderful. You came early, too," smiling, standing close to him.

He nodded. "The early bird—"

"Do I look like a worm?"

"You look—" he said, and couldn't finish the sentence. She was standing too close to him—all of her too close to him: eyes, mouth, hair.

"I look like what?"

"Like an angel."

"Have you ever seen one?"

"No," he said. "But when Gabriel lets loose that great big final blast on his horn and Peter checks the record and then opens the gate for me, he will be surrounded by lovely winged creatures all of whom will take one look at me and say, 'Link, how wonderful,' and sound as though they meant it. That is the Williams version of heaven."

"Golly! That's what you were supposed to say but I didn't know it could sound like that."

"Good?"

"Like a poet."

"That's because I was thinking 'come live with me and be my love.' It was in the back of my mind. There's something contagious about the stuff." She stiffened as though from an electric shock and he wanted to grin, and didn't; instead he said, slowly, carefully, so that she could not be certain whether he was issuing an invitation or whether he was idly quoting, "Make me immortal with a kiss."

He thought, Honey, your back can't get any straighter, if it does it'll break. You'll have to duck out of this some other way, indicate your displeasure by boxing my ears, or by saying, Sir, how dare you. If you didn't expect me to give some indication of interest in you, why did you come back here?

She said, coolly, "Now that we've got that out of the way, I want to make a suggestion."

He said, "'Her lips suck forth my soul.'" Voice soft, voice caressing.

She skipped that one. "I thought—"

"Is it the necktie? I spent two hours selecting this tie. I thought it was a pretty good job. Sort of enhances the beard. Gray tie. Gray beard."

"They're both beautiful. That's not the suggestion. I came early because I thought it might be fun to drive to New York, see a movie, and then go somewhere and eat."

"To New York?" He thought, Lady, you go so fast. You should have been an executive. The female doesn't usually direct the movement of the troops, at least not right out in the open. The female normally deploys her forces from ambush in order that the beginning of the attack shall be concealed.

"Why not? Two hours going. Two hours coming back. Why should we waste our Sunday afternoon costumes, your tie, your beard, my wings, and my halo, on The Moonbeam—"

"Okay."

When they reached the car, he said, "I'll drive."

"Why? Don't you trust my driving?"

He waited until he had started the car before he answered her. Then he said, "To be truthful, no. You drive too fast. You ignore the intersections. You act as though you were driving a royal coach, with outriders clearing the way. The peasants, taking the air on the Merritt Parkway, heading for New York, in their Fords and Chevrolets, might not recognize the royal coach, might not know they were blocking the royal route. Therefore, I will drive."

"Why did you say that?" she said sharply, frowning.

"I have watched you drive off in this crate. Twice. Both times you made my hair stand on end. I do not like to have my hair stand on end and my hair does not like to stand on end because it knows that human hair is not supposed to do that. My scalp is outraged by the unnatural action of my hair and cries, Halt, Stop, Cut it out."

"You're laughing at me," voice muffled, angry.

She was silent as they left Monmouth. Dear me, he thought, this is a temperamental little one and I have no liking for the silent treatment. I do not respond to it properly. My hackles rise. I will have to practice walking on eggshells. I have no experience, no previous experience, in eggshell-walking and therefore I will not be able to give a good performance. They skirted New Haven, entered the Parkway and she still hadn't said anything.

He increased the speed of the car, then he said, softly, "Did you ever hear a very old saying to the effect that where there was no offense intended, no offense should be taken?"

"No. But it sounds reasonable."

He let it go at that, said, and he'd been wanting to say it, "Whenever I see a sky like this one, brassy color rioting all over it, I always wish I could paint. Show the sun going down incredibly hotlooking, and show, too, that the air is cold, make the whole thing look as though the sun were throwing down a gauntlet to winter, shoving it down the throat of the long cold nights."

"You could write it," she said.

"Writing's inadequate. It's not fast enough. A gaudy winter sunset done up in color straight out of the tropics, the whole thing set down in the brutal cold of New England, calls for paint. You see you've got to get it across in the first glance, show the impossible, incredible contrast, bare branches of trees, gaunt, grayblack, silhouetted against that smashing color—all across the horizon—" He took his hands off the wheel, made a wide all-encompassing gesture, using both hands, and the car swerved to the right. He pulled it back on the road quickly.

Camilo said, politely, "Quote. I do not like to have my hair stand on end. My hair does not like to stand on end because it knows that human hair is not supposed to do that. End quote." She laughed. "I'm sorry, but I really couldn't help it."

"Just for future reference, what was wrong with what I said about your driving?"

"I can't bear to be laughed at."

"I was teasing you. I wasn't laughing at you. Even if I had been—why can't you bear to be laughed at?"

"It makes me feel as though I were fourteen again, and back in boarding school, and so fat that I have to wear size forty-two clothes, and a girl named Emmaline is holding up one of my nightgowns, laughing, laughing, laughing, and saying, 'It's like a tent. I bet three of us could get inside it and there'd be room left over. Look! It's like a tent.'"

He said, "In one way or another, it happens to everybody." He thought, I was ten, and they called me Sambo, and I died a little, each time. Well, we have a little more information. You went to boarding school. I didn't think they turned 'em out of Monmouth High School with your stance.

"It's a funny thing," she said. "But when you're that young, people think you haven't any feelings. We were weighed every month, and every month part of me shriveled up and died because I weighed so much it was a joke. Everybody laughed, the nurse, the doctor, the other girls. I wanted to look like Garbo-Cleopatra and I looked like Dickens' fat boy but with pigtails, and wearing a size forty-two tent, not a dress, but a tent. So at night I escaped from the ridicule and the fatness by reading poetry; then after the lights were turned out I would stay awake a long time, making up a dream lover, a dark, handsome man who would recognize the beauty of my soul and fall in love with me, not with any of the pretty, emptyheaded, thin ones.

"In every boarding school, there's a girl with the face of a Botticelli angel and the tongue of an asp, to let you know exactly how awful you look. The one at the school where I went was Emmaline Rosa May Carruthers. In my dream world, Emmaline always died of jealousy, because the dark, handsome lover jilted her and ran off with me."

He thought, listening, how wonderfully complicated the female is, even at fourteen. Fourteen, fourteen, fourteen. What was I like at fourteen? I was damn near being a professional football player, baseball player, basketball player; and I was hellbent on swimming the English Channel. Somebody must have conquered the Channel about then, otherwise I wouldn't have been practically living in The River Wye, covered with grease. Weak Knees and Bill Hod, on the dock, egging me on. Nobody could have paid me to go near a girl. I thought they were dumb, none of 'em could dive.

Camilo said, "I hated those girls, all those pretty curlyheaded girls. But I bought them candy and cake and silk stockings, hoping that if they were in my debt they wouldn't laugh at me. They ate the candy and the cake, and wore the stockings and laughed at me just the same. It was a brandnew, unpleasant experience. Even now, I get angry if I'm laughed at."

"I can't somehow picture you as a fat little girl. But you must have been beautiful." Certainly the hair, the eyes, the mouth, must have been exactly the same.

"I wasn't though. No child can be dreadfully fat and still be beautiful."

"How long have you been looking the way you do now?"

"Ever since I was eighteen."

"What happened then?"

"I was in college by then. In my second year at Barnard. Nobody laughed at me there. But all the girls had boyfriends. I did, too, but mine were the toofat ones who wore thicklensed glasses, or the toothin ones, whose backs were hunched over from studying. So I went on a diet and for the first time in my life I learned what it was like to be hungry, all the time. When I'd got thin enough to wear size fourteen clothes I had my hair cut off. In June, one of the fat boys peered at me, then his eyes opened, wide, and he said, 'Why, you're beautiful!' I felt like the Count of Monte Cristo because I'd dug my way out of what amounted to a tomb of fat, and done it alone, unaided."

She was silent and then she turned toward him and said,

"You know, when you told me about going to your first movie and how you believed that the world was yours, I was startled. Because the same thing had happened to me. When that boy said, 'You're beautiful,' I believed the world was mine, all I had to do was reach out and take it."

He asked her the same question she had asked him. "Do you still believe it?"

"Of course not. I was awfully young at eighteen, terribly young."

"You still are."

"Not in the same way. It's all right to believe that the world is yours when you're eight. If you're eighteen you're liable to run into trouble."

In New York, he paid a buck and a half to park the car in a midtown parking lot. The attendant looked at Camilo, looked at Link, blandly, incuriously. Link thought, In New York all the black boys who go in for what they like to call Caddies also go in for white girls. So this is old hat to him. He figures that if I'm rich enough—numbers or women or rackets of one kind or another—to drive one of these crates, then almost any goodlooking white girl is going to find me acceptable. Money transforms the black male. Makes him beautiful in the eyes of the white female. Black and comely. No. It was black *but* comely. Black and comely, take it for granted that blackness and comeliness were not only possible but went hand in hand. A taken-for-granted condition. The other was an explanation and an apology. He thought, That far back. They started that far back. Ah, well.

"Which movie, honey? It was your idea."

"I've got reservations for Radio City," she said.

"How much?"

"Oh, these are Annie Oakleys. I'm always getting tickets to this or that because I write about fashions."

He made no comment but he didn't quite like the idea. He sat beside her in the brilliantly lighted vastness, the elaborateness, of the Music Hall at Radio City, thinking, Well, it's a new experience. I've never been took to the movies before. I must say she's a rather highhanded little female.

The lights went down, and his resentment vanished, because there was always a moment, in any theatre, just before the curtains opened, when he could convince himself that he would, once again, experience that disembodied feeling he had known, at his first movie, when he was eight years old. He never did. Yet, even here, where he knew in advance pretty much what he was going to see, he leaned forward, watching the curtains part, half convinced that this time the magic would work, and he would behold a new and wonderful world.

He saw a stage full of dancing girls, wearing fabulous costumes, and he sat back in his seat. He glanced at Camilo. She was watching the stage, completely absorbed, leaning forward, as though she were alone here, as though this particular show had been staged for her, for no one else. She had removed the white gloves. The soft brown fur that she'd worn around her shoulders was in her lap, mounded in her lap. His hand brushed against it. He resisted an impulse to touch her hand, to say something, anything, that would turn her attention from the dancing girls on the stage to the man sitting beside her.

Finally, the dancing girls moved off the stage, kicking high. They were so exactly alike, the legs, ankles, thighs, breasts, so exactly alike, that they might have been turned out of a mold. Even the high kicks, high kick and turn the head, high kick and turn the head. Maybe they had some kind of meter machine in the rehearsal hall that measured the height of the kicks. It could be simpler than that, maybe they'd worked out something like the automat, put in a nickel, in a giant machine, located on Forty-Second Street, and out would come a girl, or girls, who would meet the requirements as to size and shape, and would be kicking up her legs, just so far, and thus they could trot her right up to this theatre, without any further effort on the part of the dance director.

The dancing girls were followed by a pair of dancing colored comedians. He thought, Why, this is the minstrel show again. I'm right back in the Arsenal School on Franklin Avenue and Miss—pause—Dwight is saying, "We won't have to use any burnt cork on—pause—Link."

On the way down, Camilo had said, "It's a funny thing but when you're that young, people think you haven't any feelings." She was fourteen then. Well, he was ten when Miss pause Dwight, who was his teacher, must have come to the conclusion that he didn't have any feelings.

It wasn't just Miss Dwight either. As Dumble Street changed, and more and more colored kids began to go to the Arsenal School, he learned about a new and different kind of insecurity. He was never certain whether the white kids would let him play with them. Sometimes, after school, they played baseball and the kids shouted, "Throw it to old Link, throw it to old Link, Link's good!" Then again the white kids would band together in a tight invulnerable group, welded together by their whiteness, and he, the outcast, the separate one, would be turned on suddenly, ostracized by a gesture, a look, a word.

He kept his fears to himself. They were varied, peculiar. He was afraid of pigeons, afraid of those fat, outrageously breasted birds, that fed on the school lawn, waddling across the grass, in groups, murmuring to themselves, Look at the coon, Look at the coon, Look at the coon, until finally it sounded like one long word, Lookatthecoon.

At least that's what the white kids told him the pigeons were saying. They laughed when they told him. If he grew sullen, furious, and showed it, they said, "Lookit old Link. We ain't talkin' about you. That's what them pigeons say," and then the pigeons and the kids would say, Lookitthecoon, Lookitthe-coon, Lookitthecoon, over and over.

He hated crows and grackles and starlings—all the black birds. Because the kids giggled, their eyes sliding around to him when they saw these big black birds, "Blackbird!" they said, and meant him. He hated storms too, thunderstorms, rain clouds, wind clouds, any big black cloud that piled its darkness in the sky. "Storm comin' up," the white kids said. They said it easily, with laughter, innocent-eyed as they looked at him, "A big black cloud's around so a storm's comin' up." "Link's here. A storm's comin' up."

Then, just as suddenly, they welcomed him, accepted him. But he was wary of their acceptance. He never knew at what moment he would be betrayed, thrust out, because of the pres-ence of some other dark creature like himself, perhaps a star-ling or a crow or another colored boy; betrayed by the gross redlegged pigeons, calling, Lookitthecoon, Lookitthecoon.

Even his name betrayed him. His teacher, Miss Dwight, managed to make it a peculiar name; she hesitated before she said it, made it laughable, and her eyes rejected him, "Speak up—pause—Link." The pause before the name turned it into something to be ashamed of.

It was Miss Dwight, Miss Eleanora Dwight, who decided that his class would give a minstrel show, to raise money, to help raise money for the Parent Teachers' Association. She gave him a part in the show. When the other kids heard her read the lines that would be his, they laughed until they almost cried. He was the butt of all the jokes, he was to say all of the yessuhs and the nosuhs, he was to explain what he was doing in the chicken house, Ain't nobody in here, boss, but us chickens; he was to be caught stealing watermelons; he was to dance something that Miss Dwight called the buck and wing; he was to act sleepy and be late for everything. His name in the minstrel was Sambo.

He could dance better than the other kids. But Miss Dwight and her pause—Link made him ashamed of his ability to dance.

"You know the buck and wing, don't you, pause, Link?"

"No, ma'am," he said politely and let his answer lie there unadorned, no explanation, just the denial.

Miss Dwight said, "Oh, well, any of the dances you know will do," and waited.

Link said nothing.

"What other dances do you know?"

"I don't know any dances, Miss Dwight, except the ones they teach us here in school."

"I thought—" Miss Dwight said and frowned. "Well, we'll make up something. Perhaps your father could teach you the buck and wing or some dance like it." When he didn't reply she said, "Answer me. Can your father teach you the buck and wing?"

He said, "Miss—" then he had a sudden inspiration. He paused before he said "Dwight" just the way she paused before she said "Link." He gave his voice the same intonation as though the name were very strange, very foreign, very funny, and the other kids giggled. Miss Dwight's face turned red, the red seeped into her neck, up to her hairline. "My father's dead," he said; and her face turned even redder. Silence in the room. Stillness.

She went on reading the lines that would be his, and her face stayed red. He felt triumphant. He had beaten her at her own game. But when she finished reading, the kids laughed. It wasn't quite as spontaneous, not quite as hearty as it had been before—but they laughed. She looked around the room, not looking at Link; and he thought, She's going to do something to show I'm different from the rest of the kids.

Miss Dwight said, "Of course this is to be done in black face. You know, like Al Jolson in *Mammy*." She studied Link's face. She said, "We won't have to use any burnt cork on Link though."

For the first time in his life he was ashamed of the color of his skin. He decided that he would get sick. He would go to all the rehearsals and two days before, no, on the very night of the minstrel show, he would get sick, so sick that he wouldn't be able to be Sambo. None of the kids would be able to take his part on such short notice. So there wouldn't be any minstrel show.

Abbie read the *Chronicle* every night after supper. "I see they're having a minstrel show at school," she said.

Link said, "Uh-huh."

"Are you in it?"

"In a sort of way," he answered and left before she could ask him any more questions. Storm clouds, black birds, gross pigeons strutting on the school lawn, but infinitely worse than any of these—minstrel shows, minstrel shows gotten up by teachers named Miss pause Dwight, teachers who took your name and made it a thing to laugh at, changing it.

At rehearsals he kept getting clumsier and clumsier, bumping into tables and chairs, falling over his own feet.

Miss pause Dwight laughed and choked and coughed and laughed again. "Oh, he's wonderful!" she said. "He makes the show."

The kids began calling him Sambo, during school hours, after school hours, on Saturdays. When they met him on the street, they said, "Hi, Sambo," in chorus, and waited, eying him for some sign of anger. He muttered, "Hi," and walked away.

On the stage, in Radio City Music Hall, one of the dancing colored comedians, slowed his furious pace, lay down, flat on his back, sleeping, sleeping, sleeping. The other dancing colored comedian annoyed him, tormented him, moving about him with the swift darting motion of a mosquito or a fly or a gnat. The sleeping one brushed at the dancing one, slapped at him, moved an arm out of range, moved a leg, shook himself, refusing to wake up. The pantomime was skilful, carefully thought out, comic.

He smiled, as he watched this rhythmic performance, thinking, Well, well, Sambo is still sittin' in the sun. He glanced at the girl. She was laughing, head flung back, revealing the long line of the throat; possibly because she had changed her position he was more than ever aware of her perfume. He thought, I have come a long way. If it hadn't been for Bill Hod and Weak Knees, the color of your skin would disturb me as I watch you laughing at Sambo sittin' in the sun.

9

HE COULD STILL REMEMBER some of the things that Sambo was to say: Yessuh, ain't nobody in here but us chickens; nosuh, watermelon's mah favoritest vegittible; ah'm Sambo, yessuh, Sambo, just sittin' in the sun, suh; just catchin' up with mah sleep, suh.

Ten years old. And on the day of the minstrel show, he woke up feeling hot, suffocated. His head ached. Abbie called and called for him to come and eat his breakfast. She came in his room and said, "Why, Link," and put her hand on his forehead. Her hand felt cool, dry. He was sweating.

Abbie said, "You get right back in bed."

He went to sleep and when he woke up, Dr. Easter was leaning over him, saying "Hmmm—" Then Dr. Easter was gone but it couldn't have been as fast a visit as that because he kept remembering the cool hard feel of a thermometer under his tongue.

He went to sleep again. The ringing of the telephone woke him up. He heard Abbie say, "He's very sick, Miss Dwight." Silence. "Oh, no!" Her voice was crisp, cold. "Absolutely impossible. He can't get out of bed."

He stared up at the ceiling. He had forgotten about the minstrel show. Was he really sick or had he made himself sick? Could you make yourself sick, not really meaning to? Not really meaning to? Then you could make yourself go crazy, too.

He sat up, frowning. He hadn't made himself sick. It had just happened. Maybe he had the mumps. But he didn't ache anywhere. He felt strong, cool, comfortable. He wanted to get out of bed; he felt like going swimming.

If he wasn't sick any more, he ought to get dressed, and go down to the school auditorium and be Sambo, sittin' in the sun. He'd sold out, hadn't he? Sold what out?

He got dressed. He went out of the front door very quietly so Abbie wouldn't hear him. Miss Dwight would be happy. He would be unhappy. But he had to be Sambo, sittin' in the sun. He walked slowly, up Dumble Street, over to Franklin, down Franklin to the school.

He stood still. People were going up the long walk, in through the front door. Cars were parked on both sides of the school driveway. He couldn't be Sambo sittin' in the sun in front of all those people. Ain't nobody in here but us chickens.

If Abbie knew about this, she'd say that he'd let The Race down. She said colored people (sometimes she just said The Race) had to be cleaner, smarter, thriftier, more ambitious than white people, so that white people would like colored people. The way she explained it made him feel as though he were carrying The Race around with him all the time. It kept him confused, a little frightened, too. At that moment The Race sat astride his shoulders, a weight so great that his back bent under it. When he turned away from the school, he was walking fast.

In school, the next morning, Miss pause Dwight said, "I thought you were sick, pause, Link."

"I was," he said.

"You know you ruined the minstrel show. We couldn't have it. On account of you. I should have known that you'd fail me at the last minute."

He knew what she meant about failing her at the last minute. There wasn't much about The Race that he didn't know. Abbie kept telling him all the things he could, and could not, do because of The Race. You had to be polite; you had to be punctual; you couldn't wear bright-colored clothes, or loud-colored socks; and even certain food was forbidden. Abbie said that she loved watermelons, but she would just as soon cut off her right arm as go in a store and buy one, because colored people loved watermelons. She wouldn't buy porgies because colored people loved all the coarsefleshed fish, and were particularly fond of porgies. She wouldn't fry fish, she wouldn't fry chicken, because everybody knew that colored people liked fried food. She was always on time, in fact, way ahead of time, because colored people were always late, you could never count on them, they had no sense of responsibility. The funny thing about it was that when Abbie talked about The Race she sounded as though she weren't colored, and yet she obviously was.

All of this was why Miss pause Dwight had known that he'd fail her at the last minute. But she couldn't have known. He had been sick, really and truly sick. Then he got better. He had got out of bed, and come all the way down to the school, yesterday; but then when he got here he just couldn't be Sambo sittin' in the sun. Not in front of all those people.

All that morning Miss pause Dwight said: "I might have known"; "Sit still"; "Stop wriggling"; "Answer me!" "Are you asleep?" "Stand up!" "Sit down!"

By the time the noon bell rang, he knew he wasn't going back to school. Not ever. He spent the afternoon down on the dock. He found there were three other colored boys, older than he, who were playing hookey too. They figured out that if they showed up for meals, and got home just about the time the other kids came from school, and left their houses in the morning when the other kids were leaving, their families wouldn't know they were playing hookey. The mail was delivered in the morning before they left for school, so if the principal sent a notice home, they could get it first, tear it up and that way—well, they'd stay out for a long long time.

During that long wonderful week, F. K. Jackson and Abbie and The Race and Miss pause Dwight disappeared from his world, dispelled by sun and wind and fog. He forgot there was something wrong, bad, about the color of his skin. When it rained they went, all of them, single file, quietly, quickly, around the back of The Last Chance, and sat inside the old unused chicken house, and played cards and read comic books. Even when it was raining they went swimming in the river.

Abbie found out, finally, by the most unforeseen, the most appallingly unforeseen, of accidents. She went to see the principal, without saying anything to Link, suddenly, on impulse, because she wasn't satisfied with Link's reading. She kept telling him that when she was ten years old she could read and understand poetry, the Bible, Shakespeare; and he said that he could read better than any kid in his grade; and she said, "Well, in that case they must all be morons and idiots because you can barely spell out the words in a primer, and you can't write so that anybody can read what you've written." They usually stopped right there—but he felt so free, the river seemed to have soaked into his bones and blood, he felt like air and water and sun, and The Race no longer sat astride his shoulders, Miss pause Dwight no longer prodded him and The Race, at one and the same time, that he said, "Well, Aunt Abbie, other people can read my writing. Maybe you need to get new glasses."

And she got mad and went to the principal's office to find out if something couldn't be done to improve his reading.

About three-thirty in the afternoon, he came in through the back door, as usual, so he wouldn't muddy up the front hall floor, came in through the back door, whistling, not a care in the world, feeling as though there were a grin inside him that was spreading, spreading, and he kept telling himself to be careful so the grin wouldn't show in his face.

Abbie and F. K. Jackson were waiting for him, in the sitting-dining room, dining-sitting room, both looking as though they were sitting up with a corpse; he knew instantly that he was the corpse and that they had been waiting for his arrival. He could tell by the way Abbie sat in the Boston rocker, her hands folded in her lap, and she never sat still like that, she was always crocheting or knitting, as though she would not, could not, waste even so much as a moment of time; and F. K. Jackson was leaning against the marble mantel; one bony elbow on the mantel. They were both frowning. F. K. Jackson's pince-nez had more glitter than usual.

Abbie said, "Link—"

F. K. Jackson interrupted her. She said, "Why haven't you been in school this week?"

He went straight to the point, just like F. K. Jackson, and said, just as abruptly, "I got tired of it."

That was a mistake. F. K. Jackson said that his staying away from school was an evasive dishonest action which could lead to other larger kinds of dishonesty, far more serious than this; that it already had because he had tampered with the United States mail; and thus he had taken the first step straight toward the door of a reform school. She kept walking up and down, and frowning at him, as she talked. Finally, she shook one of her long, bony, forefingers, practically under his nose, and said, "You're an ingrate. That's what you are—an ingrate!"

Then Abbie talked and talked and talked. About The Race. She said that there had been a time (she always avoided mention of slavery) when it was a crime in this country to teach a colored person to read and write; and, because of that period in the history of The Race, it behooved all persons of color to take advantage of the free education now available to everybody. (He smiled because he thought about Fishmouth Taylor and Fishmouth's comment on practically everything: free

schools, pretty white teachers, and dumb niggers. Abbie must
have got mad because he smiled; otherwise she would not have
said what she did.)

She said it particularly behooved Link Williams, *orphan*,
adopted out of the goodness of the Major's heart (she wiped
away a tear) and her heart, to go to school, every day, and
learn, and learn, and learn, so that he would stand at the head
of his class, in everything, so that he would be a credit to The
Race.

The stage show came to an end in a whirling spectacular finale, composed of dancing girls, and dancing colored comedians, brilliant lighting, and music that sounded as though it
had been lifted whole from the swoop of the "William Tell
Overture," and the curtains closed. The lights came up, all over
the theatre, then went down. The curtains opened again. The
movie started.

He watched it for a few minutes. It bored him. He wondered why women liked movies. What had Camilo said, on
the trip down? Something about the dark handsome lover.
Maybe the female was always hunting for him, maybe in
the back of the female mind was the belief that he could be
found, even after the female was married and had six children.
Hollywood knew this. So the demon lover, the dark, handsome, rapacious lover, showed up in all the movies; and the
females could believe he was theirs for about an hour and a
half. So right after they finished the supper dishes, they went
around to the neighborhood theatre, and sat there, legs apart,
mouths open, panting a little, because now they were young
again, and there was no fat around their waists, no varicose
veins marred the flawless beauty of their legs, and the demon
lover took them in his arms. They always looked dazed when
the picture ended and the lights came up.

Camilo was watching the screen just as she had watched the
stage show, with the same degree of concentration. He wondered how she could identify herself so completely with the
action that took place in a movie. When he was eight, a movie
could carry him straight into another world but he'd seen a hell
of a lot of different worlds since then, and he'd had far more at
stake in all of them than he'd ever have in anything they cooked
up in Hollywood. Demon lover, he thought. Was Camilo still

hunting for one? It seemed doubtful. But if a theory was going
to hold water, wouldn't you have to try applying it? Abbie?
Had she hunted for one? She found one, in the person of the
Major. She lost him when he died, and she was never quite
the same afterwards. F. K. Jackson? Impossible to think of her
hunting a mate, handsome or otherwise. She was too brusque,
too selfsufficient. Perhaps she, in her own person, was the dark
handsome lover, and to her Abbie had been the ChinaCamilo-
Williams that the male hunts for and rarely ever finds; and even
if he finds her, never quite manages to capture her.

Ah, the hell with it, he thought.

Ten years old. And he played hookey. A week later he was
back in school, feeling ashamed and resentful. He wasn't an
ingrate. Nobody had told Abbie and the Major to adopt him.
He would have been better off if they hadn't.

Miss pause Dwight was still mad about his ruining the minstrel show, was furious because he'd played hookey. All day
long, or so it seemed, she said: "I might have expected it";
"Link, will you please wake up?" "Are you deaf? I asked you a
question."

He stopped trying to learn anything. There wasn't any use.
He thought she might forget about him if he acted as though
he were deaf, dumb, blind. So she told the principal that he
was totally unresponsive. The principal sent for him and urged
him to make an effort, "You're a bright boy, Link. You can do
anything you want to do."

Miss pause Dwight complained about him again, saying that
he could no longer stay in her class. The principal sent for
Abbie, and sent for Link too; and told them both that Link
would soon have to go in the class for the mentally retarded,
the dummies as the kids said, because he was now behaving as
though he were halfwitted. He kept right on acting as though
he were deaf, dumb, blind.

Abbie cried. F. K. Jackson scolded. They talked about him,
discussed him, all the time, even when he was in the same
room with them.

Abbie: Maybe he's sick.

F. K. Jackson: I don't believe it. He eats like a horse. If he
were sick he wouldn't eat like a horse.

Abbie: I'm going to send for Dr. Easter.

F. K. Jackson: Don't be foolish. Take the boy around to his office. It costs a dollar less. Besides there isn't a thing wrong with him.

Dr. Easter poked at him, pried at him, weighed him, measured him, said: He's as fine a specimen as I've ever seen. Not a thing wrong with him, Mrs. Crunch.

Abbie reported this to F. K. Jackson and said, a quaver in her voice: Maybe there's something wrong with his mind, Frances. Do you think there's something wrong with his mind?

F. K. Jackson snorted: It's just stubbornness. He's just like a mule. Somebody ought to—and didn't finish whatever she was going to say.

He wasn't supposed to go in The Last Chance except on Saturdays, because of some kind of compromise that F. K. Jackson had worked out with Bill Hod. But he went anyway. On a Wednesday. Late in the afternoon.

Weak Knees said, "Hiya, Sonny. You got here just in time. I got red rice in this here pot. In the middle of the afternoon, like now, a man could eat up all this rice and then turn around and start in all over again." He put a plate of red rice on the table. "Come on, Sonny, start layin' your lip over it, just start right in." Then he looked at Link, really looked at him and he said, "Whatsamatter, Sonny? You don't look so good."

The rice cooled on his plate while he told Weak Knees about the pigeons and the black birds, about Miss pause Dwight and the minstrel show and Sambo sittin' in the sun; and Bill came in and scooped up an enormous plateful of rice, pulled up a chair and sat, listening, not saying anything, just eating red rice, as Link told about The Race, and how he was responsible for all other members of The Race even though he did not know them; and how he couldn't do it any more, it sort of paralyzed him because he never knew whether he was doing something because he, Link, wanted to do it; or whether he did something because of the undesirable color of his skin, and that meant he had no control over what he did—it just happened.

All of a sudden Bill started talking. He was talking about the Chicago riots. Link leaned forward, listening, listening. He'd never heard anything like this before.

Bill told about Ma Winters, an old woman who ran a rooming house on the South Side, in Chicago; and how white men broke down the door and surged into the downstairs hall; and how Ma Winters stood at the top of the stairs with a loaded shotgun in her hand, not shouting, not talking loud, just saying, conversationally, "I'm goin' to shoot the first white bastard who puts his foot on that bottom step." And did. And laughed. And aimed again. "Come on," she said, "some of the rest of you sons of bitches put your white feet on my stairs." And they backed out of the door, backed out of the door, kept backing out of the door, and left a white man, a dead white man, there in the hall, lying on his back, a bloody mess where his face had been.

It seemed to be just a story, a good story, an exciting story, yet he was certain it had some other deeper meaning that he couldn't quite grasp. Certainly the old woman who stood at the head of the stairs firing the shotgun, killing a white man, threatening to kill other white men, didn't carry The Race around on her shoulders. The burden of race lifted a little from his own shoulders.

The next day Abbie told him that if he wanted to he could go back to The Last Chance to live. He didn't know why this should be so but he gladly moved back across the street.

Shortly after that, Bill visited the school. Right after that Link noticed that Miss pause Dwight started being nice to him; oddly enough she referred to Bill as his uncle, Mr. Hod.

Weak Knees and Bill re-educated him on the subject of race. After supper Weak Knees sat down at the kitchen table and read the newspaper, a tabloid newspaper. He spread it out flat in front of him, fingering his way down the columns. When he found something that was especially interesting, he picked the paper up. Link could see the pink outer sheets, the big black type, and Weak Knees' dark hands like a pattern on the pink paper. "Name-a-God, Sonny, lissen to this. Here's a bank teller, just a ordinary smart white boy, free of course 'cause he's white so he done stole hisself thirty-five hunnerd dollars. Done fixed himself so he ain't goin' to be able to cuddle any little gals and he's goin' to have to eat that slop they throw at 'em in jailhouses for the rest of his natural—all for thirty-five

hunnerd dollars. White folks sure is smart. Tee-hee-hee." The
kitchen was filled with his highpitched cackling laugh. Link
had never heard white people laughed at before and it made
him uncomfortable at first.

Weak Knees bought a bird feeder, and hung it in a tree in
the yard in back of The Last Chance, hung suet in the tree,
scattered crumbs.

"That's for my black boys," he said. "Watch them black
boys, Sonny. They drives all them other birds away. Tee-hee-
hee. Bestlookin' birds of any of 'em. Look how them tail feathers and them breas' feathers shine in the sun. Lookithat big
one peck that other bird. Lookithat! Lookithat! Tee-hee-hee."

Black was bestlooking. It was a new idea. He mulled over
it. Not possible. Black is evil. Satan is black. Abbie said, Black
people, and there was disapproval in her voice. Black was undesirable. Black sheep—the bad one. Black cat—bad luck. Black
was ugly, evil, dirty, to be avoided. It was worn for funerals. It
meant death, too.

They proved to him, Weak Knees and Bill Hod, that black
could be other things, too. They did it casually. Ebony was the
best wood, the hardest wood; it was black. Virginia ham was
the best ham. It was black on the outside. Tuxedos and tail
coats were black and they were a man's finest, most expensive
clothes. You had to use pepper to make most meats and vegetables fit to eat. The most flavorsome pepper was black. The
best caviar was black. The rarest jewels were black: black opals,
black pearls.

After a month of living with Bill and Weak Knees he felt fine.
He felt safe. He was no longer ashamed of the color of his skin.
One morning when he went to school he carried a rock in his
hand. When he reached the lawn, he aimed at, and hit, the fattest of the pigeons. Squawks. A fluttering of wings. The rest of
the pigeons flew up, were gone. The fattest one lay on its side.
It too tried to fly, fluttered its wings and lay still.

He knew then what that story of Bill's meant: If you were
attacked you had to fight back. If you didn't you would die.

The long full curtains covered the screen at Radio City Music
Hall. The lights went up.

Camilo turned toward him. "You weren't looking at the picture," she said. "Didn't you like it?"

He shrugged. "Sometimes I look at my own movies." He helped her put the long soft brown furpiece around her shoulders, stood up, waiting, while she put on the white gloves. "Where would you like to eat?" he asked.

"I know a place not too far from here. The food is wonderful. Suppose we go there."

They walked up Fifth Avenue. Even at this hour he thought that the people who passed them seemed, even in walking, to buck their strength against the city, against the concrete sidewalks, against the skyscrapers, and the steam heat inside them; always that suffocating dry heat inside the buildings and outside in the streets the same bone-chilling cold there was in Monmouth—damp, penetrating.

He supposed all these people they passed were hellbent on the same thing, hurrying after the same dream, chasing it up and down Fifth Avenue. He thought of Wormsley, G. Granville Wormsley, who had been his classmate at Dartmouth. Once he and Wormsley had walked along Fifth Avenue, stopping now and then to look in the store windows, just as Camilo was doing now. Only Wormsley was always hunting paintings and books; Camilo was hunting dresses and shoes and jewelry —at least that was what she looked at longest, standing, head cocked on one side, looking.

Link said, "About five years ago I walked along here with a friend of mine, a guy named Wormsley. After he'd looked in some of these store windows he said, 'This is what brought my father here, this is what keeps me here. I look in these windows, go in these stores, and I begin to believe all over again that I can conquer this city. It's the sight of the loot in these windows that keeps people in New York.' About a year after that he came to Monmouth, to say goodbye to me. He said it was hopeless, nobody could win against New York City, and that it wasn't what he wanted so he was going to London. Six months later he was back. He said he didn't know why he had left, that he never intended to leave again, because if he lost, and now he was no longer certain about the outcome, he would rather lose in New York, in the midst of the cold and chill, in the midst of the only other kind of

weather the city offered, heat and heat and heat, than to survive, let alone win, anywhere else in the world."

Camilo had stopped to look at a red evening gown, displayed on one of those incredibly thin, very natural-looking
figures they use in the windows of department stores. A seated
figure, the long thin legs crossed, the trunk bending forward.
Link looked too, and thought, Well, Sambo may still be sittin'
in the sun, sleepin' in the sun in Radio City, but Mrs. Sambo
now sits in the windows of the specialty shops, the exclusive
dress shops. Some skilled and skilful hand makes all these store
window dummies look like colored women, the hair frizzed,
the skin color no longer pink and white but the offwhite of a
high yaller. O wondrous world.

Camilo said, "What did your friend Wormsley want to win?"

"I asked him that. And he said, 'All of it. All of this city. I want
to control it.' Then he said, 'I want to be a kingmaker, not a
king you understand, but a kingmaker.' Kingmaker Wormsley."

"Why he's a fascist at heart."

"No," Link said slowly. "That doesn't allow for his other
quirks. Fascist in his desire for power—but then aren't we all?
Even you and I? Eventually won't you want to control me?
And I, of course, already want to control you." You've got a
terrific drive, an urge, toward and for power, little one, though
you evidently don't know it. "That doesn't make us fascists."

She said, "*Is* he a kingmaker?"

They turned off Fifth Avenue, started walking east.

Link said, "In a smallish way. If he lives long enough he will
be one in a largish way."

"What does he do?"

"He's a psychiatrist and a damn good one."

He studied the street ahead of them. Let's see, he thought,
where would this little exquisite be likely to think the food
was wonderful? It will be the place where the striped awning
extends over the sidewalk, offering protection to the silk hats
and the poodle cuts emerging from the limousines and taxis,
where the evergreens squat in little red pots, where the doorman in the plum-colored costume stands like the keeper of the
gate, even to the stance, separating the sheep from the goats
before they get close enough to bang on the gate. Yea, verily,
many are called, but few are chosen.

He was right. She said, "Here we are," and tucked her hand under his arm, steering him so that they turned in under the striped awning.

The headwaiter, no, manager, no, owner, well, whatever the hell he was, stood just inside the door, short, swarthy, dressed in evening clothes, greeting the customers also dressed in evening clothes. He bowed practically to the floor at the sight of Camilo, saying, "*Mademoiselle!* What pleasure! We have missed you!" He had a French accent, like Old Madame Tay-tay's, who for years was the only colored Catholic in The Narrows.

Link remembered how he used to watch her sitting on her doorstep, muttering under her breath, as she fingered her beads. She nodded her head, at frequent intervals, so that the long gold earrings she wore, dangled back and forth, making a tinkling sound. The kids said she was born in New Orleans; and that she was creole, and therefore neither colored nor white. Later, they also told him, that when she was dying, she had said her prayers in French. For a long time afterwards, he had wondered how God, whom he had always assumed to be a Protestant and an American, had been able to understand her; and didn't dare ask Abbie lest his question be dismissed as blasphemous.

Camilo said, "I've been away, Georges. In Dallas."

After a quick shrewd glance at Link, Georges bowed again, though not quite so near the floor, said, "*Monsieur!* What pleasure! This way."

Georges personally escorted them the length of the restaurant, past the tables, flowers on the tables, lighted candles on the tables, past the shaded wall lights and the muted voices and the muted laughter. It was warm inside the restaurant. Link caught whiffs of perfume from the females in evening clothes. They went past a small bar and there was the faint smell of alcoholic beverages, alien smell in this warm perfumed room, old familiar smell of The Last Chance, of The Moonbeam, in this restaurant for the very rich. All cats bee gray—

They went up a flight of stairs into a small room where there was a table set for two.

Georges said, "I hope everything will be of a perfection, *mademoiselle, monsieur.* Your waiter will be here at once. Aha, here he is."

The menu cards were big, elaborately decorated. Link thought, You could mat 'em and have 'em framed and they'd make a splash even on the walls of Grand Central. And this tall thin man, in a tail coat, who is our waiter, makes me understand how Weak Knees feels when he says, "Get away, Eddie. God damn it, get away." If he doesn't stop breathing down my neck I shall say the same thing.

Camilo said, "Roast duck, and a salad, and a vegetable. Broccoli for the vegetable."

Link handed the outsize menu back to the waiter. He said, "Steak and whatever your chef thinks an American ought to eat with steak."

The waiter left and Link said, "Did you reserve this?"

She smiled at him. "Yes, I did. Is it all right?"

He nodded, thinking, It's all right from your point of view and in your world. It's all wrong from where I sit.

The food was good though M. Georges's chef wasn't in the same class with Weak Knees, which was only to be expected. He didn't know as much about vegetables, didn't know anything at all about the possibilities of the humble potato. But he knew a good deal about steaks.

While they ate, he told Camilo about Weak Knees, about the new receipt for spaghetti, and how Jubine had said there'd be a shortage of salt pork if all chefs started using it, not really thinking about what he was saying, just making talk, while he studied her face. In the flickering light of the candles, the blue of her eyes was a dark unidentifiable color; the pale yellow hair had an added gleam, it fairly shimmered in the dancing flickering light.

"Jubine?" she said. "The photographer? I know him, too."

Pleasure in the light musical voice, pleasure in her face, because Jubine linked them together, common acquaintance, their worlds came closer because they both knew Jubine. He thought, Motorcycle, GI shoes, cigar in mouth, inquisitive eyes—how did she meet Jubine?

She said, "Sometimes he takes fashion pictures for me. They're absolutely wonderful. But he doesn't care much about photographing models and clothes."

When they finished eating, he said, "I'll ask for the check now so that we can get out of here sometime in the next hour."

She said, "Oh, there isn't any check. It's almost the other way around. If Georges could, he'd pay me to eat here."

"Look!" he said. "If Georges would like to pay you to eat here why that takes care of you. It doesn't take care of me. I'm going to pay for my part of this meal."

"Oh, no, you mustn't."

He rang for the waiter, took his wallet out of his pocket.

"Link," she said, "don't make a scene."

"A scene?" he said. "A scene? What do you mean by that? What kind of a scene do you think I'm likely to make in here?" Sambo was still sittin' in the sun in Radio City Music Hall, maybe he was still sittin' in the sun in Camilo's mind, honing his razor.

"If you insist on paying for something that isn't supposed to be paid for why you'll have to be unpleasant about it. Georges isn't going to take your money. You'd have to force him to take it—and—"

He put the wallet back in his pocket. Georges isn't going to take your money. Why wasn't Georges going to take his money?

The tall thin waiter said, "Yes, sir?" and hovered, again bending down, over Link's shoulder.

Camilo said quickly, "We'd like some hot coffee."

Now that she had got her own way she smiled at Link. She said, "Let's do this again. Next Sunday."

"Go to the movies and then afterwards come here and eat?"

She nodded. "Then you did enjoy it!"

"And when we come here again, next Sunday, I suppose you will already have ordered what you want me to eat."

"Of course not. Why would I?" She stared at him and the laughter, the gaiety, went out of her face. "You mean I'm—"

"The only reason I've put up with this—" he gestured toward the table, the flowers, the candles, the covered silver dishes, the wine glasses, "is—well—I think I'm in love with you. But either we play this my way and ride in whatever hay wagon or tractor or freight car I can provide, or—we quit."

"I think we'd better quit," she said evenly.

As they were leaving, Georges said, "Was everything all right, *monsieur*?"

Link said, "Oh, quite. Everything was of a perfection," unconsciously imitating the accent of Madame Tay-tay. Two on the aisle provided by the lady. Dinner afterwards. Private dining room reserved by the lady. Meal obviously paid for by the lady. Plantation buck. How many generations back? Oh, possibly four. Jump four generations and he shows up as a kept man. Objective about race? Hell, no. Nobody was. Not in the USA.

Georges glanced at him, sharply. "*Monsieur* has an excellent memory."

Camilo said, "Everything was perfection, Georges. Thank you very much, and, good night."

"Good night, *mademoiselle*. Good night, *monsieur*."

They were silent, both of them, all the way back to Monmouth. He stopped the car on Franklin Avenue, got out, closed the door. He had been trying to figure out something to say ever since they left New York. And ended up saying, simply, inadequately, "Goodbye," though he was certain that he would not see her again.

Four nights later. Midnight. He came out of The Last Chance, turned his coat collar up, frowned, listening to the wind keening in the branches of The Hangman, thinking, It's too damn cold to go prowling through these streets again tonight. The Weather Bureau had been predicting this sudden change in temperature, attributing it to a cold mass that was moving in from Canada. Said cold mass had been signaling its arrival for three days, mercury in the thermometers dropping, dropping, wind shifting, shifting; had obviously moved in now and brought all the relatives, including the great grandpappy and the kissin' cousins.

He glanced down Dumble Street. It was as bleak and deserted as a street in a small town where a curfew has rung. Everything closed down, shut up, all the lights out. The other streets in The Narrows would be just as dark, and silent as this one. He knew because he had been walking through them for the last three nights, not going anywhere, just walking, in the hope that when he went to bed he would be so dogtired he would go to sleep instantly and not dream about the girl.

He had walked and walked, listening to the sound of his own footsteps, echoing behind him on the sidewalk, as though in violation of the imaginary curfew that had long since sent everyone else scurrying home. No matter how far he walked, how tired he became, he never achieved the dreamless sleep that was his objective.

He always had the same dream. It came toward morning. It was so real that he could have sworn the girl was lying beside him, that she had her arms around him, and he thought he could feel the warmth from her body, and so turned on his side, turned toward her. A haunting, beautiful dream. The unpleasant part came when he woke up. The dream was so vivid, dream and desire and reality so inextricably mixed up, that as he lay there in the early morning grayness that was neither daylight nor dark, he extended his hand, expecting to find her beside him, within hand's reach.

Each morning, when he awakened, and found that she was not there, he had known a sense of loss, so real that it was painful. He had tried to assuage, to allay, the pain by re-creating her in his mind's eye, the shape of her face, the silkiness of her hair, the arched eyebrows, the deep blue eyes, the absolute perfection of the mouth and nose, the way her face lighted up when she smiled, the haunting fragrance of the perfume she used. Then he would scowl, wanting to forget her. Instead of forgetting her, putting her out of his mind, he went on remembering her, the way she walked, the light musical sound of her voice.

He knew he would never forget her. He would go on dreaming about her at night, thinking about her during the day, forever and ever. Or stand, motionless, bemused, on a cold windy street, just as he was doing now, because he was suddenly assailed by the memory of her.

He heard the creaking of the branches of The Hangman, and thought, It's too damn cold to stand here and play the mooncalf, and there's no moon, and you're a big boy now, but your wits are out, your wits are out, like Hans Kraut, and crossed the street, moving quickly, going toward Abbie's house, listening to the sound of his own footsteps, hearing the creak-creak of The Hangman so loud that he looked up, saw the bend and sway of the great branches high overhead, thought, Heavy

heavy hangs over thy head, what wilt thou do to redeem it, redeem it, never can redeem it, lost it, not lost it, threw it away, own volition, nobody made you, you stiffnecked—

He started to go up Abbie's front steps, and put his hand on the old wrought-iron railing, felt it cold under his hand, and then turned and glanced in the direction of the river, and saw the girl's car parked under the street light at the corner, and so walked toward Dock Street.

The girl got out of the car, and he stood still watching her as she came toward him. The wind was blowing her hair about her face. He felt his throat constrict, so that he couldn't swallow, could not at that moment have spoken if his life had depended on it. As she came nearer he felt a thickness rising in his throat, filling his throat.

"Hello," she said, her face alight, alive, glowing. "I came back."

"I've missed you." He put his hands on her arms. He had never touched her before and she looked up at him, the eyes darker than he had remembered them, or perhaps it was due to the darkness of this winter's night.

She said, "Link—" and it sounded like a question.

He pulled her close to him, looking at her face, thinking, Win or lose, all or nothing, Hobson's choice. Then he leaned down and kissed her, and felt her lips respond to his, felt her mouth soft, warm, slowly opening.

She said, finally, "Shall we go back to where we started—to The Moonbeam?"

"All right." He hoped he sounded matter of fact, though he doubted it. Win or lose. And he had won. He had taken a long running jump and landed on his feet. He had won MamiePowtherChinaCamiloWilliams for keeps. He knew it and he couldn't quite get his breath back.

Inside the door of The Moonbeam, they both stood still, not saying anything, just looking. He saw Old One-One ploughing across the big smoke-filled room, heading toward two young men, two dark young men, who might have been embracing each other, passionately; swaying from the force of the emotion that made them hug each other in a tight, close, hot embrace. Was this a sudden access of love, he wondered. No. It was hate. One of them had a knife and—

"Let's not go in," he said and turned the girl around, shepherding her out of the door, pushing her gently out of the door, controlling an impulse to bury his face in her hair, thinking, That's too long a jump for anyone to have to make, from the private dining room of a French restaurant in the Fifties in New York to Old One-One and The Moonbeam Café on Franklin Avenue in Monmouth.

"Where will we go?" she said. She was looking straight at him, studying his face, just as he had studied hers, in the moment before he kissed her.

He was silent, watching her, because she was deciding something. "Well?" he said.

She took hold of his arm, put her hand in his. They retraced their steps, walking slowly along Franklin Avenue, then down Dumble Street. He could smell the perfume that she used, faint, sweet. He thought, Rooms, Dollar and Half a Night, shabby hotels, dingy rooming houses, rent a room on Franklin Avenue, one-night stand, smell of kerosene, dogs, people.

He said, "This way."

They turned into Number Six Dumble Street, went up the steps. He unlocked the door. There was no sound at all, not even a faint click as the tumblers turned in the lock. Then they were standing in the hall, the only light came from what Abbie called the night lamp, an oldfashioned oil lamp, marble base, wired for electricity. In the dim light you could see the long carpeted staircase, the curve of it, see the polished parquet floor, he turned a little and he could see the gleam of the Major's goldheaded cane in its usual place in the hatrack, gleam of the Major's silk hat which Abbie brushed every morning, gleam of the walnut backs on the pair of Victorian chairs, chairs silhouetted against the striped wallpaper. He remembered how F. K. Jackson appeared to be addressing the wallpaper when she said, "The Major is dead—"

He thought there was a movement, thought his eye caught the tailend of a motion, something moving, some gesture, something, in the deep shadows of the landing, and he looked up quickly. There was nothing. There was no sound at all, anywhere in the whole house. Perhaps it was the stillness that lay over the house, perhaps it was the careful way he had opened the door, but the girl had said nothing, still said nothing, even after he opened the door of his room, turned the lights on.

Then she said, "I love you, I love you, love you."

They were in Harlem on Christmas Eve. It was snowing. They stopped to buy a newspaper and he turned and looked at her, at the snow falling on the soft brown fur coat, on the tip of her nose, on the pale yellow hair, on the scrap of black velvet that was her hat. Right there on 125th Street, corner of Seventh Avenue, he kissed the tip of her nose—because he couldn't help it. The redfaced news vendor, who had been watching them, leaned out of the newsstand and said, "Mister, you got all the Merry Christmas a man could want standin' right there by you."

Camilo smiled at the man and said, "Merry Christmas to you!"

Link thought, We're both at the stage where we love everybody, news vendors, and elevator men, and bus drivers, and charwomen, and beggars—anybody and everybody who doesn't have the hold on ecstasy that we have. We keep wanting to spread it around.

He reached in his pocket just as though he were a millionaire, just as though he plucked five-dollar bills from The Hangman every morning just before breakfast, and handed five bucks to the news vendor and said, "Buy yourself a drink. As a matter of fact, here's another one, Mack. Buy yourself two drinks."

He said, "Christmas present," to Camilo and kissed her again.

She said, "Merry Christmas, darling!" and handed him a small square package, wrapped in dark green paper. It was tied with a silver ribbon, and there was a red poinsettia smack in the middle of the package.

He held it in his hand, lightly, balancing it on the tips of his fingers.

"Camilo, will you marry me?" he asked, voice soft, voice caressing.

He wondered afterwards why he'd asked her. Was it the absolute envy in the eyes of the news vendor, as he leaned forward, watching them, his elbows on a pile of newspapers, his bulky figure silhouetted against the gaudy covers of the pulp magazines, hung all around the inside of the newsstand? Or was it the snow? Snow everywhere, even on the sidewalks, coming down so fast that it obliterated a footprint almost as soon as it was made, snow softening the brilliant redgreen of the stop lights, snow muffling sounds; turning Harlem into a place of enchantment, straight out of Grimm's Fairy Tales, no, Andersen's, because the snow and ice were in Andersen. Few people on the street. No traffic. Everyman is at home with all the lights turned on; all the houses and the apartments are full of something strangely like hope, like delight, like love, and there are children—and Christmas trees—and piles of presents.

He said, again, "Camilo, will you marry me?"

She touched his cheeks with the tips of her fingers, then put both arms around his neck and whispered, in his ear, "One of these days. Come spring. Time of the singing of birds. Yes."

"Why not now?"

"People would swear that I'd married you to keep warm," she giggled, "to keep my feet warm. And they'd be right."

They stood on the corner of 125th Street and Seventh Avenue, laughing; the snow was wet on their faces, the snow was cold on their faces.

In love with love, he thought. Was that it? No. In love with CamiloWilliamsChinaMamiePowther? No. In love with Camilo Williams.

SATURDAY, and Malcolm Powther was off for the evening, off early, too. He stood in the doorway of a side entrance to Treadway Hall, trying to raise his umbrella. The wind kept shifting, blowing the umbrella back against him and then swooping under it so that he very nearly lost his grip on the handle.

He braced himself against the door in preparation for a further struggle with the umbrella. It was a strong wind. Almost a gale. The big-leaved ivy on the walls of the house rippled, moving back and forth in the wind. The electric lights on each side of the door gave the ivy a strange yellowgreen tinge. The color of the ivy, and the constant back-and-forth motion of it, suggested that moths, millions of them, had been pinioned to the walls, and were fluttering their wings in a desperate effort to free themselves, painful to watch because it was a silent struggle.

Something eerie about the ivy tonight, he thought. First I think of moths but if I keep watching it with the wind making it quiver like that I shall begin to believe that it is not the ivy that's moving but the thick stone walls of the house.

He began his struggle with the umbrella again and then stopped because he saw Al coming up the driveway, heading for this same entrance. Al had his chauffeur's cap on the back of his head, which meant the Madam wasn't ready to leave yet.

"You goin' now?" Al asked.

Powther nodded.

"Come on, I'll drive you to the car line, Mal. I'd take you all the way but the Widow's goin' to feed her face in Bridgeport tonight and I gotta have that crate waitin' at the door of the shack the minute the outside air hits that mink."

They walked down the driveway together. The town car was parked in front of the house. Powther hesitated before he got in.

"Do you think—" he said.

Al interrupted. "I ain't goin' to let you walk to the trolley, not in no nasty weather like this. Come on, get in. I got time enough. The Widow'll be gettin' her tiara fixed on her head for a good ten minutes yet."

It was warm inside the car. He leaned back against the soft upholstery, listening to, and enjoying, the faint hum of the motor, the swish-click, swish-click of the windshield wipers. He was glad that Al had insisted on giving him a ride. A cold rainy night. Windy, too. He probably wouldn't have been able to keep his umbrella up.

Al went down the milelong driveway, fast. The big entrance gates were open so that he didn't even have to stop to toot his horn, just slowed a little, and then went straight out onto the highway. A trolley was just coming to a stop. They watched the conductor get out and change the position of the trolley pole.

Powther thought, Well, now this is very nice. Drummond is the conductor tonight. We'll have a chance for a visit.

"That's a job I sure wouldn't want," Al said. "Specially on a night like this."

"Neither would I." Powther started to get out of the car.

Al leaned toward him. "Wait a minute, Mal," he said. "I got somethin' I been wantin' to ask you."

There was something unusual about the tone of his voice, something of relish, of gloating, that made Powther turn and stare at him. He said, "Yes?"

Al lowered his voice. "You noticed anything funny goin' on at the shack lately?"

"Funny?" Powther repeated and frowned. None of the plate was missing, he always counted it himself. The maids? They were all doing their work and doing it very well. None of them was in the family way. "What do you mean?" he said sharply.

"Well," Al said and stopped. "Well, if you ain't noticed nothin' I ain't got time to go into all of it right now." He shoved the chauffeur's cap straight on his head. "I gotta go, Mal. I'll tell you about it the first chance I get. I gotta go pick up the mink cargo."

Powther stood in the rain, watching the red taillights of the town car diminish in size, grow smaller, then disappear, just as though they had been swallowed up by this dark rainy night. What was Al talking about?

He ignored the rain, the wind, while he inventoried the rooms. Gainsboroughs in the dining room, yes, all of them; the

Cellini peacocks and the Da Vinci trays, the Bateman tea set and the Paul Revere in the dining room; yes, all there; prayer rugs in the library, yes; Aubusson in the music room, yes. He thought of spots on rugs, irreparable damage to fine wood, moths in upholstery or rugs, snagged draperies. Perhaps some-one had marred the photomurals in the entrance hall. No, they were perfectly all right.

I should have gone back with Al and gone over the entire downstairs to see that everything was as it should be. Wine cellar? He was down there in the afternoon, right after lunch, checking the Château d'Yquem, the only wine the Madam really liked. But surely Mrs. Cameron, the housekeeper, would have noticed anything wrong or anything missing. They held a conference every morning. She had said, when was it? yester-day, that the house had never been more beautiful than it was this winter.

Drummond, the conductor, stuck his head out of the trolley. "Mr. Powther," he said, "is that you?"

Powther said, "Yes." He boarded the car, dropped a nickel in the coinbox.

Drummond said, "It's a sour night, ain't it?" and looked a question at Powther.

Powther said, "Yes. Funny, isn't it? It's pitchdark so all of us talk about the night though it's only five o'clock." He's won-dering why I was standing out there in the rain, ruining the crease in my trousers. "Rain in January is always worse than snow. It's so devilish cold. Warm in the trolley though."

He helped Drummond reverse the seats. He could think bet-ter when he was doing something, and he liked Drummond, a talkative kind of chap, full of odd bits of information about the people who rode on his trolley.

"How are you, Drummond? I haven't seen you for a couple of weeks."

He only heard part of Drummond's answer. Al had said, "You noticed anything funny?" Funny. Funny. But Al wouldn't notice a scarred floor or a chipped porcelain vase. Al wasn't interested in anything but cars. Al's domain was the garage. There must be something missing in the garage, something queer in the garage. That was Al's affair. Al was responsible for the garage.

He thought, Isn't it funny how you can get all upset about something that concerns you, but the instant you find out it's the other fellow's misfortune, you can relax, and look at it from a long way off, and think, Now isn't that too bad. He had just used the word funny. Queer. Strange. Unusual.

Drummond said, "When you get past fifty your legs kind of bother you."

"It's good you've got a sitting-down job, on a trolley," Powther said.

Past fifty, he thought. He was past fifty but his legs didn't bother him. He could walk that mile from the Hall to the car line, easily. He enjoyed it. Even in the rain. The driveway was always lighted at night, and it was like walking alone down a broad tree-lined boulevard. It offered beauty, fresh air, exercise, and time in which to think, all at once. In winter, snow clung to the arbor vitae, and the hemlocks, and it was like walking through a forest, a snowcovered forest; and in the spring, when the rhododendron and the French lilacs were in bloom, it was like walking through a florist's dream of heaven. Al would never be able to understand why he liked that long walk. He was always insisting that he ride, would stop his own work to take him in one of the cars, often took him all the way to Dumble Street.

Drummond said peevishly, "Trolleys are all right." He started the car and he had to raise his voice against the clang-clang so that he sounded angry. He almost shouted, "But they sure beat the hell out of your kidneys after a while."

"I suppose so," Powther said. "But I should think a bus would be worse. I hope it'll be a long time before they get around to putting busses on this line."

"Same here. You got room on a trolley. The air's better too. Sometimes I wonder what I'm goin' to do when they get around to puttin' the busses on. You're lucky, Mr. Powther. You don't know how lucky. Here I am gettin' along on the other side a little further every day, and liable to be out of a job any time. But you're set for the rest of your life."

Powther hoped another passenger would get on soon. He didn't like to listen to a man feeling sorry for himself. It was probably the weather, that cold, fine rain, and so much wind. You couldn't see anything out of the window. Pitchdark outside. Trolley rocking and swaying. A sour night. Lucky, he thought. I'm not lucky. I worked and studied and worked and studied to get where I am. Get where I am. Where am I? He frowned. He was about to do the same thing Drummond was doing, about to start feeling sorry for himself.

Drummond brought the trolley to a stop. A big slowmoving man got on. He had a metal lunchbox in his hand. Powther thought, You rarely ever see a workman with a lunchbox any more. When you did you wondered why he had to pinch his pennies, wondered what kind of misfortune forced him to deny himself that small extra sum per week with which to buy his lunch. The big man sat down near the front, right behind Drummond, and they started talking.

Drummond said, "How is she?"

The big man said, "Oh, I don't know. She ain't no worse but she ain't no better either. I don't know what to think, Drummond. Here I am gettin' older every day and I'm spending my old-age money for doctors and sicknesses."

"But if you didn't have it," Drummond said halfheartedly.

"If I didn't have it then I could get her treated free," the big man said.

Powther stopped listening to them. It was this unpleasant weather that had got them down. This sour night. Now that Drummond had someone to talk to, he could go back to thinking about Al and the garage. Perhaps something had happened to the old Rolls. It must be twenty-five or thirty years old, at least; and Al was always working on it, tuning up the motor, polishing it. He even replaced the side curtains every two years.

He'd seen Al start the motor of the old Rolls and then get out, lift the hood, and stand listening to it, head cocked on one side, eyes half closed, just as though he were listening to a concert.

Al had said, "Lissen to her, Mal. Lissen to her sing. They don't make nothin' like this no more. Nobody gives a goddamn what's under a hood no more just so they're ridin' in a shined-up crate that's long as a hearse. This baby will outlast all them Caddies them rich bastards is so crazy about."

Powther had nodded agreement. The car looked unfashionably high to him, though he supposed the lines were still good considering its age. Certainly you wouldn't turn around and stare at it if you saw it being driven along a highway. He knew absolutely nothing about motors so he couldn't agree or disagree as to the quality of what was under the hood.

"You know," Al said, and he put his hands on his hips, still looking at the car, still listening to the motor, "even if I wasn't workin' here no more, I'd come back here for just one thing."

"What would that be?" Powther asked. He knew what he himself would come back to Treadway Hall for, it would be to rub up the Cellini peacocks just for the sheer pleasure of handling them once again. But Al, who did not know one rug from another, one type of silver from another, one flower from another, what would he come back for?

"I'd come back here, Mal, just to watch the Widow drive this crate through the park at the Fourth of July picnic. She sits in it, drivin' it, and she's listenin' to the motor all the time. I've watched her and I know. She's almost as crazy about motors as me. Only woman I ever see that was."

Yes, Powther thought, comfortably, something must have gone wrong with the old Rolls-Royce. But Al was a good mechanic. He would soon have it back in running order again. He liked Al, but there was a coarseness, a vulgarity about his speech that Powther found unpleasant. Al constantly disparaged the Madam, in small ways, without ever giving direct expression to his dislike. Powther felt that if you didn't like the people you worked for, you shouldn't take their money, you ought to find another job. Al referred to the Madam as the Widow; called Treadway Hall, that great stone mansion with its park and formal gardens and its magnificently furnished interior, the shack; and all of the Madam's cars, the limousines and town cars, the station wagons and convertibles, were crates; and the Madam's friends, whether they were gentlemen or ladies, were always rich bastards.

Despite his disapproval of Al's way of talking, they were friends. Al had given him a nickname, the first one he'd ever had, and he liked it. If anyone had told him that he and Al would be friends, he wouldn't have believed it because when he first went to the Hall to work, Al was openly hostile. He was always staring at him. He had pale blue eyes that bulged, and those pale eyes showed they did not like what they saw when they rested on Powther. His hair was blond and cropped close to his head, revealing the roundness of his skull, emphasizing the roundness of his skull. A big man with a big tough face.

He had never been guilty of violent reactions against people, but he found himself referring to Al, mentally, as the Nazi. The Nazi never spoke to him. If Powther had to give him a message from the Madam, the Nazi stared at him with those pale, cold eyes, did not answer, turned his round hardlooking head away.

One morning, the Nazi did not show up when he was supposed to take the Madam to the munitions works. She waited in the hall, tapping her foot, while Powther rang the garage and rang and rang and got no answer.

"Where could Albert be?" the Madam said. "What on earth is the matter with him?"

"I'll go and see what the trouble is, madam," Powther said.

Al lived in quarters over the garage. He ran to the garage, climbed up the inside stairs, quickly, knocked at the door of Al's bedroom, got no answer, and went inside. Al was in bed, eyelids covering the pale blue bulging eyes. He seemed drowsy. He was muttering under his breath.

He touched Al's forehead lightly. It was hot. He was obviously running a temperature. He looked somehow vulnerable, lying there, pajama coat unbuttoned, thick blond hair covering his chest, a big man with broad thicklooking shoulders, formidable when dressed and on his feet, but diminished now, weaklooking.

He said, "Al, Al. Who else drives?" and had to repeat it, "Al, who can drive for you?"

"Jenkins," Al said, with an effort.

In a few minutes the limousine was at the door, Jenkins was at the wheel wearing one of Al's caps. The Madam said, "You managed this so quickly, Powther. Thank you."

He managed more than that. He nursed Al through a four-day illness and looked after his own work as well, running out to the garage to sponge him off, to give him the liquids and the medicine the doctor had ordered. Al was grateful, he was more than grateful, he insisted that Powther had saved his life.

He said, "Mal, I got to explain to you. I never had worked with a colored feller before. And you was the butler and that meant you was over me. And I didn't like it. But you're just like a white man, Mal. That don't sound right." He rubbed his forehead. "I mean you're okay, Mal. You musta knew I didn't like you but you come in there and looked after me like you was my mother. Anybody ever bother you, you let me know. Anything you ever want, you let me know, Mal. I mean that."

Ever since then Al had been driving him to the trolley line or all the way home.

They were getting near the small factories now. Workmen were boarding the car; and every now and then a pretty young woman would get on. He liked to watch these little stenographers and typists and bookkeepers. If a workman in overalls with heavy jacket and cap was sitting in a seat, the girls would move along until they found an empty seat, or one occupied by a fairly well-dressed man or another woman. It amused him that they should maintain some sort of class line on a trolley, a class line based on appearance, because the workmen unquestionably earned twice as much as the stenographers. You didn't see many workmen on the trolleys anyway. Most of them drove their own cars to and from the plants. Al was always suggesting that he buy a car.

"You get yourself a car, Mal, and I'll keep it in firstclass shape for you. You ain't even got to buy a new one. I'll help you pick out a good second. A man oughtta have a car when he lives as far from his work as you do."

He said, "Thanks, Al. But I can't afford one." And maybe for a month or so Al wouldn't say anything about it.

It wasn't that he couldn't afford a car. He could. But if he had one, Mamie would use it, and he would never know where she was, never know. As it was, he often found Kelly and Shapiro and J.C. in the house by themselves. He'd say, "Where's your mother?" The answer was always the same, "Mamie's out."

She liked to go to the movies, and she loved to go shopping but— He sighed, and then frowned, wondering if Mamie was still on a diet. He hoped not.

Once again he reminded himself, as he always did whenever he felt a little low in his mind, that though he was constantly defeated at home, he was a conqueror, a victor, at Treadway Hall. His predecessor at the Hall had been an Englishman, and though he knew he was the equal if not the superior of the

Englishman, he also knew that he would have to fight and win a war against the other servants before he was accepted. Mrs. Treadway had never had any colored help, which made it a little difficult at first.

But he had worked for Old Copper, who was just about the richest man in the country. Thus he could, in all truth, look at the Treadway plate, the Treadway porcelain, the Treadway Aubussons and prayer rugs and Persian carpets, the Treadway mahogany with a slightly contemptuous air because he had seen better, handled better, and the other servants knew it. A war of the kind that he was involved in had to be won quickly, and the ammunition consisted largely of a way of looking down one's nose, and a good stock of stories about the tremendously rich, fabulously rich, families one had worked for.

He won hands down. It wasn't really a war. Just a skirmish or two. Except, of course, for Al. The housekeeper, Mrs. Cameron, who was Scotch, made it clear that she liked and admired him. She was always saying, "Now, Mr. Powther, that youngest Copper, whatever became of him and the coal miner's daughter he married. She was Polish, wasn't she?"

Then Powther, sure of his audience, would tell all over again the world's favorite fairy story, how Cinderella (twentieth century so she was the daughter of a coal miner) and the prince (youngest son of the richest man in the United States) were married. The housekeeper and the maids, all the female help, would lean forward, listening, listening.

Fortunately, Old Copper was not only rich, he was eccentric too, so that Powther was never at a loss for a good story about his racehorses, his airplanes, his yachts, his adulteries, his private railroad car, his town houses and country houses. Treadway Hall seemed a thin, anemic sort of place by comparison; just the Madam and the one young lady, Miss Camilo, in the family. Then Miss Camilo got married, so that left just the Madam.

Old Copper had five sons. The five sons married big buxom women; and in an age when most women felt they had made the supreme sacrifice if they had one child, let alone two, the women who married Old Copper's boys had five and six children apiece. So the town house in Baltimore was filled with life, fecund, uproarious life.

The trolley stopped at the corner of Dumble Street. Powther got off. Drummond said, "Good night, Mr. Powther." Powther said, "Good night, Drummond," and hurried down the street. He always hurried down Dumble Street, hurrying home to Mamie. Uncertainty urged him on. He was afraid that some time, some night, he would open the door of that apartment upstairs in Mrs. Crunch's house, and find that Mamie had gone, leaving no note of explanation, nothing, just darkness, silence, emptiness. He could picture himself blundering around in the rooms, searching for a note that he knew he would never find because Mamie was not the kind who would write a note. Writing didn't come easy to her, and even if it had, she would have preferred the direct contact offered by speech, not the impersonal business of using a pen or a pencil to inscribe an explanation or an apology, or an apologetic explanation, on a piece of paper, thus foregoing the pleasure and the excitement of an explosive violent scene.

And so, hurrying home through this early winter night, darkness already set in, cold in the street, the kind of night when J.C. would be able to "see" his breath, wind blowing straight from the river, blowing the fine rain against his face, cold sting of the rain making him lower his head, he stopped when he got near the house, and looked up toward the windows, to see if they were lighted.

When he saw, through the bare branches of The Hangman, that familiar pinkish light, warm, glowing light, in the windows of that room he shared with Mamie, he knew a sense of delight, of anticipation. He felt as though he could see into the room, see Mamie, laughing, her head thrown back, see all the soft brown flesh waiting for him, see himself laying his head between her breasts, soft, soft, soft, and smell the strong sweet perfume she used.

That strong sweet smell came from a stick, a graywhite stick, wrapped in tinfoil, the whole thing encased in a round glass bottle. He loved to watch her uncork the bottle, carefully unwrap the tinfoil, and then smear the stick perfume on her wrists, her elbows, the lobes of her ears, the back of her neck. Everything smelt of it, her clothes, her body, her hair, the sheets and the pillowcases. He could never separate the smell of that perfume from Mamie, the two inextricably entwined;

and all he asked in life, really, was—well, not to keep his job, not long life and good health for himself and his family, not sufficient food, or ample clothing, all he asked was that Mamie would, as long as they both should live, let him sleep with her on those nights when he was not at Treadway Hall, let him sleep with her so that he could go down, down, into sleep with the strong, toosweet perfume all around him, tangible assurance of Mamie's presence.

Now that he had seen the pinkish light in the bedroom windows, he started moving faster and faster, until he was very nearly running when he went up the outside back staircase. In the back entry, he stood still for a moment. He could smell pork chops frying on the stove, thought he could hear the spit-spatter of grease as the chops cooked, could smell kale being cooked.

He opened the kitchen door, stepped inside, and had to shut his eyes for a moment, half blinded by the brilliant light from the hundred-watt bulbs Mamie used in the kitchen; and it was hot, steam came from the open pot where the kale was cooking, bubble, bubble, bubble, smell of kale. Mamie was leaning over, bending over, opening the oven door, yams in the oven, corn muffins in the oven, fragrance issuing from the oven; and over it all the smell of her perfume, strong, heavy, toosweet, overriding the food smells, and he looked at Mamie bent over like that and could hear Old Copper's big voice, roaring, "Get one with a big ass, Powther, get a big wench with a big ass, and by God, you'll be happy for the rest of your life," could see Old Copper slapping his knee, could hear him laughing, and there was Mamie, bent over, and he looked away, because of the desire that rose in him, a sudden emotion, that made him feel as though he were going to choke, and he couldn't think straight, couldn't see, he wanted to be on top of her, and he told himself there was a fresh baked cake on the kitchen table, and he heard J.C. whining, "I want cake. I want cake. I want cake."

Mamie closed the oven door, cuffed J.C. away from the cake.

Shapiro yelled, "Hit him over the head again, Mamie. Give him a good one this time."

"Ah, shut up, Shapiro," Kelly yelled back, "you big mouth, you—"

"Whose a big mouth? Whose a big mouth?"

"You—you—you—"

They rolled over on the floor, over and over, clutching at each other, shouting, faces contorted with anger.

Mamie hummed under her breath, turned the pork chops in the frying pan with a longhandled fork, apparently unaware of the noise, the brilliant light, the sound of food cooking, smell of food cooking. She was impervious to it, Powther thought. No, a part of it, not ignoring, but enjoying, liking, the heat, the light, the confusion, the noise, the boys scuffling on the floor, J.C.'s yelps of rage.

Suddenly they were all looking at him, all silent, J.C., Shapiro, Kelly, Mamie. He supposed that he had brought the cold wet air from the street in with him, the darkness of the street, the silence of the street, brought it straight into the hot, brilliantly lighted, filled-with-food-smell, noisy kitchen; and their eyes questioned him, challenged his right to enter this place that was the heartbeat of the house, heartbeat pulsing with heat, sound, life.

Mamie said, "Powther, you sure gave me a turn. Come on in. Come on in and close that door. Supper'll be ready in a minute."

He went through the kitchen, down the hall, into the bedroom. He always hurried to get here, inside the house, home, and yet he always felt as though he were an alien, a stranger, strangeness, a sense of strangeness, in the kitchen, here in this bedroom. It was always the same room no matter what the address, the room where a pink-shaded lamp shed warm pink light on the bed, on the table by the bed, on the pink taffeta spread, not too clean. Cupids on the bed.

He put his hat on the closet shelf, hung his overcoat on a hanger in the one closet—a closet jammed full of dresses which were paid for by Bill Hod. His coat would smell of Mamie's perfume, just as all these dresses did. He got a clothesbrush out of the one drawer of the chest which was reserved for his use, brushed his hat, his overcoat, then rehung them in the closet, and in a petty unreasoning kind of anger, born of what he could not say, he pushed the newestlooking dress from its hanger and watched it fall, in a heap, on the closet floor.

Tomorrow morning, if he had time, he would rearrange the closet before he went to work. Mamie liked having him fix up her clothes. He pressed her dresses, sewed on buttons, repaired the split seams under the arms. He couldn't leave that dress on the floor of the closet. He reached down, picked it up, shook it out, examined it for split seams, from force of habit. Mamie had put on quite a few pounds lately. Was she still dieting? He hoped not. True she lost weight, but she was so cross, so irritable, when she was dieting, slapping the children, swearing at him, that nobody could stay in the house with her. Two weeks ago, when he was off, he went to the movies and sat there dozing away the hours, those precious hours, of his days off, trying to think of something that would be so good to eat, so appealing, that she'd taste it and then eat it, and would be off the diet. He sat through two shows and then went home, walking warily around the side of the house, going quietly up the back stairs, sniffing the air, thinking that if she was cooking, at so early an hour, in the afternoon, she was still on the diet, still not eating.

When she went on these starvation diets, she seemed impelled to torture herself by handling food, by cooking food that smelled to high heaven. She would sit at the table with a cup of black coffee and a package of cigarettes in front of her, sit there and sip the coffee; and smoke one cigarette after another, and watch them eat, watch forkfuls of the great round crusted roast of beef, and the browned potatoes and the beautiful fresh vegetables and the rich buttery dessert go into their mouths; her eyes followed the course of their forks and spoons from the plate to mouth, mouth to plate, her eyes eating the food with them, her lower lip thrust out, mouth a little open.

He imagined he saw saliva at the corner of her mouth, and would stare, fascinated, knowing that he was imagining it, but knowing, too, that it ought to be there, that the saliva glands were working overtime. Then Mamie would catch him staring and turn her belligerent baleful hungry eyes toward him, and he would look away, eating faster and faster, eating more than his stomach could possibly hold, afraid to stop eating.

It was a horrifying business to come home and find that Mamie was still on a starvation diet that might last anywhere from two days to a month. Once she'd held out for a whole month, a month during which she watched them eat cream puffs, chocolate éclairs, strawberry shortcakes piled up with whipped cream, all the rich sweet fattening food she loved most, while she drank black coffee, and wolfed down some kind of dry hard tasteless crackers.

For a whole month, they tiptoed around her, almost whispering, and she cooked from the time she got out of bed in the morning until she went back to bed at night, using up pounds of butter and quarts of cream and God only knew how much sugar and flour and vanilla. Kelly and Shapiro began to look like small round young pigs being fattened for the kill. J.C. gorged himself to the vomiting stage every night.

Night after night, Powther sneaked out to the corner drugstore for a large dose of sodium bicarb and oil of peppermint, afraid to mix it on the premises, even in the comparative privacy of the bathroom, because Mamie would have smelt the peppermint and known he'd eaten too much and been furious, with that quick unreasoning fury of the starving.

When she was hungry like that she couldn't sleep. He remembered the tenseness of her, lying there motionless beside him, flat on her back, as though she did not have the energy to turn over, not moving, tense, stiff, hungry. And he lay there beside her, afraid to touch her.

He had looked forward to this Saturday night, unexpected time off. A cold, rainy night. The kind of night a man needed a woman's arms around him. And now—

Hot in the house, he thought. Hot in the bedroom. He was sweating. Forehead wet with sweat. He'd get a clean handkerchief, mop his forehead. One of the old handkerchiefs. They were at the bottom of the pile in the top drawer of the chest.

Someone had been in the drawer, had mussed up the handkerchiefs, had put them back every which way. J.C. was getting completely out of hand, he would tell Mamie to get after him. He didn't ask much but he simply could not, would not, stand having anyone paw through his things. He'd rearrange them. He took them all out, turned the pile upside down, started to put them back, one by one. His hand touched something cold and metallic. He stood on tiptoe, looked in the drawer. There was a cigarette case in there. It had been under the handkerchiefs.

Perhaps it was a present, a surprise, from Mamie. He took it out, wondering why she had given it to him, because he didn't smoke. He turned it over. There were initials on it. L.W. picked out in brilliants. Who was L.W.? What was his cigarette case doing in this drawer?

He took the case over to the light. He turned it over, moving it back and forth, and the stones that formed the initials flashed, seemed to wink at him. It said Tiffany & Co. on the inside. A gold cigarette case. The initials were formed by small absolutely perfect diamonds. No question about their being diamonds. He used to see Old Copper's collection. Night after night the old man sat in the library holding a few of the stones in his hand, letting them trickle between his fingers. Old Copper told him about them, told him that finally you got so you could pick out the perfect ones without a glass, but a man ought always to carry a glass with him, just in case, just to verify what his naked eye told him. He went over to the closet, got a jeweler's glass out of his coat pocket, looked at the stones through it. Oh, yes, absolutely perfect, flawless, small stones. A gold cigarette case initialed in diamonds. L.W.

L.W.? Link Williams. Link Williams. Mrs. Crunch's nephew, or whatever he was, the tall arrogant young man who did not look like Bill Hod but resembled him, the way he held his head, the way he talked, even the eyes.

Bill Hod was no threat. At least he told himself that all the time; he told himself over and over again, as he hurried home on his days off, that Bill Hod would never encumber himself by permanently annexing a woman, not even Mamie Powther. And the closer he got to the house, the more convinced he became that Mamie had now, finally, gone off with Hod. But she hadn't. And then he would be certain that she never would, and the knowledge would last about a week or ten days and then he would begin to wonder and to doubt, and hurry home to make certain. But Link Williams, Mamie—

He shivered. Perhaps she was telling him in this curious, subtle, not really to be understood, business of the cigarette case, had placed it where he would certainly find it, and thus would know that she and Link—

He put the case back in the drawer, piled the handkerchiefs on top of it, slowly, carefully, force of habit making him square them up, line them up, one on top of the other, taking a long time to do it because his hands were trembling. Mamie laughed whenever she saw him carefully arranging the contents of a drawer, "Law, Powther," she said, "you musta spent half your life in the army, must spent half your life puttin' things in piles."

He would pretend the cigarette case was not there. It would be the easiest way for everybody. It meant Mamie would have to figure out some more direct way of telling him whatever it was she was trying to tell him about herself and Link. If he had seen Link Williams before they moved in here, if Mrs. Crunch had said, "I have a very handsome young nephew, if you cherish your wife, your life, if you have a susceptible, loving wife, do not, under any circumstances, do not live under the same roof with my handsome unscrupulous young nephew."

Link Williams belonged to the Copper breed, so did Hod. You could tell by looking at them, by listening to them, that they weren't to be trusted, that no woman was safe around them, not really. Mamie. For instance, it wouldn't have been safe to leave Mamie around Old Copper. What the dickens was he thinking about anyway, mind all in a jumble.

If Mrs. Crunch had only said, well, that day he stood wiping his feet so carefully on the doormat, instead of saying, "How did you know about the apartment?" she should have said, "I have a very handsome, very lawless young nephew."

Even if she had said it, he wouldn't have believed her. Because looking at her he would have said that her nephew— Was Link Williams her nephew? He couldn't be, not with that handsome closed arrogant cruel gambler's face, with those expressionless gambler's eyes, he couldn't be her nephew, couldn't have in his veins any of the same blood that had produced short, plump, hawknosed, kindly faced, kind-but-proud-faced, expressive-eyed Mrs. Abigail Crunch. It was a mobile face, a dead-give-away face, give away of whatever she was thinking, so were the plump, moving, always-in-motion, always gesturing hands. With that white hair piled on top of her head, with the very black eyebrows—well, it was a face and head you couldn't easily forget. She had New England aristocrat written all over her, in the straight back, in the quick but not hurrying short steps she took that meant she covered a lot of ground but was never guilty of striding down the street, in the Yankee twang to her speech. She wore the kind of clothes he liked, simple, unadorned and yet completely feminine, white gloves on Sundays, small black leather pocketbooks, carefully polished shoes, pretty small hats, a feather the only gay note on her best felt hat, and the seams in her stockings always straight.

He had met her, walked along Dumble Street with her, when she went marketing in the morning, tan cotton gloves on her hands, the fingers so neatly, so cleverly darned, the darning so beautiful that only an expert would notice that the gloves had been darned; a market basket over her arm, and her pocketbook in the basket; and he knew just as though he had looked inside it that it contained a clean linen handkerchief that would smell faintly sweet (violet or lilac or lavender), the front doorkey, and a billfold and small pencil with a pad; and on the pad would be a list, the grocery list, containing all the items that she would want that particular day, so that this one trip, early in the morning, would take care of all her needs.

In Mrs. Crunch's house, there would not be, say at five o'clock, that harumscarum running to the store for the thousand-and-one things that had been forgotten as there always were in his house. Mamie never knew what she was going to have for supper until the very last minute. She would start for the store, forget her purse and hurry back to the house to get it, laughing at herself, as she came in. He had seen her change her mind about an entire meal at the sight of a choice cut of meat at the butcher's; she would hurry home with the meat and ten minutes later she'd send Shapiro scurrying to the store for potatoes and before Shapiro could get back in the house, Kelly would be sent out to get butter and bread. The only reason J.C. wasn't employed in this marathon to and from the store was because he couldn't be trusted on an errand with or without money; J.C. just never bothered to come back at all and was usually found hanging over the dock, looking down at the river, with that awful concentration of the very young.

Breakfast was the same way; at least two members of the family had to go to the corner store and back before the Powthers could break their fast in the morning. He should have married a woman like Mrs. Crunch, who never had to diet, who would never under any circumstances have permitted familiarities from a man to whom she was not married, whose every word, every look, every gesture told you that.

Then Mamie was standing in the doorway of the bedroom, tall, all soft flesh and curves, all soft warm flesh, saying, "Powther! Pow-ther! I've called you two times already."

"I was just getting—" he started to say getting a handkerchief, and said, "I was just getting ready to come out to the kitchen."

He watched her walk down the hall toward the kitchen, watched the rhythmic motion of her legs, her arms, and thought, Yes, if I'd married Mrs. Crunch or someone like her I would never have wondered if I'd come home and find that she'd run off with another man; but then neither would I have known the absolute ecstasy and delight of Mamie, in the dark, in bed, the soft flesh yielding, yielding, the feel of those curves, the pressure of her arms around me.

He would never give her up, never, never. He was going to act as though Link Williams did not exist, as though that cigarette case with its sparkling monogram did not exist, as though— Why had she put it under his handkerchiefs? Link Williams. What was he doing with a cigarette case like that? Why not? Hod probably gave it to him. Or a woman. Some rich, dissolute, white woman. Link Williams was the type they fell in love with, it was the way he was built, it was his height, and the breadth of his shoulders, and it was his face, he looked like a brute, and women, white and colored, loved men with faces like that. Let's see, he thought, this is the middle of January. So some rich dissolute white woman probably gave it to him for a Christmas present.

Mamie said, from the kitchen, "Come along now, Powther. Supper's ready."

In the kitchen he blinked, the light was so brilliant. It was hot. Steam came from the plates on the table. Mamie always piled food on plates. J.C.'s plate was just as full of food as Shapiro's or Kelly's or his own. And Mamie was still on a diet because there was nothing at her place but a cup of black coffee.

Shapiro and Kelly ate in silence. J.C. tried to talk with his mouth crammed with food, so that no one understood what he was saying, thus he carried on a monologue, a mumbling mouth-full-of-food monologue, that was also an indication of contentment because he swayed from side to side as he ate and mumbled.

Mamie sat and glared at them as the pork chops and the yams and the kale and the corn bread disappeared from their plates. Occasionally she took a sip of the hot black bitter coffee.

Powther threw small secret appraising glances at the coffee cup, lipstick all around the edges, brown stains on the side where the coffee had dripped and spilled over, the saucer splotched with a whole series of dark brown rings. She used the same cup all day long, picking it up, sipping from it, refilling it with hot coffee when the stuff cooled off.

J.C. said, "Missus Crunch—" and the rest of the sentence was lost because he had crammed his mouth full of corn bread and went on talking and chewing, talking and chewing.

Powther wondered how he could bring the conversation around to Link Williams, how introduce his name, so that he could see how Mamie acted when his name was mentioned.

J.C. pushed his chair away from the table, backed the length of the room, still chewing, eying Mamie as he edged toward the hall door, then he was through it, gone.

Powther said, "I don't think you ought to let J.C. go downstairs to Mrs. Crunch's so much." He heard J.C.'s footsteps, thud, thud, on the inside staircase. It wasn't what he had planned to say, he hadn't really planned to say anything, he was just feeling his way, if he could get a conversation started about Mrs. Crunch then perhaps he could mention Link, easily, naturally.

Mamie glared at him. "Why not?" she said.

"Mrs. Crunch will get tired of him."

No answer. Perhaps she hadn't heard him. "Mrs. Crunch will get tired of him," he repeated. "I don't think you ought to let him go down there so much. It's late. He ought to be in bed."

"Oh, for God's sake, Powther, why don't you shut up?" She pushed the coffee cup away, with a sudden violent jerky motion, and got up from the table.

He watched her as she left the kitchen. She slammed the bedroom door and he listened, and could not tell whether she had turned the key in the lock.

Kelly said, "Mamie been like that all day, Pop. Me and Shapiro been outdoors in the rain the whole afternoon."

"It ain't safe to talk to her," Shapiro said. He stuffed his mouth full of cake, and cut himself another large wedge-shaped piece.

"J.C. left because he knew he'd get in trouble if he stayed around here," Kelly said. "Mamie been awful mean to him." He watched Shapiro gulp down the cake. "Mamie say he's got a tapeworm." He pointed at Shapiro.

Shapiro said, "I have not."

"You have too. Mamie say nobody could stuff their gut like you unless they got a tapeworm."

Shapiro picked up a fork with the evident intention of stabbing Kelly with it. Powther said, "That's enough of that."

He got up from the table, took a key out of his pocket, unlocked a cupboard high over the kitchen sink. "Here," he said, and handed them each a new comic book. He didn't approve of comic books but as he evidently was going to have to contend with the boys until bedtime, he didn't know of anything else that would keep them from killing each other while he did the dishes.

He found an apron, tied it tight around his waist, and set to work, clearing the table, washing the dishes, scouring the pots, then scouring the sink, boiling the dish towels. He swept the kitchen and then mopped it, mopping carefully around Shapiro and Kelly, who were lying flat on their stomachs, totally absorbed in the comic books, thinking that if he'd been Old Copper, he would have taken the mop handle and pushed and prodded them out of the way.

J.C. poked his head in through the door, looked around the kitchen, "Where's Mamie?" he demanded.

"Gone to bed," Powther said. "Come on in and I'll tell you a story."

J.C. loved fairy stories, and Powther, feeling suddenly sorry for him, feeling that J.C. needed a mother and didn't have one, and that he must therefore be both mother and father to him in this storytelling, said, "Here, you sit on my lap and I'll tell you a new story."

Powther cleared his throat, said, slowly, "Once upon a time," and Shapiro and Kelly looked up from the comic books, and he thought, It's got to be extra good to hold their attention.

"Once upon a time," he said again, "there was a princess with golden hair who was kept chained deepdown in a dark cold dungeon. The guardian of the door that led into the dungeon was a wicked giant who was blind in one eye. The princess cried all the time because she was hungry and the giant beat her and the only food he gave her was dry hard bread and water. But he brought her precious jewels to play with, great diamonds and emeralds and rubies and sapphires and pearls; and beautiful clothes to wear. When the giant left to go about his dreadful business of robbing innocent people who passed through the woods, he would leave his dog to guard the princess. The dog was a ferocious white bulldog, also blind in one eye, and if anyone ventured near the castle he would growl; and his growling was so fearful that they went on their way again.

"One day, Gaylord, the valet in the king's palace, a man who was small in stature but quick of movement, and noted for his kindness and the quickness of his thinking, was walking through the wood. As he neared the castle, he thought he heard sobs. He tried to enter, but he could not gain entrance because of the ferocious dog who guarded the entrance. He turned and walked away, puzzled, and he made up his mind to return again and explore the place when he had the golden needle with him. Gaylord was a persistent man, and not to be discouraged by danger or the threat of danger, for he was really a prince in disguise. He had been kidnaped and taken away from his kingdom at the orders of a jealous uncle. He was severely beaten and left for dead but an old peasant woman who lived on the edge of the forest where he had been left, found him, and nursed him back to health. After he recovered his health, he looked after the old woman, took such good care of her, that on her deathbed she gave him a small round silver case, almost like a tube, but heavily and curiously carved.

"'Open it,' she said. 'Careful, now.' To his surprise he found a very fine golden needle inside the case.

"'It will sew by itself,' she told him. 'You say, Stitch, Needle, stitch this leather, and it will stitch for you. It will stitch anything, water, wine, soap, wood, stone, fire. Guard it well. It has been in my family for five hundred years. I have no children to pass it on to so I will give it to you. You have been like a son to me. And whoever has this needle will always have whatsoever he wants.'

"A week later, Gaylord returned to the castle. This time he had the needle with him. The dog growled and would not permit him to pass the entrance. Gaylord said, 'Stitch, Needle.' The needle looked like a small flaming sunset flashing about the eyes of the dog, stitching up both eyes, just in case the blind eye was not blind, as so often happens in real life where a blind eye is often a fake, based on an old rumor that nobody knows whether or not it is true and it possibly isn't true, because most rumors are started by someone who has something to gain by it, and to be thought blind in one eye when you weren't would give a person an advantage over other people.

"The dog emitted piercing cries of pain, and ran and ran, put his head down to the ground and rubbed his eyes on the ground and the needle stitched the dog's heavy leather collar to the stone wall.

"Gaylord said, 'Well done, Needle,' and held out the small round silver tube and the needle came flashing through the air and settled inside the tube.

"He then went unmolested into the castle, and followed the sound of the sobs, and went down into the dungeon and found the beautiful goldenhaired princess chained there, with a great golden goblet beside her, half full of water. She said, 'Save me, save me, kind sir!'

"At that moment the giant entered the dungeon and lunged toward Gaylord. Gaylord said, 'Stitch, Needle! Stitch both his eyes, Needle!' and held out the small round silver tube and the needle flashed through the air, and stitched both the giant's eyes. The giant let out a roar of rage and pain; and started blundering around in the dungeon, hands outstretched before him. Gaylord said, 'Stitch, Needle! Stitch hand to stone!' The needle flashed through the air and when the giant blundered near one of the walls of the dungeon, the needle stitched the giant's hand to the stone.

"Gaylord said, 'Well done, Needle!' and the needle came flashing through the air and settled inside the small round silver tube that Gaylord held out.

"Gaylord then took the keys from the giant's girdle and unlocked the padlock, and released the beautiful princess with the long golden hair.

"They left the castle together, their arms clasped around each other's waists. Then they returned to Gaylord's rightful kingdom where they were married and lived happily forever after."

J.C. said, "Tell it again! Tell it again!"

Shapiro and Kelly had long since left the comic books on the kitchen floor. They were leaning against Powther now, and they said, together, "Whew! Tell it again, Pop. Tell it again."

"Not tonight. It's too late," Powther said. He felt a little glow of pride, of accomplishment, it was a good story. But he wouldn't tell it again.

He washed all three of them, helped all three into their night clothes, tucked them under the covers, opened the window, turned out the light. When he closed the door of the bedroom J.C. was saying, "All gold. She was all gold. She came right in the front door— Stitch stone to leather." But because he left the "s" sound off words, he was really saying, "Titch tone to leather."

POWTHER TOOK his shoes off in the living room. He padded quietly down the hall in his stocking feet and tried the door of the bedroom that he shared with Mamie, turning the knob, slowly, cautiously. It was locked.

He had no blanket, nothing to cover himself with. If he should sleep on the sofa in the living room, with his clothes on, his trousers would be wrecked by morning. He undressed down to his underwear and went back to the boys' room and got in bed with J.C.

It was like trying to sleep with a dynamo. J.C.'s feet and knees were in his stomach, his chest, his back. He seemed all bone, all knobby knees and sharp elbows and hard round head, no flesh on him anywhere, though he was a plump child, his body putting a strain on every seam of his clothing.

Powther turned and twisted, trying to get comfortable, thinking of Old Copper, "Get one with a big ass, Powther, makes for happiness." Did it? The boy, the old man's youngest son, Peter, beat his wife, the miner's redheaded daughter, with a horsewhip. Did it? Mamie Powther locked Malcolm Powther out of the bedroom.

He remembered that the newspapers somehow got wind of that story about Peter and his wife and when the reporters came, Old Copper sat in his big leather chair in the library and laughed at them; and ordered whiskey and soda for them, whiskey and soda, whiskey and soda. That afternoon Powther mixed drinks, passed drinks to the thirstiest set of men he'd ever seen.

Old Copper kept bellowing, "True? How in hell do I know if it's true? Hope so, gentlemen. I certainly hope so. Ha, ha, ha. Funniest thing I ever heard. Ha, ha, ha."

The reporters were in a deliciously rosy state when they left, laughing, talking. Powther wondered when they would realize that they didn't have a story, that Old Copper had neither denied nor confirmed the story; and he supposed they would hold long confused discussions as to whether they should print his statement, "How in hell do I know?"

One of them, a short sharp-eyed young chap, who had politely refused the whiskey and soda, cornered Powther in the hall and said, "Look here, old man, what's this all about anyway?"

He had sidestepped out of the corner. He said, "I hope the whiskey was satisfactory, sir," and walked fast down the hall, the great hall lined with those tremendous oils of monstrously outsized, monstrously pinkfleshed females painted by a Dutchman. Old Copper was standing in the doorway of the library. He was grinning, looking up at one of the paintings, grinning at it. At that moment it occurred to Powther that those paintings belonged to Old Copper in a peculiarly intimate sort of way. He was always leering at them, and the big nude women in the paintings seemed to leer back at him.

He shoved J.C.'s knees out of his stomach again, and thought, Makes for happiness, and pursed his lips. The Copper boys fought with their big wives, filled the house in Baltimore with the sound and fury of their quarrels. And yet, because of the paintings, because of the blatant lecherousness of the old man, but especially because of the paintings, he, Powther, fell in love with a woman who might have been painted by the Dutchman.

One of the sons, the oldest one, came home for a visit, accompanied by his wife and his four-month-old son, and the wife's personal maid, and the baby's trained nurse, a lean fortyish looking and acting and sounding woman in a starched white uniform and cap. Old Copper met them in the hall. The nurse was holding the baby. The old man let out a roar, like a maddened bull, "Who's that?"

They stood there, in the hall, all of them, the oldest son, and his wife, and the nurse, and the maid, and Powther, all motionless, all frozen, frightened by the roar. The baby, probably sensing the consternation of the adults, began to wail.

Young Mrs. Copper, the mother of the child, said, bewildered, "Why it's the baby, Jonathan Copper Four."

"Dammit I know that," Old Copper roared. "Who's that lean-shanked witch that's holdin' him?"

"The nurse. His nurse. A trained nurse."

Old Copper bellowed, "Give me that baby." There was a kind of seesaw movement for a moment, the nurse trying to retain hold on the baby and Old Copper pulling at him, and the baby bellowing too, now.

"Powther," Old Copper shouted, "where's Powther?" He held the baby in his arms, glaring, cursing. "God dammit, why don't none of these people have any brains? Powther, go get a nurse for this baby. Go get a big fat colored woman." He turned on the nurse. "Here, you. You're fired. Get out."

The nurse said, "Mr. Copper, you can't, you mustn't. Give me the baby. You haven't washed your hands." She got quite excited and said, "Germs, germs, germs," as though she were talking to an idiot, and had to repeat one word, over and over, in the hope that something would trickle through the idiot's mind. "Germs," she said again.

Young Mrs. Copper said, "Oh, no. You can't do that. You can't do that. You mustn't. She's so wonderful."

"Shut up!" Old Copper shouted. "Powther, stop standin' there with your mouth open. Go get a big fat colored woman to look after this brat, a big fat colored woman that can sing. Don't stand there—"

He walked out the front door, hatless, thinking, A big fat colored woman. He was supposed to pull one out of thin air. Where in the city of Baltimore was he going to find a fat colored woman who was suitable? She had to be suitable.

He went, finally, and logically enough, to an employment agency. He explained to the thinfaced white woman who was in charge of the agency what type of nurse Mr. Jonathan Copper II wanted. She searched through the files and found a Mamie Smith who sounded promising.

The thinfaced woman called the number listed on the filing card and asked to speak to Mamie Smith. There was quite a delay, at least fifteen minutes, during which the employment agency woman grew impatient, threatened to hang up, bit her lip, tapped her foot, muttered under her breath something about colored people being so slow, until apparently Mamie Smith came to the phone; also apparently she explained with suitable apologies that she had a job, but that there was a lady who was highly suitable, who lived in the same rooming house, that said lady, a Mrs. Drewey, was expected back in a half-hour, and was listed at the agency under nursemaid's work. The thinfaced woman conveyed this information to Powther. He said he'd go right out there and interview her himself.

It was a big frame house, in need of paint, in need of repairs, in fact, as he rang the bell, he studied the house, and decided that what it really needed was to be torn down and rebuilt. It even needed a new foundation.

A lean, light-colored female opened the door a cautious crack. He knew instantly that she was the landlady, because of her eyes. She summed him up, all his potentialities and possibilities in one quick shrewd glance. He asked for Mrs. Drewey. Mrs. Drewey was out, and the door started to close. Then he asked for Mamie Smith, and explained hastily and untruthfully that he had come about a job for Mamie Smith, and the door opened and the landlady said, "Step inside, and I'll call her."

He stood in the uncarpeted hall, waiting. He heard footsteps upstairs, somewhere; and then a woman came down the stairs. He stood, not moving, looking up at her. She came down the stairs, slowly, the uncarpeted badly-in-need-of-paint stairs, of a rooming house in the least desirable part of Baltimore, and his heart started beating faster and faster, and he wished he had brought his hat with him, he needed something to hold in his hands. If he had brought his hat, he could have turned it around and around, as though shaping and reshaping the brim, brushing it off, because his hands needed something to do with themselves, desperately needed something to do, because there in front of him coming down the stairs, in the flesh, was a woman exactly like the women in the great oil paintings with the ornately carved frames that hung in the long hall of Old Copper's town house.

This woman was clothed, of course. She had on a dress, sleeveless, and short of skirt. She was wearing shoes, a flimsy kind of sandal, runover at the heel, but no stockings. The dress was a rather awful shade of brown. And her skin was brown, deep reddish brown, skin as smooth and flawless as that of Jonathan Copper IV with the same dewy quality, and it was just as though one of those big women in the paintings was coming down a staircase, the curve of the leg was the same, and the deepbosomed, bigbosomed look of her was the same.

"Yes?" she said. "You wanted to see me?"

Her voice was like music and it confused him even more, excited him even more, so that he swallowed twice and cleared his throat before he could answer her. "I'm Malcolm Powther," he said. "I'm the butler at the Coppers'. We need a nursemaid and the employment agency where I made inquiries phoned here about the job just a little while ago. I came straight here from the agency because a Miss Smith suggested a Mrs. Drewey."

"I'm Mamie," she said. "I was the one who suggested Drewey. She's good. She's about the best in the whole of Maryland. Come on in and sit. She'll be along pretty soon."

He couldn't get over her voice, and he kept asking her questions, just to hear her talk. It was more like listening to singing than listening to someone talk. He knew he shouldn't stare at her, that he ought to look away, and he tried to keep his eyes focused on some part of the room. But who could keep looking at a shabby, cheap rocking chair, at soiled badly fitted slipcovers on horrible overstuffed chairs, at sagging curtains in need of laundering, at a dreadful newlooking machine-made rug, all garish colors, and at dusty beaded lamp shades, when Mamie Smith was sitting on a sofa with her legs crossed, leaning her head back? He thought, I've got to have her. If it takes me the rest of my life, if it costs me my job, if it costs me all my savings, my life savings, I've still got to have her.

He asked her questions, just to keep her talking, just so he could keep hearing that voice that was like music. She lived in one of the upstairs rooms, across the hall from Mrs. Drewey. She had been married and was divorced. She didn't like Baltimore, it was too Southern a city for anybody like her who had been born in the North. She wanted to live North again, and as soon as she could leave, had enough money saved to tide her over the business of finding another job in a new place, she would go live in a small Northern city, any small Northern city.

He thought, Enough money. I'll be back here again. I can spend money, I've saved it all my life but I'm going to spend it now, spend and spend and spend, until I can buy Mamie Smith.

He said, "Miss Smith—"

"Oh," she said, and waved her hand in the air, waving his words away, "don't be so formal. Everybody calls me Mamie."

"Mamie, will you, could you have dinner with me this coming Thursday? Go out to dinner with me?"

"Sure," she said easily. "Any night you say. Thursday's fine."

He was about to set the hour, when the front door opened and Mamie said, "There's Drewey. Come on in, honey. I got a job for you. Powther'll tell you all about it."

Drewey sat down in the parlor with them, on one of the worn, sagging chairs. He thought, Suitable. Highly suitable. She was more than that. She was exactly what Old Copper wanted. She looked clean but not starchy. She was big, with a lap made for sitting on and a feather-pillow bosom made for laying the head on, and arms big enough to enfold and cuddle the young Jonathan Copper in, for five or six years.

"Can you sing, Mrs. Drewey?" Powther asked.

"Sing?" Drewey repeated, frowning, "Course not. Is this a singin' job? I didn't put in for no singin' job at the agency."

Powther explained about the job, about how he felt that she was exactly what was wanted. He carefully avoided using the old man's phrase "big fat colored woman," because after all— Then he said, "I mean, can you, ah, sing enough to say, sing a baby to sleep while rocking him in a rocking chair?"

"Lord, yes. I don't call that singin'. That's just a little hum-a-byin'."

"Would you mind sitting in that rocking chair over there, just, you understand, so I can get an idea, and do a little hum-a-byin'?"

Mrs. Drewey looked as though she were going to refuse and Mamie said, in that voice that was like singing, "Aw, go on, Drewey, hum-a-by for Powther. It could mean a lot to you workin' for them stinkin' rich Coppers."

Mrs. Drewey sat down in the shabby, cheap rocking chair, her hands stiff on the arms, and glared at them. Then she began to rock, back and forth, back and forth, and the chair creaked a little every time she rocked. The glare subsided in her eyes, and she closed them, her hands relaxed in her lap, and she began to hum, and the humming, at some point, Powther didn't know just when, became a soft singing. If there was a tune, it was not one he had ever heard before, if there were actual words they made no sense whatsoever, and he thought it was the most comforting, relaxing, beautiful sound he had ever heard.

His eyelids drooped over his eyes, and for the first time in his life he must have gone sound asleep sitting in a chair because when he opened his eyes Mrs. Drewey was no longer in the rocking chair, she and Mamie Smith were sitting on the sofa, both of them looking at him, both of them laughing. It was evidently the sound of their laughter that woke him up. He felt like a fool, going to sleep like that in a chair, and he wondered if his mouth had been open, wished that he had teeth like Mamie Smith's, big, strong, evenly spaced teeth, very white in that coppery brown face.

He sat up straight. "I'm sure you'll do, Mrs. Drewey. Can you come for an interview right away?"

When Old Copper saw Mrs. Drewey, he promptly roared an order for a rocking chair, roared another order to the effect that Jonathan Copper IV be placed in Mrs. Drewey's lap. Young Jonathan was still howling his head off, and the instant Drewey tucked his head into the fleshy part of her arm, covered his little feet up with a blanket and started rocking and hum-a-byin', he stopped howling, sighed, and promptly went to sleep.

Mrs. Jonathan Copper III stared, amazed. "Why, he's asleep. He hasn't been asleep for six hours. He's done nothing but cry. I've never seen anything like it."

"Just wanted a big fat colored woman," Old Copper said. "Don't never give no male Coppers to no bony white women to bring up."

Powther told Mamie about Drewey and the baby when he took her to dinner on Thursday night. While he talked he studied her, trying to analyze her weaknesses. He decided that she would never be able to save the money to tide her over until she got a job in a small Northern city, that there would always be something that she wanted to buy. After all, the Northern city was an intangible, and the gaudy costume jewelry or the flimsy shoes were tangible, touchable, seeable, right there in a store window.

He knew, too, just by looking at her, that if she married him, he would always find gentlemen callers in his home. He couldn't foresee Bill Hod, and the general shape and size and viciousness of him, because he had led a life in the houses of the very rich which prevented him from being aware of the existence of the Bill Hods, but he could foresee jealousy and insecurity. Knowing this, he still intended to marry Mamie Smith, and so directed all his resources toward that end.

Whenever he saw her he talked about the disadvantages of living in rented rooms, about the luxury it was possible to enjoy in a small place of one's own.

He bought presents for her. Just before Christmas he sent to

New York for three nightgowns, three such nightgowns as he was certain she had never dreamed could possibly exist. There was a gray one, because he knew the color would surprise her; a flaming red one, because she had a passion for red; and a peculiar yellowish one that would bring out the coppery tones of her skin. They were more like expensive evening gowns than like anything to sleep in.

But they were worth the price he paid for them because on Christmas Eve when she opened the box, she stared, and said, "What on earth—"

She took the nightgowns out of the big beautiful box, out of the layers of tissue paper, and sat with them in her lap, holding them, hugging them, spreading them out so that the long full pleated skirts foamed over the floor, covering part of the cheap, garish, machine-made rug.

He thought, If I had my choice I'd ask her to put on the yellowish one.

Mamie said, "Powther, you want me to try one of them on for you?"

He was suddenly overcome by emotion, a kind of shyness, and he nodded, holding his head down because he couldn't look at her.

"Which one?"

He pointed at the yellowish one, the almost mustard-colored yellow one, but not quite mustard, it had more green in it than that, a peculiar color. She swept all the gowns up in her arms, and he heard her going up that long uncarpeted staircase, walking swiftly.

A few minutes later, she said, "Powther!" from somewhere upstairs.

He stumbled on the stairs, striking his knee so that it hurt unbearably, and the pain halted him, halfway up. She called again, "Powther!" and he hurried up the stairs, his knee aching, stiff; and there she was standing in the doorway of a room, and the nightgown was made of a fabric so sheer that he could see through it, see all of her, and yet it was as though there were veiling over the flesh, and the flesh was so beautiful, that his eyes filled with tears; and that moment seemed to sum up all of his future relationship with Mamie, rapture, but pain, too.

After that he set to work to make himself indispensable to her. When he went to see her he brought choice crackers and old cheeses and beautiful fruit, in case she wanted something to eat late at night. He slipped the landlady ten dollars so that Mamie could cook in her room, which was against the rules. He bought a small electric icebox and an extremely efficient small electric stove so that she could bake and fry as much as she wanted to. He used all of his efficiency, all of his knowledge of the luxurious, and most of his bank account, in his courtship of Mamie Smith. He transformed that rundown dismal bedroom into a very comfortable one-room apartment.

Finally, he went to New York and registered with a high-class employment agency, explaining optimistically that he was going to get married, that his fiancée preferred to live in Connecticut. The Treadway job was offered to him and he went to Monmouth for an interview. He explained to Mrs. Treadway that his wife preferred not to live on the premises. Though he was certain Mamie would have gentlemen callers, he did not intend to have the Treadway chauffeur, cook, gardener included in their number. It would make for an impossible situation, all of them being white. Before he went back to Baltimore he rented an apartment for Mamie in the colored section of Monmouth. It wasn't what he wanted but it would do until he could locate something better.

When he told Old Copper that he was leaving, the old man let out one of those roars that made people jump back from him, startled, awed.

"Whatsamatter?" he bellowed. "I'll raise your pay. Is that the trouble? You want more money? You want more money?"

"No, oh, no, sir. It's just that I'm getting married."

"You are? Good God!" Old Copper looked at Powther half questioningly. "Has she got a big—"

Powther said hastily, "My fiancée don't like Baltimore, sir. The only way I can get her to marry me is to offer her the chance to live in Connecticut."

Old Copper snorted, "Connecticut! Of all the godfosaken swampy places to live," he shuddered. "It's got the god-damndest climate, the goddamndest weather in the whole United States. They got drought in August, flood in MarchApril, hurricanes in the fall, winds howlin' down the chimneys all winter long. The goddamndest—I know what I'm talkin' about,

Powther. I was born there." He sighed, sank deeper in the leather chair. "When you leavin'?"

"In three weeks."

"I'll give you a weddin' present, Powther. Bring her around before you leave and I'll give you a weddin' present. And if those goddamn farmers you're goin' to work for in Connecticut don't treat you right, you come back here and I'll pay you twice what they been payin' you."

Powther nodded, thinking, I may never go to Monmouth. I may be wrong about Mamie Smith. He stayed away from her until the day before he was to leave, stayed away for three weeks, hoping that she would wonder about him, miss him, become aware of the disorder in which she lived without him.

When he finally went to see her, he carried two big packages of food with him. He walked through that shabby downattheheels crooked street where she lived, thinking, Too many people, too many dogs, too many smells. Spring of the year but already hot. Heat waves rising from the sidewalk, nearly naked children toddling down the street, crawling up and down the highstooped steps in front of the houses.

He would tell her about spring in Connecticut, about the dogwood and the laurel, about the smell of the river, the curve of the river, sunlight on the River Wye, about the grass, and the birds, the pigeons that strutted on every available patch of grass, about the friendliness of the people, about how clean Monmouth looked, how the houses, many of them, were painted white and the blinds were green, so that even though it was a city, it looked like a toy city compared to Baltimore with its dingy streets and its gray old buildings.

He wondered what Mamie had been doing these past three weeks while he had been completing his carefully thought out campaign. Had he made himself indispensable? He soon found out that in one way he had, and in another, perhaps more important way, he hadn't. The bleak furnished room that he had turned into a colorful, rather luxurious, one-room apartment was in a state of dreadful disorder. He took off his coat, rolled up his shirt sleeves and set to work, washing dishes, making the bed, cleaning the room.

She must have been going to the movies rather often because there were innumerable stubs of tickets from the colored theatre, on the floor, on top of the chest of drawers. She hadn't bothered to fix a decent meal for herself because there wasn't a scrap of food in the icebox. She'd had a caller, or callers, there were six empty beer cans on the floor, and she didn't drink beer; two empty whiskey bottles, and several sticky glasses and innumerable empty ginger ale bottles. He found a man's socks, large size, loud red and green stripes, medium-priced, under the bed. Indispensable? For some things. Not needed for companionship though. He held the socks in his hand, wondering, conjecturing, and then tossed them into the dustpan with the rest of the rubbish.

He had set the table, one of his gifts, a card table, very expensive, actually a folding table, heavy, unshakable, and the steak was just about ready to serve when Mamie came home from the restaurant where she worked.

She had a parcel under her arm, wrapped in brown paper, almost the color of the brown dress she wore. No stockings. No hat. Perspiration on her forehead. She looked hot and tired and so beautiful, so big and beautiful, that he swallowed twice, in an effort to get rid of the lump that rose in his throat. He didn't say anything to her because somehow he couldn't.

"Powther!" she said, pleasure in her voice. "My God! Ain't it hot!"

She looked all around the room, looked longest at the table set for two, at the white tablecloth, the carefully folded napkins, made no comment. He watched her cross the room, sit down in the chair by the front window, slip her feet out of her shoes, and then he turned back to the stove, stuck the French bread in the oven, served the plates, poured wine in the wine glasses.

She ate in silence, ate with a relish that made him wish he hadn't stayed away so long. She must have been hungry. He watched her with a tender, yearning feeling, and thought, surprised, That's the way mothers feel about their children. She ate four of the pastries he'd brought with him, drank coffee, and then nibbled at the white grapes.

"Powther," she said. "I haven't eaten a meal like this since the last time you was here. Where've you been?"

He leaned forward, grasped the edge of the table. "I've been getting a new job. In Monmouth. A small city in Connecticut. I've got an apartment there. And all you've got to do is to say the word, just say the word, and you can go with me. I leave tomorrow." He opened his wallet, took out two railroad tickets. "One's for you and one's for me."

"I couldn't," she said. "It was right sweet of you to get the ticket for me but I haven't got a job in Monmouth. I've tried and tried to save the money so I'd have enough to tide me over but I haven't got ten dollars to my name and that's the God's truth."

"That's just it," he said eagerly. "You won't need any job. I thought, well, will you marry me? I earn enough money to more than take care of both of us."

She threw her head back and laughed. "You're a funny little man," she said. "Here I been thinkin' I'd done something to hurt your feelings and you been away makin' plans." She was silent for a moment. "Suppose I said no?"

"I—" he began, and stopped. What would he do? He'd die. That's what he'd do. He couldn't live without her. "I'd—I'd just turn the unused ticket in when I got to the station tomorrow afternoon."

"You mean you'd go anyway? Without me?"

"I have to," he said. "I have a job there. I have to go."

She looked around the room again. He wished, afterwards, that she had looked at him, appraised him, studied him, but she didn't. She looked at the room, at the stove, at the table, at the chairs he'd bought, at the comfortable bed. He supposed she was weighing the comfort and luxury, the good food, the cleanliness, against the disorder and discomfort of the past three weeks. He knew that people got accustomed to luxury very quickly, accepting it finally as their due, and no matter what strain and struggle, what utter poverty they may have known, they soon forgot it, they soon reached the point where they could not survive whole without comfort, luxury. It softened them up. He knew that. He had used it to win Mamie with, but he couldn't help wishing that he, as a person, had been the one important factor in her decision.

Picking up one of the tickets, she started humming under her breath. "I'll wear that new navy hat," she said. "And that new navy suit because it'll be cool up there and I've got some new navy suedes and I've got a big red pocketbook that'll go good with it. Let's see, what time's this train go anyway?" She frowned at the ticket, examining it.

It was as simple as that, as quick as that. He couldn't quite believe it, even while he packed her things, and made arrangements to have a moving van pick up the furniture.

On their way to the railroad station, the next day, they stopped to see Old Copper. He stared at Mamie a long time and to Powther's great discomfort, Mamie stared right back.

"You done well, Powther," Old Copper said. "If I was younger I'd give you a run for your money." Then he got out of the big leather chair, in the library, sat down at his desk, wrote a note, made out a check, put the note and the check in an envelope, and handed it to Powther. He handed the envelope to Powther, but he kept looking at Mamie, staring at Mamie, and Mamie was staring right back. Powther felt more and more uncomfortable, embarrassed.

Old Copper said, "Well! Good luck!" and shook Powther's hand, and patted his shoulder and said, again, "If them goddamn farmers you're goin' to work for don't treat you right, you come straight back here."

He followed them to the door, and once outside Powther looked back and Old Copper was still staring at Mamie, watching her go down the steps, and he knew a sudden rush of sheer maleness such as he had never felt before, suddenly hated the old man because of his wealth, the whiteness of his skin, wanted to go back and punch him in the jaw. When Old Copper saw Powther looking at him, he closed the door suddenly.

While Mamie was in the ladies' room, on the train, he opened the envelope. Old Copper's check was for a thousand dollars, and the note, written in that bold heavy hand, sounded as though the old man had spoken to him:

> Watch what I tell you. Someday she'll leave you for another man. If you're ever broke, ever need a job, ever need anything, just let me know, because God damn it, Powther, there's nobody else in the world can look after me like you done.

He was tempted to tell Mamie, after all they were married now, that he had to go back to Old Copper, that now that he had left, he knew he couldn't stand a new place, new people. And there was, too, the old man's warning, "She'll leave you for another man." In a new place it was much more likely to happen than in Baltimore.

It was all a dreadful mistake. He had spent money like a millionaire and his bank account had practically vanished. But he had Old Copper's check. That would serve as a stake, a kind of cushion against disaster. He folded the check and put it in his wallet, tore the letter into tiny pieces and thrust the pieces far under the seat.

Mamie came swaying down the aisle, swaying partially because of the motion of the train, but also because it was the way she walked. And he thought, Well, I can't go back to Old Copper's, not with Mamie. They had looked at each other, stared at each other, just as though they were testing each other out, as though they had immediately recognized some quality they had in common and were instantly defiant, instantly jockeying for position for some final test of strength.

He knew that he would have rivals, knew that he would find gentlemen callers in his house, but he could not, would not, make it possible for Old Copper to be included among them.

And now as he lay in this bed, beside J.C., turning and twisting, in vain, wasted effort to avoid the child's knees, elbows, head, he asked himself if he regretted that decision he'd made on the train. Should he have gone back to Old Copper? More important still, was it a mistake, the whole thing? Wouldn't he have been better off if he hadn't married Mamie? No. He had never known such delight as he had experienced with Mamie.

J.C. moved for the millionth time, turning over, and then inching up in bed. He put his arm around him thinking to restrain his movements, and J.C.'s head caught him under the chin, hard, heavy, the impact was such that Powther thought his jaw was broken, then that he had cracked his bridge, but he had only bitten his tongue, viciously, painfully. It felt swollen and he lay there, pain along the edge of his tongue, moving it back and forth cautiously, exploratively, expecting to feel a gush of blood at any moment. J.C. muttered darkly to himself, under his breath. Kelly and Shapiro echoed his mutterings. They were talking in their sleep, repeating words, phrases. Then they turned over, sighed, groaned, kicked the covers off. He could hear their feet rejecting the covers, getting free of the covers.

I will never get to sleep, he thought. And I have to be at the Hall early tomorrow morning. He heard the clang-clang of the last trolley that went up Franklin Avenue. It seemed like a long time after that that the lights went off in The Last Chance. This room in the front of the house became suddenly darker, the pinkorange light from the neon sign went out suddenly; and just before it went out, there was a little eddy, a gust of talk in the street below, suggesting wind, eddying, gone, as the last of the beer drinkers, and the seekers after Nirvana, left The Last Chance, heading reluctantly toward home.

The Last Chance. The Last Chance. Last chance to do what? Get a drink? Burn in hell? Look at Bill Hod?

He sat up in bed, listening. He thought he heard footsteps in the hall, then the click of a lock. He really couldn't tell, not in this room with its restless sleepers.

Getting out of bed, he covered J.C. carefully, closed the door of the boys' room behind him, and went down the hall, slowly, quietly, in his bare feet, the floor cold to his feet. He stood outside the door of the bedroom, listening, and he thought he heard Bill Hod's voice. But he wasn't certain. He couldn't see anything except a thin thread of pinkish light under the door.

The thread of pinkish light disappeared from under the door and there was silence, no sound at all, nothing, just the darkness and the cold floor under his feet. He stood there waiting for some further sound. There was nothing at all, no sound of voices, no movement. Silence.

He went back down the hall, opened the door of the boys' bedroom, and got in bed with J.C., refusing to think about what he thought he'd heard, thinking instead, I will not sleep on that damn sofa in the living room, I will sleep in a bed, a rightful bed, even if I cannot rest. I am not a refugee. I have a right to a bed. I work all day and half the night, and come home to—Bill Hod? Link Williams? Cigarette case incrusted with diamonds.

At five o'clock the next morning he was dressing in the living room. The boys were good for another two hours at least. While he was putting on his shoes, he thought he heard the thud-thud of the percolator in the kitchen, was certain that he smelt coffee. But he didn't know how to greet Mamie this morning, so he finished dressing and then went down the hall. The bedroom door was open, the room was empty.

Mamie called from the kitchen, "You up already, Powther? Set the table for me, will you? Mebbe we can eat without them starvin' Armenians sittin' in our laps."

He decided that he must have dreamed that business last night, had a nightmare, a night horse, as his father used to say. She was so gay this morning, her eyes sparkled, her lips kept curving into a smile, and she sang as she turned the bacon in the frying pan, cooked the pancakes.

"Soup's on," she said. He thought even her voice was lovelier this morning, there was more music in it than ever. And she was off the diet. She ate everything in sight.

When they finished eating, she leaned back in her chair, sighed and lit a cigarette. "Let's leave the dishes," she said. "And go get back in bed. It's too early for any poor black sinners to be up."

He nearly tripped over his feet getting there, and later, he went to sleep, relaxing into sleep, easily, quickly, contentment seeping all through him, so that he smiled in his sleep, aware just before he slid down into the total darkness, the blackout, the delicious oblivion of sleep that Mamie's soft warm naked body was pressed tight against him, and the strong sweet perfume was all around him, like a cloud.

When he woke up he looked around the room, trying to remember where he was, and how he got there, and then he smiled, remembering. He sat up in bed and saw that Mamie was up, and getting dressed.

She always put her shoes on first, she never wore any stockings in the house, and now she was leaning over, back turned, putting on a pair of green highheeled sandals. He liked to tease her about putting her shoes on first, telling her that she must have been born in the South, must have been a little barefoot pickaninny, and then she finally acquired a pair of shoes, sign of prosperity, mark of distinction, that set her apart from the rest of the black barefoot tribe, so precious a possession that she slept with them under her pillow, her hand resting on them, like an old-time prospector with a small bag of gold dust never out of reach of his hand. When she woke up, she felt under her pillow for her shoes, and then got up, and put them on, just as she was doing now.

He changed the story each time he told it, changing the
emphasis, changing the details, embellishing it, sometimes the
shoes were scarlet, sometimes they were gold, sometimes she
lost them and could not find them, but always on the morning
when she first got them, she went around singing, "All God's
chillun got shoes."

Mamie straightened up and the new story about the first
pair of shoes went out of his mind. She was shaped almost like
a violin, like the base of a violin, big beautiful curve, and as she
turned toward the bed, he thought, If she were standing inside
a frame, naked like that, with that look of expectancy on her
face, all the museums in the world would sell their Da Vincis
and their Manets and their Rubens in order to own this one
woman.

He said, "Mamie."

"Powther!" she said. "You awake? Here I been tippin'
around—" She crossed over to the bed, sat down on the side
of it, put her arms around him, hugged him close to her, and
kissed his cheek.

He thought, I, I, I, cuckolded as I am, worried as I often
am, after a night with you, you, you, soft warm flesh, smell
of perfume, toosweet, toosweet, toostrong, deep-soft-cushion
feel of you, feel of the arms, the legs, the thighs, me incased
in your thighs, all joy, all ecstasy, all pleasure, not caring, forgetting, completely forget, not forgetting, not caring, who else
does this to you, defying Bill Hod, conquering Bill Hod and
you and the world, even I, an old man, sorrowful sometimes,
frightened always, living forever afraid that you will leave me,
don't ever leave me, even I can, could, walk for miles, could
sing, could shout, could believe that I will live forever and ever,
that I will never die, I am too alive, too filled with joy to die.

He had to get up, get dressed, get back to the Hall. He left
Mamie, sitting on the side of the bed, singing:

> Tell me what color an' I'll tell you
>   what road she took,
> Tell me what color an' I'll tell you
>   what road she took.
> Why'n'cha tell me what color an' I'll
>   tell you what road she took.

SUNDAY. Quarter past twelve. Powther put on his overcoat and his hat.

"I've got to speak to Albert for a few minutes," he said to the second man, who was his assistant.

It would be at least a half-hour before he started to set up the dining room and he had just finished checking the entire downstairs. Everything was in order, everything polished, spotless, gleaming. Flowers everywhere.

Al was not in the garage. He heard the slush-slush of water from somewhere behind the garage, so he walked outside to the area where Al washed the cars. Al was hosing down one of the station wagons, his face was red, and there was something violent in the way he manipulated the hose, as though he were beating the car with it. Powther wondered why he was washing it.

He said, "It's a nice sunny morning, Al." Sunny but cold. Very cold. Too cold to be washing cars outdoors.

Al looked up. "Hi, Mal," he said and turned the hose off. He kicked at one of the tires, scowling at it. "Rogers must carry horse shit around in this crate all day. He's got a stink in it that would choke you to death. It's got my garage stunk up like a stable. So I'm out here, in January, hosin' it down."

Rogers was the head gardener and Powther wasn't the least bit interested in whatever it was he carried in the station wagon.

He said, "I haven't got much time, Al. I've got to get back and set up my dining room. What did you mean last night, when you asked me if I'd noticed anything wrong?"

"Not wrong, Mal. Funny. Funny ha-ha and funny boo-hoo, too." Al lowered his voice. "You know where my room is? Right in the front part of the garage? Upstairs, right over the doors?"

Powther nodded. It wasn't the Rolls-Royce, it couldn't be, though people often began to tell you something by introducing the extraneous, the obvious, but he couldn't somehow connect the location of Al's room with the Rolls-Royce.

Al laid the hose down. He said, "Well, from them front

windows I gotta view of the drive, a clear straight view. And I been seein' Camilo's car come up that straight stretch of drive, night after night. For weeks on end now, she's been stayin' out half the night." He hesitated for a minute. Then he said, "She must be doin' eighty when she comes up that drive. Somebody oughtta tell her, Don't drive like that, or she's sure goin' to have a smashup."

"How do you know it isn't the Captain coming in late?" Scandal, Powther thought. Al isn't interested in the rate of speed, it's the scandal.

"How do you know it isn't the Captain?" he repeated. "Are you sure it's Miss Camilo?"

"Am I sure? Listen, Mal, she puts the car up herself. She always puts it up herself. She ain't like some of them rich bastards I've worked for who could drive just as good as me but would leave their cars out in front of their shacks for me to put up because they were scared they wouldn't get their money's worth out of me if they put a car in a garage themselves.

"For two nights straight I thought it was lightnin' flashin' through them Venetian blinds upstairs. It woke me up. Two nights straight. So the third night I decide it ain't lightnin' flashin' in my face, not in December, three nights in a row, so I get out of bed and look down, out of the window. And there's Camilo in the car. She's got to wait for them doors to open up. Them automatic doors ain't hooked up to go up in no split second.

"Ever since then I been lookin' at her, out of the window, three or four nights a week. She comes in later than ever on Saturdays. I seen her, even in bad weather settin' down there at the wheel of her car, the top down, her head lifted watchin' them doors go up. Ain't nobody else looks like her, or got hair like hers. It's Camilo all right. On Saturday nights, she comes in about four or five in the mornin', drivin' like a bat out of hell." He stopped talking and frowned.

Then he said, "She—well, if I was the Captain, I'd, well, she looks like an angel, sittin' down there in that car with her face lifted, watchin' them doors open up."

Powther thought, No wonder the Captain has been looking so discontented. Even when Miss Camilo was away, the Captain had dinner with the Madam on Sundays. Lately the expression on the Captain's face had made Powther wonder what was the matter with him. Now he understood what caused it.

He, too, knew what it was like to lie awake wondering where a woman was, what she was doing, knew what it was like to pretend to be asleep when she came home at some ungodly hour, came home from God knows what, God knows where, and undressed and got in bed and relaxed into sleep almost instantly, knew what it was like to prop himself up on his elbow, cautiously, so as not to disturb the sleeping woman, to examine her face, study her face, try, in a room dimly lighted by the street light outside to figure out from that placid, relaxed, beautiful face where she had been, what she had been doing, because he would never dare ask.

Al said, "Where's she go?"

"I don't know," he said sharply. "I wish I did know. I'll probably never know." Then he remembered that Al was talking about Miss Camilo. "I'm sorry," he said, "I was thinking about something else. I haven't any idea where she goes."

"This town closes up tighter'n a drum after ten o'clock. There ain't no place for nobody to go. What's Camilo doin' out in a closed-up town till all hours of the mornin'? In all kinds of weather. She don't know nobody in Monmouth."

"She probably goes to New York," Powther said. He felt impelled to steer Al away from this affair which was none of his business. "Her friends all live in New York. Or Boston. Young people like to drive a hundred miles or more, to a party or a dance."

"No, she don't," Al said.

"How do you know?"

"Because I measure the gas. I don't question she's in New York on the weekends. But the rest of the time she ain't. She don't use a half-gallon of gas from here to wherever she goes and back here again. She goes somewhere right here in Monmouth. And she don't know nobody in Monmouth."

Powther sighed. "Look, Al," he said, "maybe she plays Canasta or goes to the movies or—"

"There ain't no movies open at three in the morning," Al said stubbornly. "The Treadways ain't never had nothin' to do with the town. I been with them for twenty years and the widow don't even buy her clothes in the town. Camilo don't even know the names of the streets. There ain't nothin' there for her. What's she doin' there, Mal?"

"She's probably got friends in Monmouth," he said firmly. "Well, I've got to set up my dining room now. I'll see you later."

"Come on out when you get through and I'll drive you to the car line, Mal."

"Thank you, Al," he said. When they were driving to the car line he would have to somehow convince Al that whatever Miss Camilo did or did not do was none of Al's business. He wondered why if Al had known this, "for weeks on end," he had kept it to himself up until now.

He liked Miss Camilo. In many ways she was like the Madam, younger, of course, but with the same kindness and kindliness about her. Good people to work for. Thoughtful.

As he moved about the dining room, he forgot about Al and Miss Camilo. He always set his own tables, because he enjoyed doing it. He prided himself on the result. For this intimate family dinner, he placed a small round table in the great bay window. The dining room faced west and by dinnertime, the winter sunlight would lie across the table like a spotlight. In his early days, he had trained under an Armenian, a peculiar man, totally unreliable and unpredictable but an artist at heart. He was always saying, "Now the food it is important, yes. But the dining room is even more so. You must set it up like a stage, Powther, like a stage. You must vary the setting to go with the food, and the hour of eating so that everything fits itself together."

So for these Sunday dinners, in winter, served at the unfashionable hour of three o'clock, he always used the Crown Derby and the old silver goblets, and the Versailles flatware. For the centerpiece he selected an Imari bowl, and filled it with chrysanthemums, because the reds and tawny yellows were like the coloring of the Crown Derby china. By the time he announced dinner there would be sunlight on the table, reaching into the room, shining on the Gainsboroughs, on the mahogany paneling, on the fireplace brasses, so that the entire room would seem to pick up and echo the colors used on the table.

At quarter of three, he lit the fire in the dining room fire-place, and stood watching it, to be sure it was going to burn evenly. He kept thinking about Miss Camilo, found himself shaking his head, saying, Dear me, under his breath. He should have known this would happen eventually.

One morning last summer he was walking past the garage, going toward the house, when he saw her backing that long red Cadillac out of the garage. She turned her head, watching where she was going, and he saw that her face was sharply im-patient, set, not smiling.

She waved at him, and said, "Oh, oh, oh. Where've you been, Powther?"

"Home with my wife," he said, and then, "It's going to be a beautiful day, Miss Camilo."

She had looked up at the sky. "I suppose so," she said. "Yes, I guess it will. Though sometimes they seem pretty much alike."

He had thought, Oh, dear me, as he watched her drive off, at your age and looking the way you do, with that shining silky hair and that lovely smile, you ought to be saying, Oh, it's good to be alive on a morning like this, it ought to show in your face, the morning, the joy at being alive. You look as though you were neither dead nor alive, sort of half of each.

It was one of those mornings when he felt like singing, like shouting, because Mamie had held him in her arms, half the night, and he had watched the car go down the driveway too fast, going faster and faster, flash of red disappearing around the curve, top down, silky yellow hair blowing back in the wind, not dyed, people thought she dyed it, but she didn't; thinking, Oh, dear me, why can't that youngest Copper's wife die, so Miss Camilo can find the man she's looking for.

One minute of three. He opened the doors of the dining room, took one quick backward glance, sunlight in the room, fire burning quietly in the fireplace, red damask draperies in even folds at the windows, Gainsboroughs all straight on the walls, Persian rug free of lint. He'd done a good job. Big as the room was, your eyes went straight to the table, even at this distance away. All the sunlight was concentrated on the table, even the wood of the Adam chairs gleamed in the sun.

At exactly three o'clock, he entered the drawing room, and announced dinner. He got the impression that all three of them, the Madam, Miss Camilo, and the Captain, welcomed the announcement, that they had been sitting there together, saying nothing.

As he moved quietly about the dining room, serving them, he thought about the Captain, wondering why he had written the Captain off, that day last summer when he watched Miss Camilo go down the driveway. Written him off, just as though he didn't exist. But then everybody did, all the servants, even the Madam.

The Captain was handsome, a big young man, with a fine looking head and face. He was unquestionably a gentleman. But— Al said he was a tame cat. For once, Al's description of some one really fitted. The Captain was too nice, too gentle, too wellbred. Powther thought, Well, he came from an old New York family, perhaps the blood line ran out, got too thin. Some of his ancestors should have married into lusty peasant families.

But Miss Camilo— He studied her as she sat at the table, talking and laughing. She has become a raving beauty. There is a gleam about her, a gleam that competes with, no, it surpasses the gleam in this room. It's in her flesh, her hair, her eyes. I know what it is, he thought, I saw the same thing happen to Mamie.

He rarely ever followed the trend of a dinner table conversation, unless it was something very unusual; he was more concerned about the smoothness of the service. But today he listened to them.

The Captain (poking at the nearest flower in the centerpiece with a forefinger, not looking at the flowers, but at Miss Camilo): The chrysanthemums are lovely, Mrs. Treadway.

Once again Powther thought how strange it was that the Captain should call his mother-in-law Mrs. Treadway, not Elinor, not Mother, always Mrs. Treadway.

The Madam: Rogers says it's because we've had so much sunlight this winter. Everything in the greenhouse is flourishing.

The Captain (still looking at Miss Camilo): Let's go for a ride after dinner, Cammie.

Miss Camilo: A ride?

The Captain: Yes, let's go as far outside of Boston as we can go and still get back to Monmouth at a decent hour tomorrow morning.

Miss Camilo: You mean spend the night?

The Captain: Of course. At the first likelylooking inn we come across. We'll play hunt-the-inn until we find a place that's absolutely perfect, even to the Windsor chairs and the fireplaces (the tone of his voice changed, grew softer), the way we used to.

The Madam: You'll probably find snow along the way and the countryside is beautiful in the snow.

Miss Camilo: You come too, Mother. You've never been on a trip with us.

Powther watched the Captain's face and he decided that the Captain was holding the muscles of his face in the exact expression it had had when he first spoke, but the eagerness, the young eager look, left it, the glow went out of his eyes.

The Captain: Good idea. You come too, Mrs. Treadway.

The Madam: I really can't. I've got a nine o'clock appointment at the plant. Thank you for inviting me.

Miss Camilo looked at the Captain, and Powther frowned, not meaning to, unable to prevent the frown, because the look Miss Camilo gave the Captain was a caressing, lingering kind of look, and Powther thought, She has a lover and because she is so happy, she is going to let a little of her happiness spill over on the Captain, and he will believe that it is he who has made her happy, but some day, some day—

In the butler's pantry, he waited for them to finish the second course. He thought about himself and Mamie.

A year after he and Mamie were married he knew that there was something wrong, but he did not know what it was. He could read the evidence in the droop of her mouth, the infrequent laughter when laughter had been as natural to her as breathing, now there was a languor and an indifference that disturbed him. He had thought, If we had children, and she agreed. After Kelly and Shapiro were born she was like she used to be but by the time they were two years old, she was bored with them, cross with them, impatient with them, and then, about a year after that, she was a Rubens female again, her flesh glowing, the house always filled with the rippling sound of her laughter. She was always singing, and her voice acquired an added depth and richness, a beauty of tone that he explained to himself by saying that childbirth wrought wondrous changes in women.

He would have let it go at that except for the new clothes. He knew the contents of Mamie's closet far better than most husbands do, he was always brushing her dresses, cleaning and pressing them, making minor repairs. He kept finding new dresses, new coats, new suits. The drawers of the chest were filled with new underwear and stockings, stockings by the dozen.

He knew deepdown inside him that she had a lover, that some man had entered her life, came home unexpectedly one afternoon and found a man sitting in the kitchen. In his shirt sleeves. Starched white shirt. No necktie. Collar open at the throat. Sleeves rolled up. He was drinking a glass of milk. When Powther entered the kitchen, the man stood up, getting up quickly, all in one motion.

Mamie said, easily, unselfconsciously, "Powther, meet my cousin, Mr. Bill Hod. Bill, this is Powther."

He saw a man put together like a statue, no fat on him anywhere, tall, broad of shoulder, narrow of waist, a man with a quick graceful body and a face like the face of one of the early popes, in a small dark oil painting that hung in Old Copper's library, a cruel face, with eyes that saw everything and disclosed nothing, with a narrowlipped, cruel mouth, a shark's mouth.

He gave Powther one swift, all-inclusive glance, nodded, sat down again, and finished the glass of milk. He left right afterwards.

Powther made cautious inquiries about Bill Hod and learned very little about him that any discerning person couldn't have guessed just from looking at his face. In the barber shop, they said he was the owner of The Last Chance, that he was a gambler, an operator of houses of ill fame, a numbers king, probably nearer the truth, that nobody really knew what illegal enterprises he directed or controlled but that he was unquestionably a racketeer. He was reported to be blind in one eye but nobody knew which eye, both eyes looked equally blank, and nobody knew how he had lost the sight of the eye, assuming that one of them really was sightless. No one knew how old he was; looking at his face, just his face, you could safely say that he was an evil old man of eighty, but he had the thick black lustrous hair of a young man in his twenties.

He couldn't prove that Mamie had a lover, or that if she

had one, it was Bill Hod. For all he knew, Hod might really and truly be her cousin. But he had to find out. So he took to playing that most dangerous, most hazardous, of all the games that husbands and wives play with each other. He had to find out, to make sure, he had to know, could not live without knowing, so he finished his work at the Hall as quickly as he could, arriving home at unexpected hours, entering the house quietly, unannounced.

Sometimes Mamie was alone in the house, sometimes she was not there at all. Once he found Bill Hod sitting in the kitchen, drinking milk, sleeves of the white shirt rolled up, collar of the white shirt open at the throat, and Mamie was seated across the table from him, drinking coffee and eating doughnuts.

Mamie said, "Have one, Powther. Weak Knees made 'em. He's the cook at Bill's place."

Powther ate one of the doughnuts, drank a cup of coffee, moving nervously back and forth, in front of the kitchen sink, thinking, There's something about him, what is it, it's not just the face, it's more than just the face, I don't know what it is, but I'm afraid of him. His hands began to shake so that he put the unfinished cup of coffee down in the sink, afraid he would drop it, and nibbled at the doughnut, not really conscious that he was eating, and yet aware that the doughnut was incredibly good, better than any he had ever eaten, and that on the strength of those doughnuts, Weak Knees, whoever he was, could cook in the White House. Though the best cooks sneered at the White House as a place to work, prestige, yes, but a pinchpenny kind of place, you couldn't really let yourself go there as you could in, say, the kitchen of any millionaire in the country.

He glanced in the dining room to see how near finished they were. And then went all the way inside and started removing plates. The Madam and the Captain were about to start another argument about politics.

The Madam: Oh, Bunny, you talk such nonsense. If all the wealth in this country were divided up, in less than a year's time the same people would be rich and the same ones would be poor.

The Captain: I doubt it. Because—

Miss Camilo (she gave the Captain another one of those long-lingering caressing glances that Powther was certain were not directed at the Captain but inspired by someone else and therefore directed at the other man even though he was not there): Let's drive north for eighty miles and then go east for twenty miles and see what we find.

Miss Camilo had changed the subject, so abruptly, so quickly, Powther didn't see how the Madam and the Captain could possibly bring it up again. He could tell by what the Madam had been saying that she and the Captain were heading straight for one of those long unpleasant arguments about Roosevelt. No matter where they started they always ended up arguing about Roosevelt, and the Madam always managed to call the Captain a fool.

Powther served the dessert, brought in the coffee service. They were talking about the projected ride again.

The Madam: Did you ever find anything wonderful that way?

Miss Camilo: You'd be surprised at the things you find when you're just out riding and don't know where you're going. Even here in Monmouth.

The Captain: You're right. Monmouth's full of surprises. Especially if you follow the river.

The Madam: What kind of surprises?

The Captain: Views of the river. Maybe it's because of the mural in the entrance hall, perhaps the mural made me really see the river. But you can catch the most marvelous glimpses of it, looking down some of the side streets, and then when you actually come to it, and follow its course, you feel as though you had made a personal discovery, come on a secret that no one else has ever found.

Miss Camilo: That's the way I feel about it, too. It's almost as though you had finally found something you'd been hunting for all your life without really knowing that you'd been looking for it. And then you see that it's there, the thing you've been hunting for is there, in the river.

Powther passed the coffee cups as the Madam filled them. He was a little surprised when Miss Camilo again urged the Madam to go for a ride with them.

Miss Camilo: Mother, you come with us. It's such fun to go somewhere, not knowing where you're going or what you'll find when you get there.

The Captain, quickly: We'll all go exploring. Do come and play hunt-the-inn with us, Mrs. Treadway. Each and every-man-Jack of us will be Christopher Columbus. No. You can be Cortez, he was a better man than the rest of them. Cammie will be Ponce de León. I'll be, well, I'll just go along for the ride, and keep the log.

The Madam gave Captain Sheffield a funny sharp look. Powther looked at him, too, and couldn't decide whether the Captain was joking, teasing the Madam and Miss Camilo in some fashion that he, Powther, could not understand or whether he was angry, anger born of fear that the Madam would ignore the fact that three's a crowd and go with them, and so was being sarcastic.

The Madam: Thank you for asking me but I really can't go with you. Besides even if I could, I don't like the idea of hunting for a place to spend the night. I honestly prefer my own bed in my own room, or a bed that's equally as comfortable in a hotel room that's been reserved for me in advance.

Miss Camilo: Well, we tried, didn't we, Bunny?

The Captain: You'll go with us some other time, won't you?

The Madam: Not when you're going to play hunt-the-inn. But some time when you know where you're going, and you let me know beforehand, I'd love to go along.

Miss Camilo: Okay, Bunny, we'll start as soon as I can get a toothbrush in a bag.

Al backed the car out of the garage. He said, "Camilo musta took her Cadillac. I didn't see her get it."

Powther said, "She and the Captain are going away for the weekend."

"Camilo and Bunny?" Al said, and he sounded surprised.

"That's right."

"You mean they went off together some place?"

"That's right."

Al was strangely silent. Powther glanced at him a couple of times. He seemed to be thinking about something, puzzling over something. When they reached the car line, Al slowed down, then said, "Ah, what's the differ? I'll drive you all the way, Mal. I ain't got nothing else to do."

At one point Al got stuck behind a trolley car, and was forced to follow it block after block, going slowly through the streets, unable to pass it, because of all the Sunday traffic. Because of Miss Camilo and the Captain, Powther kept thinking about the day he rode on a trolley car from early morning until late at night. It was a hot day, too, it had started off hot, early in the morning, and the Madam suddenly decided to go to Newport to visit friends for a long weekend.

As soon as he had organized the Hall for the day, and conferred with Mrs. Cameron as to who would be off and when, he hurried home. He kept mopping his forehead with a handkerchief, trying to hurry the trolley car along, and the effort he put into it, the hurry, hurry, hurry, made him feel hotter and hotter. He was still going home at unexpected hours because he had to find out whether Bill Hod was Mamie's lover, or whether he was her cousin just as she said.

He entered the apartment house quietly, tiptoeing up the stairs, though he knew that there was no reason to move quietly in the hall, but the moment he entered the street door he began to feel like a spy, a conspirator, and so he walked on tiptoe up the stairs of that old building where they had lived before they moved into Mrs. Crunch's beautifully kept, fine, old brick house on Dumble Street.

He had been in and out of that building hundreds of times, but for some reason, perhaps because he was extra sensitive to everything that day, the heat was dreadful, he was sweating, the hall impressed him as being singularly ugly. He paused on the second floor, just standing there, on the landing, thinking, Why couldn't whoever painted this hall have made it two-thirds green and one-third tan, or three-quarters green and one-quarter tan? His eye kept following the dividing line between the two colors, hunting for some break in the evenness. It was so damn monotonous and he was under some peculiar and inexplicable compulsion to touch the design stamped in the metal of the wall, his fingers kept seeking it out. It was repeated over and over again, at the exact same interval, the metal cool under his hands, his hands hot, too hot. He tried to figure out what the design was. A leaf? A fleur-de-lis? Just

a conventionalized pattern, senseless, unrecognizable. But repeated, repeated, repeated.

Ordinarily when he walked up the stairs he chose the side
next to the wall, avoiding the banister, for fear he might
brush against it, it was always greasy. He had never stopped to
study the wall. His heart was beating faster and faster, and he
thought, There's something wrong upstairs. Perhaps Mamie
isn't there. Perhaps she's left me.

He kept reaching toward the wall, his fingers seeming to
find some sort of satisfaction in verifying the distance between
the designs stamped in the metal. He drew his hand away,
and it would reach out again, apparently of its own volition,
as though something in his hand needed to find this senseless pattern always in the same place, the place where it ought
to be.

Mrs. Adams owned this building, he thought. She was responsible for this ugly hallway. She must be seventy and yet
she had only a few gray hairs, and the effect of the black thick
woolly hair above the face with the dark brown skin, deep lines
at each side of the mouth, was all wrong. One eye went off at
an angle, so that he was never certain whether she was looking
at him or something over his head or to his right.

Mrs. Adams had a silly kind of manner. When she wasn't
whispering, she talked in a thin whining voice. An arch and
silly manner. He was certain the pearl earrings she wore were
real ones, and he had thought she would verify this when he
admired them. But she didn't. She arched her long neck, and
bridled, and said, "They belonged to my Grandmother Williams." And that was all.

Whenever he thought of her, he thought of the pocketbook
she carried. She never let it out of her hand, out of her arm,
actually, because not only did her hand rest on it, but it was
always tucked under her arm as well. She never put it down,
no matter what she was doing. She collected the rents herself,
counting the money carefully, and then opening the pocketbook just wide enough to push the bills and the coins inside
and then snapped it shut, the whole thing done awkwardly, the
bony hands clutching and fumbling with the powerful clasp,
because she never really let the pocketbook get out from under
her arm all the time she was opening and closing it.

She was thin all over, arms, shoulders, legs, feet, long lean feet. But she had a tremendous, pendulous, belly, the sag and sway of it suggested a big tumor inside. She walked with a slow, stiff-legged gait, as though her legs were brittle, and she had to plan each step in advance lest one of them snap.

Right after he and Mamie moved into the apartment, he met Mrs. Adams in the hall, just coming in, pocketbook clutched under her arm, hand resting on the clasp, and he told her that he'd like to have the apartment painted.

"Everything's so high, Mr. Powther," she had said, leaning toward him. Her manner became highly confidential. She began to whisper. "What it costs me to keep this place heated, and a new furnace last year, and now they've just made me buy new garbage cans. The Board of Health made me buy them and the old ones was perfectly good except the covers was gone. Those little niggers runnin' through the street all the time, steals all the covers off the garbage cans. The big niggers steals the handles to use as blackjacks, and the little niggers steal the covers, for what I don't know. And what it cost me to buy those new cans I could have put that money by for a rainy day, and it woulda carried me for a long time to come. And then I bought chains and chained the covers on. I told that man from the Board of Health, 'Listen, I'm just a poor black woman and a widow, and I can't throw money around like that,'" she paused, sighed, moved a little closer to Powther. "Well, it didn't do any good."

The eye that wandered seemed to find something of interest behind him, on the stairway, halfway up, anyway it focused there and the other eye seemed to be studying the top of his head. Dear God, he had thought, why did I ask her anything about paint? Why did I ask her anything at all?

Mrs. Adams moved a little closer, and her great belly brushed against him, soft, huge. She smelt old and musty, and most unpleasantly of some kind of perfume. He moved away, and her belly followed him, pressed against him.

"As for paint. Well, I rent these apartments as is, Mr. Powther. I can't pay out a single penny for paint. Not one penny. You might as well say I'm the janitor for all the good I get out of this place."

So he paid the painters himself, hired them himself, and then right after that had new plumbing fixtures put in the bathroom, though he knew if he and Mamie ever moved, Mrs. Adams would get double the rent for it because of the money he'd spent improving it.

He didn't know why he should have thought about Mrs. Adams, didn't know why he was standing motionless, on the landing, the second floor landing of Mrs. Adams' rundown house. He'd done everything for Mamie, given her everything, let her do exactly as she pleased. He didn't have to live in this colored slum. If it hadn't been for Mamie, he would have lived at the Hall, in his own quarters, as fine a setup as any man ever had. But Mamie wouldn't have fitted in with the life there. It was bad enough to come home and find Bill Hod in his house, it would have been unbearable to have found Rogers, the gardener, Al, the chauffeur, the French chef, the men he worked with every day on intimate terms with Mamie.

Besides, Mamie was always saying, "Powther, there is things about white people that I never will understand. And to tell you the God's honest truth, I don't intend to try. I am a hell of a lot more comfortable, and it gives me a lot more honest-to-God pleasure just to write 'em all down as bastards and leave 'em strictly alone. Live and let live is what I say. I don't bother them and they don't bother me, so we get along fine. If they say the same about me, it's perfectly all right. That means we're even Steven."

Then she'd start to sing, and you couldn't talk, couldn't argue with her when she was singing, you had to listen. Perhaps that was why she sang, it meant he couldn't discuss anything with her that she didn't want to discuss. She began to sing that song he didn't like. He thought it was a spiritual, but she made it sound like the kind of song they banned on the radio, banned on records:

> Same train carry my mother;
> Same train be back tomorrer;
> Same train, same train.
> Same train blowin' at the station,
> Same train be back tomorrer;
> Same train, same train.

If it hadn't been for Mamie, his life would have been as tranquil and as satisfactory as anybody's life could be. He was doing the kind of work he loved. He did it superbly and knew it, he was well paid for it, all the help liked him, respected him. So did the Madam. She even confided in him. Not even her personal maid had as much of the Madam's confidence as he had. When he first went to Treadway Hall he was certain she had qualms about him, wondered if she hadn't made a mistake, she'd never had colored help before so he supposed it was understandable. He could tell by the way she watched him, something skeptical in her gaze. But by the end of that first year he had turned in such a magnificent performance, that she forgot all about his being colored. Finally, she told him that she had never known how beautiful the house could be, until he took it over.

Yes, everything would have gone smoothly without Mamie. But he couldn't live without her. He would die. He would shrivel up and die if she left him. He had felt suddenly old, horribly old, and so sorry for himself that for a moment he thought he was going to cry. It's this goddamn hallway, he thought. It's just like Mrs. Adams', it's enough to depress a saint. He started tiptoeing up the stairs again, going quickly.

Once inside the apartment, he found out what he had already known, deep inside him, found out because he saw the evidence there in the bedroom he shared with Mamie, Mamie, Mamie.

He had furnished the room with simple, unadorned, soundly constructed furniture made of good wood, carefully finished. Mamie had slowly replaced it with overornate imitations of period furniture, horrible, cheap stuff, not cheap in price, they charged enough for it, but it was the kind of furniture that was despised by people who really knew fine things, the sort of stuff sold in poor neighborhoods to Italians and colored people and Puerto Ricans. The bed was a copy of a copy of a Louis Something-or-Other, the wood, God knows what the wood was, stained and varnished and the headboard and footboard covered with cupids and doves and flowers, all turned out by machine and glued on.

Mamie and Bill Hod lay there, side by side, in that fake Louis Something-or-Other bed. Mamie asleep. Bill Hod, lying on

his side, back to the door, something in his position suggesting that he was not asleep. Both of them naked. Hod's body
bore absolutely no relation to his face, his body was young and
beautiful and with no knowledge of evil.

Powther told himself that he was a coward, that he was a
fool. He tried to think of more searing descriptions of himself
and couldn't, as he went down the stairs, softly, afraid of being
heard, afraid of Bill Hod, of Mamie, of himself, half blind with
fear, and with rage, and something else, something that made
his eyes fill with tears. He couldn't see where he was going, and
his throat was filling with mucus, so that he couldn't swallow,
thickness in his throat.

He got on a trolley car, more by instinct than because he
actually saw the car coming and decided to board it. Anyway,
there he was, standing in the front of the car, dropping money
in the coinbox and he did not remember how he got there. He
rode to the end of the line, and paid another fare and rode to
the center of the city, and got a transfer and boarded another
trolley, going in another direction.

All that day and part of the night he rode on trolleys, the
clang-clang of the car, the rattling, covering up the sound of
the sobs that kept bubbling up in his throat, the sound of the
groans that kept forming in his throat, the swaying of the car
covering up, concealing, helping to conceal the convulsive
heaving of his chest.

At ten o'clock that night, he went home. His only concern was whether he would find Mamie there, because he had
reached a point in quiet despair, in which he knew that it did
not matter who Mamie slept with, so long as she let him sleep
with her, so long as she did not leave him. That was all he
asked, all he wanted.

Prideless. Pride gone. Even that last vanishing traditional
male right of ownership gone. Even that vestige of it which
had been nourished by his final meeting with Old Copper was
gone, never to return. He had faced and acknowledged the
fact that Mamie was all he wanted in life. If Bill Hod was what
she wanted then he would accept Hod, go on day after day
pretending that Hod was her cousin.

Mamie was waiting for him when he got home. She had supper ready. She seemed so happy, humming under her breath,

laughing, talking, that the sheer music of her overwhelmed him.

It was a wonderful supper, shrimp salad and hot biscuits and a soup so flavorsome that he ate two bowls of it. He hadn't had anything to eat all day. He hadn't stopped to eat breakfast that morning, hurrying, cutting every possible corner, as he had done for weeks, hurrying through his work at the Hall so that he could arrive home unexpectedly, in order to find out, find out, what he had finally and dreadfully found out, and then knew that he had been better off when he didn't know, when he only suspected.

He had said, "This is good. This is wonderful. This is like the salad the Frenchman makes at the Hall."

Mamie said, "Weak Knees fixed it up. You know he's the cook at Bill's place."

He went on eating, chewing carefully, putting measured forkfuls of the shrimp salad in his mouth, avocado and garlic in it, the flavor so perfect, chewing, making himself chew at the same rate, not pausing, not stopping, feeling sick, his throat rebelling against the idea of swallowing.

He laid the fork down and looked at Mamie, the redbrown skin, the big soft breasts, the flimsy elaborate-with-lace pink nightgown, that he had not bought, that Bill Hod had bought, not of course in the sense that he had gone into a store and said, I will have that one, saying in his mind, for the wife of another man into whose bed I sneak, sneak, no, for the wife of another man into whose bed I walk boldly, unafraid, not caring whether he knows it or not.

He said, not meaning to, "I don't like Bill Hod coming here so much."

The expression on her face did not change. She sat in the same position, elbows on the table. She said, in a matter-of-fact voice, "I'm right fond of him. If you don't like his comin' here, Powther, I can always go live somewhere else."

He had said, hastily, panic in his voice, "I didn't mean that. It's all right. As long as you want him here, it's all right. I thought maybe you didn't want him here so much. It's all right."

She must have known that his reply was senseless but she didn't bother to say so. She just sat there, elbows on the table, humming under her breath, "Same train carry my mother, same train be back tomorrer . . ."

He thought sullenly, She speaks of going to live somewhere else just as though she were talking about buying a new pair of shoes. What about Shapiro and Kelly? What about me? She would probably never even think of us again, never mention us, even in casual conversation, just as she had married him, and left Baltimore, never looking back, never questioning the advisability of what she planned to do, just doing it, marrying him, getting on the train, because it was convenient, it suited her plans, fitted in with her desire to live in a small Northern city. If he hadn't packed her clothes she would have left them there in that rooming house in Baltimore, left everything behind her, and never regretted the leaving. She had never mentioned Baltimore since they'd been living in Monmouth.

Al stopped the car at the corner of Dumble Street and Franklin Avenue.

"Say," he said, almost reluctantly, "say, Mal, you live down that street, don't you?" He pointed toward Dumble Street.

"Yes," Powther said. He hoped Al wasn't fishing for an invitation to spend the afternoon. He liked Al, yes, but he didn't think he could bear watching Al's pale blue eyes travel over Mamie's curves. As he waited for Al's next words he tried to think of a plausible excuse for not inviting Al to go home with him. Sickness. Mamie. He would say his wife was sick, and everybody knew that the husband didn't bring his friends home to visit when the wife was sick.

"What's down that way?" Al pointed again.

"Nothing. The street ends at the dock. The river's there. You can see it. That's all."

"I shoulda told you before, Mal. One night last week I followed Camilo's car. You see I kept thinkin' to myself, night after night, I'd pay out good money to know where she goes all the time. So I parked outside the gates, way down, and when she come out on the road drivin' like a bat out of hell, I followed her."

Al stared down toward the river. "She come right in this street. I lost all trace of her right here in this street. I shouldn'a done it, followed her like that, it ain't none of my business where she goes but I had this curiosity about her."

"Here?" Powther said. He shook his head. "You must have been drinking too much beer, Al, and followed the wrong car. I live on this street, my family lives here, but this isn't, well, Miss Camilo might go a lot of places in Monmouth but Dumble Street wouldn't be one of them. It's the toughest, noisiest street imaginable. I don't walk along here myself after ten o'clock. It isn't safe. Anything could happen on Dumble Street, even in the daytime. If I know I'm going to be late getting through at the Hall, I spend the night there."

"Whyn't you and your wife live at the Hall?"

"Mrs. Powther doesn't want to," he said, stiffly. "She prefers her own place."

"She's right," Al said. "When the husband works in service and has a wife and they live in, the Madam is always hellbent on puttin' the wife to work. Last place I worked before I come to the Widow's, the old maid I worked for was always sayin', 'Albert, whyn't your wife do the upstairs? We need another upstairs girl.'

"That's why me and my old woman broke up. She said she wasn't goin' to do no chambermaid work for nobody no matter how rich they was. She said handlin' other people's dirty sheets all day long was her idea of nothin' at all, even if they was so fine they felt like silk between the fingers, they was still dirty sheets. She blamed me, but hell, Mal, I figured like the old maid, there she was settin' round on her can all day, she might as well be doin' somethin' to earn herself her beer money.

"Well, anyway, I was wrong. After two weeks of doin' the upstairs she quit me cold, just walked right out of the house. She got up one mornin' and cooked me my breakfast. Best meal I ever ate. And I said so, and she said, 'Well I'm leavin', now, Al, I can't stand this place no more.' She had called a cab and it was waitin' right outside and she got in it with a coupla suitcases and was gone. I ain't never seen or heard of her from that day to this."

Powther said, "I'm sorry to hear it, Al."

"I don't know what made me start shootin' off at the mouth, but sometimes, on my day off," he shook his head. "Well, see you in church if not before."

Powther waved his thanks to Al and walked down Dumble Street, thinking, If I knew the Captain better, if there was between us something approaching friendship, only there isn't and never will be, I would tell him to let Miss Camilo alone for awhile, let this love affair of hers run its course. Run its course? Bill Hod and Mamie, that love affair had never run its course. It was like an ocean, limitless, unexplored.

But he would still tell the Captain, if he could, to let Miss Camilo alone for awhile. It would be hard, the waiting, the fear, the anxiety, the nights. During the day it wasn't so bad. But at night, the nights, when your mind worked overtime, painting pictures, making up dialogue between yourself and Bill Hod, between Bill Hod and Mamie, the nights are indescribable, Captain, too long, too dark, too full of sounds.

What's the matter with me, he thought. The Captain isn't the one who has to make up conversations with Bill Hod. It's me. Why do I care what happens to them, why should I worry about them, about the Captain, and Miss Camilo and some man who lives in Monmouth. They're rich and they were all three born holding the world by the tail.

He shook his head. "That's not enough," he muttered.

He looked around quickly to see if anyone had heard him because he was horrified to think that he'd been walking along the street, talking to himself. He wished that he had someone to talk to, someone to whom he could explain his very real concern about the Captain and Miss Camilo. The fact that the Captain was white and rich could not in any way diminish the feeling of outrage he would experience when he found out what he must already suspect. If only the Captain wouldn't try to find out whether she had a lover and who he was, wouldn't try to make certain, it was better to just go on suspecting, much, much better.

Nice little man, Al thought, watching Powther hurry down Dumble Street. Runs just like a rabbit, all the time. Just like a rabbit, all day long. I'd pay good money to know what in hell his wife is like, must be some reason why he's never asked me to go in his house, probably just like him, and runs right along side of him, Momma Rabbit and Poppa Rabbit. Never saw a colored feller just like him before, never knew there was any

just like him. Now why did I tell him about my ex? Something
about his face. And he listens good. I wish I could find me a
little whore, a nice little whore, beddy-by with a nice little—
My! My!

He honked his horn at a curvey colored wench, who was
just turning into Dumble Street, curving into Dumble Street,
swaying into Dumble Street. She turned and smiled straight at
him, showing all of her white even teeth.

"Hey," Al called out, tooting on the horn again, dum-dee-
dah-dah-dah, "come on and get in here with Poppa."

She shook her head but she kept smiling. "My God!" he
thought as he watched her, "I'da paid good money for a piece
of that."

He could have followed her and argued with her, tried to
persuade her, but this was a colored neighborhood and many a
white man had been found on a roof with his pants, his shoes
gone, and his skull split wide open, in neighborhoods like this.
He sighed, and drove off, following Franklin Avenue until
he found a good place to turn the crate around in, thinking
about that big one who had just gone down Dumble Street, he
wasn't sure but what it wouldn'ta been worth getting his skull
split open to have a piece of that.

Mrs. Mamie Powther said to herself, as she walked toward
Number Six Dumble Street, Wonder where that big one came
from. A smile kept appearing around the corners of her mouth,
and in her eyes.

13

ABBIE CRUNCH was ostensibly adjusting her best winter hat, looking in the sitting room mirror as she settled it on her head at what she thought was the most becoming angle; actually, she was admiring the shine of the black coq feathers that adorned the hat, blueblack feathers that were astonishingly effective against her white hair. Sealskin cape, sealskin muff, plain black wool coat, white gloves. It added up to an extremely smart winter outfit, if she did say so herself. If she hadn't been looking in the mirror, she wouldn't have seen J.C. enter the room. He came in through the door, sideways, walking on tiptoe, which was unnecessary because he was wearing sneakers and she wouldn't have heard him come in.

He stood in back of her, touched the sealskin cape, tentatively, gently, and then stroked it.

"Is dat fur, Missus Crunch?" he asked.

"Yes, it is."

"Fur," he repeated. "Her's got one, too."

"J.C., take your thumb out of your mouth. Where will you get a new one when you've got that one all chewed up?" To her surprise, he actually took his thumb out of his mouth.

Is that fur! she thought. It's Alaskan sealskin. Cape made from the Governor's wife's old sealskin coat. The Governor's wife had given it to her in the fall of the year the Major died, saying, "Mrs. Crunch, I brought this to you because I thought you might be able to get collars and cuffs out of it."

When Abbie took it to Quagliamatti, the tailor who used to be on Franklin Avenue, and explained that she wanted a cape and a muff made out of it, he held the coat up, turned it around and around, muttering, "Rump sprung. Rump sprung. Have to cut around it." He was such an expert and so inexpensive that she did not reprove him for his unnecessary vulgarity for fear that he might refuse to work on the coat. He had turned out this rippling cape and the fat round muff. By treating them with care, having them stored, and worked over every year, they would last as long as she did. She turned slightly so that she could see the way the cape flared in the back, and thought, as she always did, that the cape would have done credit to a Fifth Avenue furrier.

J.C. said, "You goin' out?"

"That's right." She was going to Deacon Lord's funeral.

"Kin I go wid you?"

"No."

"What'm I goin' do?"

"You're going right back upstairs to your own part of the house and talk to your mother or play with your brothers."

"Mamie's out. Them bastids Kelly and Shapiro is in the movies, 'n they wouldn't let me go. What'm I goin' to do? They told me to stay down here."

"Good heavens!" she said. He was standing close to her, looking at her, his thumb in his mouth, his round hard head on one side, something speculative in his black eyes. I knew it was a mistake to let that woman stay in my house. I've changed. I knew I would. A woman like that always changes things, her mere presence is like water working on stone, slow attrition, finally a groove, stone worn down. I no longer state my objections to the child's language. He uses the word "bastard" and I say nothing, because if I do he'll just repeat it again and again. He's watching me, waiting for me to do something about him. He knows I won't leave him alone in the house.

She'd known Frances for twenty-five years. Or was it thirty years? Anyway, in all that time Frances had never once said, Abbie, will you do something for me? Never asked a favor. Until yesterday morning. The phone rang, and Frances, who was usually quite clear about what she wanted had sounded excited, and what she said didn't make sense.

Frances had said, "Howard's a fool—"

Howard? Abbie had thought. Had something happened to him? He was Frances' assistant, a tall, softlooking man, not young, not old, with reddish hair, and skin almost the same color as his hair.

"Funeral tomorrow afternoon. Deacon Lord's funeral," Frances had said, talking faster and faster.

What does she want me to do? How does that involve me, she had wondered, frowning.

"Go to South Carolina. Bring back the body of the Smith boys' mother," Frances said, and she'd sounded as though she were barking into the mouthpiece.

She remembered having said, "Wait a minute, Frances. Wait a minute."

She had been completely confused. Did Frances want her to go to South Carolina? Pretty Boy had been asleep in the Boston rocker, white paws tucked under him, so mounded up, so curled up, that he looked like a big gray and white cushion.

While she was standing there in the sitting room, holding the receiver, trying to think, J.C. had suddenly appeared in the room, edging in, not there one minute, there the next. He pulled the cat out of the rocker, tried to make him walk on his hind feet. Pretty Boy had clawed at him, and J.C. let him go. Then he tried to sit on Pretty Boy's back, saying, "Dis a horse. Dis a horse."

"J.C., leave that cat alone," she had shouted, right into the mouthpiece of the telephone, "Leave him alone! You go back upstairs. Did you hear what I said, J.C.? I'm trying to talk on the telephone. Now go on upstairs! Go on!"

J.C. had backed out of the room. He was always backing away, perhaps because he was conditioned to sudden violent attack from the rear. She had watched him. Did Frances want her to go to South Carolina? Pretty Boy had jumped back in the rocker, curled up again. The cyclamen were in bloom now. The white geraniums were resting. Dormant. Cyclamen almost too brilliant, too vivid, almost red. When Mr. Powther had stopped in to pay his January rent, he had looked at them and said, "What beautiful plants, Mrs. Crunch!" He noticed everything beautiful, appreciated everything beautiful. How he ever came to marry that careless young woman, she couldn't imagine. Frances gave her the cyclamen at Christmas, every Christmas, plants. How long would she have to stay away? Who would water the plants?

"Yes," she had said firmly into the telephone. Frances had never asked a favor.

"They don't want her buried there. They say they won't even leave their dead in the South, nothing of theirs will they leave there. They never could get her to come North to live but they hate the South so they won't let her be buried there."

South Carolina, she had thought. Not buried there. Somebody's mother. What difference would it make? South or North, if you were dead, you were dead. Where you were buried didn't matter. She hadn't traveled that far, alone, in years.

What did she think would happen to her? But she couldn't go. What would she do with Pretty Boy? And there was J.C. always wandering around, always poking and prying into things. He had the awful curiosity of the very young. She was certain Link hadn't been like that at that age. J.C. looking under Pretty Boy's tail, asking, "Where does his bowels move?" or standing staring at her, "Where does you wee-wee?" And Link—Link out all night—

"Will you come over tomorrow afternoon? Funeral at two. If you'll just see that everything goes all right. Howard's a fool," Frances said.

"You mean at your place?"

"Of course."

"Oh. I thought you wanted me to go to South Carolina."

Silence. Then, "South Carolina? And you were going?"

"Certainly."

"Abbie," tenderness in Frances' voice, the voice pitched lower, "why, Abbie—" Laughter. Then, "Abbie, you're wonderful. I wouldn't dream of asking you to go to South Carolina. I wouldn't go myself but they're paying me so much money that I can't very well refuse."

So much money, she thought. "Who are they?"

"The Smith boys. They're numbers bankers. So they can well afford to spend as much as they want to on a funeral or anything else."

Frances had said, "I wouldn't ask you to come over but Howard's such a fool. I'll be back tomorrow afternoon. Not in time for the service. Right afterwards though. And we can have tea over here."

So here she was, dressed in her best clothes, on her way to attend the funeral of a Baptist deacon that she had never known except by sight, because some numbers bankers whom she had never seen did not want their mother buried in South Carolina. That was complicated enough in itself; in addition, here was this child of Mamie Powther's, standing in front of her, sucking his thumb. She thought, Of all the unprepossessing sights—his overalls were torn at the knees and he was standing on one foot, and there was a hole in the toe of one of his faded blue sneakers. They were too short for him. His big toe had made that hole. Hole in his sock, too. At that age their toes were always freeing themselves, in fact, the big toe was like a separate aggressive appendage, an added something on the foot which was impelled to keep working its way toward light, going through fabric, leather.

She said, indignantly, "Well, you'll have to change your clothes."

He ignored the indignation, took his thumb out of his mouth, looked up at her, his eyes sparkling, his lips curving into a smile. She thought, He has a lovely smile, and she patted his shoulder.

"I kin put 'em on, all alone, Missus Crunch. And I be right down de tairs." Voice eager, face eager.

She waited for him in the hall, smoothing her gloves over her fingers, with a nervous impatient motion, because she was certain that she would have to dress him. Then he came clumping down the stairs, wearing new brown shoes, different overalls, dark gray, newlooking, too, and a bright red jacket that was much too big for him, the sleeves so long they covered his hands.

"Are you going to be warm enough?" she asked, fingering the material of the jacket. It seemed to be wool but what a dreadful color for a little boy.

"I be warm enough," he said. He sniffed. "Smell it?" he asked, head cocked on one side.

"Smell what?"

"It's the printhess," he said. "It's her smell."

"Come," she said. "We'll have to hurry or we'll be late." You in your red jacket, and I in my sealskin cape, you looking like a thumbling and I looking like Mother Goose. She wondered why a man as sensible, as businesslike, as efficient as little Mr. Powther told fairy stories to his children. J.C. was always muttering about robbers and giants and a princess who was all gold.

They were halfway down Dumble Street, J.C. trotting along beside her, holding on to her hand, when she stopped, said, "J.C., did you go to the bathroom before you left?"

"Yes, Missus Crunch," he said meekly. Silence. Then he said anxiously, "Ain't they got no wee-wee chairs dere?" He tugged at her hand, "Missus Crunch," he said, "where we goin'?"

"We're going to Washington Street. In the next block. To— uh—" she paused. What was she going to do with him during the funeral service? "We're going to Miss Jackson's house."

"Ain't they got no wee-wee chairs dere?"

"Yes," she said absently.

She looked back, down the street. The Hangman, leafless now, was a darker gray than the sky. In fact the lower end of Dumble Street looked like a steel engraving, dark gray river, and sidewalk and buildings. All the buildings looked gray this afternoon. Except Number Six which was a dark red. She did not look at, but was aware of, the redorange neon sign in front of The Last Chance. She shivered, feeling suddenly cold, remembering Bill Hod's black fathomless eyes, for no reason at all, thinking, Full fathom five thy father lies—

Was the child warm enough? She used to walk along the street with Link, just like this, holding him by the hand. Their hands always felt so hot.

They turned into Franklin Avenue. Smell of kerosene. From the newsstand on the corner. Woman in the newsstand, so wrapped up, so bundled up, dark blue knit cap pulled down over her forehead, bundled up to the eyes, like a Mongolian, layers of clothes, and the little kerosene stove right near her.

Franklin Avenue was filled with people. Curiously enough there were no children in sight. She saw just one woman with a small child by the hand. But there were countless young women wearing red coats and highheeled shoes, and long gold earrings that dangled against their brown cheeks. Voices. Laughter. Most of the older women were milling around in Davioli's market, talking and laughing, too. Street suddenly warm, because of warm air from the Five-and-Ten, revolving door, going around and around, people going in, coming out, blend of frankfurters, coffee, mustard, perfume.

No wonder there were so few children on the street. They were all queued up in front of the Franklin Theatre, in a crooked, constantly in motion line, a line that suggested a caterpillar, inching along. Argument going on—young, determined voices.

"Dat's my place."

"It ain't."

J.C. stood still, studied the line.

"Dat's my place."

"It ain't."

"You git out."

The line that was like a caterpillar swayed, violent motion in the center, broke in two, became two separate parts, and then bent in on itself. Small boys and girls, all looking. Some in coats too long, some in coats too short, some with no coats, shivering, bent over, hands in their pockets. All watching two small boys who were pushing each other.

"Git outta the way."

"Git outta the way yourself."

J.C. said, delight in his voice, "That's them bastids Kelly and Shapiro." Two small boys rolled over and over, on the sidewalk, shouting at each other, their voices muffled.

"Kick him in de ass. Kick him in de ass," J.C. yelled, jumping up and down.

"J.C.!" Abbie said sternly, pulling him along. "How many times have I told you that you simply cannot use that kind of language when you're with me. I simply will not have it."

"Yes'm," he said.

Then she pulled him across the street, crossing Franklin Avenue though they would only have to recross it when they reached the corner of Washington Street. But she had seen Cat Jimmie propelling himself along on his little wooden wagon. She couldn't bear to walk near that creature on the wagon, it wasn't just the smell of him, it was the whole horrible degenerate look of him, his eyes, and the mutilated flesh on the stumps of legs and arms, exposed even now on this cold windy afternoon. Pass by on the other side, she thought. "If you believe the Lord looks after and cares about a sparrow, then you must of necessity also believe that He looks after and cares about Bill Hod." That's what the Major had said. And she supposed that he would feel the same way about Cat Jimmie. The Major had a capacity for including all men in his sympathy, his understanding, that had sometimes annoyed her, sometimes surprised her. But Cat Jimmie—"there came down a certain priest that way: and when he saw him, he passed by on the other side. And likewise a Levite, when he was at the place, came and looked on him, and passed by on the other side. But a certain Samaritan . . . when he saw him, he had compassion on him."

Fall of a sparrow, she thought. Bill Hod? Compassion? For Hod? And that inhuman creature on the wagon? Mouth open, eyes like the eyes of a trapped animal, fierce, crazed. She turned and looked back, and he was lying down on the wagon, looking up under a woman's skirts, and the woman jumped away from him, went running up Franklin Avenue. Oh, no, she thought, he is no longer human, he is an animal, and it does say, "A certain man went down from Jerusalem to Jericho, and fell among thieves—" fall of a sparrow—Bill Hod—compassion— Cat Jimmie.

Once she'd stopped to speak to that creature on the wagon, something in her, pity, compassion, something, made her stop. She saw his eyes, horrible, the whites were red, and she turned away, mounting the steps of her house, and looked back and the pity, the compassion, vanished, replaced by revulsion, because he had propelled himself close to the bottom step and was looking up, trying to look under her skirts, panting, his mouth working, the eyes fierce, vengeful. For a moment she was so overcome by nausea that she couldn't move, and then she ran up the last two steps, hurried inside the house, and slammed the door.

They walked as far as Washington Street and then crossed Franklin Avenue again.

J.C. said, "What we cross over Franklin for, Missus Crunch?"

She hesitated, thinking, Evasion? outright lie? the truth? Truth. She said, "I didn't want to walk near that man on the little cart."

J.C. looked back, down Franklin Avenue. "Aw, him!" he said, contempt in his voice. "Mamie say he don't hurt nobody. She say he can't git it no other way but lookin'. And she say seein's dat's the only way he can pleasure himself, best thing to do is just let him go ahead and look."

I know what I'll do with you, young man, she thought, I'm going to leave you with Miss Doris. Miss Doris was Frances' maid, housekeeper, cook, whathaveyou, and Miss Doris' husband, whom she called Sugar, mowed the lawn, looked after the garden, and made all the repairs. Miss Doris could have a white cloth tied around her head, and have on very worn, very faded, but very clean, slacks, and be down on her hands and knees weeding a flower bed, and when she looked you over, she could make you feel as though your hair were uncombed and there were runs in your stockings.

When they turned in at the F. K. Jackson Funeral Home, J.C. tugged at Abbie's hand, again. "Is we goin' to a funeral-izin', Missus Crunch?"

"I am," Abbie said. She looked down at his upturned face. His eyes were sparkling with excitement, pleasure. "But you're not. You're going to stay with Mrs. King until I come back."

Hand in hand, they climbed the front steps. Abbie rang the bell. The door opened almost immediately.

"Good afternoon, Mrs. Crunch," Miss Doris said. She had a white cloth wrapped tight around her head, a shorthandled dust mop in her hand.

Abbie thought she looked more than ever like a statue, short, wide, not fat, but bulky. Her flesh had the hard look of metal, and her voice was hard, cold, suggesting metal, too.

"I were not told to expect you so soon," Miss Doris said, reproach in the hard metallic voice. "Or I would have been in a state of preparation."

Abbie said, apologetically, "I'm early, Miss Doris. But I wanted to ask a favor of you. Will you look after this little boy for me, until after the funeral?"

Miss Doris and J.C. eyed each other with suspicion. Miss Doris said, "All right, boy. Come in." She frowned. "I see you brought your lollipop with you."

Abbie looked at J.C. He was sucking his thumb again but he didn't have a lollipop.

J.C. took his thumb out of his mouth. "Ain't got no lol-lipop," he said indignantly. Then put the thumb back in his mouth.

"What's that in your mouth?" Miss Doris said, sharply.

No answer. Scorn in his eyes. He cocked his round, hard head on one side, studying her.

"Come on, boy. I can't stand here all day," Miss Doris prod-ded J.C. with the shorthandled mop, pushing him inside the door.

Abbie turned away, quickly. She heard J.C. say, "You take dat mop off my clothes," and then the door closed.

The F. K. Jackson funeral parlor occupied the basement floor of the building where Frances lived, a building that reminded Abbie of the brownstone-front houses in New York. She and the Major had spent their honeymoon in a house very much like this one, same long flight of steps leading to the first floor, same type of basement with a separate entrance, at street level.

Howard, Frances' assistant, was standing just inside the door of the office.

Abbie said, "Miss Jackson asked me to see that everything— to—asked me to come over," faltering, remembering Frances' brusque voiced statement, "Howard's a fool."

Looking at him now, as he hovered in the doorway, she thought he was built like a eunuch, or what she thought a eunuch would be built like, very tall, very fat, soft fat, too broad across the hips, and he had a waddling kind of walk. He came waddling toward her, holding out his hand, and he bowed over her hand, then straightened up and looked into her eyes. He said, gravely, "Ah, yes, Mrs. Crunch. So very kind of you. Miss Jackson couldn't have found a more impressive representative."

The skin on his face was like a baby's skin, a kind of bloom on it. Amazing skin. A peculiar color. Almost the exact color of the fuzzy redbrown hair, not much of the hair left, he was getting bald, hairline receding, so that seen close to, without a hat, and she had never seen him hatless before, he appeared to have a high domeshaped forehead, a forehead that just never ended. And he had a moustache, a feather of a moustache, which seemed to have just taken rest, for a moment, over what in a woman would have been an incredibly pretty mouth. Baby's skin. Woman's mouth.

He said, "There are always so many details. I almost forgot your gloves. We'll put them on in Miss Jackson's office." His manner confidential, his eyes widening a little.

Abbie smiled at him, feeling as though he had just shared a delightful secret with her. She leaned toward him, ever so slightly. Then she checked the bend of her body, stiffening, straightening up, no longer smiling, frowning a little, thinking, Why the man's a hypnotist.

The glistening of his eyes told her he was waiting for this leaning response of her body, had known it would come, that he was practised in this business of subtly conveying the idea that here were his strong masculine shoulders, and the whole long smooth-skinned length of him, for widows, for orphans over sixteen, to lean on, to find solace in the leaning.

In the office, he helped her put on a pair of black gloves. He smelt ever so faintly of liquor and she thought of the Major—and that day he died. Frances' hands were long and bony and hers were short and plump. But they got the black gloves on and then he escorted her to a seat midway in the chapel. She sat staring at the ends of the glove fingers, black, empty, wiggled them once, thought they looked like the armless sleeves of a scarecrow, that a child would be frightened by these empty glove fingers, wondered what J.C. and Miss Doris were doing.

But she was here to see that everything was all right, went all right. The chapel was filling up with people, there were flowers in the embrasure where the casket stood in front of the windows, drawn curtains and shaded lights that cast a mournful pinklavender light. An airless room. Too hot. And filled with the heavy toosweet smell of roses.

The family came in. The widow was heavily veiled, there was a uniformed nurse in attendance, pallbearers in gray gloves. Everything seemed in order. Everything in order except the pressure, the feeling of tremendous pressure about her head.

The service started on time. Then the Baptist minister, Reverend Ananias Hill, grown older these last years, gaunter, slower of movement, even his voice had changed, the thunder had gone out of it to be replaced by a quality that was sad, sorrowful, spoke of the late Deacon Lord, and prayed for his immortal soul, and read from the Bible: "Thou shalt love the Lord thy God with all thy heart . . ."

A tremulous old man with an old man's voice. Mamaluke Hill's father. Queer the things you remembered about people. For years The Narrows had conjectured about Reverend Hill's wife, trying to decide whether she was white or whether she was colored. Nobody ever really knew. They said Reverend Hill didn't know himself whether she was white. The child's name, Mamaluke, would suggest that she was colored. She finally died in a rooming house, on Dumble Street. The fact that she left Reverend Hill, no longer lived with him, was a minor scandal.

Abbie heard Reverend Hill say that the late Deacon Lord had loved God, and had loved his neighbor as himself, and then she stopped listening to him. She began thinking about Dumble Street. About Link. About the night the Major died.

The Major had said, "Abbie, the house, the house." And she could smell the morning, the river, see fog blurring the street, feel it wet and cold against her face, drifting in in waves from the river, fog undulating, blurring the sidewalk, and once again she leaned over, blinked her eyes, wiped her eyes, so that she could read what had been written on the sidewalk, in front of her house, "At her feet he bowed, he fell—"

Reverend Hill said, again, "Thou shalt love the Lord thy God with all thy heart." And the pressure, the feeling of pressure increased. All of us, she thought, young and old, all of us here in this funeral chapel were brought up on the King James version of the Bible, all able to quote it, part of our thinking, part of our lives, and we keep moving away from it, forget about it. Even though we go to church. But we attend a funeral and something in us is fascinated, and afraid, and we keep going back into the past, trying to find ourselves or what we believe to be ourselves, a part of us lost somewhere back in the past.

Someone screamed. She thought for a moment that it was she who had screamed. Then she saw that the relatives, the family, were filing past Deacon Lord's coffin. It was the widow who had screamed, not so much screamed as wailed. She was a large woman, dressed in black, wearing a black veil so long, so thick, that it was like a curtain, a drapery over her face. Abbie thought of the Major and his favorite joke, "When I mourns, I mourns all over."

"I won't let him go," Mrs. Lord wailed. "I won't let him go, I won't let him go. Hubborn, come back, come back." The "come back" sounded as though it were being sung, on one high note, sustained, repeated.

Mourn all over, she thought. People do, in one way or another.

Then, very quickly, they were all outside on the sidewalk, standing there, and Howard and two other men were shepherding the people into the proper cars, darting in and out, just like sheepdogs, impatiently nosing a group of slowmoving and very stupid sheep over a stile.

Howard turned to Abbie, "Ah, yes, Mrs. Crunch," he said, taking her by the arm. "Miss Jackson always rides in front with me. So if you'll get in here. But first," he opened the back door of the car, "Mrs. Lord, this is Mrs. Crunch. She's Miss Jackson's personal representative. She'll be riding in the front seat with me."

Mrs. Lord said, "Glad to meet you," and reached out a blackgloved hand and shook Abbie's blackgloved hand. It was a surprisingly firm handshake.

"And this is Mr. Angus Lord," Howard said. "Deacon Lord's brother."

"My compliments," Mr. Angus Lord leaned forward, bowed. Then he sat back and sucked his teeth.

Abbie sat in the front seat of the car, close to the door. She was waiting for Mrs. Lord to start that weird wailing sound again, the back of her neck cold with waiting, her hands in the long-fingered black gloves clenched into fists, hands tense with waiting. Howard started the car, pulled off, following close behind the hearse. Silence in the back seat.

Then Mrs. Lord said petulantly, "Angus, I can't remember whether I locked my back door."

Mr. Angus Lord said, "I locked it. It don't matter anyway. That big dog would keep anybody out ceptin' a blind man, who was a deaf man, too. A deaf blind man wouldn't be robbin' nobody's house." Pause. "A lot of folks at the funeral."

"I didn't see his cousin. Was she there?"

"I dunno. I ain't seen her in years." Pause. "By the way, I'd like his gold watch. For a keepsake."

"I'm keepsakin' it myself." Reproof in Mrs. Lord's voice. "I figure to keepsake it the rest of my life. Hubborn never give me nothin' while he was alive and now he's dead, he can start in. I aims to keepsake his gold watch and his diamond stickpin."

"He ain't in his grave," Mr. Angus Lord said, voice scornful. "You can wait awhile before you start puttin' bad mouth on him."

Abbie wondered if the scorn was due to disappointment or to fear of disparaging a dead man, fear so old no one really knew its source. Mrs. Lord had criticized the deacon, "Hubborn never give me nothin' while he was alive—" Speak no evil of the dead.

She turned her head to look at Mrs. Lord. The heavy black veil still concealed her face, but she had removed the black gloves, had rolled them up into a ball, and was kneading them with one hand, just as though the gloves were a ball of black dough. Mr. Angus Lord was staring out of the window, watching the traffic.

When they slowed down in order to turn in between the gates at the entrance to the cemetery, Abbie found herself thinking about the Major again, and his story about Aunt Hal who had ridden to a funeral astride the hearse, and how the rest of the Crunches shouted, "Whip up them horses! Ride her down! Ride Hal down!"

Then the Reverend Ananias Hill was intoning, "Ashes to ashes—" voice sorrowful, voice sad, voice old, and Mrs. Lord wailed again, "Hubborn, come back, come back to me," and Reverend Hill went right on intoning, "Dust to dust—"

About five minutes afterwards, Howard was helping Mrs. Lord into the long black car, the nurse was hovering close by. Howard said, "Here, drink this—no—drink it right down— and you'll feel better—it's brandy." Then they were off, leaving the cemetery, going faster and faster.

Mr. Angus Lord said, "I'll have a little of that likker, young man." He sucked his teeth, waiting.

Howard stopped the car, reached in the glove compartment, got out the flask, a package of paper cups, handed them back to Mr. Angus Lord, and then started the car, driving even faster now.

Mr. Lord said, "Ah!"

Abbie turned, saw that he was drinking out of the flask, and that he was apparently emptying it; he paused for a moment in his drinking, and then said "Ah!" again.

"Now what might that have been, young man?" he asked.

Howard glanced at Mr. Angus Lord in the mirror. "Hennessy's Five Star brandy."

"Five stars. Stars. Thought so," he said. "Tasted like it." He smacked his lips. "Was that a colored cemetery, young man?" he asked companionably.

"No," Howard said. "But in another ten years or so we'll have that, too. We've got two practically colored schools and we've got a separate place for the colored to live, and separate places for them to go to church in, and it won't be long before we'll work up to a separate place for the colored to lie in after they're dead. It won't be long, brother. Then you'll feel right at home here in Monmouth. It'll be just like Georgia except for the climate."

Howard must be angry about something, Abbie thought. That's no way to talk to a customer. Customer? The customer was dead. They'd just left him there under the hemlocks. Well, it was no way to talk to the customer's family. Surely Mrs. Lord would resent the reprimanding, sarcastic voice Howard had used. Howard. What was his last name? How many people have I ever known that I called by their first names? What's his last name? I'll ask Frances. Maybe he didn't have one. Maybe he came into the world, broad of hips, fullgrown, fullblown, in his cutaway coat and striped trousers, with his flask of brandy and his derby hat and his gray gloves, and his feather moustache, above that delicatelyshaped, moistlooking, thirstylooking mouth. What had made him angry? Why, the brandy, of course. The late Deacon Lord's brother had drunk up every drop of Howard's Five Stars. Then she thought, This whole thing has made me lightheaded, because she was rhyming again, saying over and over, Stars in his crown, to his renown, stars in his crown, to his renown.

The late Deacon Lord's brother must have been mellowed by the brandy, warmed by it, slightly intoxicated by it, because just as Abbie turned to look at him, he laid his hand on Mrs. Lord's large wellfleshed knee and said, "I spose you'll be lookin' around for another man—"

Mrs. Lord snorted. "Another man? Me? Another man? I could tell you things about Hubborn that would make your hair straighten out just like white folks' hair." Pause. "And I'll thank you to take your black hand off'n my leg."

Howard said smoothly, "Mind if I turn on the radio?" Music filled the swiftly moving car, jazz music, loud, strongly accented.

By the time they pulled up in front of Mrs. Lord's house, on the edge of Monmouth, a one-story shingled affair, glassed-in porch across the front, she had removed the black veil and the black gloves. She got out of the car, unassisted, handed Howard a white box edged with black.

Abbie thought, That's where she put the veil and the gloves.

Mrs. Lord said, "Goodbye, Mrs. Crunch, and thank you. Tell Miss Jackson everything was fine," and walked heavily toward her front steps, the late Mr. Lord's brother trailing along behind her.

Howard turned toward Abbie. "Drop you at Number Six?"

"No, thank you. I'll go back to the funeral parlor with you. I want to see Miss Jackson. She said she'd be back after the service."

She wondered what J.C. and Miss Doris were doing. Something intractable about Miss Doris. Even the way she used the word "were," pronouncing it as though it were "wear," and using it constantly. She was short but not stout, bulky, bulk of a statue. Her face and body looked like wrought iron, both as to color of skin, and an almost metallic hardness of the flesh. Flesh on the face, flesh on the forearms, like iron. Thin legs. Splay feet. She planted her feet flat on the ground when she walked. Even the voice hard and cold.

J.C. and Miss Doris? He'd be all right. If he could survive Mamie Powther and Shapiro and Kelly, he'd survive Miss Doris too.

"Tell me," she said to Howard, raising her voice against the sound of the radio. "Why did Mrs. Lord call Deacon Lord 'Hubborn.' I thought his first name was Richard."

"She couldn't say 'husband.' Hubborn was the nearest she could come to it in that loosepalated, liverlipped speech of hers." He turned the radio off.

He's still angry about his Five Stars, she thought. "Was she really upset? She seemed so calm, and then all of a sudden she was shrieking like a banshee."

Howard said, "Yes and no. She didn't want him back. If by lifting a finger she could bring him back, she'd tie her hands together, bind them, so the fingers couldn't move, even by reflex action. He was an old devil and she'd been married to him for forty years, married to a little black man who was mean and stingy and malicious. That was Hubborn. Mean.

"When her old mother died, a few years back, he wouldn't pay for the funeral. The city buried her. He knew a couple of ward heelers and he hollered poor mouth so Mrs. Lord's mother was dumped into what amounts to an open lot. The old lady had insurance. All these old folks have enough insurance to give 'em a pretty good funeral. They save pennies and nickels to pay for their insurance, pay for it by the week. Well, anyway, Mrs. Lord's old mother got a pine box, no extras, just a box. The city paid for it and we took care of the arrangements. That's how I know about it. The old lady got a plain pine box and the box was put in potter's field. Hubborn took the five hundred dollars from the insurance and bought himself a diamond and had one of the local jewelers set it in a gold stickpin.

"He was a great man for gold, Hubborn was. He was a thirty-third-degree Mason, too, and he kept the colored Masons in such a state of confusion and muddlement that they've never been able to buy a home. They rent one of those storefronts one night a week, and on the other nights the members of the I Will Arise and Follow Thee Praise the Lord for Making Me Colored and Not White Church sing hallelujah in it.

"No, she wouldn't bring him back. But he was alive one minute with his gold teeth flashing, and his gambler's cufflinks gleaming, ten-dollar gold piece in each one, and his diamond stickpin glittering, and his bright yellow ties shining and the next minute he was dead. So Mrs. Lord now has his gold cufflinks and his undeaconly diamond stickpin and his gold watch tucked in her black bosom—for keepsakin'."

He stopped talking, lit a cigarette, and Abbie thought he had finished. Then he said, indifferently, "Maybe she screamed because she was afraid she was dreaming, afraid that she would wake up and find that Hubborn was still alive. Or perhaps she saw herself as she would ultimately be, very dead, very cold, lying in a coffin, a satin-lined one, of course."

He gave her a sly sidewise glance, and she thought, This is an assumed callousness and I shall ignore it. He is trying to give me the impression that he is so accustomed to the idea of death that he can speak of coffins and satin linings, and go on smoking, and looking around him as he drives, as though none of it really mattered, as though it had nothing to do with him.

They were going down Franklin Avenue. The street was still filled with people, mostly women, all of whom were carrying bundles, or packages. They had finished their Saturday shopping, had finished exchanging a week's wages for clothes, groceries, liquor.

When he stopped the car in front of the F. K. Jackson Funeral Home, she got out quickly, before he could help her, deliberately ignoring his outstretched hand.

"By the way," she said abruptly, "what is your last name?"

"Thomas. Good old Anglo-Saxon last name. All of us black sub rosa Anglo-Saxons are named Stevens, Jackson, Williams, Smith, King."

"I'll tell Miss Jackson how well you managed everything, Mrs. Thomas." Heavens, what kind of a slip of the tongue was that? She started to say, What could I have been thinking of, I mean Mr. Thomas; but he appeared not to have noticed. He was kicking one of the front tires, trying to dislodge the mud that had spattered on its white walls.

"Muck," he muttered. "Graveyard muck."

Then he opened the door of the car, reached deep inside the glove compartment, took out a package, tore off the green paper wrappings, then the thin white paper underneath, clawing at it in his haste, got a corkscrew out of his pocket, pulled the cork out of the bottle.

"Can't do this on the job," he said, "but if you'll excuse me." He gave a slight shudder and poured half the contents of the bottle down his throat in one great swallowless draft. She walked away from him so that she would not see the second great draft go down his throat, the draft that would unquestionably empty the bottle.

14

FRANCES JACKSON leaned over and kissed Abbie. Then she said, "Abbie! Come in, come in. Are you all right?"

"Why, of course. And you? Are you all right?"

"Never been better. Come in the living room. Let me take your coat and your cape. And your hat. Take off your hat, Abbie. Here, give it to me." Holding the coat, the cape, the muff, under one arm, she took the hat in her hand, turned it around. "You know, this outfit makes you look like a duchess."

"The Ugly Duchess?" Abbie said, and laughed.

"No. The Duchess of Kent. But older and mellower. Don't sit there, Abbie. Sit in the armchair near the fire. It's much more comfortable."

Abbie watched her quick, nervous movements, and thought She's wound up like a spring from the hustle and bustle, the ordering around that she experienced in South Carolina. She's even dressed to suit this ordering-around mood. Straight black skirt. White blouse. The blouse cut almost like a man's shirt. French cuffs on the blouse. Cufflinks in them. And the gray hair brushed back, away from her forehead, the pince-nez set perfectly straight on her nose. President of the corporation. An austere face. Bony, distinguished. The eyes behind the glasses looked small, shrewd, very wise. Tall bony body. Unrelaxed body. She keeps walking up and down because she's still traveling, still managing the family, offering advice, remembering all the details, the insurance papers, the will.

Frances placed the coat, the cape, the muff, the hat on the horsehair sofa. "I feel just like a world traveler," she said. "I flew down and came back on the train. Do you know, I enjoyed it? It was like a twenty-four-hour holiday, a vacation spent in a different part of the world. Everything different. The customs. The people. The language. On the train, coming back, I began to wonder whether it's a good idea to read as much as I do, to see as many plays, because I don't think I really saw the city of Charleston, even though I was there. I kept seeing Crown and Porgy and Bess and Sportin' Life and Catfish Alley. Isn't that funny?"

I wish she'd stop walking up and down, Abbie thought, she'll never unwind if she doesn't sit.

"And if I ever go to London, I know I won't see the English people as they really are. I'll see Oliver Twist and Fagin, and David Copperfield and Little Nell," Frances said, still pacing.

"What about Monmouth? What do you see in Monmouth, Frances?" She'll have to sit down to answer that. I keep seeing Link as a little boy, keep hearing the Major talk, keep using his phrases. Bulletheaded. Meriney. "When I mourns, I mourns all over."

"Monmouth?" Frances said, and sat down in the wing chair on the other side of the fireplace. Wing chair upholstered in a velvet that reminded Abbie of the dark green plush used on trains.

"Monmouth?" Frances repeated, and leaned back in the chair. The light from the fire was reflected in her glasses. "I see my father. I see myself walking down Franklin Avenue, holding on to his hand, and he's saying, 'Frank, you know you've got a man's mind.' Anywhere I go here in Monmouth, I can always see myself—too tall, too thin, too bony. Even at twelve. And too bright, Abbie, and unable and unwilling to conceal the fact that I had brains. When I finished high school I went to college, to Wellesley, where I was a kind of Eighth Wonder of the world because I was colored. I hadn't been there very long when the dean sent for me and asked me if I was happy there. I looked straight at her and I said, 'My father didn't send me here to be happy, he sent me here to learn.' I have always remembered the look of astonishment that came over her face. Then she said, 'I would like to know your father.'"

Abbie thought, We're both getting old. We tell the same stories, over and over again. We've influenced each other in the telling. Shared experience, I suppose. Tell it and retell it. And finally act on it. Happiness not important. It's the learning, the education. Magic wand. Golden key. I thought it would be that for Link, too. And he works in a bar. And stays out all night. Playing poker. And doing what else? Where does he go?

"Twenty-two, and I was back in Monmouth. A college graduate. All hung over with honors and awards and prizes. And I knew I'd never get married, never have any children. So I was going to be a doctor." She laughed, and the pince-nez trembled on her nose, glittering and trembling there. "But by then my mother had been dead for three years. My father was alone here, and I couldn't bear to leave him, and there was the business that he had built up so slowly and so carefully. So I became an undertaker too. What do I see in Monmouth, Abbie? I see myself, lonely and a little bitter until I met you," a barely noticeable pause, and she added, "and the Major. I see myself at twenty-five going to the casket company to pick out my father's casket and I hear the Irishman who owned the place saying to his pimplyfaced clerk, 'That nigger woman undertaker from Washington Street is here again, see what she wants.' At the time it happened I found it unbearable. Now I feel indebted to the man because the sound of the word nigger has never bothered me since then, though I have never been able to share your enthusiasm for the Irish."

Abbie knew that story, too. She thought, On how peculiar, and accidental, a foundation rests all of one's attitudes toward a people. She loved the Irish. Part of her faith, her belief, came straight from the old Irishwomen she had known, in those early years on Dumble Street. Their faith, unwavering, firm, unmoving, despite drunken husbands, drunken sons, wanton daughters, despite idiot children who crouched, hunched over in rocking chairs, always in the kitchen near the big black iron stoves, babbling endlessly, having to feed, diaper, croon to, a fullgrown human being. She, too, like the Irishwomen, had made it a habit, when she was downtown, to go in the cathedral, saying her Protestant prayers humbly in the dim cool interior, sitting there afterwards, refreshed, her faith renewed. When she left, walking slowly down the aisle, it was with the sure knowledge that death is only a beginning.

Frances hears the word Irish and thinks of her father and hears the word nigger. I hear the word Irish and I think of a cathedral and the quiet of it, the flickering light of the votive candles, the magnificence of the altar, and I see Irishwomen, strong in their faith, holding a family together. Accident? Coincidence? It all depended on what had happened in the past. We carry it around with us. We're never rid of it.

Dumble Street, she thought, remembering a Sunday morning, years ago. She had met Mrs. Abe Cohen, weeping, and there was a wail in her voice, as she told Abbie that her little boy had been to the Christian Sunday School, and came home, reciting, Matzos, Matzos, two for five, that's what keeps the kikes alive—wail in her voice, overtone of despair, as she said, "Mrs. Crunch, what kind of people is that to be teaching him a thing like that, to be telling him to come home and say it to his own mother, what kind of people—what kind of thing is that to be teaching my Abie in the Sunday School?" What kind of people—she tried to convince Mrs. Cohen that no one could possibly have taught Abie to say that—not in Sunday School. Hopeless.

Frances said, "Here I've been babbling like a brook, Abbie, and I never once thought to ask you about Deacon Lord's funeral. Was everything all right?"

"Yes, indeed. Mrs. Lord asked me to tell you that everything was fine."

Should she mention the shrieks and screams? The cold sweat that broke out on her own forehead? Talk about the spattering sound of earth on the coffin? Speak of the artificial grass used to conceal, conceal, cover up, the earth that could never be covered up, the earth where what was left of the deacon would slowly disintegrate? No. Frances would lean forward in that wing chair that looked as though it ought to be on a train, thrust her legs straight out in front of her, gesture with her bony hands, and talk of immortality, of hysteria, of selfpity, of overidentification, of catharsis. Frances could be unnecessarily voluble on the subject of death and all that it meant. She would be even more disturbing than Howard Thomas: Probably she saw herself as she would ultimately be, very cold, very dead—satin-lined coffin, of course—

Abbie said, "Your assistant, Howard Thomas, seems quite self-assured. Very capable."

"Howard's a fool. He's half educated. And there's no bigger fool in the civilized world than a half-educated colored man. He was going to be a lawyer and he ended up an undertaker. From law court to mortuary is a long jump. Anyway, he drinks brandy to keep from thinking too much about how and why he made the jump. I'm always afraid he'll show up at a funeral so far gone in drink that he'll do something outrageous."

"Is he married?"

"Married!" Frances snorted. "Good heavens, no! He doesn't like women. But women respond to him on sight. They want to rub up against him. Just as though he were catnip and they were cats."

Including me, Abbie thought, remembering how she had leaned toward him. But never again. And I wouldn't have described it like that.

"He makes a good assistant." Frances got out of the wing chair. "You make yourself comfortable while I go and see about tea." She was going out of the room, and she turned back, and said, "Sometimes I wish his behind didn't wiggle quite so much."

Abbie wondered why Frances thought the jump from lawyer to undertaker was any longer than the jump from doctor to undertaker. We all take these jumps. I went from schoolteacher to coachman's wife, from wife to widow, from widow to needlewoman-landlady. Accident? Coincidence? No. It all depended on what had happened to you in the past. And as you grew older, the sharp edges were rubbed off, rounded, blurred, so that the big things that happened to you were finally reduced to stories that you told, and the stories became fewer and fewer. Even though it was a commonplace, ordinary, story, enough of the emotion you had felt, came through to make it a good story. Frances talks about her father. I don't talk about the Major because I trained myself not to. Selfdiscipline. But I think about him. I talk about Link. Link talks about Bill Hod.

The fire crackled in the fireplace. Fortunately Miss Doris liked fires in fireplaces. She must have liked brass fenders, too, because she saw to it that Sugar kept this one polished so that it shone like gold. Miss Doris must have approved of Frances' living room, because she hadn't changed anything in it, same heavy draperies at the windows, same massive furniture, same Turkish carpet, all dark red, horsehair sofa still against the far wall. A highceilinged room. Dark woodwork. Dark floors. Sugar, who was Miss Doris' husband, waxed the doors and the floors and baseboards. A tall thin man. Face of a Brahmin. Look of hauteur. He talked exactly like Miss Doris. Miss Doris. Where was J.C.?

Frances came into the room carrying a tray.

Abbie said, "Where's J.C.?"

"I was wondering when you'd remember him. He's in the kitchen with Miss Doris. They've been making cookies."

"Really?" They must somehow have declared a truce. "I'll take a look at them while you're pouring."

She went through the dining room, bowl of artificial flowers in the center of the dining room table, because Miss Doris refused to "mess with fresh flowers," straw matting on the dining room floor because Miss Doris said colored people didn't know how to eat, and were always spilling food, Frances' mother's silver tea set on the lowboy, looking as though it had just come out of a jeweler's window because it had been lacquered because Miss Doris said she couldn't spend all of her good time polishing silver, because—and then pushed open the kitchen door, and looked in.

Miss Doris was saying, in that hard cold voice, "And were I surprised? He were coming right through all that traffic, hand over hand, and I told Sugar afterwards, Sugar, he were the nearest thing to the ape I have ever saw in human form."

Miss Doris was sitting by the kitchen table, her hands in her lap, talking to J.C. J.C. was quite close to her, perched on a high stool, his feet twisted in the rungs. Nothing had been changed in the rest of the house, but in the year that Miss Doris had been working for Frances, the kitchen had been radically changed. It now looked like a model kitchen in an advertisement, even to the plants on the long window sill under the battery of windows that had been placed over the sink—and the long counters on each side of it.

J.C. said, "Is them cookies done yet?"

"Well, I picked up that umbrella, the one with the long handle, and I give him a poke, and that took care of him."

J.C. said, "Miss Doris, ain't it time to take them cookies out?"

It would be a shame to disturb them, Abbie thought. I'll stand here long enough to find out whether Miss Doris ever answers him about the cookies.

Miss Doris said, in her cold hard voice, "Another time, I said to Sugar, Dressin' gown? Mr. Orwell ain't never owned no dressin' gown, what color is it? And Sugar said, It's a kind of light tan color and it's kind of tight on him, it's kind of squeezin' him in the shoulders and arms. And I said, Sugar, you go right up there, he's done put that woman's new spring coat on, that's what he's done, you go right up there and get it off him, Mr. Orwell ain't never owned no dressin' gown; and Sugar went up and he come back down to the kitchen and he said, Sugar, you were correct, he were layin' up there in that bed dead drunk wearin' that woman's new spring coat that come from Carnegie and cost two hundred dollars, that's just what he had on. There's nothin' worse, Jackson, than a multonmillionaire who is far gone in drink."

"Miss Doris—" J.C. started.

Miss Doris said, "Mr. Orwell were a old devil, Jackson. One time he come in my kitchen and he et up all the lemon meringue pies I had fixed for the dinner dessert and I told him, I said, Mr. Orwell, when my menims is fixed for the day I can't start in fresh at seven o'clock at night for no seven-fifteen p.m. dinner and make no new dessert. It were in the summer and with that daylight time it were still like afternoon and the sun were right in his face and he were a terrible sight in that strong sun, he were all red-eyed from drink and his skin were full of little small broken veins so that he were purplefaced. And Mrs. Orwell were sittin' right close by on the sunporch and he went right out there and I heard him say, What is the matter with old Doris, she's out there in the kitchen just as black and evil.

"And I were mad, anyway, Jackson, so I picked up one of them long thin meat-carvin' knives, and I went right out there on that sunporch and I said, Excuse me, Mrs. Orwell, for breakin' up the peace like this but I got something to tell Mr. Orwell and there were strong sun on the porch and I said, Mr. Orwell, I been workin' for multonmillionaires all my life and I were never insulted by any of them up until right now, and I were holding this long thinblade meat-carving knife behind my back and I snatched it out and I held it right under his nose, and moved it back and forth and that strong sun made it shine like a switch blade, and I said, You come in my kitchen with your drunken self and you et up all my pies and then you come out here and insult me and I'm goin' to stand right here and take this knife and cut your nose off even to your face, I mean that, Mr. Orwell.

"Mrs. Orwell she let out a little scream and she said, Miss Doris, don't, put it away, don't do that to Mr. Orwell. And Mr. Orwell, he said, Miss Doris what have I done, what have I said, I didn't mean it whatever it was, and I will never do it again, I will never eat all your lemon meringue pies up again, Miss Doris, I promise, and I will never go in your kitchen again, Miss Doris, I mean that, just move that shinybladed butcher knife away from my nose, Miss Doris. And he never did either, Jackson. He would stand in my kitchen door, his face all purple from drink, and say what he had to say, but he never set his drunken feet in my kitchen again."

J.C. said, firmly, "Miss Doris, them cookies were done now."

Abbie thought, Why he hasn't been with her two hours and he pronounces "were" the same way she does, as though it were "wear."

"No, they were not, Jackson. I were cookin' thirty or forty years before you were born and I know when cookies is done."

"Where were I before I were born?"

Miss Doris gave him one of those hard appraising stares. "You were sittin' around under a rosebush waitin'."

"Waitin' for what, Miss Doris? I ain't never sat under no rosebush. I sets under The Hangman."

"In that case, Jackson, you were settin' around under The Hangman waitin' to be born."

Silence in the kitchen. They both seemed to be meditating. Abbie knew the tea must be cooling in the cups, but—

J.C. said, "Miss Doris, is all printhesses white?"

"How's that?"

"Is printhesses always white?"

"I ain't seen one recently. Last one I seen was black."

"Powther say they're white."

"Who's he?"

"My daddy."

"Well," Miss Doris said, "maybe your pappy's only seen white ones. Folks only see what they want to see. I see black ones. He sees white ones. If there were a law about it either way the law would be wrote down in a book somewhere."

"Is them cookies ready now, Miss Doris?"

"Not yet. Now there were another time when Mr. Orwell—"

"Is there a thin shinyblade knife in this one?"

"No. This one's about the time Mr. Orwell seen a buffalo on the train goin' Pullman to New York. And I were ashamed to be with them, it were just like travelin' with a zoo because Mr. Orwell didn't have no decent suit to wear so he put on his tuck, everything else were et up by the moths and covered with gravy drips and Mrs. Orwell were wearin' his beaver hat, and they both smelt like moth balls and likker and they were goin' dressed like that to Mr. Orwell's brother's funeral and Mrs. Orwell had on a diamont necklace and had practically took a bath in Guerlain's and what with her havin' on Mr. Orwell's beaver hat I said to Sugar, Well, Sugar, I just hope they'll let us get on that train. Well anyway, just outside New Haven Mr. Orwell got up and went in the gentlemen's rest room, and he come out real quick, all purplefaced, and he let out a high scream, he came out fast, and he kept lettin' out this high scream, and he said, Miss Doris, come quick, Miss Doris, there's a buffalo in there. And I said to Sugar, Sugar, he's lost his mind, I always knew he were goin' to and here he's gone and done it while he's ridin' on this Pullman of all places. And I said real firm but not loud, Mr. Orwell, you come and sit down. And he said, Miss Doris, where are you, come quick, Miss Doris and get this goddamittohell buffalo out of the toilet. And he let out another one of them high screams, and he said, Please come quick, Miss Doris, before I lose my mind.

"So the ladies and gentlemen on the train were all lookin' at him standin' up there in his tuck in broad daylight and kind of murmurin' to each other, and the porter were not around, they are just like policemen if you need one you cannot lay hands on one, so I got up and I said to Sugar, Sugar, you get Mr. Orwell sat down while I go and see. And Mr. Orwell said, That's right, Miss Doris, you go in there and scare the shit out of that buffalo, and I said, Mr. Orwell, you stop usin' that bad language, you're not at home. You go sit down and be quiet. And he turned more purple and went and sat down when Sugar told him to.

"And I went in the gentlemen's rest room and there were a woodchuck in there. And at first I thought I had stayed with Mr. and Mrs. Orwell too long, I were always telling Sugar, Sugar, we must not stay here too long or we will lose our minds, too, just like these crazy rich people, but we are poor and so they would put us in confinement, but if you are rich and crazy, you can run loose.

"But that woodchuck were so big and so fat and he looked at me so fresh and made a noise, a kind of a big grunt noise, that I knew he were real, and I were mad anyway, goin' Pullman to New York with them Orwells lookin' like they had just been let loose from a zoo or a circus, so I snatched that woodchuck up by the tail and by the neck, and I come out of the gentlemen's rest room, holdin' him and somebody had sent for the porter and he were one of them little wiry old black men been a porter so long he thinks he owns the Pullman and he come sloofootin' it up to me and said, What you doin' in there, woman, and I said, I'm Mrs. King to you and to everybody that ever knew me, and you can call me that. Here, I said, this is your Pullman so this must be your buffalo, too, and I tried to hand him that fat sassy woodchuck, clawin' and gruntin', and he let out a high scream just like Mr. Orwell and jumped back and Mr. Orwell yelled real loud, That's right, Miss Doris, you scare the shit out of him, too, and I said to Sugar, Sugar, put your hand over Mr. Orwell's mouth, and I went and opened up the train door and turned that woodchuck loose."

Silence.

J.C. frowned. "How did de buffalo—" He paused, appeared to think. "I mean, how'd he get down in de toilet?"

Abbie thought, I was wondering the same thing. And the tea must be cold, stone cold, by now, and Frances will be wondering where I am, but Miss Doris hadn't said the buffalo, that is, the woodchuck was down in the toilet— She held the swinging door open a little wider.

"Mr. Orwell he were so drunk and so scared he couldn't tell a woodchuck from a buffalo. Some of them fresh Yale boys had put that woodchuck in the gentlemen's rest room while the train were waitin' at the New Haven station, where they changes over the engines, for ten minutes."

She let the door swing to, gently, and went back to the living room.

Frances said, "Were they all right?"

"I should say so. Doris was talking about the Orwells, and J.C. was talking about his princess, and asking when the cookies would be done, and neither one was really listening to the other. That's the way all conversations, really satisfying ones, are carried on."

While they drank their tea, they talked about Link. They always talked about Link. Abbie thought of all the conversations, the discussions, the endless arguments, they had had about him. They had to explain to him, somehow, about his being a Negro, and there was the awful business of sex, and religion, and the problem of where to send him to college, and the more complicated problem of how to finance his education, and that job with the Valkills. It seemed as though he were always making too much noise, and he played football and went swimming in the river. Both equally dangerous. So many things to be explained and avoided and circled around. And he survived. He survived Bill Hod and pneumonia, and the redlight district, and the Navy. Tall, now. Shoulders broad, now. Speaking voice like the low notes of an organ. If only—

"I wish he'd get married," Abbie said, "and settle down."

"Isn't he settled down?" Frances asked.

"He isn't really settled down until he's married. No young man is. Lately, well, he stays out half the night and I don't dare ask him where he goes or what he does. And it worries me. He's always in New York. He stays there two or three days at a time. I suppose he has a girl. I'd like to see her, to meet her. I don't know how to ask him about her, to tell him to bring her home for tea. I'm afraid he'll think I'm interfering."

She had picked out a house for him, a brick house, on the other side of town. The instant she saw the For Sale sign on it, she'd managed to marry Link to a nice girl, and get them moved into the house, all in her mind. There were lilacs in the dooryard, big old lilacs, and orange lilies, great clumps of them, in bloom there, last August. And a fence across the front, one of those iron fences that you rarely ever see any more. She didn't know who Link's girl was. She was sure he had one. All young men had girls. But she'd never seen him with a girl, never heard him mention one. He seemed to have skipped the girl-crazy stage they go through in their teens. When he was seventeen and home from Dartmouth for the summer, he saw girls every Sunday after church, and sometimes he talked to them, briefly, laughed with them, briefly, and turned away from them quickly. She didn't know that she blamed him. They fidgeted so, and their heads seemed to have been turned out by some kind of machine, all exactly alike, all slick with grease, and they used too much perfume, apparently the same kind of perfume, so that they smelled alike; most of them had pimples under the powder and rouge. They perspired easily, their dresses darkening under the armpits, beads of perspiration appearing on their wide, bridgeless noses, as they teetered toward Link on their highheeled shoes, shoes that made their thin straight legs look brittle, teetering toward seventeen-year-old Link after church, and perspiring as they talked to him.

But those were the good girls, the ones who went to church, the ones who wanted husbands and homes and children. And they were absolutely all wrong for Link. The ones who didn't go to church were the ones with the shapely legs and the smooth brown skins that didn't need any heavy concealing layers of powder, the ones with the artfully curled hair, the ones who didn't want husbands and children and wellkept homes. They wanted boyfriends, an endless succession of boyfriends and a perpetual good time. And they were absolutely all wrong for Link too.

"He'll get married one of these days," Frances said easily. "Most of the things we worried about never happened. Now that he's grown-up, we have to remember that he is grown-up. He'll be all right."

Link had said that Frances was right, ninety-nine point nine times out of a hundred. She could be wrong, though, one one-tenth of the time. That afternoon she had hurried to tell Frances that she couldn't have Mamie Powther living in her house, Frances had laughed at her. She couldn't make her understand how shocked and frightened she had been when Mamie Powther told her that Bill Hod was her cousin, couldn't make her understand that moment of pure terror she had known because Bill Hod came down the back stairs, no sound of footsteps, but the sound of a whistled tune, the tune of the song that Mrs. Powther had been singing when she was hanging up clothes in the backyard, the whistled tune coming down the stairs, high, sweet, down, down the stairs, no sound of feet descending, just the whistle, so that it seemed to descend by itself, and then Bill Hod went past the back door, went around the side of the house, still whistling, the same Bill Hod who had supported the Major down the street, who for a space of sixty seconds, probably less time than that, had glared at her, shouting as no one had ever shouted at her before, "You fool—you goddam fool—get a doctor!" His face, so contorted, his voice, so furious, that she had picked up a poker, with the intention of striking him with it if he came any nearer, and his face had changed, and he shrugged and walked away. Cold, cruel face. Face of a hangman. Frances either couldn't or wouldn't understand why she was so disturbed by the knowledge that Bill Hod was Mamie Powther's cousin.

Frances had listened, that afternoon, and said, impatiently, "Sooner or later, Abbie, you'll have to make up your mind to accept defects in your tenants or else stop renting the place. You'll never find a perfect tenant. There's no such thing. If you stop renting the place you'll cut off a big important part of your income. It's unfortunate that Mr. Hod should be Mrs. Powther's cousin, bad for your peace of mind, but there isn't anything you can do about it."

Mamie Powther. Just listening to her, not seeing her, but listening to her voice, you could tell what kind of woman she would be, the big soft unconfined bosom, the smooth red-brown skin, the toosweet strong perfume, it was all there in her voice. Emanation of warmth, animal warmth, in her voice.

Abbie sighed. "I can't tell you how much I wish Link would fall in love and get married."

Lately his getting married had taken on an urgency in her mind. Because of Mamie Powther. She was afraid of Mamie Powther. Afraid of Bill Hod. She had always been afraid of Bill Hod but at least there had been the street between them; now it was just as though he had moved into her house. "Hi, Mamie, what's the pitch?" Didn't this fear of Mamie Powther suggest a doubt about Link? Why should she expect him to succumb to the blowsy charms of a married woman, mother of three children, a big young woman, a careless young woman, who went gallivanting off, with never a thought as to who would look after her children?

"It's getting late," she said. "I'll go and get J.C."

In the modern, lightfilled kitchen, Miss Doris was wrapping up a package. J.C. stood watching her. He had a cooky in each hand. The kitchen was filled with the fragrant, delicate, buttery smell of freshbaked cookies.

Miss Doris said, in that cold hard voice, "Now here you is, Jackson. This here's your midnight snack. If'n you should wake up in the middle of one of them night horses you were tellin' me about, you eat one of these cookies. And you carry this package, careful."

"Yes, ma'am, Miss Doris," J.C. said.

Abbie said, "I forgot to tell you, Miss Doris, but his name is J.C."

Miss Doris gave Abbie a swift, hard stare. "Yes, Mrs. Crunch. I know that. He told me. But I don't plan to have no children around me without no Christian names. So I named him. When he's here with me, he's Jackson."

She woke up, suddenly. Pitchdark in the room. She felt cold. No covers over her chest, her arms. And an outing flannel nightgown, even a longsleeved one, was no substitute for blankets. Wind blowing, too.

It must have been the sound of the metal screen banging, back and forth, against the window that had awakened her. She pulled the covers up, way up, under her chin, remembering how the Major slept, on his side, a big man, a Teddy bear of a man, so that the covers were lifted by his shoulders, forming a tent, and drafts blew about her shoulders, her neck, all night long.

She ought to get up and put the window down. But she couldn't sleep in a room that was all shut up, but then, neither could she sleep with that ventilating screen rattling, banging, moving back and forth against the window. She wondered if it was still foggy, if J.C. was awake and eating his midnight snack. Thought of Deacon Lord's funeral, remembered that fog was just beginning to drift in from the river when she and J.C. left Frances' house. Thought of Frances' New Year's Eve party. She gave it every year, a kind of mass entertainment that took care of all her social obligations, a big buffet supper, set up in that dark gloomy dining room, and Sugar, who was Miss Doris' husband, did the carving, served the plates, and Miss Doris carried trays, too, and managed to convey her disapproval of the proceeding just in the way she walked, slapping her feet down on the floor, slap, slap, slap. "Coffee?" Slap, slap, slap.

Thought of Mamie Powther, appearing suddenly at the back door, two weeks ago, with a fruit cake, "Missus Crunch, you been so nice to J.C. I thought it bein' New Year's Eve, and all, you know, if you was havin' friends in, this'd be nice to have in the house," smiling, affable, easy-voiced. Mamie Powther had been wearing another new coat, a purple coat, fitted, with brass buttons in a double row down the front, the big bosom making the buttons look as though they were ascending and descending a hill. She had so many coats. Not a badlooking woman. But so much bosom, always so unconfined, even under the coats you knew it was there. Taller than little Mr. Powther. How had he ever come to marry her? The past. The answer in the past. Miss Doris and the Orwells. Frances and her father. Howard Thomas went from lawyer to undertaker because of his past. Abbie Crunch went from schoolteacher to coachman's bride to widow to landlady-needlewoman, now able to go to funerals, to smell liquor without shuddering, to be tolerant of the occasional, unexpected vulgarities that crept into Frances' conversation, "Rub up against him just as though he were catnip and they were cats." "I wish his behind didn't wiggle—"

She had the queer disconcerting feeling that a hand, or hands, had come at her out of the dark. Vague, directionless, groping hands were pulling at the blankets, at the sheet, at the woolfilled comforter. She edged away, thinking, I always knew this would happen, all my life I've been afraid of this, waiting for this, always known that something would come at me out of the dark, feeling, groping, for me. It's my imagination. I'm always picturing disaster.

King of England. King of England. He said it on the radio at Christmas, a few years ago. What was it? I saved it. I never can quite remember it. Safer than a known way. Better than a light. Anonymous. Put your hand into the hand of God. Reach out your hand. Into the darkness.

She put her hand out, reaching out, into the darkness. Something brushed against it. She jerked her hand back, away from whatever it was, and tried to scream, and couldn't. She said, "Oh," and it was like a sigh.

J. C. Powther said, "Missus Crunch—"

For a moment she couldn't answer him, still thinking, I always knew—always in the back of my mind was the fear, formless, shapeless—that something dreadful would come at me, out of the dark. I was certain that that small hand, J.C.'s hand, was the—

"Yes?" she said.

"She's here, Missus Crunch."

"Why aren't you in bed?" Abbie asked.

"Not sleepy."

"Of course not. You don't get up until noon. What kind of way is that to bring a child up? Up all night. In bed all day. It's bad enough for grown people."

J.C. ignored her. "She's here," he repeated.

"Will you please go back upstairs and get in bed and go to sleep. Why do you walk around all hours of the night? Why does your mother allow it? You walk in and out of here and most of the time I don't even know you're in the room."

"Mamie's out," he said.

"That's no excuse. Aren't Kelly and Shapiro in bed?"

"Yes," he said, something very like impatience in his voice. "Missus Crunch, the printhess is in Link's room."

"I've asked you not to tell lies. It's wrong. It's a bad thing to do. I don't know why you make things up."

"She's all gold," he said, his voice dreamy. "'N she and Link walk gumshoe when dey come in through de door. Dey gumshoe in, through de door."

"Have you got to go to the bathroom?" He didn't answer. "J.C., have you got to go to the bathroom?" That woman didn't have sense enough, or was too lazy, to get up and take him to the bathroom. It was the only way to keep them from wetting the bed when they were that young, and it was probably why he walked around at all hours of the night. He was uncomfortable.

"I just wet. I don't need to."

"Very well. Now go upstairs and go to sleep."

"It's dark in here," J.C. said. "You want a light on?"

"No, I don't. Don't you touch that lamp! Go on, J.C., go on upstairs." Silence. But he was still there, right by her bed. She could hear him breathing.

"Missus Crunch," he said.

She didn't answer. If she didn't answer, he'd go.

"Missus Crunch," he said softly. "I gotta go to de bathroom."

"You haven't. You told me you just went." Oh, dear, she thought. I'm sure he hasn't got to, he's just saying so to get me out of bed, and yet, he might have to.

"I gotta go to de bathroom, Missus Crunch," he whined.

She turned the light on by her bed. He was wiggling, standing first on one foot and then on the other. And he must have dressed himself in the dark. He had his overalls on backwards, the pockets in the back, the stubbed brown shoes were on the wrong feet. She reached for her heavy gray bathrobe, put on her slippers, and then looked at the clock. It was four in the morning.

In the bathroom, J.C. said, "I had to," triumph in his voice, "You hear dat?"

She looked away from him, down the hall. It was better to ignore some things. The night light was still burning. Link wasn't home yet. Where did he go? Four o'clock in the morning. Oh, dear, if it isn't one thing, it's another. She'd turn the light out. It would be daylight soon, and there wasn't any point in wasting electricity.

"I'm going to turn this hall light out, J.C. You go up the stairs before I turn it out so you can see where you're going."

J.C. followed her obediently. He stopped and sniffed. "It's her smell," he said. "It's the printhess smell."

Smell of perfume in the hall, faint, sweet, lingering there.

"Run along before I turn the light out."

"Mamie said don't tell," J.C. said. "Mamie's a robber. Her took de pretty-pretty. It was all gold and her took it and wouldn't give it back. I'm goin' to tell. Her's in dere," he said, pointing at the door of Link's room.

Abbie was suddenly angry. "There's no one in there. Link's not home yet." Where does he go? What is he doing? "There's no one in there. I don't know what's going to become of you if you don't stop making things up." There were times when J.C. was absolutely unintelligible, she doubted if his own mother knew what he was talking about. Cold in the hall. She'd never get rid of this bulletheaded little boy.

"Here," she said and flung open the door of Link's room.

And stood still. Light on. Link in bed. In that bed that didn't look like a bed, the one the decorator put in there when he did the room over, and threw out the walnut bedstead, this bed just some kind of rubber mattress that stood on legs, no headboard, no footboard, and when she said, "How perfectly dreadful," Link had said, "But try it, Aunt Abbie. It's comfortable. It's the most comfortable bed I've ever slept in," and even now whenever she looked at it, all these years afterwards, she felt resentful, to think of the way in which her perfectly good furniture had been tossed out as though it were—

A girl there in bed with Link. Both naked. The girl's head, the hair yellow, head on his chest, yellow hair on his chest, his shoulder. A white girl. How dare he? In her house, her house, "Abbie—the house—the house—" speech thickened, light gone out of the Major's eyes, as though he were blind, and inside she had already started to cry, a faint smile about his mouth, the effort, desperate, to sit up and Frances helped her prop him against the pillows, and then that awful, horrible-to-watch struggle to talk. "The house, Abbie, the house—"

For a moment she could not speak, could not move.

Then she was shaking the girl, shaking her, shaking her back and forth, trying to talk, no control over her tongue, her throat, having to talk, having to let the girl know, let Link know how she felt. Something seemed to explode inside her head. Spots dancing before the eyes. Heat and heat. Pressure, unbearable pressure, up and down the back of the neck, the head, pressure behind the eyes, the ears, the face. Ringing in the ears. A roaring, a pounding, inside her head.

"In my house," she said, "in my house, hussy, plying your trade, get out, get out of my house."

She looked for something, anything, grabbed a newspaper, not even knowing what it was, brandished it about the girl's head. "Get out before I kill you."

Hands aware of the newspaper. Mind remembering the newspapers under the chair where the Major sat. *Monmouth Chronicle.*

"Abbie," Link protested. Asleep, she thought. He was asleep. He sat up, then reached for the sheet, and pulled it over himself.

"Don't," Link said.

She pushed and pulled the girl out of bed, pushed her into the hall. Went back in the room, picked up the girl's clothes, picked up a coat, a fur coat. Coat soft, silky. Her hands aware of it, and her mind ignoring it. She flung the coat at the girl. She opened the front door. Fog outside. She threw the girl's clothes, dress, slip, stockings, out on the sidewalk. Hall filled with fog.

The girl stood in the hall, bending over, trying to pick the coat up, trembling with rage or fear or shame. Abbie pushed her, so that she stumbled, half fell down the steps.

Fog outside. Fog obscuring the sidewalk. Fog billowing up from the river. Lean over and see what was written on the sidewalk. Cesar the Writing Man. Moment of confusion in which she stood in the doorway, lost, not here, not anywhere. Don't let him die. Fog cold against her face.

Fog billowing up from the river. Where am I? She heard laughter. Someone was laughing, outside, standing in the street, laughing.

J.C. said, "Was she a bad printhess?"

Abbie turned toward him, waved the newspaper about his head. "Go upstairs. Go to bed. Go away." The girl was taller, younger, stronger than she was, but she could have strangled her, killed her.

"Go before I kill you," she said to J.C.

He scuttled up the stairs.

Someone was laughing, outside, on the street. Dumble Street. She slammed the front door, banging it shut. Where am I?

She went back into her room, closed the door, still wanting to shout at the girl, even though she was gone, How dare you, dare you, in my house, tramp, in my house, yellow hair on my pillowcases, the bridal ones, the ones that I made with my own hands, as part of my trousseau, with lace edges, filet lace, that I crocheted, smiling, dreaming about my wedding day. Schoolteacher, teaching at the Penn School, children of the Gullahs, beautiful, the first time I knew that black people could be beautiful, the fathers and mothers and the children, and I teaching, and dreaming of my wedding day, fifty years ago, dreaming of the white brocaded satin that cost three dollars a yard, and that I didn't make up because I decided that we didn't need a big wedding, the Major and I, it would be too expensive, and it is still wrapped in black paper, thin black paper between the folds, black tissue paper, rustles when you touch it, wrapped up, in the back of the middle drawer of my bureau, and I thought if I had a daughter, she would have it made up, we would make it up together, for her wedding, and then later, that the girl Link would marry would have it made up.

Girl Link would marry. Harlot. In my house. I put the pillowcases on his bed by mistake. Saturday morning. Change the beds. I always have, and I had pillowcases for my bed and his bed and I started in his room and I had the bridal pillowcases with the others because I had washed them and ironed them, I do it every three months, linen, kept and not used, yellows, and gets stains on it, hard to get out, sometimes impossible, and I was going to put them back in the linen closet.

And J.C. was underfoot, he always is and I wasn't paying any attention to what I was doing because he kept wandering around, as though he were looking for something, and he kept watching me, and it made me nervous, he weaves back and forth like some kind of little animal, in a cage, always under my feet, or he comes and stands and leans against me, all his weight, as though I were a wall or a tree, and he leaning against it for support or protection and so I tried, was hurrying, trying to finish quickly, and he came and leaned against me, almost knocking me down, and then he started wandering around again, and he kept watching me with those inscrutable black eyes, and it made me nervous and he said, "It's her smell."

He'd been saying it for days, and I said, "Whose smell?"

He didn't answer me. He said, "You smell it, too?"

"No."

"It's the princthess. It's her smell."

That made me hurry even faster, not paying any attention to what I was doing, and I must have put the bridal pillowcases on Link's pillows without noticing, then later I couldn't find them, and I spent most of the morning, Saturday morning, yesterday morning, looking for them, looking everywhere, and J.C. following me around, and finally I accused him of taking them.

"I did not," he said, "you got 'em yourself."

"You must have taken them."

"Yeah," he said, finally, and he laughed, and I never saw a young child before who had malice in his eyes and in his laughter. Malice. He said, "I ate 'em all up. I put on season' and butter and ate 'em all up. Yum-yum," and made that humming sound he makes when he's eating, and rocked back and forth just as though he were eating, "I ate 'em pillowcases all up."

How do I know he's in love with her, I knew it the moment I went into that room and saw them lying there naked, because I saw the immorality, the license, the wantonness, but I saw and remembered, just that quickly, their bodies, the perfection, he on his back, one arm extended, so that it was around her shoulders, and she turned toward him, curving toward him, and the young rounded breasts, and he lying there, and the big curve of her hips and the long line tapering down to the knee and then curve again from calf to ankle, small feet, arched feet, with the toenails painted, I think it was not so much the white nakedness of her, not just the shock of finding them there like that, it was the hair, pale yellow hair, not tousled or tangled, but curling about the bare shoulders, pale yellow hair, under his chin, it was the sight of her hair, that pale yellow hair, yellow hair, and Link—Link—

Yellow hair. Yellow chalk. Writing on the sidewalk early in the morning. Pink, yellow. Decorative, elaborately patterned writing, an adornment and a decoration on the sidewalk. Fog coming in.

Up until the time of the Major's death, no situation ever too much. In her what the Major laughingly called the benign persistence of the Jew, laughed, and meant it, though he laughed. She knew the phrase wasn't his, it came straight from the Governor, who probably laughed when he said it, and meant it, too, just as the Major did. The Major's death had been too much for her, vanquished by death, beaten by it. Then surmounted it.

Emptiness. For years afterwards. Sometimes the feeling that he is very close. Nearby. That if I reached out my hand I would find his big strong warm hand. Never again, in anyone, anywhere, that total acceptance, the adoration.

Dumble Street. What kind of people, Mrs. Cohen crying, Matzos, matzos, two for five. Dumble Street. Christian Sunday School. That nigger woman undertaker from Washington

Street. See what she wants. I sets under The Hangman. You fool. You goddamn fool. Get a doctor.

Fog coming in, blowing in from the river, sidewalk obscured, light from the hall, on the steps, swallowed up by the fog, and somewhere someone laughed, somewhere outside on the street, laughter. Someone standing there, watching and laughing, ripple of laughter, vaguely familiar sound, not the laughter, the tone, the pitch of it, laughing, laughing, laughing. Fog undulating up from the sidewalk, in waves. She had closed the front door, slammed it. Thick sound. Lid on a coffin. Final sound. Deacon Lord's funeral. A man who loved God. Mean . . . that was Hubborn . . . a great man for gold.

Link? She would ask him to leave, to live somewhere else. A white girl. In my house. In bed with Link. Tramp of a white girl. Pale yellow hair on the bridal pillowcases. Sweet smell in the hall. In Link's room. He would bring a tramp into my house. I am a fool. Frances, "Howard's a fool." You fool. You goddamn fool. Get a doctor.

HE WAS so damn tired, so damn tired. He never got
enough sleep any more. And now someone was trying
to wake him up, kept trying to wake him up. The room was
full of confused movement, senseless movement. He thought
at first that he was in The Hotel in Harlem with Camilo,
The Hotel where the elevator jerkrumbled outside the door,
all night, where the street music of New York, cacophony of
pneumatic brakes, of gears, of sirens, played all night, eight
floors down, on 125th Street.

Then he decided that they weren't in that suite, on the eighth
floor, they were in the lobby, and he was signing the register,
Mr. and Mrs. Lincoln Williams, Syracuse, New York, and all
this movement, confused, violent movement, was due to the
arrival and departure of the hasbeens and the wouldbes who
were The Hotel's patrons. He was signing the register in The
Hotel and nobody believed what he wrote, the clerks, the el-
evator boys, the bellhops. Nobody. Male and female certainly.
But not Mr. and Mrs. Anybody. Not from Syracuse, either.
New York markers on the car, so from somewhere in New York
State. Not Syracuse. From Rabbit Hollow or Sycamore Creek.
En route to Shangri-La. Heaven bound.

But they weren't in New York. They couldn't be. He had
told her he was too damn tired to drive down and back in that
fog and she had said, "I'll drive. I just drove up. It took me
about an hour and a half. Even in the fog."

"Not me, honey. You won't drive me to New York. You drive
too fast."

"I do not," quickly, impatiently, blue eyes darkening with
anger. Hair-trigger temper all set to blow. Then, "Don't look
at me like that," imperiously.

"Like what?"

"As though you wanted to bite my head off."

"It's a lovely head. I wouldn't bite it off, ever. I have occasionally wanted to knock it off." Like right now. When you
sound like the lady of the manor ordering a poacher off the
place. "In fact, every time I've watched you tear off in that

crate I have wished that I could get my hands on your head, or some other perhaps more appropriate part, for about five minutes."

"For what?"

"For to teach you not to pass stop lights when they are red, honey. For to teach you to hang on to your temper, too. It would be a very pretty kettle of fish if we both lost, couldn't find, dropped our tempers, at one and the same time. One of us would get hurt and it wouldn't be me."

"You—" she said, "you—"

He had kissed her, not letting her talk, pressing his mouth hard on hers, feeling her mouth moving, still trying to form words, trying to protest, and he kissing her, holding her and kissing her, until she stopped trying to talk, and relaxed against him, leaned against him, put her arms around his neck.

Later, in his room, mouth on his chest, mouth moving against his chest, she had murmured, "Don't ever leave me," hair with a shimmer, perfumed hair, under his chin, "I can't live without you, I love you, love you, love you, oh, Link!"

They must be in The Hotel because almost every weekend, since sometime in December, they'd been in The Hotel in New York. Except that Sunday when he waited and waited at the dock, and she didn't show up, staying away for a week, and then the following week she was there, and he, by then, ready to kill her, swearing to himself that when he saw her again he would throttle her for making him wait, for not calling up, or writing, and when he saw her crossing the street, saw the long lovely legs, the ballerina's walk, the innocent lovely face, he didn't even ask her why she stayed away, and she didn't bother to explain, they were both hellbent on one thing, the same thing, fast, because they couldn't wait, couldn't wait. She had said, "Link, put your arms around me. Put your arms around me, hurry," shivering. Ecstasy.

There was confused violent motion, in the room, all around him. He couldn't wake up enough to protest against this un-seemly disturbance, whatever it was. Abbie was in the center of the confusion, creating it. She was standing by the bed, leaning over, pushing and pulling at the bed, arms violent, short stout body, violent, long white braids downdangling, violent, too. She's gone crazy, he thought. I have, too. I'm eight years old again and the Major is dead and Abbie is wearing that Aunt Mehalie dressing gown, not a brack or a break in it, wearing slippers all day long, not brushing her hair any more, letting it hang in two long braids. But the braids should be gray. And they are white.

So he was dreaming this. She was leaning over the bed, shouting, pushing and pulling, glaring, shouting, not really shouting, her voice was hoarse, muffled, but the effort she put into it, the energy, was like that which produces a shout, it was a kind of hoarse, furious talking, something about her house, and she was waving a newspaper, the black eyes that he had described to himself as valorous, were the eyes of a virago, a termagant.

"Get out of my house," she said.

He sat up, said, "Abbie—don't." He thought she was about to attack him, with that rolled-up newspaper, and he pulled the sheet up for protection, because he was half asleep, and moving with the illogic of a dream.

New York. Had they gone to New York? Where was Camilo? Nightmare. Abbie went out of the room, and then she was back again, still talking in that hoarse muffled voice, which could not produce a shout, she picked up something, bundled it up, and went out into the hall. He caught a glimpse of Camilo. Abbie was pushing her.

Oh, damn, he thought, what's the matter with Abbie? What has happened to the censor that sits in her brain, controlling her actions, directing her thoughts. If she were anyone else I would say she was drunk. He found a T-shirt, put it on, pulled on a pair of slacks, stuck his feet in his slippers. The night light was still burning, in the hall. No sign of Abbie anywhere.

He walked toward the dock, never enough sleep, life filled with crazy women, one back there in the house, and he out here chasing another one through the fog, cold out here, why hadn't he stopped to put on a jacket, no socks on, feet cold in the slippers, fog in Dumble Street, cold in Dumble Street.

Camilo had turned on the headlights of the car. She was trying to put on her clothes, shivering, furious, frightened. He helped with stockings, helped with shoes, with slip, with dress, she still shivering, eyes blazing, not saying anything. All cats bee gray? All cats bee crazy.

They sat there, in that car with its smooth, coldfeeling up-holstery, he talking to her, trying to apologize, thinking, Explain Abbie? Impossible. Queen Victoria turned shrew, turned virago. Turned. Changed. Why the fury? Why the violence?

"It was my fault," he said. His fault? Whose fault? Why anybody's fault? How his fault? "I'm awfully sorry."

No answer.

Cold in the car. Fog outside. Fog in the car. He had no coat on. Dumble Street was silent, asleep, closed up for the night. Fog in the street. Fog in him. He was asleep, closed up for the night.

"I'm awfully sorry," he repeated. He would have to explain Abbie. But he couldn't. He'd never been able to explain her even to himself, how explain her to someone else.

He said, irritably, "Say something."

She kept staring straight ahead, hands gripping the steering wheel, refusing to look at him. He thought, You're in the dog-house, Bud. You're in the doghouse. Why not stay there? Why not stay there for keeps? He put his hands on her shoulders, forced her to turn so that she was facing him.

"Camilo, listen to me," he said.

"You bastard," she said, "you knew—you—knew, leave me alone," turning and twisting under his hands. "That woman, laughing at me, laughing at me," twisting, turning, pushing him away, "Get out of my car," voice imperious.

They all carry eviction notices around with them, typed up, ready to use. Abbie: Get out of my house. Mr. B. Hod: Get the hell out of my face. Camilo: Get out of my car.

"Let's fix it up for keeps," he said savagely. Cold in the car. In love with love? In love with Camilo Williams? Wait for you on the dock, two weeks ago, on a Sunday night, and you not come, when you do show up, you not say anything, you not explain, you not apologize, you bitch, you, you keep me on a seesaw, now up, now down.

Camilo said, "Let go of me."

He tightened his grip on her shoulders.

"You black bastard," she said, voice furious. "Let go of me."

Something exploded inside his head. I never understood, he thought, I never could quite understand Mr. B. Hod. But I do now. I never could figure out what happens to him, what goes on inside him that turns him into an executioner. But I do now. It is just this. It is an explosion inside his head. Will you marry me? Yes, come spring, and the time of the singing of birds, you black bastard.

He held her hands, soft hands, usually warm, cold now to the touch, he held the cold hands in his left hand, and slapped her, with his right hand.

If we were not here, in this car, on Dock Street, I would kill you. Just this way, just by slapping you, just by working on your face. Love. Hate. No one in the USA free—from, warfare, eternal war between the male and the female. Black bastard. White bitch.

She tried to bite his hand, and he kept slapping her, slapping her, remembering a conversation out of his past:

Dr. Easter: You're okay, eh?

L. Williams: Yes, sir.

Dr. Easter: Let's have a look. (pause in the examination and then the sudden question) Who did it?

L. Williams (unprepared for the question. Dr. Easter had been treating him for three weeks and had asked no questions): Did what?

Dr. Easter: Beat you with a rawhide whip until he very nearly killed you.

L. Williams: I don't know.

Dr. Easter: I see. I suppose it was a dark night and you were waylaid by four or five total strangers and you can't identify any of them because you couldn't see their faces. Or did they wear masks? Where did it happen? Here in The Narrows?

L. Williams: I don't remember anything about it.

Dr. Easter: "Don't know." "Don't remember." You must have been studying those gangster trials. You mean you're not telling.

L. Williams: I don't know what you're talking about.

Dr. Easter: A man capable of doing this sort of thing to a sixteen-year-old boy ought to be put in prison. If I were Mrs. Crunch, I would have him arrested. He's a mad dog. He ought to be locked up.

Weak Knees (quickly): Sonny's comin' along fine, now, ain't he, Doc?

Dr. Easter: So we talk about something else, eh?

Kill you, he thought, just by working on your face. Face
that he had dreamed about, held between his hands, kissed,
rubbed his cheek against, traced the line of the eyebrows with
his fingers. Expressive face. Gay, laughing face. Innocent face.
Ruin it.

He let go of her hands. Got out of the car, slammed the
door.

He stood on the dock, thinking, Bill Hod: I'll cripple you for
life. It was, somewhere, in everybody. It was in Abbie, which
shocked him. It was in Link Williams, which didn't shock
him at all because he had always known it was there. It was in
Camilo Williams. You black bastard. Fury rose in him again,
and he thought, I ought to go back to that car where you sit
shuddering and slap you and keep on slapping you until I have
killed you. I can't live without you. You black bastard.

Far down Dock Street he heard the putt-putt of Jubine's
motorcycle, like a series of small explosions, coming nearer.
Fog over the river, fog over Dumble Street, lapping of the
river under the piling, and over it all the sound of Jubine's
motorcycle. The red car was still there, fog obscuring it, but he
could see the headlights. Putt-putt of the motorcycle, nearer
and nearer. It would be daylight in another hour or so, or what
would pass for daylight in this fog.

He heard her start the motor, and then the grinding sound
of a car not in gear, was now though, roaring down the street
in first, she'd forgotten to shift, now in second, now in high,
she must be doing eighty. "I'll cripple you for life." He thought
the fury had died in him. It hadn't. Because he kept thinking,
You'll have to explain it, you're going to have trouble explaining the way your face looks, to whoever it is you have to explain things to, to whoever it was you were with that Sunday
night when you didn't show up. I wish I had not stopped.
Come spring, and the singing of birds. You black bastard. Who
did it? I don't know.

The putt-putt of the motorcycle stopped. Headlight turned
off. Footsteps on the dock. Jubine. Any other night, any other
time, but not now. Face of a snoop. Stand still, don't say anything, and the bulging eyes and the cigar will go away. Hear all,
see all, smell all will go away.

A long beam of light cut through the fog, sweeping the length of the dock, beam of a flashlight, moving, Oh, goddamn him, he thought, the light now directly in his eyes. Then it was turned off.

"Sonny!" Jubine said. "Jesus, what're you doin' here at this hour?"

For a moment he didn't answer, couldn't. Then he said, angrily, "I don't know." Who did this to you? I don't know. Where did it happen? Here in The Narrows? I don't remember anything about it.

Jubine was peering at him, trying to see his face.

"I've missed you, Sonny. Where've you been? No poker game. Nobody to talk to. Nobody who speaks my language. Mr. Hod and Mr. Weak Knees and I have been desolate. For a thousand Saturday nights. How come you've divorced us?"

Link was silent.

Jubine said, "Why do you no longer sit out the late watch at The Last Chance? It disturbs all of us. Mr. Hod tries to kill his customers, nightly, instead of just once in three months, as was his wont. Mr. Weak Knees keeps brushing Eddie away, pushing him away. And I, Sonny, I watch for you, wait for you." He lit a match, held it in front of his cigar, too far away from the cigar, held it high, staring at Link, and said, "Did the canary get out of the cage?"

Sound of the river lapping against the piling. Fog. Girl running, running, running down the dock. It began here. It ended here. Fury dying in him now. I want her back, I want to hold her in my arms again, I want her, I want her. Smell of stock. Walk like a ballerina's. Long neck of a ballerina. Blue eyes, innocent, candid. Warm, sweet mouth. What made me—

Jubine said, in his soft, compassionate voice, "Was it your canary, Sonny?"

I like him, Link thought, I like his snoop's face, and his jeering talk, but if he doesn't move off—I, executioner. The river. What more appropriate than Jubine and his cigar, and his inquisitive eyes, his snoop's face, placed finally and irrevocably in his river. Abbie: Out of my house. Camilo: Black bastard. Bill Hod: I'll cripple you for life. And Mamie Powther? Sure. She hung little Mr. Powther from the sour apple tree, a long time ago, and keeps him there, not only refusing to cut him down, but rehanging him, three or four times a week, so that he will dangle, in perpetuity. China? Sure. Stand in a doorway and pull a curtain aside, watching and licking her lips while Mr. B. Hod tries to break my spine. Executioners, all.

Jubine turned the flashlight on. The sudden light blinded him, and he thought, Got to know, got to see what I look like, got to find out. Was it your canary? And how does a man look, what can you see in his face, what would you have had if you could have taken a picture of him at the moment when he lost his canary? Recording angel with a camera? Hangman with a camera.

He headed straight into the long blinding beam of light. "You son of a bitch," he said, "I'll throw you in the river."

The flashlight went off. Jubine turned and ran. Thud, thud, of his feet in the GI shoes. Then the putt-putt of the motorcycle.

He did not go back to Abbie's house to live. He stayed at The Last Chance. He tried not to think about the girl. He could sit in the kitchen of The Last Chance, drinking a cup of coffee, listening to Weak Knees talk, hear what he said, and see, not the stove, or the copper hood, or the bare whitish wood of the table, or the pots and pans like a decoration on the wall, but see, instead, Camilo lying next to him, light from the street, even that far up, eighth floor of The Hotel, powerful enough so that the room was never completely dark, see her lying next to him, wearing a thin thin nightgown, pale pink stuff like gossamer, like cobwebs, pale pink ribbons at waist, at neck, at wrists, longsleeved cobweb, sleeves an artful accentuation of nakedness, like Olympia, with the shoes and the ribbon tied around the neck, seeming more naked than without them, Camilo like Olympia in this pink cobweb of a nightgown, see right through it; and the feet perfect, toenails painted with pale pink polish, hair tied back with a black ribbon, tied back in a kind of horse's tail, pale yellow horse's tail.

Night after night he sat in the kitchen of The Last Chance and listened to Weak Knees, and saw Camilo in his mind's eye.

End of February and he was doing the same thing.

Finally, on a Friday night, Weak Knees said, caution in his

voice, curiosity, too, "Sonny, you had a rumble with somebody or somep'n? Not that it's none of my business, but I couldn't help noticin' you don't never go anywhere no more at night."

Link put his feet up on the kitchen table, tilted his chair back against the wall, consciously assuming Mr. Bill Hod's favorite position. "I guess you'd call it a somep'n." It sure to God wasn't a fight. "I don't know exactly what it was."

"You goin' to be here for the game, tomorrow night?"

"Yeah." I have let Mr. Hod bait me, four Saturday nights in a row, while we played poker, I have let Mr. Jubine photograph me with his eyes, watched him record in his mind's eye how a man looks who has lost a canary, while we played poker; both gentlemen seem quite aware of the fact that I have lost something, though only one of them is certain that it was a canary. Tomorrow will be the fifth Saturday night, in a row, that I have let Hod wave red capes under my nose, and ignored them. By the sixteenth or seventeenth Saturday night, in a row, I will stop feeling as though I had lost an arm or a leg, the sickness will have gone out of me. Sickness, anger, regret, fury, ebb and flow of all four.

Weak Knees poured coffee into a mansized white mug, "Here, Sonny," he said, not moving away from the stove, "lay your lip over this."

"Don't make me move, Weak. I'm too damn comfortable. Bring it over and put it on the table."

"Name-a-God, Sonny, I got a sauce cookin' on this stove. I can't leave it. Come and git this coffee. Wassamatter with you, anyway?"

Bill attacked the swinging door, announcing his arrival in the kitchen.

Weak Knees said, "Boss, make him git up off his can and come and git this cup of coffee. Wassamatter with him anyway?"

Bill put the coffee cup down on the table, in front of Link. "You in some kind of trouble?"

"No, Mr. Boss."

"What's the matter then?"

He didn't answer that one. He watched Weak Knees turn away from his sauce, turn away from the stove, to stare at them. He's always afraid of trouble, afraid he'll be an eyewitness to trouble between me and Mr. Hod. But Mr. Hod and I are at peace, for the moment. I can tell by Mr. Hod's face, by his eyes. No warfare tonight.

"Are you broke?" Bill asked.

"Thank you, sir, I am not. My funds are ample for my modest needs. At the moment. I hasten to add that qualifying phrase because I never know when they may run completely out. Funds have a way of doing that at the most—"

"Don't talk that crap to me. If you're not broke and you're not in some kind of trouble, whyn't you go out at night any more?"

"I have no place to go, friend. I got an eviction notice." And now we'll end the audience, we'll switch over to you. "Did you ever get one, pal?"

Bill said, "Yeah," and walked out of the kitchen.

"Ain't no way to fight a eviction," Weak Knees said, relief in his voice. "Man says he wants his property why he's got a right to it. Ain't nothin' nobody can do about it 'cept let him have it."

"Yeah," he said and thought, At night, in The Hotel, in that queer, reflected light that reached into the room, she looked like something out of a store window, dreamed up by an artist who quit painting and took a job decorating store windows before he got so hungry he started eating grass in Central Park, grazing like a horse in Central Park, and the starving boughtandsold talented painter transformed what had been a dummy in a window, breathed life into it, created a female to haunt a man's dreams. Haunt his dreams? Haunt him for the rest of his life, waking or sleeping, in his bloodstream like a disease.

"Girls?" he had said. "Other girls?" They always wanted to know, who they were, were you in love with them—

"Only you. You only," he had said.

"Really and truly? Link, I don't believe you."

"You shouldn't. I had 'em by the hundred. I had 'em by the thousands. I had 'em by the millions, millions and millions of 'em, honey, round ones, square ones, triangular ones, up to and including the octagonal—"

She had poked him sharply, in the side, with her elbow.

"Ouch! That hurt."

Male and female horseplay.

"It was supposed to." She had traced the line of his torso, with the tips of her fingers, and he thought he could feel the blood pulse down his side, in the wake of her fingertips. "Hey, you're tickling me. Stop it!"

"You are the most beautiful color," she said. She kept running her fingers up and down his side. "I remember the first time I saw a colored woman. When I was a little girl. I wondered if the color would wash off, and then I wondered if she was that color all over. Or was it just the face and hands."

"Yeah," he said. "All the missionaries who come back from Africa or India tell that same story, in reverse. I used to listen to 'em, on Sundays, in the colored Congregational Church, and us dark folks whose black souls had been saved practically at birth, would titter when we heard about those ignorant black Africans, those ignorant brown Indians, who were hellbent on finding out if the missionaries were white all over, or was it just the face and hands, we rocked back and forth tittering when we heard how those heathen dark folks peeked at the white missionaries when they took their baths." Silence. "Even a missionary, a fisherman of souls, is aware of, and proud of, his white skin."

"I'm not."

"You're not a missionary. Or are you?" He remembered that he had turned over on his side, remembered that The Hotel's too-soft bed had been long since replaced by a kingsize bed, the suite changed, from week to week, in subtle ways, comfortable, then positively luxurious. He had turned over on his side so he could look at her. "Did some beneficent Board of Missions send you into the jungle to save me from perdition?" She didn't answer. He said, "What are you thinking about?"

"I wish I was colored, too."

"Why?"

"I've begun to be afraid—"

"Afraid of what?"

"I'm afraid that sometime you'll fall in love with a colored girl."

The wheezegroan of the elevator was an overture, a prelude, a finale, playing on and on, outside in the corridor.

You black bastard.

He remembered thinking, She sleeps like Bill Hod, like a cat, all of her relaxed, stretched out, remembered Hod walking barefooted, in a room full of sunlight, full of cold air, Hod, making no sound as he moved, air-borne, creature from another planet, Mars, perhaps, looked at her and thought of Bill Hod.

Weak Knees was no longer talking about eviction notices. He was talking about people—religion—but he was still stirring the sauce: "When they're young they don't go to church. Then when they gets false teeth and they waterworks run all the time, they gets scared, they think that well, after all, everybody's got to die some time and so mebbe they could, too. It's a funny thing but when they're young, Sonny, they don't believe they can get old or die. Then one mornin' they gets up and looks in the mirror and they got gray hair and a bald spot and they kind of adds themselves up, and they got a full set of uppers and lowers and two sets of glasses and some kind of funny crick in the middle of they backs and they begin to figure mebbe they better start goin' to church. I used to stand out there on that sidewalk in Charleston and watch 'em go by. Sunday mornin'. All them baldhead white Christians."

That first night in The Hotel he had looked out of the window, thinking, Well, yes, the sheets are clean, and there's a view from the windows of these rooms which pass for the royal suite, view at night, mostly neon signs, harsh red, harsher blue, and there's the night music of New York, sound of busses and cars, whine of siren on ambulance and fire engine, and police emergency squad, but it is hardly a place that I would choose to spend much time in. The bed's too soft; and the slipcovers on those chairs and the sofa outside in the sitting room are covered with the grease marks from the heads of the Jacksons and the Johnsons, the kind of place where you put a quarter in the radio, and it plays for exactly a half-hour and then dies on you, without warning, slowing down, the sound fading out, a horrid sound like a death rattle.

Suite on the eighth floor of a downattheheels hotel, hot water faucet in the bathtub dripped, dripped, and when you turned it on you got a gush of lukewarm water, place operated on the principle that noise would serve as a screen for shabbiness, as a cushion for the high prices. Yet he had to admit that the view was, well, it was New York, a crosstown street, extending and extending, lights in the buildings, street stretching away and away, and up, slight rise in the ground, small hill, so that the lights were not only strung out but seemed to rise, ascend, and if you didn't know what the place was like in daylight, saw only that, the lights reaching up and up, you could say it was beautiful. New York at night.

Mr. and Mrs. Williams, Syracuse, New York. Hotel maid came in at six in the morning and closed the windows, turned the heat on in the radiators, and then left. He got up, dressed, and found breakfast for one in the sitting room, and wondered how come in this fifteenth-rate hotel—and remembered that Camilo had slipped Room Service a neatly folded bill the night before, Room Service, with the face of a pimp, face of a whore, a could be bought, could be paid for, all of him for sale, and would see nothing and tell all any time, and Camilo knew how to get service even in a fifteenth-rate hotel, all front and no behind, all lobby and the rooms, rundown. No hot water that night, but the next morning it was damn near boiling when he took a shower.

Weak Knees finished whatever he had been doing at the stove, came and sat down at the table, with a cup of coffee, stirring it with vigor. He said, "You know, Sonny, I get sick of all these whafolks askin' me first thing, first drop of a hat, what do I think about Paul Robeson. The meat man he come in here this mornin', a brokedown dogass white man if I ever see one, all bandylegged from carryin' carcasses, and he come in here with my order, and before he gets the meat put down on the table good he wants to know what do I think about Paul Robeson. So I made him happy, I said I thought he oughtta hightail it back to Russia where he come from, and that softened him up, and I waited awhile and I give him a cup of coffee, and then I says, The reason he oughtta have stayed in Russia, mister, is because over there if he went around talkin' about the changes he wanted made, why'd he get hisself shot full of holes, but nobody over there would be goin' around about to piss in their pants because he was a black man talkin' the wrong kind of politics.

"And if his boy went and married hisself a little white chickadee over there in Russia, the whafolks wouldn't waste their time runnin' to all the colored folks they see askin' 'em what they thought about it. I says over there they wouldn't give a damn, mister, and I don't give a damn over here. Any country where the folks can't marry each other when they got a heat on for each other why—"

On Saturday nights, Link thought, sitting here in the kitchen, you could hear, faintly, far-off, because of the weight of the door between, a murmur from the bar. The only time you could hear it. The rest of the week, nothing at all. The door cut off sounds. Friday nights—no sounds at all, a good night in which to think, to remember, to taste regret, to stand off and look at yourself—

The door opened suddenly. Mr. B. Hod, he thought, the only man in the world who could make a swinging door perform in that fashion, make it erupt, not open, erupt. Bill Hod stood still, just inside the door. What in hell's the matter with him? Murder writ all over his face for any man to see, usually only in his eyes when he's about to sap somebody up, this time, all over his face, what's happened in the bar to make him look like that?

He stood up. It's me, he thought, and I always knew that someday you would look at me like that again, and I would decide, finally, that I could take you apart, piece by piece, and find out whether you're a son of a bitch all the way through, or just in sections.

Bill said, "You're wanted out front, Bud."

"Wanted?" he said, glaring at him, not moving, thinking, Stallions? Bucks. Find the antlers in the underbrush, years afterwards, still locked.

"Yeah." Hod turned, went out through the swinging door.

Weak Knees said, "Old Gruff and Grim's got his habits on. Don't you go lockin' asses with him, Sonny," pleading note in his voice. "You leave him be, Sonny. You hear? He's spoilin' for a fight. You leave him be, Sonny—"

The bar was comfortably full, Friday night crowd, yeasty smell of beer, fruity smell of rye, bourbon, blue haze of smoke, strangely quiet though, no male voices lifted in song, in tall storytelling, in laughter. He looked along the length of the bar, seeking Old Man John the Barber, the barometer, the weather vane. Barber had his back turned to the street. At night the old man always stood near the front window, studying the street (man in his private club, watching the world go by), stood where he could catch the street sounds, see the car lights, movement of people, watch the women's legs, all legs redorange under the neon sign, accept or reject them as they passed, play kingemperormaharajahsultanshah standing in The Last Chance watching the women's redorange legs, estimating their rumps, no good, off with her head, fair to middlin', decision reserved, let her live awhile, this one, but definitely, I will take this one for tonight, you could tell when the old man picked one because his fierce old eyes lit up, he bent forward, the thrust of his jaw accentuated, I will take this one, an old man with shaggy eyebrows playing a game.

Old Man John the Barber had turned his back on the street.

Wanted, Link thought. Wanted for what? What goes on here? Why has Old Man John the Barber quit playing his favorite game?

Then he saw that she was standing at the end of the bar, that she had her back turned, facing the street. He walked toward her, moving quickly. In Moscow, he thought, why in Moscow, because of whatever it was Weak Knees was talking about back there in the kitchen, if I walked along a street in Moscow, street filled with kulaks and Commissars and Robesons and whatever else walks the streets of Mr. Stalin's dream city, and you were standing with your back turned I would know you, and it's not the coat either, if you had on rags, had a bag tied over your head covering the pale yellow hair, I'd still know you, recognize your back.

He said, "Hello," softly.

She turned, "Link—I—"

He said, "Camilo," and held out his hands, both hands, "I—"

As they went out, he was aware of a restless movement, a stir, along the length of the bar, and he looked back. Bill Hod's face had changed. He was behind the bar, way down, near the door, looking at them, face expressionless now but the eyes were hooded, like the eyes of a snake.

WEAK KNEES was sitting at one of the tables in The Last Chance, reading the weekend edition of a New York tabloid. He had it flat on the table in front of him. As he read he moved a finger back and forth across the printed column. His lips moved, too, forming words.

"Name-a-God, Sonny," he said suddenly, voice sopranohigh. He turned toward the bar, holding up the tabloid, arms thrust out as though he were handing it, opened out like that, to someone who was taller than he, someone who was standing armlength away from him.

"Lissen to this," Weak Knees said. His dark supplefingered hands were silhouetted against the pink outside sheets of the feature section. Link thought, That's a shot Jubine would eat up, Weak with that tall chef's hat on his head, and only the top part of the white hat visible behind the newspaper, and the dark hands, holding the paper far away.

"Here's another one of them white boys done robbed a bank, tee-hee-hee." Weak Knees' arms and hands moved as he laughed, and the newspaper made a dry, rustling sound.

Link leaned over the bar, staring, frowning at the newspaper. There was a picture of a girl on the front page of the feature section.

"Say," he said.

"Wassamatter?"

"Let me see that paper for a minute." It felt brittle, dried out, in his hands.

Sunday feature section. Story on American heiresses, one of a series of stories about young women who owned, controlled, were heir to the great American fortunes—vast, unspendable fortunes. Picture of Camilo Williams, laughing. Only that wasn't her name. Her name was Camilla Treadway Sheffield. Internationally known heiress. The Treadway fortune was described as being like that of Krupp or Vickers. Young wife of Captain Bunny Sheffield. Blownup picture of Camilo on the front page. Small picture of Camilo and her

husband on the first inside page. Bunny and Camilo at Palm
Beach, lounging on the sand in bathing suits. "The Treadway
Munitions Company is located in Monmouth, Conn." Yeah,
he thought, you can hear the noon whistle blasting all over the
place; hear the seven-in-the-morning whistle, every morning,
all over Monmouth, everybody says, "She's up, you get up,
too," because Mrs. John Edward Treadway ran the plant, the
Chronicle always carried stories about her, and how she took
over the plant when her husband died; and how she'd geared
it up, speeding up production, even changing the time when
it opened up, used to open at eight o'clock, she changed the
time to seven o'clock, "She's up, you get up, too."

Why didn't he know that she was the Treadway girl? How
could he? He didn't even know there was a Treadway girl.
They inhabited different worlds, you could tell even from
this scissors-and-paste-job feature story, this patched together
story that wasn't news, story that said Camilla went to a boarding school in Virginia, private school, picture of it, could have
been somebody's old Georgian mansion, covered with Virginia
creeper; story said she actually worked, had a job on a fashion
magazine; story said she had an apartment at Treadway Hall
(picture of that, all stone and ivycovered too) but rarely ever
used it because she lived in New York and London and Paris;
story said her husband was a New York broker, Captain Bunny
Sheffield.

Story said the Treadways were the conservative, credit-to-
the-country kind of millionaires, no scandals, no divorces;
story contained a description of the library, the museum, the
concert hall the late John Edward Treadway gave to the city
of Monmouth.

Why didn't she tell me who she was—probably got a charge
out of the setup, rich white girl shacked up with a dinge
in Harlem, in The Narrows. Why not? If you were that rich
you could have your cake and eat it too, if you were that
rich you could keep all the exits covered. I was just another
muscle boy in a long line of muscle boys. Tell by this story.
She grew up on the nursemaid, governess, private school,
Palm Beach, Hot Springs, Paris, London circuit, and that
circuit doesn't normally impinge on Dumble Street—The

Last Chance, The Moonbeam, F. K. Jackson Funeral Home, Church of I Am The Master, Get Your Kool-Aid Free—unless you're out hunting for a new muscle boy.

It's not true, he thought. But it was. It was the same girl. Same laughing, innocent face. Pale yellow hair, silky hair, with a shimmer. Visible even in the smoky cavelike interior of The Moonbeam. Beautiful body. The skin luminous. (Will you marry me? Yes, come spring. You black bastard.) Captain Sheffield's young wife.

Dry rustling of the paper, again, as he turned the page. Brittle. Why brittle? Heat did that to paper, dried it out. He looked at the dateline, automatically, looked again, not believing it, last year's paper, January 1951. There's a mistake somewhere. No. The boys set this one up for me. Not Weak Knees. Bill Hod had used Weak Knees to convey this information. Bill set this one up. Bill never forgets a face. How do I know he never forgets a face? Never heard him say so. It's got something to do with a permit for a gun.

In that bedroom of his, front room, full of sunlight, walls painted white, windows always open, no curtains, see the branches of the trees in winter, look down into the greenleaved heart of the trees in summer, hear voices from the street (he's still mixed up in my mind with sun and wind and trees), in that front room, pile of old tabloids on the table by the bed, a telephone on the table and a gun and a pile of old tabloids, dating back three or four years, and in the kitchen on top of the radiator, radiator big enough to heat all of Grand Central, and what with a coal fire going in that chef's range, and the steam in that big radiator, could be cold as hell outdoors in winter, and the kitchen like the inside of a boiler room, B. Hod wearing nothing but shorts, torso completely naked, can see him now grabbing up a couple of old newspapers from the radiator, then sitting at the kitchen table, reading them, newspapers dating back three or four years, not reading, looking at the pictures. "He don't never forget a face." Careful search through old newspapers until he found this one because Mr. Hod knew he'd seen the face before. How do I know he never forgets a face? Weak Knees said so.

It was about a permit. I was a knowitall, home from Dartmouth for the summer, just finished my sophomore year, so I knew everything, biology, sociology, history, psychology, math, everything, and I could outrun, outjump, outski, outshoot, outswim anything on two legs my own age, and damn near anything any other age, too. I was on the track team. I was right tackle on the football team. So I was always baiting Bill, still scared to tackle him head on, but always baiting him, always hunting for an opening. I tried it head on before the summer was over and he laughed at me, just before he threw me down that long flight of stairs that leads into the kitchen.

Anyway I was always looking for a weak spot, I knew I couldn't win but I was always giving the thing a whirl, so I said to Weak Knees, "Why does King Hod walk around The Narrows with a gun strapped under his armpit? He's got a permit for these premises but he hasn't any permit that says he can walk through his empire with a gun on him."

"You wanta bet, Sonny?"

"Sure."

"How much?"

"Five bucks."

"Okay. Leave it lay right there on the kitchen table. Because it's mine." Weak Knees went out of the kitchen, came back and waved the permit right under my nose. "What's that?" he said.

"All right. So it's a permit. How'd he get it?"

"He's got a friend high up in the police department who give it to him. He's the one who put all them pansy college boys on the force. They got to pass some kind of tests in Latin now before they can walk a beat in Monmouth."

"Fine. But how'd he get to be friends with a highranking cop? I thought he was the guy you said could smell a cop a mile away, whether he was in uniform or not, and that every time he got a whiff of that cop smell he had to leave fast because if he stayed around he'd try to kill the cop."

"That's right. But one time he was hangin' around New York. And he come through a street and he see a kid being worked over by a couple of cops. It was one of them side streets where the folks strictly minds their own business and they wasn't a soul in sight because the folks always moves off when a cop comes along. There wasn't nobody around but Bill and a priest. He'd a moved off too but this priest comes along.

The kid's got blood all over his face and he sees the priest and says, 'Father, help me!'

"Bill's always been interested in folks' religion so he stops to see what the priest is goin' to do. And the priest he looks at the boy kind of dreamylike and says, 'Pray, my son, pray!' And goes on about his business and the biggest cop brings his stick down on top of the boy's head so hard you can hear a crackin' noise for damn near a block. The priest don't even turn his head, he goes shufflin' on down the street, even his skirts movin' kind of pious. Well, in those days Bill never give quarter to no cop. So he pours a little somethin' on the back of the neck of the biggest one, and he starts screamin' and jumpin' up and down and he tosses a little of the same thing on the face of the other one and he starts screamin' and jumpin' up and down.

"They get all mixed up with each other and forget about the kid. The kid, he couldn't have been more than seventeen, nothing but a kid, can just about walk and that's all. Bill takes him to where he's roomin' and gets him fixed up. The kid hadn't had nothin' to eat since God knows when and he had stole himself something to eat, and these big fat cops caught him at it and Bill said the thing about it that made him sore is that there these cops had worked over this kid for stealin' a lousy loaf of bread and every brokedown whore on the block is payin' 'em off, and so are the pimps and the boys who are runnin' a game in the back of the pool hall and the ones who are makin' book. When some of the boys cleaned out Izzie's pawnshop them same fat cops stayed way down at the end of the block where they won't see nothin' or hear nothin' because they're gettin' a cut on the deal. Them was the days, Sonny. These book-readin' cops ain't in it.

"Anyway this white kid is grateful. He's a good kid run into a streak of bad luck. He stays with Bill about three weeks, till he's back on his feet. He writes Bill's name down real careful in a little notebook he's got and just before he leaves he says someday he'll be able to do somep'n for Bill. Well Bill forgets all about it. After he come to Monmouth he was lookin' through the paper one mornin' and there was a picture of this same kid, he's grown bigger, and older, and filled out a lot, but it's the same face. Bill don't never forget a face, Sonny.

"This kid is way up in the police here. Bill goes to see him and he remembers Bill and asks him if he don't need anything, a permit, or anything. That's how Bill got the permit."

Link remembered feeling a vague dissatisfaction with this story. He supposed the story was true but Weak's stories always left him with the feeling that he'd left something out, something important. He remembered asking him what it was Bill had sprinkled on the fat cops, and that he had said, carelessly, "Oh, a little somep'n he used to carry around with him."

And now he handed the pinksheeted tabloid back to Weak Knees, went behind the bar and poured himself a drink and kept the bottle in his hand.

Bill Hod came out of his office, came and stood behind the bar, too. Link thought, You didn't have to come out here to check, Father Hod, it worked, I walked right into it.

"How come you're drinkin'?" Bill asked.

"The weather."

"The weather?"

Bill glanced out the front window, Link did, too. Bright strong sunlight on the snow outside. The kind of sun that you got in March, on a good day. A couple of weeks ago the thermometers at the back doors, fastened outside the north windows, registered zero, today they registered fifty-two and the sun was warm, the street was filled with women pushing baby buggies; water was dripping from eaves, running down gutters, rivulets of water gurgling down the drains, and small boys were floating bits of wood and paper in the water that collected in pools at the street crossings.

Sun on Dumble Street. Sun shining on the brass knocker at Number Six, sun on the brick of Number Six, turning it pink, sun on the dark gray bark of The Hangman, making it lighter gray, sun on the river.

Bill turned away from the window. Link supposed he had confirmed whatever his original impression of the weather had been, couldn't see that it had changed in any way.

"Are you broke?" he asked.

"Broke?" Link said. "Oh, Christ, no! I own custombuilt Cadillacs and yachts. I have them in pinks and blues and yellows and purples. Purple Cadillacs in the morning. Yellow yachts at night. Any time you want to take a cushioned ride from here to hell and back, I'll be glad to loan you one."

What to do now, Uncle George? he thought. Where'd I get that from? One of those kids next door, years back, when the Finns lived next door, before the colored folk, the dark folk, engulfed Dumble Street, in the days when the drunken riotous Finns jumped out of the windows every night, good way to live, from oblivion in the morning to oblivion at night. Money on the table. No complications. One of those kids that belonged to the Finns, weaving back and forth in the strip of driveway next door to Abbie's house, looking for new worlds to conquer, demanding adult direction, adult inspiration, as to the nature of the world to take on next, said, "What to do now, Uncle George?" Yes, indeed, what to do now, Uncle Link? What to do now? How gracefully and tactfully withdraw, retreat, because the position is no longer tenable, it is untenable and ruinous.

Don't ever leave me, come spring and the singing of birds, you black bastard, wait here in the hall.

Why hadn't she told him that she had a husband. The hell with the husband. It was the money. The hell with the money. This was just another variation on the theme. You wait here in the hall. Variation on the theme. Bill Hod and China.

Before I went in China's place he thought, remembering, I used to walk by and sometimes the door opened and it seemed to me that light and laughter and music came out of the door, spilled out into the street, yes and the smell of incense. Incense. China burned incense in the hall, burned it in a bowl under an imitation Buddha, a plaster of paris reproduction, hideous, evil, not peaceful, contemplative, but evil, as though the nature of China's business was summed up there in the hall, summed up in the Buddha. It was the first thing you saw going in and the last thing you saw coming out. The smell of the incense was everywhere in the hall. There was a heavy curtain over the door that led from the hall to what he supposed was the parlor, velvet-surfaced stuff, and while he stood there, waiting, he touched the curtain, inadvertently, and his pants leg must have brushed against it, because when he left he could still smell incense, it seemed to be in his hair, his clothes, and the Buddha became in his mind a symbol of evil, of treachery, indelibly marked in his memory along with the smell of incense. "You wait right here in the hall."

He was sixteen when China told him that. Sixteen, and school was out, and there was a whole long glorious stretch of hot sunny days and hot nights, and the river sparkling in the sun, and the trees in leaf, The Hangman so full of leaves it was like a green roof over the sidewalk, and girls in thin summer dresses everywhere he looked.

He didn't know when he first noticed that Bill was riding herd on him. But he never had a chance to linger in the street, never had time to lounge around the dock, to watch, and listen to the girls who went by, walking in twos and threes, arms linked together. Bill always had something for him to do, he sent him on errands in other parts of town, or else he discovered some back-breaking piece of drudgery that needed to be done inside The Last Chance. He was forever saying to do this, or stop doing that, quit brawling in the street, stop hanging out on the corner, get the lead out.

He never had time for anything but work, work, work. And so at night, it was still daylight at eight o'clock, he'd stop in The Moonbeam, the beer parlor on Franklin Avenue; at first he only stopped in there to talk to some of the guys he knew, and to crack jokes with them about the girls who came in without escorts. But two nights running he had some beer and it seemed to him he had never felt quite so adult, nor quite so sick, as when he drank half the beer at one swallow and then laughed too loud with the rest of the guys because one of them said something funny and obscene about a fat girl in a short thin dress who sat at one of the tables with her legs crossed.

Two nights straight he drank beer in The Moonbeam and sneaked in Abbie's house afterwards, the taste of the stuff still in his mouth, bitter, nauseous; sneaked home and called down the hall to Abbie that he was tired and going to bed early, not feeling tired, but sleepy, relaxed, getting in bed early just as he said and lying there drowsing and thinking about girls and wondering what they were really like and if he'd ever have one.

The morning after the second night of beer drinking, of lounging in The Moonbeam, laughing in The Moonbeam, he was polishing the brass rail on the bar, seven-thirty in the morning, and that's what he was doing.

Weak Knees said, "The boss wants to see you."

"To see me?"

"That's right."

"What's he want to see me for? Christ, is he going to send me to the other end of town again to buy a bar of soap or a stick of chewing gum or something? What's the matter with him lately anyway?"

"I dunno, Sonny. But he's kinda mad."

"Where is he?"

"In his office."

Link stuck his head inside the office door, they called it the office, though there wasn't a thing in it but a desk and a chair and a telephone. "Weak Knees said you wanted to see me."

"Yeah," Bill jerked open the drawer of his desk, shoved a pile of papers in it, and watching him Link thought, He always opens the drawer of that desk as though someone had just yelled "Fire" and he was opening an exit door and he shoves it shut the same way, and he jerks doors open and shut the same way.

Bill said, "You stay out of that beer parlor up the street. You go in there one more time and I'll come up there and smack you all over the place just as though you were a twobit whore."

His mind jumped away from the word whore. He wondered if his face had revealed what he had been thinking about. For weeks now he had been wondering what they were like and how much it cost, and—

He said, "Oh, for Christ's sake, Bill, all the guys—"

"All but you, Sonny. You stay out of that dump unless you want to be embarrassed."

He stayed away from The Moonbeam after that though he deliberately walked past the place, slowing down so that he could look in through the open door; after all Bill couldn't very well stop him from glancing inside as he went by. He didn't intend to give Bill the chance to maul him in front of a lot of guys, so he didn't go in. And always there were the girls in the thin summer dresses, laughing and chattering. He eyed them when he passed them in the street, and a kind of yearning would come over him.

It seemed to him that this phase, this stage of his life was impossible, hopeless, and that it would never pass. He was always being told that he was too young for this or that; and too old for certain so-called childish pleasure. It wasn't just Bill either. It was all of them, Bill and Weak Knees and Abbie and F. K. Jackson. They kept him on what Abbie called the straight and narrow path; Bill called it minding your own business; and Weak Knees called it staying away from trouble; and Miss Jackson, who had no handy, easy-to-use categories for right and wrong, spoke in terms of infantile reactions and pulled her glasses up and down on the thin gold chain to which they were attached by a sort of button arrangement pinned to her flat chest.

And all the time he ached for what Abbie called the Broad Path that leads to Destruction, the Primrose Path. Primroses. Why primroses? He wondered about that, too, and then went back to thinking about girls, girls in thin dresses, whores, whores who sat around in The Moonbeam. Wherein lay the difference? How did you find out about them?

And so finally he went to China's Place, the place the guys talked about, that very respectablelooking house that looked like all the other houses on Franklin except that the lights burned late in the windows, and sometimes the lights went out very suddenly, but other than the laughter and the music and the smell of incense, drifting out into the street when the door was opened, there wasn't anything which told you exactly what went on inside.

He walked into China's Place one evening, fairly early, around eight. China, vast, fat, yellow of skin, opened the door, looked him over, smiled at him, said, "Come on in."

But once inside she studied him, from head to foot, kept looking at him, until he was so uncomfortable that he started to walk out of the place, without saying anything.

"Baby, you're too young," she said, finally. "I'm an old woman," licking her lips, tip edge of her tongue, delicately moistening her lips, tip edge of her tongue going in and out. "I'm an old woman," she said again. "But you wait here in the hall. I'll be right back."

And he believed her. He stood there in the hall, not able to think, excitement mounting in him, excitement and a quiver of fear, and he forced himself to look at the hallway, in which he was standing, right near those dark green velvetylooking curtains behind which China had disappeared, she had pushed the curtain aside, a thick fabric, falling back in place, slowly, deep folds in it, smell of incense, a Buddha on the table, dim light in the hall, and the Buddha right near the curtained doorway, absolute silence, and he believing, waited, not thinking, just waiting.

Someone pushed the street door open, violently, suddenly.

Bill said, "Get out of here."

He didn't move. Bill walked toward him, took hold of his arm, twisted it, kept twisting it, so that he had either to bend toward him or resist him by not bending, and resistance meant the bone in his wrist would snap, he could have sworn he felt it give, and so he bent toward him, and the pain that shot up his arm took his breath away.

He said, "Don't."

Bill said, "Get out of here."

And twisted his arm again, and the pain ran up his shoulder into his neck, reached into his spine, and he thought he's trying to break my back, break my spine, and the dark green curtains moved, and he saw that fat yellow woman standing there watching. He said, "For Christ's sake, Bill."

"What are you waiting for? Get going."

In the kitchen of The Last Chance, he sat down at the table, touched his wrist, gingerly, with the tips of his fingers.

Bill came in and sat on the edge of the kitchen table, swinging one foot back and forth, and he looked at Link so long that Link thought, If there was anything around here in reach, I'd throw it at him.

He had said, finally, still swinging his foot, back and forth, "I catch you in that whorehouse again, I'll kill you."

Link turned his head away, touched his wrist again, tenderly, with his fingertips and winced.

"You hear what I said?"

"Yes."

"You better soak that wrist in some hot water," Bill said, mildly, and stood up.

The war between them started like that, and it never really ended. He still gave the thing a whirl, now and then. So did Bill.

Bill was giving it a whirl, now. He said, "You got somethin' on your mind?"

"Just the human race, friend. I have complications to straighten out with it. In New York. This afternoon."

"Any time you get tired of this job, Bud, all you got to do is say so. You been playing footsie with it for months now. Saturday night is the night all the Dumble Street punks have to swill enough liquor to be able to forget their troubles for the rest of the week. We'd take it kindly if you could bring yourself to stay around and do a little honest labor some Saturday night."

Complications, he thought. Stevedore and the lady. Prizefighter and the lady. Both parties white. Sometimes the rich white ladies married the big-muscle white boys, the penniless, body-beautiful white boys. And the marriages wouldn't work, couldn't work, because the wenches had too much money, and the penniless muscle men couldn't control them, couldn't keep them in line because they didn't have anything to keep them in line with except the good bones and the long smooth muscles, the fighter's heart and the dockhand's vocabulary, and after a while the novelty of the whole thing wore off, the rich white lady called quits, until she ran across another one with bigger muscles, a stronger back.

But if you were a black barkeep, a black barkeep, and the girl was white, and a multonmillionaire as Weak Knees called the very rich, the filthy rich, the obscenely rich, something so wrong with having millions that there must always be the clearcut, clearstated word about money being dirty, if you were a black barkeep: Stud.

"As a matter of fact, pal, and come to think about it," he said, "I will be here for the late watch tonight. It will take longer to dispose of the body than to actually commit the murder."

Part of his mind parroted, I bid two hundred; look at his teeth, make it three hundred; the gentleman says five hundred; look at his muscle, look at his back; the lady says one thousand dollars. Sold to the lady for one thousand dollars. Plantation buck. Stud.

He had been in love with her, wooed her, won her, thought there was between them that once in a lifetime kind of love. He remembered the snow falling on her hair, on her face, on the tip of her nose, and that he had been filled with tenderness, with a yearning tenderness, known once again what complete and utter surrender was like, felt responsible for her, felt protective toward her, standing on that cold windswept corner in Harlem, Christmas lights everywhere, in store windows, in houses, strung across the streets, yellow, red, blue lights, and that he wanted to marry her, thinking of her as the mother of his children, thinking of a home and a continuing, enduring love, not this all at once and clearly, not clearly, incoherently, illogically, but all of it inside him when he kissed the tip of her nose, and asked her to marry him.

Bought and sold, he thought. Bought at an auction, sold again at the death of the owner, part of an estate to be disposed of at the death of the owner, along with his horses and cows. Presents. She was always giving him presents. Lisle socks, English imports, and cashmere sweaters, English imports, too, handpainted neckties, first editions, mint condition. Diamond-studded cigarette case. He didn't even know where the hell it was. Kept man. The wrist watch. Chronometer. Kept man. Stud.

He took the watch off and laid it down on the bar.

Weak Knees got up from the table. "Wassamatter, ain't it workin'?" He leaned over and looked at it. "Hey, Sonny, what's a watch like that cost?"

"A piece of your life." He pushed it toward Weak Knees. "Here, you want it?"

"You kiddin', Sonny?"

"No. You take it. I'm making you a present of it. I've got five more just like it."

Weak Knees hesitated. "You sure you don't want this watch?"

"No. It's contaminated."

"What's that mean?" Weak Knees poked at it with his forefinger.

"It means it's got 'I cost too much' written all over it."

"I don't see nothin' on it."

"Such things are in the eyes of the beholder, old man. If you don't see nothin' on it then I would say there wasn't nothin' on it. So it's yours."

"I can't take it, Sonny."

"If you don't want it, leave it on the bar and let one of the lushes palm it. Then it'll end up at Uncle Abraham's place of exchange. Where it belongs."

He parked the car in front of The Hotel, parked the long red Cadillac, custombuilt, red leather upholstery, a thousand gadgets on it, all polished metal, gleaming car, multonmillionaire's car, right in front of The Hotel.

His distaste for everything, the girl, the car, The Hotel, everything, himself included, was so great that he looked at the doorman and thought, He ought to be in a zoo, with that longtailed dark red coat flapping around his legs and that permanent fixed purchasable grin on his ape's face, grin that only changed the shape of his mouth, did not reach to his eyes, eyes keep estimating the contents of pants pockets, automatically and accurately.

The doorman leaped toward the car, like a kangaroo.

"Mr. and Mrs. Williams," he said, smiling, bowing, opening the door with a flourish. "Let me have those keys, Mr. Williams, and I'll get that trunk open and get those bags out for you. You jus' go right on in—"

Camilo said, "Thank you, Ralph."

The elevator man said, "Good afternoon," the instant he saw them, and pushed the button for the eighth floor without having to be told. Regular customers. You always know where they get off, it flatters 'em to be taken automatically and without being told, to the floor where they hold their assignation, it means a bigger, fatter, juicier tip.

"How are you, John?" Camilo said.

"Fine, ma'am. Just fine. Nice to have you back again."

The elevator creaked and groaned and sighed just as it always did.

Elevator man all smiles. So was the bellboy who practically met them at the door of the suite with all the pigskin luggage, overnight bags and suitcases, that she had bought and paid for, bellboy all smiles, too, all bought and paid for, too.

The bellboy said, "It's good weather to be in the city. Won't be long before it's spring. You both been all right?"

"We're fine," she said. "How about you, Roland?"

"I'm fine, ma'am. Just fine. My mother's all right too. The doctor you told me to get for her fixed her up good. Her back ain't bothered her since she went to him." He was still holding the bags, looking at Camilo with a mixture of awe and gratitude that infuriated Link, his eyes were like the eyes of a setter, soft, liquid, undemanding, humble.

"We can't ever thank you, ma'am. Ain't there somethin' we can do for you?"

Camilo's eyes widened. The incredibly blue, candid, innocent eyes, widening, in surprise. "Why—I—"

"We been tryin' to think of somethin', ma'am, but—"

Link said, "Okay, Bud. Put the bags down and scram."

Roland looked around for the bags, saw that he was still holding them, looked confused and put them down hastily, said, "Oh," and left quickly.

Camilo gave Link a long, direct, meaningful glance, and he thought, I've seen married women give their husbands that same kind of dirty look and you know that as soon as the door is closed, that the gentleman is going to catch hell and when the gentleman has caught all the hell the lady can throw at him, under the inspiration of the moment, the lady would really go to work on him and when she got through, the gentleman was going to wish that the female had never been dreamed up by whatever Machiavellian intelligence had created females as a means of ensuring the propagation of the species.

He picked up the bags, all of them, all the pretty cream-colored pigskin bags, and deliberately slammed them down on the floor of the bedroom, heard the clink of glass, and thought, Well, here we go Miss Multonmillionaire.

"I bet you've broken all my little bottles," she said.

"You can buy some more."

"I can't buy them here in The Hotel, and besides you're being awfully rude. What's the matter?"

She called it The Hotel, just like the rest of Harlem, easily, casually, taking it for granted that you would know that she was talking about this one particular hotel, not needing to identify it by name. She makes everything hers, he thought. Part of that easy adaptability which he had once liked and admired and even envied in her, and which he now found irritating.

She owned everything: people, cars, houses, establishing her ownership quickly; she bought bellboys, desk clerks, elevator men, doormen. Bought 'em up fast. Had bought him, too.

"What's the matter?" she repeated.

He wanted to say, I have thought of myself in many ways, called myself many things, but I have never thought of myself as the toy, the plaything, of a rich white woman. Even if this thing between us were over, ended, finished, long since dead and buried and the grass growing over the grave, even then if I had found out who you are, I would still feel as though I had been tricked, used, played with.

"Link! You're angry. What have I done? Tell me."

"You haven't done anything." He took off his jacket, took off the handpainted Bronzini necktie, the shirt from Sulka. "Come on, get in bed."

"Why are you acting like this?" she said softly.

She put her hand on his arm, and the sweet smell of her perfume seemed to come from her skin, from her hair, smell of nightblooming stock in the moonlight, smell that evoked images of females, roundhipped, globular-breasted, luminous of skin. "Tell me what's wrong," she said.

"I said you were to get in bed."

"What's the matter? Don't let's spoil what we had. It was so beautiful and so wonderful—"

"It's gone down the drain," he said savagely, and then forced her down on the bed, something raging inside him, furious now, and enjoying his fury, thinking, Everywhere, everything, even this bed, that first night we came here, the bed was the one provided by The Hotel for people who thought toosoft mattresses were comfortable, were the last word in luxury, and The Hotel knowing that these rooms would be used for assignations, for the consummation of illicit relations between males, beween females, between males and females, for rape, for seduction, sexes arranged and rearranged, mixed up, mismatched, and so charged Waldorf-Astoria prices for thirdrate fourthrate accommodations, but the next night, ah, miracle of wealth, miracle of gun money, miracle of being an heiress, the next night he noticed, only vaguely of course because he was heavenbound, in a state of ecstasy, prolonged and wonderful, the bed was wider, longer, bed with no mounds and hummocks of softness, bed designed by someone who knew what a bed should be like. Kingsize bed. Sheets made to order. Blankets made to order.

Millionaire's bed.

And now, he thought, now, I will get even with you for being rich, for being white, for owning bellboys, for owning one particular bellboy named Roland, Knight of the Bags, for knowing his name, and remembering it, for knowing that the Knight of the Bags had a mother, for helping his mother with your vast unspendable unspeakable fortune.

Rape her? He couldn't.

He got dressed in a hurry, put his shirt on, knotted the Bronzini tie, yanking it, put his jacket on, the jacket she had picked out, made him buy ("We'll both wear gray flannel") in a fancy store on Fiftieth Street, and the clerks had eyed them, speculation in their faces, and word must have been passed around because every time he looked up there was another sheepfaced one standing nearby, staring, eyes round, speculative, astonishment on their faces, bewilderment, until finally, he had roared at the sheepfaced one who seemed to be in charge, "Look, mister, I'm not Public Exhibit Number One. That is not yet. Find something for these flunkeys to do, will you?"

"Where are you going?" she said.

"Don't you know, hasn't anyone ever taught you that you're not supposed to ask a gentleman who is leaving, who is taking a runout powder, where he's going?" He put his hands in his pockets, leaned against the door jamb. "So you won't waste any time hunting for me or worrying about me—would you worry I wonder—I'm going to get myself about five fast drinks, and then get on a train for Monmouth."

He went downstairs to the bar in The Hotel, drank whiskey and soda, not wanting it, kept drinking it though the stuff tasted like hell, and he felt as though he were already drunk and had been drunk for days. But he had accomplished something, he had finally achieved understanding of this bar. You have to be on the offside of a binge to understand it, he thought. They come in here to drink, come in here with memory perched on their shoulders, memory pecking at their vital organs, and after they drink enough of this amber-colored stuff, pour enough of it down their throats, they get the critter hooded and chained as though it were a falcon.

Hooded and chained? That toofat female over there, just five people down from me, same color as China, same kind of skin, yellowish, about fifty pounds lighter though, comes in here to get a hood on the falconmemory, tell by her eyes—the whites bloodshot, eyes swivel on an axis which eyes should not do, the good clean line of the jaw obscured by rolls of soft fat.

The woman said, "Mike," to the bartender and pushed her empty glass toward him.

The bartender reached for a bottle of brandy, filled the glass. "You getting a head start, Mrs. Cumin."

"I need it."

Her voice was harsh, flat, with a forced tone, unpleasant to the ear. She emptied the glass quickly, and shoved it toward the bartender again, and Link thought, Mrs. Cumin, I wonder if you know what you're doing drinking brandy at this hour in the afternoon, you already have most of the symptoms of a lush and one of these days they'll call the wagon for you and your spotted dress and your small shortfingered plumpfingered grubby little hands and your small and very nice feet will enter the wagon first. Feet first. He looked at the woman's hair, dyed a queer redbrown, and thought of Camilo, no spare flesh and yet not bony, the hair clean, fragrant, silkysoft, the cleareyed innocence of her.

He thought, Maybe I'm wrong. No. I couldn't be. He could remember exactly how it went. They were going to have dinner with Wormsley and his wife, and the conversation went like this:

Camilo: I forgot your tie.

L. Williams: Tie? I've got one on.

Camilo: Not that one. This one. I had it made for you. It matches my dress.

L. Williams: My God! I can't wear that. I've never worn a green tie in my life.

Camilo: But it matches my dress. And I had it specially made for you.

Total identification, he thought. I wore white shirts when I was fifteen because Bill wore white shirts. So I had to wear a green necktie because she was wearing a green dress—but how could she—

L. Williams (looking in mirror, after the tie was knotted

around his neck, she having knotted it): Honey, I sure must love you an awful lot to let you do this to me. I look exactly like a goddamn pansy.

Camilo: You do not.

L. Williams: Well I feel like one. Same thing.

He thought, Necktie, green necktie, made of the same stuff as a fullskirted dinner dress, or wear white shirts because the enthroned one wears white shirts, or put a black man in the family tree, like Lena Wormsley, make him up, and put him in the family tree, because Wormsley is black. Total identification —that's what he thought, then and now—now—kept man— toy—plaything—

Camilo (in the hotel, after the dinner party): I wish I was colored too.

L. Williams (no longer startled, having heard this before): Whyn't you make yourself up a black grandfather like Lena Wormsley did?

Camilo (sitting up in bed): That woman! I could have killed her. She couldn't keep her hands off you. (frowning) How do you know she made herself up a black grandfather?

L. Williams: Wormsley told me so.

Camilo: When?

L. Williams: Why the cross-examination? Oh, I see, you think that at some point Lena and I went into a huddle. No. When we two gentlemen were sitting in the dining room, English fashion, and you two ladies had gone into the good doctor's drawing room, also English fashion—

Camilo: Why did she do that?

L. Williams: Wormsley seems to be just a fat black man but he is an Englishman at heart, an English gentleman, Victorian English gentleman, at that. So after dinner the ladies retire to the drawing room while the gentlemen—

Camilo: I'm not talking about that. I want to know why that woman claims to have a black grandfather, when she's obviously white, obviously French.

L. Williams: Lena Wormsley? A black grandfather? (intoning) "Thy people shall be my people, and thy God my God: Where thou diest, will I die, and there will I be buried: the Lord do so to me, and more also, if ought but death part thee and me."

Silence.

Then he had heard the wheezegroan of the elevator outside in the corridor.

Camilo: Oh, Link! (face buried in his chest; sat up) If she's in love with Wormsley, why did she find you so irresistible?

L. Williams: Doesn't the female always take what she wants and at the same time try to hang on to what she already has? Maybe it's the collector's instinct. I don't know what it is. You tell me.

He had thought of Mamie Powther and Bill Hod. Mamie in The Last Chance at five o'clock, winter, so it was already dark, cold outside, "Bill, mix me a long tall one," warmth of a tropical country in her voice. Same train. Same train be back tomorrer. Same train waitin' at the station. Dusk, not yet dark, the light of day fading, fading. L. Williams about to leave The Last Chance stopped and watched Powther, a small hurrying figure in his creased pants and shined-up shoes, scuttling through Dumble Street, watched him, convinced that he'd take a watch out of his waistcoat pocket and mutter, "Oh dear! Oh dear! I shall be too late!" just before he disappeared down the rabbithole.

Bill, mix me a long tall one.

Same train.

The female wasn't complicated, it was the male who was complicated. The female was simple, elemental, direct, primordial.

L. Williams: Honey, haven't you ever kept your pretty little left hand on the lead rope you'd put around the neck of one male while you put your pretty little right hand to work fastening a lead rope around the neck of another male?

She had blushed. Deep rosyred color had suffused her face, her neck. He could have sworn that all of her body changed color, turning faintly pink.

Camilo: I love you, love you, love you (silky perfumed hair on his chest, under his chin).

And now Camilo was saying, "What are you drinking?" She put her hand on his arm, and he felt himself assailed, defeated, by the clean lovely line of her, by the smile, by the sweet smell of her.

"Whiskey and soda. Want one?"

The fat yellow woman in the tootight purple dress glanced at him, at Camilo, at him again, and then turned her back, deliberately, and he saw by the motion of her hand, the backward tilt of her head that she had drained the glass in one long swallow. He heard her say, "Mike," and thought, Fat lady in the purple dress you must have had complications, too, at some time in the past, the not toodistant past. Mr. B. Hod and Mr. B. Franklin are in many ways right. There are degrees, however. Degrees.

"Not at this hour, thank you," Camilo said. Then softly, a coaxing note in her voice, "I want to talk to you, sweetie."

Wifely admonition. "Not at this hour." They can't help it. Gentle, wifely admonition.

He shook his head. "If we talk, we'll fight. And I don't, and it's funny, I don't want to fight with you and ten minutes ago the one thing in the world I wanted to do was beat the bejesus out of you. And if we go back upstairs to that, that suite—I am afraid I will forget all the reasons why I shouldn't do it. Because you will say something that will make me forget."

"Come on," she said, and took the whiskey glass out of his hand, set it down on the bar, tucked his arm in hers, and led him, unresisting, out of the bar, into the lobby.

"I see you found him, Mrs. Williams," the elevator man said, grinning, exuding friendliness.

Mountebank, Link thought, bought and paid for, paid to grin, will stand on head, will wave feet in air, will make noises like a human being for one quarter, for one dime, for one penny.

"Well, of course," Camilo said, and grinned back at John-RolandJoseph and his long line of bought and paid for ancestors, as friendly and unselfconscious as though all her life she had been looking for men, black men, big black men—plantation bucks (stud) look at his thighs, look at that back, look at his dingle-dangle—as though all her life she had been looking for colored men to whom she was not married, to whom she would never be married because she was already married to a nice young white man, as though all her life she had told uniformed monkeys who pulled elevators in rundown colored hotels, in Harlem, that she couldn't find, had lost, misplaced, a gentleman of color named Williams.

"They say that if you keep working at it, you'll always find what you want. So—knowing I'd find him, there he was, in the bar, looking into a tall tall glass of whiskey and soda." She laughed. Light, musical, gay sound of laughter. "Besides, you said he'd gone toward the bar."

All of it good clean fun. Lighthearted. Gay. The elevator man JohnJosephRoland, and his long line of bought and paid for ancestors, was still laughing, showing all his teeth, including two gold ones in the lower jaw when he brought the elevator to a stop at the eighth floor, dead-level stop on the first throw.

Having closed the door of the sitting room, he stood with his back against it. Checker game, he thought, it's your move. But there's one thing in all this that puzzles me. How can you look so innocent? How can your eyes still retain that expression of absolute honesty, of purity? Perhaps I wasn't one of a long line of muscle boys, maybe the line is just forming, and I'm only the third or fourth. Or maybe I'm wrong. Maybe you don't live with Captain Bunny Sheffield any more. Maybe you've divorced him. I wouldn't know that either. The checker games they play on the mink circuit aren't likely to come to my attention.

"I'm going to know right now what this is all about," she said.

"It's about you. You and your money. You and who you really are."

"My money?"

"Yeah. The Treadway billions or whatever the total is. I'm running out on it, or quitting, doing whatever it is that a merry-go-round does when it can't be wound up any more."

"There isn't anything I can do about the money, Link. It isn't my fault. It isn't anything I can help or that I planned."

"Of course not. You're just a fashion expert, and you work for a living, don't you? And you're in love with me, aren't you?"

"Yes, I'm in love with you," she said quietly. "As for the money, well, once people find out that I'm a Treadway, they don't see me any more. All they see is money. They either hate the money or love the money but not me. It's just like being covered with a solid gold sheet, nobody cares what's under it, because they can no longer see that there's anything there in front of them but gold."

She waited for him to say something, and when he didn't, she said, "You're doing the same thing. But it doesn't usually make people angry when they find out who I am. They may hate me but they're not angry. I don't understand that. Why are you angry? I'm the same person. I'm really and truly in love with you. I always will be. What's changed? Oh, Link, let's not—"

He interrupted her. He said, "You're not married either, are you? Just for the record, honey, why do you still live with him? What do you do, take notes on us—for Kinsey?"

"You're horrible," she said.

So she was still married to him, still living with him.

"I haven't finished—"

"Well, I'm not going to listen to you."

"You will—" he said.

But she moved too fast. She went into the bathroom and slammed the door, and he heard the click of the lock.

He went down in the elevator, listening to the asthmatic wheezing, thinking, Even the bathroom, she could fix anything, change anything, buy anything. The water was always boiling wherever they were. The thin worn towels had been replaced by thick big ones. Nobody would believe it was the same place, everything changed, everything fixed up.

Leave it all behind you, the silk pajamas and the brocaded dressing gown, the china and the silver, the pigskin suitcases, and the television set that replaced the putinaquarter and get a neatly, exactly apportioned piece of listening-time radio, leave it all behind, the grinning doormen and the bellboys and the elevator men, the one who peddled numbers and this one of the gold teeth who keeps an apple and a pear on a little shelf, just over his head, this one who was a goddamn fruit eater.

On his way through the lobby, he stopped at the desk, to get one final piece of information.

"Let me take a look at the record for a minute, honey," he said to the girl behind the desk, girl with slant eyes and mascaraed eyelashes, brown girl wearing a crisp white blouse, very white, virginal-looking blouse, girl obviously no virgin, couldn't be.

He stood right beside her and started hunting up the record for himself.

"The guests aren't supposed to go through the account book, Mr. Williams," the girl said, standing up, reaching toward the record book.

"It's okay, honey. Here," he fished a five dollar bill out of his pocket. "You buy yourself some nylons for your lovely legs the next time you're downtown." The girl smiled at him and located the Williams' account in the record book for him, and he smiled right back at her thinking, You can buy any of 'em, they're a dime a dozen.

At the 125th Street railroad station, he had to wait half an hour for a train to New Haven. He stood on the platform, above the street, listening to the foul, noisome racket of New York, car horns blasting, roar of airplanes overhead, rumbling of passing trains, thinking, It's a wonder the people who live here don't have a continual vibration going on inside their heads. They do but they don't know it. Camilo lives here, in New York. So her head is filled with vibrations too. That's what's the matter with her. There's nothing the matter with her. It's me.

Some of Abbie's oldfashioned morality spilled over on me, a long time ago, and I'll never be able to wipe it off. Nuts. It's the husband, it's the continuing continued relationship with Captain Bunny Sheffield and with me at the same time that puts a label on me—MECHANICAL TOY. Put a quarter in the slot and it'll dance for a half-hour.

She paid for that suite in The Hotel by the month. She has been paying for it, by the month, ever since we started going there in December. I thought I paid for it at so much per day. Will stand on head, will wave feet in air. For one dime.

I used to dream about her on the nights when I didn't see her, dream that she was lying beside me, the soft warm naked flesh, the curves, the sweet, sweet curves, within hand's reach. Will make sounds like a human being for one penny.

Captain Bunny Sheffield probably dreamed the same thing, on the nights when he didn't see her.

In New Haven, he had to wait another half-hour for a train to Monmouth, and went in a bar and had three more drinks, one right after the other.

I get a little farther along in it each time I take a drink, he thought. True, Abbie's morality, some of it, spilled over on me, but the portion of it that I retained isn't exactly like the original stuff. It changed a little when it hit me. If I ever get so I really understand all of this, I'll be too drunk to know it. Mr. B. Hod is going to be voluble and vulgar on the subject of one of his hired hands showing up well on the way to being soused to the gills.

He ignored the taxis at the Monmouth Railroad Station. Taxis were for the rich, the filthy rich, the rich who had pale yellow hair and wore mink coats and cheated at cards. He boarded a Franklin Avenue car, the same car he rode on when he worked for the Valkills, those other fine rich people he had known when he was very young. The streetcar put him where he belonged, back with the poor, the peons, the poor, black peons.

17

"I WANT de pretty-pretty," J.C. said. "You give me de pretty-pretty. Mamie, you give me dat pretty-pretty."

"What'sa matter with you, J.C.? Come in here waking me up like this." Mamie Powther stretched, yawned, sat up in bed, thinking, Pretty-pretty, he means Link's cigarette case. She looked around the bedroom to see what it was that had made him remember it. Sometimes she could figure out what made him remember a thing, and sometimes she couldn't. Sunlight in the room, on the rug. It was the sunlight. He had been sitting on the floor, in the sun, playing with the cigarette case, when she took it away from him.

"You give me—" he began.

She leaned back against the pillows, sank deep into the pillows. "You don't get out of here and leave me finish my sleep out I'll give you whatfor."

"I want de pretty-pretty," he whined.

"Well, I ain't going to give it to you. See? You go on now because if I have to get out of my bed to make you stop pulling at the cover, I'll wear you out. You go on downstairs and see if Crunch's got anything for your breakfast. You hear? Go on now."

He glared at her and she laughed because he looked just like Bill when Bill was being pure nigger.

"You go on now, J.C.," she said, still laughing.

"You got some Kool-Aid, Mamie?" he asked, not moving, still glaring, holding his round hard head on one side.

"I'll get you some this afternoon. You go on downstairs and get your breakfast."

She listened to the thud, thud, thud of his feet as he went down the hall. He put his feet down hard just like he had planted seeds and was using his feet to tramp them down in the ground. Kids never had any control over their feet. They clumped along just like they were clubfooted. But when he wanted to, he could walk like Bill, just like he was a cat, sneaking up on a robin, and the robin don't know he's coming until the cat's got him between his paws. She pushed the pillows away, lay flat on her back, not asleep, not awake, eyes closed, aware of the sun shining in the room, like something red laid over her eyelids.

She didn't intend to do a damn thing all day, just laze around, not even get dressed, not even bother to fix herself something to eat. She'd get herself some coffee pretty soon. Around five or so she'd go over to Bill's and get a sandwich for herself and have a drink with him. Powther would be home tonight and tomorrow night too.

But I got to get that Kool-Aid, she thought. I promised it to J.C. And when you promise a kid something he would wear you out until he got it. But a kid could promise you something and forget it just as easy. It didn't work both ways. Kool-Aid. Crunch got all upset when she saw J.C. licking something off his hand. Crunch saw him shake some powder out of a package, shake it in his hand, and then lick it off, and she had come out in the backyard, head held up high, "Mrs. Powther," she said, "what's J.C. taking?"

I was hanging up the wash and I didn't know what she was talking about and I said, "Taking?" I thought he'd been stealing some of her things, he don't exactly steal, he just picks up anything that's real shiny, anything that looks like it was gold or silver, on account of them dumb fairy stories Powther's always telling him.

Crunch said, "Does he take narcotics?"

I thought she'd gone out of her mind, and then I started laughing because he was standing there in the yard right behind her licking some of that Kool-Aid powder out of his hand, and she must have figured he was sniffing coke and he only three and a half, and I explains it to her and she looked mad and said, "Well, that probably accounts for his tongue being that peculiar bright red. I thought he had some kind of unusual disease. Anyway I shouldn't think it would be good for him, anything that color couldn't be good for the inside of his stomach."

And I got kind of mad and I shouldn't have and I said, "Well, Mrs. Crunch, I had three children and they all licked up that Kool-Aid and they're all in good health and never had no sicknesses and so I would think that would show that it don't do nothing to the inside of their stomachs. Besides if it did, it wouldn't be sold everywhere all over this country. And besides I imagine I know more about kids than anybody who never had none."

Her head kind of went down, for a minute, and then she held it right up again, and looked at me the way she always does, as though she smelt something bad, and went back in the house. And on the way to the house she must have got mad too, because she banged the door shut.

Crunch is different from anybody I ever come across. But she is awful good to J.C. I hope she never finds out Bill comes over here so much.

She opened her eyes, and laughed, lightly, under her breath. He's a crazy man, Bill is. Two nights ago he come busting in here like all hell was after him, and when he left he looked like an angel, well, a kind of wornout halfgoat angel. He was put together better than any man she'd ever seen, except maybe for Link Williams, and that only because Link was younger.

Link Williams. She still had that cigarette case. She'd forgotten all about it. It was on a sunny morning, just like this one, and she was lying in bed half asleep, just like now, and the sunlight shifted and changed, flashing almost like lightning across her eyelids. When she sat up, leaning on one elbow, looking around she saw that J.C. was sitting on the floor, by the window, the early morning sun shining on him. He's cute, she'd thought. He looked awful clean. Powther must have given him a bath. Powther was always fondest of 'em when they were still young enough to need a lot of care. Or maybe Crunch had washed him. Crunch was always washing him.

J.C. had muttered, "All gold, and the robbers came, bang! bang! You're dead, you bastid."

So he was interested in something that would keep him out of her hair, out of her way, for a long time, and she could lie in bed not moving, half dreaming. The light had flashed again. He was playing with something that glittered in the sun, flashed in the sun. What on earth had he got hold of? She remembered that she had sat all the way up, eyes wide open. He was still talking to himself, turning something around and over, holding it on the palm of his hand, then turning it again so that it glittered and flashed.

"She was all gold, all gold," he'd said.

If she asked him what he had, he'd hide it, behind his back and run out of the room. So she got out of bed and walked right up to him without his hearing her, thinking that when a kid is interested in something he's just like he's blind and deaf too. J.C. was holding the glittering object flat on the palm of his hand, and she had approached him so quietly, had picked it out of his hand so quickly, that he was too surprised to move, just sat there, staring at his empty palm.

When he looked up and saw her, saw that the glittering object was there in her hand, he let out a roar, and threw himself at her, grabbing her around the knees, clawing at her legs, so angry that he couldn't do anything but holler. Then he had said the same thing over and over again, panting, "Give me dat, dat's mine, give me dat, dat's mine."

She had pushed him away, "Stop that," she'd said. "You, J.C., you stop that noise."

She had ignored the noise to study the thing she was holding. It was a cigarette case. There was a monogram on it, picked out in brilliants that caught the light, the stones winking in the sun, flashing red, green, blue, yellow.

"L.W." she murmured. "Some woman musta give this to Link."

How did she know whose it was, right off, like that? Because she had been thinking about him, because she wanted, just once, once would be enough, to try him out. She had turned it over and over in her hands, finally held it flat, on the palm of her hand, just as J.C. had done. Then she opened it, read the fine print, eighteen-carat gold, Tiffany & Co. Not brilliants. Diamonds.

"Great day in the morning!" she'd said. "Diamonds!" What woman— J.C. had dived at her legs again, nearly knocking her off balance and she reached down and whacked him across the seat. "You J.C., you stop that. You better be glad I'm feeling good, you J.C. you, get up from there," and she whacked him again.

"Let me tell you somethin'. You stay outta Link's room. That's where you got his cigarette case."

J.C. had howled and she had leaned over to give him another whack, and missed him, dropped the cigarette case, and had to race toward it, before J.C. got it, a form of exertion in the early morning which she'd resented, and she put the cigarette case down on the bed, grabbed J.C., and held him and cuffed him.

"There," she said, breathing hard from the effort, "that'll hold you."

She remembered how he had sat crosslegged on the floor, silent, his thumb in his mouth, watching her, waiting to see where she was going to put the cigarette case, his glance followed hers as she looked around the room for a good hiding place.

"You had your breakfast, J.C.?"

He shook his head.

"You go downstairs to Crunch's. It's about time she was having herself a second cup of coffee, though it sure surprises me that she should have a weakness like coffee drinking, and she'll be feeling real good and she'll give you some leftovers. You run along now."

She supposed she shouldn't have beat on him like that, but sometimes he looked at her just like Bill, and there were times when Bill made her mad but she never'd worked up nerve enough to let him know it, and she supposed that she took it out on J.C. She had followed J.C. to the door, watched him go slowly, reluctantly, down the hall, heading for the front stairs, then she'd locked the door of the bedroom. Sometimes he moved so quiet that he was right in the room with you, standing behind you, and you never knew he was there till he said something. She didn't intend that he should come creeping back up the stairs and catch her in the very act of hiding the cigarette case. She should have taken it back right then and given it to Crunch but she didn't feel like listening to Crunch being holy that early in the morning.

Instead she had decided that some morning she'd wake up feeling so good or so evil that whatever Crunch had to say on the subject of thievery wouldn't bother her at all. So she had thought, Let's see, where's the best place to keep this until I can get it back downstairs where it belongs. Who could have give it to Link? A woman, yes. But what woman? What made me think he was going to sit around on his can somewhere waiting until I could get around to him? And was I going to get around to him? Sure. He was ready, willing, and able and his eyes kind of sparkled whenever he saw her, though he only nodded, very formal, the formal nod was funny because it didn't match his face, didn't match the devilment in his eyes when he said, "Good evening, Mrs. Powther."

She had tucked the cigarette case under a pile of Powther's handkerchiefs in the top drawer of the tall chest, and afterwards, stood running her fingers over the fronts, the behinds, of the cupids carved on the handles, smiling, liking the roundness of them. Powther didn't like the furniture she'd bought. He wouldn't. He liked things plain, ordinary, and she liked things fancy, dressed up. She had glanced in the drawer, still smiling, at the neatly rolled-up socks, gray cotton socks, black cotton socks, that he washed himself and when they were dry, rolled them up in these little balls. He only had two drawers in the chest. He kept his shirts in the second drawer, shirts done by the Chinaman and taken to the Chinaman every Monday morning, just like clockwork, and picked up every Friday. Powther was always carrying packages, under his arm. Had to have everything lined up in rows, everything folded, even that oldfashioned knit underwear he wore, what'd they call 'em, union suits, even the union suits folded up.

She'd tried to get him to wear shorts and undershirts like a human being, but, no, he couldn't get used to the idea, he had to wear those funnylooking things. Bill was the only man she'd ever seen looked good in his underwear, just shorts he wore, and he looked good in them. Link Williams would look good in just his underwear.

Powther looked kind of like he belonged in a glass case with a label on it when he stepped out of his pants and shirts and stood around in one of those union suits. She always wanted to laugh, had to swallow the laughter, because she wouldn't hurt his feelings for anything, he was such a funny, serious little man, so she always said, "Come on, honey, hurry up and get in bed," because she knew if she kept looking at him, she'd start laughing and wouldn't be able to stop and men couldn't stand being laughed at.

She had decided that the top drawer was a good safe place. J.C. couldn't reach the top drawer and besides there wasn't anything in there to interest him. And she'd give the cigarette case back to Crunch sometime soon.

Now she traced the outline of a bunch of grapes on the headboard of the bed, round fat grapes, then looked at her hand. I need to do my nails, she thought. Pretty soon I'll get up and do my nails and make myself some coffee, and bring it back to bed and drink it. Wonder if Powther made the coffee before he left. Sometimes he does, sometimes he doesn't. I never ask him about it. He knows I love to laze around in bed, in the morning, drinking coffee, and that I hate to get up and make it, and I got the feeling that when he's kind of mad at me, why he don't make the coffee.

It was late in the afternoon when she got up. She dressed slowly, carefully, spending a long time fixing up her face, studying it in the mirror of the dressing table, turning her head this way and that, thinking, I've seen better faces but it's mine and it ain't too bad. Then she took the cigarette case out of the top drawer of the tall chest, put it in the pocket of her purple coat. She liked that coat better than any she'd ever owned. It really showed off her figure, and the brass buttons dressed it up, and at the same time let you know that there were some fine breasts underneath that purple cloth.

If Crunch was out she'd just stick that case somewhere in Link's room and not say anything about it. She was only kidding herself if she thought there would be any time soon when she could hand that case to Crunch and tell her that J.C. took it, because Crunch would look at her as though she thought she smelt bad and her eyes would shoot sparks, and her back would get like she had a bedpost down it. She wouldn't give it to Link Williams because men always got mad when people went through their things, and Link looked as though he could pitch one just like Bill, he looked like Bill, younger, browner, but the eyes and the walk and the stayonyourownside of the street expression exactly the same.

She was dressed and ready to go out of the room, and she thought, Powther don't like to have people go through his things either. So she spent about ten minutes lining Powther's handkerchiefs up in neat piles, all the edges even, smiling and humming under her breath as she worked. "There," she said when she finished, "I bet I could learn the Army something about putting things in piles. Powther couldn'ta done a better job himself. Real pretty."

She went straight across the street to The Last Chance with the cigarette case still in the pocket of the purple coat because she heard Crunch moving around in the kitchen, rattling pots and pans. She thought, Well, I'll get a drink and a sandwich and then go downtown and buy myself a pair of green suede shoes, high heels, open at the toes and the heels, sandals, really, and a red-and-white-striped dress, a silk one, because spring's on its way, I can feel it in the air, it's still cold but the air smells fresh, and I need some new clothes anyway. By the time I get back Crunch may have gone out.

At first glance, there wasn't anyone in the place but Bill. He was standing behind the bar looking as evil as Satan. Then she saw that Old Man John the Barber was in there too, sitting at one of the tables, crouched over a glass of beer looking as though he hated himself. He had a fixed scowl between his bushy eyebrows, and his beard always had a kind of stuckout look, as though he kept thrusting his jaw out, and so the beard stuck out too. She nodded to Barber, said, "Hi, babe," to Bill.

"You want a drink?" Bill said.

"Yeah. A long cold drink."

Weak Knees stuck his head out from the kitchen door. "You want me to put a record on, Mamie? I got a new one that'll send you."

"Sure."

Weak Knees put the record on, and went back to the kitchen.

She didn't pay any attention when the street door opened because the drink was good, cold in her mouth, slow warmth seeping through her veins, and the record on the jukebox was better than anything she'd ever heard, not too fast, not too slow, and the bird doing the singing had a sweet kind of voice, it had a lilt in it, and she wondered who he was because most of them couldn't sing, they messed a song up, but this one was really singing, it was like being in bed, stretched out, waiting, because something good was about to happen, something very good and very wonderful. Like Bill Hod.

She never looked at Bill's customers anyway. They were a rough hungry crew, not good to look at, not good to listen to, dockhands and cooks off the oil barges, hunkies and Swedes and sometimes a foreign nigger off a river tramp, an old tramp loaded down so heavy that she really wasn't safe any more, sitting too low in the water, and the guys looked and sounded as though they'd come right off a tramp, not too clean, wanting to drink fast, get a load on fast, get a woman fast. But she turned and looked toward the door because Bill's expression had changed, not his expression, his eyes, they narrowed down until they were slits, and she felt a funny kind of thrill run all through her, a kind of tingling, because she was afraid of him when he looked like that, afraid of him and more nearly in love with him than at any other time, when he got that got-you-cornered-trapped-beat-you-to-death look in his eyes. And he couldn't cover it up. He could keep his face perfectly still but not his eyes.

She turned to see who had come in through that big door that should make Bill look like that and saw a girl, a white girl in a mink coat. She was looking for someone, not Bill, because she glanced at him and then looked away, looked along the length of the bar, glanced at the tables, at Old Man John the Barber, and then toward the back. Weak Knees had come out of the kitchen and was standing near the jukebox. He started that creepy motion of his hand, and she couldn't hear him say it but she could tell by the way his lips moved that he was saying, "Get away, get away, Eddie. God damn it, get away from me." Then he ducked back into the kitchen.

This was Link's girl, the girl with the yellow hair, girl with a mink coat, the one that Crunch pushed down the front steps, and she felt laughter well up inside her, all over again, and told herself sternly, Don't start laughing again because you'll never be able to stop, you're such a fool you'll never be able to stop. Besides, why should a white girl have Link Williams? When you thought about all the white men there were for this girl to climb in bed with it wasn't fair that she should cheat some colored girl out of the chance to go with him.

The girl acted as though she were going to turn around and go out, she looked around as though she couldn't make up her mind, and then she walked right up to the bar and said, "Scotch and soda."

She drank it fast. She kept turning her head toward the window. Mamie wondered why. You couldn't see nothing out of the window, nothing but Dumble Street, the front of Crunch's house, the knocker on the door, well you knew it was there, you couldn't really see it in this halflight, even though Crunch kept it polished up like it was gold, and the front steps and the iron railing. Those steps made her think of Baltimore where the front steps were painted white, and the housemaids scrubbed them down every morning. That's what she did when she was eighteen, scrubbed down the steps every morning, and a white guy used to be going by when she was down on her hands and knees, she used to know it was him, because he'd start whistling "Yankee Doodle" when he got near that house where she worked, whistling and laughing, and she laughed, too, because she figured she looked like an elephant all turned up to the street like that, scrubbing away at steps that would be dirty before nightfall, and finally they got so they kind of talked to each other and she got tired of doing those same steps every morning, and she went and lived with him and stayed for three years.

She didn't know what made her think about him, it was a long time ago, he was a conductor on some railroad line, and she didn't even remember now how they came to break up.

The girl was still looking out of the window. Nothing to see, except Crunch's front steps and that iron railing on each side of the steps, looking at it from here if you half closed your eyes, it looked like a cock, repeated over and over, though nobody else would probably think of it but her.

"Fill it up, please," the girl said.

Mamie looked at the girl sharply, thinking, She's got half a jag on. I can tell by her voice—sounds like she'd swallowed a lot of fuzz. And she's hanging around here looking for Link. They must have broke up. She reached in her coat pocket for a package of cigarettes and her fingers touched something cold, hard, not cigarettes. What did I put in my pocket, you mean to say I come out without no cigarettes and if there's anything Bill hates it's to have me bum some from him, he's pure nigger about 'em. No, I've got 'em, a full pack. But what else? The cigarette case. She'd forgotten all about it. She was going to put it in Link's room only Crunch was home and it was still in her pocket—and she felt kind of funny about its being there, because this girl must have given it to him—and the girl was looking straight at her—

Weak Knees stuck his head out through the swinging door in the back. The record had stopped playing and he said, louder than he would have, but he must have thought the record was still going, and he had to make himself heard, "Say, Mamie, you wanta ham sandwich, like I make for you and Link, what you say, Mamie, you wanta ham sandwich?"

The girl's face crumpled up. Why she must be in love with Link, Mamie thought, in love with him, I thought she was just fooling around with him, I ought to say something, I ought to explain about what Weak just said. He talks so dumb sometimes. He made it sound like me and Link are always in here together eating ham sandwiches and it wasn't like that. One afternoon I came over to get a drink and Link was in here, behind the bar, and Weak made a sandwich for me and Link said it looked so good he'd have one and he went out in the kitchen and as far as I know he ate it out there.

"You wanta ham sandwich like the kind I make for you and Link?" Weak Knees repeated.

"Sure," she said, and she knew that her voice sounded funny and that she had a funny look on her face. But the girl was still looking at her, just as though she could see right in the pocket of the purple coat, see that gold cigarette case in there, and Weak talking simpleminded like that.

"How much do I owe you?" the girl said.

Bill said, "Three-fifty."

"Three-fifty?" the blurred, fuzzy sound of her voice was awful. "Why—" The girl didn't finish whatever she was going to say. She laid a five dollar bill down on the bar, a brandnew five dollar bill. Bill laid the change down, almost absentmindedly, and Mamie wondered if he had deliberately selected that dirty crumpled dollar bill out of all the bills in the cash register, anyway he laid it down with an absentminded air, along with fifty cents.

The girl picked up the bill and put it in her pocketbook, her fingers poking at it, as though she really didn't want to touch it, and left the fifty cents on the bar.

She wanted to say, For Christ's sake, honey, pick it up, don't leave a tip, can't you look at him and tell he's not the kind you tip, he's got all the earmarks of being about to pitch one, pick it up, honey.

Bill picked up the fifty cents, put it in his pocket.

She glanced at the girl again. She looks sick. She looks half out of her mind. And she's pretty, she's pretty as a movie star. I never felt that way, not even about Bill. I don't think I could. He's a good guy and all that but, they all got the same thing between their legs and they're all hellbent on handing it around, one way or another, and there's none of them I've ever seen that I'd go looking for, not even Bill.

She watched the girl's slow progress toward the door. There ought to be something I could say. Well, why don't I say it. I could call her back and tell her it wasn't the way it sounded but did the girl remember me, remember me? Fog. Fog so thick the street lights couldn't cut through it. Dumble Street quiet except for the sound of the foghorn. Crunch's front door open, light from the hall reaching a little way out into the fog, and Crunch pushing this same girl down the steps. Fog outside. Fog. Crunch pushing the girl down the steps, white girl in a mink coat, nothing under it and I laughed because I couldn't help it, laughed because of the look on Crunch's face.

Crunch was standing in the hall, in a nightgown and felt slippers and an old gray bathrobe, hair in braids, white braids, that fell forward as she leaned over to give the girl a final push, saying "Out of my house, get out of my house." And I stood there, laughing, laughing, laughing because Crunch looked the way a person would look if they woke up in the middle of the night and found a tiger in one of the beds, and then Crunch threw some clothes out of the door, and stood there, peering out, looking down at the sidewalk. Then the door slammed and the girl put her shoes on and I stopped laughing because it was cold enough to get pneumonia and the girl was shivering and shaking and I remembered how the girl's face looked there in Crunch's front hall, in the light, and I could tell she'd never been thrown out anywhere, never, not anywhere.

She cleared her throat, "Say, miss—" she began, voice too husky, voice too low in pitch to carry, voice too soft to reach the girl's ears, knowing it, even as she said it, and not raising the pitch, not increasing the volume.

So that the girl kept going straight ahead toward the door, was through the door. I could catch her outside on the sidewalk and tell her that Weak just talks backwards. Girl walking up Dumble Street now, head up, back as straight as Crunch's.

She was hopped up like a cokie, I could tell by her eyes, by the size of the pupils, by the way her mouth was trembling, everything would seem bigger, louder, sounds, smells, the feel of things, everything outsize. Light would hurt her eyes. She probably heard something in my voice that wasn't there, so she's sure I'm gone on Link, and he on me. How do I know that? Tell by looking at her, tell by the way her face crumpled up when Weak was talking about me and Link eating ham sandwiches. She believes Link and I—I ought to go catch her and tell her. Aw, she's white. It's no skin off my back.

"Give me another drink, Bill. And where's that ham sandwich?"

They'll straighten it out, Link and the girl. A rich white girl. She don't need no help. Link musta laid it on her for keeps. I always heard once a white girl got herself a colored feller she wouldn't give him up, got a perpetual heat on for him, followed him around.

"Where's Link, anyway?" she asked.

"Canada. For two weeks."

"In this weather?" Smell of spring in the air, or maybe she just thought so because she wanted some new clothes, but it was cold out and there was plenty of snow still on the ground.

Bill shrugged. "Maybe he'll get cooled off. In a snowbank."

Canada, she thought. He must have had a heat on, too.

Bill said, "Somebody ought to tell that little white bitch to stay away from here. She's been in here five nights straight now."

"I told him," Weak Knees said. He put the sandwich down on the bar. "I said to him if a man's got to have a piece of white tail then he oughtta go live in some other country, some country where they don't give a damn about such things. Get away, Eddie, get away," he made a nudging movement with his elbow.

Old Man John the Barber gave a prefatory grunt, lifted his head, glared toward the door, "Tell her to go do her huntin' in her own part of town, Bill. Tell her to stop stinkin' up the place with perfume. Tell her to stop haulin' her long hot lookin' legs in and outta that car out in front of here. Who's she think she is?"

Mamie listened, thinking, She's got them talking to themselves just like a bunch of old women. Not one of them is listening to the other. I come in here for a quiet drink, nicest part of the day, and I got to run straight into the tailend of somebody else's hurricane and if there is anything I can't stand it's a whole lot of mess about who is sleeping with who as though it made any difference to anybody.

"What's Link doin' in Canada?" she asked. The place has a creepy feel, like being in the house on a night when it rained and you had to stay home, by yourself, for some reason, and the radio wouldn't work, and you sat around listening to the rain as it hit the windows. Creepy.

"Tryin' to break his neck on some damn ski jump," Bill said, still looking out of the window.

"What's he want to do that for?" she asked, just to keep some talk going about something other than that white girl with her face all collapsed, pretty girl, too. And young.

Barber lifted his head again. "He's just one of them young squirts that's got to try out different ways of breakin' his own neck, got to keep tryin' to find out will it break. Tell by lookin' at him and listenin' to him. Tell by all that fancy talk he does. Talks so you don't know what he means because he's still tryin' to find out will his neck break. If he keeps talkin' that stuff to me I'll help him find out what he wants to know, I'll show him that his neck—"

Mamie thought, Let me get the hell out of here before they start fighting with each other. She said, "Did you ever try breakin' yours, Barber?"

"Not since I was sixteen. You only try out different ways of breakin' it when you're young and the hookworm hustle keeps you runnin'."

"You ain't old, Barber," Weak Knees said.

"Nine years older'n God," the old man mumbled and picked up his glass of beer.

It was Weak Knees who started on the white girl again. He said, "Any brokedown whore'll give a man a better time. No complications. I told him that, I said, Name-a-God, Sonny—"

Mamie left, left before she'd buttoned up the brass buttons on the purple coat and had to button it up outside, standing on the sidewalk, wind from the river blowing around her neck, thinking again, She's got them talking to themselves just like a bunch of old women, I wish I hadn't, oh, well.

Crunch was still home. She heard her moving around downtairs, heard her talking to somebody, heard J.C.'s voice, answering her. I'll leave the case in my coat pocket and put it in Link's room some day soon, when she's out.

Old Man John the Barber had said, Who's she think she is? He came nearer to saying the right thing than the other two. I'll fix Powther something special for his supper, and where are those little devils, Shapiro and Kelly. I bet they're sitting in the movie house. Well, they got to do somep'n to pass the time.

When she lit the oven in the kitchen, she started moving with a deftness and speed that could only have come from long practice. Late as it was, by the time Powther and the boys got home, supper would be ready and the table set, just as it would have been if she had been the kind of housewife who planned her meals long in advance and stayed home working in the kitchen all day.

"Oh, Jesus," she said suddenly, "I gone and forgot J.C.'s Kool-Aid." She put on the purple coat, ran down the backstairs, laughing at herself, moving so fast that the long full skirts of the coat whirled about her legs.

HE INSERTED his key in the front door of Number Six Dumble Street, put his bags down in the hall. It was good to be back. Two weeks on a long slope of mountain was enough. After two weeks of snow, gleaming like mica in the sun, shadows of trees bluepurple on the snow, wind, coldhot, like a cat-o'-nine-tails across the face, it was good to be in a house that was warm inside, that smelt of floor wax and lemon oil; good to be where the gleam of a goldheaded cane, shine of a silk hat, hung on a hatrack just inside the door, set the tone, prepared you, for the spitandpolish look of the hall, the big curve of the winding staircase, smallscale repetition of the curve in the legs and backs of a pair of Victorian chairs.

Abbie said, "Who is it?" There was a tremor in her voice. "Who's there? Is there someone there?"

He thought, embarrassed, I came in here like a homing pigeon. I just plain forgot that I don't live here any more—not since that night—

"It's me, Miss Abbie," he said. He went toward the sitting room, thinking, It's all there in her voice, the fear of robbers lurking under the beds, the fear that hordes of Mongolians (though I never knew why Mongolians or why they should always attack in hordes) will appear suddenly at the windows, the expectation of disaster that makes her hide the silver butter dish, and the silver cake basket, the one with the grapes on it, if she's going to be away from home more than an hour or so. It's the thing that makes her check the doors and windows, at least three times, to make certain that they're closed and locked.

Once she lost the front doorkey and sent me hightailing over to Franklin Avenue to get Penfield the carpenter, in the hope that he could jimmy a lock somewhere, so we could get back inside the house. Penfield kept tapping a screwdriver against his overalls, as he walked around the house, trying doors and windows, muttering, "Got it locked up like it was a fort." Then he turned to me and said, "Say are you sure she's married, she's got this place bolted up just like an old maid bolts up a place."

He tried another window, in the back. "Christ," he said, "anybody'd think she kept gold bricks in the cellar. Old maids keep the houses bolted up because they're always scared of rape, even when they're ninety, got it on their minds. But you say she's married. Must be she keeps gold bricks."

She was sitting on the narrow Victorian sofa, in the sitting room. J. C. Powther sat beside her. There was a card table in front of them, books and paper, a bottle of ink, and a pen, on the table. She must have been teaching him something, or trying to. What a game old girl she is, sitting there dressed up like a duchess, in that gray dress, darker gray leaves printed on it, white hair piled on top of her head, head up in the air, and a gold necklace around her neck, and that little street urchin right beside her, and she scared out of her wits but it only showed in her voice, no trace of it in her eyes.

"Link!" she said. "You'll never know how much I missed you." There was still a faint tremor in her voice. "I thought I heard somebody come in, but I wasn't certain. Ever since that night—" her voice slowed, faltered, "that night you left," she said, voice firm now, "I've been hearing a key turn in the lock. I'd wake up and think I heard your key in the lock, think I heard you walking down the hall. I'd get up and look out in the hall. But there was never anyone there. It was just my imagination. It was just that I so desperately wanted you back. I never knew how empty a house could be until you left."

She's more than game, he thought, she's one of the last of the species known as lady. She isn't even going to mention the fact that I absolutely outraged her, violated her moral code, offensively, unforgivably.

"I am most awfully sorry," he said, slowly. "Sorry about all of it. I owe you an apology. I somehow overlooked the fact that you had a point of view, too, and that—"

"I don't want you to apologize," she said quickly. "I was more in the wrong than you, or—" her voice faltered again, "or anyone else."

She still can't mention the girl. Well, that's ended too, so it doesn't matter. He leaned over and kissed her forehead, and thought of Camilo, of the perfume she used, of the silky softness of her hair, of the color of it, and didn't know what it was that had reminded him of her. Not Abbie's hair, silkysoft like

Camilo's, not the clean, fresh smell of the eau de cologne she used. It's the way she sits, with her back so straight, her head up. Camilo sits the same way.

As he straightened up, he saw that J. C. Powther was staring at him. He said, "How are you, pal?"

J.C. blinked his eyes, and kept on staring. He seemed to be studying Link's throat and neck.

"I've been teaching J.C. the alphabet," Abbie said, and patted one of J.C.'s grubby hands.

"Yeah?" Link said, noncommitally, thinking, As round and hard as his head appears to be, I doubt that even you could teach him anything. He could probably teach both of us things we never knew, or heard of, or dreamed existed. What in hell does he see on my neck that makes him keep staring at it?

"Mamie say you was tryin' out new ways to bust up your neck. Did you bust it up?" J.C. asked.

"Not yet, old man." So that was it. "How did Mamie know that I was trying to bust up my neck?"

"Bill told her. Mamie say that white girl keeps lookin' for you over in Bill's place, and she say that if that white girl had good sense she'd stop goin' in there. Bill don't like her comin' in there and he—"

"J.C.!" Abbie said severely. "That's enough. You must not repeat things you've heard. I've told you that time and time again."

"It's my fault, Miss Abbie. He was working his way around to answering a question." Camilo has been looking for me? For what? Maybe she hasn't found Muscle Boy Number Four yet. God help him. And God damn him.

"I didn't finish yet," J.C. said. "So Mamie asked Bill where you was and Bill said you was tryin' out new ways to bust up your neck. Old Man John de Barber said you had to keep tryin' out new ways to see would it really bust or not because you was young. He say if he had to listen to that funny talk you do all the time he'd bust it for you. He say he can stand it days but if you was in Bill's place nights too, he couldn't stand it."

Abbie looked at J.C. and then at Link because Link was laughing. "There are times when I don't understand a word he says. It's just as though he spoke another language. What did he say that was so funny?"

"He was repeating what was said in The Last Chance when Bill Hod told Mamie Powther that I was up in Quebec, trying out a ski jump." Well now, wait a minute, he said to himself, leave us make a fast switch here because sooner or later Abbie is going to mull this over in her mind, and get on a very high horse because Mamie Powther is a patron of Mr. Hod's sink-hole of iniquity.

"Can you make an 'A,' old man?" he asked.

"I ain't no old man," J.C. said waspishly. "I kin make all de letters. But I didn't finish yet. I ain't told you what Weak said."

"Don't, old man, don't," Link said, hastily. "I'll see you later, Miss Abbie. I'm going across the street to see if I can grab a seat in a poker game."

"All right, dear," she said. "Don't stay out too late."

Come the revolution, he thought. We have blown up on our lines, or else the script's been changed. She should have said: Those poker games, that man, you get in so late, alone in the house, hear noises, someone walks through the backyard, knocks over the ashcan, you ought to wear a coat, Dumble Street not safe, people knifed, held up. So that I could say: Know everybody for blocks around, safe in Dumble Street, safe as a church, my end of town.

He changed his exit line. He said, "Do not worry, honey," and patted her firmskinned, clearskinned brown cheek. "I have few fish to fry tonight. Few and small. And they will fry easy."

He heard laughter from outside in the street, girls' laughter, gay, musical, the pitch high enough to reach into the sitting room. Abbie heard it too, because she looked straight at him as though she were asking a question.

She wants to know what became of the girl, only she wouldn't ask a thing like that. I couldn't answer her anyway. I don't know and I wish I could say I don't care. But I do.

After he left the house he stood outside on Abbie's front steps, looking at Dumble Street. He watched a group of girls walking arm in arm, heard a male voice lifted in song, caught a whiff of perfume, of aftershaving lotion. There were lights in all the houses. He saw the shadows of women, moving back and forth against the lighted kitchen windows, in the frame house next door. Thursday night. The tempo of the street was not as fast as on Saturdays, night music of the street, softer, slower, because this was the maid's day off, cook's day off, handyman's day off, so it was a courting night. Almost eight o'clock so all Dumble Street would soon be en route to the movies. Two by two. Go home afterwards. Two by two. Or like L. Williams, one by one.

The Last Chance was giving off muted Thursday night noises, too. The boys lined up at the bar were drinking lightly, companionably. They looked extra clean, extra scrubbed.

Wertham, the night bar man, a big, dark young man, lifted a hand in salute, when he saw Link. "Hi, Jackson," he said.

"Hi, Johnson," Link answered. They used to say Hi, stud, to each other. But not any more. Not since the night Camilo showed up at the bar looking for L. Williams.

"Where's the boss?"

"In the office, Jackson," Wertham said and grinned. "Peace, it's wonderful."

"Great God Almighty! What's he been eating?"

"I dunno. Could be Weak is sprinkling saltpeter on his food. Anyway, he hasn't whipped a head for six whole days. Maybe he's savin' himself for you," Wertham said, hopefully.

"Leave us hope not, Johnson. Mine doesn't whip as easy as it once did." He turned away and looked at Old Man John the Barber. The old man was playing his favorite game, staring out the front window, watching the girls go by. He said, "How are you, John?"

Barber looked at him, glared, looked away.

"Not yet, Barber," he said. "See?" He held his neck up as if for inspection then leaned over and half chanted, half sang, in the old man's ear, "Oh, de muscle bone connected to de shoulder bone; and de shoulder bone connected to de neck bone; and de neck bone *still* connected to de head bone; cryin', didn't it rain, chil-lun, mah Lord, didn't it rain?" Saying it so fast that it sounded like gibberish.

"Ah!" the old man snorted in disgust.

Peace, it's wonderful, he thought, as he looked in Bill's office. I bet if I returned in the year two thousand, he would be sitting with his feet up on that desk, wearing a white shirt, the sleeves rolled up, the collar open at the throat, and his hair would still be black, and he'd have on a pair of brown shoes with a mirror shine on them, and the light from that desk lamp would not be on him but it would still be swiveled around so it would blind whoever comes in through this door.

"How are you, Boss Man?" he said. And moved away from the light.

"Jesus," Bill said. "I thought we'd have to use bloodhounds and a posse."

"Thursday, remember? I said I'd be gone two weeks. It's two weeks, pal. On the nose."

"Yeah. But how was I to know you hadn't broken your neck, Sonny."

"You and J. C. Powther and Barber the bastard," Link said, irritably. "Whyn't you make book on it?"

"Because I don't make book on crazy sons of bitches," he drawled. "If I did, I'd be out of business in twenty-four hours." He crossed his legs so that one shined-up brown shoe was higher than the other, shoe practically covering his face.

Clink of glasses from the bar. Voices. Snatch of song. Thursday night quiet. Peace all broke up in little pieces and strewn around the office floor.

"You hungry?" Bill asked, amicably.

"Yeah. I could eat a horse. Stewed, fried, or picked fresh right off the vine." Peace, again.

"Weak's sitting out a movie. But he's got enough filet mignon stacked up in the icebox to even take care of you. Come on in the kitchen and I'll fix it for you."

After they finished eating, he said, "Boss, you're not in the same class with Weak but you're damn good. I haven't eaten a meal like this for two solid weeks."

"I figured you were making noises like a maneating tiger because you had an empty gut."

"You were about eighty per cent right."

"Sonny—" Bill said, and stopped.

Here we go, he thought. Poppa is about to tell Junior the facts of life as they concern white women and gentlemen of color.

He was wrong. Bill reached in his pocket, took out his wallet, and counted out a fairsized stack of very pretty new bills, and laid them on the kitchen table. He watched him, thinking, I forgot that he lets every man bury his own dead unless the other man's dead happens to get mixed up with some of his dead. But he's always willing to drop something in the hat to help out with the funeral expenses.

"Two weeks' pay. I thought you might be broke."

"Thanks," he said. Gentlemen, all. "It isn't necessary, but thanks, anyway. I'll give you a chance to get it back. How about a game tonight?" They all have cures. Abbie's is a cup of hot tea. Weak's is a cup of hot cawfee. Mr. B. Hod's is cold hard cash. Mine is snow on a mountaintop. Cold, too. Maybe Mr. Hod and I are blood brothers. Some like it hot. Some like it cold. Some like it in the pot. All one-shot prescriptions are alike. They don't work.

"Yeah," Bill said, "can you get hold of Jubie?"

"I'll try to flush him around midnight. At the dock."

"Okay. Let me go break the news to Wertham that what he really wants to do is work until closing time instead of laying that nappyheaded high yaller from midnight on."

He said, "Hold on a minute, Bill. Don't do that." Maid's night off. Courting night. The high yaller would be waiting for Wertham. "Tell him to go on home and come back at midnight. I'll take the bar over until he comes back."

"You feel like it?"

"Sure. I'll go take a shower and change and be downstairs in five or ten minutes."

At midnight he was still behind the bar, talking to Weak Knees. The door opened and Wertham came in. He said, "Hi, Jackson, and thanks."

"Don't mention it, Johnson, the pleasure was all mine," Link said. "Come to think of it though I guess it was all yours."

"It was all mine, Jackson," Wertham said, solemnly.

Weak Knees said, "Sonny, you know—" and then his voice hit high C and died away, almost like a siren, the tailend of the wobble of a siren, because the door had opened again.

Link turned to see who it was and saw Camilo walking straight toward him, smiling. He thought, I'll never get her out of my blood. All I managed to do was just forget how beautiful she is. She still walks as though she owned the world, and come to think of it, she does. That's why she walks like that.

"Link!" she said. "Where've you been?" smiling, holding out her hands, reaching across Bill Hod's bar, long mahogany bar that came out of an old New York hotel, the pale yellow hair looked like silk, same kind of gleam and shine, back straight, head up, either unaware of, or ignoring the silence, the stares. Well, of course, he thought, not moving, pretending that he didn't see her hands, if you're a multonmillionaire and white, you don't give a damn what the black peasants think.

Wertham nudged him. "Here's your coat," he said. "Give me the monkey jacket."

"Okay, stud," he said. When Wertham glared at him, he laughed. "Thanks, pal. I'm going to get you over a barrel someday just like this."

He put the coat on, said, "Come on, honey," to Camilo and held the door of The Last Chance wide open. "Leave us go bay the moon."

They walked toward the dock. Both silent.

She said, "Darling, where've you been? I've been looking for you."

Darling, he thought. I've been sweetie, and you black bastard, but—darling. "Quebec. Washing the gold dust out of my hair. Off my skin." Angry again. Sorry again. In love with her again.

She moved closer to him, and he could smell liquor mixed with the old familiar smell of her perfume. You've been drinking, he thought. You're just this side of a binge, lee side of a binge. And I shouldn't have said that business about gold dust but I still react to you, and I don't like the smell of whiskey, smell of The Moonbeam, smell of The Last Chance, smell of the twobit whores, mixing and blending with the smell of your perfume.

"I'm in love with you," she said, softly. "I'm so in love with you that nothing else matters. You can't even insult me."

"Camilla—" he said.

"Don't say it like that."

"Isn't that your name? Camilla Treadway Sheffield? How should I say it? You tell me. Perhaps I shouldn't say it at all. I really ought to call you Mrs. Sheffield. I ought to say, Mrs. Sheffield, you picked the wrong man. Or did your husband, the captain, pick me out to keep you happy? I've heard of things like that being done—only among the very rich, though."

"Don't—" she said. She tried to light a cigarette, and the wind blew the match out. Tried again, and the match illuminated her face. Her eyes were filled with tears. Blue eyes. The innocence still there, intact, the lovely mouth trembling. After the match went out it was darker on the dock. The sound of the river lapping against the piling was louder, more insistent, in the sudden darkness.

"You can't stop being in love with me," she said, voice shaking, voice blurred, as though her throat were filled with tears too, "any more than I can stop being in love with you. I tried it and it doesn't work."

Her hand was shaking, both hands probably, but the one that held the cigarette was shaking because the lighted end was bobbing up and down like a buoy in the river, a warning signal, bobbing up and down.

"Listen, honey," he said carefully. "You keep forgetting that there are two sides to this. From your point of view it was just good clean fun, and it still is. You were shacked up with a dinge in Harlem, or here in The Narrows. You were rich enough to keep all the exits open, to have your cake and eat it, too. But from my point of view—"

She interrupted him and the blur was gone from her voice, there was sharpness in it and something like anger. "You know it wasn't like that," she said. "Why do you keep harping on my money? What's that got to do with it? Everything was fine until you found out—"

"Yeah. Until I found out I was just one of a collection. Back in the eighteenth century I would have been a silver-collar boy. Did you ever hear about them? The highborn ladies of the court collected monkeys and peacocks and little blackamoors for pets. Slender young dark brown boys done up in silk with turbans wrapped around their heads and silver collars around their necks, and the name of the lady to whom they belonged was engraved on the silver collar. They were supposed to be pets like the peacocks and the monkeys, but in the old oil paintings, the lady's delicate white hand always fondled the silkclad shoulder of the silver-collar boy. So you knew they were something more useful, more serviceable—"

"It wasn't like that," she said angrily.

"Wasn't it? Isn't it?"

"No. And if there weren't something wrong with you, you'd know it. We had something wonderful."

"Yeah. You had a platinum collar and a diamond leash and I

had a neck. But that kind of collar doesn't fit my neck any better than the imitation-leather ones people have tried to buckle around it from time to time."

"You're just making up excuses."

"No, I'm not. I'm trying to show you how this thing looks from where I sit. You think there's something wrong with me because you tagged me for your collection of muscle boys and I stood up on my hind legs and shook the tag off—"

"Collection?" she said. "Collection of muscle boys? What are you talking about?"

"Stevedores. Prizefighters. Big-muscled chauffeurs. The he-men boys with the big muscles that the little millionaire girls lay up with overnight or for a weekend, after they begin to get bored with their husbands but still don't want to divorce them."

"You don't mean that," she said, slowly.

"But I do. You're not in love with me. You think you are because I ran out on you. And it should have been the other way around. So you're kind of frantic. That's all. Apparently I had the right build for the muscle boy role but my mental equipment's all wrong and, curiously enough, I've got the wrong kind of moral equipment, too. You know, even the white muscle boys run out on the little rich girls, eventually. Even with them the gold finally and awfully sticks in their throats."

"Weren't you in love with me?" she asked.

"Sure." And I still am.

"Well—"

"Look," he said. "Much as I loved you, and may still love you, I'm just not built to be anybody's shack job. Yours or anybody else's. No matter how you slice it, honey, that's what I was."

She put her hands on his arms, hands trembling, body trembling. Anger, he thought. No. Frustration? Perhaps. Love? No. Too much whiskey.

"Can't we go somewhere and talk?" she asked.

"There isn't anything to talk about."

He pushed her away, gently, firmly, thinking, We started here much like this, with me pushing you away. Difference in time, and in degree, of course. We have made love to each other, we have lived together, I suppose you could call it living together in that suite in The Hotel that you turned into a replica, smallscale, of course, but a replica of Treadway Hall, where you footed the bills, creating a silken bower for the silver-collar boy. I lay beside you and thought you were like a pink and white figure straight out of one of those Fifth Avenue store windows, thought, looking at you, that even sleeping was something you did completely, totally involved in it, relaxed all over, as though nothing else existed but you and sleep, you surrendered to sleep. Total involvement.

It would have ended anyway, eventually, not this soon, not this way, but even without the Treadway Gun, and the husband, the poor bastard of a husband, it would have ended because with you love is like sleep or dancing or driving a car, everything you do, you do too hard. You dance as though that was all there was in the world, you and me, the only dancers, the music playing for us, you creating an atmosphere of the dance, just the two of us, so that we had all the fluidity of motion, the matched rhythm, seemingly spontaneous, not rehearsed and worked over and sweated over, but the perfection of rhythm of a professional dance team, so that no one could say who led or who followed. Making love to you was almost like that, too.

He frowned, remembering the warm perfumed skin, the rounded softfleshed arms that clasped him, held him, the slender body arching up toward him, the absolute and complete surrender, the abandonment to surrender. It is at the moment the Treadway Gun and the husband, but it would eventually have been a matter of survival, a refusal to be suffocated, owned, swallowed up. He supposed she inherited this trait from her father, John Edward Treadway, the mild little mechanic, softspoken, dreamylooking, who set up shop in an old barn on the outskirts of Monmouth and tinkered and puttered, and puttered and tinkered with guns, until he perfected and patented the Treadway Gun just before the First World War. The story of the Treadway Gun was drilled into the students at Monmouth High School as an outstanding example of a rags-to-riches success story. American success story. The one goal. The total involvement in it.

Camilo had the same trait. Never give up. In spite of ridicule and insult and—

She said, "It's not really the money, is it, Link?"

"What?" he said, voice blank, face blank.

"It's not just the money," she said.

"I suppose you're right," he said, slowly. "It's not just the money."

"I thought so. The money's just an excuse, isn't it? It's that woman."

"Woman?" Abbie? Did she think that Abbie had ever really had any influence over him. He could see her in his mind's eye, sitting on that narrow little sofa, wearing a dress of some sort of printed material, a tracery of gray leaves on a darker gray fabric, the white hair piled on top of her head. There was something indestructible and wonderful about Abbie, impossible to live with, impossible to please, starchy, prideful, full of fears, afraid of thunder and lightning, of sounds in the night, of wind. Deeply religious and yet as superstitious as an Irish peasant. The week before the Major died, a hoot owl sat high up in the branches of The Hangman, for three nights straight, his repeated who-o-o-o-o like a moan in falsetto. Years afterwards she told him that she lay in bed listening to the owl, for two nights, and on the third night she got up and turned her right slipper over, leaving it with the sole turned up, and that she was ashamed of what she'd done and said a prayer, had not finished praying when she reached down and turned the left slipper over too, leaving both of them with the soles turned up, to propitiate the powers of darkness. Acting like a heathen while she prayed like a Christian, because the turned-over slippers were a snare, a trap for the evil spirits evoked by the owl.

"Woman?" he repeated. "What woman?"

"Mamie," she said.

"Mamie?" He threw his head back and laughed.

"I won't stand for it," Camilo said. "You're still in love with me. I know you are. I'll never let her have you—"

He walked away from her, walked slowly, steadily away, and heard her footsteps behind him, heard the lapping of the river, slow, soft, monotonous, against the piling, against the dock. A clear night. Stars hung low, in the night sky. He was suddenly aware of her loneliness, and of his own, and of something else, a feeling of defeat, his, not hers. He still wanted her, but on his terms—not hers. He stopped, under the street light so he could see her face, and he saw despair in it, and in her eyes, in the down droop of her mouth.

"Don't follow me, little one," he said gently. "You get in that pretty red crate and run along home and don't come back. It's all over. Finished. Done with. If I thought it would work I'd say let's start in all over again, clean slate, just as though we'd been reborn. But it wouldn't work. You know it and I know it." I, executioner. Why do it this way? I could say I've just got back, long train ride, need sleep, have to go to work. See you tomorrow or next week or next month or just, see you later. Why this way? I, executioner.

"I'll get even," she said. "I'll hurt you just like you've hurt me."

"You couldn't. It was done a long time ago. By professionals. You're only an amateur." He leaned over and kissed her, lightly, on the forehead. "Honey," he said, and he felt something like regret, "you're drunk. Lay off the stuff. It never solved anything. It doesn't even fuzz up the edges good. I know because I tried it, too." You run along now, run along and play, Link.

It may have been the finality with which he spoke, he didn't know, he never would know, whether it was the actual words or his manner of saying them, but it got through to her. She knew either from the expression on his face or the tone of his voice that it was over, ended.

She slapped him, hard, across the face, an attack so sudden and so unexpected that he didn't move, he stood looking at her, too surprised to move, and she tried to slap him again, aiming for his eyes, and he grabbed her hands, pinioning them by her sides, saying, "Not even from you, little one," and shook her and then pushed her away from him, thinking, Defeat? Are they ever really defeated? Don't all of them when it comes to the end decide to scorch the earth, If I go you will, too, if I go down I will take everything with me. Had Abbie's rejection of him been all due to shock, couldn't part of it have been the subconscious urge to destroy everything, the Major gone, she would go too, and she would destroy the eight-year-old Link, as well.

She screamed, suddenly. He looked at her in astonishment, not believing that that fullbodied sound, born of terror, came from her throat, unrehearsed, that it had always been there, waiting to be called forth, terror, outrage, fury, all there in the throat, emerging when needed. He winced, listening to her, thinking, Now I understand all of them, this Dumble Street sound is in all their throats, the potential is there, and when the need arises they emit this high horrible screaming. When the candles bee out, all cats bee gray.

I know so much about them now, he thought, I believe I could convince Wormsley that I was right. They used to argue about women when they were at Dartmouth, started doing it when they were freshmen, and by the time they reached their junior year they regarded themselves as experts, because of their vast knowledge of biology, therefore they always said the same thing:

Wormsley: Aves. The human female has the nesting instinct of the bird.

L. Williams: Felis. The human female has all the characteristics of the cat. The claw technique is congenital, it's there at birth, perfected, ready to use. The human female is a predatory animal like the cat, because the hunting instinct is congenital too. Treacherous, too. Like the panther, the leopard. She always attacks from the rear, without warning, for the sheer pleasure of it.

Wormsley: Aves. The nesting instinct is the strongest instinct in the female. They build nests, first, last and always. The other, the claws, the chase, the immorality—none of that is important. The female is always immoral. Nature makes her that way to assure the propagation of the species. Man is the moral animal. That's what makes the endless trouble between the male and the female. But above all, the human female builds nests.

L. Williams: Felis. Once the cubs, the kittens, are weaned the catleopardpanthertigerhumanfemale rejects them, tries to destroy them. Felis.

Wormsley: Aves. They build nests. It transcends the cat in them. They built nests in caves, in slave quarters, in covered wagons, on barges, in shanties. They will always be builders of nests.

Camilo screamed and screamed. He heard the thud of feet, on the sidewalk, feet running toward them, coming down Dumble Street. He stood, not moving, watching her open the expensive mink coat, watched her wrench at the front of her dress, give it up, reach inside, wrench at her slip, the lovely delicatelooking hands strong from tennis, golf, badminton, trying to tear the fabric, and the fabric not giving, the fabric used in the clothes made for a multonmillionairess not easy to tear, impossible to tear. The hands gave it up, the hands were now rumpling the pale yellow hair. Hair disordered, disarranged, but the clothes intact.

Felis, he thought. And drunk.

"Hey, what's goin' on here?" It was Rudolph, the cop, the colored cop, and Mickey, the cop, the white cop. Not safe for one cop, all alone, all by himself on Dumble Street after midnight. Two of 'em assigned to this beat. A fat white one and a thin colored one. Rudolph and Mickey. Straight from Mack Sennett, except that both of 'em belonged body and soul to Mr. B. Hod. He wondered what the soul of a cop who belonged to Mr. B. Hod would look like in a photograph. Scrambled like an omelet, no visible design, just scrambled.

"Wassmatter here?" Mickey, the fat, white cop asked.

Camilo was panting. Could pass for fright, he supposed, and not a mixture of spoiled rich girl who lost her mechanical toy, and found John Barleycorn no substitute.

"He—he—" she said, panting, pointing at L. Williams. "He tried—"

Rudolph looked at Link. Mickey looked at Link. "Him?" they said together, staring at Camilo, staring at Link, looking at Link for confirmation or denial, for direction. Tweedledum and Tweedledee. Never around when needed. Always around when not needed, not wanted.

"Arrest him," Camilo said. "I want him—locked—up."

Link still said nothing. Rudolph and Mickey looked confused, embarrassed. Situation impossible. Situation implausible, incredible. How take Mr. B. Hod's boy? How take Mr. B. Hod's right-hand man? How take the junior Mr. Hod to the lockup?

Ah, what the hell, he thought, let's play it all the way out. I, executioner. You, executioner.

He said, "If it will give the white lady any pleasure, boys, and it seems that it would, leave us retire to the Franklin Avenue jailhouse."

He called Bill Hod at three in the morning, and listened to him curse, and held the receiver of the jailhouse telephone away from his ear, far, far away, and said into the mouthpiece, "Okay, Boss. I'm all those things but I'm also in the jailhouse.

Come on down and get me out of here. What?" He laughed. "A white lady says I tried to rape her," and he laughed again. "Oh, they did, finally, and with great reluctance, write it down in the book as attempted attack," he said, and banged the receiver down on the hook, still laughing.

It was four in the morning when he and Bill got back to The Last Chance. Bill followed him to the foot of that long flight of stairs that led from the kitchen to the second floor.

"What happened?" he demanded.

"Just as I told you, pal. A white lady said I tried to rape her." He started up the stairs.

"You dumb son of a bitch," Bill said. "The next time you decide to cat around on the dock, and get caught, don't call me up at three o'clock in the morning to get you out of jail."

"Okay, Poppa," he said, over his shoulder.

He was halfway up the stairs and Bill yelled, "Go take a shower. Quit stinkin' the place up with that white woman's stink—with that jailhouse stink."

He looked down at him, at the white shirt visible under the loose tweed coat, at the black hair, at the young-old face. He thought, This is as good a time as any to find out if I can really knock your teeth down your goddamn throat.

"White woman's stink?" he said softly, and came back down the stairs. "Is Mrs. Powther's any sweeter, friend?"

Bill looked at him with murder in his eyes, on his face, in the thinlipped mouth, and then turned away, went out of the kitchen, toward the bar.

He waited at the foot of the stairs, waited for him to come back with an appropriate weapon, meat axe, or jagged end of bottle, and heard the front door close, and then nothing but silence. Mr. Hod had gone out. He obviously did not intend to come back with knife or gun. Come to think of it, he didn't have to hunt for a gun, he's got one on him. Maybe Wertham was right. Weak's been tampering with Mr. Hod's food.

He sat down on the side of his bed, upstairs, in that big bare-looking bedroom in the back, took off his shoes, held one of them in his hand, thinking suddenly of the Italian shoemaker who used to chalk "Negre" on the soles of his shoes when he took them to be repaired. "Negre" chalked on the old worn leather. He was ten years old then. And he'd go back for the shoes, with reluctance, never mentioning that chalked word to anyone, rubbing it off, once he got outside the shoemaker's shop, hating Abbie for insisting that shoes be resoled when the soles were worn.

Once he took a brandnew pair of shoes to the Italian, to have rubber heels put on them, because Abbie said the rubber heels wore better and when he went to get them, there was the word "Negre" chalked this time on the new yellowbrown soles. He remembered the smell of wax, of shoe polish, remembered the dusty look of the big old machine that the shoemaker used, remembered his bent back, the curve of his back, the lined face, the calloused brown hands, the heavy accent, remembered wondering by what right that bentover man had labeled his shoes, like that, remembered thinking, Even my shoes, separated from the others, clearly marked: shoes of a black.

Not too long after that Mr. B. Hod and Mr. W. Knees started re-educating him on the subject of The Race. Part of the education of L. Williams.

He finished undressing and got in bed, and lay flat on his back, staring up at the ceiling, thinking, Maybe there's something wrong with me. What did she say? "There's something wrong with you." Something wrong with me. Why wouldn't I take her on her terms? Why did it have to be all or nothing? Muscle boy. Shack job. Mechanical toy. Stud. Fine. Keep saying all those words over and over. Keep saying, Everything she does she does too hard. Keep saying, Total involvement, Swallowed up, Suffocated, Strangled. Keep saying, Would have ended anyway, eventually. Say all of it, over and over. Fine.

Yeah, I can keep on saying all those words and yet I will never be able to forget her, will never get her out of my mind. Any more than I ever was able, wholly, to forget China, so too, I will never forget Camilo. I will be haunted by her. The ghost never laid. Not waiting for midnight. Any hour will do. Not haunting any special place. Any place will do.

I will hear the asthmatic wheezing of an old elevator, or catch a glimpse of a young woman with pale yellow hair, or walk too close to Abbie's border some night in August when the night-blooming stock is perfuming the air, or smell a perfume like it, and the ghost will walk again.

The trouble with me is—he thought, and grinned, remembering the summer he hauled ice for Old Trimble. Old Trimble hauled ice in summer, and hauled junk in winter, and summer or winter, growled and grumbled all day long, sucked on a toothpick, all day long. The summer I worked for him he kept saying, "The trouble with boys is they fathers don't break enough sticks over they backsides—" and I kept thinking, The trouble with me is a man who isn't my father tried to kill me. Because that was the summer I was sixteen, the summer I stole F. K. Jackson's gun because I was going to kill King Hod because he caught me in China's place again, and, justifiably, from his point of view, and, justifiably, according to his theory of educating a young male, damn near beat me to death.

All part of the education of one Link Williams. A longdrawn-out affair. Can now include Camilla Treadway Sheffield as part of the process, the finishingoff process. Can now say that I have taken the advanced course in the graduate school.

No one in the USA free-from—free from what? Leave it lie. No one in the USA free (*period period*).

Weak and Mr. Hod? Hardly. Hod hardly. Mr. B. Hod *in loco parentis.* Parents: blank space. *In loco parentis* write Mr. B. Hod. Preliminary course in The Race: under Miss Abbie. I failed that one but got an "A" under Mr. Hod and Mr. W. Knees.

Advanced courses: had had various advanced courses. One of the best under old Bob White, Robert Watson White who taught history in Monmouth High School. He had an absolute passion for history. Passion like a transmitter, always some kind of response to it. Even the dimwits had responded to Bob White.

Even a dimwit would respond to Mrs. Bunny Sheffield.

Bob White had a lowpitched voice, and knew how to use it, and so could make you feel as though you had been there when the Stars and Stripes went up over Fort Sumter, because he read an eyewitness account of it: "And then we gave a queer cry, between a cheer and a yell; nobody started it and nobody led it; I never heard anything like it before or since, but I can hear it now."

I felt as though I had been running and couldn't get my breath back when Bob White read those words, one afternoon, in the history class, last class of the day.

"But I can hear it now." Can hear the voice of the gun heiress now, light voice, sweet voice, musical voice, "Don't ever leave me—don't ever leave me." Time passes. The year turns. And the same voice says, "I want him locked up—"

Write it off as part of the education of Link Williams.

L. Williams took the graduate course on the subject of The Race, under Bob White, not meaning to, not wanting to.

I was fifteen then, a junior in High School, Monmouth High School, and one afternoon Bob White stopped me as I was about to leave the classroom, said, "I want to talk to you, Williams," then said, "Pull up a chair," then said, "I've noticed that you wince, fidget, get upset, every time I mention the subject of slavery." Said it suddenly, bluntly, with no warning.

Then he handed me three large books and one small one, and a notebook. He said, "Once a man knows who he is, knows something of his own history, he can rid himself of selfdoubt, of belittling comparisons. This is a special assignment. You have three months in which to complete it. At the end of that time I shall expect a monograph from you on the subject of slavery in the United States."

I picked up the books and they were heavy as all hell and I walked out of the room, and the sound of his voice followed me. He said, "This assignment should cure you of any further embarrassment on the subject."

I walked along the street, carrying those damn books, swearing that I'd never open them, never return them. Instead of going straight to Abbie's house, I stopped in the kitchen of The Last Chance. Weak was sitting at the kitchen table drinking a cup of coffee. Bill was reading a newspaper and Weak said, "Name-a-God, Sonny, what's in them big books? You'll be gradiated from the high schools and finished from the colleges, before you finish 'em."

I said I'd be through in three months and Bill stared at me and said, "Three months?"

Education of one Link Williams rested at that moment on chance, on fate, on the turn of the wheel. And the wheel turned, because I said, "Sure," boasting, trying to impress Bill with my ability, my superior knowledge.

Bill said, unimpressed, "Want to bet?"

So it was cigarettes against a desk. And the payoff date was marked on the calendar, a big calendar, new one sent out every year by some packing company in Chicago, brilliantly colored picture of a couple of heavyweights mauling each other in the ring, same picture every year, hanging on the wall near the stove. Fifteenth of January marked on the calendar, recorded there as the payoff date.

October to January of the year I was fifteen I read all the time, and went to school, and kept up in all the rest of the stuff, played football, and as the fall turned into winter, played basketball. Can remember reading during the lunch hour, gulping the food down, book propped up on the table against the water glass, and Abbie staring at me, frowning at me, finally asked what I was reading and why I was reading at the table.

When I explained that I was making a rather specialized, but very brief, study of slavery and the Civil War, she looked even more disapproving. Her frowning disapproval spurred me on. It was a race against time but I told myself I'd win it. There wasn't literally, wasn't enough time to win in, but I'd win anyway.

And I did. I handed the finished paper to Bob White on the morning of the fifteenth of January. And said, "Could you read this sometime today, Mr. White? And give me a letter or just a note, that I can show to a friend of mine, so he'll know I read these books in three months' time. We had a sort of bet about it."

He still had the letter somewhere, knew some of its phrases by heart because it was the first time anyone, other than Weak, had ever praised him, wholeheartedly, no reservations, no if's: "a flair for history," "What amounts to genius," "you write with eloquence and yet simply and clearly," "heartiest congratulations," and then, "finest monograph ever written by one of my students during the ten years I have taught history in this high school."

All part of the education of Link Williams.

When he returned those books to Bob White, he had felt self-conscious, awkward.

Bob White said, "Did you win your bet?"

"Yes, sir."

"I'm curious. What did you win or rather what were the stakes?"

"A carton of cigarettes against a desk." Bob White had looked blank and he said, "If I'd lost, I would have bought my friend a carton of cigarettes. He smokes Camels." Unnecessary piece of information, and it sounded as though Bill was a chain smoker and he wasn't, and it wasn't what he wanted to say, but he didn't quite know how to put it, and then blurted it out. "I didn't intend to read those books, Mr. White. But my friend was so—well, he said I couldn't do it, not in that length of time. A couple of times I didn't think I'd make it. But I did. And then you wrote the letter and now I've got a desk—a real desk."

And still had it. The same desk. It was that good. He had thought about it, while he was standing there talking to Bob White. The drawers worked like they were oiled, and the top was covered with dark red leather, handtooled along the edge, and the smell of it was wonderful, a clean, new, leathery smell, like new shoes, and he ran his fingers over the surface every time he went near it, sheer pleasure in the feel of it, smoothsoft.

Bob White had said, "A desk," thoughtfully. "I thought you were going to say a tennis racket or a set of golf clubs. But you're too young for golf. A desk. I see."

"Are you going to college?"

"I want to."

"I went to Dartmouth. It's one of the best. Not too big. Not too small. Superior faculty."

"Is it expensive?"

"All of them are," Bob White had said. "But there are scholarships. What do you plan to do after you finish college?"

"I don't know, sir. I'm pretty good at chemistry."

Bob White pushed three more big books toward him. "Don't hurry with these. Take your time."

That winter he lost interest in chemistry. He stopped carrying out the experiments that had made Abbie turn up her nose and say, "Those horrible smells. I don't think it's safe. Anything that smells like that couldn't possibly be safe."

Further education of Link Williams completed by Miss Abbie. King Hod and Miss Abbie. What a combination. Have to include Weak Knees and F. K. Jackson. And Bob White. And an heiress.

Go back to Miss Abbie's final part in the education of L. Williams.

Dust settled on the test tubes and the Bunsen burners and the beakers and the little bottles of acid and alkali, on the packages of chemicals and the filter papers. Abbie complained because he didn't go near the small laboratory he'd set up in the cellar.

"All that expensive equipment," she said. "Don't you use it any more?"

"I haven't had time lately." An evasion. He didn't want to tell her that he was no longer interested in chemistry, that he spent every penny for history books.

"Why not?"

"I've been reading history books."

"They don't have anything to do with medicine."

"I'm going to be a historian."

She was startled into silence. Then she said, "I thought you were going to be a doctor."

"I changed my mind."

"Oh, Link! One minute you're going to be a doctor, and you litter up the house with bandages and splints and borrow books from Dr. Easter and don't return them—"

That was when he was fourteen.

"Then you're going to be a cook, and you waste flour and sugar and butter and eggs and burn things up—"

That was when he was eleven. He had burned things up, sure, but he was a better cook than Abbie would ever be.

"Then you're going to be a chemist and for weeks the house is filled with the most horrible smells and I don't know how much money you spent for all those little tubes and bottles and packages and now it's history—"

Everywhere she looked, in his room, there was evidence of the change in the direction of his thoughts, his desires; the notebooks, the growing line of books on the bookshelves, indicated it clearly. History books. He'd been buying them brandnew until Bob White found out, and gave him the address of a place in New York where he could get them secondhand for one-third the price of new ones. The shelves were filling up faster and faster. Abbie didn't like the room anyway, never would like it. It was an offensive comment on her taste in decoration, and it was due to Bill Hod's interference, because the room had to be done over to get the desk in. She always looked around with an air of disdain. The black walnut bedroom set had been discarded and the Brussels carpet taken up, and this barelooking room was the result, all bookcases and desk and peculiarlooking bed with no headboard or footboard.

He didn't listen to what she said because he'd heard her preach this sermon before. He caught a familiar phrase here and there: "inability to stick to anything," "Negroes are incapable of concentrating on a long-term objective," "constantly changing jobs, changing moods."

Then her voice went up in pitch, grew louder, caught and held his attention. She said, "Whoever heard of a colored historian?" Head up. Eyes flashing with anger.

He was bewildered and hurt in a funny kind of way. He had looked at her thinking, Why should you who are colored try to destroy me, discourage me, and why should the history teacher who is white, encourage me, keep telling me I can do this thing? Why do you want to hurt me? How can you say that and then turn around and quote your father, "The black man can do anything if he sets out to do it, if he's willing to work at it, night and day, can do anything, can do anything."

All right, he thought, I will do the impossible. I will be the impossible. Because of you. I wasn't certain I could, I had doubts about it, but not any more. It's like those books Bob White handed to me, that I never intended to read, and if it hadn't been for Bill's amused, I-knew-it-all-the-time, gambler-betting-on-a-sure-thing, fifteenth-of-January-ha-ha-ha attitude, I would never have read them, never have written the paper.

When he went to Dartmouth, he majored in history. He thoroughly enjoyed the closed off, artificial, kindly, paternal world that composed that particular college. His faculty advisor approved his choice of a career, praised his ability, took it for granted that he would be what he wanted to be.

After four years of Dartmouth he ended up with a Phi Beta Kappa key, the Major's diamond stickpin and the Major's solid gold watch, and a brandnew Cadillac, special job, that had never belonged to anyone else. "Mark of esteem, Sonny, I didn't think you'd make it."

In less than two months after he graduated, he was in the Navy. After four years in the Navy, Abbie no longer loomed on his horizon like a dreadnaught. Didn't loom at all. When he was discharged, he headed for The Last Chance.

Weak Knees said, "Boss, Boss, Boss, come quick. Sonny's back. Sonny's home," and his eyes were filled with tears.

"Jesus Christ," Bill said. "What'd they feed you? You look like Louis the night he knocked out Carnera," and patted his shoulder, grinning at him.

Not too long afterwards he told Bill that he wanted a job.

"Yeah?"

"Here. Days. Behind the bar."

"Why here?"

"Because like everybody else, I have to earn a living but I don't want to have my mind all cluttered up with somebody else's business when I sign off for the day."

He didn't tell Abbie that he was working on a history of slavery in the United States, and therefore found it convenient to work for Bill Hod because the pay was good, and the hours were short, and that nowhere else would he have so much leisure in which to do the necessary research for the books he wanted to write. He simply said that he had taken a job as day man behind the bar in The Last Chance.

Abbie went off just like a firecracker. He had grinned at her, enjoying the expression of outrage on her face, the crackle in her voice.

"A bartender? What did you go to college for? It was a waste of time and money. A bartender—in that place?"

Off and on ever since.

Everything was fine until that night the fog spewed a girl with pale blond hair smack into the middle of his life. Even now I'm not sure that I was right. Maybe she was in love with me. Maybe I know too much about the various hells the white folks have been cooking up for the colored folks, ever since that Dutch man of warre landed at Jamestown in 1619 and sold twenty "Negras" to the inhabitants, just as though they were cows or horses or goats, to be able to accept a gift horse, even if it was a palomino, without a microscopic examination of the teeth.

Blame it all on China, with her tremendous buttocks, and big breasts, the layers of fat under the smooth yellow skin of the arms and throat, and the skin on the face not the same, swarthy, coarse-pored, and the hair not gray but brown and probably would be until she died. She couldn't say, Run along, kid, or you'll get in trouble. Not even that second time when I went back anyway. It took me about six months to figure out that she called Bill up both times and told him I was there. She couldn't say, Kid, Bill owns a whole string of whorehouses and this is one of them, couldn't say, Bill owns a whole string of whores and I am one of them, so you run along. No. She said, Wait right here, and went and called up Bill and then stood in the doorway and pushed that dark green curtain aside when she heard him come in so she could have a front row seat from which to view the kind of trouble I was in.

Come spring and the time of the singing of the birds, and the Treadway Gun and the black barkeep will be united in the bonds of holy matrimony. I believed that one, too.

You wait here in the hallway.

You black bastard.

I should have laid one on her jaw—for luck.

19

MALCOLM POWTHER laid a copy of the *Monmouth Chronicle* down flat on one of the long wide counters, under the cupboards in the butler's pantry, placing it there as carefully as if it had been an old illuminated manuscript. Putting on a pair of hornrimmed spectacles, he leaned over the paper, one elbow resting on the counter, and using his forefinger as a guide, went down one column and up the next, in a rapid scanning of the front page.

His posture, the hornrimmed glasses, the quick co-ordinated movement of finger and eyes gave him the appearance of a middle-aged accountant who was rapidly reviewing the financial report of a bank. His clothing would have been suitable for such a role, too: the sharply creased trousers, starched white shirt, carefully knotted black necktie, highly polished black shoes suggested conservatism, neatness. Even though he was alone in the pantry, he was wearing a coat.

When he finished with the front page, he straightened up for a moment, thinking that the news didn't vary much from day to day, from year to year. There was a stalemate in the war in Korea. The Democrats were peevishly blaming the Republicans for the state the country was in; and the Republicans were peevishly blaming the Democrats for the same thing. As far as he was concerned, this was just another case of the pot calling the kettle black; but political parties preferred to hurl the words venal and stupid at each other. Another airliner had crashed in the Midwest, in a mountainous area, which was only to be expected. After all, it was March and high winds and big snowstorms made flying hazardous. And that bony lady manufacturer whom the Madam had entertained at a dinner party last fall, the night Captain Sheffield made a scene at the table, was still waging her private war with the Treasury Department. He doubted that he'd ever get the details of it straight in his mind, but a story about her was always featured somewhere in the *Chronicle*.

He turned the page, slowly, carefully, because this was the Madam's copy of the paper, and he prided himself on the delicacy with which he handled it, intending to go up and down the columns again, just as he had on the front page. But a story far over to the right on page two seemed to come at him, leap at him, so that he began reading it at once, not reading, absorbing it, frowning, not believing it.

He read the story again, his mouth slightly open, the frown deepening between his eyebrows. A mistake, he decided. A stupid mistake. The newspaper had transferred Miss Camilo's name and her New York address, from some other story, so that it appeared here in this short item where it did not belong. Mistakes like this happened so often in newspaper offices that he was convinced they were due to malice rather than carelessness.

Having finished with the first section of the paper, he refolded the whole thing. The second section wasn't worth bothering with. There was never anything in it but sports news and inch-high stories about Ladies' Aid meetings and church suppers, accounts of weddings and funerals that had taken place in the little towns all over the state.

He placed the *Chronicle* on top of the *New York Times* on the Madam's breakfast tray. When the Madam got through with the newspapers they would be carefully folded, the pages all in order, as they were now, but after Rita, the Madam's personal maid, read them, they would look as though they had just blown in from the city dump, crumpled, the pages mixed up.

How could he most effectively annoy Rita on this gray, windy morning? She couldn't keep the resentment out of her eyes, her face, when she saw the Madam's breakfast tray. He enjoyed varying the china, the silverware that he used. Yesterday had been warm, so he'd used the Lowestoft because it had a cool, fresh look. But this cold morning called for warmth. He decided that the English bone china with the rose-colored decorations would offer a cheerful contrast to the weather. And there were just two white roses in the icebox, and he'd put them in a small crystal and silver vase, and he'd use some of that thin finely woven Belgian linen, not white but cream-colored, the napkin and place mat embroidered in white. A combination that should make Rita's nose go straight up in the air, as though she'd received a personal affront.

What a pity that Miss Camilo's name should have appeared in the paper like that, he thought, as he plugged the percolator in. She had been staying at the Hall for the last two weeks, dining with the Madam every night. He didn't think she was very well. She was too quiet, almost depressed, and drinking more than any young lady should. Just recently he had noticed that when she wasn't smoking a cigarette, or holding a glass of liquor, her hands were clenched tight, the fingers enfolding, covering the thumbs. It had startled him when he noticed how her thumbs were enclosed by the fingers, because that was a sign of a depression deep enough to be interpreted as a death wish in a grownup. When he saw the telltale position of the thumbs, he decided that her lover had left her, though he could not imagine how or why it could have happened.

Picking up the *Chronicle* again, he laid it flat on the counter, turned to page two, and reread the story. The Captain was in New York, so he wouldn't see it. The Madam wouldn't necessarily see it, and even if she did, she would recognize it for what it was—a mistake in the name and address.

It was a queer story. Link Williams, twenty-six-year-old Negro of Number Six Dumble Street, had been accused of attempted attack by a Mrs. William R. Sheffield of Park Avenue, New York City. Incident occurred at the corner of Dock and Dumble Street, about midnight. Names of the arresting officers. Link Williams out on bail. That predatory young nephew of Mrs. Crunch's must have been drunk or temporarily out of his senses, to attack a woman, almost on his own doorstep.

Sometimes he and Mamie tried to figure out, just from a short item like this, what had really happened, just for the fun of it. That is, when life was normal and she wasn't on a diet, and the house was a comfortable, warm place to be in, and she was laughing and singing and telling jokes. Though he basked in this after-supper warmth and gaiety, he was uneasily aware that Bill Hod's visits had a direct connection with Mamie's obvious sense of well-being, but not dwelling on it because it was better not to. She didn't do much reading but she liked a magazine called *True Crime*, and she was quite clever about figuring out ways in which a crime might have been committed. She was always saying that the way a detective solves a crime is to make himself think like somebody else, put himself in somebody else's shoes. She knew a lot about it because she was always going to movies that had to do with murder and detectives. She couldn't stand the ones that had to do with love.

He'd try to figure this story out by pretending that he was an average reader of the *Chronicle*, say a bank clerk, riding to work on the Franklin Avenue trolley. Bank clerks were about the only ones who rode on trolleys. What would he make of it?

I'd read it again because I would be puzzled by it, intrigued. How did this woman who lived on Park Avenue, in New York, richest street in the world, most expensive place to live, come to be walking about on Dock Street, at midnight? Park Avenue meant wealth, penthouses, liveried servants, elegance. Dock Street at the corner of Dumble meant poverty, colored people, tenements, whether you called it Dark Town, Little Harlem, The Narrows, or The Bottom.

Perhaps she was driving through Monmouth, en route to New York, stopped to ask for directions, and this young Negro immediately attacked her. But how could he attack a woman sitting in a car, engine running, he standing on sidewalk, woman leaning out of car, window down, "Could you tell me—"

Undoubtedly the woman got out of the car. It's a lonely street, Dock Street, at midnight. It was the kind of street you stumble into in a dream, a street that runs parallel to a river, and you're always falling when you reach a street like that in your dreams, you know there's a river nearby though you can neither see it nor hear it, and you keep falling, falling, falling, toward the river. The lights are so few and far between that they can't penetrate the darkness, they only serve to make the street longer and darker than the inside of a nightmare, and there's never any traffic, nobody walking by.

So this woman, this stranger from Park Avenue, got out of her car and asked directions of the first passer-by, who happened to be Mrs. Crunch's unscrupulous young nephew, and he immediately attacked her.

Nonsense, he thought. Besides I've accepted the Park Avenue part of this story as being correct. But so would a bank clerk. He would not know that Mrs. William R. Sheffield's name and address appeared erroneously in the story; nor would he know that Camilla Treadway Sheffield and Mrs. William R. Sheffield were the same person.

Having replaced the *Chronicle* on the Madam's tray, he unplugged the percolator and busied himself making toast, squeezing oranges. He couldn't waste any more time puzzling over this conundrum. This was one of his busiest days. They were having a tea, a high tea, in the afternoon, for three hundred young women from the plant.

It would have been understandable if the Madam had said, They're just little working girls, anything will do, just the fact that they're asked out here for tea is enough, no need to fuss, give them some little sandwiches and small cakes and that will do very well. But she didn't. That first year he worked for her, she had told him that this annual tea was to be handled with as much care as though they were having the President of the United States in for tea, well, any of the presidents before Roosevelt.

Under his direction it had become more than tea, it was a kind of open house, which called for the best silver and china and the finest napkins, oak logs burning in the fireplaces, two waiters from the Monmouth Hotel to help keep the service smooth, and honest-to-goodness food: sandwiches with wonderfully flavored fillings—chicken, anchovy, cheese, lettuce, pâté; toasted muffins accompanied by slivers of Virginia ham; bitesize cakes as well as loaves of cake, candies, mints, salted nuts—all of this set out in the dining room.

At seven-thirty when Rita came into the butler's pantry, he was rubbing up the trays that he was going to use that afternoon.

"Good morning, Mr. Powther," she said, yawning, patting her hair, giving the small pleated apron she wore a kind of jerk, as though she'd like to take it off.

"Good morning, Rita." She looked sleepy and so her clothing didn't sit properly on her. The white dress was clean, unrumpled, but because she was sagging with sleep the uniform sagged too. Lately she'd been having an affair with Al of which Powther disapproved. She didn't keep her mind on her work any more. Right now she was leaning over the sink, staring out of the long window, in hope she'd catch a glimpse of Al as he came toward the house for breakfast.

He started to say something to her about the unfortunate mixup in names in the paper, but didn't. She was much too fond of gossip, especially if it concerned the family. She was about twenty-five pounds heavier than the Madam, and so couldn't wear her clothes, always a source of irritation to a personal maid. As a result, she constantly disparaged the Madam. Al did the same thing but he went in for an all-inclusive large-scale vulgarity, that not only included the Madam, but the house, the other servants, the garage, the cars, everything. Rita went in for a highly personal, smallscale cattiness directed exclusively at the Madam.

"She's in her bath," she said, turning away from the window. She opened her eyes very wide, as she always did whenever she was about to say something unkind. She had large brown eyes, and the sudden widening of them underlined, pointed up whatever she said.

"She can get in and out of a bathtub faster than anybody I've ever seen. I don't think she's clean. In one minute and out the next—"

"You'd better run along then," he said coldly. "Or the coffee will be cold."

She picked up the tray, and he held the door open for her. He was quite near her when she looked down at the tray, really looked at it, and he saw sullenness, resentment come into her face, changing it, as though a mask had been placed over it.

"Roses," she said, a sneer in her voice. "White roses! I suppose she'll be wanting them pinned on that mink coat when she leaves for the plant."

"They should look very well on it," he retorted, thinking, You'll feel more spiteful than ever when you get your first look at the downstairs part of the house this afternoon. Rita was pressed into service, taking care of coats, under Mrs. Cameron's direction, and he always judged the degree of perfection he had achieved by the quick resentment that came into Rita's face when she looked around.

By eleven o'clock he felt that the entire downstairs had the burnished look of a house ready for a high tea. Rita would not know that a week's work had gone into the making of the gleam and shine that included windows, the fine wood of the furniture, the floors. Rogers had sent his men over with oak logs for the fireplaces, had personally delivered daffodils and tulips from the greenhouse, and had included some of the poets' narcissi because of their wonderful fragrance.

He had persuaded Rogers' men to help Jenkins move a pair of sofas and ten Sheraton armchairs from the morning room upstairs down into the entrance hall, in order to increase the amount of sitting space. The east drawing room was as big a room as he'd ever seen but three hundred people could not possibly find seats in it. There was always a moment, about five o'clock, when all three hundred young women were drinking tea at one and the same time, no matter at what hour they had arrived.

After he finished arranging the flowers, he went toward the kitchen for a second cup of coffee. He would have to drink it quickly because he still had a lot of details to work out with Jenkins, but he hated to miss the midmorning coffee that the Frenchman made especially for him and for Al.

It never failed to amuse him to watch the transformation that took place in Al when Mrs. Cameron came into the kitchen. Al would be lounging in the doorway, coffee cup in hand, chauffeur's cap on the back of his head, and at the sight of Mrs. Cameron, he snatched his cap off and stood up straight. Like any firstclass housekeeper, she could be very sharp on the subject of what she called disrespectful behavior, and could, by a skilful choice of words, make Al take on the appearance of an overgrown schoolboy being sharply reprimanded by the teacher, face red, head hung down.

He pushed open the swinging door between the butler's pantry and the kitchen, and then stood still, shocked into stillness. He was totally unprepared for what Al was saying. It had never occurred to him when he was pretending that he was an average reader of the *Chronicle* that there was still another angle, another way in which people would react to that story about Link Williams.

Al was saying, "You don't believe me, huh? Well, then, what was she doin' on the dock in Niggertown, at three o'clock in the mornin'? Just like she was askin' to be raped by a nigger— -" He saw Powther standing half in, half out of the kitchen and he stopped talking.

Powther sipped the scalding hot coffee, wishing that it was

cold so that he could drink it fast, and leave the kitchen. He tried to pretend he hadn't heard what Al said, pretended not to see how red Al's face was, or the way his pale blue eyes were blinking. I always forget about race, he thought. I forget that other people think about it. I didn't think of Link Williams the way a white man would think of him. I thought of him as another man, that was all. To hear him spoken of like that hurts me.

He had never given any thought to the way the *Chronicle* identified Negroes. He had never reacted to it, one way or another. Now his reaction was a purely personal indignation, not even indignation, a kind of fretfulness. If they had just put Link Williams' name in the paper without saying he was colored, he, Powther, would not be in this awkward situation, sitting across the table from the Frenchman, who would not look at him, pretending not to see that Al's pale blue eyes were still blinking, that his big face was redder than ever, that he had pushed his cap so far back on his head that the short cropped blond hair was visible, and that the position of the cap emphasized the roundness of his skull.

Silence in the kitchen. He thought, We're all embarrassed. The Frenchman keeps stirring his coffee, the spoon clinking against the cup, stirring it though he doesn't put sugar or cream in it, and I keep sipping mine though it's so hot it burns my lips. Al keeps pushing that cap farther and farther back on his head, and it will soon fall with a soft plop on this brick floor. The Skullery keeps peeling potatoes at the kitchen sink. He must have his face almost in the sink, he was holding his head so far down, revealing his embarrassment by presenting a view of the seat of his bluejeans to them.

The Frenchman said, "Watch it there, blockhead. Watch the peels. Watch the peels."

"Yes, sir. I am, sir," the Skullery said meekly.

Powther thought his face must now be resting on the stopper, his head was so far down in the sink, the rear of the bluejeans so far up.

"You are not. Scrape. I said, scrape. Not peel."

The Frenchman was trying to fill the kitchen with talk again. By himself.

"Coffee's good, Frenchie," Al said.

Al was trying to help out, too.

Then Mrs. Cameron came in the kitchen and Al straightened up, and took his cap off, fast, as though at the unexpected approach of a five-star general.

Well, she should have been a general, Powther thought, watching her, and if she had been a man she would have been. In many ways she reminded him of Mrs. Crunch. They were both short, they had the same erect carriage, and they wore their hair in the same fashion, piled on top of their heads. Mrs. Cameron had a small neat figure, not that Mrs. Crunch's figure wasn't neat, but it was a little more ample than Mrs. Cameron's, and Mrs. Cameron was pink-cheeked, whereas Mrs. Crunch's skin was brown, skin on the face alike though in the firmness of the flesh, and the lack of wrinkles. They both had the same uncompromising manner.

She said, "Good morning. Have you seen the paper?" Brisk, don't beat about the bush, bring a thing right out in the open, don't whisper about it, talk about it, clear it up, straighten it out, all there in those few words.

She kept walking up and down, looking first at Al, then at the Frenchman, then at Powther. She was wearing a long-sleeved gray dress, and he decided it was cotton and stiffly starched, because the skirt rustled as she walked. Her expression was so severe and her lips were compressed in such a thin tight line that if she'd had a birch rod in one hand and a book in the other, she would have looked exactly like a caricature of a schoolteacher.

"Well?" she demanded.

The Frenchman said, "Yes."

"I thought we'd talk about it now. The four of us. And work out a point of view, so that when the others—"

The Frenchman held up his hand. "Wait," he said. "Empty the garbage cans, blockhead." As soon as the Skullery left the kitchen, he said, "Now—"

"What is there to discuss, or work out a point of view about, Mrs. Cameron?" Powther asked. "Obviously the *Chronicle* made a mistake. There's a mixup in names. They transferred Miss Camilo's name from some other story. It's an easy thing to do in a newspaper office. A line of type is picked up and transferred—"

"I thought about that too, Mr. Powther. But there isn't any story in the paper about the family, or about Miss Camilo, from which a line of type could have been transferred to this story. That theory just doesn't fit. I wish it did," she said.

"Then—" he faltered. It's true. But how could it be? What would Miss Camilo be doing in The Narrows at that time of night? Much as he disliked and distrusted Link Williams, he couldn't quite picture him attacking a woman, a stranger. Especially a woman as beautiful and as obviously aristocratic as Miss Camilo. He must have been terribly drunk.

Al said, "She's been runnin' with him for months. Ever since December—"

"That's enough of that, Albert," Mrs. Cameron said. Her cheeks were no longer pink, they were red. "There will be no loose talk about Miss Camilo in this house. If I hear of any, I shall take immediate steps to put an end to it—permanently. I will not allow any malicious gossip about her or any other member of the family."

Powther left the kitchen first, understandable because of the tea that afternoon, and he had so many things to do, and so little time in which to do them. He saw Mrs. Cameron go through the hall shortly afterwards, skirts rustling, head up in the air, the severe expression still on her face. He went into the butler's pantry, pushed the swinging door open about half an inch, holding it like that because he wanted to hear what Al and the Frenchman were saying. He had never listened outside a door in a household where he worked, but he had to find out what Al had been going to say when Mrs. Cameron interrupted him. *Who* had been Miss Camilo's lover ever since December?

The Frenchman was talking. He was always excited, always outraged, screaming and swearing half in English, half in French, a prima donna of a cook. He didn't sound a bit excited now. He sounded cold, matter of fact, and perfectly horrible.

The Frenchman: She's a whore. A whore ought to work in a whorehouse.

Al: Bunny oughtta take her out in the garage and strip her down and beat her every morning.

Powther thought, Why are they saying these things? There is nothing in the newspaper to make them talk like this. Then

he remembered Al, sitting behind the steering wheel of the
town car, studying Dumble Street, looking down the length
of Dumble Street, "It would be just about here—what's down
there—followed her—lost her right here in this street—she
come up that driveway like a bat outta hell—somebody oughtta
tell her, Mal—smash that crate up—if I was the Captain—she
looks like an angel—"

So Al has told the Frenchman about Miss Camilo staying out
late at night, staying somewhere in Monmouth, he thought.
Then too they both know, just as I do, that she stays away from
the Captain as much as six months at a time, and has ever since
that first year they were married. Six months or a year in Paris
or London or Quebec or Chicago, and the Captain always in
New York. Naturally they believe that so young and beautiful
a woman must long since have found a lover whom she preferred to her husband.

Al: Everybody in Monmouth's goin' to be askin' what was
she doin' on the dock in Niggertown, three in the mornin', just
askin' for that nigger to rape her.

The Frenchman: She's a whore.

He let the door swing shut, tight shut. He supposed it
would never be called attempted attack, though that was the
charge. There would always be the suggestion of rape. People
would say three o'clock in the morning, when it was midnight.
On the dock, when it was not the dock itself but Dock Street,
corner of Dumble. It said so in the paper. But when the people
in Monmouth told the story, they would always make it sound
as though Miss Camilo was held down, flat on her back, on
the dock, held down by a Negro, but they would say "nigger."
Miss Camilo held down by a nigger.

It made him feel sick inside. That was another thing he forgot when he read the paper, pretending he was a bank clerk
trying to figure that story out. He forgot that the staff at the
Hall would know instantly that Mrs. William R. Sheffield of
such and such an address in New York was Camilla Treadway Sheffield. But other people wouldn't know it. The newspaper didn't know it either. There was no reason why they
should. People in Monmouth didn't know the Captain or
Miss Camilo. They knew the Madam but not Miss Camilo.
But they would. All Monmouth would know it eventually. You

couldn't keep a thing like that quiet. The story would spread slowly, slowly, just like ink on a blotter. Mrs. Sheffield is the Treadway girl. Scandal. Story enlarged upon, embroidered, even to the nighttime trips, until Miss Camilo would sound like a common streetwalker, subject to attack, one of the weak ones to be preyed upon.

There wasn't anything that Mrs. Cameron could do to stop the progress of this scandalous story. He could tell by the way the staff avoided all mention of it at lunch in the servants' dining room, that the whole thing had been thoroughly discussed. Al had undoubtedly told every one of them about Miss Camilo coming up the driveway like a bat outta hell, had used the word nigger as though it were his own personal invention, over and over again. Mrs. Cameron, sitting at the head of the table, looked more severe than ever, and Rita, who sat midway, had a sly kind of smile that kept coming and going about her mouth. Al talked pointedly and constantly about cars, and the weather, and how he had spent the morning tuning up the old Rolls-Royce.

Powther contributed nothing to the conversation. He made himself think of something else. The Frenchman was a prima donna of a cook, not a cook, a chef—not a chef, an artist. Better than Old Copper's Angelo, the Italian, because his flavoring was more subtle, and at the same time more unexpected. If Old Copper had ever had the chance to taste the Frenchman's food, he would have kidnaped him. Old Copper always took what he wanted.

The cook at The Last Chance was even better than the Frenchman, his skills seemed to range over a wider area, included a greater variety of foods. He remembered the doughnuts, crisp outside, tender inside, flavor spicy, and not sweet. The wonderful texture had stuck in the roof of his mouth, in his throat, like glue, as he looked at Bill Hod, looked at him once, and not again, but dreadfully aware of him, and afraid of him.

He had never been able to forget that moment when he saw Hod sitting at the kitchen table, across from Mamie, not laughing or talking or caressing her, not eying her, just sitting there in his shirt sleeves, drinking a glass of milk. He had tried to drink a cup of coffee and had put the cup down because his hands had begun to shake, because of that man in a white shirt, sleeves rolled up, shirt open at the neck, not looking at him, but aware of the predatory tomcat look of him, back alleys and caterwauling fights, claw your way up and out, use tooth and nail, knife and gun, written all over his face. Like Old Copper. You looked at Old Copper's face, his eyes, his mouth, the lines about the mouth, and you knew that anything you could imagine about his past would not be as evil or as cruel as it must really have been to write the story on his face like that.

Yet he had liked Old Copper and Old Copper had liked him. That is, before he married Mamie, before Old Copper stared at Mamie. Then he had hated him, been afraid of him. He knew now that he had liked the old man only because he had never before had anything that Old Copper wanted, anything that Old Copper might take away from him.

Perhaps if it hadn't been for Mamie, he, Powther, and the idea startled him, perhaps he and Hod might have been friends. He and Al were friends, incredible as it seemed. Under different circumstances, just possibly, he and Bill Hod might have been friends—could you be friends with a man like that?

Al said, "You put two and two together and it always makes four."

"What do you mean by that, Albert?" Mrs. Cameron asked.

"I mean I got to go to work on Miss Camilo's Caddy. It sure has took a beating these last few months."

Powther watched Al get up from the table. "Put two and two together . . ." Al's voice matched his size, his appearance, his personality. It was a big voice, slightly hoarse, because he smoked cigarettes all day long; an insistent voice, you could tell by the sound of it that once he got an idea in his head, it would be impossible to get it out. "It would be about here . . . I measured the gas . . . what's down there?"

The River Wye was down there, in the direction that Al had been looking. So was the dock. So was Number Six Dumble Street. Oh, no, he thought. Impossible.

Why impossible? Put two and two together. After Al mentioned the nighttime trips he, Powther, had decided that Miss Camilo was in love, she seemed to have come suddenly alive, her face was animated, she was always laughing, her flesh had a kind of gleam. If Al was telling the truth about those trips, then her lover lived in Monmouth. Al had seen her car in Dumble Street. Sometime during the last two weeks, the love affair had ended. Miss Camilo was unhappy about it. She was too quiet, drinking too much. According to that senseless story in the *Chronicle*, she had accused Link Williams of attempted attack. "She's been runnin' with him for months now." Add all of this up and "him" was Link Williams.

A shiver ran down his spine.

He had forgotten he was still sitting at the table in the servants' dining room. Mrs. Cameron's quiet voice startled him. She said, "Mr. Powther, you're having a chill. Have you caught a cold?"

"It's these sudden changes," he said, shaking his head. "Yesterday was almost like spring, and today is like the middle of January. I've felt frozen all morning."

Attempted attack, he thought. Midnight, corner of Dock and Dumble, no traffic, no passers-by. They would have heard the lapping of the river, and the street would have been dark all around them, in spite of the light at the corner. They were within sight of that red neon sign in front of The Last Chance, but they wouldn't have been able to see the pink light in that upstairs bedroom at Number Six, and The Hangman would simply have been a dark bulk against the night sky, not really distinguishable as a tree.

Miss Camilo and Link Williams, painful to think of those two being connected in any way, stood on that corner, quarreling. Miss Camilo with her young trusting eyes, innocent face, pale blond hair, he wondered if she wore that ring with the diamond in it like the headlight of a car, a ring that said she had no business anywhere near Dumble Street, standing near Link Williams, who would have been hatless, probably coatless, too. The street light should have thrown a shadow across his face, a shadow like a scar, to emphasize the way in which his face with its thin-lipped cruel mouth resembled the face of a pirate, of an outlaw.

They must have quarreled to the hurting point. Miss Camilo was the hurt one. So it was about another woman. She probably threatened to ruin him, to get even, and he laughed, and then she stood there under that street light that could not dissipate the deadly darkness all around them, and screamed. The police came and she made the accusation and they arrested him. But he was already out on bail. The paper said so. Even if the charge was proved, and he doubted that it could be, he and Mamie had read so many of these cases in the papers, a charge like that, attempted attack, no witnesses, late at night, was too flimsy to hold up in court, and with Bill Hod's influence, he wouldn't even get a suspended sentence or a fine. Nothing.

I don't believe it, he thought. Even now I don't believe it. There's some other explanation. Link Williams couldn't have been her lover.

Al had said to the Frenchman, "You don't believe me, huh? Well, what was she doin' on the dock in Niggertown—"

Sweat broke out on his forehead.

He reached in his pocket for a handkerchief, mopped his forehead, asking himself why he kept refusing to believe that Link Williams had been Miss Camilo's lover, why he so desperately wanted it not to be true, and remembered the feel of old, soft, worn handkerchiefs, handkerchiefs that he kept at the bottom of the pile in the top drawer of the chest, in the bedroom that he shared with Mamie.

He could see that tall imitation-mahogany chest, with grapes and tendrils, and roundbottomed cupids glued on the front of the drawers, chest he didn't buy, didn't pay for, see himself reach in the drawer. His hand had struck something cold, metallic, square, shaped like a box.

L.W. The initials picked out in small flawless diamonds. Even when he held the cigarette case flat on his hand, the stones had quivered, as though the blue-red-yellow sparks they encased were trying to free themselves, and so were never still. The gold of the case was beautifully worked, obviously made to order, by a master goldsmith.

"Put two and two together."

Miss Camilo had given that cigarette case to Link Williams. Link had handed it on to Mamie. Monogrammed. Obviously his. He didn't care if the husband saw it, the husband who didn't count, didn't matter, and never had or would; because he was a fool, and a coward, and everyone who ever saw him immediately recognized him as such, even Old Copper, a lecherous old man, knew that the husband would stand for anything, telling the new husband to his face, "If I was younger I'd give you a run for your money."

Link Williams knew that the husband would put up with anything. So he told Miss Camilo, I've got another woman, a better woman. Powther supposed that Mamie was a better woman than Miss Camilo. Then he thought, appalled, This thing has already changed me. It would never have occurred to me to compare them, because Miss Camilo moved in a separate different world. But Link Williams had made these separate worlds coalesce, collide. The princess of the fairy tales, all gold, was not gold at all, was flesh, human flesh, all too human, all too weak, capable of jealousy, of vengeance, capable of being ruined, like any other woman.

He was overwhelmed by a sudden sense of urgency. If Miss Camilo could fall in love with Link Williams, then Mamie—Mamie would run off with him. They might already have gone. He had to find out. Now. Tea or no tea. Nobody had as much at stake in this dreadful business as he had.

He went straight to the garage, leaving the table so abruptly that Mrs. Cameron frowned.

"Al," he said, "would you do me a favor?"

"Sure. Just you name it, Mal."

"I've got to go home in a hurry, home and back so fast that I still have everything ready for the tea this afternoon. The Madam is having the office girls in for tea." Al knew that but he was much too upset to be able to think clearly. "And I have to be back, right away, but I've got to go home right now. I've got to go home."

"Sure, Mal. Any time. You know that."

"I'll tell Mrs. Cameron that I'm going—"

"Ah," Al said, and waved his hand, back and forth, dismissing Mrs. Cameron. "You ain't got to tell that old bag nothin'. Just hop in one of them crates. Come on, I'll use one of them goddamn convertibles. You can run like hell in 'em for the first fifty thousand miles. After that the motors ain't worth a good goddamn."

"No," he said quickly. "She'll have to keep an eye on Jenkins for me while I'm gone. It's a big tea. We've quite a lot of people coming. It won't take me a minute to tell her—"

He almost ran down Dumble Street, and up the back stairs, and into the kitchen. Just inside the kitchen door he stood still, astonished. Mamie was ironing a small blue shirt, either Kelly's or Shapiro's, humming under her breath. Just like any other wife, housewife, mother. She had a brilliant red scarf tied around her head, so she must have washed her hair. He had never seen her look quite so beautiful, so young, so appealing. She was wearing a green-and-white-checked dress, a fullskirted dress, that made her waist look very small, and made the curve of her breasts something to stare at in disbelief. A sigh rose in his throat.

"Pow-ther!" she said, smiling, mouth curving over the white even teeth, the smile enhancing the dewy look of her skin. "How come you're home?"

"I forgot my keys," he said, and gulped. "I went off without my keys. The keys to my wine cellar."

"Now ain't that a shame. You want me to help you hunt for 'em?"

"No," he said, hastily. "I know where they are. They're in my other pants." He felt humble and apologetic. It seemed as though he ought to say so, to explain how he'd been falsely accusing her in his mind, picturing her as a destroyer of other people's love affairs, tell her how he'd expected to come home and find the house cold and empty because she'd run off with another man. Instead here she was ironing in a warm clean kitchen, no dirty dishes in the sink; and she had mopped the linoleum, and waxed it afterwards, because the blue and white squares had a sheen, a kind of luster; and she had made gingerbread, he could smell it baking, spicy, fragrant, and over the smell of the gingerbread there was the strong, toosweet smell of her perfume.

He lingered in the kitchen, watching her, loving the big-bosomed look of her, thinking, I used to take it for granted that a married woman who has an affair with another man will have a depraved, wornout look. But they don't. They grow younger and there is an emanation of happiness from them that can be sensed and felt by other people, and it makes them more beautiful. Like Mamie. Like Miss Camilo before Link Williams left her.

Then he remembered that Al was waiting for him over on Franklin Avenue, in the Lincoln, remembered the tea, and all the last-minute business of fireplaces, be sure about enough spoons, get the candles lighted, and the pianist had to be fed when he arrived, he was coming from New York.

He went into the bedroom, and opened the top drawer of the dresser, to make certain that that damnable, expensive, worth-a-king's-ransom cigarette case was still there. After that night he discovered it, he had forced himself to stop thinking about it, stop conjecturing about it; he had never once permitted himself the luxury of finding out if it was still there.

It was gone. Mamie, who never bothered to put anything straight in a drawer, had lined up his handkerchiefs when she removed the cigarette case. It couldn't have been anyone else.

Perhaps it had never been there. Of course it had been there. Nobody could dream up the existence of a golden geegaw that looked like a crown jewel.

He shoved the drawer shut with a blow of his hand, trying to smack as many of the cupids as he could. A childish thing to do. But they seemed to be leering at him, mouths open, eyes sunk deep in their heads, and he struck at them again. If furniture could talk, these fat hideous little figures could tell him what Mamie had done with that cigarette case. Perhaps she had returned it to its owner. Perhaps she hadn't. Perhaps she kept it tucked inside the front of her dress, so that she would have something that belonged to Link always near her.

When he went into the kitchen, she took one look at his face, and laid the iron down. "Aw, Powther, you didn't find 'em, did you? I'll go look too."

For one incredible moment he thought she was talking about the cigarette case, and he felt as though his face and neck had been enveloped in steam. Heat was rising all about him.

Then he remembered. "I've got them," he said and pulled a bunch of keys out of his pants pocket. Her voice had sounded exactly like Drewey's voice, like the voice of that big fat woman, sitting in the creaking rocking chair, in a rooming house in Baltimore, doing what she called hum-a-byin', voice as soothing as a warm bath—now, now, now, everything is all right.

"I've got to hurry," he said. He had to get back to the Hall, and check the number of napkins, make certain about the brand of tea—one of the smoky dark ones—and yet he wanted to stay here, to put his head down in her lap, to—

"You feel all right, Powther?"

"A little indigestion. It's just that I came so fast." And that ever since Bill Hod came into our lives, I have felt as though I were stumbling around in the dark, in a strange house, hunting for a door, fumbling for a door in an unfamiliar house that has no doors. More and more, of late, I have wished that Old Copper's lust for women had not infected me, because it did, finally, so much so that I could not stop, would not stop, would not heed the warnings of my common sense, but went ahead and married you anyway. Because of that old man, who sat huddled in a red leather chair, licking his lips, staring at his paintings, oil paintings of bigbosomed, softfleshed women. And yet— I would really never have lived if I hadn't married you because I would never have known what ecstasy is like.

"I'll fix some soda for you."

"No, no. I haven't got time. Really. I've got to get back."

"Okay, sugar."

He couldn't leave like this. He ought to say something else, but he didn't know what. She had picked up the iron, was moving it back and forth, across another small shirt. "Where's J.C.?" he asked.

"J.C.?" she laughed. "Crunch took him to the liberry with her. I think she's educatin' him but I bet it's goin' to work out the other way. Time she listens to that jaybird jabber of his, especially walkin' right along the street with him for a half-hour, she'll be talkin' the same way he does. He come runnin' up the stairs, tellin' me Crunch said for me to change his clothes because he was goin' out with her, and for me to put his new shoes on him, and that Crunch said for me to hurry up because she couldn't wait. I told him, I said, Listen, J.C., I'll change 'em this time, but you come up here just one more time tellin' me what Crunch said I got to do and I'll fix your seat so you won't be able to sit on it for a week. He looked real cute when he went back downstairs."

She laughed again, head thrown back, round brown throat pulsating with laughter; and kept on laughing as though she were enjoying the rich mellow sound bubbling up in her throat. But she gave him a queer, sharp glance that made him wonder if the laughter were a screen for whatever she was thinking.

"Oh, my God!" she said suddenly, and put the iron down and hurried toward the stove. "I'm cooking with my ass again." She took the gingerbread out of the oven. It was just beginning to singe along the edges. "I guess I got up off it just in time. Them two starvin' Armenians are always looking for something to eat when they come home from school. So I stirred this up in a hurry, and then plum forgot about it."

As he went down the stairs, hurrying again now, almost running, he heard her singing, not that song he hated about some kind of train her mother took, the words of this one didn't make much sense but the tune was lovely and so was her voice, slow, clear, true, and he could hear the slap thump of the iron:

> Tell me what color an' I'll tell you what road she took.
> Tell me what color an' I'll tell you what road she took.
> Why'ncha tell me what color and I'll tell you what road
>   she took.

When he got in the car, Al looked at him queerly, too.

"Is there somep'n the matter, Mal?"

Without thinking, he said, "It's my wife."

"She sick?"

"Well—" he hesitated, "not exactly."

"What'sa matter with her?"

He shook his head, frowning. "It's—it's her heart."

"She probably runs too fast, Mal. Just like you do. Probably works too hard. People got to give themselves a break, you know. Ain't no rich bastards standin' around handin' out new tickers when the one you got quits on you."

On the way back to the Hall, Al talked about cars, about heart trouble, about the Madam and how mean she was to Rita, about Mrs. Cameron and how mean she was to Rita.

Powther ignored Al's conversation. He was trying to reorient himself to the atmosphere of the Hall, trying to forget about Mamie and Link Williams and Miss Camilo and a Tiffany cigarette case, with which Mamie was playing hide-and-seek, so that he could think about the tea, concentrate on the tea. If he didn't, he might drop a tray, step on someone's foot, do any of the hideous, awkward things a butler could do when he didn't have his mind on his work.

He succeeded fairly well, too. By five o'clock, when the east drawing room was filled with young women, all wearing print dresses and little hats with flowers on them, some seated, some standing, all talking and laughing, drinking tea, eating, thoroughly enjoying themselves, he was able to admire the scene in front of him, to the exclusion of any private worries.

Mischoff, the pianist, had arrived on schedule and was now playing the Steinway grand, so that under the talk and the laughter there was music. There was a wonderful blend of smells: tea, faint smell of cedar from the fires where he'd sprinkled cedar chips, the girls' perfume, the poets' narcissi. As he looked about him, he thought, if you stood in the doorway of this white and gold room, and took just one hasty glance, at the lights over the oil paintings, at the flickering light from the candles, and from the open fires, listened to the sound of the piano, watched the constant movement of the girls, you would want to go inside and share the warmth, the gaiety, the hospitality.

The Madam belonged in this room. She looked like a *grande dame* because of the pearl choker around her neck, because of the soft smoky blue of the afternoon dress she was wearing. The girls' faces lighted up, glowed, as she talked to them, and the glow lingered even after she'd moved away, to speak to someone else. Her hair was almost as pretty as Miss Camilo's. From a distance she seemed to be a platinum blonde, but when you got close to her, you saw that it was because the pale blond hair was mixed with gray. She was as erect and as slender as Miss Camilo. They had the same deep blue eyes but there was a difference in the expression. Miss Camilo's eyes were very young, very innocent. The Madam's eyes were the eyes of a woman in her late fifties, a little tired, eyes of a woman who had played a man's role for years. She actually managed the plant, and when you studied her eyes you saw that sometimes she had achieved the things she wanted, and sometimes she hadn't; but you also saw determination in the eyes, and the face, and you knew why she was so successful.

As he was crossing the room, to pick up some empty tea-cups, she came up to him, put her hand on his arm. She said, "It's perfect. Everything is perfect. Thank you, Powther."

He was tremendously pleased. She paid him to see that everything was perfect, and it would have been understandable if she took perfection for granted. She never did. She was always thanking him for doing his job, as though he were an old friend who had done a favor for her.

There's a glow in me now, he thought, just as there is in these girls. She has restored my confidence, made me believe in myself again. I can look at this room and feel sorry that the weather will soon be too warm for lighted candles, for fires in the fireplaces, and that we won't be entertaining on a scale like this until next year.

There was the summer picnic though. But that was handled by an outside crew. He had nothing to do with it, and he disapproved of it, anyway. Every Fourth of July, the Madam invited workmen from the plant, and gave a kind of mass entertainment for them and their families. It was more like an invasion than a party. The men wore T-shirts and their fat wives came in shorts and slacks and bathing suits. The men and women and their stickyfingered, badly behaved children ate hot dogs and crackerjack and ice cream, drank Coca-Cola and beer and lemonade, and shot off fireworks. Even the children drank beer, so that he referred to all of them, contemptuously, in his mind, as the beer drinkers.

The Madam hired special guards for the occasion, but they didn't have the family's interest in mind, weren't ever really on their toes. He was always afraid that some of these undesirable people would wander into the house, tracking it up, fingering the tapestries, smearing the upholstery.

Last summer, an unshaven young man who smelt of beer and sweat, actually got as far as the front door. When Powther opened the door, the young man said, in a loud, truculent voice, "Just wanted to see if the inside of the palace stinks like the plant."

Fortunately, one of the hired guards came up just then and led the young man away. That beer-soaked young man would always epitomize the summer picnic in Powther's mind, just as these attractive, perfumed girls in their spring dresses epitomized this late-winter tea.

Ah, well, he thought, as he crossed the room to tell Jenkins to collect the empty teacups piled up on one of the mantels, you can't make a silk purse out of a sow's ear. He paused, just behind the sofa, in front of the fireplace, to admire two girls who were sitting close together on it, watching the fire. The mandarin red silk of the sofa formed a striking background for the yelloworange tones in the print dresses they wore.

One of the girls sitting on the sofa said, in an undertone, "Don't you know who she is?"

"No." The other voice went down, lower. "Who?"

He started to move away, and the prettier of the two girls said, "Mrs. Treadway's daughter. Camilla Sheffield."

His attention was caught, held.

"I didn't know she had a daughter."

"Sure. Mrs. William R. Sheffield is Mrs. Treadway's only child. Camilla Treadway Sheffield. Now isn't that something?" The voice went up.

"How did you know?"

"I heard my boss say so. I heard him talking to somebody about it just this morning, over the telephone."

"Mrs. Treadway's daughter? What was she doing in The Narrows at that hour?"

"That's what he said, too. My boss, I mean. He said, 'What was she doing on the dock with a nigger at that time of night?'"

"She wasn't really on the dock with him, was she? I mean it didn't say that in the paper. Wait a minute," relish in the voice, curiosity, "do you mean she was—"

"Shhh!"

The Madam was coming toward them, and both girls turned toward her, smiling, faces glowing, and then stood up, to talk to her.

Powther thought incredulously, That fast! By night, all Monmouth would be asking the same question. Now he looked around the room with distaste. These girls smelt of perfume, their hair was curled, they were wearing their new spring dresses, but they were exactly like the sweaty, beer-drinking workers who invaded the park in July. They, too, resented the fact that the Madam belonged to the millionaire class.

The beer drinkers expressed their hostility in vandalism. Rogers said that every year, after the picnic, it took a crew of men a whole month to put the park back in shape, what with the mutilation of trees and shrubs, and the empty beer bottles and crackerjack boxes, and Coca-Cola bottles, and exploded firecrackers, thrown into the lake, despite the fact that he put the biggest refuse cans he could find less than ten feet apart all through the grounds.

"I finally got smart," Rogers said. "It took me three years to get smart. I move the swans back in a place where they can't find 'em. I made another little lake for 'em. For three years I found my swans with their necks wrung, or their crops so bloated up they died two or three days later. And I string an electric wire all around the rose gardens. Used to be I'd go out there and find it stripped, and some of the bushes dug up. But I got it fixed now so they can't get at it."

The beer drinkers wrecked the grounds, or tried to. And the tea drinkers, as he now called these girls from the office, were just as hostile. They welcomed the fact that the Madam's daughter was mixed up in a scandalous situation. By the time this tea was over, they would have reduced Miss Camilo to the level of a prostitute, simply because her mother was a millionaire. They couldn't take the Madam's wealth away from her, but they could destroy her daughter, just by whispering about her, while they drank a smoky dark tea, out of the Madam's best teacups, while they clinked the Madam's Versailles spoons against the saucers.

20

PETER BULLOCK, editor, owner, publisher of the *Monmouth Chronicle*, was drinking a glass of milk, in The Swiss Steak, a small restaurant on Centre Street. He watched Rutledge, head of Monmouth's police department, who sat across the table from him, as he worked his way slowly, steadily, through a steak, French fried potatoes, Parker House rolls; watched him wash his food down his throat with beer, big drafts of beer.

He tried to keep his eyes away from Rutledge's plate, and couldn't, any more than any other starving man could keep his eyes away from food. He told himself that this was unappetizing unhealthy fried food that Rutledge was stuffing in his mouth, and the beer he was pouring down his throat was little better than poison; and the smell of the steak, smell of the beer, the vast growling emptiness in his stomach made him feel as though his head were going around and around, revolving on a private Ferris wheel of its own.

"That Treadway girl sure messed herself up," Rutledge said, chewing steak. "Couldn't have done a better job if she'd been paid to do it. She was drunk when she accused Link Williams of attempted attack. Drunk again this afternoon when she ran that kid down." He signaled the waiter with his fork.

There was a big piece of steak speared on the end of the fork, and Bullock wondered what Rutledge would do if he should lean forward, mouth open, and snatch the meat off with his teeth.

"Maybe she's competing for the title," Rutledge said.

"Title? What title?"

"The rich bitch title," Rutledge said, grinning. He turned to the waiter, said, "Two pieces of apple pie. No, not for him. Just for me. And cover the whole thing over thick with ice cream. Put about a pint of vanilla on it." He popped the hunk of steak in his mouth and grinned at Bullock, chewing and grinning, and talking, "Damn if I know why I eat so much. Maybe it's because I was hungry when I was young. So hungry once that I stole a loaf of bread and—" he started in on the pie "—I've been filling my gut up ever since so I won't ever be able to remember what it felt like when it was empty."

Bullock grunted.

"She'll be in to see you."

"Who?" he asked, thinking, It's easier to be hungry when you're young. He was too old for it. Forty-nine and hungry all the time. Forty-nine and an emptiness in his stomach, a burning emptiness in his stomach, all the time.

"Mrs. Treadway. She came to see me, right after the accident. Funny thing. I felt kind of sorry for her. Imagine me feeling sorry for a billionaire. She wanted me to wipe the record off the blotter. But there wasn't a damn thing I could do about it. Hell, the girl was drunker'n a coot, passed a stop light, street crawling with witnesses—"

"What'd you say to her?" Bullock asked. He knew all the details of the accident, the story was already dummied in, already set up. Happened about five-fifteen, on Dock Street, child knocked down.

"I tried to sound as dispassionate as a judge. 'Mrs. Treadway,' I said, 'the laws in Monmouth are all written down. There are no unwritten ones. These laws apply with equal force to every resident. This is a serious matter. The child was badly injured. There is always the possibility that the child may die. There is nothing, absolutely nothing, that I can do about it.'" Rutledge paused, swallowed more beer. "She'll be in to see you," he repeated, maliciously.

"For what?"

"When the rich folks can't fix the cops, they do the next best thing, they keep the details of the mess out of the public print. You're the public print in this town, Bullock."

He shrugged. "So what good would it do to keep it out of the paper?"

"The label of rich tramp wouldn't be written down, permanently fixed on paper. It could stay where it is, up in the air, a matter of hearsay and rumor." Rutledge lit a cigarette. "What're you going to do when the old lady comes in to cop a plea?"

Casual question, he wondered. Hardly. Rutledge didn't ask casual questions. He had the cold eyes of a cop, eyes the color of lead, had the professionally expressionless face of a cop, face like a mask, only Rutledge's mask never slipped, so it was impossible to say where he stood on anything, how he felt about anything. But he didn't ask idle, casual questions.

"I don't know," he said, and pushed his chair back from the table.

The smell of steak, of French fried potatoes, of beer, accompanied him as he walked along Centre Street. It went right into his office with him, he still hungry, and the good smell of food, moving on into his office with him, tantalizing, maddening, making his head reel.

His secretary said, "Mrs. Treadway is waiting for you. I told her that you'd be right back."

"You're so goddamn efficient," he said, and let the dizziness, and the irritability born of hunger, turn into anger, and let the anger explode in the face of this old maid who was his secretary, watched her face crumple, redden. "I suppose you've got your headstone already marked, haven't you? And the coffin picked out," he said, glaring at her, and went in his office, and shook hands with Mrs. Treadway, acting as though he were pleased to see her, as though he thought this was an informal call she was paying him.

He was surprised at himself because he felt sorry for her, just as Rutledge had. She had grown older, more gray in her hair, new deep lines at the mouth, around the eyes. Not that he saw her very often. He and Lola dined with her at Treadway Hall, once a year, largely a matter of business courtesy on her part, though Lola always managed to create the impression that it was a social gesture, when she told her friends about it.

Mrs. Treadway said, "I have come to ask you not to print anything about this unfortunate accident of Camilo's."

"I can't do that," he said, just as bluntly, just as quickly. "It's on the police blotter. The child is in the hospital. There were witnesses."

"Camilo has been under a tremendous strain," she said. "That's why I am asking you not to print anything about this."

"I will make it a small story, bury it on an inside page. But it has to go in."

"There must be no story at all. On an inside page or an outside page," she said insistently.

He could understand why, anybody could understand why. That case hadn't come up yet, it had been less than a week ago, that Camilo Sheffield had charged a Negro with attempted attack. The Negro was out on bail, very low bail, and no date had been set for the trial. This accident wasn't going to help Camilo's reputation, would, in fact, polish off what was left of it.

"I'm sorry," he said, gently, and meant it. "But it will have to go in."

She stood up, and so he stood up, too, trying to think of a way to express his regret, his sympathy.

"Mr. Bullock," she said, the eyes no longer sad, the eyes determined, cold, the face grim, and the voice implacable. "If the story goes in, our advertising comes out. We have no contract with your paper."

After she left, he kept pushing a blotter around on the top of his desk, thinking, Oh, damn the woman anyway. Why couldn't she keep her tramp of a daughter under control? It was a nasty business. The girl was drunk, driving as though the devil was riding with her, sidesaddle on a fender, and she was trying to outride him, outrun him. She passed a red light. In Niggertown. On Dock Street. Why Dock Street? How did she come to be in that narrow, dingy, street composed of warehouses and stinking little factories, and old frame buildings, street that ran parallel to the river, and smelt and looked like what it was—a waterfront street.

These things were always bad. The priests and the rabbis, the jackleg nigger preachers, the union leaders, the ward heelers would holler and scream about a bought press for months afterwards. You couldn't prevent people from knowing about a thing just because you kept it out of a newspaper. It had happened shortly after five o'clock, and the streets were filled with dock workers and factory hands, going home. He had tried to tell Mrs. Treadway that, but oh, no, if the story went in, the advertising came out—permanently. And he couldn't afford to lose it, and she knew it.

So he personally pulled the story, and even as he did it knew that word of what he'd done would be all through the building, five minutes after he left the pressroom.

Back in his office, he tried to shift the blame, the responsibility, for his action. Rutledge could have wiped the thing off the police blotter. Why did Rutledge have to be so god-damn moral, or rather, he thought, why should Monmouth's leaden-eyed Chief of Police be in a position where he can afford to put his morality into practice, and the editor of the *Chronicle* shouldn't be? Is it a matter of morality? No, it's a matter of what will people say—what will people think—public opinion.

The original error stemmed from that numbskull who had picked up the story about young Mrs. Sheffield accusing a Negro of attack. He was one of those knowitalls from the Columbia School of Journalism, complete with crew haircut and more lip than John L. Lewis, and a sophomoric belief in his own judgment.

"So I didn't know she was the Treadway girl," he said, when Bullock got after him about it. "But any woman from Park Avenue on the loose in the Dumble Street area at midnight is news. Because of the sheer incongruity of her being there at all."

"You're supposed to know who people are. It's part of your job. That's what you're paid for. Or don't they teach that at—"

The crew haircut had interrupted him. "Who'd recognize her by that name? It got past the desk. It got past you. Did you know who Mrs. William R. Sheffield was? So I was supposed to know anyway, huh? That's what you pay me for, huh? All right. Even if I'd known who she was, I'd of picked the story up. A stranger could have got in that section by accident. The Treadway girl must have gone there deliberately. She's been commuting between Monmouth and New York for months now. So she wouldn't be apt to lose her way. If you ask me, that line of hers about attempted attack is absolute rot. It was a lovers' quarrel."

"What?" he roared. "Why you—"

"Listen," the crew haircut said calmly, "I looked the man up. My girl works in the plant and she told me that Mrs. Sheffield was the Treadway girl. So I got curious and looked up his record. He's a Phi Beta Kappa from Dartmouth, majored in history, honor graduate of Monmouth High School, football star, basketball star in high school and at Dartmouth. Was in the Navy for four years, censor, Navy installation in Hawaii. There's nothing in his background to make the charge believable. If you want to know what I think, I think they were in love and—"

"You goddam fool," he shouted, and his throat constricted, just as though he were choking. When he was able to talk again, his voice no longer contained the surface irascibility of the ulcer victim, it was an outraged furious voice, because the idea, the possibility that the Treadway girl could have had a nigger lover, that any rational white man could contemplate such a thought without—"You're fired," he shouted, "I won't have any irresponsible bastard like you on my payroll—"

The knowitall with the crew haircut said, cheerfully, "It's okay, pops. I felt the same way about you the first time I saw you."

He had watched him go toward the door, saw him hesitate, turn back, and thought he was going to say, I need the job, I got a wife and four starving kids, and a dying grandmother; and instead, he offered advice.

"You better get your ulcers taped up, way up out of the muck," he said, "otherwise you might get 'em mired in this Treadway case."

At eight o'clock, that night, the phone on his desk rang, and the girl at the switchboard said that Jubine wanted to see him.

"Tell him to go drown himself."

"He has a picture that—"

"Tell him to drop it in and pull the chain and—"

"He says—"

Jubine interrupted. "Bullock, you better look at this picture. See this picture."

"No."

"You'll be sorry, peon, sorry, sorry—"

"Get the hell out of my building before I call a cop."

"You'll be sorry, sorry, sorry."

Jubine's soft reproachful voice singsonged the words in his ear again and he banged the receiver down, cutting the sound off, thinking, Yes, eight o'clock at night, that's all I need is to have that bastard come in here and start yapping that line he talks, unlit cigar in the corner of his mouth, beady eyes roving all around the room, looking, looking, looking, as though he were estimating the cost of everything, putting a price on it, cost of the desk, cost of the dark red carpeting, cost of the mahogany paneling on the walls, price you paid, Ha, ha, ha, you got gypped, look at the price you paid. Restless, inquisitive eyes, moving over and around the editorpublisherowner of the *Monmouth Chronicle*, examining him, cataloguing him, summing him up by saying, "You're a type, Bullock. A state of mind. And you'll never recover from it."

He kept remembering the sound of Jubine's voice, Sorry, you'll be sorry, sorry, a singsong, tuneless, reiterated, like some brat of a child baiting another brat of a child. He stayed in his office until the presses started to roll, and he thought he could hear that singsong under the rumble and roar of the press. Heard it off and on all night, even after he got home, got in bed.

At six o'clock in the morning he woke up, feeling uneasy, wornout, as though his subconscious had been trying to get a message through to him all night, and so he had slept restlessly, aware of something wrong, but too obtuse to recognize the signal, to answer it. Pictures, he thought, what about—

He reached for the telephone by the bed, dialed Rutledge's number.

"Listen," he said, when he heard Rutledge's voice, thick with sleep; though he already knew the answer to the question he was going to ask, he asked it anyway, "Were there any pictures taken of that Treadway girl's accident? Who? Oh—Christ!"

Lola sat up in bed, not yawning, not sagging with sleep, wide awake, face as fresh as the morning, hair curling over her forehead. "What's the matter?" She watched him dress, frowning. "Where are you going at this hour? Pete, answer me—"

He was gone before she could ask him again. He backed his car out of the three-car garage, attached garage, station wagon in it, Lola's brandnew convertible in it, his slave ship, as Jubine called it, also housed in it. Why'd they need two cars and a station wagon? Because he was a sucker, he was a peon, he was a poor peon trying to act like a rich peon because he was in love with an expensive beautiful redheaded female peon, and somewhere in the twentieth century they'd both lost the use of their legs, and their minds, and their will power. So they couldn't walk any more, they couldn't—

The loft where Jubine lived, across from the Commerce Street Police Station, was empty. Door wide open. He yelled, "Jubine, hey, Jubine!"

No answer. He went inside. It was just a big, bare, practically unfurnished room, not even a room, a loft, so big that the walls couldn't define it, give it form, just unfurnished space, with a roof over it. Pictures everywhere, all the litter of photography, everywhere. Not even a bed. Probably sleeps on the floor. No, there was a cot, but no sheets, an army blanket rolled up at the foot took the place of sheets, bedspread, blanket, all in one; could serve as pillow, too, if one put one's head on it.

An old man's voice said, "You want something, mister?"

He turned toward the direction of the voice, and saw that there was a chair in the loft, and that a thin old man was sitting in it. Wrinkled face. Something satirical in his eyes, or it may have been the effect of the toobig gray cap he was wearing, peak of the cap threw a shadow over the eyes. He was sucking on a corncob pipe. His face seemed to consist of the peak of the cap, the pipe, and the wrinkles.

"Where's Jubine?"

"New York."

"New York? Jubine?" The *Chronicle* was piled on the news-stands by now, it was being distributed in the post offices of all the little towns all over the state, it was in the big bundles being tossed off trucks in front of drugstores and candy stores, and in another hour it would be on the doorsteps of the houses, boys would be hawking it on Main Street. He used to think of this hour with pleasure, with satisfaction, because his paper was being read over the breakfast tables, on the trains and busses, his personal creation, brandnew, eagerly awaited, every morning. And now—

"That's right, mister. He's been gone all night. He said ye'd be here, lookin' for him. Said ye'd be here last night. It's morning though, ain't it. Ye're later'n he said." He paused. "He left a message."

"Well?" How did this old man in his mismatched pants and coat, his toobig cap, know him. Jubine would have left a description of him. Camel-hair coat. Rich peon's coat. Of course. "Well?" he repeated.

The old man took the pipe out of his mouth, licked his lips. He spoke slowly, deliberately, as though he had been rehearsing this speech for hours, and was now enjoying the opportunity to deliver it before an audience, blinking his eyes, cat fashion, in approval of his own performance.

"He said to tell ye that he was sorry ye was goin' to get more of them little sore places in ye belly but ye would."

Curse him, Bullock thought, curse all his ancestors, curse —little sore places in your stomach. You want to be a middle peon, neither rich nor poor, and there's no such thing. That's why you swear so much, that's why you wear that rich peon's coat, that yellow camel-hair coat. All poor peons who try to be middle peons, ache to be middle peons, get those little sore places. Sure I set 'em up. I tell the poor peons you stand here, you go without food so you will look hungry, for three days you go without food. I tell the rich peons, Jubine is here with his camera, stand on your head, ride a horse up the courthouse steps, jump in your swimming pool with your clothes on. Sure, I set 'em up, Bullock.

He sat in his car on Commerce Street, waiting for the newsstand on the corner to open up, watched the slowmoving owner of the stand rip open the big bundles of newspapers, and then heave them into position on the stand.

After the papers were lined up on the stand, he crossed the street, thinking he'd have to buy all the New York papers, and hunt, until he found— But he didn't have to. The first thing he saw was Jubine's goddamn picture.

He must have mailed it in, oh, who the hell cared how he got it there. Perfectly evident he'd gone to all the trouble, taken the pains, wasted the time, to deliver it in person, speeding through the night, on that motorcycle of his, speeding, speeding, to get even, straight to New York; and one of those halfbreed mongrel newspapers that had little or no advertising, certainly was not dependent on any from the Treadway Munitions Company, one of those New York tabloids, published it.

It must have been a dull night for crime in New York, because the picture had been blown up and put on the front page. The legend under it was short, clear, concise, easy to understand. It implied, in a few, carefully chosen, easy-to-read words, that the Duchess of Moneyland, young Mrs. Money-bags, of the gun empire, while drunk on a long life of lewdness, drunk on black beluga caviar and pink champagne, drunk on mink coats and Kohinoor diamonds, while driving her golden coach (he thought, Cinderella, pumpkin coach, papers in the pumpkin, Chambers, Hiss), accompanied by eighteen outriders wearing crimson velvet, trimmed with gold braid, had ridden down a child of the poor, in the streets of Monmouth, a city which belonged body and soul (since when do cities have bodies and souls, he thought) to the dowager Duchess of Moneyland. While the child of the poor lay helpless in the street (It would have to be a female child, he thought), the outriders had beaten her with blacksnake whips.

The Duchess of Moneyland, young Mrs. Moneybags, had laughed, her lascivious lips had curled as she pulled her sable coat about her slender shoulders, shouting, "Lay on, Macduff; and damn'd be him that first cries, 'Hold, Enough!'"

It didn't actually say that though the implication was there. But the tabloid's caption writer forgot to coach Mrs. Bunny Sheffield for the role she was to play. True, she was wearing a mink coat, and you could see that on one hand she wore a ring with a diamond in it so fiery that even on the cheap grayish impermanent paper of the tabloid she seemed to be wearing a spotlight on her finger. But her face was white, eyes haunted, mouth slack, one hand lifted, as though to ward off a blow. She was leaning against one of the fenders of the car, and she was looking up, no beauty in the face, nothing human about the face, just emptiness, and the drunkenness showed in the awful slackness of the mouth.

The child of the poor looked the part, might have been dressed by an imaginative stage designer for the part. The clothes were worn handmedowns, the coat sleeves too short, revealing thin wrists and thinner arms, shockingly nakedlooking wrists and arms. The coat and the dress so short that the legs were grotesque, too long, the knees knobby, the leg bones twisted; twisted from lack of food, but one leg twisted at an angle that was painful to look at, even in a photograph, because it had been twisted from contact with that big powerful shiny car, part of which could be seen.

And in the background, surrounding the car, the girl, were people, a great crowd of people, with angry, hostile faces; women with their arms akimbo; men frowning, shaking their fists, mouths drawn back in a snarl; and a policeman taking notes, two more policemen, arms uplifted, threatening the crowd; the child of the poor, dead center in front of the car, eyes closed, face deathlike.

Lest some careless reader miss the details, it said, just above this picture, See story page 3.

"Holy Mother of God!" he muttered. There wasn't a word about this in the *Chronicle*, not a word, not a line.

He flipped the page and read the story, quickly. Goddamn Jubine, anyway, he thought, may he burn in hell, he not only took pictures, he also played reporter, slick reporter, able to convince a sonofabitching city editor that one of his pictures was front page news, and that it deserved a story, a story longer than a tabloid normally uses.

It was one of those easy-to-read feature stories, padded with local color about Jubine, the photographer (called the recording angel), about Monmouth (that beautiful, rich, conservative, typically New England city), located in Connecticut (that neat, small, rich, conservative state, unlike any other in the Union), about Cesar the Writing Man, who was poetically referred to as the city's conscience. Detail about Cesar: how he chalked verses from the Bible on the streets of Monmouth. Samples of same: "For where your treasure is, there will your heart be also," in front of the banks. "Therefore all things whatsoever ye would that men should do to you, do ye even so to them: for this is the law and the prophets," in front of the courthouse. "Physician, heal thyself" in front of the professional building. "For wheresoever the carcase is, there will the eagles be gathered together," in front of real estate offices, insurance companies, churches. "For they that take the sword shall perish with the sword," in front of the armory.

Fine. And then he cursed again, felt a spasm of pain that twisted his stomach. "Thirty pieces of silver." Chalked in front of the building that housed the *Chronicle*, Monmouth's one big newspaper. Jubine made that one up. Nobody had ever written that there. Son of a bitch, he thought, skunk, bastard.

The pain in his lower abdomen was no longer a spasm, it was a twisting, turning, spreading horror that reached into his throat. He had to sit down or he'd vomit.

He sat in his car and waited until the pain eased off into a burning sensation, hateful but bearable. Then he went on reading what he now knew was Jubine's story. Jubine said that Cesar had prophetic powers, that if one of his quotes appeared in an unusual place, he, Jubine, knew that a crime would be committed on that spot. It had happened that way many times.

So, earlier on the afternoon of the accident, Jubine had seen Cesar chalk a verse at an intersection, on Dock Street: "Like the driving of Jehu the son of Nimshi; for he driveth furiously. II Kings 9:20."

Jubine had hung around, waiting. He was there when Camilo came roaring past the red light, slammed on the brakes, too late. The street was filled with factory workers going home —Poles, Italians, Negroes formed a mob around the car. The vagueness of her manner, her halting speech, the mink coat, the delicate shoes, the manicured hands, the big diamond were like a personal insult to these people.

Camilo murmured, "I lost—I can't find—I lost—"

Jubine said, "Camilo, ah, Camilo, what have you done?"

She looked up, eyes wide, horrified, and Jubine got his picture.

Even the quotes there in the tabloid. And then the story of Camilo's charge of attempted attack against Link Williams, Negro.

Photograph of Link Williams on the same page. Bullock studied the face. You couldn't trust Jubine's pictures. He waited and waited until a building, a church or a bank or a school, or a human being, a man, woman, or child, assumed the aspect, momentary, fleeting, that he wanted, and then clicked his shutter. The result was not truth but a distortion of it achieved by tricks of light, by special circumstance, surprise or shock.

So here was this Negro standing on the dock, lordlylooking bastard, leaning against the railing, head slightly turned, profile like Barrymore's, sunlight concentrated on his left side, so that the head, the shoulders, the whole length of him had the solidity of sculpture, the picture damn near had the three-dimensional quality of fine sculpture. There was an easy carelessness about the leaning position of his body, controlled carelessness, and the striped T-shirt, the slacks, the moccasins on the feet suited his posture.

Every woman who saw this nigger's picture would cut it out, clip it out, tear it out, drool over it. Every white man who saw it would do a slow burn.

He crumpled the mongrel tabloid newspaper between his hands, tossed it out of the car window. Jubine had tried the case, handed in a verdict, with his goddamn pictures. He'd made the Treadway girl look like a whore and made the nigger look like Apollo.

It was planned, deliberate. Jubine waited three hours before he brought that picture around, waited that long so I wouldn't connect it with the accident. Even if I'd had it, he thought, I wouldn't have used it.

Not a word, not a line, in the *Chronicle*.

Those same words were thrown at him, spat at him, later in the morning. He was sitting at his desk, not thinking, not doing anything, just sitting there, when the door was flung open.

"What the hell kind of newspaper you think you're runnin' here?"

He didn't answer. He stared at the man who had invaded his office, a big angry, unshaven man, thinking, Well, well, well, I always wondered what Public Opinion would look like in the flesh, and here he is: hatless, drunken, odoriferous, brandishing a New York tabloid about his head as though it were a weapon.

"No fear, no favor, huh? That goddamn woman don't own this town yet, see? There ain't a word, not a line, in the *Chronicle* about it. Anybody'd think it never happened. Things is in one hell of a shape when you got to read a New York paper to find out what's goin' on in your own home town."

Bullock opened his desk drawer.

Public Opinion shouted, "I don't hold for niggers rapin' white women but I don't hold for no drunk rich women runnin' down poor folks' children in the street, either, see?"

Bullock said, "I don't hold for no drunken bums in my office either, see?" And took an automatic out of the desk drawer, and aimed it at the chest region of Public Opinion's dirty white shirt, and watched him deflate like a balloon, even to the

hissing sound of his breath, just before he yelped and ran out,
bumping into the door in his haste to get away.

Right after that he called in the city editor, and they planned
the details of the story of the accident for the next day's paper,
a reporter was to interview the child's parents, and another
one was to get information from the hospital on the child's
condition. The finished story was a smooth minimization of
the accident, but it contained new information: the child had
a broken leg, and a mild concussion, and was .enjoying the
special nurses, the flowers, the toys that Mrs. Treadway had
provided for her. The parents of the child were grateful for the
many kindnesses and the special attention that their child had
received at Treadway Memorial Hospital.

He thought that was the end of it. But it wasn't. He was
sitting in the dining room, eating breakfast with Lola, at eight
o'clock the next morning when the telephone rang. He let
it ring awhile, irritated that his normal-morning grumpiness
should be disturbed by a telephone bell, feeling a curious kin-
ship with his father, thinking that you had to get to be near
fifty before you arrived at understanding of a male parent. His
father had always performed like this at the breakfast table, and
his mother had been as silent and as unobtrusive as Lola, not
speaking until he downed his second cup of coffee.

Shrill ringing of the telephone again.

Lola said, "Pete—" softly.

Hush in her voice, just as though she were talking to an
old and delicate invalid. He looked straight at her for the first
time since they'd sat down at the table. She had on a white
negligee, thin, silky, long. At eight in the morning she smelt
good, looked good, red hair curling all over her head. Damn
near forty and she could have passed for eighteen, with that
handspan waist, and her breasts rising up out of that thin white
pleated stuff, soft to the touch, delicately perfumed, ah, what
the hell, he thought, she didn't do anything else but work at
looking like that, just like an actress, whose appearance is an
investment to be protected.

"Aren't you going to answer it?"

He sighed and got up from the table. The telephone was
behind a screen, in the corner of the dining room. All dining
rooms either eighteenth-century reproductions, or Swedish

modern, theirs was Swedish modern, probably because it was more becoming to a redhead, and had cost enough to buy a house, just this modern furniture where he sat down to drink the skim milk and eat the mashed potatoes at night, and to drink the two cups of coffee in the morning, coffee that he wasn't supposed to drink, but had to—like that stuff they shoot into a hasbeen racehorse, jazz him up so he can keep running.

He went behind the screen, eightfold screen of thin blond wood, with drawings or paintings of wheat or rye on it, the thin curved blades a pale green, and the grains of wheat or rye painted a deeper color than the wood; both sides decorated like that, the bend and sway of the wheat or rye suggesting wind blowing through it, and the goddamn thing had cost enough to have been a Picasso, and after he'd stared at that grain blowing in the wind for as much as two minutes, his stomach began to heave, it made him seasick, cost as much as a Picasso and it made him seasick.

He said, "Hello," and stared at the wheat, and said, "Yes, all right," voice stiff, sounding rude, and not caring because he was thinking, What the hell do you want now, have I got to let you ruin my paper, or is it just a small matter of a Chinaman you want murdered, or a simple case of blackmail or arson?

"Yes, I'll be here," he said. "Very well." And hung up.

"Who was that?" Lola asked, holding a thin white coffee cup in both hands, the scarlet fingernails like an exotic decoration on the thin china.

"Mrs. Treadway." He wondered what his mother would have thought of Lola, wondered what he really thought of her himself. Unproductive. Good in bed, sure, but aren't they all? Wouldn't it have been cheaper to set her up in an apartment, and just go on from there? "She's coming here. This morning."

"Pete," she said, face thoughtful, eyes thoughtful. "Don't do it. Whatever it is she wants you to do, don't do it."

"Why?"

"It's gotten too complicated. She's still trying to save Camilo's reputation. And she can't. It's shot to hell. She wouldn't be coming here this morning, if she didn't plan to use you. Pete, you're not listening."

He grunted his refusal to commit himself. Did she think he was a simpleton? Well, wasn't he? Lola'd seen Jubine's pictures in the tabloid, she knew the *Chronicle* hadn't mentioned the accident. She must have heard the jokes, the salacious stories being told about Camilo, on every street corner, in the markets, on the busses and trolley cars. The flavor of the stuff being mouthed in the beauty parlors and the department stores, the special domain of the female, would be subtler and nastier than what was said in the bars and the barber shops.

He'd heard a fair sample of the barber shops' opinion of Camilo when he went to get a haircut yesterday afternoon. The barber behind the chair, right next to him, said to his customer, "Rich women got some funny tastes. I've heard that some of 'em got to go with colored fellers, just like they believed—"

"I don't think—" the customer started to say.

The barber slapped a hot towel firmly over the customer's face, and said, "So what was Camilo doing up in Niggertown at that hour in the morning when she said that the colored feller raped her? My wife says someone told her Camilo'd been to a dance, or somep'n, and she got out of the car to take the air, and kinda cool off. Now we got air all over Monmouth but Camilo's got to go breathe the stink up at the Dumble dock. After I see that picture of the colored feller, I figure he's been layin' her right along."

He had wondered if Mrs. Treadway knew what was being said about Camilo, and when he opened the door in answer to her ring, and she said, "Good morning, Mr. Bullock. I want to thank you for seeing me at this hour," he knew by the strained, tired note in her voice, the weariness in her face and eyes, that she probably knew more than he did of the stories being told about her daughter. Inside forty-eight hours, her face and voice had become that of an old woman.

He ushered her into the library, a pinepaneled room, that he rarely ever sat in, let alone used. The walls were lined, floor to ceiling, with shelves filled with books that had belonged to his father, his grandfather, his great-grandfather. The worn bindings were a shabby anachronism in the artful brightness of this modern widewindowed room, with its white linen draperies and its handwoven offwhite nylon rug. A woman's room. A pretty room. Except for the dark grimy leather bindings on the old books.

It was a room in which Mrs. Treadway in her fur cape and dark gray tweed suit, small fur hat on the hair that once had been pale yellow and was now streaked with gray, should feel at home. A pretty woman in a pretty room. A woman's room.

"Won't you sit down?" He indicated an armchair near his desk, chair upholstered in some kind of nonsensical whimsical geranium-red fabric.

She sat down, but she leaned toward him, and her manner was urgent, unrelaxed.

"These stories about Camilo," she said. Then the tired voice died, came to life again. "You've got to help me put a stop to them. You've got to help me, Mr. Bullock. She's disintegrating, emotionally, psychologically, because of them."

I could tell her about the monkey and his friend, the cat, and the roasted chestnuts, he thought. I could say, These are not my chestnuts, Mrs. Treadway; and I will not thrust my paw into the fire to pull them out for you. But if I plan to keep, hold on to, that thirty thousand a year she pays out for advertising in my paper, then I will pull rabbits out of hats, I will stand, sit, beg, charge, sic 'em, and pull her hot chestnuts out of the fire—as ordered.

"They are saying horrible things about her. I didn't know people could be so cruel. Nobody believes—they're saying that she—" the tired voice faltered, stopped, refused to put in words the accusations against Camilo. "I never knew that people could be so cruel," she said again. "My own servants believe these dreadful stories. I have been to see the Judge, and he will not set a date for that man's trial. He was evasive, full of excuses. He—he managed to express doubt of Camilo's innocence—" Her face changed, still haggard, old, but the expression was angry, ruthless, coldly determined.

He thought, Juggernaut. I'm in the path of a juggernaut. It's more serious than that. He remembered having seen this same expression on his mother's face. He was ten years old, hair always hanging down over his eyes, because he would not have his hair cut, and a trip to the barber shop entailed assault with intent to kill on the part of his parents; so they postponed the necessary violence until he began to look like Rip van Winkle or a buffalo, or both. He was in that shaggyheaded state one night, at supper, and there were candles on the table;

and he stood up, bent over, long unkempt hair falling forward over the lighted candles. His hair caught on fire. His mother reached out and smothered the fire with her hands, bare, unprotected hands. As she bent toward him, reaching across the table, beating the fire out, just with her hands, the expression on her face had frightened him, so that he cried out in alarm. Years afterwards he saw a painting of The Furies, and there was the same expression that had been on his mother's face as she thrust her hands straight into his blazing hair—a ruthlessness, and a fury, and a cold determination. Same expression still on Mrs. Treadway's face.

"You've got to help me," Mrs. Treadway said. "I want—"

After she left, he wondered how it was that he came to be in a position where he couldn't say no. It was the rising cost of newsprint, it was the cost-of-living increase in wages that he had paid because it was requested, open threat behind the request. Most of the people who worked for him belonged to the Newspaper Guild, and it was perfectly obvious, though he had done everything he could to prevent it, that sooner or later his newspaper, the newspaper that had belonged to his father, and to his grandfather, *The Monmouth Chronicle*, started as an abolitionist newspaper, started by that erratic highly moral definitely crazy man, his great-grandfather, would soon be run as a closed shop.

Yes, and it was the payments on that modern horribly-expensive-but-absolutely-necessary rotary press; it was the real estate tax on the building; the interest on the mortgage on the building, and on this ranchtype completely modern and unjustifiably expensive house that Lola had had to have. Now that she had it, she was not one whit happier than she'd been when they lived in that oldfashioned three-story affair that had belonged to his father—or maybe she was, she could spend more money living out here. There was the upkeep and the payments on the two cars and the station wagon, and the income taxes, and the Social Security payments. There was Social Security to be paid for the maid, and the laundress, and Social Security to be paid for the three-times-a-week heavy cleaning woman, whom Lola facetiously called the work girl; work horse would be a better name, he thought.

Social Security for maids. Blah! People didn't want to work any more. He could remember when maids saved for their old age, worked and saved, just like anybody else, and now they didn't have to, the State would take care of them, just like in Russia.

But what of a man named Bullock? Who was going to take care of Bullock in his old age? Not the State. Just Bullock.

If Mrs. Treadway took that institutional advertising with the American flag at the top, advertising that consisted of editorials on democracy, hymns of praise to the United States, out of his paper, it would just about fold up.

Lola would have to give up the green Buick, and the maid, and the laundress, and the cleaning woman, and the new fall clothes and the new winter clothes, the new spring clothes, the new summer clothes, and the annual cruise to Bermuda. She would have to do her own washing and ironing. What the hell did she do all day anyway? There was always extra help brought in for dinner parties, for luncheons, for bridge parties.

He could remember, how well remember, that his mother had had one girl, Swedish, name of Jenny, who stayed with the family until she died, and not only had his mother's house been a pleasant, orderly place, but she'd had five children and— But Lola had to have someone to do the cleaning and the dusting, someone to do the washing and the ironing, someone to do the cooking, and they had no children, yet there were always the most terrific, the most unexplainable and unexpected bills.

Take this house, this big mortgaged completely modern house that they'd built in the most exclusive section of Monmouth, on the outskirts, near Treadway Hall, and Lola still said they were lucky to be able to buy the land because after all, only millionaires lived out here. Monmouth's tradespeople knew it, so it cost them three times as much to live here as it had to live in his father's oldfashioned house in the center of the city.

Suppose I'd said no to Mrs. Treadway. Would Lola, could Lola, do her own washing and ironing and cooking? Would she? Could she? No. Well, he supposed she could, there were women who did. Lola? Why blame it on Lola?

Mrs. Treadway had said, again, "We have no contract with your paper, Mr. Bullock."

So that night he sat in the pinepaneled library, in the mortgaged ranchtype house, and thought about Mrs. Treadway, and then about his maiden aunt, who used to say, "A lie will be all over Providence while Truth is getting his boots on," salt of the sea in her speech, on her tongue, so that she looked and sounded as though she had been pickled in brine, remembering her house with its three chimneys, and a fireplace in every room, captain's house, double house. He'd lived with her in that house during the four years he went to Brown, thought of the city of Providence, lowlying city, and yet hilly, and of the graduation exercises and the baccalaureate held in the Baptist Meeting House, long hill to go down, and the caps and gowns descending, moving slowly, might have been a procession of blackrobed priests, except for the mortarboards, except, too, for the Baptist Meeting House, sacred to the memory of Roger Williams.

"A lie will be all over Providence," he said to himself, "or Berlin, or Rome, or MonmouthConnecticut, or any other damn place, while Truth is getting his boots on."

But this that he had agreed to do, and he reminded himself that he had agreed, was simply a matter of selecting one or two stories about crimes committed in The Narrows (Why not Niggertown? Because there is in me somewhere a reluctance. Then call her up and say you won't do it, say you changed your mind; and thought, Social Security, income tax, interest on mortgages and the amortization thereof, and payments on cars, and all the different kinds of insurance) and giving them a front page spot, in the *Chronicle*, every morning. Simply a matter of emphasizing, spotlighting, underlining these stories about crimes committed by Negroes. Simple. Uncomplicated. Neither truth nor lie. But truthlie. Lietruth.

Then he thought, But the mind of man being what it is, I know, and Mrs. Treadway knows, that if the *Chronicle* keeps saying that The Narrows breeds crime and criminals, a new set of images will be superimposed over those pictures that Jubine sold to the goddamn tabloid. The face of that nigger (Why not Negro? Because of the arrogance) Apollo will change first. It will almost immediately be transformed into the face of The Criminal, and will be remembered as such. Camilo's slackjawed face, face of the eternal whore, will be changed, transformed (more slowly, of course), until it becomes the face of The Victim, and she will be remembered and spoken of as such. Truthlie? Yes.

Is this possible? Of course. And quite necessary because that highly moral man, Judge Doan, has thus far refused to set a date for the trial. Someone must have got to the Judge, must have tampered with the Judge. He suddenly remembered Rutledge's seemingly idle question, "What're you going to do when the old lady comes in to cop a plea?" Thought of Rutledge's face, the way he talked, the lack of expression in his lead-colored eyes, and decided that he had the corrupt look of a man who had been born with a dollar sign where his soul should have been.

Then thought, Who am I to appraise, evaluate, another man's soul?

But if Rutledge got to the judge, then who got to Rutledge? Who persuaded Monmouth's Chief of Police to intervene, interfere, in this case? A person or persons unknown. Person powerful enough to push a judge and a chief of police in the direction he wanted them to go, just as though they were pawns on a chessboard.

Jubine? Hardly. He is a simpleton with a monomania, a monomaniacal simpleton, and therefore powerless. Not really powerless. He has already tried the case and turned in a verdict. With his camera.

It doesn't matter who controls the Judge and the Chief of Police. What really matters is that Monmouth has a venal judge, and a venal chief of police. What of Bullock? Man named Bullock? Venal, too. The purchase price for all of us is low. We're bargain basement stuff. Marked way down.

These days people make that nasty counting gesture with the fingers, whenever my name is mentioned, whenever the *Chronicle* is mentioned. They say I sold out to the Treadway interests. Truthlie. Lietruth.

At midnight Lola came into the library, slender, redheaded, perfumed, wearing a dress of some kind of pale green brocaded stuff. Emerald earrings in her ears. He'd given them to her at Christmas.

"Whatever are you doing?" she asked. "You've been in here for hours."

"I am paying the piper," he said slowly. "I met him just the other day and he told me that I've been dancing to the tune he plays for a long time. Therefore I must pay him."

"What do you mean by that?"

"Just what I said. My business is, at the moment, inextricably mixed up with the piper's business." I wish she'd go away, leave me alone. She looks like a wood nymph.

"Have you been gambling?" she said, sharply.

"No. Nor wenching. Nor drinking. Nor contracting bad debts. Wait a minute," he said, thoughtfully. "Maybe it's the debts. No. That's not true." Lietruth. Truthlie. "I'll be goddamned if I know how my path crossed the path of the piper." He thought of Jubine, saying, "The price you paid," of Jubine saying, "You're a poor peon and you ache to be a rich peon."

Lola said, "Pete, has this got something to do with Mrs. Treadway?"

"Sure, it's got something to do with Mrs. Treadway," he said, glaring at her, thinking, All marriages are like this. The component parts are contempt and irritation because we know each other by heart, by rote; we're all graduates of the blab school for double harness. Then he looked at the redgold hair, the sweet curve of the mouth, and thought, Truthlie, because marriage is more than that. It's part hate, part love. It's remembered agony, and remembered delight.

"Sure," he repeated, leaning forward, lowering his voice, "Didn't you know that I raped Camilo? But I wore a black mask and used a bow and arrow instead of Popeye's corncob."

He leaned back in his chair, watching her, waiting for her to say, "I don't know why I go on living with you," because that's what she always said when she was angry. This time she didn't say anything, simply turned away from him, and went out of the room. He sat still, for a moment, listening to the rustling sound of her brocaded skirt, thinking of the way she looked when she first woke up, how the freshness of the morning seemed to be reflected in her face, in her eyes, and he got out of the chair quickly, and followed her out into the hallway, and put his arms around her.

Two weeks later, he sat in his office, frowning. He had been looking at copies of the *Chronicle*, all the issues, for the past two weeks, trying to determine why this crusade (If you could call it that, he thought) against crime in The Narrows had influenced his own thinking so that he had done something, finally, that he was ashamed of. His secretary had stacked the newspapers on his desk, in a neat pile, and he had crumbled them up, one by one, and tossed them on the floor.

He searched through these crumpled papers until he found Tuesday's paper, and reread the story about Miss Eleanora Dwight. On Monday night, Miss Dwight, an old maid school-teacher, retired, was walking toward the rooming house where she lived. It was dusk, and the street was filled with shadows. She saw a man, a Negro, emerge from an areaway. She said it was as though a part of the night came toward her, a moving piece of darkness. The man knocked her down. Before he could harm her, she was rescued by a passer-by. Her assailant disappeared. Miss Dwight said, "He seemed to vanish, seemed to go right back into the blackness of the night."

This story, which had nothing to do with the dock or The Narrows, had been placed on the front page. Bullock's orders. No good reason for putting it there (a thirty-thousand-dollar reason). No good reason for not putting it there (a thirty-thousand-dollar reason). It should have been buried on an inside page where it would have been read with amusement, and dismissed as the wishful thinking of an old woman, and so forgotten. Instead—he shrugged. There was something poetic and disturbing and unforgettable, about that phrase, "a moving piece of darkness."

Wednesday's paper was of no importance. He didn't bother to look for it. It had the usual front page story about a crime committed in The Narrows. A robbery.

But Thursday's paper was very important. So was Friday's. He found both papers, smoothed them out, put them on his desk. On Wednesday night, a prisoner escaped from the State Prison. Thursday morning's paper said that all Monmouth knew about his escape. Because of the wail of the siren that stood atop the gray stone walls, because of the lights, the searchlights, because of the sudden frenzied activity of the guards, who were stationed along the length of the wall. The siren sounded about six o'clock. There was a dense fog and so the foghorn was sounding at the same time. The sound of the siren and the bray of the foghorn mixed, mingled, but the siren was always louder, stronger, more terrifying, symbol of disaster, of death.

The convict, a big heavily built Negro, knocked a man down, and took the man's clothes, and thus was able to leave his prison garb behind, on the road. He headed toward Monmouth, straight toward Monmouth, running with his head down. Dogs sensed his passage and barked, and he kept going, almost unseen, because of the fog. A dangerous man, a brute, a murderer. He disappeared.

Bullock read the story twice, thinking, There's nothing to be ashamed of here. It's overly dramatic but it is all true.

He picked up Friday's paper, with reluctance. He was ashamed of this one. This one told the story of the convict's end, and it carried his picture, a front page, blownup picture of the Negrovillainconvicthero.

He thought, I did this myself, no one told me to. It had nothing to do with Mrs. Treadway or that goddamn institutional advertising. The headline is bad enough. It ought to be on a billboard. They use the same kind of type on 'em. The picture is infinitely worse. But it's been done before. It's an ugly, senseless thing to do but not unforgivable. It's the story itself. It is the outrageous lie that I deliberately put in there.

But by next week, the convict would be forgotten. People would be talking about something else. Besides it was the kind of story that didn't harm anyone. It couldn't.

He started reading Friday's paper. It said the convict disappeared. The next day hunger drove him out into the open. He circled around a solitary farmhouse, waited outside for half an hour, crouched down in the shrubbery near the house. There was no car in the barn that was now used as a garage.

He went nearer, looked in through the kitchen windows, saw a woman, alone, fixing food, and opened the kitchen door.

"Food," he said. "I want food."

The woman screamed and he put his hand over her mouth, grabbed a dish towel, and made a gag, stuffing it in her mouth, snatched up some food, and was gone. The woman was lying on the floor when her husband found her, and when the gag was removed, she began screaming, and couldn't stop.

They caught the brute, the murderer, the escaped convict,

the Negro, on the edge of the city. All the roads leading into and out of the city, leading to and from the prison, were patrolled.

Though why, Bullock thought, rereading this story that he had written himself, why any sane escaped convict would head toward those gray walls from which he had emerged, after God-knows-what struggle, God-knows-what weeks, probably months, of planning, nobody would know. But the readers of this story would not stop to question a matter of phrasing, they would shiver with horror and fright, and there would be, also, a certain delicate enjoyment, pleasure, mixed with it, because the convict was dead.

The policemen, detectives, guards from the prison, National Guard, had patrolled the roads, the streets of the city, so that everywhere you went you saw armed huntsmen, peering, walking, patrolling.

Ah, what the hell, he thought, as he threw the newspaper down on the floor of his office. He wasn't responsible for this. This had happened all by itself. Or had it? How did he know whether this man, this convict, had not somehow been influenced by the stories in the *Chronicle*? How did he know what word had seeped back inside the walls of that gray stone prison, so near the city that you could see it, yet so far away that you could easily forget that it was there, except when the siren sounded. Anyway, the man was dead. He'd been shot, riddled with bullets, the story said.

It had damn near backfired, too. Because that thin, gray-haired, overworked housewife had refused to say that the convict had tried to attack her.

The *Chronicle*'s reporter said that she had stubbornly repeated the same words, over and over again. "He didn't do nothing to me. I hollered because I didn't know he was there in the kitchen. He spoke up and I didn't know there was nobody there but me until he spoke up and it scared me and I hollered. I didn't know he was no convict. He was a big black man and the sight of him there so sudden and so unexpected in my kitchen scared me. I'da hollered the same way if he'da been a big white man showing up so sudden and so unexpected in my kitchen. He didn't do nothing to me except stuff the dish towel in my mouth, and then stuffed some food in his own mouth, and grabbed up some more food and run out the door. He didn't do nothing to me."

Her husband kept saying, "Shut up, you're nervous, you're upset, you don't know what you're talking about—"

The wife, the thin overworked past-middle-age wife, said to the reporter, "Young man, don't you write down that he bothered me. He didn't do nothing to me. All he done was—"

So Bullock wrote down simply, and untruthfully, that the black convict, the brute, the escaped murderer, had attacked the frail housewife when he found her alone in the big farmhouse. And put the convict's picture on the front page.

It was a picture which showed the convict not as a man but as a black animal, teeth bared in a snarl, eyes crazy, long razor scar like a mouth, an open mouth, reaching from beneath the eye to the chin, the flesh turned back on each side, forming the lips of this dreadful extra mouth. Bullock knew that everyone who saw that picture would remember it, and wake up in the middle of the night covered with sweat, because this terror, this black terror, had a shape, a face; and they would remember the headline NEGRO CONVICT SHOT in boldface type, headline that took up the center half of the paper, and they'd think Yes, the crazed black animal with the mutilated face is dead, but what about the others, there are others who are still alive, who are just as dangerous. White women not safe. Not safe in Monmouth.

What the hell, he thought, if it hadn't been this it would have been something else. No matter how you looked at it, it was a nervous time in which to be alive, a nervous year, what with high prices, and all the little wars that threatened to become big wars; what with people fumbling for, reaching for security, and looking over their shoulders at insecurity.

Even the State Department was acting like a harried housewife, searching out the hiding place of mice and cockroaches and bedbugs, any of the vermin that from time to time invade a house, searching carefully under beds and in bureau drawers, and on closet shelves, in cellars and in attics, peering inside ovens, and sugar bowls, looking in every likely and unlikely place for communists and socialists, for heretics and unbelievers, and uncovering so much dust, so much of what Bullock's maiden aunt, the one with the sharp vulgar tongue, called slut's wool, so much of the dirty traceries of moths, so many cobwebs that the whole country shuddered.

So what difference does it make, he thought, whether we here in Monmouth hunt down Negroes or whether we hunt down Communists. We? You mean you and Mrs. Treadway. And there is a difference, though at the moment it escapes me.

That picture of the Negro with the mutilated face—that wasn't, I shouldn't have. It is the one thing I regret. The rest of it isn't important. But I had to. I had to offset that other picture, Jubine's picture of that arrogant nigger with the Barrymore profile. I had to. I had to offset, counterbalance, outweigh that dirty counting gesture made with index finger and thumb that had become an unspoken byword, a symbol for the *Chronicle*. I had to.

But on Monday he was going to tell Mrs. John Edward Treadway to take her goddamn advertising and stick it because he was going all out in another direction. He would—

But by Monday it was too late.

21

MALCOLM POWTHER sat in the back seat of Captain Sheffield's car, on Dumble Street, and listened to the soft sound of the motor, soft sound of the motor, and the windshield wiper kept it saying, Scupper, scupper, scupper, scupper, just the one word, over and over, and it made a sound in the car, which was good, and the foghorn was sounding at intervals, Whodid, whodid, on two notes—and it made a sound outside, which was good, because they were sitting there silent, all of them, waiting.

The Madam, and that had surprised him, was in the car too, sitting in the front seat with the Captain. And the two young men, who were friends of the Captain's, were in the back seat. Waiting.

He wouldn't let himself think about why they were waiting. Though bits and pieces of the reason would float up to the surface of his mind. He approved of the rain. The early dark. Otherwise there would be more people on the street, and they would have turned to look at that parked car, people sitting in it, seemed to be a lot of men in it, and the engine running.

Last winter Al kept saying, "Whyn't she divorce Bunny?" That was before any of this had happened. He had told Al, "It's kinder. What she's doing is really kinder. When a man, all of him, is involved with a woman, I don't think the man really cares whether she has affairs with other men. So long as she doesn't leave him. He cares, yes, that is, he doesn't like it. It hurts him. But it would hurt worse if she left him. And Miss Camilo is a very kind person. A lovely person. She knows that it would ruin the Captain if she left him. It's not a perfect situation for her or the Captain. But Miss Camilo is a very great lady and perhaps she feels it's her fault that the Captain is so dreadfully in love with her, so she stays with him. She can't bring herself to hurt him, the way it would if she left him."

That was before all this other business. The Captain must have known he would have rivals. Yes, but had he been able to foresee one the size and shape—and color—of Link Williams?

Scupper. Scupper. Scupper. Link Williams. Mamie tore that picture of him out of that New York paper. It was on the kitchen table, one night when he came home. He said, "What's that there for?" not wanting to ask, but having to, afraid to know, but having to know, actually believing that she would say, "Because I got a heat on for him, sugar."

She never talked about love, always about somebody having a heat on for somebody else, and he expected her to say that, standing there in the kitchen, wearing a new red-and-white-striped dress, with no sleeves in it, and the neckline cut so low you could see the dividing line of her breasts. And the kitchen filled with the toosweet smell of her perfume, and J.C. standing there barefooted, looking at both of them, licking raspberry Kool-Aid off the palm of his hand, no expression on his face, just that bovine licking of the palm of his hand, and his tongue a brilliant poisonous red, and the acidulous smell of the stuff competing with the smell of Mamie's perfume.

Mamie laughed. She said, "That's one goodlookin' nigger, Powther. Look at him standing there on that dock, just like he owned it, and would throw anybody in the river who said he didn't. That's why I cut it out. Because he looks like he owns everything in sight. That's why."

She didn't say a word about Miss Camilo's accident with the car, and that dreadful picture of her on the front page of that New York tabloid, and the talk, the talk, everywhere, so much of it, and so filthy, that he finally asked Al to drive him home nights because he couldn't bear to listen to what people said on the Franklin trolley. Listening to the servants at the Hall was bad enough, but it was worse, infinitely worse to have to listen to strangers bandying Miss Camilo's name around, just as though they knew her and had the right, had been given the right, to discuss her. He tried to figure out why people were so malicious, why they showed such delight in saying horrible things about a young woman they'd never seen. He supposed it was the same thing that had, for years, sent thousands of people to championship fights when Joe Louis was fighting. Sure they all thought he was wonderful, was a great fighter, had the heart of a champion, but they wanted to see him knocked out. People like to see a king uncrowned, like to see a thoroughbred racehorse beaten when he's running at the top of his form and has outrun everything in sight. They wanted to see demonstrated right before their eyes that there was no such thing as invincibility, wanted to see that the king, the top dog, the best man, has a flaw, can be beaten like them, is vulnerable like them, can be defeated, unfrocked, uncrowned, knocked down, and thus brought right down to their level.

Scandal in a wealthy, important family like the Treadways served to bring the Treadways right down to the level of the trolley car conductor, the bootblack. It showed they could be hurt, wounded, ruined, just like other people.

He sighed, impatient with the waiting, wishing that some one of them would say something. As soon as he got out of the car, he would hurry across the street, go in through the front door, up the carpeted staircase, ears straining with listening, trying to determine in that dark upstairs hall whether Mamie was home, still there, or did the darkness and the silence mean that he had been too late, that she had gone off somewhere. He didn't use the outside back stairs any more, hadn't since all this crime had been going on in The Narrows, couldn't bring himself to walk around the side of Mrs. Crunch's house, head into the darkness at the corner of the house. He'd tried it and it seemed to him that his shoulder blades started to itch, in anticipation of a knife blade plunged into his unprotected back. He explained to Mrs. Crunch why he came in through the front, and she had said, "Mercy, yes, Mr. Powther. I keep expecting we'll all be murdered in our beds. I move a bureau in front of my bedroom door every night, and I've got new locks on the windows, and I still wake up frightened. What ever has happened to these people? Why are they acting like this?"

Someone came out of The Last Chance, and he leaned forward. No. It wasn't. How much longer would they have to wait?

Sunday and a quiet rain, April rain, falling in the street. Umbrellas, rubbers, raincoats. And the interminable swish of the windshield wiper, a mechanical thing, but it ought to be tired. Not time for evening church services to start, dinner mostly in the early afternoon, this was a kind of winding down of the day, of Sunday. Very few people on the street, an occasional passer-by, intent on his or her own business. No sound of voices.

He became aware of the beating of his heart, unpleasant, wanted to count it, noticed that it was not synchronized with the whodid of the foghorn, the scupper, scupper of the windshield wiper, his heartbeat faster, than the other two, and the windshield wiper faster than the foghorn, irritating, listening to, waiting for three different sounds occurring at different intervals. A car passed, and then another one, and they all shrank back, drew back, the sudden illumination of the headlights disturbing.

A man turned into The Last Chance, a man who shambled, shuffled when he walked, shapeless felt hat pale redorange under the neon sign. Weak Knees. He stood still in front of the door, looking up and down the street. Powther thought, He knows there's something wrong, he senses it, smells it, like an animal recognizes the presence of danger without knowing what it is. "Weak made 'em. He's the cook in Bill's place"— doughnuts, wonderful texture, sweet fragrant flavorsomeness sticking in his throat—

Weak Knees went in The Last Chance. Another car went by. This one going slowly, not the sudden flashing brilliance, there one moment and gone the next, this one slowmoving, so that he saw the back of the Captain's head, saw each reddish hair, the cleanlooking neck, thought he must have had a haircut in New York, before he came up yesterday; saw the back of the Madam's head, her shoulders straight, held stiffly under the tan-colored raincoat, the hair looked white in the slowmoving unfocused car lights, disturbed by it too, because she lifted her hand, beautifully manicured hand, in a vague, purposeless gesture which reached for and never touched the whitelooking curls.

Never until now had he thought of her as a person, with feelings, with emotions, always vaguely as a fine, generous, kind, great lady, a kind of separate and apart person, living and breathing, yes, but not as ever having known anger or hate or fear, not as a mother. She and the Captain didn't like each other. Or rather, the Madam didn't like the Captain. He wondered why the Captain called her Mrs. Treadway, never having had a mother-in-law he couldn't hope to figure out all the delicate posturings and nuances and half-formed vague resentments that such a relationship might entail. The Copper boys' wives all called Old Copper "Pop" easily, naturally. This formality between the Captain and the Madam was a strange thing.

He watched the doorway of The Last Chance. Nothing. Another car, and that sudden swift illumination revealing the Captain's head, the Madam's whitelooking curls. He wished someone would say something.

Two people walking past. Talking. He listened, glad to hear voices.

The man (querulously): I don't know where he is. What you keep askin' me that for? I told you—I ain't seen him for two weeks.

The woman: What kind of fool you take me for? If you don't know where he is, how come you got his wallet?

The man: He give it to me. He give it to me before he left.

The woman: 'Fore he left for where? You ain't said nothin' 'bout his leavin' for nowhere.

The man: You ain't give me chance. You been sayin' nothin' but where is he. I don't know where he is. He told me he was goin' away and he's gone. I don't know where he's gone.

The woman: You always been a son of a bitch. He ain't give you no wallet of his and you know it. What you done with him? You answer me that. Where is he? He's your own brother and you gotta know where he is—

A quiet April rain, just enough fog to blur the edges of buildings, to destroy the clean outline of The Hangman. Hangman's buds beginning to swell. No one would really be aware of the coming of spring in Dumble Street, except for The Hangman. Thought of Old Copper, "Got the goddamndest climate, in the whole United States." Old Copper and his paintings, Mamie coming down the steps, walking slowly, bigbosomed, firmfleshed, brown skin translucent, like there was a light under it, redbrown, even the smile, the expression, just like the women in the paintings. The nudes. Outsize. Pinkfleshed.

Dreadful to watch Miss Camilo, to see Miss Camilo. Unbearable. He would collapse just like that if Mamie should leave him. Sound of the foghorn, Whodid? Whodid? Whodid? Why wouldn't she go away from Monmouth? Go into the country. Country. Cows. Cool. Spring. Could remember that bellowing, that moaning mooing of a cow, night after night, day after day, nerve endings right at the surface of the skin, the sound tearing the nerves, and his grandmother finally yelling, Whyn't somebody go git a bull, whyn't somebody, nerve ends frazzled, exposed, jumping. Miss Camilo.

Wish again for voices. Scupper? Scupper? Scupper?

Then a blast of sound in the street. He jumped. And felt the men, the two men, the friends of the Captain's, the two big young men that were like a blanket on each side of him exuding heat, warmth, jump too.

The Madam said, "What was that?" in a whisper, desperate, tense.

Then a voice, magnified, huge, all about them, said, "In the beginning God created the heaven and the earth."

Then a whirring sound. Powther sighed. It was that new loudspeaker they'd installed in Reverend Longworth's church —Masters University, healings of mind and body, I am the Way, the Truth, and the Life, and then the minister's name, Dr. H. H. Franklin Longworth, F.M.B. Minister, Psychologist, Metaphysician. Everyone Is Welcome. That's about what it said on the sign.

Mamie had told him about the loudspeaker that Reverend Longworth had had installed, had said they were going to try it out this Sunday, using a record. She said, "Now ain't that goin' to be a bitch, to have to listen to that pansy preachin' and prayin', just like he was in your house."

The lights came on in the church, or rather the building that housed Reverend Longworth's followers, came on suddenly, all over the building, spotlights on the sign across the front. Powther thought, It's just as though he said, Let there be light. He could visualize Longworth's face, his figure. He was a tall thin man, and his skin should have been brown but it was a sickly yellow, pallid yellow skin, like a plant whose leaves should have been dark green but because it was untouched by the sun, the leaves were pale yellow. He had a pointed beard too, and the beard was luxurious, thick, glossy, and didn't match his face.

Well, I didn't really bring the Madam here, he thought, that is, it was her idea, not mine; but I hate to have her listen to that charlatan perform. Then he couldn't think any more because the blasting sound of the Reverend Longworth's voice not only filled his ears, it filled his mind too.

Longworth (in a highpitched, rhythmical, hypnotic voice): And the Lord said unto Cain—

Then there was music, a choir composed of male and female voices began to hum, the sound rising, falling, rising, increasing in volume, and then an organ accompaniment in the background.

Slight pause. Organ music again. So loud it hurt the ears. Then the choir picked up the pitch of Longworth's voice, uncannily, preposterously, so that the singing voices seemed to be answering him, or questioning him.

Choir: Oh my good Lord, Show me the way,
   Enter the chariot travel along—

Longworth (voice louder, slower): And the Lord said unto Cain—

Choir: Noah sent out a mornin' dove
   Enter the chariot travel along—

Longworth: Where is Abel thy brother?

Choir: That dove came bearin' a branch of love
   Enter the chariot travel along—

Longworth (voice sonorous, slower and slower): And he said, What hast thou done?

Choir: Oh my good Lord, Show me the way,
   Enter the chariot travel along—

Longworth (voice faster, louder, voice blasting): The voice of thy brother's blood crieth unto me from the ground.

Choir (faster, louder, volume increasing):
   Oh my good Lord, Show me the way,
   Enter the chariot, travel along—

There was the loud whirring sound of the record. And then the voice of Reverend Longworth filled Dumble Street again. There was a caressing note in it this time. He said, "The service starts at seven o'clock tonight. Everyone is welcome. In the beginning there was the Word." Long pause. "I am the Way, the Truth, and the Life." Then the whirring sound again. That's what he said but the cajoling, caressing voice suggested that he was saying, Come unto me, I understand everything. Come. Be Saved.

Silence in the street now. Just the soft April rain. No cars. No one walking past. Idling sound of the motor. Scupper of the windshield wiper. Foghorn. Whodid, whodid, whodid. Red-orange neon sign in front of The Last Chance. Then the clang-clang of a trolley car over on Franklin.

He was unpleasantly aware of the two big young men on each side of him, unpleasantly aware of the warmth from their bodies. Two big young male animals.

The mateless cow, bellowing.

Where is thy brother? Lost somewhere between the who-did of the foghorn, and the scupperscupper of the windshield wiper. He wasn't my brother. I have to prove he wasn't my brother. Prove to these people in this car, that all Negroes are not criminal, some of them are good, some of them are self-respecting, some of them are first class butlers named Powther.

He had looked at that picture on the front page of the *Chronicle*, picture of a black man with a livid living scar across one side of his face, picture of an escaped convict who was dead, but who lived again in that nightmare photograph. Looked at it and shuddered.

Then he had seen the same newspaper on the Madam's desk, the same picture, when she said, Will you point out, point at, point? Looked at it and started to shudder again, thinking, Why should the face of this animal be permitted to enter my world, expected to hear the Madam say, You have been satisfactory, done a good job here, but you might become, you might, after all, you belong to the same race, there must be in you whatever it was in this man that made him—and instead she said, Will you point out. Point at. Point.

Sunday morning. This morning. It seemed a long time ago. He had gone up the stairs, slowly, wondering why he was being summoned to the morning room at ten o'clock. The Madam was sitting at her desk, turning over some papers. She said, "Powther, I need your help."

"My help, madam? I'll be glad to—"

"Wait," she said sharply. "Don't say that until you know what I want you to do. Do you know the man named Lincoln Williams?"

"Lincoln Williams?" he repeated. "You mean Link Williams? Why, yes—" and he was embarrassed because he did not want to discuss Miss Camilo with the Madam.

"You see, I—that is, we, Captain Sheffield and I want to talk to him. And we do not know him when we see him. I thought you might be willing to go into that area with us, and point him out to us."

Link Williams, he thought, Link Williams, point him out, point him out, what did she mean, point him out for what, point with your finger, but why? For what? Then he thought, "That area." It sounded like a compound. Dumble Street. She doesn't know, she has forgotten that I live there.

"You undoubtedly know about the troubles we've had of late. And if you could help us, I would be extremely grateful, Powther."

In the early morning sunlight she looked old and tired and there were new fine lines around her eyes that he hadn't noticed before; and her hair was drylooking, brittlelooking, that light blond hair that had gray in it, but it didn't show up at first glance because of the color of the hair, same color hair that Miss Camilo had; most people thought Miss Camilo dyed it but she didn't, it was naturally that color. And the Madam's eyes, funny, and he didn't quite believe it, seemed to plead with him for help. He thought, Why, she's really all alone. There isn't anybody to help her. Miss Camilo is walking around in a trance, drinking too much, taking sleeping pills, Rita said the Madam had gotten after Miss Camilo about the sleeping pills, had asked Miss Camilo to go back to New York, and Miss Camilo had refused to leave Monmouth. Or so Rita said.

What did she want him to do? Point at, point to, point out. Point.

"You will do it?"

"Certainly, madam. It's a small enough thing to ask. I'll be glad to."

So here they sat, in the Captain's car, waiting, and the windshield wiper kept making that talking sound, Scupper, scupper, scupper. Sometimes he thought it was in the form of a question: Scupper? Scupper? Scupper?

The door of The Last Chance opened again. Powther leaned forward, "That's him," he said, pointing at the man who stood for a moment under the redorange sign, bathed in redorange light, redorange from head to foot, hatless, coatless.

They all watched him, waiting, to see if he was going to cross the street, move away from the door. He stood there, motionless.

Powther kept willing him to move, thinking, End the agony, the jealousy, the pain, the hurt, the outraged cries that bubble up in one's throat at night, and the nights, the dark, pitiless, endless nights, I know what it's like and so does the Captain. Link Williams and Bill Hod, mixed up in his mind, had become one and the same person in his mind.

At this moment, if it works out right, because they only plan to frighten him, make him leave Monmouth, I am helping to get rid of this creature who is worse than thief, worse than murderer, this wife stealer, and here and now in this thing the Captain and I are equals, both outraged, both victims, and so we have achieved a kind of togetherness, and in this way I have restored a little of my own long lost selfrespect.

The two young men were leaning forward, watching, too, waiting, too, and Powther thought he could feel the tenseness in them, thought of the badges they had, nickel badges that would shine just like real ones, under an electric light, thought of that white paper they carried, that could at just a glance appear to be a warrant, paper with a picture pasted on it, smooth paste job, so that it was almost like print, and that official-looking type, cut from an old newspaper and pasted on so that that, too, at first glance seemed part and parcel of a real warrant, only it said:

> Life is a mysterious and exciting affair and anything can be a thrill if you know how to look for it, and what to do with opportunity when it comes.

Rain misting the windshield, and the wiper talking to itself, it was a statement now, Scupper, scupper, scupper.

He thought, Why am I here? Why me? They couldn't trust anybody else. They can't tell one colored person from another. Link Williams and I look alike to them. They couldn't pick him out of a crowd, let alone on this street, this rainy street, at almost night, because all colored persons look alike to them.

Suddenly he said, "There."

Because Link Williams was moving away from the door of The Last Chance, walking away, toward the dock, with that easy effortless walk. He said, "That's him," again, louder, emphasizing it, with a large wide gesture of his hand.

The two big young men got out of the car. Powther saw Link Williams hesitate, saw the flash of the badges under the street light, saw the whiteness of the paper they held out toward him, warrant for his arrest, official-looking warrant.

Then he slipped out of the car, got out on the side next to the road, a little man indistinguishable in the dusk, just a small anonymous figure, moving fast, moving away fast, hurrying away from the sound of the windshield wiper, Scupper, scupper, scupper.

Once inside the kitchen, in the heat, and the light, and the smell of the food cooking, and the yelping of the boys, the sound of Mamie's singing, he started to tremble, to shake, it was more than shaking, it was a jerking of his body.

Mamie said, "Sugar, what's the matter? You look awful," and put her arms around him, pulling his head down on her big soft breasts, cushioning his head there.

22

THE MOMENT Link Williams sat down in the back seat of the car, handcuffed, he knew that these men, sitting on each side of him, were not policemen, not plainclothesmen, knew that this new black Packard was not a police car. The motor was running, and the man behind the steering wheel put the car in gear, pulled off, before the doors slammed shut, in the back.

They went down Dock Street, car going fast, faster. He thought, Kidnaping? Ransom? Have I somehow got mixed up in one of Mr. B. Hod's private wars?

He leaned back against the seat, relaxed against it, and the trenchcoated gentlemen, on each side of him, stiffened, tensed, very nearly jumped, he could feel their bodies tighten up. He wondered what they had expected him to do, a man handcuffed, sitting between two men not handcuffed.

They turned off Dock Street and went east for a block, turned again, and went down Franklin Avenue, following the trolley tracks. Couldn't be a kidnaping because the driver was staying on this through road. Yet the lady on the front seat doesn't like light. He could see the outlines of her shoulders, see whitelooking, curly hair. She doesn't like the pauses for the stop lights, she stiffens, shoulders get rigid; and these gentlemen in the back seat don't like the stop lights either, they shrink back as though they were trying to escape into the steel framework of the car. Not kidnaping. Some other dark midnight deed.

Going faster and faster, still following the car tracks. He used to ride this route, on the trolley. If they stayed on Franklin he would recognize the place where the tracks ended, just disappeared in the black of the macadam road. End of the line. Used to ride the trolley, going to work for the Valkills, an almost-but-not-quite-middle-aged, childless couple, who wanted someone just for the summer, someone to set the table and wash-wipe a few dishes. Abbie found the job for him when he was twelve years old.

He used to get on the trolley about eight-thirty in the morning, and the air was clean and clear and fresh, and still cool, at that hour. He liked the clang of the trolley, liked to watch the people get on and off, most of them knew the motorman, and everything was friendly and the people all looked early morning clean and brisk. He rode the car to the end of the line, and got out and walked a quarter of a mile to where the Valkills lived, and as he walked along, the nearer he got to the house, the more the early morning cleanness seemed to evaporate, diminish, begin to slide down into the hot tired dreary part of the day.

The Valkill house was on the edge of the river, a small weathered gray house filled with an indescribably stale, old, shutup river smell; it seemed to come from the wood, the walls and the floors. He finally got so he thought he could smell the house before he saw it, thought he could see the Valkills before he caught a glimpse of them.

They were always outside the house, lying on a narrow strip of gravelly rocky shore which constituted a beach, a mere separation of the river from the land. Mrs. Valkill wore a black bathing suit and Mr. Valkill wore khaki shorts. Even at nine in the morning, even when he was on a three-week vacation, Mr. Valkill had his eyes closed, as though he were too tired to look at Mrs. Valkill's meaty underside-of-a-flounder-white thighs. Mr. Valkill was very tanned. His eyes were blue and very wide open—when he wasn't looking at Mrs. Valkill.

Abbie said they were fine rich people. He thought they were fine slave drivers. He hated them.

He rebelled against this job that Abbie had picked out for him, rebelled against doing housework that was never finished. There were the breakfast dishes, and the last night's dinner dishes, more or less skilfully tucked around here and there, but he recognized them, knew that two people could not possibly use all those dishes just for breakfast. And he was supposed to sort of help with lunch, and while they ate in the dining room, he sat on the small porch off the kitchen, on the railing, watching the river, and wondering about these people he worked for, the Valkills.

After lunch he cleared the table, washed the luncheon dishes, swept and dusted, and dusted and swept. He'd been there about two weeks when Mrs. Valkill gave a tea, and had him wear some kind of Japanese kimono and the kimono was all peculiar colors, made of a sleazy thin material that smelled like the house, and the old tired musty river smell that clung to the material made his skin crawl.

Mr. Valkill strolled in at the tailend of the tea party, and his eyes were filled with laughter whenever he looked at Link in the kimono, and he followed him out to the kitchen and watched him as he washed the cups and saucers, and said, "Mrs. Valkill is a genius. I never would have noticed—never would have known how attractive a Japanese kimono could be—"

Mr. Valkill called him Cassius, and when Mrs. Valkill asked him why, he said, "'Yond Cassius has a lean and hungry look,' such men are dangerous," and Mrs. Valkill laughed and laughed and had to wipe her eyes. They talked about him, right in front of him, just as though he weren't around.

He hated the job, and told Abbie so, and Abbie wouldn't listen to him. She folded her mouth into a thin straight line, and said in that refusingtolisten voice, "Every boy should know how to keep a house clean. There aren't any easy jobs. You might as well find it out now while you're young—"

After he wore the Japanese kimono, Mr. Valkill took to appearing suddenly in the kitchen, watching him, leaning in the doorway, or practically lying down on one of the straight-backed kitchen chairs because he lolled on the end of his spine, but his bright blue eyes were wide open, bright blue eyes always filled with laughter.

Now when he approached the house, Mr. Valkill greeted him, from the beach. "Good morning, Cassius, what's the weather like? You want to go back to sleep? There's plenty of room." Bright blue eyes very wide open, one hand indicating the beach, the rocky little beach, hand extended in invitation.

Mrs. Valkill said, "Stop it, Henry."

Mr. Valkill ignored her. "The rocks aren't bad once you get yourself in the right position."

Shortly after that they went away for the weekend, a long weekend. He had all of Monday off, and spent it in the kitchen of The Last Chance, except when he went swimming off the dock with Bill. He told Bill about the Valkills, and Bill kept looking blank, completely blank, except when he came to the

part about the Japanese women's clothes they had him wear
when they had people in for tea, and his face changed. "Holy
Christ!" he said. "Listen, you go out there tomorrow morning
and you quit. You hear? Quit. Just like that. And if your aunt
don't like it, tell her to see me and I'll spell it out for her, in
two words."

Tuesday morning he went back to the Valkills. Just as he
opened the kitchen door, Mr. Valkill came sauntering into the
kitchen, wearing khaki shorts, his long hairy legs, his knobby
knees, thick blond hair on his tanned chest, something not to
look at, to avoid looking at.

"Well, well, well," he said. "If it isn't Cassius just in time to
fix the morning coffee." His eyes looked more alive than Link
had ever remembered seeing them.

He made the coffee and Mr. Valkill lingered in the kitchen
drinking it, and talking, and when he finished he sat on the end
of his spine, delicately balancing the cup on his fingertips. He
said, "Madam Valkill won't be home until late this afternoon."

He stopped listening to the soft drawling voice because Mr.
Valkill seemed to be talking to himself. He supposed he'd have
to wait until Mrs. Valkill came home, tell her he was quitting,
because she was the one who hired him, who paid him, and
Abbie said you always told your employer when you resigned
from a job, or if you had any complaint. You had to take the
direct approach, never the indirect approach, because colored
people invariably avoided unpleasantness, they would lie, they
would laugh, but they never faced right up to a situation,
head on.

He wondered what he ought to do when he finished the
dishes. These were the Friday morning breakfast dishes, really
stuck with food, like it was glued on, eggs on the plates like
yellow oil paint, crusted black stuff in the bottom of both coffee cups, two sticky glasses that had contained orange juice,
both of them had had toast, and there had been marmalade on
Mr. Valkill's toast, because the leftover portion had little fine
red ants on it. Mrs. Valkill didn't eat marmalade on her toast
for fear of getting fat—no, she said because of her hips.

There was a change in Mr. Valkill's voice. It was softer, gen-
tler. Link turned and looked at him.

"Did anyone ever tell you you were goodlooking?" he said, idly, not moving, still balancing the coffee cup.

"What?"

"You're a goodlooking boy, Cassius."

Link said Yeah, yeah, yeah, thinking of Weak Knees: Some things is natural and some things is against nature. Don't you never spend no time listenin' to any man who starts sweet talkin' to you. You hear me, Sonny? You always move off. If you ain't got no place to move off to, then you holler.

He hung the dish towels on the rack, carefully, taking his time about it, his movements slow, his thoughts fast, remembering Weak Knees kneading bread, one Saturday morning in the kitchen, thump thump of the dough, "Any time you smell trouble, and you kind of all alone some place where can't nobody hear you if you was to holler, why it ain't never no disgrace to turn tail and run. Even the Boss has had to hightail it a coupla times anyway. Ain't never no disgrace to turn tail and run."

The black Packard was going faster and faster. Nobody spoke in the car. Good advice. If you smell trouble. I smell trouble. How do you go about running, in the interior of a car, with handcuffs on your wrists, how do you run then?

But he'd run that other time. Mr. Valkill put his hand on his arm, Mr. Valkill's hand reminded him of Bill Hod's hand, firm warm wellcaredfor clean hand, the nails filed, but the forearm was thickcovered with blond hair, like blond fur on the forearm, forearm of a blond ape, and revulsion made him move. He'd been standing there half fascinated, half afraid, curious, too—wondering what and how—

He said "Yeah" again and moved fast, so fast, that Mr. Valkill's hand was left outstretched, reaching. He went toward the kitchen door, out on the porch, down the steps, fast, not running, but covering ground without wasting any time, so that he was outside the house, going down the road, before Mr. Valkill could possibly overtake him.

He heard him shouting, "Hey, what's the matter? Where are you going?"

Then he ran. He ran all the way to the car line, to that place where the tracks, the trolley tracks, appeared suddenly in the black of the macadam road. When he reached Dumble Street, he went in The Last Chance, and when he came out, he had a job for the rest of the summer, working in the kitchen there. And told Abbie so. Abbie said, "I won't allow it. You're going straight back to Mrs. Valkill tomorrow morning and tell her that I sent you back."

"I won't," he said, flatly, stubbornly.

He heard Abbie and F. K. Jackson discussing it.

F. K. Jackson: He can't go back to the Valkills, Abbie.

Abbie: I've already sent him back. He is not going to work in the kitchen of that place across the street.

F. K. Jackson: It's most unfortunate. But Mr. Valkill is abnormal. He likes little boys. He—

Abbie: I don't see anything abnormal about liking little boys. Most people do. I think it's wonderful that a man like Mr. Valkill should take an interest in a mere boy.

F. K. Jackson (sharply): Listen to me, Abbie. Mr. Valkill is a pervert, a sexual pervert. He will corrupt Link.

Abbie: Corrupt him how? What are you talking about? A pervert—you mean—oh—Link—oh—

F. K. Jackson: That's why he can't go back there. That's why you will have to get used to the idea of his working at The Last Chance. Mr. Hod is using this as a stick over our heads, a threat. He sent for me, summoned me, just as though he were an emperor, couldn't use the telephone or write a letter but sent his servant to tell me that he wanted to see me. When I went over there he said, "Link will be here for the rest of the summer, helping Weak Knees in the kitchen. When school starts he will be here after school and on weekends. If you can't convince his aunt that it's a good idea, I'll be glad to." He actually smiled at me, Abbie, and he looked just like a wolf, baring its teeth. He said, "There's a juvenile court in this city."

Abbie: The nerve of him. I don't care what he said. Link is not going to work there. It's against the law anyway. He's a minor. And the state liquor law says that a minor cannot be employed in any capacity on the premises of a place—

F. K. Jackson: It doesn't cover a private kitchen. He would be working in their private kitchen. Not in the bar. I'm afraid you'll have to get used to the idea. Mr. Hod claims that Mr. Valkill has a most unsavory reputation. If Hod wanted to make trouble, I think he could. He has considerable political influence and he might be able to get himself appointed as some sort of guardian for Link, on the grounds that you were no longer a suitable person, that you had placed Link in a position where—

Abbie: They seemed like such fine people and Mr. Valkill had the loveliest manners, and his wife was so sweet and they were wealthy. Fine rich people. It was Link's first real job—

F. K. Jackson (slowly): I honestly believe that he will be safer over there. There are a great many things that they know more about than we do.

Abbie: Oh, dear!

They were on the outskirts of the city now, still going fast. Used to be nothing but fields and open lots and woods out here, now all neat lawns and forty-thousand-dollar houses with attached garages. The Major used to tell him stories about when there were farms in this part of Monmouth, and people kept goats and cows and horses. Used to tell about Gleason's goat, a diabolical male animal, complete with beard, and what he now recognized as the naturally foul disposition of the male animal in a state of perpetual and unappeasable rut, who worked and worked and worked until he made an opening in Gleason's fence, and then would appear suddenly in the dooryard of one of the houses.

The cry would go up, from house to house, "Gleason's goat is out, Gleason's goat is out!" and women would run out of the houses, armed with brooms and mops and pokers and shovels, emerging from the back doors like arrows hurled from a catapult, intent on working over Gleason's goat, looking forward to the attack with a kind of furious pleasure, because the goat could destroy a prize rosebush in less than thirty seconds, because the goat headed straight for clotheslines and preferred the clean white shirts and the white dresses which represented a whole morning of backbending labor over a washtub.

The Major described the uproar and the excitement, with relish, telling how the goat would be ducking, butting, charging, retreating, silent, malevolent, intelligent, and the middle-aged women would duck and butt and retreat and advance too, but not silently, emitting an unholy screeching as they mauled the goat and then retreated.

He laughed now because he thought it wasn't the clean clothes or the rosebushes that infuriated the women. It was the goat, the sheer maleness of the goat, that they were butting, charging, mauling with intent to kill. It was the old old war between the male and the female. Laughed again under his breath, and felt the men on each side of him stiffen again, saw the woman's head turn, ever so slightly.

He could smell perfume, the woman's perfume. Perhaps because of that slight movement of her head. Woman in the front seat. Why? Woman with a straight back, shoulders held rigid. Something in his mind said, Even with a bag tied over your head, even on the streets of Moscow, I would know—would recognize—your back.

Then he lost the thought, the nudging memory, looked out of the opened window, past the trenchcoated figure on his right, watched the landscape, the houses were smaller now, postage-stamp size, matchbox size, houses of war veterans, man spend the rest of his life paying for one of these chickencoops, one right on top of the other, no *lebensraum*, no garages, park the car right near the house, near the front door, but television aerials on all the little rooftops, a tangle of wire against the dark night sky.

Car going faster and faster. What the hell is this, he wondered. Relax, Bud, and wait and see. So they went along and they went along, Henny Penny and Turkey Lurkey and Ducky Lucky and Foxy Loxy. Now which of us, he wondered, is Foxy Loxy. Most logically the lady in the tan-colored raincoat, because otherwise why would she be here, riding in this car, riding through the fine misty rain with a handcuffed man in the back seat.

The car slowed, turned off to the right, entering a driveway, not a driveway, a long wide private road with a pair of gates at the entrance, gates studded and decorated and gilded like the gates of Victoria's summer palace in the south of France, pair of stone lions, couchant, emphasized the entrance, dramatized it, guarded it. The car picked up speed again. A rabbit bounded across the road, white cottontail going hell for leather, suddenly there in front of the headlights, and as suddenly gone. The car swerved to the right, and then as abruptly to the left, straightened out. Nerves all shot to hell, he thought, even from where I sit in this back seat, he wasn't anywhere near the damn rabbit, rabbit probably in a thousand cabbage patches or briar patches at the moment when he jerked the wheel like that.

The woman sitting on the front seat said, "Bunny!" protest in the voice.

And it all fell into place. He thought, No one in the USA free from prejudice, shows up somewhere, finally got all these male and female people into this black Packard. Finally. Why after all this time? Or did she in the back of her mind know when she stood under that street light on Dock Street, corner of Dumble, screaming her head off, that it would end like this, even to the handcuffs?

He thought of that picture on the front page of the tabloid, Jubine's picture, and how he had looked at it and cursed Jubine, because the canary, the little lost one, the palomino, had the face of a drunk, a lush, mindless, insentient, slackjawed, one hand lifted in an atypical cringing. He had laid the tabloid flat on the bar, Bill Hod's mahogany bar, the wood smooth, polished by the slow motion of elbows, of hands, by the wool of coats, sliding motion of bare forearms, until the wood responded to the warmth, the friction, the oil from the skin, and acquired a patina, not a surface slickness, but a glow that came from deepdown in the wood. The bar served as a frame, polished frame for Jubine's picture. It reminded him of something. It was the cringe in the shoulder line, there because the hand was raised, it was the way the hair fell forward, the awful jaw line. If he covered the eyes, lowered the hand but left that shoulder line intact, what would he see? He'd see Toulouse-Lautrec's Harlot.

He had thought he didn't love her any more, didn't hate her any more, and felt an ache inside him, a loss, an emptiness, thought it was like losing an arm or a leg, thought it was the kind of ache you got from an old wound when it rained, dull, monotonous, and studied the face again, the horrified eyes, the pale blond hair. He had stared across the bar at the telephone booth in the corner, near the front. Could drop a coin in the coinbox, and dial a number, and the light musical voice would answer, and he would say, Let's begin again, my fault, I am a fool, let's begin again. Shack job. Stud.

And so didn't do anything. But stand still. Then started cleaning the bar, cleaning out the beer pumps.

Remembered that headline in milehigh type, NEGRO CONVICT SHOT, strung across the front page of the *Monmouth Chronicle*, remembered that blownup picture of the escaped convict who had had one side of his face practically destroyed because someone had slashed him with a razor, years back.

Could hear Old Man John the Barber, when he came for his morning beer and looked at the picture. Barber would start to drink the beer and then put the glass down, and stare at the convict as though he were hypnotized, and say, "The bastards"; start to drink the beer again and put the glass down and say, "The bastards," just as though he were a nickel-in-the-slot automaton and someone had dropped a nickel in a slot somewhere inside him, and the two words emerged from his throat, automatically, no emphasis, just the two words.

So it was Jubine Lautrec's Harlot and The Convict by Anonymous that got me in this black Packard. That is one-quarter of the explanation. The other three-quarters reaches back to that Dutch man of warre that landed in Jamestown in 1619.

And they went along and they went along and the house was a stone pile, pile of stone, huge, formless, so few lights in it that it would be impossible to guess at the architecture, nothing to define its shape to the eye, no indication of windows, doors. The car stopped.

One of the trenchcoated gentlemen said, "Come on. Get out." His voice tense, excited. The GrotonHarvard accent blurred with fear.

They went in through a side entrance. He saw ivy on the walls, wet, slicklooking on the walls, rippling in the wind. Then they were standing in a hallway, hesitating there, uncertain.

The woman said, "This way."

It was a small room, no rug on the floor. Seemed to be a small sitting room, with a stone fireplace across one end. There was a moment, awkward, fleeting, during which they looked at him, and then looked away, and then looked again.

He dismissed the three men as unimportant, all of them cut from the same tree, perhaps elm, a soft wood no good for burning. But the woman. The woman is dangerous. It's in the face, the eyes, the mouth—determination, intractability.

Danger in the shaking. There's a tremor running through her that she can't control, running all through her body. Not fear but hate.

I know because I once shook like that myself. I watch this woman shake and I am standing in that dark little corridor outside Bill's office, holding his gun, and I am shaking so that I can hardly stand up, I have to lean against the wall, because I am remembering how he caught me in China's place again. We walked back to The Last Chance together and he said, Go in my office and he closed the door and locked it and picked that rawhide up, it was on top of his desk, and when it landed I gasped, and went on gasping because he kept hitting me with it.

When I got so I could walk again I tried to kill him, was going to shoot him with his own gun, and stood, shaking and trembling, not even able to point the gun, let alone hold it up, because I kept hearing his voice, seeing his face, when he bent over me, with that rawhide in his hand, "Get up, you bastard, or I'll kick your guts out—" I went down that long flight of stairs, leading into the kitchen, stood outside his office door, shaking and trembling, because I saw him sitting there, feet up on his desk, his back to the window, sunlight on the black hair, on the white shirt, the clean starched white shirt that he put on every morning, and that F. K. Jackson said was a fetish.

L. Williams: Bill!

B. Hod (looking up, voice deceptive, mild): So you're feeling better. What's the gun for?

He lifted his arm, tried to aim the gun, and his hand was shaking so that the gun went back and forth, back and forth, as though he had reverted to infancy and was waving byebye with it, his hand shaking and trembling so violently that the gun began moving in wide loose circles. Bill got up, walked toward him, hit his arm, one short sharp blow, and the gun went out of his hand, landed on the floor.

B. Hod: I suppose you're sore because you got a licking. What're you sore about?

L. Williams: You tried to kill me.

B. Hod: I told you not to go in that whorehouse again. And you did. So I took some of the hide off your back.

L. Williams: You tried to kill me.

B. Hod: So as soon as you can walk down those stairs again, you come in here and pull a gun on me. My own gun. Get the hell outta my face.

L. Williams: You bastard. You beat me until I couldn't stand up, couldn't see, couldn't hear. What do you call that?

B. Hod (voice ugly, voice furious): I ever catch you in China's place again, I'll cripple you for life. Get the hell out of my face.

The trenchcoated gentlemen, his escorts, keepers, bodyguards, said, together, in their GrotonHarvard voices, only GrotonHarvard had not prepared them for the handcuff technique so that they sounded solemn and dimwitted at the same time, "We'll wait outside. If you want us, just call."

Just call, gentlemen. On call. Call house.

The man with the reddish-blond hair, the goodlooking face, the poor bastard of a husband, closed the door behind them, waited a moment, hesitated, and then said, "Do you know who I am?"

He didn't answer, thinking, I could have predicted that you would start off that way, at an angle. You've chosen this tortuous, adumbrative approach, out of embarrassment. Because you've been horsed into this and you don't know what to do with it. So keep on circling around it because it's still your move.

Silence.

The man said, "I think you know who I am."

The woman said, "Why don't we sit down?"

That's right, lady, he thought, because if you don't, you'll fall down. I know how that feels, too, to hold oneself up, keep forcing oneself to stand up when the bones the muscles the nerves won't co-operate, and signal their lack of co-operation by shaking, shaking, shaking, and the shaking says, Sit down, lie down, or you'll fall down.

The woman sat down but the man stayed on his feet. The man said, not looking at him, "We don't want to harm you, to hurt you in any way. We just want to talk to you—to—" and his voice stopped, died.

"Suppose we stop playing tag with it," he said. He sat down in an armchair, directly across from the woman. "What do you want to talk about, Captain Sheffield?"

The woman tried to get up, almost managed it. What did I say that caused that change in her expression? If she'd had a gun, she would have shot me, right then, at that moment. But why? Voice. It's the sound of your voice, Bud. You hadn't spoken before and she took it for granted you would sound like AmosAndySambo, nobody in here but us chickens. And it has for the first time occurred to her that you and Camilo were making the beast with two backs. An old black ram has been tupping her white ewe. She will never let you get out of this room alive, and how will she manage to keep you from being alive. She has the shakes. These gentlemen that she is depending on to help her in the blood sacrifice are weak sisters, sad sacks.

Silence again. The man was leaning against the mantel now, staring at him. He looked at the woman, she was breathing at a faster rate, and the trembling had not increased, but somehow, the expression on her face, the outrage in her eyes, had changed the feel of the room. It was like a change in the tempo of a song, faster now, the woman had made it go faster.

She said, "We want you to sign a confession."

He kept watching her face. "A confession?" he asked, slowly. "Mea culpa?" He thought, I have no weapon, I have nothing to attack you with but my voice. I will make you wait and wait and wait and wait and wonder what I am going to say, and finally tell you—tell you—

"How far back shall I go?" he asked. They were both staring at him, fear in the woman's face, tension in the man's, fear and tension, building.

He began to use his voice as though it were an instrument, playing with it, reminiscent now, speaking deliberately, letting his voice range around. "I stole a lollipop when I was five, stole it in a candy store run by a man named Mintz. I ran away from home when I was eight. I went a long ways, too, just across the street." He stopped again, thinking, well, I might as well at some point name the complication, the inflammatory complication that the choreographer rang in on the old rigadoon of adultery and cuckoldry, because The Race with his deathshead face unmasked walked right in here with us, with me. "But the distance that I went was farther away from where I had been living than if it had been the coast of Africa where your

rapacious Christian ancestors went to kidnap the Guinea niggers who were my ancestors."

He paused again, watching the uneasiness, the fear, the
hate. "When I was sixteen I tried to kill a man. Between then
and now, well, I have not always loved my neighbor as myself. I have, on occasion, looked on the wine when it was red,
looked too long, and with too tender and yearning an eye."
He grinned, remembering Old Man John the Barber, If I
had to listen to that funny talk he does— "I have been guilty,
also on occasion, of running swiftly with the hares, gambol-
ing with the hares, and at the same time running swiftly with
the hounds, baying the moon at midnight, with the hounds."
Pause again.

"How about you two people?" he said, conversationally.
"Do you want to join me in the confessional? All of us culpa?"

Captain Sheffield moved farther away from the mantel. "You
raped my wife," he said, "there on the dock. You—"

"No."

Captain Sheffield said, "You raped my wife, you—"

He watched the woman, though he addressed the man,
speaking softly, taunt in his voice, "What was she doing on the
Dumble Street dock at midnight? Why don't you keep your
wife home—at midnight? Why don't you keep her home—at
night, Captain Sheffield?"

He watched the woman. She opened her mouth, tried to say
something, and she couldn't control the trembling of her lips.
She tried to get out of the chair, force herself to stand up, and
couldn't make it, sat down again.

Shared experience, he thought. I know about that, too.
Know how it feels. After Dr. Easter's last visit I tried to get
out of the chair, sat back down again, tried again, and made it.
I walked across the hall, went in Bill's room, and got the gun
from under his pillow and went down the stairs, slow, because
I couldn't go fast because of the shaking and the trembling.
I used the wall for support, leaning against it, going down
that enclosed staircase, no railing, stairs went straight down,
no turn, walls were pine, they call it knotty pine these days,
but to me, at sixteen, it was just wood, dark brown wood, and
I leaned against it, going down three steps and then standing
with my back against the brown wood of the wall, waiting until

my heart stopped trying to jump out of my chest, and the damn gun was so heavy I was afraid I'd drop it.

There was a tremor in the woman's voice. She said, "Bunny, there's no use talking to him, there's no use, don't let him—"

He watched her try to get out of the chair again. This time she succeeded but the effort she put into it made the shaking worse. She walked over to the sofa, bent over, fishing for something under the cushions, hands shaking, groping, reaching for something. Gun in the shaking hand.

It was a forty-five. He stared at it in disbelief. Tribal law, he thought. Man who breaks a taboo must die.

One for the money. Two for the show. Three to make ready. "It wasn't rape, Captain Sheffield."

The woman tried to point the gun, and couldn't lift it. It kept slipping down, and she tried to hold it with both hands, and the weight was too much, still couldn't raise it, muzzle kept pointing down at her own feet, downdangling. A forty-five.

You'll shake like that for the rest of your life, he thought, watching her. Like you had palsy. He knew. He'd had the tremors too, that time after Bill beat him up. He hauled ice for Old Trimble, in the belief that if he got his body rockhard he wouldn't shake and tremble every time he caught a glimpse of a man in a white shirt. Stole F. K. Jackson's gun because once he got rid of that shameful trembling, he was going to kill Hod. He hadn't succeeded the first time. He was going to try again. Because he hated him. Was afraid of him.

When Abbie found she couldn't make him quit hauling ice, she froze up, refusing to speak to him, turning her back on him, acting as though he had cut off his right arm and were peddling bits and pieces of it on the corner of Franklin and Dumble.

But he wouldn't stop. He went on hauling ice, grimly, despairingly, stubbornly returning to the job, day after day, lived with an icecold woman at home, and handled ice at work, hauling it into dirty kitchens, walking through dark foulsmelling hallways, up long flights of filthy stairs. At night he collapsed into bed, and slept as though he were dead, not moving, not dreaming. Sometimes he woke up in the middle of the night, sweating, cold sweat from head to foot, shaking again, because he'd heard a sharp cracking sound outside in the street, and cringed because he thought Bill was standing over him with that rawhide in his hand, cursing him. And he'd get out of bed and reach up in the chimney, one hand braced against the marble mantel, reach up where he'd put F. K. Jackson's gun and take it out and heft it in his hand, and find he still couldn't hold it, that the trembling got worse, somehow, just from the feel of the gun.

"I want the truth from you," the man said. "We brought you here to tell the whole story of what happened there on the dock. And I want the truth."

He isn't geared for this, isn't geared for violence. But the woman is. Unfortunately, or fortunately, she's geared up so high she's practically paralyzed.

"If you won't talk, we'll make you talk," the woman said.

"I thought you said you wanted a confession," he said politely. "Sometimes there is a difference. The truth. Confession. Not always the same thing." Fight back. With what? Sitting duck. A forty-five. Never get out of this room alive. And how will she manage it? Do the boys from GrotonHarvard know what a forty-five can do?

The woman sat down. She laid the gun on a table. Too heavy for her to hold. She sat there staring at him, and shaking.

He finally got his shaking under control. After six weeks of hauling ice to those stinking airless top floors in the tenements on Franklin, on Dumble, always to the top floors, he finally stopped shaking. And Abbie got colder, and more unbearable. He began to forget that he was going to try to kill Hod—to try again.

One morning he almost bumped into Weak Knees, right at the corner of Dumble and Franklin. And was ashamed because if he had seen Weak first, he would have crossed over on the other side of the street, pretended he hadn't seen him. Weak said, "Sonny, Sonny, Sonny," over and over, and his eyes filled with tears and he patted his arm and then went off down the street, shambling worse than ever, weaving from side to side as though he were dead drunk. He saw Weak stop and brush that imaginary figure away and knew that he was muttering, "Get away, Eddie, get away!"

Weak hadn't done him any harm. Neither had Bill. Not really. They had balanced that other world, the world of starched curtains and the price of butter, the world of crocheted doilies and what will people think, the world of white bedspreads and pillow shams and behavior governed by what The Race did or did not do.

He went home and ate lunch and Abbie looked down her nose at him. When he finished eating he went straight across the street, went in through the open door of The Last Chance.

Bill was behind the bar, reading a tabloid, the clean white shirt open at the throat, the clean white apron tied tight around his lean waist.

When he looked up his gaze was as impersonal as though Link had been down the street, trotting around town on those thousand-and-one errands they were always sending him on. Impersonal and penetrating. He didn't know that he'd ever been looked at quite so thoroughly.

B. Hod: Well?

L. Williams: I came over to tell you I think you were right and I was wrong. I thought—

B. Hod: What'd they do, put you out across the street?

L. Williams: No.

B. Hod: You get tired of playing horse?

L. Williams: No. It's just that I'm not mad any more.

B. Hod: So? (reading the paper again)

He had waited, not knowing what to say next or what to do.

B. Hod: Now that we've kissed and made up, whyn't you go in the kitchen and kiss Weak, too. (not looking up)

He stood there wishing he hadn't come. There didn't seem to be anything he could say that would make Bill get over being sore. Why should Bill be sore? Then Frankie came from somewhere in the back, old then, but he jumped up on him, snuffing around him, licking his hands, slobbering on him, panting, acting like a puppy half crazy from the joy of seeing him. He hugged him and patted him and turned toward Bill, grinning.

Bill said, "Yeah. Even Frankie's been acting droopy since you quit us. And Weak has been looking as though he just came back from his mother's funeral, if he'd ever had a mother who had a funeral." He paused and then said, "I've been wearing full mourning myself."

So the next Sunday morning when the smell of Canadian bacon, yeasty smell of freshbaked rolls, drifted up into his room from the kitchen, along with the sound of Weak singing, "Give me a girl with a curl, give me a girl I can furl," he ducked under the shower, got his clothes on, and when Weak yelled, "Come and get it," he let Frankie get a head start down the hall, and then ran down the hall, sat down on the top step and kicked his heels against the riser, drumming, drumming, drumming with his heels, and then sat motionless, waiting and listening, and then drummed again, and Bill's voice, deep, outraged, furious, assailed his ears.

"For Christ's sake cut out that goddamn racket what the hell you trying to do wake up the whole goddam neighborhood," in one breath, on the same note of absolute rage.

He kicked the stairs again, drumming, drumming, drumming, and Bill came tearing out of his room, came down the hall, roaring, "What the hell's the matter with you?"

He laughed and choked and went on laughing and had to lean against the wall, choking and laughing.

Bill leaned over, "Sonny, are you all right?" concern in his voice. Bent all the way over him, put his hand on his shoulder, "What's the matter with you?"

"I just wanted to hear you carry on like a crazy man again. I missed the sound of it for six weeks."

Bill said, "You—all that goddam noise—" hauled him to his feet, lifted his hand as though he were going to clip him, drew his hand back and laughed. He said, "Go on. Hightail it down those stairs, Sonny, before I change my mind and lay one on your jaw."

The woman got up, handed the gun to the man. The man held it, gingerly, as though it were a hardshell crab, a big one, and it might turn on him.

He thought, The gutless bastard. She's using him, just as though he were a hired gunman. Let's see what he'll do with it. Gambler. You're gambling with your own life. So let's see what he'll do with it.

"We were in love," he said, casually, conversationally.

The man's face stayed the same, just the same. The woman sighed, or at least there was the sound of the exhalation of her breath. Then the man's face did change, slowly, it became still, stunned. He's gone into shock. I don't think he even knows he's standing there. He's out on his feet, not lifting the gun, not doing anything just standing there with a forty-five in his hand.

"Four to go," he said. "The black barkeep and the Treadway Gun were in love."

The woman said, "Bunny!"

He thought, It's just as though she were a steeplechase rider, and something's gone wrong with her hands and her knees, and he's the horse that's got to take the jump. She's trying to make him jump, just with her voice.

She said, "Bunny!" again.

Then, he thought, amazed, Why he's going to. He doesn't know what he's doing, he's out on his feet, knocked out, but he's taking the jump anyway.

He heard the explosion. It was in his ears, his chest, his head, at one and the same time. There was one split second in which he thought, Legacy, I have to leave a legacy, for this multon-millionaire white woman who has the tremors, the shakes.

"The truth is," he said, and felt the great engulfing thickness in his chest well up into his throat, and talked through it, in spite of it, "we were in love."

He heard the woman say, "Bunny, what have you done?"

He tried to laugh, and pitched forward on the floor.

23

WHEN SHE OPENED the door of the sitting room, the two young men were walking toward her, moving swiftly, their hard heels hitting the polished floor in unison, as though they were marching. They were still wearing their raincoats.

"He—" she said, and heard the gun go off again, and put her hands over her ears, and heard the explosive sound of it again and again. Then silence. "He—" she repeated. "The Negro confessed—and Bunny shot him."

"Is he—"

"Yes," she said and turned back into the room. Bunny was still holding the gun. She took it out of his hand and laid it down on a table. Though he looked at her, his eyes were fixed, unseeing.

One of the young men said, "I think you ought to take him into another room, Mrs. Treadway. Let him sit down somewhere—but not in here."

She guided him into the dining room, turned on a wall switch, and the Gainsboroughs on the walls, the crimson draperies at the windows, the long polished table, the chairs seemed to move in the sudden light, and then were still.

"It's all right," she said. "Everything will be all right." He lifted his hand, shielding his eyes with it, as though the light were painful. "Sit here. You'll be all right in a minute. We'll take care of everything. Bunny, do you hear me? It's all right."

Back in the sitting room, she said, "We'll have to hurry. The servants are all off this evening. There's no one here. But we'll have to do something quickly because Mrs. Cameron, the housekeeper, will be back very soon. She always goes through the house, just to see that everything—" And then she said, "The blood. There's so much blood. I can't—"

One of the young men said, "I tell you what you do, Mrs. Treadway. You get us some rope. If we had some rope we could tie the body up, use old sheets, get it away from here, in the car."

"Yes," she said. "In the garage. I think there's some out there. We had a runway for Camilo's dog. There must be some in the garage."

It was still raining outside. Quiet, gentle rain. She walked toward the garage, fumbled for the lights, turned them on. There was a coil of rope on a bench, near the back wall. She carried it to the house.

One of the young men met her at the door of the sitting room, blocking her view of the room. "If you'll turn the car around, Mrs. Treadway, we'll be right out."

"Captain Sheffield—Bunny is—he's very much upset, of course." She could see bloodstained towels on the floor. The gun was still there on the table. "I think he'll be all right in a few minutes." She took a deep breath. "There's so much blood," she said again, staring into the room. "I didn't know—"

"If you'll go and turn the car around, Mrs. Treadway," the young man repeated firmly, "we'll be right out." He closed the door.

She kept looking at the door. "But these new cars," she said. "The shift is on the steering wheel. I've never driven one of them. I couldn't—I can't turn it around. And Bunny is practically unconscious. He can't drive." She went out through the side entrance, went into the garage.

She backed the Rolls-Royce out of the garage, drove it to the side entrance, and waited with the motor running, listening to the quiet sound it made, watching the rain, falling in myriad slanting lines in front of the headlights.

When she saw them coming out of the house, their backs bent, struggling under the weight of that roped heavy bundle, she got out of the car, opened one of the doors in the back, got in and closed the side curtains and the curtain across the window in the back. Then she got out and held the door open for them.

"We found a thin old rug in one of the rooms in the back of the house," one of the young men said, panting a little from the exertion of lifting that bundle into the car. "It's better for this than sheets." Then he frowned, looking at the car, "Why are we using this ark? What's the matter with the Packard?"

"I can't drive the Packard. I'm not used to the shift—"

"But you're not going to drive—you're not—"

"Yes," she said. "Yes, I am. You can't be involved in this. Not any further. I can manage alone."

"Take Bunny with you," the other one said quickly. "The air will help bring him to. He mustn't stay there, knocked out like that. If anybody showed up, the housekeeper or anybody they'd wonder—"

"All right."

They brought him out of the house, and he staggered along between them, like a drunken man. They helped him get in the front seat.

One of the young men got in the car beside Bunny. "We decided you couldn't possibly manage alone. Rick'll clean up while we're gone."

"Oh," she said. "I couldn't remember. I've been trying to remember what your names were. The other one is Rick. I see. But you're—"

"I'm Skipper. Rick and I were in the Air Corps with Bunny. Remember now?"

"Yes. Yes, of course. It's just since—there was so much blood —" her voice died.

She seemed to be listening to the idling sound of the motor.

Then she said, talking faster and faster, "The Judge wouldn't set a date for the trial—he wouldn't bring the Negro to trial —and Camilo was going to pieces—we thought if we could get him to sign a confession it would end these dreadful stories about her." She sighed and her voice slowed, "We never intended to hurt him—we just wanted him to confess—that was all—and then when he did—when he confessed—"

"I know."

"I've stopped shaking," she said. "You know I was shaking so that I thought I'd never stop. But it's gone now. See?" She held out both hands.

"Good," he said. "Everything will be all right now. Just hold the car to the same pace. Not too fast and not too slow. Steady pace."

When she drove down the long driveway, not too slow, not too fast, out through the gilded, decorated entrance gatcs, past the stone lions, couchant, the rain was still falling in long slanting myriad lines in front of the headlights.

"Where do you plan to go?" he asked.

"To the river."

24

ABBIE CRUNCH was waiting for Frances Jackson to come out of Davioli's market. She had not gone into the market because she did not want to see the look of sympathy that would come over Davioli's face, did not want to hear the sound of heartbreak that would come into his voice, when he spoke of Link, as of course he would.

Suddenly impatient with this waiting, with standing still, she started walking down Franklin Avenue, going slowly, turned into Dumble Street. Most people were home eating supper at this hour, though there were still a great many children playing on the sidewalk, calling to each other, their voices high, shrill. The Hangman was in bud, early this year. It was a pale green, not all over, just lightly brushed with it at the top and on the sides, like a prime coat on an old house, color daubed here and there, over the old weatherbeaten wood, not a finished job, but a visible freshening.

In this fading afternoon light, light going, fading, dying, her house, Number Six, was a deep dark red; and the river was diminished in size, narrower. It looked like a band of tarnished silver, depthless, darkly gleaming, at the foot of the street.

This river, she thought, this one river, and this street, Dumble Street, and this city, Monmouth, are famous now. Or infamous. Not just The Narrows. The entire city. Famous or infamous because of Mrs. Treadway and Link and that girl with the pale blond hair, and that oldfashioned car, a Rolls-Royce, with its curtains down. I keep going over it in my mind, over and over it, and I still do not understand it.

I can see it, I can picture it. An oldfashioned car with the curtains down, side curtains and a curtain in the back. A patrol car started to follow the Rolls-Royce, and the Rolls went faster and faster, and the patrol car relayed a message to two motorcycle policemen. Then the men on the motorcycle pursued the Rolls-Royce, and finally shot at the tires. A woman was driving that carefullycaredfor oldfashioned car. There were two men sitting on the front seat. But the woman was driving. There was a body on the floor of the car in the back, a body wrapped up in a thin worn rug, tied with heavy rope.

But she had omitted that exchange of words that had taken place between the woman who was driving the car and the policeman:

Motor Policeman: What's in the bundle, lady?

Mrs. Treadway: Old clothes for the Salvation Army.

Motor Policeman (to his confrere): You better check.

The *Chronicle* had reported that the policeman who opened that roped bundle wished that he hadn't.

She thought, I mustn't begin thinking about this again, going over and over it in my mind. It doesn't do any good. And instantly thought of that picture on the front page of the *Chronicle*, a picture of Captain Sheffield and Mrs. Treadway, sitting on the side of the road, near the dock, waiting, already under arrest, but waiting to be loaded into a police car, and people all around them, behind them, and there was horror and disbelief on the faces of all those people in the background; kept remembering the girl, the Treadway girl, Mrs. Sheffield, and the pale blond hair curling, the delicately arched feet, and could see the girl lying beside Link, her head on his shoulder, both of them naked. And even now could feel rage at the memory of them in her house, and thought again, as she had ever since that night when the telephone rang and Frances told her, bluntly, almost rudely, what had happened to Link, that she could almost understand, could almost understand how Mrs. Treadway came to be driving that car.

Shock, yes, pain, and a sense of loss, and infinite regret, and the familiar feeling that if she hadn't failed Link when he was a little boy none of this need have happened. She had experienced these things when the Major died. There was nothing new in any of these reactions. But she had behaved differently this time. Because she felt as though something inside her had congealed, frozen, and that it would never thaw again, as long as she lived, as long as she remembered that question and the answer to it: What's in the bundle, lady? Old clothes for the Salvation Army.

She turned and looked back toward Franklin Avenue.

Frances wasn't in sight. What was keeping her so long? Frances had been so kind, always been so kind. I'll stand here and wait for her.

Frances had no family of her own, so she adopted us, adopted Link and me, looked after us as though we were her family. We were an outsize family, or at least we had outsize problems.

We all adopt each other, or marry each other. Miss Doris has apparently adopted Frances. On the day of Link's funeral Frances sent Miss Doris to look after me. Miss Doris looked exactly like a stone monument with a black straw hat on its head, gray gloves on its hands, but in motion, moving majestically down the steps, across the sidewalk, into the car.

She supposed that all of them were shocked, Frances and Miss Doris, and Sugar, Miss Doris' husband, and Howard Thomas, because she didn't collapse into weeping. But she couldn't. She simply felt cold and furious and indomitable. She was impervious to the stares, the comments, the photographers, getting out of the car in front of the church, unaided, going up the aisle of the church, head up, back straight, coming out of the church the same way, watching the service at the grave, as though she were a stranger who had paused for a moment to watch a group of people who happened to be listening to the burial service. She no longer cared what people thought, or what they said, she, who all her life had been governed by the fear of other people's thoughts, had acquired an armor of indifference.

On the way back from the cemetery, she talked about the murder, discussed it, tried to find the reasons behind it. She rode on the back seat of the car with Miss Doris and Frances. She had said, "It was that woman. That Mamie Powther. I should never have allowed her to stay under my roof. A woman like that starts an evil action, just by her mere presence. She doesn't have to take part in it—just her being in a place—she's a—" She had stopped talking, thinking, That isn't true. This all started long ago. It started when the first married woman whoever she was took a lover and went on living with her husband, and the husband discovered the existence of the lover and so killed him. It has always been done that way. Why do the women always go free, as though they were guiltless?

Howard Thomas murmured, "Catalyst," loud enough for her to hear him.

"It were everybody's fault," Miss Doris said in that cold menacing voice.

"It were—" Frances said, paused, corrected herself, "I mean it was the girl's fault, the Treadway girl. She seemed to forget that she was white and Link was colored, so when she made that silly charge against him—"

"It were everybody's fault," Miss Doris' hard metallic voice interrupted. "It were purely like a snowball and everybody give it a push, that twocent newspaper give it the last big push. The morning I seen that picture, that big black convict picture, with half his face gone from a razor, just a long hole where one side of his face should have were, all strew across the front page, I said to Sugar, Sugar that picture were pure murder, and this white folks twocent newspaper ought to be took out and burned, didn't I, Sugar?"

Sugar said, "That's right," automatically.

When Howard stopped the car in front of Number Six, Miss Doris gave him a cruel jab in the back, and when he turned around, she handed him the doorkey, "Go open the door," she ordered.

Sugar stayed behind to help them out of the car. They went up the steps, slowly, all of them. Inside the hall, they stopped. Because Howard Thomas was standing quite still, and as they looked at him, puzzled by his lack of motion, he started backing away, backing toward the door.

Abbie looked past him and saw that there was something squatted down on the staircase. She thought at first it was some kind of animal, the kind of thing you half expect to see materialize in the middle of a nightmare. The creature on the stairs seemed to have a body, small and partially clothed, but it was faceless. No face. It didn't have a head, either, where the head should have been there was simply a black shiny surface, smooth, rounded, and very sleek.

Howard kept moving away from it. There was a tearing sound, and Howard said, "Oh—" and his voice was as high-pitched as a woman's voice, "it's laying an egg. No, it's a foetus emerging from the womb. See?" he said, still backing away, as a round head emerged, kept emerging, and making sounds like an animal, "It's fighting to get out of the womb, and tearing the flesh."

She remembered letting her breath out in a long sigh. Because J. C. Powther's round hard head had appeared, and there was something black around his neck, almost like a bracelet, and something black and shiny far back on his head, and she had thought, Haile Selassie reduced to midget size but crowned, with a black and midnight crown.

Miss Doris said, "You, Jackson, you," in that flat toneless perpetually threatening voice.

"The Major's hat." Abbie could hear her own voice, the sound of it, again. Because there was a note of mourning in her voice at that moment, note of mourning and the sound of tears, for the first time since Link's death. They had stared at her, and she had looked right back at them, not caring what any of them thought. "It's the Major's silk hat," she said.

The round hard head, the dark brown small face, had ducked back under the tall crown of the hat, as though sensing disaster.

Miss Doris had lifted one of those powerful hands and struck the crown of the hat a resounding blow, jamming the crown down, way down, covering the round hard bullet head, the domed forehead, the black inscrutable eyes that were not a child's eyes, covering the small mouth that had opened in protest.

"You, Jackson," Miss Doris had said, in that cold metallic voice, "You set there now. That hat's yours now. You set there under it. Sugar, you stand right there and see that Jackson sets with his hat." She waited until the tall dark man said, "Yes, Sugar," in an obedient voice, and then she said, "Come, ladies, the tea were about ready, come right in the setting room."

And now Abbie thought, aimlessly, The tea were about ready, and then, What's in the bundle, lady? Old clothes for the Salvation Army.

Midway in the block she stopped and looked back toward Franklin Avenue, wondering why it should take Frances so long to buy three lemons. Then she stood still, waiting for Frances. She glanced toward the river, then at the redorange neon sign in front of The Last Chance.

While she was standing there, a man came out of The Last

Chance. She got the impression that he had been backing out. When he reached the sidewalk, he headed toward the dock and the river, moving quickly, and then turned around with such speed that he almost lost his balance, and came toward her. He wasn't running but he looked as though he were. He kept mopping the back of his neck, his forehead, with his handkerchief, and he was constantly turning his head, glancing hastily behind him, as though he expected to be followed, or thought he was being followed.

As he came nearer she recognized the striped pants and cutaway coat of Howard Thomas, Frances' assistant. She assumed that he was intoxicated, and, not wanting to listen to the meandering conversation of a drunken man, she continued to stand still, confident that he would pass her without recognizing her.

He went past her, muttering to himself, "Chinaman's chance. Not a Chinaman's chance," and then turned around again, looked back over his shoulder, then hastened on his way, almost running toward Franklin Avenue. Either he didn't see Frances, or if he saw her he couldn't control his movements, anyway he walked right into her, almost knocking her down.

Abbie heard Frances say, "Well—really—"

"Oh—" he said, "Sorry, Miss Jackson. I didn't see you— wasn't looking—"

Frances peered at him through the thicklensed glasses. "How funny you look. What have you been doing?"

"I have," he said, "I did," he said. "I'm going to— What am I saying anyway?"

"I really don't know. Have you been drinking?"

"No, no, no, Miss Jackson. I just came out of The Last Chance but I haven't been drinking. Ha-ha-ha, but I'm going to. If I live that long, what am I saying? I'm going straight home and drink three lunches and four dinners, in fact, ha-ha-ha, all my meals for the week, all at once, right now."

There was a tremor in his voice, and Abbie, listening, thought, It's as though his voice, too, was constantly looking behind it, mopping its forehead, its face, the back of its neck. And his fear, his terror, whatever it was that was making him perspire and tremble, communicated itself to her so that she, too, looked back over her shoulder, half expecting to see someone behind her, threatening her, looked back over her

shoulder and saw only that redorange sign, vivid now in the
dusk. She thought of Bill Hod's face and shivered, and turned
and watched Howard's progress, rapid, erratic, as he went on
up the street, watched him go in a drugstore at the corner
of Franklin Avenue. The door had barely closed behind him,
when he was out on the street again, then he turned around
and came back down Dumble Street.

Abbie said, "Frances, what on earth's the matter with him?
Why he's gone back in the same drugstore he just came out
of. Do come along. I can't bear to stand here and watch him."

Frances didn't move, didn't answer. She was staring at the
front door of The Last Chance, staring and frowning.

Abbie said, "Did you get the lemons?" and touched her arm,
lightly.

"Of course. It took forever. Mamie Powther was in Davioli's
doing some last-minute shopping, and I thought she'd never
finish. Davioli was in there by himself, so I waited." Frances
cleared her throat, hesitated, said, "Here, you take the lemons.
I'll be along in a minute. I think I'd better go in that drugstore
and see what's the matter with Howard. You can start the tea.
I won't be gone very long."

"All right," she said, and took the little paper bag, three lemons in it. As she walked along the bag made a rustling sound
and she thought, Bag, bundle, what's in the bundle, lady. How
they must have hated him. She shook her head, remembering
the pictures in the newspapers, picture of Mrs. Treadway sitting near the dock, face immobile, pictures of the dock, of the
car with its curtains drawn, of that bundle, open on the dock
and its awful contents revealed, exposed, and pictures of the
crowd of people that collected there, the bobtail, ragtail, flot-
sam and jetsam from The Narrows and the waterfront.

When she opened the door of Number Six, the little paper bag rustled because she pushed the door open with it in
her hand. She turned the hall light on, stood still for a moment listening, wondering if Mamie Powther were home yet.
She wished they'd move. She couldn't bear having them in
the house any more. A woman with that kind of blowsy face
and figure, all that toosoft flesh, didn't belong in any wellkept
home. When Mrs. Powther walked down the street men
turned to look at her, turned to watch the rippling movement

of hips and thighs. She was always half smiling as she walked, as though she experienced some inner pleasure from the motion of her own hips.

As she stood there in the hall, she felt old and defeated, because she started thinking about Link and the Major, remembering the fog in the street that night she pushed the blond girl out into the hall, down the front steps, remembering the sound of Link's laughter when he said, "The female fruit fly," and then went out of the house whistling that tune of Mamie Powther's, I'm lonesome, I'm lonesome.

It was Mamie Powther's fault, she thought. I'm sure of it. Mamie Powther in that purple coat with brass buttons down the front, a double row of them, coat selected to accentuate the grossness of her bosom, could and would upset the pattern of anybody's life. It wasn't her fault. Not really. It was that girl with the blond hair, and her mother, and her husband. She wondered what it was like inside that great stone mansion now. Milelong driveway. Lake with swans in it. And a park. And a picnic every Fourth of July. Perhaps it was little Mr. Powther, too. The Treadway butler. Perhaps it was his entry into my house which precipitated this, perhaps he was the one who out of some awful hideous weakness set the wheels in motion. Then she thought impatiently, It was all of us, in one way or another, we all had a hand in it, we all reacted violently to those two people, to Link and that girl, because he was colored and she was white.

Why should Link be dead, and that girl, that girl with the pale blond hair, be left alive? It didn't have to end that way. The girl was here in my house with him, lying beside him, naked, obviously in love with him, and then two months later, not much more than that, she accused him of attacking her. Why?

She took off her hat and coat, turned on the lights in the sitting room, and in the kitchen, and set about getting supper. She filled the big nickelplated teakettle with water, lit the stove, started to set the table in the kitchen, and decided that it would be pleasanter to eat in the sitting room, and so put a white cloth on the Pembroke table. While she was arranging the silver, she thought about Howard walking at that hurried erratic pace, looking back over his shoulder, mopping his forehead, his face, with a wadded-up handkerchief; thought of that blond girl, intoxicated, and driving a car too fast, running over a child; and then thought of J. C. Powther sitting on the stairs, of his round head emerging from the wreckage of the Major's silk hat.

The teakettle made a hissing sound and she went into the kitchen, turned the fire low under the kettle, rinsed the big brown teapot with boiling water, then sat down at the kitchen table, waiting for Frances, and thinking of Link and that girl. Warmth and affection when her thoughts turned toward Link. A coldness and a fury when she thought of the girl.

Who would ever know what happened between them, or why it happened. Then she thought, But I can guess, conjecture, because of that house next door, that old frame house, where the Finnish people used to live. They were the only white people on Dumble Street, for five or six years. It was a rooming house then, just as it is now, and the men who lived there were almost always intoxicated. On Sunday mornings she saw them staggering home, and there was an iron fence, an ornamental iron fence, in front of the house, and the men would lean on the fence, clinging to it, and from her windows, upstairs, they looked as though they had been impaled on those iron pickets.

During the course of the years, she got to know the Finnish woman who was landlady and janitor in that rooming house. On winter mornings, the woman emptied the ashcans, pouring the contents in the driveway, wind blowing the fine gray stuff back into her face, wind blowing strands of rough uncared for gray hair across her face, and she thrusting it away with impatience. Even on the coldest days her arms were bare, reddened from the cold, and she wore no hat.

Abbie got to know most of the tenants, just by watching them come and go. She knew what time they got up, and what time they went to work. A thin young man, and a thin young woman, occupied the front bedroom on the second floor. In the summer when the windows were open, Abbie could hear them quarreling, and toward dusk she would see the young man stumbling home. Sometimes late at night, she could hear him say, voice thickened, "Aw, I got a right, what's the matter with you," could hear the girl crying, and then the man's voice, again, "Aw, shut up, whatsamatter with you, I got a right."

The girl worked in the Five-and-Ten on Franklin Avenue. Abbie went in there once to buy something, saw the girl standing behind one of the counters, wearing a white blouse, open at the neck, revealing the bones in her neck, the hollows at the base of her throat, and felt embarrassed, and hurried out of the store, because she knew so much about this girl, yet had never seen her closeto before, though she had heard the nighttime quarrels, heard the sound of her weeping.

The thin young man did not work at all. He got up about noon. Abbie could see him moving back and forth in that front room, whose windows were so near her own bedroom windows, looking at himself in the mirror, knotting his tie, putting on his jacket, adjusting and readjusting his hat brim, finally lighting a cigarette, turning to study his profile, making another minute adjustment of his hat brim, and then a few minutes later, she would see him outside on the sidewalk, moving at a slow, leisurely pace.

One day she noticed that the girl no longer lived there. She never saw her coming home whitefaced, exhaustedlooking, any more. The woman who ran the rooming house began quarreling with the thin young man. She was always shouting at him, shaking her fist, as she said he was no good, no damn good, that he didn't work, that he had never worked, no, she wouldn't give him any money, all he'd ever done was sit on his can all day, day in day out.

His clothes got shabbier. The widebrimmed light gray hat was streaked with dirt, lost its shape. Late one afternoon, Abbie saw him coming home. It was raining but he had no coat on. He couldn't get in the house, and he stood on the steps rattling the door, then he kicked against it, then he stood outside on the sidewalk, looking up at the windows, and finally walked away.

Finally, she had asked the Finnish woman about the girl. The woman said the boy, she called him the kid, half contemptuously, was no good, he lived off the girl, and the girl was crazy about him, so crazy about him that it would make anybody sick to watch her, to listen to her, and the girl believed in him, stood behind a counter all day, stood on her feet, earning a little bit of money the hard way, and the kid was always drinking up and gambling away the money the girl earned.

Abbie, puzzled, had said to the woman, "But if she was so crazy about him why did she leave him?"

The woman had stared at her, the blue eyes, hard and cold, the red roughened hands on the hips, the mouth compressed as she said, "She find out he got another woman. Nobody stay after that. Nobody. If I find my man got another woman, I leave, too. But I got strength, see? So I break up everything first. Everything. This girl got no strength. She just go."

Abbie thought, That's what that girl with the yellow hair and the beautiful feet and hands, that's what that girl did. She had strength and so she destroyed Link. Because he had fallen in love with someone else. But he hadn't. Then she thought, How do I know? How would anyone know?

She stopped thinking about it because she heard Frances knocking at the front door, knew it was she because the knocker sounded against the door quickly, lightly, three times in succession and then there was a pause and the knocker hit the door twice. Frances always knocked like that so she would know who it was, had been doing it ever since the Major died, ever since those days when the thought of a stranger at the door filled Abbie with a senseless fear, afraid to open her own door.

She opened the door with a flourish. "I've got everything ready for supper," she said. "You might as well eat here and have tea at the same time."

Frances said, "I'd love to. But I'll have to phone Miss Doris."

While Frances used the telephone, Abbie heated the soup, a thick meaty soup, practically a meal in itself, and then made a salad, fixed the tea, and then filled the soup plates.

Frances came into the kitchen, "Can I do anything?" she asked.

"Just sit down at the table."

They ate slowly, and when they had finished, they stayed at the table, talking.

Abbie said, "Was Miss Doris angry?"

"Oh, no. It took her forever to answer the telephone. She was listening to a news broadcast, so she didn't say much of anything, sort of grunted, and then said, 'I were listening'— and hung up." Frances stirred the tea in her teacup, vigorously, and then said, "Abbie, why don't you come and live with me? Rent out this place. I've got that great big house and there's nobody in it, really, or at least not enough people in it to fill it up."

She toyed with the idea for a moment, Miss Doris would look after both of them, there would be no more household cares, never come home to a dark house, people always around, yes, and Miss Doris didn't like cats, especially didn't like tomcats, and there would be no comfortable cushions for Pretty Boy to lie on in a house which Miss Doris managed, no house plants, so the geraniums and the cyclamen and the African violets, would be left behind, or given away; and Frances was just as dictatorial as Miss Doris, and between them one Abbie Crunch would rapidly disintegrate into a doddering old woman.

She said, "Thank you very much. But I'm not that old, or that feeble. I'll be all right. If the time ever comes when I feel I can no longer live here alone, why I'll let you know."

"You've been wonderful."

Abbie thought, She's trying to find out why, and changed the subject. She said, "By the way, what is a Chinaman's chance?"

"A Chinaman's chance? What on earth made you think of that?"

"Well, when Howard Thomas passed me, fairly running along the street, he muttered something about a Chinaman's chance. That reminds me, did you find him? And what was the matter with him?"

"I don't think he knew himself. Or if he did he didn't tell me. He said he'd lost his wallet, and then proceeded to take it out of his back pocket right in front of me. I said, Why there it is, and he said, Why so it is, ha-ha-ha, Miss Jackson, why so it is. So I walked off and left him."

"But a Chinaman's chance," Abbie persisted. "Whatever was wrong with him must have had something to do with that. He kept repeating it, 'Not a Chinaman's chance,' and looking back over his shoulder as he said it."

Frances was sitting in one of the Hitchcock chairs, and when she leaned back in it it made a creaking sound, and she moved again, farther back, and said, "Ha!" and smiled and her glasses glittered as the light struck them. "That's the chance a Chinaman has when he's wrapped up in a burlap sack, tied up, with the stones, the necessary stones to weight him down, when he's to be smuggled across the border, in a boat. I have heard it said that Bill Hod used to bring them in over the Canadian border. Years ago. At a thousand dollars a head. If the border patrol stopped him, challenged the great god Hod, why he dumped the Chinese overboard. That is a Chinaman's chance."

Abbie thought that Frances was waiting for her to say something, at least she was looking directly at her. Abbie avoided her gaze. She glanced at the African violets blooming in the bay window, at the Boston rocker, and the marbletopped table, at the little Victorian sofa by the fireplace, and the card table drawn up in front of it, books and magazines on it, ready for the evening of quiet reading, saw none of these things, saw instead Bill Hod's face, the hooded eyes, the cruel thinlipped mouth, as plainly as though he were there in the room. She experienced a moment of prescience, in which she foresaw that Bill Hod would never permit that girl with the blond hair to stay alive, unscathed, in the same world in which he lived. And Howard Thomas—

"Well?" Frances asked. "Have you figured it out?"

"No," Abbie said, lying, deliberately lying. "And I don't want to."

I could be wrong, she thought. Perhaps Hod's face is deceptive, perhaps I have always misjudged him. Impossible. He has always taken an eye for an eye, and a tooth for a tooth. It is written all over him. There is no reason to believe that he has changed, or would, or could change. Miss Doris said, It were purely like a snowball, everybody give it a push. So Bill Hod must have arranged to give this dreadful business a final push. And Howard Thomas knows it. Has somehow discovered it.

Shortly afterwards, Frances went home. Abbie went to the door with her, patted her arm, kissed her lightly on the cheek. She stood in the doorway watching Frances' tall bony figure until it was out of sight, and not meaning to, not wanting to, she glanced across the street at the brilliant neon sign in front of The Last Chance.

She could go to the police and say—say what? Say that a man who appeared to be frightened came out of The Last Chance, that he went into a drugstore, that she believed he wanted to telephone to the police, meant to, but he was too frightened, too afraid of Bill Hod, therefore she had become convinced

—and they would laugh at her, not laugh, they would listen politely but they would not believe her. She had no evidence to offer.

Stepping back into the hall, she closed the front door quickly, shutting out the sight of that vivid neon sign, thinking, Even if I knew, even if I could offer irrefutable evidence that Bill Hod was planning to destroy that blond girl I would not do anything about it. I would not try to stop it.

She caught her breath, appalled by the changes that had taken place deep inside her. During this last week she had lost part of herself, irretrievably lost the part of herself that had been composed of honor and integrity, lost the ability to distinguish between right and wrong. Not lost it. It had been seeping away ever since she read those words: What's in the bundle, lady? Old clothes for the Salvation Army.

In the sitting room, she sat down on the Victorian sofa, put on her glasses, and began to read the *Chronicle*, and finally laid it aside, because no matter what she read, she kept seeing that front page picture of Mrs. Treadway sitting on the side of the road, near the dock, surrounded by policemen, her son-in-law beside her; kept seeing that signed statement of Mrs. Treadway's: "We were helping the law. Camilo was going to pieces, and we had to do something. We didn't mean to harm the Negro. We thought if he confessed it would put a stop to those terrible stories about Camilo. Then when the Negro confessed, Bunny seemed to go out of his mind, and he shot him."

We didn't mean to harm the Negro, Abbie thought. The Negro confessed. The Negro.

To them, all of them, he's the Negro. And to me—

She could remember when he was the most important player on the football team at Monmouth High. Though she was proud of his ability, pleased at the acclaim he received, she had never gone to watch him play. She'd always been too busy. Finally he persuaded her to attend one of the games.

That morning, before he left for school, he took a pencil and a piece of paper, and drew a rough diagram. "See," he said, "these are the teams, here in the center of the field, eleven men on each side—"

Men, her mind had echoed the word. Men. Link was only fifteen. True, his shoulders were broad, and he was taller than she, but he was a boy. His bones not really hardened yet. When he finished talking she said, "Is that all there is to it? Just running with a ball?"

He had seemed disconcerted. "I suppose so. It really isn't quite that simple. But you'll see." Before he left the house he said, "I wear number twenty-one. That's how you'll know me."

She had smiled, thinking that she would know him anywhere, with or without a number. Yet that afternoon, when the boys ran out on the field she couldn't tell one from another. The padded pants and the helmets made them look exactly alike. She wouldn't have known which of them was Link if it hadn't been for that big printed number on his back.

When the game started, she was dismayed by its roughness. The players were always piling up in mounds, their arms and legs every which way. She wondered if they didn't sometimes tug at a leg or try to move an arm and then discover that it was another boy's arm or leg.

Toward the end of the half they piled up again—a mass of seemingly headless bodies, the arms and legs askew. When they struggled to their feet, she saw that Number Twenty-One was flat on the ground, not moving. Her first thought was, I knew this was going to happen, I knew it. Number Twenty-One can't move. Number Twenty-One is Link.

She said, "I'll stop the game." Said it out loud. The woman sitting next to her looked at her, in surprise.

Link got to his feet, slowly, and stood up, shaking his head back and forth, leaned over and felt one of his knees. A short stout man came waddling from the sidelines, carrying a pail, and a towel, and what looked to be a sponge, and he poked at Link, prodding him here and there, and made him take off his helmet and Link kept waving him away. There was a little group of players around Link, and then they all seemed to wave their arms at once, and a whistle blew and they were running back and forth on the field again, running headlong into each other, piling up in those horrid mounds, arms and legs twisted.

Number Twenty-One seemed to be all right. He ran and fell down and got up. Her mind was full of thoughts of concussion, of fractured skulls and cracked ribs and broken legs and elbows, and she had found herself rhyming again: Twenty One is my only son. Son and one. Over and over.

Then they all seemed to move faster, to fall down oftener, to run into each other with greater violence, and suddenly Number Twenty-One had the ball, and was running down the field, evading those other fastmoving figures. Her heart started hammering in her chest, as though she were running with him, and she was filled with pride, at the sight of that swiftfooted strong young figure moving so fleetly across the green field. She didn't know enough about the game to know exactly what he was doing, but all around her people were standing up, shouting, calling out his name, chanting his name, "Link! Link! Link!" It was a deep-throated roar that increased her own excitement, made her breath catch in her throat, as though she were the one going swiftly down the length of the playing field, while a great crowd cheered her on.

Then from somewhere in the back of the stadium, an angry voice rang out, "Get the nigger! Get the nigger!"

She sat down, suddenly, on the hard concrete seat, sat down without ever having been aware that she had been standing, and the abruptness with which she sat jarred her entire body. She sat there, trembling, thinking, I will never let him play football again. Never.

When she left the stadium she went to see Frances, told her about Link's being knocked down, about that loud furious voice, calling, Get the nigger, get the nigger, told her that Link could not play football any more.

Frances had said, "Nonsense. You're not to say a word about it. You may have forgotten that he was an orphan adopted by people who were strangers. But he hasn't forgotten it. And you may have forgotten that you rejected him, completely, totally, when the Major died. But he hasn't forgotten it. He never will. Football is good for him. Every time he hears a crowd of people roar their approval of him it helps him build up a reserve of belief in himself as a person. As for the word nigger—"

It was then that Frances had told her, for the first time, that story about her father's death, and why she was never again the least bit disturbed when she heard someone use the word nigger.

And now she thought irritably, That's fine. For Frances. It doesn't help me a bit. Link and that girl, girl with pale yellow hair, girl here with him so often that she left the smell of her perfume in my house. Link running down a football field, carrying a ball, eluding all the other strong young figures. Link walking down Dumble Street with her, on Saturday mornings, carrying her market basket, swinging it back and forth, looking up at her. Adoration, devotion in the young face, in the eyes.

He was in love with that girl. In love with her—

She got up, put on her hat, her coat. She was going to the police. She was going to tell them that she believed the girl was in danger. They would not believe her over there at the Franklin Avenue Police Station. But if she used her most emphatic manner, some one of those policemen would be sufficiently impressed to suggest that special guards be assigned to that blond girl.

She was ready to leave, when J. C. Powther sidled into the room. She had not seen him since the day of the funeral, the day he had demolished the Major's hat.

He stared at her then put his thumb in his mouth, took it out, said, "You goin' out, Missus Crunch?"

"Yes."

"Kin I go with you?"

"No. You run along upstairs."

"Ain't nobody home but Powther. He's just settin' around holdin' on his head. Mamie told him it would drive a body crazy if they had to keep lookin' at him settin' around holdin' on his head like that. 'N she went out. 'N then Kelly and Shapiro went out. That's why they's nobody home. Kin I go with you?"

"No," she said firmly. "You run along now—"

She heard an echo out of the past, heard Frances' voice saying, Run along now, Link, run along and play, and saw that small desolate figure leave the room, slowly, reluctantly, and tried to call him back and could not form the words, could only huddle under that shawl with Frances and weep because the Major was dead.

"All right," she said, and patted J.C.'s shoulder. "You can come with me." Though she couldn't imagine what they would think at the police station when she arrived with this bullet-headed little boy by the hand.

"Get your hat and coat. But you go to the bathroom first. You go right now," she said. Because he was wiggling, standing first on one scuffed brown shoe and then on the other, holding his knees together.

"Where we goin'?" he asked suspiciously. "Ain't they got no wee-wee chairs dere?"

"I really don't know," she said. "I've never been inside a police station before."

OTHER WRITINGS

The Great Secret

I HAVE, to my continuing surprise, written two novels. They have both been published. This surprises me because I wanted to be a writer of short stories. I wrote short stories for more years than I care to remember. And also for more years than I care to remember the stories did not sell. I have collected enough rejection slips to paper any fair-sized room.

Finally, I sold a story. When the story was published I received a letter from Houghton Mifflin Company asking if I were working on a novel. I was not. And though the thought of writing a novel, the hours of concentrated work which it would involve, frightened me, I began writing one.

While I was struggling with this first novel, *The Street*, I came to believe that there must be some conjuring trick by which a novel is produced—a rabbit-out-of-hat stunt which the published novelist has somehow mastered and which he hugs close to his breast for fear his secret may be snatched away from him.

It was during this period that one of my friends, perhaps by accident, perhaps as part of a foreordained design, gave me a copy of Anthony Trollope's autobiography—which is called, simply *An Autobiography*. It was Trollope who revealed the great secret, in a passage which would, I think, have inspired Dickens' Fat Boy had someone read it to him:

> I always had a pen in my hand, whether crossing the seas, or fighting with American officials, or tramping about the streets of Beverley. I could do a little, and generally more than a little. I had long since convinced myself that in such work as mine, *the great secret* consisted in acknowledging myself to be bound to rules of labor similar to those which an artisan or a mechanic is forced to obey. A shoemaker when he has finished one pair of shoes does not sit down and contemplate his work in idle satisfaction. "There is my pair of shoes finished at last! What a pair of shoes it is!" The shoemaker who so indulged himself would be without wages half his time.

It seemed to me that the first rule of labor which governs an artisan or a mechanic is that he has mastered his trade; and mastered the tools of his trade. And so, while in the process of writing a novel, I tried, and I am still trying, to master the tools of the novelist's trade. I decided that the tools were, roughly: words; a better-than-average knowledge of people; and a first-class story-telling technique—this phrase to include plot, characterization, style, theme, etc.

The study of words would, of course, be a lifetime project. I still read a great deal of poetry because it is the most enjoyable way in which to sharpen one's awareness of words, to quicken one's sense of rhythm. I found three endlessly fascinating books which deal with words. There are many others but these were particularly useful: Fowler's *Modern English Usage*, H. L. Mencken's *The American Language*, Ivor Brown's *A Word in Your Ear and Just Another Word*.

I had been an avid reader of novels for a good many years. But I stopped reading for pleasure and began to study them. If a passage in Dickens made me laugh, I went back to it again and again until I knew why I had laughed; whether it was the character, the situation, the dialogue which seemed so funny. I dissected plots, analyzed style and emotional effects. I did this because I was convinced that no matter what else a novel might do, it must tell a story, preferably a believable one, if it was to hold the reader's attention.

I dissected plays, too. For the playwright is confronted by a task far more difficult than that of the novelist. He must tell his story solely in terms of what his characters say and what they do; and he performs this miracle inside the very rigid framework of a stage.

Though I was, at the time, writing a novel and learning a good deal in the process, I began to doubt the value of the advice which is so often given to beginners: write about what you know. I think this should be qualified so that it goes something like this: first find out what you know, find out what it means, and then set your imagination to work on it, transforming it, dramatizing it.

If you look at this piece of advice (write about what you know) in terms of the mechanic who has mastered his trade, the mechanic who supposedly works always within the limited area of his mechanical knowledge, you will see that it is a half-truth. A mechanic often finds himself confronted by a problem which he can solve only if he uses his imagination—for the answer lies outside his experience, outside his range of observation.

This same thing happens to writers. Certainly the historical novelist does not write about what he knows—if "know" means first-hand observation or experience. He writes about places he has not seen, about an era in which he did not live; and yet he manages, if he is expert enough, to recreate a believable 17th century France or Spain, or England.

Then, too, many a man has turned out a first-class novel dealing with the great emotional peaks in a woman's life—her loves, her hates, and her final tragic destiny. *Anna Karenina* and *Madame Bovary* are excellent examples. Can it honestly be said that Tolstoy and Flaubert, who were men, were writing about what they knew when they put on paper the workings of a woman's mind?

It is true, of course, that one can do a better job of getting the feel of a place, a small town or a big city, into a novel if one has actually lived there—the sound of the subway starting and stopping, the cattle-like stampede of people at Times Square, at Penn Station, the look of a country road in the snow, the precise pattern of trees against a winter sky. These things, yes. But there would be more novelists in the world if the first law of writing were simply to write about that which one knows.

And so I came to the conclusion that I could spend the rest of my life writing about what I knew and yet when the book was finished no one would want to read it. I had first to learn how to tell a long story; I had to deepen my understanding of people and their motives; and finally I had to cultivate my imagination, set it to work on what I "knew." Because I would frequently have to write about many things that I had neither experienced nor observed, it was up to me to start acquiring a better-than-average knowledge of psychology, of anthropology, of sociology.

Despite all my reading and study I still did not know how to begin writing a novel. It seemed far more complicated than beginning a short story. And all I had to start with was an idea, an idea that came from a newspaper clipping. I think I still have the clipping somewhere. It was a brief item about a janitor in a

Harlem tenement who had been arrested for teaching an eight-year-old boy to steal.

Finally I decided to use the same procedure that I used in writing a short story; and that was to put down on paper everything that occurred to me about the plot, the theme, the setting, the characters. I did this in longhand. In the process the little boy became Bub of *The Street* and the janitor became Jones. This did not happen all at once—their birth was a slow, uncertain process.

I pieced together a story about them, set it down in rough chronological order, still in longhand. The next step was to type it, adding more information as I went along, expanding scenes, strengthening the plot.

Once I had it typed, the whole story, or at least as much of it as I knew at the time, I divided it into chapters; and then typed these chapters on yellow sheets. This meant I now had the skeleton of a book to work with. I twisted the chapters around, changed their order, shortened some, lengthened others, always with the idea of trying to carry the reader on from one page to the next. I rewrote these chapters again and again, working on the dialogue, the characters, tightening the plot, trying to strengthen the story line.

Some of the chapters were rewritten as many as seven times —only one of them was left unchanged. By that time I had a book which had been written as well as I knew how to write it, tested and fought with every step of the way. Then I rewrote it again. This time I tried to add the something more—which was really a matter of fitting the style of the writing to the material. In *The Street* I wanted to achieve a swift-moving, almost passionate style in order to heighten the story of Lutie Johnson and her small son, Bub.

In *Country Place* I tried to *under*write, if there is such a word for writing, a word which corresponds to underplaying in the theatre. Despite the obvious violence of the storm, and the violent action of some of the characters, I tried to get into the style something of the surface quiet of a small country town —a slowness of tempo which I hoped the reader would absorb almost unconsciously.

But to get back to Trollope and his great secret. He said that he found he could always "do a little." That is, of course, the secret of accomplishing any task. But I found it extremely difficult to keep on working on that first book, hour after hour, day after day. I was always finding something else to do. I can still find any number of perfectly valid reasons for not writing, today, or tomorrow, or the next day.

And so I began using a clock as taskmaster. I decided that if I were working for someone else there would be no question about the number of hours I put in; no question about *when* I showed up for work. I placed a clock where I could see it. The hands of the clock shamed me into working, steadily, with few pauses for daydreaming; though I must confess that I still, on occasion, cheat like a schoolboy.

I discovered, too, that it was easier to maintain a more or less constant rate of production if I never stopped the day's work without a fairly accurate knowledge of what was to come next. It might only be an idea scribbled on a torn sheet of paper, but it gave me a definite starting point for the next day's work. Thus at nine in the morning I did not start out faced with a blank sheet of paper.

Once having finished that first novel, *The Street*, I began on the second one, *Country Place* (like the shoemaker at work on his next pair of shoes). In the process of writing these two books I have learned much. But when I look back it seems to me that I learned equally as much from reading E. M. Forster's *Aspects of the Novel*, Lajos Egri's *The Art of Dramatic Writing*, Phyllis Bentley's *Some Observations on the Art of Narrative Writing*, and Anthony Trollope's *An Autobiography*. For I am still an apprentice in the sense that I have not as yet mastered the tools of the novelist's trade or the trade itself, for that matter.

Despite Trollope's great secret, I cannot resist ending this with a word of warning which appears in Somerset Maugham's autobiography, *The Summing Up*:

> One should always accept what a writer says about the art he practices with reservation, for his remarks are always apt to be colored by his own practice. We none of us write as we would like to: we write as best we can.

The Writer, July 1948

Harlem

THE SHADOW OF THE PAST hangs heavily over Harlem, obscuring its outlines, obliterating its true face.

During the Prohibition era Harlem was described, usually with laughter, as a vast gin mill—a place where everybody manufactured synthetic gin in bathtubs, washtubs and kitchen sinks, where corn liquor bubbled in stills that steamed in dank basements, littered alleyways and back yards.

Those were the days when experienced pub crawlers, having made the rounds of the speakeasies in midtown Manhattan, headed for Harlem, where the joints stayed open right around the clock; when it was whispered that the cops and the Federal agents kept their heads turned the other way, and that you could buy anything in Harlem from human flesh to dope because the Dutchman (the late Dutch Schultz) paid off in crisp, new, hundred-dollar bills.

During the '30s, those lost, bitter years of the depression, Harlem became known as a city of evictions, relief bureaus and bread lines, where half of the people lived on "the Relief." Social workers complained, in those days, that Harlemites were importing hundreds of their ragged Southern relatives—their sick old mothers, their rachitic and illegitimate children—who were supposed to have been supplied with faked baptismal certificates so that they could meet the residence requirements and share in New York's comparatively bountiful relief funds. Thus Harlem was tagged, first, as the home of a dangerous underworld; then, later, as a poverty-stricken community, expert in the practice of shabby fraud.

In 1935, and again in 1943, there were "disturbances" in Harlem, disturbances that centered around 125th Street, the principal shopping section. Rioting mobs broke plate-glass windows, looted stores, causing property damage estimated in the millions. And in the process they seem to have permanently rubbed out that other hackneyed description of Harlem—the dwelling place of a dancing, laughing, happy-go-lucky, child-like people.

Harlem is now called a trouble spot, a "hot" place. Many

conservative citizens believe it to be a lawless, violent community, inhabited by just two kinds of people—the poor and the criminal. More sophisticated minds simply dismiss it as that section of New York where the Saturday nights are one long, lost, hellish week end and where every night is a Saturday night.

And yet in this place of unhappy repute an astonishing number of boys and girls have lived long enough to grow up; and some of them have even achieved international fame. Bill (Bojangles) Robinson, Walter White, Dr. W. E. B. Du Bois, Channing Tobias, Judge Jane Bolin and A. Philip Randolph live here. Duke Ellington writes music about the place, and many of his bandsmen call Harlem home. When Lena Horne, Rochester, and Joe Louis are in New York they stay in Harlem.

If a nose-by-nose count were made it would reveal that Harlem has a high proportion of distinguished residents. And if you subscribe to the theory that class distinctions in America are based on wealth, then Harlem can be said to have an aristocracy. There is a moneyed class which lives largely in and around the section known as the Hill—a high, hilly area, overlooking the Hudson River to the west and the Polo Grounds to the northeast. It is called Sugar Hill because it takes a lot of sugar to pay the rent for a swank apartment on Edgecombe, St. Nicholas or Convent Avenues.

There is no inherited wealth on the Hill. The leisure class is composed of the wives of successful doctors, lawyers, dentists, real-estate operators and businessmen. Their lives refute the picture of Harlem as a poverty-stricken community. The Hill's children are sent to experimental nursery schools, to expensive private schools, and on to the big Eastern colleges. They vacation in Canada, Mexico, New England, Bermuda, and they travel to England and France and Sweden.

Sometimes the Hill aristocrats display all of the glittering trappings of the 20th Century brand of conspicuous consumption. They drive high-priced cars. They obtain sensational divorces in Reno and Mexico and the Virgin Islands. Their women collect Persian rugs and mink coats and diamonds.

These are the people who can afford to eat the thick juicy steaks at Frank's Restaurant on 125th Street and drink Irish whisky at the Theresa Bar, or drop in at Ma Frazier's on the maid's night off to eat some of the best food to be found in New York—sizzling hot lamb chops; chicken, fried, broiled, or roasted to a turn; thick slices of ham steak.

The Hill suggests that Harlem is simply a pleasant and rather luxurious part of Manhattan. Actually it is only one of Harlem's thousand varied faces.

Harlem is also the *Amsterdam News*: "One of America's Greatest Newspapers—We Only Print the News—We Do Not Make It." This is the most widely read Negro newspaper in New York. Twice a week, the *Amsterdam* reports the births and deaths, the defeats and victories, the sins and virtues of the Negro in New York City to some 375,000 readers. It headlines the ripest scandals and the goriest murders: Man Killed For Fee of $25; Upshot of Three-Way Love Tilt Is Knifing; Nab Society Photog As Numbers Boss; Gangs Kill Schoolboy. By contrast, its editorials are as sedately written and as innocuous as those in the *New York Sun*.

Dan Burley, the former managing editor, (now managing editor of the New York *Age*, another Harlem paper) used to give a tongue-in-cheek report on the doings of Harlem's big and little fish in a column called *Back Door Stuff*. It revealed still another side of Harlem.

Burley poked fun at a curious assortment of people: fighters, singers, dancers, actors, night-club entertainers, Hill aristocrats and a demimonde composed of kept women and gentlemen with no known source of income.

He portrayed the Hill's aristocrats as selfish, stupid and un-grammatical; spavined and permanently winded from getting off to a fast start in that rat race known as keeping up with the Joneses. He pretended to believe, for example, that the folk on the Hill are so stony-broke that they cannot afford the luxury of overnight guests:

"I heard one woman say: 'Lawd, here comes old Big Foot Hattie and them kids of hers. . . . I ain't got no place for 'em to stay here and I stayed six weeks with them when I was down in Raleigh last summer. . . . Roosevelt, you pull them windows down and turn out them lights and for Gawd's sake, keep quiet till they leave. . . .'"

The *Amsterdam* is worth a look for many other reasons. Not all Harlemites spend their time carving each other with knife and razor. Sometimes they carve out a financial empire instead.

This newspaper with the big circulation and the gaudy headlines is part of the empire built by Dr. Philip M. H. Savory and Dr. Clilan Bethany Powell.

They own not only the *Amsterdam News* but also an insurance concern, Victory Mutual Life Insurance Company; a loan business, Personal Finance Corporation; a photo-engraving company, Rapid Reproduction. Doctor Savory, a general practitioner, is president of the insurance company and secretary-treasurer of the *Amsterdam*. Doctor Powell, who was an X-ray specialist until his retirement about eight years ago, is president and editor of the *Amsterdam*, a Dewey-appointed member of the State Athletic Commission, and executive vice-president of the Midway Technical School, a newly opened trade school.

But Harlem is not all Hill and wealth and empire. It is also the ugly tenements and the scarred, evil-smelling rooms in the Hollow.

The Hollow, called that only by way of contrast to the Hill, is that central area in Harlem which welcomed the first influx of Negroes at the turn of the century. When Negroes entered this area, the whites who lived there fled before them, block by block, street by street. The houses were old when Negroes moved into them; they are some forty-nine years older now.

The Hollow is as unpredictable and contradictory as the rest of Harlem. Some of the last of the Victorians live in the brownstone houses on Fifth Avenue, 130th Street, 133rd Street —one family to a house, the high-ceilinged rooms with the intricately laid oak flooring, and the carved mantels still intact. The Metropolitan Life Insurance Company's crisp new Harlem project, the Riverton Houses, sits on the eastern edge of the Hollow; and the Hill aristocrats have very nearly filled it. Strivers Row, that quiet residential street of houses designed by Stanford White, is in the Hollow, too—138th Street between Seventh and Eighth Avenues.

Parts of the Hollow, and parts of the Hill, too, for that matter, reveal something else about Harlem. In some of the side streets the law is an enemy, visible, hateful—a fat cat in a blue uniform, twirling a nightstick.

New York's "Finest" has, on occasion, been so hated, so distrusted here, that if a man was found lying in the street, stabbed, and a policeman leaned over him, a crowd would gather, instantly; and this angry crowd would believe that the *cop* knifed the man.

Fear of the police seems to go hand in hand with wretched housing. And the Hollow offers, in spots, some of the world's most miserable shelter. Many of the old brownstones were long ago turned into rooming houses. The landlord or the lessee found that he could double, triple, quadruple his income if he partitioned the big rooms into cubicles just big enough to hold a bed, a bureau and a broken chair or two. These were offered for rent as "Furnished Rooms For Respectable Tenants."

And so Harlem is also two hundred persons jammed into seventy dingy, vermin-ridden rooms, in old-fashioned brownstones without fire escapes, on Lenox Avenue, and 123rd Street, their halls lightless, their stairs, corridors and lavatories filthy. Harlem is these same two hundred persons paying anywhere from $1.50 to $3.75 a week in excess of legal rentals. It is also the fifty-seven tenements in which the New York City Commissioner of Housing and Buildings reported finding 1407 "shocking" violations.

This type of substandard housing predominates in East Harlem, known in real-estate circles as a "blighted area," the kind of section that usually harbors drug vendors and users and becomes a breeding place for gangs.

Yet one small portion of East Harlem, known as Spanish Harlem, now houses nearly half of New York City's newest immigrants—the Puerto Ricans. Thousands of them have come to New York in the last few years, and it is now estimated that 60,000 to 80,000 live in a boxlike area around 110th Street and Madison Avenue.

There is definite hostility between the Puerto Ricans and the Negroes who are in the great majority; and between the Puerto Ricans and the Italians living east of Third Avenue. And so Harlem is also a Puerto Rican child, afraid to use the swimming pools in the East River playgrounds because, "Those belong to the Italians."

Sometimes these separate, hostile, national groups rub shoulders and, for a moment, create the illusion that Harlem is a melting pot. One of the places in which they meet is known throughout the area as "under the bridge." This is the City Market which runs under the New York, New Haven and Hartford Railroad bridge, on Park Avenue, from 111th to 116th Street. Here, beneath the railroad tracks, in block-long sheds, the concessionaires, many of them former pushcart vendors, quarrel, bargain, exchange insults with their customers, in Spanish, Italian, Yiddish, and in American ranging from tough East Side New Yorkese to the soft accents of the Old South. Leaning over their stalls, they cry, "Step up, Momma, step up and buy! I got fresh fruit!"

Overhead, the trains of the New York Central and the New Haven thunder across the bridge, taking commuters in and out of the city, carrying passengers to Boston, rushing them to Chicago on the Century.

Few of these travelers are aware that at this point on their journey they are crossing bits of Spain and Italy and the West Indies, as well as characteristic bits of the United States. Much of the merchandise offered for sale under the bridge suggests the homeland of the gesticulating crowds that come here to buy.

The stalls are piled with children's clothing, underwear in vivid colors, earrings, necklaces, and a bewildering variety of food: porgies, whiting, eels, crabs, long-grain Carolina rice, Spanish saffron, chili powder, fresh ginger root, plantains, water cress, olive oil, olives, spaghetti and macaroni, garlic, basil, zucchini, finocchio, white corn meal, collards, mustard greens, black-eyed peas, big hominy and little hominy, spareribs, hot peppers, pimentos, coconuts, pineapples, mangoes.

And so "under the bridge" is Harlem too. So is the Hotel Theresa, on Seventh Avenue, where the visiting firemen stay in three-room suites; and the Schomburg Collection of Negro Arts and Letters at the 135th Street Branch Library, housed in the newest, most modern library building in the city. It is Sydenham Hospital, the only interracial voluntary hospital in the world; and the American Negro Theater, on 126th Street, which first produced *Anna Lucasta*; and the High School of Music and Art where young musical geniuses and its potential artists receive a high-school education.

The truth is Harlem is as varied and as full of ambivalences as Manhattan itself. For it is also the long-legged girls in the floor show at Small's Paradise, New York's oldest Negro-owned night club; the mass meetings and political rallies at the Golden Gate Ballroom whose barnlike interior serves as Harlem's Hyde Park and Union Square. And it is a pushcart peddler calling, "I got fish, fresh porgy, weakfish. I got fish."

It is a hodgepodge of churches, bars, beauty parlors, harsh orange-red neon signs, poolrooms, candy stores. It is a per-spiring soapbox orator shouting from the top of a stepladder at the corner of Seventh Avenue and 125th Street, on a warm night in June; a hot roasted yam purchased from a pushcart and eaten on the street on a cold windy night; and the cricket matches at Van Cortlandt Park. It is the exclusive Comus Club giving a formal dance at the Savoy Ballroom; a woman cry-ing, "Murder!" at three in the morning; a thick slice of ice-cold watermelon, honeysweet, bought on Lenox Avenue on a hot summer day; the barbecued ribs browning on a spit in the window of a Seventh Avenue restaurant. And it is a real gone gal on stage at the Apollo Theater, so gone that the audience stamps and whistles, beating out the rhythm until the Apollo's old walls tremble. It is a furtive man dropping numbers slips into the eager hands of a syndicate; and a calypso singer, at a Trinidadian carnival, in the spring of the year, half-talking, half-singing, "Always marry a woman uglier than you."

Harlem is all these things, yes. But it is primarily George Jackson, American Negro, neither rich nor rags-and-tatters poor. He is a typical New Yorker in that he was born some-where else.

The chances are that the place he calls home is a small, dark apartment on Seventh Avenue, that broad through street which bisects the heart of Harlem and is neither Hill nor Hol-low but a combination of both. If he lives in a large dark apart-ment then he takes in roomers to help out with the rent. He is always trying to close that ever-widening gap between what he earns and what he spends for food and clothing and shelter for his family.

His worries and his dissatisfaction with the place in which he lives have turned him into one of Manhattan's most sophisticated voters, crossing and recrossing party lines, voting for issues and men, ignoring party labels.

Rep. Adam Clayton Powell, Jr., played an important part in George Jackson's political education. In 1941 Powell announced his candidacy for the City Council from the pulpit of Harlem's 140-year-old Abyssinian Baptist Church. Sunday after Sunday, he stood in the pulpit of his church shouting: "If you want to change Harlem, then you've got to vote, vote, vote! And you've got to register in order to vote. And if your old grandmother can't vote because she can't read, then bring her to Abyssinian and we'll *teach* her to read."

Powell's 14,000 faithful church members trudged up and down the streets of Harlem, ringing doorbells, urging people to "vote for Adam." They rang George Jackson's doorbell too. And Powell was elected to the Council by the third largest majority in the city. Ever since, his congregation has been regarded as one of the most formidable vote-getting machines in New York. When Reverend Powell ran for Congress, George Jackson helped elect him, and re-elect him. This same George Jackson has twice helped to elect Benjamin J. Davis, Jr., a Communist, to the seat that Powell held in the City Council. This hardly meant, however, that our Mr. Jackson had become a member of the Communist Party. It was likely he was pursuing his usual political course and voting for a man, not a political party. The chances are that he voted for Ben Davis because he felt Davis would never sell Harlem down the river.

George Jackson is a man with deep religious convictions. On Sunday mornings, he dons his best suit and goes to church. He walks through quiet streets. The stores are closed; the bars and grills are shut down. He meets other churchgoers: scrubbed kids, women wearing white gloves, men dressed in their best dark suits. One Hundred and Twenty-fifth Street, which the day before was overflowing with housewives seeking bargains, with children and sight-seers and beggars, is now as deserted as a village street. The long lines of people waiting to get inside the Apollo Theater have disappeared. There are so few street noises that the chimes atop Bishop Lawson's Refuge Temple on Seventh Avenue can be heard for blocks.

As George Jackson walks slowly to and from his church, he tries to arrive at an honest conclusion about Harlem. He knows there is too much fear around—fear of the police, and an equally great fear of one's neighbors, as evidenced by special locks on the doors of the apartments and iron bars at the windows that open on fire escapes. He admits, uneasily, that there are too many children playing in the streets, night and day—his own and other people's children. His final conclusion might be contained in one short sentence: "Hawkins is here."

You can hear these same words all over Harlem when a bone-chilling wind sweeps across the town, hiking down from the North, intensifying the damp cold of the Island. On all sides people say, "Hawkins is here," or "Old Man Hawk is out there."

Whether George Jackson lives in the clutter of the Hollow or the comparative luxury of the Hill, he shivers as he looks around him; even on a hot day in August when the heat waves are rising from the sidewalk and the roads go soft and gummy underfoot, he shivers and says, "Hawk is here."

I do not know who Hawkins is or how he became a symbol for cold weather. But he could represent the chilling statistics on Harlem: the high death rate, the incredible population rate per city block. In that sense Old Man Hawkins stays in Harlem, huddled in the doorways, perched on the rooftops.

Can he be run out of this end of town? I think so. One of my favorite stories about the Rev. John Johnson suggests how the job might be done. Reverend Johnson was a police chaplain, the minister of Harlem's St. Martin's Protestant Episcopal Church, and a special advisor to the late Mayor Fiorello LaGuardia on the doings, the troubles, the needs and the demands of the people of Harlem.

The Little Flower, so the story goes, used to send for John Johnson about twice a week; and, leaning back in his chair, fiddling with his black-rimmed spectacles, the mayor would say, "Well, Johnnie, what do they want now?"

Johnnie Johnson always gave the same answer. "More houses, Mr. Mayor. More houses."

They still want more houses, need more houses.

And there is something else involved. Harlem has been studied and analyzed by sociologists, anthropologists, politicians. It has been turned and twisted, to the right and to the left; prettied up and called colorful and exotic; defamed and labeled criminal.

Sometimes its past has been glorified; more often it has been censured. But looked at head on, its thousand faces finally merge into one—the face of a ghetto. In point of time it belongs back in the Middle Ages. Harlem is an anachronism —shameful and unjustifiable, set down in the heart of the biggest, richest city in the world.

Holiday, April 1949

The Novel as Social Criticism

AFTER I had written a novel of social criticism (it was my first book, written for the most part without realizing that it belonged in a special category) I slowly became aware that such novels were regarded as a special and quite deplorable creation of American writers of the twentieth century. It took me quite awhile to realize that there were fashions in literary criticism and that they shifted and changed much like the fashions in women's hats.

Right now the latest style, in literary circles, is to say that the sociological novel reached its peak and its greatest glory in *The Grapes of Wrath*, and having served its purpose it now lies stone-cold dead in the market place. Perhaps it does. But the corpse is quick with life. Week after week it sits up and moves close to the top of the best-seller list.

It is my personal opinion that novels of this type will continue to be written until such time as man loses his ability to read and returns to the cave. Once there he will tell stories to his mate and to his children; and the stories will contain a message, make a comment on cave society; and he will, finally, work out a method of recording the stories, and having come full circle the novel of social criticism will be reborn.

Its rebirth in a cave or an underground mine seems inevitable because it is not easy to destroy an old art form. The idea that a story should point a moral, convey a message, did not originate in the twentieth century; it goes far back in the history of man. Modern novels with their "messages" are cut from the same bolt of cloth as the world's folk tales and fairy stories, the parables of the Bible, the old morality plays, the Greek tragedies, the Shakespearean tragedies. Even the basic theme of these novels is very old. It is derived from the best known murder story in literature. The cast and the setting vary, of course, but the message in *Knock on Any Door*, *Gentleman's Agreement*, *Kingsblood Royal*, *Native Son*, *The Naked and the Dead*, *Strange Fruit*, *A Passage to India*, is essentially the same: And the Lord said unto Cain, Where is Abel thy brother: And he said, I know not: Am I my brother's keeper?

In one way or another, the novelist who criticizes some un-desirable phase of the status quo is saying that man *is* his broth-er's keeper and that unless a social evil (war or racial prejudice or anti-Semitism or political corruption) is destroyed man cannot survive but will become what Cain feared he would become—a wanderer and a vagabond on the face of the earth.

The critical disapproval that I mentioned just above is largely based on an idea that had its origin in the latter part of the eighteenth century, the idea that art should exist for art's sake —*l'art pour l'art*, Poe's poem for the poem's sake. The argu-ment runs something like this: the novel is an art form; art (any and all art) is prostituted, bastardized, when it is used to serve some moral or political end for it then becomes propaganda. This eighteenth century attitude is now as fashionable as Dior dresses. Hence, many a critic who keeps up with the literary Joneses reserves his most powerful ammunition for what he calls problem novels, thesis novels, propaganda novels.

Being a product of the twentieth century (Hitler, atomic energy, Hiroshima, Buchenwald, Mussolini, USSR) I find it difficult to subscribe to the idea that art exists for art's sake. It seems to me that all truly great art is propaganda, whether it be the Sistine Chapel, or La Gioconda, *Madame Bovary*, or *War and Peace*. The novel, like all other forms of art, will al-ways reflect the political, economic, and social structure of the period in which it was created. I think I could make out a fairly good case for the idea that the finest novels are basically nov-els of social criticism, some obviously and intentionally, others less obviously, unintentionally, from *Crime and Punishment* to *Ulysses*, to *Remembrance of Things Past*, to *USA*. The moment the novelist begins to show how society affected the lives of his characters, how they were formed and shaped by the sprawl-ing inchoate world in which they lived, he is writing a novel of social criticism whether he calls it that or not. The greatest novelists have been so sharply aware of the political and social aspects of their time that this awareness inevitably showed up in their major works. I think that this is as true of Dickens, Tolstoy, and Dostoevski as it is of Balzac, Hemingway, Dreiser, Faulkner.

A professional patter has been developed to describe the awareness of social problems which has crept into creative writing. It is a confused patter. Naturalism and realism are terms that are used almost interchangeably. *Studs Lonigan* and *USA* are called naturalist novels; but *The Grapes of Wrath* is cited as an example of realism. So is *Tom Jones*. Time, that enemy of labels, makes this ridiculous. Dickens, George Sand, Mrs. Gaskell, George Eliot, Harriet Beecher Stowe, wrote books in which they advocated the rights of labor, condemned slums, slavery and anti-Semitism, roughly a hundred years ago. They are known as "the humanitarian novelists of the nineteenth century." Yet the novels produced in the thirties which made a similar comment on society are lumped together as proletarian literature and their origin attributed to the perfidious influence of Karl Marx. This particular label has been used so extensively in recent years that the ghost of Marx seems even livelier than that of Hamlet's father's ghost—or at least he, Marx, appears to have done his haunting over more of the world's surface.

I think it would make more sense if some of the fictional emphasis on social problems were attributed to the influence of the Old Testament idea that man is his brother's keeper. True it is an idea that has been corrupted in a thousand ways —sometimes it has been offered to the world as socialism, and then again as communism. It was used to justify the Inquisition of the Roman Church in Spain, the burning of witches in New England, the institution of slavery in the South.

It seems plausible that so potent an idea should keep cropping up in fiction for it is a part of the cultural heritage of the West. If it is not recognized as such it is almost impossible to arrive at a satisfactory explanation for, let alone classify, some of the novels that are derived from it. How should *Uncle Tom's Cabin*, *Germinal*, and *Mary Barton* be classified? As proletarian literature? If *Gentleman's Agreement* is a problem novel what is *Daniel Deronda*? Jack London may be a proletarian writer but his most famous book *The Call of the Wild* is an adventure story. George Sand has been called one of the founders of the "problem" novel but the bulk of her output dealt with those bourgeois emotions: love and passion.

I think one of the difficulties here is the refusal to recognize and admit the fact that not all of the concern about the shortcomings of society originated with Marx. Many a socially conscious novelist is merely a man or a woman with a conscience. Though part of the cultural heritage of all of us derives from Marx, whether we subscribe to the Marxist theory or not, a larger portion of it stems from the Bible. If novelists were asked for an explanation of their criticism of society they might well quote Richard Rumbold, who knew nothing about realism or naturalism and who had never heard of Karl Marx. When Rumbold mounted the scaffold in 1685 he said, according to Macaulay's *History of England*: "I never could believe that Providence had sent a few men into the world, ready booted and spurred to ride, and millions ready saddled and bridled to be ridden."

Similar beliefs have been stated in every century. Novelists would be strangely impervious to ideas if a variant of this particular belief did not find expression in some of their works.

No matter what these novels are called, the average reader seems to like them. Possibly the reading public, and here I include myself, is like the man who kept butting his head against a stone wall and when asked for an explanation said that he went in for this strange practice because it felt so good when he stopped. Perhaps there is a streak of masochism in all of us; or perhaps we all feel guilty because of the shortcomings of society and our sense of guilt is partially assuaged when we are accused, in the printed pages of a novel, of having done those things that we ought not to have done—and of having left undone those things we ought to have done.

The craftsmanship that goes into these novels is of a high order. It has to be. They differ from other novels only in the emphasis on the theme—but it is the theme which causes the most difficulty. All novelists attempt to record the slow struggle of man toward his long home, sometimes depicting only the beginning or the middle or the end of the journey, emphasizing the great emotional peaks of birth and marriage and death which occur along the route. If it is a good job, the reader nods and says, Yes, that is how it must have been. Because the characters are as real as one's next-door-neighbor, predictable and yet unpredictable, lingering in the memory.

The sociological novelist sets out to do the same thing. But he is apt to become so obsessed by his theme, so entangled in it and fascinated by it, that his heroes resemble the early Christian martyrs; and his villains are showboat villains, first-class scoundrels with no redeeming features or virtues. If he is more pamphleteer than novelist, and something of a romanticist in the bargain, he will offer a solution to the social problem he has posed. He may be in love with a new world order, and try to sell it to his readers; or, and this happens more frequently, he has a trade union, usually the CIO, come to the rescue in the final scene, horse-opera fashion, and the curtain rings down on a happy ending as rosy as that of a western movie done in technicolor.

Characterization can be the greatest glory of the sociological novel. I offer as examples: Oliver Twist, child of the London slums, asking for more; Ma Joad, holding the fam'ly together in that long westward journey, somehow in her person epitomizing an earlier generation of women who traveled westward in search of a promised land; Bigger Thomas, who was both criminal and victim, fleeing for his life over the rooftops of Chicago; Jeeter Lester clinging to his worn-out land in futile defiance of a mechanized world. They have an amazing vitality, much of which springs from the theme. People still discuss them, argue about them, as though they had had an actual existence.

Though characterization is the great strength of these novels, as it is of all novels, it can also be the great weakness. When society is given the role of fate, made the evil in the age-old battle between good and evil, the burden of responsibility for their actions is shifted away from the characters. This negates the Old Testament idea of evil as a thing of the spirit, with each individual carrying on his own personal battle against the evil within himself. In a book which is more political pamphlet or sermon than novel the characters do not battle with themselves to save their souls, so to speak. Their defeat or their victory is not their own—they are pawns in the hands of a deaf, blind, stupid, social system. Once the novelist begins to manipulate his characters to serve the interests of his theme they lose whatever vitality they had when their creator first thought about them.

And so the novelist who takes an evil in society for his theme is rather like an aerial trapeze artist desperately trying to maintain his balance in mid-air. He works without a net and he may be sent tumbling by the dialogue, the plot, the theme itself.

Dialogue presents a terrible temptation. It offers the writer a convenient platform from which to set forth his pet theories and ideas. This is especially true of the books that deal with some phase of the relationship between whites and Negroes in the United States. Most of the talk in these books comes straight out of a never-never land existing in the author's mind. Anyone planning to write a book on this theme should re-read *Native Son* and compare the small talk which touches on race relations with that found in almost any novel on the subject published since then. Or reread Act I Scene 1 of *Othello*, and note how the dialogue advances the action, characterizes the speaker and yet at no point smacks of the pulpit or of the soapbox. When Iago and Rodrigo inform Brabantio that Desdemona has eloped with Othello, the Moor, they speak the language of the prejudiced; but it is introduced with a smoothness that hasn't been duplicated elsewhere.

One of the most successful recent performances is that of Alan Paton in *Cry the Beloved Country*. The hero, the old Zulu minister, wrestles with the recognized evil within himself, and emerges victorious. Yet the miserable existence of the exploited native in Johannesburg, the city of evil, has been revealed and the terror and glory of Africa become as real as though one had lived there. It is written in a prose style so musical and so rhythmic that much of it is pure poetry. *Cry the Beloved Country* is proof, if such proof is necessary, that the novel of social criticism will have a life as long and as honorable as that of the novel itself as an art form. For this book is art of the highest order, but it could not possibly be called an example of art for art's sake. It tells the reader in no uncertain terms that society is responsible for the tragedy of the native African.

In recent years, many novels of social criticism have dealt with race relations in this country. It is a theme which offers the novelist a wide and fertile field; it is the very stuff of fiction, sometimes comic, more often tragic, always ironic, endlessly dramatic. The setting and the characters vary in these books but the basic story line is derived from *Uncle Tom's Cabin*; discrimination and/or segregation (substitute slavery for the one or the other) are evils which lead to death—actual death or potential death. The characters either conform to the local taboos and mores and live, miserably; or refuse to conform and die.

This pattern of violence is characteristic of the type for a very good reason. The arguments used to justify slavery still influence American attitudes toward the Negro. If I use the words intermarriage, mixed marriage, miscegenation, there are few Americans who would not react to those words emotionally. Part of that emotion can be traced directly to the days of slavery. And if emotion is aroused merely by the use of certain words, and the emotion is violent, apoplectic, then it seems fairly logical that novels which deal with race relations should reflect some of this violence.

As I said, my first novel was a novel of social criticism. Having written it, I discovered that I was supposed to know the answer to many of the questions that are asked about such novels. What good do they do is a favorite. I think they do a lot of good. Social reforms have often received their original impetus from novels which aroused the emotions of a large number of readers. *Earth and High Heaven*, *Focus*, and *Gentleman's Agreement* undoubtedly made many a person examine the logic of his own special brand of anti-Semitism. The novels that deal with race relations have influenced the passage of the civil rights bills which have become law in many states.

I was often asked another question: *Why* do people write these novels? Sometimes I have been tempted to paraphrase the Duchess in *Alice in Wonderland* by way of answer (I never did): "'Please would you tell me,' said Alice a little timidly . . . 'Why your cat grins like that?' 'It's a Cheshire cat,' said the Duchess, 'and that's why.'"

Behind this question there is the implication that a writer who finds fault with society must be a little wrong in the head. Or that he is moved by the missionary spirit or a holier-than-thou attitude and therefore is in need of psychiatric treatment. I think the best answer to that question, on record, is to be found in Robert Van Gelder's *Writers and Writing*. He quotes Erich Remarque (*All Quiet on the Western Front*, *Three Comrades*, *Arch of Triumph*) as saying that people cannot count with their imaginations, that if five million die in a concentration camp it really does not equal one death in emotional impact and meaning—the death of someone you have known and loved: "If I say one died—a man I have made you know and understand—he lived so, this is what he thought, this is what he hoped, this was his faith, these were his difficulties, these his triumphs and then he—in this manner, on this day, at an hour when it rained and the room was stuffy—was killed, after torture, then perhaps I have told you something that you should know about the Nazis. . . . Some people who did not understand before may be made to understand what the Nazis were like and what they did and what their kind will try to do again."

It is with reluctance that I speak of my own writing. I have never been satisfied with anything I have written and I doubt that I ever will be. Most of what I have learned about writing I learned the hard way, through trial and error and rejection slips. I set out to be a writer of short stories and somehow ended up as a novelist—possibly because there simply wasn't room enough within the framework of a short story to do the sort of thing I wanted to do. I have collected enough rejection slips for my short stories to paper four or five good sized rooms. During that rejection slip period I was always reading the autobiography of writers, and in Arthur Train's *My Day in Court* I found a piece of rather wonderful advice. He said that if he were a beginning writer one of the things that he would do would be to enter Mabel L. Robinson's course in the short story at Columbia University. Needless to say I promptly applied for admission to the class.

I spent a year in Miss Robinson's short story class. And during another year I was a member of the workshop that she conducts at Columbia. What I didn't learn through trial and error I learned from Miss Robinson. She taught me to criticize what I had written and to read other people's creative efforts with a critical eye. Perhaps of even greater importance she made me believe in myself.

As partial payment for a debt of gratitude I am passing along Arthur Train's advice. If the walls of your apartment or your house are papered with rejection slips I suggest that you apply for admission to one of Miss Robinson's classes.

The Writer's Book, ed. Helen Hull (1950)

CHRONOLOGY

NOTE ON THE TEXTS

NOTES

Chronology

<table>
<tr>
<td>1908–1912</td>
<td>Born Anna Houston Lane in Old Saybrook, Connecticut, on October 12, 1908, the younger of two surviving children of Bertha Ernestine James and Peter Clark Lane. Mother, thirty-three, is a recently licensed barber and beautician who later starts her own business, Beautiful Linens for Beautiful Homes, producing handmade linen and lace tablecloths and napkins. Father, thirty-five, has owned and operated the local drugstore at 2 Pennywise Lane since 1902; the family lives above it. Their first child, Bertha Harriet Lane, died of pleurisy as an infant, in 1905; their second, Helen Louise Lane, was born December 14, 1906. The Lanes are one of four black families in Old Saybrook, "a picture-postcard of a town" (as she later describes it) but also "an essentially hostile environment for a black family." The 1910 census lists paternal uncle Warren Lane, a thirty-three-year-old livery driver, and maternal aunt Helen James, a thirty-year-old grade school teacher, as members of the household. Aunt Anna Louise James arrives in 1912 and works in the family drugstore; the previous year, at age twenty-five, she became the first licensed African American woman pharmacist in Connecticut.</td>
</tr>
<tr>
<td>1913–1917</td>
<td>Enters Old Saybrook Elementary School at age four, along with her older sister. The two girls are bullied by boys who hurl rocks and racial epithets. The next day, their uncles accompany them to school, confront the boys, and the bullying stops. Reads Louisa May Alcott's *Little Women* in the second or third grade; feels "as though I was part of Jo and she was part of me." In 1915, mother graduates from New York School of Chiropody in Harlem and begins practicing next to the family drugstore.</td>
</tr>
<tr>
<td>1918</td>
<td>Father takes job with a drug wholesaler in Hartford, Connecticut, boarding with relatives during the week and returning home on weekends. Aunt Anna Louise James takes responsibility for the family pharmacy, and within a few years becomes its owner.</td>
</tr>
</table>

787

1919   Becomes an "omnivorous reader," she later remembers, after her encounter with Wilkie Collins's *The Moonstone*.

1920   In May, family moves from their apartment above James Pharmacy into a new house in Old Saybrook.

1921   Father writes letter to NAACP magazine *The Crisis*, not published, describing problems with a racist eighth-grade teacher in Old Saybrook: "I want my daughters to have a good education and they want to get one also. I am a laboring man and have got to have some one to help me to get my girls through this school."

1922–1923   In May 1922, is confirmed as a member of the Old Saybrook Congregational Church, which her family attends. Remains active in the church for the rest of her life, helping to organize the Sunday school and collecting books to be sold at annual church fairs.

1924   Sister is accepted at the Woman's College in Brown University; arriving on campus with her family, she is told she cannot live in school dormitories because of her race and must find private accommodation.

1925   Graduates from Old Saybrook High School.

1926   Attends Hampton Normal and Agricultural Institute in Hampton, Virginia; takes courses in meal preparation and domestic economy.

1927   Leaves Hampton in the fall in the wake of a strike in which students demand an expanded role in the administration, more African American faculty, and a higher quality of teaching.

1928–1930   Attends Connecticut College of Pharmacy in New Haven beginning in 1928. Sister graduates from Brown with a degree in English the same year, and goes on to teach.

1931–1935   Graduates from Connecticut College of Pharmacy in 1931 and begins working in the family business, first in Old Saybrook and then as manager of a second store in Old Lyme, Connecticut. ("I worked seven days a week," she later recalls; "the only time that the drugstore was closed was on Christmas in the afternoon and on Thanksgiving in the afternoon.") Sends short stories to magazines, receiving many rejection letters. Meets future husband George David Petry during a trip to Hartford, where both are visiting friends; about a year her senior, Petry moved to New York City during the 1920s from New Iberia, Louisiana, to continue his education, ultimately completing two years of college while managing a restaurant. He also played football, and wrote detective fiction.

1936–1937　On March 13, 1936, marries Petry in Mount Vernon, New York, keeping the fact secret from her parents. Acting Mayor William E. Hughes, Jr., officiates. A week after the ceremony, supplies false information for a story in *The Amsterdam News* ("Connecticut Druggist Likes Shows, So She Comes Here," March 21), which reports that Miss Anna Houston Lane has been staying at the Emma Ransom House, a women's residence at the Harlem YMCA, to attend Broadway shows with her friends. The reasons for her secrecy remain obscure.

1938　On February 22, marries George Petry publicly in a ceremony officiated by the Rev. Herbert P. Wooden in her parents' living room in Old Saybrook; gives 1938 as the date of her marriage in subsequent accounts of her life. The couple lives at 2 East 129th Street in Harlem with George's older sister. Works briefly as an advertising copywriter for a wig company, then begins career at New York's *Amsterdam News* in the advertising department.

1939　Publishes first short story, "Marie of the Cabin Club," in the Baltimore *Afro-American* on August 19, under the pseudonym Arnold Petri; receives a check for $5.

1940　Performs in the role of newspaper editor Tillie Petunia in the American Negro Theater's production of *On Striver's Row*, written and directed by Abram Hill, which opens on September 11 at the 135th Street Library Theater (now part of the Schomburg Center for Research in Black Culture) and runs for five months. Later helps to raise funds for the theater company. Publishes story "One Night in Harlem" in the *Afro-American* on November 16, again under the pseudonym Arnold Petri. In December, helps to organize and serves as temporary chair of the Consolidated Housewives League, a Harlem consumer group "determined to put a stop to the shady practices of unscrupulous merchants."

1941   In February, the Housewives League protests a planned
        New York screening of D. W. Griffith's film *The Birth of
        a Nation*. Leaves *The Amsterdam News* to work for *The
        People's Voice*, founded by Adam Clayton Powell, Jr., and
        the most radical of Harlem's three weekly newspapers,
        serving as women's editor. Reports on "everything from
        teas to fires, with births, deaths and picket lines inter-
        spersed," as she later puts it; some of her journalism in-
        spires her later fiction. Takes painting and drawing classes
        at the Harlem Community Arts Center.

1942   With Dollie Robinson, a trade unionist and political ac-
        tivist, establishes Negro Women Incorporated, described
        as "a Harlem consumer's watch group that provides
        working class women with 'how-to' information for pur-
        chasing food, clothing, and furniture." The organization
        also encourages participation in the war effort, mobilizes
        the vote, and teaches black women to recognize them-
        selves as political agents. Begins a regular weekly column
        for *The People's Voice* on March 7; titled "The Lighter
        Side," it discusses art, literature, music, the comings and
        goings of Harlem's elites, and other topics of the day. In
        August, joins a Negro Women Incorporated picket line
        protesting New York *Daily News* coverage of Harlem;
        writes article "Harlem Women Wax Indignant over Lat-
        est 'Crime' Campaign" for her paper. Volunteers for the
        Laundry Workers Joint Board, developing educational
        materials for the children of laundry workers, and hosts a
        tea to benefit Hope Day Nursery in Harlem. Is admitted
        to Mabel Louise Robinson's celebrated writing workshop
        at Columbia University; studies with Robinson for two
        years, later crediting her with having a profound influ-
        ence on her literary development.

1943   In April, with other journalists, helps to organize a vari-
        ety show to benefit Harlem Neighborhood Clubs, which
        provide "wholesome activities for the boys and girls of
        Harlem." Loses her full-time position at *The People's
        Voice* amid staff cutbacks, publishing her last column on
        May 8, but continues to contribute occasional articles.
        On July 3, husband enlists in the U.S. Army; he enters
        active service on July 24 at Camp Upton, New York.
        Works in several part-time or short-term positions: for
        the Harlem-Riverside Defense Council, preparing press

releases as assistant to the secretary; for the National Association of Colored Graduate Nurses, as publicity director; and for Harlem's Play Schools Association Project at Public School No. 10, as a recreation specialist. In the latter role she helps to develop programs for the children of working parents at the school, focusing on the problem of "latchkey" children, who return from school to empty apartments because their parents work long hours. Receives $20 for the story "On Saturday the Siren Sounds at Noon," which appears in the December issue of *The Crisis*; an editor at Houghton Mifflin, reading the story, asks if she is working on a novel, and encourages her to apply for the Houghton Mifflin Literary Fellowship.

1944   Starts writing *The Street* in the fall. Toward the end of the year, submits outline and chapters of the novel to Houghton Mifflin Literary Fellowship. Organizes Negro History discussions at P.S. 10 on St. Nicholas Avenue and 116th Street. In October, Negro Women Incorporated holds voter registration mass meeting at Abyssinian Baptist Church, located at 132 West 138th Street. Story "Doby's Gone" appears in *Phylon*, a journal established by W.E.B. Du Bois in 1940.

1945   In February, wins $2,400 Houghton Mifflin Literary Fellowship to work on *The Street*. Publishes "New England's John Henry," about Venture Smith, a slave who purchased his freedom in 1765, in the March issue of *Negro Digest*, followed by stories "Olaf and His Girl Friend" and "Like a Winding Sheet" in *The Crisis*. Is honored by Negro Women Incorporated at an April testimonial tea at the 135th Street Public Library. Moves to a new apartment in the Bronx sometime before June; spends summer vacation with family in Old Saybrook.

1946   On February 7, Houghton Mifflin publishes *The Street* with notable fanfare; 20,000 copies are sold in advance of its release (the novel will eventually sell over one million copies, the first book by an African American woman to do so). Publisher hosts a book party at the Hotel Biltmore attended by Owen Dodson, John Dos Passos, Lewis Gannet of the *New York Herald Tribune*, Harold Jackman, Grace Nail Johnson, Bucklin Moon, Isabelle Washington Powell, Orville Prescott of *The New York*

Times, and Cornelia Otis Skinner, among others. Friend Frances Reckling hosts more intimate gathering in her Harlem studio. Corresponds with prominent Harlem Renaissance intellectual Alain Locke about her plans for a second novel. In April, is featured speaker at a New York conference of the Play Schools Association. Describes a personal encounter with racism for the *Negro Digest* series "My Most Humiliating Jim Crow Experience" in June: at age seven, she and her classmates had to leave a Connecticut beach because she was black. Is honored for "exceptional contributions to the life of New York City" by the Women's City Club. In September, reviews Margaret Halsey's *Color Blind: A White Woman Looks at the Negro* for *PM*, a liberal-leaning New York daily. Husband George is discharged from the U.S. Army at Camp Pickett, Virginia, on October 4. *The Crisis* publishes her story "Like a Winding Sheet" in November; it is included in the year's *Best American Short Stories*, which editor Martha Foley dedicates to Petry.

1947   Article "What's Wrong with Negro Men" appears in the March issue of *Negro Digest*; reviews Laura Z. Hobson's novel *Gentleman's Agreement* in *PM*. In June, *The Street* is optioned for film by a former Warner Brothers publicist. *Country Place*, her second novel, is published by Houghton Mifflin in September; some reviewers compare it unfavorably to *The Street*. Friend Frances Kraft Reckling hosts book party at her Harlem studio. Moves to Old Saybrook with husband George, "beleaguered," as she later puts it, "by all the hoopla, the interviews, the invitations to speak" that follow her fame as a novelist. They purchase an old house, originally built for a sea captain around 1790, which they gradually renovate. Furnishes the house with local antiques, becoming a lifelong collector of china and silver and frequenter of estate sales. Donates manuscripts of *The Street* to the James Weldon Johnson Memorial Collection at Yale University. Publishes stories "The Bones of Louella Brown" in *Opportunity* (October–December), "Solo on the Drums" in *'47: The Magazine of the Year* (October), and "In Darkness and Confusion" in the anthology *Cross Section*, edited by Edwin Seaver.

1948   In May, attends Harlem book party for publication of Dorothy West's novel *The Living Is Easy*. Donates letters, photographs, and the manuscript of *Country Place* to James Weldon Johnson Memorial Collection at Yale.

1949   Daughter Elisabeth Ann Petry is born on January 28 in Middletown, Connecticut. Photo-essay "Harlem" appears in the April issue of *Holiday*. Reviews Bucklin Moon's novel *Without Magnolias* in the *New York Herald Tribune*. Father dies of cancer on August 27. Publishes first children's book, *The Drugstore Cat*, with Thomas Y. Crowell in November; it is illustrated by Susanne Suba.

1950   Essay "The Novel as Social Criticism" appears in *The Writer's Book*, edited by Helen Hull. Reviews novels *Stranger and Alone* by J. Saunders Redding and *Taffy* by Philip B. Kaye for the *Saturday Review of Literature*. Lectures at Morgan State College in Baltimore.

1951   Works intensively on third novel *The Narrows*, for which she had begun making notes around 1948.

1952   Speaks at a February conference of the U.S. National Commission for UNESCO, at Hunter College in New York.

1953   *The Narrows* is published by Houghton Mifflin on July 30; for many reviewers, it confirms and extends the promise of her debut. *The Boston Globe* praises the novel as "a story filled with dramatic force, earthy humor, and tragic intensity."

1954   In April, speaks to the Essex (Connecticut) Women's Club on the business of publishing. *The Narrows* is published in England by Victor Gollancz. Reviews John Oliver Killens's novel *Youngblood* in the *New York Herald Tribune*.

1955   Addresses the Old Saybrook Women's Republican Club in February on "The Origins of Constitutional Government." ("In order to have a say in local governance," her daughter later explains of her mother's politics, "one joined the Republican Party," but "with the possible exception of Dwight Eisenhower, I know she never voted for a GOP presidential candidate during my lifetime.") Also in the mid-1950s, joins the League of Women Voters and is elected to the Old Saybrook Board of Education. After uncle Fritz James suffers a stroke in March, takes responsibility for overseeing the family's Old Lyme pharmacy. Publishes *Harriet Tubman: Conductor on the Underground Railroad* on June 30. In December, delivers opening address at Hampton Institute Book Fair, "How To Write."

1956   Signs American Civil Liberties Union's "Statement on Censorship Activity by Private Organizations and the National Organization for Decent Literature" along with other writers; the NODL had included *The Narrows* on its lists of books recommended for censorship. New plans for a film version of *The Street* are widely publicized beginning in August. To be produced by Harold Robbins, who completes a screenplay, the film will potentially feature Leigh Whipper, Rosalind Hayes, Diahann Carroll, or Lena Horne as Lutie Johnson; Joe Louis, Earl Hyman, and Nat King Cole are mentioned in male roles, Gerd Oswald as director, and Duke Ellington as contributor of an original score. Mother dies in Old Saybrook on September 2.

1957   In December, speaks on "The Problems of Writing Fiction and Biography" at a Columbia University event honoring her former teacher Mabel Louise Robinson.

1958   Spends two months in Hollywood in the fall working as a screenwriter for Columbia Pictures, adapting Charles Williams's 1951 novel *Hill Girl* as "That Hill Girl," to star Kim Novak. The Chicago *Defender* notes: "It's the first time a Negro writer has been employed . . . to do a screen adaptation." The film is never produced. Story "Has Anybody Seen Miss Dora Dean?" appears in the October–November issue of *The New Yorker*.

1959   Chairs an Old Saybrook town committee tasked with appointing representatives to oversee construction of a new elementary school. Harold Robbins makes a second attempt to find financing for his screenplay of *The Street*, but the film is never made.

1960   Recounts her experiences in Hollywood for the Old Saybrook Women's Club. *Harriet Tubman* is published by Methuen in London under the title *The Girl Called Moses*.

1961   Attends celebration of detective writer Rex Stout's 75th birthday at Sardi's in New York.

1962   Spends part of the winter in Puerto Rico, taking an un-
            accustomed vacation trip. "I never felt that at home any-
            where I have been," she writes in her journal; "the curves
            in the roads, the mountains, the rain forest—the beat of
            that Spanish music—the brilliance of the sun—the color
            of the flowers."

1963   On February 12, Lincoln's birthday, attends White House
            reception celebrating the first century of emancipation.
            Novella "Miss Muriel," described as part of "a larger
            work now in progress," appears in anthology *Soon, One
            Morning: New Writing by American Negroes, 1940–1962*,
            edited by Herbert Hill.

1964   Criticizes plans for the construction of a new high school
            in Old Saybrook at a March town meeting, calling them
            "inefficient and wildly extravagant." *Tituba of Salem
            Village*, a young adult historical novel, is published by
            Thomas Y. Crowell on September 4. In November,
            speaks on children's literature at the New York Public Li-
            brary; titled "The Common Ground," her lecture is pub-
            lished in *The Horn Book Magazine* the following April.

1965   Along with writers Russell Baker and Nathaniel Bench-
            ley, speaks at Baltimore Book and Author Luncheon
            in April. Story "The New Mirror" appears in *The New
            Yorker* on May 29. Reviews historical novel *I, Juan de
            Pareja* by Elizabeth Borton de Trevino in *The New York
            Times Book Review*.

1966   Purchases a television set, the family's first. Reviews nov-
            els *Canalboat to Freedom* by Thomas Fall and *David in
            Silence* by Veronica Robinson in *The New York Times
            Book Review*. Daughter Elisabeth graduates from Old
            Saybrook High School as valedictorian and enrolls at
            Vassar College in Poughkeepsie, New York.

1967   Story "The Migraine Workers" appears in the May issue
            of *Redbook*. Over the summer, speaks at a symposium
            on children's literature at the University of California at
            Berkeley. After aunt Anna Louise James breaks an ankle,
            helps run and eventually close the James Pharmacy.

1968   Testifies before Old Saybrook Planning Commission
            to protest proposed alterations to the town's cemeter-
            ies. Donates papers to the Mugar Library at Boston
            University.

1969   Speaks at a conference of English teachers at Hartford
            Public High School.

1970   In January, gives presentation to Old Saybrook Histor-
            ical Society on witchcraft in seventeenth-century New
            England. Publishes *Legends of the Saints* on August 27.
            Illustrated by Anne Rockwell, it retells the legends of ten
            saints, some well-known and some obscure: Christopher,
            Genesius, George, Blaise, Catherine of Alexandria, Nich-
            olas, Francis of Assisi, Joan of Arc, Thomas More, and
            Martin de Porres. Writes biographical article on Harriet
            Tubman for the *Encyclopedia Britannica.*

1971   Story "The Witness" appears in the February issue of
            Redbook. On May 17, Houghton Mifflin publishes *Miss
            Muriel and Other Stories*; it gathers thirteen stories,
            twelve originally printed in magazines from 1945 to
            1971 and one, "Mother Africa," appearing for the first
            time.

1972   Travels to Oxford, Ohio, over the summer as a guest
            of the creative writing program of Miami University. Is
            elected secretary of the Cypress Cemetery Association in
            Old Saybrook.

1973   Presents lecture "This Unforgettable Passage," on her
            life and works, at Suffolk University in Boston; it inau-
            gurates new African American literature program there.
            Also speaks to public school library volunteers at a con-
            ference in Fairfield, Connecticut, and to the Women's
            Club in Essex, Connecticut, on "How Not to Write a
            Book."

1974   Appointed visiting professor of English at the Univer-
            sity of Hawaii for the 1974–75 academic year. In Au-
            gust, daughter enrolls in law school at University of
            Pennsylvania.

1975   Reads her story "The Migraine Workers" at a University
            of Hawaii event in March, and in April gives a public lec-
            ture on the art of writing; is interviewed by *The Honolulu
            Advertiser* and appears on local television.

1976   Publishes her first poems—"Noo York City 1," "Noo
            York City 2," and "Noo York City 3"—in the journal
            Weid: The Sensibility Review.

1977   Challenges Congressman Christopher Dodd, at an April public meeting in Old Saybrook, "to simplify the forms and instructions so that any literate person could fill out his own taxes"; declares she will rewrite the instructions for IRS form 1040 herself. Aunt Anna Louise James dies on December 12; takes responsibility for cleaning out and selling the James Pharmacy building.

1978   Receives Literature Fellowship from National Endowment for the Arts.

1979   In March, reads her story "The Witness" during "Women in the Arts Week" at the University of Connecticut in Storrs. Attends a "Meet the Authors" event at the Waterford (Connecticut) Public Library.

1980   Harold Robbins, who attempted unsuccessfully to produce a movie adaptation of *The Street* in the 1950s, seeks investors to take the novel to Broadway as a musical, again without success.

1981   An adaptation of her story "Solo on the Drums" airs on PBS television in March, as an episode in the series *With Ossie and Ruby*; Ossie Davis and Ruby Dee read from the text while Billy Taylor accompanies on piano and Max Roach on drums. Publishes poems "A Purely Black Stone" and "A Real Boss Black Cat" in *The View from the Top of the Mountain: Poems after Sixty*. Sister Helen Bush is diagnosed with bone marrow cancer.

1982   Delivers fourth annual Richard Wright Lecture at Yale, "The Making of a Writer." Reads from her work at The New School in New York City and Brandeis University in Waltham, Massachusetts.

1983   Receives honorary Doctor of Letters degree from Suffolk University. Talks with students in the class "Black Women and Their Fictions" at Yale, at the invitation of Henry Louis Gates, Jr.

1984   Visits the College of Pharmacy at the University of Illinois–Chicago, where students perform a play taken from a section of her novel *Country Place*. Speaks at a symposium on "Black Women's Literary Traditions" organized by the writing program at MIT, along with historian Dorothy Sterling and novelist Dorothy West.

1985 Gives lecture at University of Massachusetts symposium "Writers Speak III: New England as Region and Idea"; meets James Baldwin, who is teaching at Amherst.

1986 Reads new story, "The Moses Project," at Hampshire College in Amherst, Massachusetts; it is published in *Harbor Review*. *The Street* appears in a new edition from Beacon Press.

1987 In January, reads her work at the Afro-American Historical and Cultural Museum in Philadelphia.

1988 Sister Helen Bush dies in Old Saybrook on May 16. A week later, receives honorary Doctor of Letters degree from the University of Connecticut. Publishes an appreciation of Langston Hughes's and Roy DeCarava's *The Sweet Flypaper of Life* in *Rediscoveries II*, edited by David Madden and Peggy Bach. *The Narrows* and *The Drugstore Cat* appear in new editions from Beacon Press. In October, lectures and reads from her work at the University of New Hampshire in Durham.

1989 Is presented with a Lifetime Achievement Award by Philadelphia mayor Wilson Goode during a Celebration of Black Writers in February. Later that month, joins sculptor Selma Burke and artist Margaret Burroughs to discuss "Coming of Age in Post-Depression America" at the Wadsworth Atheneum in Hartford. Attends commencement at Mount Holyoke College in South Hadley, Massachusetts, where she is given an honorary doctorate.

1990 With playwright Alice Childress and poets Gwendolyn Brooks and Sonia Sanchez, reads from her works at Hartford College for Women conference "Prophets for a New Day."

1991 HarperCollins publishes a new edition of *Tituba of Salem Village*.

1992 Houghton Mifflin reissues *The Street* in February, prompting wide, career-retrospective review coverage. In May, gives keynote speech for twenty-fifth anniversary of Old Saybrook Library. Receives Connecticut Arts Award from the Connecticut Commission of the Arts in October. The following month, attends day of programming devoted to her work at Trinity College in Hartford; organized by Farah Jasmine Griffin, the event includes a scholarly symposium, an evening tribute by novelist Gloria Naylor, and a dinner in her honor. Reads from her works on Connecticut Public Radio as part of the "Connecticut Voices" series. Contributes story "My First Real Hat" to *When I Was a Child*, published by the Children's Literature Association.

1993   Receives honorary degree from Trinity College. Donates autographed copies of all her works to the Ann Petry Collection at the African American Research Center at Shaw University in Raleigh, North Carolina.

1994   The James Pharmacy is listed in the National Register of Historic Places.

1995–1997 Donates aunt Anna Louise James's papers to Radcliffe College in 1995. On February 7, falls down the stairs and breaks her hip. Following surgery is transferred to a nursing home to undergo rehabilitation. Dies on April 28, and is buried in Old Saybrook's Cypress Cemetery. Husband is interred beside her after his death on December 7, 2000.

Note on the Texts

This volume contains Ann Petry's novels *The Street* (1946) and *The Narrows* (1953), along with three related short essays, "The Great Secret," "Harlem," and "The Novel as Social Criticism." The texts of the novels, both first published by Houghton Mifflin, have been taken from their first printings, and the text of the essays from their original magazine and anthology appearances, as described below.

The Street. By her own account, Petry's decision to begin *The Street* was prompted by an editor at Houghton Mifflin, who wrote to ask, after reading her story "On Saturday the Siren Sounds at Noon" in the December 1943 issue of *The Crisis*, if she was at work on a novel. Encouraged to apply for the Houghton Mifflin Literary Fellowship, Petry drafted five chapters and an outline during the fall of 1944, submitting them to the Fellowship competition at the end of the year. In February 1945 she was notified she had won the $2,400 award, and by June she was able to tell a reporter from the *New York Age* that she was "near completion."

Houghton Mifflin published *The Street* on February 7, 1946, in an edition that quickly went through multiple printings. The novel has been described as the first book by an African American woman to sell over a million copies: it was reissued in February 1947 by the World Publishing Company in Cleveland, in an edition prepared from the original Houghton Mifflin printing plates; in April 1947 by Michael Joseph in London, newly typeset for British readers; in 1949 by Signet/New American Library in New York, as a newly typeset paperback; and in numerous editions since. Petry is not known to have corrected or revised her novel after its initial appearance in print, and she declined invitations in subsequent decades to add new introductory material, believing her work was complete. The text of *The Street* in the present volume is that of the February 1946 Houghton Mifflin first printing.

The Narrows. Petry started writing *The Narrows* soon after the publication of her second novel, *Country Place*, in September 1947, and worked on it almost exclusively for about five years; it was published by Houghton Mifflin on July 30, 1953. As in the case of *The Street*, she is not known to have sought corrections or revisions after the novel's initial printing, though it was subsequently reissued by Victor Gollancz in London (1954), Signet/New American Library in New York (1955), and other publishers thereafter during her lifetime. The text of the novel in the present volume is taken from the July 1953 Houghton Mifflin first printing.

Other Writings. The texts of the three essays that follow *The Street* and *The Narrows* in this collection have been taken from their first appearances in print: "The Great Secret" from the July 1948 issue of *The Writer*; "Harlem" from the April 1949 issue of *Holiday* (where it was illustrated with photographs by George Leavens); and "The Novel as Social Criticism" from *The Writer's Book*, an anthology edited by Helen R. Hull and published by Harper in New York in 1950. It is believed all three essays are reprinted here for the first time.

This volume presents the texts of the original printings chosen for inclusion here, but it does not attempt to reproduce features of their design and layout. The texts are presented without change, except for the correction of typographical errors. Spelling, punctuation, and capitalization are often expressive features and they are not altered, even when inconsistent or irregular. The following is a list of typographical errors corrected, cited by page and line number: 35.23, it's; 76.15, moving The; 94.20, Jones's; 140.34, policemen; 174.6, you when; 187.2, Run; 191.10, Hey,; 196.33, stop She; 205.35, him It; 226.29, you all.; 236.30, further He; 265.13, super's; 266.2, drew; 337.34, imperturably; 349.24, hod; 362.33, heat" in; 363.38, blubs; 364.19, gorilla; 404.15, herself.; 408.7–8, suprised; 408.26, said.; 417.14, morning',; 419.3, front'; 422.24, said.; 423.40, afternon,; 434.33, bar keep; 439.7, coffe; 442.13, Same Train; 442.20, gaity; 442.28, Camillo; 456.18, mantle.; 475.15, that it; 475.27, devilsh; 477.25–26, happend; 482.4, aways; 486.15, peperment; 488.30–31, expressived-eyed; 496.11, dyamo; 505.6, goddam; 519.6, to."; 519.23 (and *passim*), captain,; 528.21, Adams,; 529.14, coming, and; 538.7, staring her,; 540.7, afternon; 541.9, voice.; 548.8, Crunches,; 561.36 (and *passim*), gentleman's; 561.37, thougth; 563.15, now,; 579.10, free-from; 589.20, quickly,; 594.11, Se he; 597.10, had chance; 605.34, Waldorf-astoria; 615.2, J.C.,; 633.35, and arm; 641.25, heather; 644.11, Mr. B.; 646.16, Knees,; 649.27, flare; 702.13, Negrovillianconvicthero; 710.16, bout; 721.1, every; 725.18, tabliod; 756.28, now—; 764.30, sty e; 765.25, *The Novel*; 776.33, *any.*

Notes

In the notes below, the reference numbers denote page and line of this volume (the line count includes chapter headings but not blank lines). Quotations from Shakespeare are keyed to *The Riverside Shakespeare*, ed. G. Blakemore Evans (Boston: Houghton Mifflin, 1974). Biblical references are keyed to the King James Version. For further information about Petry's life and works, and references to other studies, see Keith Clark, *The Radical Fiction of Ann Petry* (Baton Rouge: Louisiana State University Press, 2013); Hazel Arnett Ervin, *Ann Petry: A Bio-Bibliography* (New York: G. K. Hall, 1993); Hazel Arnett Ervin, *The Critical Response to Ann Petry* (Westport, Connecticut: Praeger, 2005); Hazel Arnett Ervin and Hilary Holladay, eds., *Ann Petry's Short Fiction: Critical Essays* (Westport, Connecticut: Praeger, 2004); Farah Jasmine Griffin, *Harlem Nocturne: Women Artists and Progressive Politics During World War II* (New York: Basic Civitas, 2013); Hilary Holladay, *Ann Petry* (New York: Twayne, 1996); Alex Lubin, ed., *Revising the Blueprint: Ann Petry and the Literary Left* (Jackson: University Press of Mississippi, 2007); and Elisabeth Petry, *At Home Inside: A Daughter's Tribute to Ann Petry* (Jackson: University Press of Mississippi, 2009).

THE STREET

46.3 Ben Franklin and his loaf of bread.] See Franklin's *Autobiography*, first published in English in 1793.

103.29 "Swing It, Sister."] Song performed by The Mills Brothers in the 1934 film *Strictly Dynamite*, with lyrics by Harold Adamson (1906–1980) and music by Burton Lane (1912–1997).

104.28–30 "Darlin' . . . no fun, Darlin'."] Ballad by Lucius Venable "Lucky" Millinder (1910–1966) and Petry's friend Frances Kraft Reckling (1906–1987), first recorded in May 1944. Continuing the song after it has finished playing, Lutie extemporizes new lyrics.

113.18–19 Night and Day. . . . Let's Go Home."] "Night and Day" was written by Cole Porter (1891–1964) for the 1932 musical *Gay Divorce* and subsequently performed by many artists. "Hurry Up, Sammy, and Let's Go Home," written by Dan Burley (1907–1962) and Frances Kraft Reckling (1906–1987), was registered for copyright in 1943 but is not known to have been recorded. For "Darlin'," see note 104.28–30.

175.30 Sugar Hill] See Petry's description of this section of Harlem on page 767 of the present volume.

218.13 Rock, Raleigh, Rock.] This musical title is obscure and may be Petry's invention.

THE NARROWS

308.2 *Mabel Louise Robinson*] Robinson (1874–1962), an author of fiction for children and young adults, taught creative writing at Columbia University. Petry was her student for two years beginning in 1943.

314.29 Poro Method] As taught at Poro College, a St. Louis school of hair care and cosmetology founded by Annie Turnbo Malone (1877–1957).

319.28 old Aunt Grinny Granny] See "Old Grinny-Granny Wolf" in *Nights with Uncle Remus* (1883) by Joel Chandler Harris (1848–1908) and "The Charmer" (*Saturday Evening Post*, May 29, 1909) by Harris Dickson (1868–1946).

341.17 WCTU] Woman's Christian Temperance Union.

347.4 "Goin' Home."] 1922 song by William Arms Fisher (1861–1949), adapted from the Largo theme of Antonín Dvořák's Symphony No. 9 (1893).

351.8–9 "'How beautiful . . . daughter—'"] Song of Solomon 7:1.

369.34 clinker tops] Women with natural, kinky hair.

374.19 Marlene] Marlene Dietrich (1901–1992), German actress who began a Hollywood career in 1930.

374.28 the Sadler's Wells] A London theater, home to prominent ballet companies beginning in the 1930s.

376.29–30 packed a punch like Old Man Louis . . . Joe] Joe Louis (1914–1981), world heavyweight boxing champion from 1937 to 1949.

396.40 CIO] Congress of Industrial Organizations.

397.27 Dietrich] See note 374.19.

399.21–24 Come when you're called . . . chid.] An English nursery rhyme.

409.40–410.2 "'How many goodly creatures . . . in't.'] *The Tempest*, V.i.182–84.

439.28–33 Same train carry . . . same train.] A traditional spiritual.

441.36–442.1 monologues and soliloquies . . . Frankie and Johnnie.] See "Maud" (1855) by Alfred Lord Tennyson (1809–1892); "The Passionate Shepherd to His Love" (1599) and *Doctor Faustus* (1592), V.i.93, by Christopher Marlowe (1564–1593); *Romeo and Juliet* (1597), III.v.6, by William Shakespeare

(1564–1616); *Doctor Faustus*, V.i.93; "The Passionate Shepherd to His Love"; and the American folksong "Frankie and Johnnie."

445.32   Dickens' fat boy] See *The Posthumous Papers of the Pickwick Club* (1837) by Charles Dickens (1812–1870).

447.23   black *but* comely] Song of Solomon 1:5.

468.34–36   play the mooncalf . . . Hans Kraut] The Moon-Calf and Hans Krout (*sic*) are characters in *The Garden Behind the Moon* (1895), a children's story by Howard Pyle (1853–1911).

469.23   Hobson's choice] A "take it or leave it" choice, named after English stable owner Thomas Hobson (1544–1631).

512.34–39   Tell me what color . . . she took.] From "Ticket Agent Blues" (1935) by Blind Willie McTell (1898–1959).

517.38   Adam chairs] Chairs designed by or in the manner of Scottish architect Robert Adam (1728–1792).

527.34–39   Same train . . . same train.] See note 439.28–33.

540.11   Full fathom five thy father lies] *The Tempest*, I.ii.397.

541.33–37   "there came down a certain priest . . . on him."] Luke 10:31.

553.34–36   the city of Charleston . . . Catfish Alley.] Crown, Porgy, Bess, and Sportin' Life are characters in the 1935 opera *Porgy and Bess*, adapted from Dorothy Heyward and DuBose Heyward's 1927 play *Porgy* and ultimately from DuBose Heyward's 1925 novel of the same title. All three works are set on the fictional Catfish Row, in Charleston, South Carolina.

554.9   Meriney] A term for skin color, possibly from the light brown of merino wool; also spelled *meriny*.

567.32–36   King of England . . . the darkness.] In his 1939 Christmas broadcast, George VI quoted from the poem "God Knows" by Minnie Louise Haskins (1875–1957), published in her collection *The Desert* (1912): "And I said to the man who stood at the gate of the year: / 'Give me a light that I may tread safely into the unknown.' / And he replied: / 'Go out into the darkness and put your hand into the Hand of God. That shall be to you better than light and safer than a known way.'"

582.30   Olympia] Painting by Edouard Manet (1832–1883), first exhibited in 1865.

587.24–588.4   what do I think about Paul Robeson . . . can't marry each other] Robeson (1898–1976), who first traveled to the Soviet Union in 1934, made laudatory statements about Soviet racial attitudes, and sent his son to school there; his controversial pro-Soviet statements after another visit in 1949 led him to be blacklisted in the United States.

589.23   kulaks] In late imperial Russia and the early Soviet Union, farmers who had achieved a degree of prosperity above that of ordinary peasants.

608.37–40 "Thy people shall be . . . thee and me."] Ruth 1:16–17.

612.10 take notes on us—for Kinsey?"] Alfred C. Kinsey (1894–1956) and his coauthors obtained information for the best-selling Kinsey Reports (*Sexual Behavior in the Human Male*, 1948, and *Sexual Behavior in the Human Female*, 1953) from interviews and questionnaires.

644.9–10 Mack Sennett] Sennett (1880–1960) directed and produced slapstick comedies including the Keystone Cops series (1912–17).

644.17 John Barleycorn] A personification of alcoholic liquor.

647.33–36 an eyewitness account . . . hear it now."] See Mary Cadwalader Jones's *Lantern Slides* (1937).

653.8 like Louis . . . Carnera] Joe Louis (1914–1981) defeated Primo Carnera (1906–1967) in a New York boxing match on June 25, 1935; Carnera outweighed Louis by more than 60 pounds.

674.10–13 Tell me what color . . . road she took.] See note 512.34–39.

683.12 more lip than John L. Lewis] Lewis (1880–1969), president of the United Mine Workers of America (1920–60) and leader of the Congress of Industrial Organizations (1935–41), was widely known for his eloquent and aggressive advocacy of workers' rights.

688.5–6 papers in the pumpkin, Chambers, Hiss] Having accused former State Department official Alger Hiss (1904–1996) of Communist affiliations in widely publicized testimony before the House Un-American Activities Committee in August 1948, Whittaker Chambers (1901–1961) subsequently retrieved evidence against Hiss that Chambers had hidden, among other places, in a hollowed-out pumpkin.

688.16–17 "Lay on, Macduff . . . Enough!'"] *Macbeth*, V.viii.33–34.

698.9–14 the Baptist Meeting House . . . Roger Williams.] Williams (1603–1683) founded the First Baptist Church of Providence in 1638.

719.13–14 "'Yond Cassius . . . dangerous,"] *Julius Caesar*, I.ii.194–95.

724.19 *lebensraum*] Literally "living space," a German word associated with Nazi expansionist ideology.

744.7–8 Haile Selassie . . . crown.] Selassie (1892–1975) was crowned as emperor of Ethiopia on November 2, 1930.

OTHER WRITINGS

761.23 Dickens' Fat Boy] See note 445.32.

766.15 the Dutchman (the late Dutch Schultz)] Born Arthur Simon Flegenheimer (1901–1935), Schultz was an organized crime figure who ran speakeasies and, after Prohibition, the Harlem numbers racket.

767.10–12 Bill (Bojangles) Robinson . . . A. Philip Randolph] Robinson (1878–1949) was a dancer and actor; White (1893–1955), head of the NAACP from 1931 to 1955; Du Bois (1868–1963), a prominent author, editor, and civil rights leader; Tobias (1882–1961), senior secretary of the Colored Work Department on the YMCA from 1924 to 1946; Bolin (1908–2007), the only female African American judge in the United States, appointed to the New York City Domestic Relations Court in 1939; and Randolph (1889–1979), a prominent labor organizer and civil rights leader.

767.14 Rochester] Eddie Anderson (1905–1977), a prominent radio comedian, played the role of Rochester, Jack Benny's butler, on *The Jack Benny Program* from 1937 to 1965.

772.2 *Anna Lucasta*] 1944 play by Philip Yordan (1914–2003); after opening at the American Negro Theatre in Harlem, it ran for over two years on Broadway.

772.23–24 real gone gal] Title of a 1951 song by John Lee Hooker (1912–2001).

772.29 "Always marry . . . than you."] Lyrics from the calypso song "Ugly Woman" (c. 1933) by Roaring Lion (Rafael De Leon, 1908–1991).

774.35 The Little Flower] Fiorello La Guardia's nickname: a translation from the Italian of his first name, and a reference to his short stature.

776.12 *The Grapes of Wrath*] 1939 novel by John Steinbeck (1902–1968).

776.33–35 *Knock on Any Door . . . A Passage to India*] See *Knock on Any Door* (1947) by Willard Motley (1909–1965); *Gentleman's Agreement* (1947) by Laura Z. Hobson (1900–1986); *Kingsblood Royal* (1947) by Sinclair Lewis (1885–1951); *Native Son* (1940) by Richard Wright (1908–1960); *The Naked and the Dead* (1948) by Norman Mailer (1923–2007); *Strange Fruit* (1944) by Lillian Smith (1897–1966); and *A Passage to India* (1924) by E. M. Forster (1897–1970).

777.10 Poe's poem for the poem's sake.] See Poe's posthumously published essay "The Poetic Principle" (1850).

780.11–18 Oliver Twist . . . mechanized world.] Characters in *Oliver Twist* (1839) by Charles Dickens (1812–1870), *The Grapes of Wrath* (1939) by John Steinbeck (1902–1968), *Native Son* (1940) by Richard Wright (1908–1960), and *Tobacco Road* (1932) by Erskine Caldwell (1903–1987).

781.36 *Uncle Tom's Cabin*] 1852 novel by Harriet Beecher Stowe (1811–1896).

782.17–18 *Earth and High Heaven . . . Agreement*] Novels first published in 1944, 1945, and 1947, respectively, by Gwethalyn Graham (1913–1965), Arthur Miller (1915–2005), and Laura Z. Hobson (1900–1986).

This book is set in 10 point ITC Galliard Pro, a face designed for digital composition by Matthew Carter and based on the sixteenth-century face Granjon. The paper is acid-free lightweight opaque that will not turn yellow or brittle with age. The binding is sewn, which allows the book to open easily and lie flat. The binding board is covered in Brillianta, a woven rayon cloth made by Van Heek–Scholco Textielfabrieken, Holland. Composition by Dedicated Book Services. Printing and binding by LSC Communications. Designed by Bruce Campbell.

THE LIBRARY OF AMERICA SERIES

Library of America fosters appreciation of America's literary heritage by publishing, and keeping permanently in print, authoritative editions of America's best and most significant writing. An independent nonprofit organization, it was founded in 1979 with seed funding from the National Endowment for the Humanities and the Ford Foundation.

1. Herman Melville: Typee, Omoo, Mardi
2. Nathaniel Hawthorne: Tales & Sketches
3. Walt Whitman: Poetry & Prose
4. Harriet Beecher Stowe: Three Novels
5. Mark Twain: Mississippi Writings
6. Jack London: Novels & Stories
7. Jack London: Novels & Social Writings
8. William Dean Howells: Novels 1875–1886
9. Herman Melville: Redburn, White-Jacket, Moby-Dick
10. Nathaniel Hawthorne: Collected Novels
11 & 12. Francis Parkman: France and England in North America
13. Henry James: Novels 1871–1880
14. Henry Adams: Novels, Mont Saint Michel, The Education
15. Ralph Waldo Emerson: Essays & Lectures
16. Washington Irving: History, Tales & Sketches
17. Thomas Jefferson: Writings
18. Stephen Crane: Prose & Poetry
19. Edgar Allan Poe: Poetry & Tales
20. Edgar Allan Poe: Essays & Reviews
21. Mark Twain: The Innocents Abroad, Roughing It
22 & 23. Henry James: Literary Criticism
24. Herman Melville: Pierre, Israel Potter, The Confidence-Man, Tales & Billy Budd
25. William Faulkner: Novels 1930–1935
26 & 27. James Fenimore Cooper: The Leatherstocking Tales
28. Henry David Thoreau: A Week, Walden, The Maine Woods, Cape Cod
29. Henry James: Novels 1881–1886
30. Edith Wharton: Novels
31 & 32. Henry Adams: History of the U.S. during the Administrations of Jefferson & Madison
33. Frank Norris: Novels & Essays
34. W.E.B. Du Bois: Writings
35. Willa Cather: Early Novels & Stories
36. Theodore Dreiser: Sister Carrie, Jennie Gerhardt, Twelve Men
37. Benjamin Franklin: Writings (2 vols.)
38. William James: Writings 1902–1910
39. Flannery O'Connor: Collected Works
40, 41, & 42. Eugene O'Neill: Complete Plays
43. Henry James: Novels 1886–1890
44. William Dean Howells: Novels 1886–1888
45 & 46. Abraham Lincoln: Speeches & Writings
47. Edith Wharton: Novellas & Other Writings
48. William Faulkner: Novels 1936–1940
49. Willa Cather: Later Novels
50. Ulysses S. Grant: Memoirs & Selected Letters
51. William Tecumseh Sherman: Memoirs
52. Washington Irving: Bracebridge Hall, Tales of a Traveller, The Alhambra
53. Francis Parkman: The Oregon Trail, The Conspiracy of Pontiac
54. James Fenimore Cooper: Sea Tales
55 & 56. Richard Wright: Works
57. Willa Cather: Stories, Poems, & Other Writings
58. William James: Writings 1878–1899
59. Sinclair Lewis: Main Street & Babbitt
60 & 61. Mark Twain: Collected Tales, Sketches, Speeches, & Essays
62 & 63. The Debate on the Constitution
64 & 65. Henry James: Collected Travel Writings
66 & 67. American Poetry: The Nineteenth Century
68. Frederick Douglass: Autobiographies
69. Sarah Orne Jewett: Novels & Stories
70. Ralph Waldo Emerson: Collected Poems & Translations
71. Mark Twain: Historical Romances
72. John Steinbeck: Novels & Stories 1932–1937
73. William Faulkner: Novels 1942–1954
74 & 75. Zora Neale Hurston: Novels, Stories, & Other Writings
76. Thomas Paine: Collected Writings
77 & 78. Reporting World War II: American Journalism
79 & 80. Raymond Chandler: Novels, Stories, & Other Writings

81. Robert Frost: Collected Poems, Prose, & Plays

82 & 83. Henry James: Complete Stories 1892–1910

84. William Bartram: Travels & Other Writings

85. John Dos Passos: U.S.A.

86. John Steinbeck: The Grapes of Wrath & Other Writings 1936–1941

87, 88, & 89. Vladimir Nabokov: Novels & Other Writings

90. James Thurber: Writings & Drawings

91. George Washington: Writings

92. John Muir: Nature Writings

93. Nathanael West: Novels & Other Writings

94 & 95. Crime Novels: American Noir of the 1930s, 40s, & 50s

96. Wallace Stevens: Collected Poetry & Prose

97. James Baldwin: Early Novels & Stories

98. James Baldwin: Collected Essays

99 & 100. Gertrude Stein: Writings

101 & 102. Eudora Welty: Novels, Stories, & Other Writings

103. Charles Brockden Brown: Three Gothic Novels

104 & 105. Reporting Vietnam: American Journalism

106 & 107. Henry James: Complete Stories 1874–1891

108. American Sermons

109. James Madison: Writings

110. Dashiell Hammett: Complete Novels

111. Henry James: Complete Stories 1864–1874

112. William Faulkner: Novels 1957–1962

113. John James Audubon: Writings & Drawings

114. Slave Narratives

115 & 116. American Poetry: The Twentieth Century

117. F. Scott Fitzgerald: Novels & Stories 1920–1922

118. Henry Wadsworth Longfellow: Poems & Other Writings

119 & 120. Tennessee Williams: Collected Plays

121 & 122. Edith Wharton: Collected Stories

123. The American Revolution: Writings from the War of Independence

124. Henry David Thoreau: Collected Essays & Poems

125. Dashiell Hammett: Crime Stories & Other Writings

126 & 127. Dawn Powell: Novels

128. Carson McCullers: Complete Novels

129. Alexander Hamilton: Writings

130. Mark Twain: The Gilded Age & Later Novels

131. Charles W. Chesnutt: Stories, Novels, & Essays

132. John Steinbeck: Novels 1942–1952

133. Sinclair Lewis: Arrowsmith, Elmer Gantry, Dodsworth

134 & 135. Paul Bowles: Novels, Stories, & Other Writings

136. Kate Chopin: Complete Novels & Stories

137 & 138. Reporting Civil Rights: American Journalism

139. Henry James: Novels 1896–1899

140. Theodore Dreiser: An American Tragedy

141. Saul Bellow: Novels 1944–1953

142. John Dos Passos: Novels 1920–1925

143. John Dos Passos: Travel Books & Other Writings

144. Ezra Pound: Poems & Translations

145. James Weldon Johnson: Writings

146. Washington Irving: Three Western Narratives

147. Alexis de Tocqueville: Democracy in America

148. James T. Farrell: Studs Lonigan Trilogy

149, 150, & 151. Isaac Bashevis Singer: Collected Stories

152. Kaufman & Co.: Broadway Comedies

153. Theodore Roosevelt: Rough Riders, An Autobiography

154. Theodore Roosevelt: Letters & Speeches

155. H. P. Lovecraft: Tales

156. Louisa May Alcott: Little Women, Little Men, Jo's Boys

157. Philip Roth: Novels & Stories 1959–1962

158. Philip Roth: Novels 1967–1972

159. James Agee: Let Us Now Praise Famous Men, A Death in the Family, Shorter Fiction

160. James Agee: Film Writing & Selected Journalism

161. Richard Henry Dana Jr.: Two Years Before the Mast & Other Voyages

162. Henry James: Novels 1901–1902

163. Arthur Miller: Plays 1944–1961

164. William Faulkner: Novels 1926–1929

165. Philip Roth: Novels 1973–1977

166 & 167. American Speeches: Political Oratory

168. Hart Crane: Complete Poems & Selected Letters

169. Saul Bellow: Novels 1956–1964

170. John Steinbeck: Travels with Charley & Later Novels

171. Capt. John Smith: Writings with Other Narratives

172. Thornton Wilder: Collected Plays & Writings on Theater

173. Philip K. Dick: Four Novels of the 1960s

174. Jack Kerouac: Road Novels 1957–1960

175. Philip Roth: Zuckerman Bound

176 & 177. Edmund Wilson: Literary Essays & Reviews

178. American Poetry: The 17th & 18th Centuries

179. William Maxwell: Early Novels & Stories

180. Elizabeth Bishop: Poems, Prose, & Letters

181. A. J. Liebling: World War II Writings

182. American Earth: Environmental Writing Since Thoreau

183. Philip K. Dick: Five Novels of the 1960s & 70s

184. William Maxwell: Later Novels & Stories

185. Philip Roth: Novels & Other Narratives 1986–1991

186. Katherine Anne Porter: Collected Stories & Other Writings

187. John Ashbery: Collected Poems 1956–1987

188 & 189. John Cheever: Complete Novels & Collected Stories

190. Lafcadio Hearn: American Writings

191. A. J. Liebling: The Sweet Science & Other Writings

192. The Lincoln Anthology

193. Philip K. Dick: VALIS & Later Novels

194. Thornton Wilder: The Bridge of San Luis Rey & Other Novels 1926–1948

195. Raymond Carver: Collected Stories

196 & 197. American Fantastic Tales

198. John Marshall: Writings

199. The Mark Twain Anthology

200. Mark Twain: A Tramp Abroad, Following the Equator, Other Travels

201 & 202. Ralph Waldo Emerson: Selected Journals

203. The American Stage: Writing on Theater

204. Shirley Jackson: Novels & Stories

205. Philip Roth: Novels 1993–1995

206 & 207. H. L. Mencken: Prejudices

208. John Kenneth Galbraith: The Affluent Society & Other Writings 1952–1967

209. Saul Bellow: Novels 1970–1982

210 & 211. Lynd Ward: Six Novels in Woodcuts

212. The Civil War: The First Year

213 & 214. John Adams: Revolutionary Writings

215. Henry James: Novels 1903–1911

216. Kurt Vonnegut: Novels & Stories 1963–1973

217 & 218. Harlem Renaissance Novels

219. Ambrose Bierce: The Devil's Dictionary, Tales, & Memoirs

220. Philip Roth: The American Trilogy 1997–2000

221. The Civil War: The Second Year

222. Barbara W. Tuchman: The Guns of August, The Proud Tower

223. Arthur Miller: Plays 1964–1982

224. Thornton Wilder: The Eighth Day, Theophilus North, Autobiographical Writings

225. David Goodis: Five Noir Novels of the 1940s & 50s

226. Kurt Vonnegut: Novels & Stories 1950–1962

227 & 228. American Science Fiction: Nine Novels of the 1950s

229 & 230. Laura Ingalls Wilder: The Little House Books

231. Jack Kerouac: Collected Poems

232. The War of 1812

233. American Antislavery Writings

234. The Civil War: The Third Year

235. Sherwood Anderson: Collected Stories

236. Philip Roth: Novels 2001–2007

237. Philip Roth: Nemeses

238. Aldo Leopold: A Sand County Almanac & Other Writings

239. May Swenson: Collected Poems

240 & 241. W. S. Merwin: Collected Poems

242 & 243. John Updike: Collected Stories

244. Ring Lardner: Stories & Other Writings

245. Jonathan Edwards: Writings from the Great Awakening

246. Susan Sontag: Essays of the 1960s & 70s

247. William Wells Brown: Clotel & Other Writings
248 & 249. Bernard Malamud: Novels & Stories of the 1940s, 50s, & 60s
250. The Civil War: The Final Year
251. Shakespeare in America
252. Kurt Vonnegut: Novels 1976–1985
253 & 254. American Musicals 1927–1969
255. Elmore Leonard: Four Novels of the 1970s
256. Louisa May Alcott: Work, Eight Cousins, Rose in Bloom, Stories & Other Writings
257. H. L. Mencken: The Days Trilogy
258. Virgil Thomson: Music Chronicles 1940–1954
259. Art in America 1945–1970
260. Saul Bellow: Novels 1984–2000
261. Arthur Miller: Plays 1987–2004
262. Jack Kerouac: Visions of Cody, Visions of Gerard, Big Sur
263. Reinhold Niebuhr: Major Works on Religion & Politics
264. Ross Macdonald: Four Novels of the 1950s
265 & 266. The American Revolution: Writings from the Pamphlet Debate
267. Elmore Leonard: Four Novels of the 1980s
268 & 269. Women Crime Writers: Suspense Novels of the 1940s & 50s
270. Frederick Law Olmsted: Writings on Landscape, Culture, & Society
271. Edith Wharton: Four Novels of the 1920s
272. James Baldwin: Later Novels
273. Kurt Vonnegut: Novels 1987–1997
274. Henry James: Autobiographies
275. Abigail Adams: Letters
276. John Adams: Writings from the New Nation 1784–1826
277. Virgil Thomson: The State of Music & Other Writings
278. War No More: American Antiwar & Peace Writing
279. Ross Macdonald: Three Novels of the Early 1960s
280. Elmore Leonard: Four Later Novels
281. Ursula K. Le Guin: The Complete Orsinia
282. John O'Hara: Stories
283. The Unknown Kerouac: Rare, Unpublished & Newly Translated Writings
284. Albert Murray: Collected Essays & Memoirs
285 & 286. Loren Eiseley: Collected Essays on Evolution, Nature, & the Cosmos
287. Carson McCullers: Stories, Plays & Other Writings
288. Jane Bowles: Collected Writings
289. World War I and America: Told by the Americans Who Lived It
290 & 291. Mary McCarthy: The Complete Fiction
292. Susan Sontag: Later Essays
293 & 294. John Quincy Adams: Diaries
295. Ross Macdonald: Four Later Novels
296 & 297. Ursula K. Le Guin: The Hainish Novels & Stories
298 & 299. Peter Taylor: The Complete Stories
300. Philip Roth: Why Write? Collected Nonfiction 1960–2013
301. John Ashbery: Collected Poems 1991–2000
302. Wendell Berry: Port William Novels & Stories: The Civil War to World War II
303. Reconstruction: Voices from America's First Great Struggle for Racial Equality
304. Albert Murray: Collected Novels & Poems
305 & 306. Norman Mailer: The Sixties
307. Rachel Carson: Silent Spring & Other Writings on the Environment
308. Elmore Leonard: Westerns
309 & 310. Madeleine L'Engle: The Kairos Novels
311. John Updike: Novels 1959–1965
312. James Fenimore Cooper: Two Novels of the American Revolution